Burn

Tedd Hawks

Burn

Copyright © November 2018 by Tedd Hawks
ISBN: 9781731569004

Cover design by Adam Velasquez

All rights reserved.
No part of this book may be reproduced or transmitted in any form or by any means, electronic or mechanical, including photocopying, recording, or by any information storage retrieval system, without written permission from the author.

Tedd Hawks
www.teddhawks.com
teddhawks@yahoo.com

This is a work of fiction. Any resemblance to persons living or dead is entirely coincidental.

Dedication:

For Marshall, Mitch, and Tom, my three gay wise(ish) men.

Table of Contents

City Lights 7
    One 9
    Two 15
    Three 23
    Four 30
    Five 38
    Six 46
    Seven 54
    Eight 63
    Nine 70

The Exodus 77
    Welcome to the Pity Party 79
    Tomorrow Comes Alive 85
    That Gala Feeling 92
    Into the Woods 105
    Grindrella 116
    Dog Days 132
    B-I-N-G-O 142
    Hard to Get 154
    Flip or Flop? 162
    Everything Is Probably Fine 170
    A Farewell to Oz 177

An Interlude 185
    I. 186
    II. 191
    III. 205

IV.	212
V.	222
VI.	229
VII.	238
VIII.	248

Judges *253*
    2015: Prologue 254
    2000: Interior Hearts 257
    2005: Men in a Maze 279
    2010: Judges 301
    2015: Epilogue 325

A Modern Ruin in Deep Focus *333*

Dramatis Personae *334*

Act I *335*
    SCENE I – PILLARS OF CLOUD 335
    SCENE II – REVELERS 353
    SCENE III – THE MAGNIFICENT YOUTH 362
    SCENE IV – XANADU 368
    SCENE V – WORLDS AT WAR 374

ACT II *383*
    SCENE VI – THE WHISPERING WAVES 383
    SCENE VII – THE OPEN TABLE 391
    SCENE VIII – THE SOUTH END OF THE WORLD 400

Act III *410*
    SCENE IX: A TOUCH OF EVIL 410
    SCENE X: A TOUCH OF GOSPEL 419
    SCENE XI: THE END IS THE BEGINNING 427
    SCENE XII: PILLARS OF FIRE 441

Appendix: Sal's Poetry *446*
Reading Notes *448*
Acknowledgments *452*

City Lights

"It was always the becoming he dreamed of, never the being."
- F. Scott Fitzgerald, *This Side of Paradise*

Summer 2015

One

Sitting in his cousin's living room across from a new acquaintance, Nick suddenly thought of his father. It was a flash from just a few years before, a memory of the old man's wiry frame lording over Nick as he sat on the sofa. Pants pulled high, decrepit spectacles shining like stars in the glow of fluorescent lights, his father was deathly serious and deeply focused. The advice given to Nick at that moment, right before his first day of classes at community college, had been in response to his choice to stay close to home to attend school. His father's advice rambled for some time, but the theme was one of pride in Nick realizing that staying at home was the wise and pragmatic decision. It was the family's belief that going outside of the bounds of their small town, their cornfields, their static lives, was a prelude to pain and failure.

It struck Nick as an especially poignant memory sitting in the bright, early afternoon sunshine of his cousin, Peter's, Chicago condo. It was an early Saturday in May and the windows were thrown open, the world throbbing around him. Outside there was laughter, shouting, and the beeping of car horns. The scene was a far cry from his parent's living room, the alleged security of shag carpeting, dusty curtains, and peeling wood paneling. Likewise, the actor in the scene was immensely different from his aging, conservative father. Before him was an immaculately dressed gay man sipping a glass of champagne. The man, Jordan, smiled at Nick and lowered his glass, setting it delicately on the table. Nick's cousin, Peter, was older, grayed in many respects, but he and his partner, George, had solicited their younger friend, a protean Boystown gadabout, to be a guide for Nick as he began his college career in the big city. It was their hope that Jordan, in his jaunty, freewheeling way would show Nick the ins and outs of their gay world. Far away from the blustering speech of his Puritanical father and the waving fields of corn, Peter and George wanted to be sure their young ward was in the right hands.

Jordan put his hand behind his head and smiled, a perfect flash of white in his tanned face. He drew a long breath, as if in preparation for a grand speech, his young countenance alive with manic energy and amorous interest in the boy across from him. "Division," he said leaning forward, "the story of all people, but for our people its source is Halsted Street." He placed his hands under his chin. "I mean, you need to know these things since you're new to us. Halsted is the primary fissure, the source of all the cracks between age, race, ethnicity, and types. You see bears and otters, twinks and A-gays, blacks and Asians, gaymers and jocks. You think everything is just 'gay', but Halsted divides us – it makes these differences clear."

Nick nodded haphazardly and turned his attention to the window. Jordan hesitated, fearing he was losing the chance to make an impression on the young man, a man that tacitly had been offered to him as a love interest by the couple. He had come to provide aid in getting their young family member adjusted to the city but had been pleasantly surprised by his looks. It was a very real possibility that he could cultivate a summer passion in this youth, a passing fancy, a lesson in love for the boy from the rural wastelands. Jordan was one of those who never settled down, never let anyone get particularly far under his skin. His history was one of dodging other's judgments and slipping on masks to avoid scrutiny. In doing so, the relationships he fostered ended up being constructed of the same protean substance as his own personality. An effect was that the real joy cultivated from his amorous entanglements was drawn from the chase, the seduction, smoke and mirror games that netted him another conquest to discuss at future cocktail parties.

This latest notch in his belt, however, seemed to be in jeopardy as Nick looked longingly out the window and into the streets that bustled with herds of gay men moving from the lethargy of hangover to the bright din of brunch. Jordan licked his lips and threw himself forward, fearing he may lose his chance to impress the young man and secure a sexual conquest.

"I suppose you should know about Hedley," he said quickly.

"What's Hedley?" Nick looked up quizzically. From the kitchen they heard the crack of warm liquid poured over ice.

"Hedley is a kind of celebrity in Boystown – *the* celebrity. He's our poster boy, you know. He's a legend around here."

Nick, who had returned his gaze to Jordan's, turned away and focused his attention on the steel and glass coffee table in the center of the room.

Jordan sighed, putting his finger to his temple. He bit his lip, as was his habit when brushed aside, and stared toward the kitchen. A shuffle of feet and the clank of tableware stirred the silence.

"What else is there to do?" Nick stood and walked to the window. The condo's view was average; at two floors up, the picture windows faced the roof of a low-standing structure split into a number of bars and sex shops. "Peter said there is a lot to do in the summers here."

Jordan turned his gaze to Nick. A power shift had occurred and made him feel like being less pleasant. Rather than being the wizened domesticate, he was a distanced other. "There is a lot to do. There's the beach, volleyball, brunch – my god, the drinking. You may not spend a moment sober."

Footsteps interrupted them as Peter and George entered the room. They both stood erect, their starched shirts pulled taught across their lean, middle-aged bodies.

Although different human beings, there may have been no two men more alike in look and personality outside of genetic twins. Behind their broad, toned backs, many described both as banal in nature and bland in conversation. They used the same chestnut hair dye and groomed their swirling brown and silver chest hair in the same obsessive ways. Their partnership and proximity made shopping for two items instead of one a natural occurrence, the result being they dressed in shirts of the same cut and brand in a variety of different colors. In many of their social settings, liquor flowing and lights dimmed, the couple simply merge together and become Geter or Peorge. It was a regular occurrence upon the arrival of one without the other that they would be met with the searching, hesitant greeting, "Hello…you!"

"I hope you're not corrupting our rural transplant!" Peter clasped his hands behind his back. "He's a sweet boy from among the cornstalks, Jordan."

Jordan turned to Nick and arched his eyebrows. "My guess is he's already corrupted in some way; he's just hiding it from us."

Nick shyly smiled, melting some of the discomfort and rancor Jordan had felt at his perceived earlier disinterest.

"I guess you'll have to wait and see." Nick shyly leaned over to pick up a magazine from the coffee table. With a coquettish smile, he flipped through its pages.

"Well, if you're not there, you can start right now," said Peter. "Brunch is on! Veggie quiche and fruit salad, strategically designed so that all calories will be from the booze and not the brunch."

"Jesus." Jordan stood up. Nick's eyes drank in his new acquaintance's tall, lithe body as it stretched upward. The form of his chiseled lower abdomen peeked out as his shirt lifted. "You queens and your aversion to meat. Our 'transplant' won't know what to eat."

"He'll figure it out!" George had now taken over speaking duties as Peter urged them into the dining room.

Wind lapped at the lace tablecloth as they took their seats at the refinished oak table. Large windows faced east across Halsted, letting in vibrant May light that sparked their flutes of champagne, transforming them into dazzling, bubbling glasses of fire. Around them food spilled about the table, perfectly organized around an overflowing vase of fresh daises. The wind circled around them teasing their olfactory senses with the perfume of spring and food and flowers.

"Isn't it lovely?" asked Peter. "It's beautiful, isn't it?"

Jordan raised his glass to his lips. His eyes tripped about the room in an envious sweep. "It's very nice. You boys know how to throw a party."

"You think? Really?" George asked.

"We invited Kinsey and Byron," began Peter, but rather than concluding he looked down to the floor. When he lifted his eyes, he looked directly at Jordan. It was if he had been asking a question rather than beginning his own statement. "Well..." he said quietly and tapped his fingers on the table.

"I was telling Nick a bit about Boystown," Jordan said. "He was telling me he hasn't been to our corner of the world."

Nick hadn't spent much time outside of his hometown, the pervasive advice of his father and a number of other factors pinning him in, making him unsure of moving outside the boundaries of their conservative hamlet. He had spent the past two years in a small community college on the far rings of Western Illinois. He edged that far out after high school, a period that was a tangled web of denial, fear, and self-loathing. Afternoons spent indoors added to his physical girth and complex knowledge of online role-playing games. In his small town, gay had been an abstract concept, a specter that haunted certain families. The liberalization of the country to the queer community was a distant knocking that he felt, but not the gale force that he had hoped would sweep him up and carry him to acceptance and confidence. His weight increased, as did his fantasies of a life in a different place; in this world, he was one with the beautiful, enigmatic community of gays that he worshipped in *Queer as Folk* YouTube compilations. The disjunction between reality and fantasy was completed in the hours of pornography he devoured late at night when his parents were abed. He saw the beautiful, toned bodies of his fantasies engage each other. But just as ephemeral as the witches and elves in his gaming adventures, these men remained pixelated versions of reality – digital dreams that twitched at the edge of his imagination.

The mounting depression and isolation meant that as he paced the halls of his high school, instead of jeers pointing to his homosexuality, he was met with slurs and epithets against his great weight and timidity. The sloth, the monster, the slug: his schoolmates' messages rang in his ears. The poison, rich and plentiful, took its effect, its black bile filling him up, an untapped reservoir of spite and hatred.

It was not until he blundered into community college, a thirty-minute drive from his home, that the great wall between reality and fantasy began to erode away.

"It is a triumph, Nick," Peter said spooning a small portion of quiche. "From the great wilds of Western Illinois to the halls of DePaul, what an absolute success story."

"And the weight, of course," George offered. "It's so good to see you looking so healthy. When we saw you for your high school graduation you looked so grey and tired. So heavy."

"You used to be fat?" Jordan asked incredulously. "I would never have guessed. You have such a thick, toned physique." Jordan, already feeling the bubbling of the champagne effect his brain, giggled to himself. He let his own spindly leg splay out and surreptitiously touch Nick's under the table.

Nick's heart beat quickly the moment Jordan's leg brushed against his own. The disinterest Jordan had imagined earlier from Nick's actions had been from timidity, not rejection. In Nick's mind, he had not imagined he could provide anything that would pique the interest of the older, handsome man across from him.

Nick had been about to speak but his voice caught in his throat as he felt the heat of Jordan's skin. In a bumbling, panicked manner he said, "I'm excited to start – um – school... Meet people. I'm going to keep studying business." He then quickly added: "Finance."

"A good choice!" Peter bellowed raising his glass. "A future titan of industry!"

George smiled, his lineless face pulled taught. "You remember when we were his age, Peter?" he sighed. "The world was so endless then – around every corner was possibility, endless hope."

Initially, Nick planned to move in with his uncle upon coming into the city, however, after some thought, his parents, more out of fear of Peter's gay influence than anything else, convinced Nick that he needed his own space in his first year away from home. His parents secured him a small studio apartment at Wrightwood and Clark. While pricey, they liked the largely heterosexual population that milled about at the corner restaurants and 7-11. It was far enough away from DePaul's campus to offer some solitude, but close enough to make tardiness to class inexcusable. The small box now seemed a veritable hovel as Nick felt the kiss of afternoon sunlight on his cheek and admired the bourgeoisie art that bedecked Peter and George's walls.

The afternoon hours moved by insouciantly. The sun burned hot and high as the glasses of champagne followed each other in rapid succession. Food was eaten, pushed around plates, as gossip and anecdotes filled their ears. Jordan, the lead raconteur, spun tales of the past winter. As if a Biblical line of heritage, his list went on and on in drunken celebration: Horace fucked Brian who fucked Steven who fucked Tim, Nial, and Nial's gay stepfather at the St. Patrick's Day party.

Nick watched him with keen interest, the touch of Jordan's skin against his own lighting a fantasy in his mind. As stories followed each other, Jordan's hand inched closer to Nick's thigh. Nick's whole person trembled under the soft caress.

"Isn't this a lovely party," Peter said rising to turn on music. "It's beautiful. Take a picture," he garbled fumbling for the on switch. "This is beauty."

Music played as the whisperings of evening climbed up the ivy on the building's red brick front and flooded into the small room. George and Peter embraced each other and danced. Their steps remained in time, but they looked to the window, to the awkward courtship beginning at the dining room table. Both older men, by rote, kept time to the music, but their own hearts beat to the cadence of an earlier rhythm, a raucous dance hall, a nightclub, their younger bodies pressed against each other. These imaginative rustlings were disturbed only by the feel of their own aging hands cusped together. If they were to close their eyes, they were again young and beautiful.

Hours bled together, the sun sinking lazily into the western sky, turning the dining room the color of cabernet.

"Well," Jordan said standing up, "we should probably be thinking about going out." He looked directly at Nick. The younger man's face was bathed in the scarlet light of dusk. "You boys think you'll come?"

George and Peter had been sitting on the sofa drinking glasses of wine. The sound of Jordan's voice woke them as if from a dream.

"Is it that time?" asked George. "Already?"

"How time flies," said Peter.

"Well, Kinsey is having a few people over for a little pre-game, then to the bars."

Peter flinched slightly at the name of Kinsey, the one who had so glibly rejected the invitation to brunch.

George seemed to have forgotten entirely. "What is it? Saturday? What's tonight?"

"The circuit," Jordan said starting to cross the room and get his bag. "Start at Sidey, of course, then probably Progress. I think the boy," he said motioning to Nick, "needs a Berlin night to christen his arrival in Chicago."

Nick looked between the three men, hoping these foreign references would be translated for the sake of his understanding.

"Well, why don't you boys have fun at Kinsey's and then let us know when you go to Sidetrack? Is that...?" Peter's eyes went to George.

"That's fine," George said.

"Do that," Peter said lifting another drought of wine to his lips.

"Most excellent!" Jordan reached out his hand to Nick. "Let's go!" he said smiling.

Nick took the hand, feeling its warmth, its calloused grip in his own. Again, his heart began to slam in his chest. Sweat visibly formed along his brow.

The two men exited the condo, leaping down the steps. Alcohol circulated in their systems, pumping to every extremity. Their brains were dulled; their hearts were pounding. In their champagne-glazed eyes, the reflection of the evening lights glowed brightly.

"Division!" Jordan laughed raucously in the street. "That's where we started!" He slung his arm around Nick's shoulders. "We are a divided people, Mr. Nick – what's your last name?"

Nick opened his lips to answer.

"Shh! Shh!" Jordan tittered. "Let's keep it a mystery. Yes, I think that's fitting. But we are divided – all over." He pointed east to a bar beginning to fill with men in garish spring costumes, then west to the warm lights in George and Peter's condo above them. "We all have to find our place in that in-between space: this void, this street, your new home." His arm hung over Nick's shoulders. Gently, he squeezed his new friend's bicep. The champagne rising, Jordan leaned in and gently kissed the base of Nick's neck. He then breathed in deeply. "You're lovely," he said, his voice soft and gentle, blending into the quiet murmur of the night around them.

  Nick felt his body set fire, his desire flowering under the heat and intimacy of Jordan's erotic touch. Around them the night was beginning: couples sauntered out of restaurants, groups of young men burst from apartments along the street, taxis roared by bringing gaggles of queens to their night's starting point. The neon lights of Halsted bled together, formed a luminous artery, feeding the shuddering heart of his new city. As Jordan pulled him down a side street, Nick smiled to himself, the dream, his dream of life and freedom, finally coming to fruition. Ahead the sky blazed orange as they walked toward the horizon, the great globe of fire, the setting May sun.

Two

It was two blocks later that Jordan and Nick's course was interrupted by a man in a suit. The gentleman's ash-grey hair sat perfectly quaffed in a pompadour. He had called out to Jordan from across the street and run to catch up.

Nick smiled and took his hand as Jordan introduced him with slight edge in his voice. "Nick, this is Lawrence Soot. He's a well-known Boystown fixture; he somehow finds himself at every party."

As Nick shook his hand, he couldn't help but notice the slight aberrations in Soot's appearance, the traits and qualities about his face and eyes that strangely defied expectations. His grey hair signaled age, however, his skin stretched tightly across his tanned face. There again, coming to Chicago in May, the warm air signaling spring, his rust-colored complexion signaled days and weeks bathed in sunlight on a tropical beach. His pale, grey, watery eyes rested under highly manicured eyebrows, their arch and thinness almost too controlled, too corrected from their natural forms. It was as if, to Nick, the real Lawrence Soot lay somewhere else, and this poor reflection was all that had been able to catch up with them.

"I didn't think I'd catch you boys!" Soot panted, gently tucking his tie back into his suit jacket. "I just had to talk to you, though." He smiled and pulled out cigarettes. "Do you mind? Do either of you want one?" A smooth, manicured hand held out the package of cigarettes.

Jordan took one and held it up to be lit. Nick politely declined. The lighter clicked, a jet of flame issuing forth.

"News, darling." Soot smiled, his teeth a blinding white in his orange face. "I ran into The Set last night."

Jordan laughed. "'Ran into,' Sooty? I feel like 'hunted' is more appropriate."

"Well," Soot smirked, "whichever, but guess who was flitting about with them last night?" Soot held up his phone and checked his reflection. Gently, he patted his perfect hair, a slight dust of product and hairspray rising up in the motion's wake.

"Someone new?"

"Someone old!" Soot tapped his cigarette, a volley of ash plummeting to the sidewalk. "You know Jonathan Kearns? He used to be with David."

"Yes." Jordan's eyebrows raised. "I remember Joe introducing them to me at Hedley's Gala last year."

"Well, he's been busy in the gym and with a stylist, I should say." Soot turned to Nick and pantomimed a V-shape. "His body is chiseled now. *And* he's running about with The Set."

"Really?" Jordan seemed genuinely surprised. "I haven't seen him this winter at all. I assume he and David…?"

"Completely broke it off – much needed, if you ask me." Soot coughed, an oddly staged act, his hand in a fist, his pinky extended. "Sorry," he said quickly. "I think I may be getting a cold. I'm getting too old for all these parties – last night was Alvin's, you know…"

Soot proceeded to tell an elaborate story of a cocktail party from the previous night. The list of names and bars referenced was enough to put Jordan's previous anecdotes to shame. At the story's conclusion, he again coughed and tapped the ash from his cigarette. The silver and white piece of flame drifted up, circling around him in the vernal wind.

"Well," said Jordan impatiently, "Sooty, we're off to Kinsey's."

Soot shook with laughter. "Oh! Oh!" He removed his handkerchief and dabbed his eyes. "That will be a treat!"

"What does that mean?" Jordan asked.

"What – what?" Soot's eyebrows lifted to the extent his face allowed. "You haven't checked the Boystown feed, have you?"

"I haven't been on Twitter today."

Soot again laughed. "Well, I suggest you read up. There is a great deal of news!" He winked at Nick. "I won't spoil it for you."

Jordan immediately dug into his pocket to pull out his phone. Soot put out his cigarette and gracefully bowed. "Ciao, ciao to you both! Jordan, I hope we will be seeing you out and about more that the weather is better. And," Soot turned and once again extended his hand, "be sure to bring this delicious one with you when you do."

The older man drifted away as Jordan frantically tapped at his phone. Upon arriving at his Twitter feed, his hand flew to his mouth.

"Oh, my," he chuckled. "Kinsey's place is going to be interesting."

"How so?" Nick asked.

"Well, he's gotten into trouble." Jordan continued to read and then smiled broadly. "Oh! And Hedley's Gala is announced!" Jordan slung his arm around Nick's shoulders. "What an exciting time for you to join us in Chicago!"

The two men walked further down the street. As they drew closer to a bright intersection, the trees thinned slightly and a huge billboard became visible at the corner. It erupted out of nowhere, a luminous, monstrous white board decorated with the bodies of two preternaturally beautiful men wrapped in an embrace. It stood as a monument to advertise a gay dating site, the name writ large in masculine scrawl along the bottom of the board.

Jordan caught Nick's eyes looking up, admiring the two, toned men lording over them.

"Sexy, right? The model on the left is actually from Chicago, one of Hedley's exes, of course." Jordan laughed. "Funny thing, it used to be for a church, some really conservative and awful place in The Loop. It was replaced a few months ago with these two beauties. It's much nicer to look at, if you ask me. They say God is dead – let's hope his grave always brings forth such beautiful flowers."

#

Whatever electricity had passed between Nick and Jordan diminished as they drew closer to the apartment of Cedric Kinsey. Jordan's manner went through a process of resetting; his face relaxed into a more somber expression, his body language became cryptic and unreadable. Nick even noticed his voice alter, dropping slightly to affect a more masculine, staccato rhythm rather than the fluid, florid speech of Peter and George's apartment.

They came to the back of Kinsey's apartment building, the wrought iron gate ajar, a bouquet of fresh roses tied to the bars of the fence. Jordan led them up the back staircase at a rapid pace, eager to get in and see the fallout from Kinsey's most recent adventure. The wooden stairs creaked under the weight of their feet. The entire way over Jordan had been trying to explain the situation, a stream of names, dates, locations piling up in Nick's mind. Nick tried to hold them in his memory, fix each name with an imaginary face, but it was of little use as the deluge of people, places, and things overwhelmed his ears and imagination. They paused briefly outside the back door to knock. From inside the sound of laughter, voices, and music streamed through the windows, a homey soundtrack to the quiet night around them.

"This will be interesting. Kinsey should be in a state. Oh, and if Myrtle is here, you'll want to stay away. She's in a constant state of drunkenness."

At that instant, the door flew open. Light spilled out onto the porch as the figure of a woman staggered to greet them.

"Jesus, Jordy, you scared me! Scared me right out of my mind! Out of it!" The woman smiled in the darkness. With the backlight of the doorway framing her teased out brown hair and the subtle glow of the moon illuminating her classical features, Myrtle resembled a silent film star in dramatic close up, caught in the romantic glow of first love. Her dress fit her full figure too tightly, her plentiful breasts pushing out against the fabric. The makeup caked to her face, visible as she presented her profile to the men and motioned them in, was too thick, too stagey, adding to the quality of her being called too late to the era of early cinema.

"And who is this stud with you?" she asked taking a slug from the drink in her hand. "He looks divine! A new pet, Jordy? So soon after the last one, too. I guess maybe not that soon – a few months? Six? I get it confused, you're about so much. Was it August?"

As she teetered on her heels, crossing the threshold from the apartment to the porch, she took another drink from her glass and extended her hand to Nick.

"Myrtle," she said dramatically. Her glass rose above her head and she bowed slightly as if presenting herself to a head of state. "I like to consider myself kind of the queen of this little group of gays. The real queen, you know – the lady!" She cackled and tottered over to the edge of the deck. Her hand dove into her purse, pulling out a pack of cigarettes. "You want to smoke with me?" She pushed a cigarette into her mouth. "Everyone but Soot has given it up, you know. It is the healthy thing to do, but it's no fun, is it? None!" She finished lighting the cigarette and looked at Nick as if seeing him for the first time. "Who are you again?"

"Nick."

"Nick is Peter's cousin, Myrtle. He just moved to Chicago."

"Peter is the one with the… Or George? I can never remember the difference."

"Peter has the slightly grayer hair around the temples."

"I think he's my favorite." Myrtle sucked on her cigarette for a brief moment before she suddenly jumped as if she had been frightened. Her hand dove into her purse, pulling out her cellphone. Myrtle ceased to be present, her universe became only the screen in front of her.

Quickly, Jordan pushed Nick inside the apartment.

"I told you," Jordan said raising an eyebrow. "Absolute mess, that one."

They went down a hall and came out in Kinsey's large living room. The scene that met them appeared specially set for their entrance. All figures looked frozen, as if in tableaux, waiting for the next bodies to enter before the action could play out. Seated on the sofa were two men, seemingly a couple, their knees touching, their eyes locked in a knowing gaze. In a recliner, directly to their right was an older man, a nest of brown-grey hair circling his bald head. His face held some of the mystery of Soot's, the disjunction of youth and age, in his tightly pulled features. At the head of the room was what had to be Kinsey, the most beautiful and well-dressed of all the party, leaning against the wall, his face twisted into a look of anger and, what seemed to Nick, a proud, arrogant smile, flashing intermittently behind the guise of rage.

"Well," Kinsey said coming to life at Jordan and Nick's entrance, "someone had to tell someone. It doesn't just come out of thin air, does it? Was it one of you? Who'd you tell?"

The two men on the couch put their heads down. The older man crossed his arms and groaned.

"Oh, Kinsey," the old man purred in a warm baritone, "you know these things just come out. Who knows who told who…" He paused briefly. "Who told whom, is it?"

"Kinz," one of the couple said quietly. "These things always come up. You can't think it will be a secret forever." He turned to his partner on the couch, expectantly. The partner jumped to life and nodded.

"Yeah," the partner said, "you can't think you can do anything with The Hedley Set without everyone finding out about it. We kind of told you when you were with Lloyd that you shouldn't – I mean, he's married…"

Kinsey scowled. "I assumed they were open. You'd think they'd have to be with the way Lloyd comes onto everyone." Kinsey smiled and playfully pulled at his shirt collar.

Jordan took this time to enter. Like an actor making his entrance, he crossed into the living room, going straight to Kinsey. "I'm glad Nick could see all of you at your finest," he said. "Always some kind of drama."

"Always drama," Kinsey said smiling. All sense of rage melted in the presence of his new guests. "You saw Twitter about me and Lloyd, I suppose. I think Terrence had a fit about it."

"I don't think I've ever seen Terrence upset," Jordan said turning to those seated on the couch. "He's one of the nicest people I've ever met."

"Well," the old man said shifting his weight in his chair, "we all know Lloyd – I suppose it's just his indiscretions have never been made public before."

"Thankfully, it's all been dusted under the rug by the announcement of Hedley's Gala," Kinsey said moving to the couch. "I heard more details. It's going to be next Saturday night up in Winnetka. Word is some DJ from LA is coming in for it."

Even the subdued couple came alive with this smattering of news about the party. Kinsey paused in his movement to the couch to extend his hand, which Jordan took and clasped excitedly. Again, the scene took on the look of a stage play. There was a brief drop in momentum, however, as it seemed whoever had the next line was failing to enter the scene. All gathered kept their looks, their smiles, their excitement for just one beat too long.

The awkward moment broke when the older gentleman stirred slightly and directed his gaze at Nick. "Boys, where are our manners?" He lifted himself from the recliner, crossing the room and taking Nick's hand. "I'm Clive."

"Hello," Nick smiled shyly.

"This is Nick," Jordan said disinterestedly. "Nick – this is Aaron and Todd." The couple on the couch waved politely. "And Kinsey, the Homewrecker." Jordan looked to Kinsey. They exchanged knowing smiles.

Clive put his hand behind Nick's back and gently pushed him out of the living room. "I'm going to take Nick to get a drink!" he said playfully. "He seems far too sober for all this gossip and drama."

The older man guided Nick to the kitchen. Like the rest of the apartment it was meticulously put together. Everything was neat and clean. The counters reflected the bright fluorescent lights in sharp stars on the stainless-steel counter. Around the cabinetry Kinsey had cultivated an ivy plant that curled perfectly around the ivory panels and cascaded down the sides, framing them in a beautiful, lively green. The only object out of place was the bedraggled figure of Myrtle, holding a bottle of wine and staring intently out of the window above the sink.

"They're coming," she said quietly, checking her phone and then turning her gaze to the darkness of the window.

Clive faked a smile at Myrtle before focusing his attention on the wet bar that was placed on a small wooden cart in the center of the kitchen. "What do you drink?" he asked smoothly, taking a bottle of whiskey and twisting off the cap.

"I don't really drink much…" Nick said.

"Oh, my, well we'll change that!" Clive's eyes twinkled. "You remind me a bit of me when I came to the city."

Myrtle laughed, a loud braying sound. "Oh, Clive," she said vacantly, "you wish you were as cute as this one. You were always kind of a toad."

Clive's lip curled. "Well, Myrtle, believe it or not, I was handsome in my day. I had my hair and my figure." Clive jokingly shook his belly. "I wasn't always this ghastly." His voice fell on the last word.

"I didn't mean ghastly," Myrtle said after taking a drink from the wine bottle. "I just meant you aren't as pretty as this one." She motioned to Nick. "Sorry if that was rude." Myrtle looked at Nick and rolled her eyes.

"It's too bad Sal isn't around too much anymore," Clive said looking at Nick. "He owned a bookshop down in Lake View. It was kind of a halfway house for young gay men. He's a good man. Back in the 70's he was a father figure for those of us kicked out of our homes."

Myrtle's face softened. "Clive was disowned when he was sixteen. His parents didn't like the gay thing."

"I'm too afraid to even tell mine," Nick said softly.

In truth, some part of Nick believed that transforming his person, his friends, his life, and returning triumphantly to his home would cushion the blow. In his imagination, he thought that the more beautiful the boyfriend he brought to his parents, the less heartbreak and anguish would rise from the occasion. No matter how great his homecoming would be, however, over the scene clung the shadow of his father's presence, the towering figure that lectured him about the safety of their rural existence.

"Well!" Clive put his arm around Nick. "You have support here. Grass is greener and now…" He took his arm from Nick's shoulders and refocused on the bottle of whiskey. Filling three glasses he passed them to Myrtle and Nick and held one himself. "We'll guide you into this brave new world!"

Clive raised his glass; the three of them toasted.

"You came at the perfect time. Hedley's party is next weekend. You'll see and meet absolutely everyone." Clive smiled.

"Oh, it's incredible." Myrtle leaned forward and almost fell doing so. She braced herself on the sink. "Lights and music and color. Every year it's more beautiful than before!"

Clive and Myrtle exchanged a look of reverence.

"Who was it that they were talking about in the living room?" Nick asked. "Terrence or something?"

"Ah." Clive drained his glass of whiskey and set it on the counter. "You know about the Twitter account?"

"Not really," Nick said.

"It posts all the rumors and gossip from around Boystown. No one knows who runs it, but it just broke a story about Kinsey."

"Can't keep his pecker in his pants," Myrtle added.

"He was caught cheating." Clive coughed slightly. "I mean... we all know Lloyd cheats, but it's always been clandestine affairs. It's never really been made public like this."

"Drama," said Myrtle, chasing her whiskey drink with a drag from the wine bottle.

"We also found out that Hedley's party is happening next weekend."

"I'm devastated," Myrtle was again pulling out her phone. Her manicured nails tapped the screen. "I have a wedding that weekend and won't be able to make it."

Clive shook his head in grief, as if Myrtle had confessed that her family had been executed. "That's a true shame." Clive turned to Nick excitedly. "They all come," he said in a whisper. "All the beautiful things two-by-two, descending upon Hedley's great, glittering ark."

"Where are they?" Myrtle asked looking from her phone to the dark window. Her eyes were vacant, her mouth twisted into a look of disappointment. "They should be here..."

Clive guided Nick back toward the living room.

"All this Boystown drama aside," Clive said, "you will really love it here in Chicago. There's so much history here. I suggest reading up on it. Go on an architecture cruise and find out about crazy Streeter." The old man turned and earnestly stared into Nick's eyes. "And trust me, all of us know the pain of coming out. Sal told me something about The Great Chicago Fire once. He said, 'It's why the city is such a great sign of hope – all of it, everything can burn down and yet something beautiful and new will rise up.'" Clive's eyes had grown damp. "Isn't that nice?" he asked. "Isn't that hopeful?"

"It is." Nick nodded politely.

Clive took Nick's hands and stared at him with collaged eyes. Through their grey screens emotions clustered in different forms, junctions, combinations. Here was longing, hopefulness, sadness, loss. Unlike the stage play of Kinsey's living room, this moment was filled with life. Nick barely felt the force of the odd connection before Clive dropped his hands, wiped his own eyes, and they bounded toward the living room.

Upon reentry, they noticed the party had grown livelier. Jordan was at center stage, recounting his run-in with Soot.

Between the laughter and drinks, the night slipped into a kaleidoscope of light and activity. The world faded into a silvery blur as the little group drifted from the apartment and made their way between the bars on Halsted. The wall between Jordan and Nick erected in the presence of Kinsey gave way. Drinks loosened Jordan's hands. They found themselves placed on Nick's body, his hand on his thigh, his arm, drifting finally to rest on his crotch.

Bars bled together as they weaved down Halsted Street. Nick fondly recalled the first night later, the cornucopia of different spaces that Jordan guided him into. In a few weeks he would put names on these places – Roscoe's, Sidetrack, Progress, Mini – but in that moment, it was a voyage to new worlds. Crossing each threshold brought him to a new, unknown territory. At Roscoe's drunks danced in the neon lights of the back room; under Progress's bubble-lighted ceiling, he saw a plethora of beautiful men in tight shirts, gripping each other and heading into the dark spaces beyond the DJ booth.

Berlin was their terminus. There in the darkness, under the dim lights and blaring music, Jordan firmly took what was his. It was subtle, but one arm wrapped around Nick's back initiated the bond that would build steadily throughout the summer. Nick felt his emotions stumble, lift, shudder, and tremble with the movement. In front of him he saw one of the new worlds. Beautiful men were wrapped up in each other, tongues lashing wildly between their faces. Some queens were stumbling through the dark, dropping drinks, roaring with empty laughter, speaking to no one at all. It was all much and nothing, a dazzling oblivion that pushed and pulled him at the same time.

The first hints of daylight met them as they emerged from the amber glow of Berlin's depths.

They briefly hesitated outside Jordan's apartment building. The early morning light falling on Nick's face illuminated his insecurity about following Jordan upstairs. But Jordan drove out the fear. Lightly, he placed his two hands on his young ward's cheeks. As if waking him from an enchanted sleep, he pressed his soft lips to Nick's. All fear, all wavering feelings ebbed away under the impressions of this boy's lips. Nick forcefully pulled himself into Jordan, the light touch of mouths becoming a flurry of tongues and staccato breaths.

Upstairs Jordan laid Nick on his bed. Their eyes briefly locked, Jordan asking for permission in the early daylight hours. Nick answered his searching stare with a voracious kiss.

The sexual act, Nick's first, twisted together both romance and violence. He felt Jordan enter him, the pain of first contact, evolving as Nick's own breath slowed, as Jordan playfully ran a hand through Nick's hair, ran his fingertips over his taught skin.

The sun was above the horizon when they both came to the full force of their passion. Nick looked out the window at a bright, new world. In his mind the pain of the sex had been a sacrifice. Whatever version of him had come before had been immolated. Out of the flames, emerging in the pale dawn light, a new creature was born. This being, who in the dark of Berlin had had his first full taste of life in Halsted's neon incubator, was ready to spread his wings and make an imprint on the partitioned world which Jordan had shown him. As with all newly born, he ached with the desire to feed – a savage hunger, becoming stronger, desiring more, everything, all.

Three

The manor attained for Hedley's Gala was a soaring, Grecian structure with expansive wings and additions folding out from the central, Corinthian-arched entryway. Floodlights illumined the ivory facade bathing it in a celestial glow. Ivy growing up and down its blank columns caught the white flood lamps and shone as waxy, glowing points in the crepuscular light. Removed enough from the main road, the ubiquitous building stood as a ghostly, otherworldly ark in the middle of a verdant, rolling lawn. All around the circular, cobblestoned drive, cars were parked, a menagerie of persons climbing from their vehicles, making pilgrimage to the front entry which glowed with welcoming light.

When Jordan, Nick, Peter, and George arrived after ten, the drive was already packed with cars. They had to leave George's BMW at the far edge of the cobblestones, near the dirt track that led through the small copse of trees at the house's western side.

"What do you think, Nicky?" Jordan asked hopping out of the car. He caught his reflection in the window and immediately checked his hair. "Ever seen such a thing?"

Nick's response came in the form of a slack jaw, his only reaction to the gliding, tumbling, and clopping crowd of guests getting out of their vehicles and making their way to the shining house. Beautiful gay men in suits led slender, attractive females up the walkway. Some men were wearing only tight shorts and no tops, opting for suspenders or body paint. A few yards ahead of them a drag queen in a flowing gown roared with laughter, her heels clapping up the rough cobblestones. The sea of guests flowed forward, blended in color, style, and texture, moved grandiosely toward the home's gaping, golden maw.

In the lush glow of this May evening, Nick thought of his father, thought of what sort of judgmental frown would cross his weathered features as the cacophony erupted all around them.

It was this thought and the scrutiny of all the eyes that appraised him as he approached the house that filled his young heart with an ominous feeling. Everyone was watching, and the stares were not benign, but transmitted judgement, calculated estimation. This was not simply a frivolous party but a test, even the white, blank home had eyes. Spectral pupils watched from every angle, from every shadow. Sweeping, judging, sizing up all those who crossed the threshold into The Gala. There was an unseen scale, putting all in attendance on a spectrum of good, better, best. The whole gay world seemed to be waiting, watching for Nick to prove his place among the gilded crowd.

This tense feeling was muted upon entering the foyer. The air trembled with the anticipation of the evening. Voices swirled in a symphony of laughter, song, popped champagne bottles, and raucous club music from the back porch.

The singular group, Jordan, Nick, Peter, and George, stayed just one moment together in the entry before they broke off in all directions. Nick watched anxiously as Jordan waved goodbye and disappeared down the hall. This particular evening his iteration was of a frat boy. He wore a loose, button-up shirt, open at the collar, exposing stray reddish-brown chest hairs. A backwards hat covered his thick mane of brown curls. His voice registered deeper than with Kinsey or Peter and George. Nick saw him stop near a group of athletic looking men and join their conversation. Peter and George disappeared like vapor into the throng around them.

Nick was alone for just a moment before his interest was pulled to the adjoining room. An intermittent pounding on a baby grand piano drew his attention to a group of men and women already deeply in the throes of their alcoholic spirits. They looked as if they had been rented with the house, natural extensions of the sofas and ottomans. Unlike the main foyer, blasted with golden light, this small sitting room was drenched in red furniture and draperies; the only light came from two small lamps at either corner of the room. Among the company, the odd one was the gentleman plucking at the piano. His interest in it was erratic, almost as if he kept forgetting the object was in front of him and upon recognizing its presence, found it impossible to avoid trying to play. The group did not illuminate the space like the visages of some of the others that Nick had seen making his way up to the house. Every one of their faces was bland and forgettable. Their clothes were dim and insipid, blurring into the darkness around them. Like pale ghosts they muttered incomprehensible incantations, their speech slurred and undulating under the burden of vodka, bourbon, and wine.

One of this party, a man in tweed sport coat and bowtie, called over to him. "Hey there," he said, teetering on the edge of the sofa. "How about getting us a few more drinks, kid?" He reached into his pocket and withdrew a five-dollar bill. "I'll give you a little tip!"

A woman, emerging from a crying fit, heavy mascara flared out around her eyes, snapped her fingers. "Don't harass the poor kid, Sid." She extended a jeweled hand outward. "Come sit with us!"

Nick inched into the room and stood on the outside of the dim little circle. All gathered turned in unison to see the new visitor to their marginalized corner of the celebration.

"You know Hedley?" the mascara woman asked. "I can't say any of us do."

"He's a wonderful guy!" A man in a fluorescent tank top cackled and fell forward off the ottoman on which he had been seated. His martini glass crashed on the floor, a sparkling, wet mess left on the marble tiles. "Oh – I need another one, don't I?" he asked matter-of-factly, not bothering to rise up, but crawling out of the room.

Mascara didn't seem to notice the crash or mess. Her eyes stared intently at Nick. "You know Hedley?" she asked again.

Nick shook his head.

"We've been trying to figure out which one he is, you know." She took a sip from her drink. "We heard he's remarkable, the son of some rich family out east. I guess he came to Chicago on business. Investments or something – finance?" The woman's eyes flicked behind Nick. "Excuse me, sweetie," she said clopping forward in stiletto heels. "Excuse me!" she called to a man standing in the foyer. "Hello! Do you know Hedley?"

Mascara otherwise engaged, Nick took the chance to escape, drifting silently out of the room and making his way down the main hall that Jordan had vanished down earlier. From behind him, he heard the odd man discover the piano again. The mashed chords of "O Come All Ye Faithful" provided the soundtrack for his exit.

The main entry hall ran straight back into a massive, open kitchen, beyond which was the party's featured event, the outdoor grand balcony and dance floor. Nick strove to get to through the raging kitchen crowd, a mess of men and women in varying states of drunken oblivion. Movement forward was slow and painful, the mash of bodies knocking him around. Twisting and weaving, he cut a small path through the tangled mass. When he passed the long, granite island in the middle of the room, he noted a young, shirtless gay trying to climb on top of it; his friends laughing maniacally were pulling him down. Around him people laughed, shouted, sang. Drinks were spilled with reckless abandon. Nick smiled, feeling the sticky contents pour over him. The pain of the crowd was ebbing as the infectiousness of the chaos began to take hold of him. French doors led outside to the massive, two-storied marble patio overlooking Lake Michigan. When Nick threw them open, the energy outside overwhelmed him.

All was darkness, mystery, and music. Other people were reduced to shadows, the only lights glow sticks and flashing strobes near the DJ. The sound of bass and thundering club music swallowed the voices of the enthusiastic crowd. The patio looked out on a rolling green lawn that plunged into the azure face of the lake. A group of muscled, bathing suit-clad men moved up the lawn from the cool water. Although all was dark on the back patio, below soft flood lamps shone, illuminating the bathers' wet bodies, giving their outlines a haloed, angelic appearance.

"Drink?"

Nick turned to face a handsome man wearing only a bowtie and underwear. His face was hidden behind a black mask.

"Um, yes, I –" Nick stammered.

The man handed him a flute of champagne and withdrew into the crowd. As he disappeared, he saw Jordan with another group of men, this entourage all wearing only suspenders holding up lycra shorts. He and Nick locked eyes and Jordan tipped his glass in salute. Nick raised his in response and smiled.

Beyond the physical, Jordan's tight, tawny body, rubbed against his own, there was something intriguing and genuine about his first gay friend in Chicago. Despite his choir of voices, his protean form around different people, the essence of Jordan remained constant. He was glib, sarcastic, and yet also allowed moments of emotional insight. After their first night together, he had kissed Nick on the cheek. "We'll call this the beginning of your gay education," he said throwing open his curtains, letting in the blaring May sun. "I never had a guide, so I would like to be yours as you get a footing in this weird, Halstedian World. Don't expect much from me in the way of a relationship, but I can be your friend."

They had slept together one other time that week. Completely spontaneous, they were watching television when Nick let his hand fall onto Jordan's knee. In moments they were peeled free of clothes and wrapped up in each other on the floor.

Nick had been with other boys, not to full consummation as he had with Jordan, but he had kissed and blown and writhed with other men. In the beginnings of his coming out, he still had the girth accumulated in high school and messaged people from the dark, secluded corner of his bedroom. In his first semester of college he started to use Grindr. His specialty had been blowjobs for older, closeted men in the small town in which he attended classes. These were decadent, shame-filled treats he cultivated every few weeks, when his libido was able to overthrow the shame of his hidden sexuality.

It was towards the end of his first year of college that he began to see the possibility of a life without this shame. He discovered that there was a group of young gay men with a club on campus. He found their website and clicked through the event photos. While not the sex gods he pleasured himself to on YouTube and in pornography, they were cute and, most importantly, living, breathing gay men. Under his searching touch he could imagine their bodies trembling, twitching and coming to life.

A photo in May of the graduating seniors with their event speaker triggered the beginning of Nick's transformation. Stewart Johnson, a stunningly beautiful graduate, had given a speech about life after graduation. Three years out of school he was a paragon of the hope of gay existence beyond the confines of their tiny town and college. A Facebook search revealed that Stewart had also once been overweight. The stunning monument of physical perfection was once as homely and encased in fat as Nick was staring at him on the computer. For Nick, it was an idea that an incarnate fantasy could have walked in his shoes, traced the same halls as him and breathed the same air, that set him free. It was a man with his history that proved his life could be rewritten. A wall collapsed and gave way. Nick had a glimpse of a new future, a new possibility of what he could become.

Over the course of months, pounds shed away. The fat of his face melted to reveal a strong jaw and bone structure. His diet was regulated fiercely and in time, his portly frame turned firm. Hidden beneath the layers of fat, Nick had the hearty build of a linebacker. He came to Chicago at the conclusion of his sophomore year of community college, his entire second year dedicated to fitness and grades. With an acceptance to DePaul in his pocket and his new body tightly fitted in tank tops, he considered this summer his debutante ball.

The mass of forms on the balcony began to shiver with life. Pounding rhythms thundered from the speakers on the side of the house, mixing with roars and shouts of laughter. Around Nick the percussive music of a party night added its track to the melee around him: the shatter of champagne flutes, sighs and mutters from passersby, and the faint, barely audible sparkle and fizz of the drinks around him.

Peter and George emerged from the swarming mass. Their shirts were unbuttoned, exposing their matching, manicured chests. Sweat streaked down their faces; the droplets twinkled like diamonds.

"Having fun, Nicholas?" Peter asked grabbing a drink from a passing waiter.

"This party is always the big explosion of summer!" George took the drink from Peter's hand and downed it himself. As the cool liquid flowed down his throat, his eyes followed a burly, hairy man who was weaving through the crowd.

"It's heaven, isn't it?" Peter continued. "Fireworks at midnight and on and on – I believe they don't end. They just go on all night!"

"Boom!" shouted George.

"Pow!" shrieked Peter.

They howled with laughter and vanished in a wave of bodies writhing to the music.

Nick turned his attention toward the lake again. The moon was a beautiful, pale white in the eastern sky. Its pure glow was reflected in the dark water. Above him stars shone down, creating ribbons of light that rippled across the lake's stern face.

"Beautiful, right?" A voice came from the darkness beside Nick. It tickled his ears, a masculine, susurrus barely audible in the din of music and human voices.

"It is. It's incredible…"

Nick turned to see the figure. Cloaked under the hood of a sleeveless sweatshirt, only half the man's face was visible in the moonlight. His arms were thin and toned, the sinew rippling as his fingers tapped the glass of champagne he held in his hand. In the half-light, Nick made out a bow-like mouth and glittering, green eyes. They glimmered from the hood with the deep, wild shine of leaves in a rainforest canopy.

"I wish the parties didn't have to be so deep in the night, though," the hooded man continued. "It's nice to be able to swim. When you're coming up out of the water toward the estate, the mansion takes on an entirely different look. She's less grandiose, more bucolic and haunting. Her face stares longingly at the lake." The green eyes swept over Nick's face and body. "I don't recall seeing you around before."

Nick stared at the man in silence.

A smile shone from the darkness of the hood. "New in town? You look young." He raised his champagne glass and took a short sip. "You're quite nice to look at. How do you know Hedley?"

"I don't," Nick said shortly. "I mean, my friends do. I just – have never had the chance to meet him." Nick hesitated; the brief silence filled with the rush of pulsing club music. "I am new in town. Just moved about a week ago."

"College?"

"Yes. I'm starting DePaul in August. I'll be a junior."

"Twenty-one?"

"Just turned a few months ago."

The man nodded, a knowing smile turning up the sides of his mouth. With a quick motion, he snapped off his hood, his full faced exposed in the moonlight. It was a striking visage. High cheekbones led down into a strong, virile jaw line. The structure of his face, neck, and body all appeared to be masterfully carved rather than compiled by the wild and entropic hand of nature. Although his corporeal form was sharply defined, it was his wild, verdant eyes that gave his presence the mysterious life that so enchanted all those he met. His eyes rippled with transient states of being – sadness, wisdom, mirth, judgment.

Nick swallowed, unable to remove his eyes from the man before him. "You're – you're him then?"

"Who him?" The man asked mockingly.

"Hedley him."

Hedley nodded almost imperceptibly and locked eyes with Nick. The younger man was entranced by their steady stare. Around him, the whole party faded away, the only things that existed in that moment were Hedley and himself, the look of Hedley's green eyes an enchanted thread that had pulled Nick out of the roar of the crowd.

"A little advice, friend," Hedley said softly, his voice barely audible in the jubilant roar of The Gala around them. "I think I should like to see you around more. However, you must not become static." Peter and George were in Hedley's periphery; a subtle gaze in their direction said more than any cutting remark about his cousin could. "What I mean to say is that you look like you could be one who is more than a side player in this little game." His fingers again twitched, tapping against the side of his glass. "You need to find the right people and cultivate your highest self. There are a number of ways to describe evolution: transfiguration, ascent, becoming. Think of it as transforming your mind, vision, and," his hand extended taking hold of Nick's arm, "body." A faint smile appeared over Hedley's pale face.

The statement was barely finished before Hedley vanished back into the crowd, his ghostly presence replaced by the warm touch of Jordan.

"Oh, my stars!" Jordan laughed exuberantly. His hand shook, spilling champagne on Nick's shirt. "An audience with Hedley! What did he say?" His eyes flashed, their normal tawny brown, but glazed with drink.

"What?" Nick looked after Hedley, the hooded man's words ringing in his ears. "Nothing. He just said hello."

"Hedley never just says hello."

"He said I was 'lovely.'"

Jordan laughed. "Our newbie! I can't believe it!" He crossed his arms and seemed to be deep in thought. "Well, I think maybe you need another lesson then." He looked around, grabbed Nick's hand, and proceeded to pull him through the crowd.

They reentered the illuminated mansion. The gay who had been trying to get atop the island in the kitchen had succeeded. He was dancing and pouring shots of liquor into awaiting mouths. In the main foyer the party's flotsam and jetsam were arranged in various poses around the room. Already this cast of characters was consumed in drunkenness. A man on the floor vomited in a pool at the foot of a stranger. His female companion roared with laughter.

"Messes," Jordan said raising an eyebrow. His eyes scanned the room and halted at the front entry. A group of four men had just entered. Jordan clutched Nick's arm, his lips pressed against his young friend's ear. "The coterie. If Hedley spoke to you, you may as well meet the rest."

Three of the men stood together. In Nick's head they brought to mind paper dolls all cut from the same mold but accessorized and colored in different iterations. They wore different colored tank tops and multi-colored pants of varying shades. Two of them had sunglasses, while the third was wearing a green scarf that circled his neck like a gossamer serpent. Their hairstyles were a few degrees different between them, the part and point of their sculpted ends facing in different directions. One of them looked slightly larger, his face darkened by slight stubble.

The fourth of the men stood somewhat to the side. He appeared a shade darker, almost a shadow of the other three. While the others' style and molding were cut with exact precision, this separated one had rougher edges. His thick frame seemed out of place in the chiseled, thin stalks of the others.

"That's The Hedley Set. Well," Jordan gently moved Nick to the side and out of the view of the four men, "the fourth one is new. Sooty mentioned him when we ran into him last weekend – Jonathan. He's made some strong moves up the social ladder."

"That's who you all are always talking about?"

"Yes." Jordan put his arm around Nick and began to steer him back out to the patio. "Skyler, Stephen, and Samson are the main three – the ones who seemed all connected together."

They came back outside to the dance. The crowd had regressed further, a mass of shirtless, sweaty bodies mingling on the dance floor. Nick was already able to pinpoint a few players from the Boystown World – Aaron and Todd gyrated in the middle of the exuberant crowd, Kinsey sat in a chair, fawning over a beautiful man with perfect, flowing hair. Night was fully around them, the stars and moon at full light, showering the gathered crowd in an alien glow. Nick briefly looked around for Hedley, but he was nowhere to be seen. The conversation with him had further fueled that appetite that had erupted after his first night with Jordan. This hunger had its beginnings in the first time he had seen Stewart Johnson and realized the possible trajectory of his life as a gay man. And now he had been chosen by Hedley. This stunning man had found him and opened up the sky, let Nick know he could rise, climb up, and sit among The Set and the other glittering jewels of the Boystown scene.

Lost in thought, he collided with a man in a baggy green shirt, spilling his drink all over the stranger's clothes.

"Oh! Sorry…" Nick instinctively reached out and patted the man's shirt with his hand.

"No, don't worry." The man gently tapped Nick's shoulder. "It's fine. Thought that would happen so I wore older clothes." He winked jovially at Nick and dabbed at the growing stain. "It always turns into a mess here."

"Hello, David." Jordan nodded politely.

"Oh! Jordan! It's good to see you." The chubby man reached out and gripped Jordan's hand. "I guess we've all been hibernating this winter. Time to come out of the woodwork and be sloppy."

"Yeah, how are…things?" Jordan asked coyly.

"Things are fine. Going."

David and Jordan locked eyes for a moment and then turned away. David's gaze flicked to the door as The Set entered the party. He covered his mouth as if to cough. "I should go," he said quickly. "You boys have fun!"

In an instant, he had disappeared into the crowd.

"That's Jonathan's ex," Jordan said raising and eyebrow. "Jonathan obviously used to have a little different standard."

Nick watched David as he disappeared into the crowd. Jordan lightly touched Nick's arm, grazing his skin with his fingertips.

"Why don't we enjoy the party together?" He leaned in closer, his lips barely touching Nick's ear. "Follow me."

Jordan led Nick into the heart of the pulsing mob. Deftly, he reached down and plucked the buttons open on Nick's shirt, exposing his chest to the summer breeze. He then leaned in grabbing Nick in a tight embrace.

Nick still felt the words of Hedley in his ears, tracing down his spine, fusing into him, rippling in his heart, his bones, his blood.

Transfiguration.

Ascent.

Around them the lithe bodies of others gyrated to the music. Some of the party was gone, lost in a haze of molly and ecstasy. Others fell onto each other, their faces locked in feverish and carnal kisses. As Jordan moved closer, Hedley's words reverberated through Nick's body. He began to look around and see the others, differentiate them one by one. In the quivering mob he saw men, more beautiful, more striking than Jordan. By the light of the moon, Jordan's form diminished in these other men's light. In the mysterious shadow of Hedley's cloak, the darkness and the fierce, wild eyes, Nick had glimpsed his future. The sounds of the lake and the quiver and sigh of the stars were lost in the forceful rush of music and screams and bodies.

Four

Post-Hedley's Gala Nick's social circle burst open like a firework, a great cacophonous and variegated herd of new gays entering his life in the brunches and golden afternoons of early June. Some of them carved out niches and others left, ghosts in the shimmering lights of Halsted Street.

Throughout those opening weeks, he met Simon and Jordan Jenkins, once important in Chicago, but they migrated to New York to take their place in the more elite social circles of the Upper East Side. Simon and Art Goldberg informed him of the small but very forceful and boisterous Jewish community thriving under the "yuppie pretentious mass" of Minibar and Progress. Sam Clemens, Jorge Gonzalez, and Marshall Finnerman were an establishment to the further northlands of Uptown and Edgewater. Their Fourth of July party was of particular importance; they would take out Sam's older brother's boat for an afternoon on Lake Michigan.

Jack Freeman was new on the scene, a senior at Northwestern in journalism. He penned articles for the local gay rag magazine and hung about the outskirts with a group of gays of marginal importance in occasional Boystown drama. Deborah Marth was a mother hen in her early forties. A figurehead at all the biggest gay parties, she had the body of a twenty-year old, and high, blond hair that made all the local drag queens jealous. Donnie and Tibbs were a Tweedle Dee and Tweedle Dum pairing that prowled bars at closing time. In those wild wastes, they would be waiting, like wolves, to take the night's refuse home. Between all of these figures, Lawrence Soot was ever-present, always peeping his wide eyes out from the fringe; there was nary a party that summer Jordan and Nick attended that his presence wasn't noted.

While Nick's life had become subsumed by social obligations, Peter and George had secured him a job at a gym in the heart of Boystown to pay bills and keep him entertained during daylight hours. The staff had proven to be a microcosm of the entire gay world that he had come to inhabit: a small group of trainers, the elite, mixed amongst lesser beings, who strived to be noticed by the trainers' cold gazes. With their gym-hardened bodies, the trainers passed by Nick at his check-in desk, no recognition on their faces as their blank, white keycards passed over the turnstiles to allow them in. These small rebukes built up in Nick. The words of Hedley at The Gala, recognition of Nick's beauty and potential, turning over and over like a leaf in a fall wind: transfiguration, ascent. He watched all of the boys at the gym, the pawns in this great game of gay chess, entering the turnstiles, working out, sweating, driving themselves toward the pinnacle of some great abstraction of aesthetic perfection. The goals of this constant upward momentum had become clear to Nick in the corners and stages of Mini, Progress, and Scarlet – in wild, cheap-drink infused Sunday afternoons at Roscoe's. He watched, with his searching green eyes, the others, their stares, their sighs, their admiration. When one entered, one was seen, registered, and calculated. The eyes of Hedley's Gala House didn't disappear with the ending of the party, but rather diffused, spread, and took on life in the shadows of the bars up and down Halsted.

Through their gaze the world of Halsted became a ledger, with those men in the black and those in the red. People like his cousin, Peter, were doomed to be smoke and support on the stage of this Boystown drama. Their age and partnership limited them from fulfilling any greater destiny. The toothing and clawing of others in Peter and George's social caste to retain their power and prestige was manifested in Soot, his pulled face and manicured hands. It was a constant state of motion that kept this kind of man within the relevant social spheres, while others had merely to exist, to spin, their gravity pulling on all those around, them.

In light of Hedley's speech, Nick had begun to see himself as one of these sources of gravity. Like in one of his online adventure games, the sage had spoken to him and given him a quest. Despite this, the subtle sleights of Nick by the gorgeous men at the gym had made him very aware that, while his physical transformation had been substantial in the past year, it wasn't enough. Satisfaction with his current physical iteration was an open admonition that he was satisfied with support and stagnation; it was not motion, ascent. In the back of his mind, he continued to build the perfect idea of himself; what had begun with Stewart Johnson, now morphed, swelled into something larger, uncontrolled. He had work to do to meet the expectation that he was slowly building within himself, the standards set by all those judgmental eyes that reflected light from Halsted's darkness. Until he arrived at the fulfilment of this vague dream, he knew he had to remain to the side, biding his time until he was ready to unveil something perfect.

With this in mind, he put his machinations to work, pulling closer to a number of the trainers who did not exist so centrally in the gay social circle. These men with thick, muscular bodies, smiled at him as they entered and talked about their partners and family in small exchanges between the beeping of the keycard and the spin of the turnstile. In a matter of a week he had secured a workout partner, a taught, mid-twenties spin instructor. The instructor doled out workouts, helped push Nick in the gym, and prescribed food choices that would build up his physique.

In tandem with the physical, Nick was absorbing all he could culturally from Jordan during their evenings together. The cultural aspect of his Halsted life was bifurcated between the cultures of the community of Boystown and the Gay Community proper. It was Jordan, who between their physical engagements, watched Drag Race and Top Model, who put on Kylie and also made him aware of the pulsing, sonic rush of EDM. Whenever they went out, Jordan put a hand behind Nick, propelled him forward to meet and exchange kiss-cheek greetings with the endless, overlapping circles of the Boystown social scene. At the conclusion of these greetings Jordan would pull him to the side, giving his standard heritage listing of relationships and team connections, and ultimately, their scaled proximity to Hedley:

"You met Alex, who is actually Daniel's ex, but if given the choice, which you will be, you will have to choose Alex. He's a bartender and knows all the members of The Set. If you get in with him, I can guarantee you free drinks at Replay all day."

All the while, Tweets coming through the Boystown feed became moments of instruction as Jordan listed out the importance of each tagged person. In the weeks between The Gala and Pride, the newsfeed had dried up slightly, however, it began to pick up again as June faded and summer came to its full climax.

"I assume whoever runs it has been permanently drunk since Memorial Day," Jordan said one morning when a Saturday night had unveiled no new information or gossip.

As Jordan and Nick drew closer, Nick became aware of Jordan's own precarious orbit, his shimmering, tentative existence within the transient universe of Boystown. At twenty-six, he had already shown signs of weakening resolve within the social circles. Aware of everything, he did not seem particularly connected to anything. On evenings when Peter and George would text about the next themed night at Sidetrack, there would be moments of hesitation. Jordan would look briefly out his small window into the maudlin glow of Boystown's neon lights.

"Tuesdays should be a night for staying in..." he'd say, doing his signature lip bite. But the phrase would barely be uttered before he quickly dove into his closet for a perfect pair of shoes to match his neon tank top. These pauses, these hitches forced Nick to re-estimate his closest companion. Hedley had made it clear to him that devotion to the scene must be total.

One afternoon, after an intense two-hour workout with the spin instructor, Nick stepped out of the gym and into the street. The early June sun was smoldering in the eastern sky, the wind of summer rustling the leaves and potted flower boxes of hydrangeas that flanked Broadway Street. Staring intently into his phone at a message from Jordan, he didn't notice that he was on a collision course with Myrtle.

"Oh!" she shrieked.

Nick looked into her face, still covered in the smatterings of makeup from the night before. She wore a heavy, grey sweatshirt selected to cover a tight top and short skirt worn to go out the previous evening. Her left hand was extended, holding a cigarette, her mascara-streaked eyes blinked twice as they looked at Nick. Gone was the faded movie star of their first meeting, in her place was the dancer who had let herself go, shuffling across the stage of an Off-Off-Off-Off-Broadway production. A fog of hangover clouded her malformed sentences.

"Look at you! The little one." She took a drag and smiled. Her eyes rolled to the horizon. "Hot," she said shortly.

"It is."

"Isn't it?" She licked her lips. "What are you doing? Interested in brunch? It's just me and Sooty. You know Soot?"

"Yes."

"Come!" Myrtle looked at her phone. "No one else is coming. You should come." Her eyebrows lifted slightly. As if just realizing she was in the sunlight, she plunged a hand into her purse and pulled out a pair of dark sunglasses. Once upon her face, she again looked at Nick. Her expression pulled itself into a pathetic, pleading manifestation: raised eyebrows, a quick flick of her tongue over her lips, tensed knuckles. The subtle yet sad gesture convinced Nick to join.

Myrtle grabbed his arm, guiding him down the street about a block to where her car was illegally parked. It was a small, eco-friendly sedan in butterscotch. Its paint still gleamed, however, along the side, small dents and scratches were cut into the pleasant surface, marring its starry shine. Three tickets wavered under her windshield. Myrtle tsked as she retrieved them and tossed them into the back of the car.

"Fuckers," she said tossing down her cigarette. "Fucking fuckers."

Her body fell into the car as Nick slid into the passenger seat. With a soft whir the engine purred to life and pulled them onto Lake Shore, the emerald waters of Lake Michigan sparkling in the late morning light.

"Thank gawd I ran into you," Myrtle said bracing the steering wheel between her knees so she could draw out another cigarette. "I love Soot, of course, but one-on-one he is so," she paused in lighting her cigarette to ponder. No thought came, however, and the sentence ended in ambiguous silence. "Hedley was supposed to meet us," she continued abruptly, "but he had something come up. A dick up his ass, I believe." Myrtle chirped – her laugh a piercing array of notes. Her eyes flashed to Nick to be sure that he had found the comment amusing.

The mention of Hedley caused his heart to lift momentarily in his chest. His breath slightly quickened. "Where are we going?" he asked.

"Oh, Tweet. It's fabulous." Myrtle signaled, and swerved into the far-left lane. "Delicious, gluten-free options, an 'absolute must' for Soot." She scornfully shook her head. "He's on a diet, I guess. He wants a beach body. Can you believe the old fart wants to look good on the beach? He should just pack it in."

On the right, they passed a golf course, just further on a harbor with small boats gently rolling with the movement of the lake. A large black tower stared at them sinisterly from further down the coast, while beside them, on the median, trees shook in the wind, their leaves spasming in the breeze, glittering silver and green in the bright June light.

"Tweet's kind of between Edgewater and Uptown," Myrtle said. "Have you ever been this far north? It's almost Wisconsin." She cackled and whipped her car around a cab moving slowly in the far-left lane.

Edgewater, to Nick, was a foreign country, some large tract of forgotten territory on the city's north side. It stood as a faraway haze beyond the drunken, debaucherous glow of Wrigleyville's neon lights and the wild, whispered crimes of Uptown. As they pulled off the exit, Nick looked at the cornucopia of characters: a gaggle of gays in pinks and yellows, an old woman with a walker, shuffling resiliently across the street, an African-American woman standing with groceries waiting for the traffic light to change. The buildings themselves were a many-colored coat of diversity. An Art Deco building stared contemptuously at a McDonald's across the street.

"It's a mess up here," Myrtle said dumping cigarette ash out the window. "Gays retire. Some kooks from the closed nuthouses wander around screaming. I hear some girl was robbed, shot in the head right off of Bryn Mawr a few years ago."

The light flashed green and Myrtle slammed on the accelerator. After only a block she hit the brakes, parking in a small spot between a Mercedes and an old minivan.

Soot was waiting for them inside the restaurant. Despite the June heat, he wore a suit jacket and scarf tied around his neck. His smile pulled tightly at the corners of his chemically injected face.

"Darlings!" His papery lips touched their cheeks. "Such a divine pleasure. Dee-vine!" He took Nick's hand and pressed it in his clammy palm.

"Sorry we're late. I'm so hungover," Myrtle said.

"Not a worry!" Soot handed out the menus. "We'll get you fixed up in no time. And you!" Soot leered at Nick. "It's been a bit. It looks like you're beefing up. I like it." Soot licked his lips. "Ronny said he's been seeing you at the gym."

"I work there," said Nick.

"How wonderful! You probably know Marly, Zaxston, and Frederick then."

The names struck harshly against Nick's ears. He knew these boys, the taut, rippling forms that passed by him, silently, disinterestedly, with the click of the turnstile.

"They are all people to know," Soot went on. "We all gather 'round Hedley when it's possible. We have so much fun together."

"You and Hedley are close?" Nick asked. Soot and Hedley's orbits overlapped, always crossing but never quite connecting.

"Oh." Soot dabbed his mouth with his napkin. "We go back quite a while. He's such an amazing person." The old dandy looked down at his phone. Gingerly, he tapped the screen, hiding the most recent notifications.

Myrtle sighed. "Can a girl get some coffee?" she asked.

"Take mine." Soot slid his mug across the table.

The waitress came and took their orders. Soot peppered the conversation with a vast cornucopia of names, places, and events:

"But you know I ran into David at The Gala. He doesn't look so good, if you ask me...Kinsey is still talking about the Lloyd thing, you know, offhandedly, like the little ornery girl he is...I can't believe we're creeping toward the middle of summer, there's so much to do and I'm on a committee for one of the Market Days booths..."

At the first possible break in conversation, Myrtle rose. "Now it's time to shit," she said standing and quickly staggering toward the restroom.

Soot watched her leave. As soon as she was out of earshot, his neck twisted with alarming speed. A tight smile spread over his waxy features.

"Nicky! I'm so glad to run into you. What are you doing the second weekend in July?"

Nick and Jordan had briefly discussed a trip to the botanical gardens around that time, but those plans vanished under the eerie glow of Soot's smile. "I don't think anything," Nick said.

"Oh, well, how would you like to help me out?"

"How?"

"There's a little fundraiser in Lake View. It's to raise money for," Soot paused and looked slightly confused for a moment, "an important cause," he abruptly finished. "Anyway, it's a white party and we hire servers to go around and take orders. Would you be interested in being a server?"

"Sure."

"Well, it's..." Soot winked, "a white party, so you'd be asked to wear a white Speedo and a bowtie. And that's it."

Nick's eyebrows arched.

"I mean, you can think about it. But everyone is going to be there, and it'd be a wonderful opportunity to help a good cause and meet some new people."

Nick slid his hand over his stomach feeling the slight bulge. In his gaining of muscle, a small layer of fat had accumulated around his midsection. "You think I'd look okay?" he asked hesitantly.

"Oh, darling," Soot dramatically threw back his head and laughed. "You're gorgeous. You'll be young and perfect."

When Myrtle reappeared at the table, the discussion turned to other events of the summer. A brief recap of Hedley's party and fond reminisces of the evening brought Soot's time to end.

"I must away my ducklings," he said leaving a twenty on the table. "Important business to attend to!" He rose, a cloud of light dust from his hair product rising into the air as he adjusted his quaff. "Ciao, ciao!"

Once he was gone, Myrtle relaxed, her shoulders drooping and her mouth forming into a contented smile.

"I do like Soot, but brunch with him is so much work," she said. "He must have been out last night with Hedley and them, he wasn't probing me for information like he usually does."

"You know Hedley?"

"Better than any of these other queens. We went to high school together."

Nick's ears perked. "So, you're really good friends?"

"Yes," Myrtle's smile grew wider for a fleeting moment. "I mean, we were closer in high school. He wasn't *Hedley* then."

"What do you mean?"

"He wasn't always like he is now." Myrtle raised her hand at the passing waitress. Once another Bloody Mary was set down in front of her, she leaned back in her chair and began.

When Myrtle had been young and in Hedley's circle, he had been Hank Turner from Kokomo, Indiana. In his earlier days, he had been a rather unimpressive and innocuous character within the local high school. He and Myrtle had become fast friends in the marching band, him playing the trumpet and her the clarinet. During those adolescent years, his family had been very Catholic. Hedley was in the closet, very aware of his predicament and confiding in Myrtle their junior year that he was gay and intended on coming out and living free as soon as he started at Indiana University.

Their friendship remained consistent throughout their university days. In their third year, Hank invited her over to a party at his parents' home. It was at this fete that he introduced her to his first boyfriend, a very handsome boy with blond hair and wireframe spectacles. The boy was from New York and had met Hank in a history course. As young Hank droned on about his beloved, Myrtle realized she had never seen him in such a state of ecstatic happiness. He had deified the boy during their short courtship and spoke of his great deeds and acts as if he were some Biblical hero. It was in that short time that Hedley confessed that he had only been with the boy for a short time, but it wasn't out of the realm of possibility that this boy was the one. The only one.

Months passed with Myrtle not hearing much from her high school friend. They discussed meeting just before school started, but their schedules never lined up, and Hank was going to visit his boyfriend in New York. As the school year started, she began to miss his presence. During Christmas break she tried relentlessly to get a hold of him: email, phone, Facebook, all avenues proved to be dead ends. She noticed that his Facebook account had gone silent several weeks before she had tried to reinitiate contact. After almost a month of sporadic attempts to contact him, she finally called his parents the weekend before Christmas to see if perhaps he had changed his phone number or grown ill.

Hank's parents responded that, while Hank had been fine, he had a rough time with the break up with his boyfriend. They would most definitely let him know to call whenever he had the chance.

A few more months passed and there was very little news from Hank or his parents. No call had ever come and Myrtle sensed that this was the end of a friendship.

She tried a few more emails and texts and when she was met with silence, she was incensed and decided it was best to leave him alone and bury their friendship.

It was almost five years later that Myrtle moved to Chicago and their paths crossed again. She and a gay coworker had become Facebook friends, and one of his comments had appeared in her newsfeed. The comment was regarding the cobbled torso of an attractive male.

Looking good!

Myrtle, wondering who this man was, clicked on his profile and was bewildered when the picture came up full size on her screen. Gone was the short, thin boy that played trumpet in her high school band. In his place was a chiseled, statuesque man, abs clearly defined, face framed by a perfect quaff of auburn hair. At first, she had assumed that this man was a Hank look-a-like, but one profile picture gave the game away, a family shot with his mother, father, sister, and nephew. The rest were a variety of pictures of Hank, now Hedley, in various revealing outfits, showing off his perfect body. A link to Instagram soon revealed him posing in various scenes around the globe, his perfect torso exposed, his radiant smile shining out of groups of similarly perfectly constructed men.

She immediately messaged him, saying how wonderful and happy he looked and asked if they could get coffee. They did a few weeks later, Hank/Hedley a vision of calm. The goofy boy of youth had been replaced by a serious, driven man.

"But it was weird," Myrtle said shaking her empty Bloody Mary glass. "Even though we were getting coffee, even though he was there – Hank – it felt like it was someone completely different." Her eyes clouded as she looked into the distance. "When I went home that day I felt like I'd lost someone. I never expected him to text a week later and invite me to his first Gala. When we met there, he hugged me and said it was nice to see me, but it wasn't him, you know." Myrtle put down her glass and looked into Nick's eyes. "It just felt like I had met someone new. He didn't mention anything about home or our high school times. Everything was present and what was happening then." Myrtle shrugged. "We still never talk like we used to, but we see each other. We visit."

At the conclusion of her story, Myrtle played with the ice at the bottom of her glass. Her eyes lifted and searched Nick, expectantly.

"Hedley seems like an interesting person," he said.

Myrtle appeared not to hear. In an erratic movement, her hand flew across the table and gripped Nick's. Her mouth formed into a crooked smile, the expression cutting a pained line in her pale face.

"What do you say we live like Hedley then? We let memory be memory. The only line that cuts forward is here and now." Her eyes glazed and lost focus. Releasing her grip, she fell back into her chair. "I mean the past is just a wound, anyway, isn't it?"

Nick thought briefly of the shadows cast by his father, by others, the undulating skyline of his past: valleys, troughs, deep, jagged cuts in a naked sky. He thought of his own form, nebulous, disgusting, of his new shapely figure, lithely flowing through a crowd of beautiful men at Soot's party. It seemed right to let that pained, formless history fall away. In its place appeared a horizon flooded with the light of a blood red dawn.

Nick tenuously extended his hand and lightly gripped Myrtle's. "History is bunk," he said smiling.

Myrtle responded by squeezing his hand. The act, in that moment, the signature on some sacred pact forged between them.

Five

Jordan and Nick's relationship unfolded leisurely as the summer moved on. Many afternoons and evenings were spent together; sex became a ritual in their social interactions. With coaching and practice, Nick began to understand more mechanics. While Jordan started the summer viewing their affair as light and airy, Nick took each moment as a serious chance for learning, an opportunity to experiment and probe the mysteries and depths of Jordan's lithe body. It was a surprise to Jordan that in the early mornings of Saturday and Sunday, Nick's small, dense body not beside him, that a pang of some unknown and illogical emotion rippled through him, like a drip of rain on a placid lake. At the Pride Parade he felt a sense of propriety over Nick as he strutted in front of a group of gay men in the volleyball league. There was a rush of unchecked emotion that swept across his visage as he admired the newly formed cuts and contours in Nick's gym-hardened body. It was at the parade that he, for the first time, noted that over the six weeks since he had known him, Nick had altered greatly. It wasn't just the transforming physique, but a new confidence, an air and quality that he had not noted the first time they met. In their quiet moments together at his home, Jordan had not picked up this tremor in the landscape. It was only staring at him from afar, his drink raised to his lips that he noted the new swagger, the puffed chest and purposefully masculine stance.

Jordan's eyes were locked on Nick and an early-thirties gentleman as they conversed quietly at the Pride party; it was the same man that had been hurt in the infidelity discussed at the Kinsey party Nick's first night in Chicago. Terrence, cuckolded, but forgiving, had only recently come back to the gay scene. He and Lloyd had mended their relationship. Terrence confided in Nick that it had been a mistake on Terrence's part to get upset. They were part of the new era, the new age, when sexual promiscuity was no longer a moral impropriety but a right exercised by a male in a homosexual relationship. Even though same-sex marriage was just made the law of the land, it didn't mean they had to follow the same patterns as the previous generations.

"It makes sense, I suppose," said Terrence, looking between Nick and Soot. "We are evolving – morality is evolving and it was very Victorian of me to get so upset." Terrence said this, his eyes glazed and far off. It hadn't been his topic of conversation, but Soot's, who had been dying to find out the whole story since it was discovered that, during the course of the affair, Kinsey and Lloyd had spent an entire week together in Cabo with the excuse that Lloyd was at a conference.

Nick stood with Soot and Terrence by the window of a newly renovated condo off of Broadway. It was a very small and elite party that had been invited. It was just shy of noon, the parade only beginning. Outside the roars of drunken revelers pulsed against the brick buildings.

"We all couldn't believe you weren't furious," Soot goaded. "I mean a friend and within the same circle." Soot pulled out a handkerchief and delicately rubbed his nose. "I mean, regardless of morality, it's the propriety of it, you know. You don't shit where you eat." Soot raised his glass and chuckled merrily.

Terrence turned his attention to Nick. "It's complicated, the whole gay thing, isn't it?"

Soot smiled his cadaverous smile. "He wouldn't know, Terry. He's a newbie. Little Nick just moved to Chicago this summer to start school. He's not quite as submerged in the gay life as you or me."

"Oh," Terrence's face brightened slightly. "So, you're not really in the scene yet?"

"He's been to quite a few events this summer," Soot interjected.

Terrence appeared not to hear this interruption. "Nick," he said purposefully addressing the younger man, "how do you like it? Chicago?"

"It's been good. Jordan has shown me around. We went to Hedley's party a few weeks ago."

"I heard it was fun – overdone, but it's Hedley, of course."

"It was a triumph!" Soot raised his hand as if to begin a long discourse.

Terrence, gently, interrupted. "That seems a grand claim, Sooty," he said, without looking at the older man. "Nick, what did you think?"

A look of dejection flickered over Soot's face. With an arch of his manicured eyebrows, he turned away. "Looks like I could use another drink..." he mumbled crossing out of the room.

Terrence watched him leave. "Soot loves being the center of all things."

Nick nodded in understanding. Soot had always been an innocuous part of their social gatherings. In party situations he hovered and contributed vague insights and brought up new restaurants and bars that everyone should try. Everyone realized that Soot stood in a precarious position, teetering on the edge of obscurity. Most recently he had rushed into CrossFit classes, a rabid attempt to tone up and get further in, further entrenched in the kingdom in which he had so long been at court.

"So, Nick, you just came out?" Terrence asked earnestly.

"Kind of," Nick said. "I'm out here but my whole family doesn't know."

"I struggled in my own coming out," Terrance said. "Father..." he trailed off.

"Luckily my cousin is Peter Gentry. He lives on Halsted. He's out and has been helping me get used to it."

"Yes!" Terrence smiled, recovering from his brief melancholy. "I use to play softball with Peter. He and George are very nice."

Nick nodded. In the tableaux of the party, Terrence's glimmering eyes, his rebuffs of Soot, made a small tremor in the otherwise stagnant fresco of their surroundings. This divergence could have been the reckless acts of the cuckold. Terrence had been marked in the community by his boyfriend's actions and now stood unsexed, humiliated, in front of them all. Already separated, he perhaps had begun to relish his newfound deviance from the tight social strata.

"Have you had a chance to meet Sal yet?" Terence asked, his eyes sparkling. "Peter and George know him very well. He's a really wonderful older gay man. He's seen it all, really. He was a teacher in Chicago in the 70's. Came out... You can imagine what that was like."

"Someone at Kinsey's mentioned him, I think. Clive, maybe."

"Hmmm," Terrence put his finger to his lips. "Are your days very busy this summer?"

"Not too busy. I work at the gym three or four days a week."

"Would you want to do coffee with me next week? We can go up to Andersonville into Sal's shop. It's a wonderful little bookstore." Terrence flicked his eyes to the window; the din of the earlier crowds was growing into a roar. "I think you'd like Sal."

Nick felt indifference regarding the invitation. In the weeks since Hedley's party his understanding of the social world had transformed. Hedley's words and the vision of male beauty and movement at The Gala had catalyzed a transformation in his spectrum. People now pulsed at the frequency of their social class, their form and function within the microcosm of Halsted Street. Terrence had only recently arrived and had not generated any esteem. If anything, his difference, his recklessness seemed dangerous to Nick's rapidly evolving vision.

"Let me give you my number," Terrence said getting out his phone. "You ready?"

The two exchanged numbers and then Terrence politely withdrew from the room. Upon his exit, Jordan sidled up to Nick, putting his hand on the small of Nick's back.

"Hey," he said into his ear.

The stir of warm breath brought Nick to arousal.

"Hey," Nick said.

Jordan kissed Nick's neck and then playfully nipped his ear. "Saw you talking to Terrence. Are you two banging?"

The question hung in the air for just a brief moment. Jordan's hold on Nick's back loosened slightly.

"No," Nick said after the pause had grown heavy. "He wants me to grab coffee with him next week."

"Probably revenge on Lloyd for his indiscretion." Jordan had taken a step back. He bit his lip.

"We're supposed to meet some guy named Sal," Nick said. Sensing Jordan's awkwardness, he drew closer.

"Sal…" Jordan said softly. His eyes looked up and met Nick's. He had felt a slight tremble in their connection, a cloud passing over the sun he believed shone on their coupling. Something in Nick's eyes, however, calmed his beating heart, emolliated the small wound that opened in the pregnant pause. "Well," Jordan said regaining his composure, "he can tell you more about gay history in Chicago than anyone else. He's lived it. He's a walking memory."

Outside the noise of the parade thundered. Screams and shouts filled the space around them bounding through the open windows.

"You know," Nick said, gently tracing a finger over Jordan's chest, "this would be a good time for me to kiss you."

Jordan looked into Nick's eyes. It was a brief moment of peace in a relationship that was beginning to churn with the motion of the two bodies within it. Even in the glitter of Nick's green stare, Jordan perceived darker times ahead. But with the touch of their bodies, the soft caress of Nick's lips, the phantom moment was gone. In its place was love, fleeting and trembling, but present in the space around them. Its tepid music drifted from their embrace, its melody all but consumed by the thunderous screams of crowds celebrating the holiday of gay liberation.

#

At Jordan's urging, Nick met with Terrence to make the acquaintance of Sal. They arrived at Sal's shop on a Wednesday afternoon. The unpredictable Chicago summer had turned cool again, the boiling heat of the end of June transformed into a chilled, windswept July day. Sal was outside his small bookshop, his full rear raised to the sky as he sorted through a pot of geraniums on the front stoop of the store. When the old man heard their approach, he turned, his wrinkled features bursting into a wide smile. Enthusiastically, he opened his arms and pulled Terrence into a close embrace.

"Terrance! How are you?" His voice, to Nick's surprise, still held its fair notes of youth. Its timbre trembled, but the tones were soft and light. It sounded as if it were lifted, musical, despite the sagging weight age and time had waged on the rest of his heavy body. "And," he turned to Nick, "this must be the new one." Sal took Nick's hand in his own. "Sal," his eyes twinkled. "It's very nice to meet you."

Nick felt his face crack into a smile, the indifferent mask he had begun to wear in the social circles of Boystown flaking slightly under the luminous visage of the older man. Just like Sal's voice, his smile and face held the notes and graces of youth. His eyes, especially, seemed to transcend time and space, shining orbs that echoed Sal as he was, as he had been, as he would be.

The smile opened more broadly across Nick's face. "It's nice to meet you," he said.

Dusting his hands on his khaki trousers, Sal waved them inside. "Please!" he called. "Let's go in. I've got tea waiting for us."

The three entered a small, dusty room. Although aged and generally unkempt, the space was filled with light from the windows. The bookshelves were crowned with ivy, their green leaves cascading down, twisting and writhing over tomes of ancient leather and faded paperbacks. Mixed amongst the piles of books other plants were scattered – huge, overflowing potted flowers in a variety of scarlet, cerulean, and lavender. From the back of the shop a radio played soft notes of classical music. A strong breeze blew from front to back, making a few of the books open, their pages dancing in the dim light.

"Sugar? Honey?" Sal's slow steps clopped from behind the counter where he poured from a hotpot, yellowed with age. "I've got everything, so just tell me what you want."

"Milk and honey," Terrence said. He turned to stare at a vase of daisies. "The place looks nice, Sal. Are these flowers new since the last time?"

"Yes! You know I switch them every few weeks. The old ones I take to the retirement home over on Ashland and Foster." He turned and winked at his guests. "I'll be there soon, so hopefully I'm paying it forward."

Staring at the piles of books, the thought of anyone shopping in the ancient store seemed a farce to Nick. A fine coat of dust hung over the volumes entombed in the old bookshelves. The glimmering shine of a cobweb was visible in one corner of the room, its sparkling threads slung over a stack of old coffee table books. The windows alone were clean, a blast of July sun breaking into the room and lighting the dusty floorboards.

"Nick, how about you?" Sal asked, shuffling between the hotpot and his grand desk. "Would you like anything extra in yours?"

"I don't want tea, thanks."

"I suppose I should have some...what? Spritzers? Cocktails? I hear there was quite the array of drinks at Hedley's last month."

"I wouldn't know," Terrence said indifferently. His eyes were absorbed in deciphering the faded lettering on an old book's spine. "Nick was there."

"How was it, Nick?" Sal's asked. "Was it the extravaganza it always is?"

Nick rubbed the dust off of a book with his finger. "It was really cool. I've never seen so many gay men anywhere. Compared to where I'm from it was like being on the moon."

"I suppose it would be." Sal shuffled over to Terrence with his cup of tea. "I like Hedley. He is a modern gay but maintains some of that wild, extravagant, old-school queen in him. Probably not in appearance, but in function. His parties are camp."

"Camp," Terrence smiled. "That's a good word. It's like they're pretending to be themselves. They want to be the party they already are – they try so hard. It's a reflection of a reflection."

Nick thought for a moment on Terrence's observation. The idea of the party being anything other than itself, a perfect form of a party, was incomprehensible. In his mind, he tacitly added this to the list of items already against Terrence: his rebuffs of Soot, his detached air, his cuckolded standing at the Pride party.

"But it was fun, Nick?" Sal asked earnestly. "You had a good time?"

"Yes," Nick said. "I met a lot of people."

"Sooty and The Set and a bunch of others." Terrence took a sip of tea. His eyes caught Sal's for a moment, their exchange a silent, earnest commiseration.

"They're a fun group." Sal motioned for them to follow him. "Come on out back. There's at least a place to sit."

The three paraded around the old desk and out a back door that lay concealed behind a faded wall hanging. The colors worn, it displayed The Birth of Adam from The Sistine Chapel.

Sal caught Nick looking and chuckled softly. "One of my favorite pictures – meaningful and artistic. But also, let's face it, Adam and God are kind of hunks."

He pinned the hanging back so that he could clearly see into the store, should there be visitors.

Outside there was a small patio drenched in the perfume of flowers. The sun was blocked by a large, rainbow-colored parasol. It was in an alley, the small deck surrounded by garbage cans. The scenery was a cobbled wall of variegated bricks; the alley led down to a vanishing point of square blue sky.

"It's not much," Sal laughed, "but it will let us feel the breeze."

Sal let his weight come to rest on a small wrought iron chair, looking into the store. Nick and Terrence took seats to his right and left.

"Sal, I thought Nick would get a kick out of some of your old stories. He's already seen Halsted. He probably doesn't know much about what it used to be."

"Oh," Sal laughed. "Nick, you know how the bars down Halsted have all those manicured garden boxes and awnings roped in glittering lights?"

Nick nodded.

"Imagine walking down that street – blacked out windows and unmarked doors. No one wanted to be seen. In the 1970's it was all a secret, a well-known one, but a secret. When Sidetrack opened in 1982, everything was still sign-less. They had beer cases for seating, for heaven's sake." Sal looked thoughtfully into the dimness of the store. "With marriage equality and all the celebrations last weekend, you wouldn't think of that old Sidetrack. You wouldn't know it was a bastion of that forgotten time, with its new bleached floors and shining, stainless fixtures. But it was." The old man sighed. "It was."

Something in this history, the blacked-out windows and boarded facades, reopened Nick's own story. It awakened the girthy boy of his distant youth; the echoes of history turned on the light of that secluded room that he had longed to forget. The shame of those dark bars told a story that spoke to his sunken self. A voice that vibrated at a pitch that the isolated, rebuked high school soul understood more clearly than the gilded, bass-thumping roar of Hedley's lakeside Gala. The history he had agreed to bury with Myrtle rose, undead, and paced a tenuous path through his whole being, left small, shadowed footprints on the case of his heart.

"I can imagine..." he said softly. "It must have been awful."

Sal shook his head. "Oh, it was bad in its way, but we all found each other, made new families. I lived in Lake View, that's where the bookshop used to be. It was a place for kids to come visit, ones who didn't have a home after they came out."

"I know you know Clive," Terrence said. "That was a story."

"A sad one." Sal glanced at Nick. "How did your family take it? The whole coming out thing."

"Don't know yet," Nick said softly. "Haven't gotten to tell my parents."

"Most of us can commiserate. Clive..." Terrence turned and looked meaningfully at Sal.

"Clive came to me in the middle of the night," Sal said. "His face was bloodied, his eye so swollen it wouldn't open."

"His father," Terrence whispered.

"Beat him almost to death," Sal continued. "It was his brother that dragged him out of their front lawn, drove him into the city, and left him on my stoop."

"Jesus," Nick's eyes fell to the blacktopped alleyway.

"We all survive that." Terrence had steepled his fingers. "I feel we all were abused in some way. It's why we gays strive for perfect bodies, perfect jobs. We have to annihilate those abuses – we spend our whole lives disproving lies."

"Not just strivings, though," Sal sighed. "It's why we return to our own abuses over and over again. We feel empty, confounded when we're actually happy."

Sal looked hard at Terrence. Terrence briefly let his eyes make contact with his old friend, their gazes locked in an unspoken argument.

"I think I'm going to go pick up some gardening things at Gethsemane, Sal." Terrence rose and politely bowed his head. "Nick just text when you're ready to meet up. Sal," Terrence said without looking at the older man, "why don't you show him your little cupboard? I think he'd rather like it."

Terrence did not wait for an answer, but drifted off, down the alley and around the corner.

Sal sighed and stretched.

"Sorry about that, Nick. Terrence and I have been arguing for a bit about his home situation." He shook his head and took a small sip of tea. "But! Now that the old biddy is gone, we can gossip. How do you like the city?"

"It's good." Nick paused. "There's a lot to learn."

"About Chicago?"

"About everything: Chicago, gays, school, work. I've never had so much going on. When I was younger I didn't have many friends."

"Did the other kids tease you?"

"Yes."

"It seems it is adolescents' jobs to be abusive. When I taught in the 70's it was the same. Now that men no longer have knighthood, we have to suffer the slings and arrows of high school."

Nick nodded and turned to the horizon. He thought briefly again of the dark, cavern-like room of his teenage years. In this moment, he felt submerged again in that painful cave, felt the dull angst of those days spent alone. In some ways it felt good, the memories, the thoughts of blacked out bar windows and the image of Clive on the street, a welcoming door opening and enveloping him in an oasis of kindness.

But inside him, unfolding from the same store of loneliness and isolation, a dark, viperous stalk had climbed and been nurtured in the glow of Boystown's neon lights. This tentacle twined down the gay main street and crawled toward that flaming sunset of his first evening. It grew from no place of history. Creeping forward, it cast off the shadows of his years of girth, his heavy body hiding up in a chapel of isolation. It strove only forward to the new Boystown ideal cultivated in the depths of Nick's imagination: his own taught body dressed in a tight Speedo for Soot's white party. This new iteration of himself, an idol, a possibility formed when he first discovered the opportunity for a new gay life at community college, was nurtured in the celestial glow of The Gala, in the whisperings of Hedley that one, fateful night.

It was in this tension of past and future that Sal led Nick upstairs to his small apartment. The twisting wooden stair at the back of the building spiraled up to his modest home.

"My castle," the old man chuckled as they emerged from the stair and into the cozy living room. "It's not much, but it's home. I have everything I need here."

Nick surveyed the room, its small nooks lit by amber-colored lamps. It was decorated with old photographs and pictures. A number of the frames were occupied by a younger Sal. Several contained snapshots of a man a few years his junior; Sal and the man were not in any pictures together. The other man had chestnut hair swept to the side. In most of the photographs, his expression was unreadable, only a ghostly smile on his face.

"Is this your...?" Nick hesitated thinking of the right word. "Partner? Husband?"

"Hmmm," Sal smiled, he placed a finger to his lips. "Yes. That's Arnold - Arnie."

"Where is he now?"

"About six feet under." Sal laughed once, a low, macabre note. "He passed away about thirty years ago now."

"These pictures seem old."

"His last years weren't the best," Sal said quietly shuffling forward. "I like these old pictures best."

Nick looked at the rest of the room. An old leather sofa, cracked with age was the centerpiece. In one corner an old rocking chair glided forward and backward, the breeze of an open window guiding its ghostly movement. A soft creak filled the silence as the rockers slid over the hardwood floors. Next to the old chair was a record cabinet; a Righteous Brothers album sitting on top of it looked like it had recently been listened to.

Sal moved into the adjoining room, a dining area with a china cabinet in one corner. The east wall consisted of two large windows. Their dressings were pulled back, allowing the room to be flooded with light. Strung across the lower portion of the window were a number of old shirts, yellowed with age, drifting in the breeze.

"I like to dry my laundry in the open air," Sal said crossing the room and sitting at a small table. "It's an old habit from when Arnie and I lived together."

Nick walked over to the window and gently ran his hand over one of the oxford shirts. The coarse, aged fabric felt brittle in his hands. The light, filtered through the swinging shirts, fell on his open palm, calloused from his time in the gym.

"You and Jordan should come by some time," Sal said looking out the window. "We could have coffee or dinner."

Nick nodded politely. "Yeah, that would be nice."

"Jordan's a good kid. I don't think he quite knows who he is yet, but most don't at twenty-five."

"Six," Nick answered looking at the yellowed shirts absently.

"Ancient!" Sal laughed. "You want any other snack? I should get back down to the store."

"I'm fine, thanks."

Sal clapped his hands and rose. "I'll skip the tour of the bedroom. It's not as exciting as you may think."

Nick followed him out of the dining room and back through the living room. As Nick's feet climbed down the narrow stairs, his thoughts wandered lecherously through other spaces. The veil of the old oxfords lifted and he saw the glittering chandeliers of Hedley's lakefront estate. His mind drifted to the writhing bodies throbbing under the drumming of the club music, the dark stalk twisting toward that blood-red sunset. As Sal closed the door on the back stair, Nick felt the click shut of two spaces: the one above, and that dark space of his youth. Something in the patina of those hanging shirts made him resolutely sure that he didn't want the burden of that crushing history. He was a heavenly body with his own gravity. His end would not come in the back of a cramped bookshop. Soon those queens at the gym who clicked through the turnstile would notice him. He would shine.

Ascent. Transfiguration.

He said good-bye to Sal and headed into the street. Terrence texted him to meet up the block at Gethsemane. He was holding a potted plant, his sunglasses over his eyes when Nick approached.

"How'd you like Sal's hideaway?" he asked.

Nick, without hesitation, shrugged. "Very cozy," he said. "Covered in dust."

Six

Early July brought a story about Hedley in *The Windy City Times*. It was written by Jack Freeman, in what Soot called a very "Freemanian style."

"He's very gifted, that one," Soot opined of Jack. "I think he captures that certain *je ne sais quoi* of Hedley's quite romantically."

While the entire focus was not devoted to Hedley, it consisted of erratic diatribes into the mysterious background of its central figure. The main story was about a large grant given by a Chicago gay foundation (The Red Tie League) to a literacy program on the South Side. Hedley was the head of this venture and had devoted Herculean efforts to see it come to fruition.

While it is rare to see Mr. Renault at the Literacy Accord's central offices, his presence is ubiquitous in the place. It is in the whispers of gratitude and thanksgiving of its workers that Renault's apparition is palpably felt.

Freeman wove the Boystown rumors of Hedley throughout his piece: a modeling career, a childhood in the fields of a large Kentucky horse farm, a rumored shot at competing in the Beijing Olympics in 2008, a bit part in the film *Titanic* as a child. He only put into text all the rumors and web-like lies the men of Boystown had been repeating since Hedley first appeared on the scene a few years earlier.

His true story was obscured in mystery. Tiny truths lay buried in great pillars of mendacious rock. Chunks were known by individuals like Myrtle, who could pin him to one place and time, but for large pieces of his history, these individuals lost the thread completely. A select few were in his strictest confidences and could tell you the full truth, but such status was hard fought and held tightly enough to keep the full, burgeoning truth from breaking into the light of day. His history was preciously guarded, hid away in the obscure cave of rumor, its guardians not really the keepers of his secrets, but the fawning dilettantes who fueled the fantastic rumors of his forgotten past.

Nick would come into these confidences toward the end of summer, gathering the pieces of Hedley's story, each anecdote and hushed truth, a precious piece in the Hedley puzzle. It may have been Hedley's own genius to bring only those hungry, rabid few into his graces that would feed on the stories as sustenance. Each tale of truth would only magnify its whorish lie of a counterpoint to build his esteem in the eyes of those who worshipped him so devotedly.

"I believe it was at a gala opening in New York that I met George Clooney," he would say nonchalantly, his feet resting languidly on the banister of a boat deck. "Perhaps it was actually in London, though."

These vagaries suspended a tower that the others climbed with keen and avid interest. The zenith of this climb was to seize Hedley, have him, to be devoted to him and win the precious prize that no one had seemed to ever capture: his love. But this peak, in its Babelian glory, remained obscured, out of reach. He kept his disciples believing that only a few more tidbits, one more revelation, would reveal the heights of his tower's lofty peak. It was this calculated unveiling of his life's tragedy that won Nick, bathed Hedley in the halo of wonder that would bind them together.

The initial story Nick would hear was the tragedy of Hedley's first love. It filled in the gaps left by Myrtle in her story spun after the brunch with Soot. It was during college that Hedley first met Cedric, a blond, bespectacled cheerleader who attended the same university. They met in class, Development of Civilizations, and locked eyes across the room the first day.

"He was glory," Hedley would say mellifluously, sipping on wine. "Imagine having your entire past broken by one man's eyes. He looked into me and the guilt, the lurid fascination with the closet, with appeasing others and acting straight, was eradicated with one beaming smile."

The two quickly became inseparable, their love budding in an Indiana spring. In afternoon light, motes of dust from their dorm room floating in the breeze, they would lie down next to each other and divulge their deepest selves, the parts that they had buried during their time in the closet. In those moments, outpourings of dreams, hopes, and aspirations ran like an electric current between them. As the full beauty of summer emerged in May, their love came to full flower.

Hedley, self-admittedly, was nervous about their first time. Among all the things he shared with Cedric, the most intimate, holy part of him lay sequestered in fear, loathing, and Midwestern Catholic guilt. Cedric was calm and helpful, letting limbs fall in the right places and gently guiding him to an open, calming space to lay claim to his virginity.

One early summer night, as the school year was coming to a close, Cedric's hands drifted to the belt wrapped around Hedley's cargo shorts. Deftly he tugged at them, drew down his underwear, and looked upon the full purity of Hedley, bathed in pale moonlight.

"I was terrified," Hedley would say, nimbly cutting tomatoes for quiche. "It was a moment I had dreamed of for so long and we were on its precipice. I looked into his eyes, gaping, loving, waiting, and knew that this was an irrevocable and disastrous moment. In all my years of catechism, the ideas of purity, holiness, the sin of sexuality lay spread upon me like some heavy chain. This man held the key. I guess, not key, really, but cutters. He had the power and the desire to set me free. But I knew," Hedley's eyes would dart up, locking his auditor in a fervent stare, "I knew that this was the death of me; there was this person, this human that I had tried to be that I was stepping away from – murdering! In the moonlight, I could almost see the blood on my skin, feel the shuddering pulse of my heart coming to its end. But it was an awakening, too, a moment of splendid rebirth – gospel."

Only the moon watched over them as they made love in the tall grasses of an Indiana field. At the conclusion, Cedric pulled Hedley closer, wrapping him in one of his muscled arms.

"It was love," Hedley would say returning to his wine, his quiche, his boat. "It was ecstatic, voracious love."

The two parted ways that summer. On a trip to New York to visit Cedric right before their senior year started, Hedley discovered that he had been cheated on. As summer turned to fall, the leaves tumbling to their demise, Hedley found himself laid bare, dropped slowly, morosely into the earth.

"It was a dark time, but we all have them. Whatever darkness, whatever hopelessness the closet had in its depths, it is nothing to the pain and horror of heartbreak."

With one year left at school, Hedley picked up the pieces of his life. There was no need for love, no need to find someone else.

"That year I found myself," he would say, a graceful note of finality in his husky voice. "After death, there is life."

#

Nick began his foray into Hedley's confidences about the same time that the article was published in *The Times*. The inciting incident occurred one warm Sunday afternoon at a garish, jubilant garden party hosted by Peter and George.

Fresh orchids from the local florist covered their dining room table, the air crisp with their redolence. The dining room hummed with voices engaged in the summer's latest gossip. Toned bodies gleamed in the afternoon light, their owners bedecked in tank tops, open cotton shirts, and light summer scarves. Soot alone wore his typical blazer, ascot, and polyester shirt. At frequent intervals he would reach into his jacket pocket to pluck out a handkerchief and lightly dust his moistened forehead.

Jordan sat idly on the same couch on which he had first seen Nick. In his hand, he cupped a glass of chardonnay garnished with rose petals. His mouth was drawn into a tight line of judgment as he watched Nick stand with three other men: Skyler from The Set, Jonathan, and an unknown, fawning attendant.

Only a few weeks prior he had looked on his date with a nascent wonder; the boy who had arrived in Chicago wide-eyed and awkward only a while before had come to blossom into a member of the Boystown elite. As summer quietly drifted into its full, dazzling glory, this blooming had only continued to grow more opulent and daring. Standing with one of The Set in a shirt that hugged the contours of his burgeoning body and a pair of shorts that barely concealed their precious cargo, the boy of a month earlier had come to draw forth an acrid spite from Jordan. The one who had once thrilled him with his soft, hushed confidences now stood erect in the center of a private circle, his mouth pulled into an arrogant, cockeyed smile.

"Can you believe it?" Peter (or George) asked taking a seat next to Jordan. "Our small, country ward has transformed into a mature, gay man." The older man sipped a glass of pink champagne. He dabbed his face with a cocktail napkin, his recently botoxed visage attempting an emotion.

"Yes," Jordan said swatting away the comment. He drank the remnants of his glass in one quick motion. "You expecting more people? This party is a bore."

"Oh, don't be catty with me, Jordan. Just because you're little Nick is flying the coop, doesn't mean you can blame me."

"I didn't mean to be catty. I meant to be bitchy."

"Well, it needs some work."

The other member of the couple not present (perhaps Peter) took a seat in the middle of the two men and sighed dramatically.

"What are you two hens on about?"

"Nicky."

"Oh, he's doing quite well." Peter laughed girlishly. "Did you see him at Soot's event last night? He drew some stares in his little get up."

"Oh," Jordan turned and looked venomously at the old queens, "Soot's little bash. I heard it was another wonderful event – raising hope and awareness for…what was it?"

Peter and George both touched their index fingers to their lips. Their eyes rolled back in silent contemplation.

"I think it was a cancer," George said finally. "Colon?"

"I grow weary of all of you." Jordan rose, his tall frame gliding from the room. His bare feet causing the polished floorboards to creak.

"Who let the cat out?" Peter giggled into his napkin.

Nick saw Jordan leave the room but showed no sign of interest. His eyes were fixed on the handsome face of Skyler, the youngest Set member, as he clutched firmly to a glass filled with vodka soda. He was in the middle of a meandering story about a party earlier in the week. The content mattered little to Nick. He would follow its threads, its divergences into unrelated tales of sexual conquest, but its source was his only interest. Each time the speaker formed the open, soaring sounds of his oration, the high, precise mode of his speech ebbed into the pulsing rhythms of Hedley's Summer Gala. Nick was again in that sea of bodies twisting in time to raging club music. But now he had begun to pull away from the formless mass and take shape in the throng. He was on his way to becoming one of those shining beacons of manhood that his eyes ravenously devoured that wild night weeks before.

Skyler glanced disinterestedly at his phone as it chirped to life. His eyes, normally holding a scornful glance, fell into round, tawny pools as he stared at his screen. "Hedley," he said quickly, "is coming."

The skinny man next to Nick and Skyler put his hands over his mouth in a look of wonderment. "Here?" he said in a whisper. "Hedley is coming…here?"

Skyler arched his eyebrow. "No, he's coming to Minnesota, Klipspringer." The tiny man looked confused for a moment, anxiously biting his thumbnail. Skyler shook his head and began to walk away. "Jesus, of course here. He'll be here in five."

Whether it was by Hedley's design or not, the word of his impending arrival had just circled the party when he appeared at the door, sunglasses on, wrapped in a silk scarf and holding a garish, leather bag. The confluence of his hyper-masculine physique with the feminine accouterment was a newer surprise of this season. Appearances of Hedley varied widely on the masculine scale, from backward baseball caps and cargo shorts in the 2012 fall season, to his brief stint in studded leather leggings and heels during the spring of 2013.

Jordan had another full glass of chardonnay, his eyes fixed on the newly arrived party, which included the remaining members of The Set. Hedley's blazing smile flashed, illuminating the room in its ivory glow. Peter met them at the door and embraced Hedley.

"I'm SO glad you could come!" he cooed.

"What a nice party!" Hedley took a step to the side, his shining green eyes tracing over the warm interior. Flashes of interest intermittently flowed over his cool features as he assessed the furnishings.

Despite his recent pouty mood, Jordan couldn't help but stare at Hedley's face. Whatever loathing was in him was muted by its verdant eyes, its chiseled jaw and cheeks. The emollient of his beauty faded as his eyes shifted across the room to Nick. Holding a glass of champagne, his young friend stood eagerly waiting for his turn at Hedley's court.

Jordan sulkily withdrew to the kitchen where he stared idly out the window. From its vantage point he could see down the street. His mind wandered to that first evening he had met Nick, their first kisses and embraces. It was on that street across the way that they had run into Soot, his black suit forming out of the darkness to greet them, smoke from his cigarette coiling in the air. Cutting through the middle of his view and the memory was the lofty billboard staring down the street, the two beautiful men in a tight embrace.

"Hello," a voice called from the kitchen door.

Jordan turned and beheld Hedley's flotsam, just arrived. "Myrtle," he said coolly.

"Where's the gin?" she asked staggering to the cabinets. "It's for Hedley. He wants a little splash in his chardonnay."

"If you're looking for booze, why not just distill your breath? That should be enough to get more than one party going."

Myrtle slumped down and began digging through a cabinet. "Someone must have upset Jordy. He's in his waning bitch phase."

"Not waning. Waxing." Jordan walked over to the window and leaned next to the screen, drawing in the warm, heavy air. His thoughts grew hazy, muddled. Not in a drunken state but alive with the emotional pulsings he had tried to bury in his youth. As the clatter of bottles filled the room from Myrtle's pawing, his mind reeled back to high school, his moments standing awkwardly and feeling the spur of his fellow student's words digging into his flesh.

Faggot.

Queer.

Not always the butt of the jokes, but at their periphery, the odd one who took the lashings when there were no one else queenier or faggier to take them. It was not a conscious decision, but more of a survival tactic that made him cold. It was armor in the form of wit and humor with which he girded himself. In those middle teen years, he became protean, forming into whatever a new clique or group demanded of him, always quick to a joke, asserting himself in a group setting, but never standing out.

Now, somehow, Nick had found a way into the armor and Jordan felt the old stings. It wasn't Nick himself, so much as his becoming one of The Set, that made the wound ache with so much ferocity. His transformation from the quiet boy on Peter and George's couch to the peacocking soldier in the room next door, made him tremble, think that perhaps everyone, underneath, was a bully in disguise. With enough power and force even the softest, most effusive spirit could transcend into a demon, a creature that would stand at the edge of the party, eyes alert and scanning, littering tacit judgments on those around him.

What plagued Jordan more than anything about Nick was the possibility that something had been real, at least initially: his eyes, for instance. Their first night together, he had woken up to Nick's gaze. The boy smiled as Jordan stretched his long arms. It was as if, in the whole world, the one thing Nick wanted was for Jordan to open his eyes and look into his own.

Now, sitting on the couch, he had felt the same gaze turn arctic in the summer heat of Peter and George's living room. No longer was Jordan an object of affection, but an other, some distant, loathsome spirit, a hated doomsday prophet in a flowering empire. While at their first meeting Jordan had confused his shyness for disinterest, now there was no question that Nick was looking on him with opprobrium. The garbled noise of the room turned to a rush of voices, mutedly tearing at Jordan, just as they had in his adolescent days: "queer" and "fag" transmuted into "ugly" and "dull."

"Who does he even know?"

"Did he come with you?"

As was his typical reaction to these feelings of rejection, he bit his lip. The coarse, raw emotions of childhood hit him, dampened, but still aching due to his own inferiority, his falling short of the standardized ideal. He had grown to know this model of excellence was vaporous, arbitrary, but its power was transcendent. What had once been the ideal of the straight, jock football player of his high school, evolved, iterated, into the form of Hedley – chiseled, shaved body gleaming in a designer scarf and overpriced denim.

Sighing, Jordan walked out of the kitchen having traded his glass of wine for a bottle of tequila Myrtle had dug out of the liquor cabinet. The alcohol had taken him over. He hobbled toward the dining room table, landing heavily in a chair.

The seat happened to be next to a young man, huge spectacles falling off his thin nose. The glasses were the largest part of his person, the rest being composed of spindly limbs enjoined to a sparse trunk. His brown eyes were only magnified by his huge, round eye accessories. Upon further scrutiny Jordan was sure they served no ophthalmological use at all.

"I wonder what Hedley's drinking," the glasses youth said softly. "I was drinking the chardonnay, but it looks like he's got a spritzer or something. It looks delectable."

Jordan looked at Hedley. He held a goblet, conspicuously large and gaudy, filled with a shimmering, gold-tinted liquid.

"It's gin and chardonnay," replied Jordan brusquely.

"How refreshing!" the boy squeaked. With determination, he rose and sped to the drink table, where his dainty, trembling hands poured a splash of gin into his wine. His features betrayed him as he downed the first sip, his gag reflex reacting to the mishmash of flavors.

Jordan smiled to himself and looked again upon Hedley. The Head of The Set stood, as he always did at these events, as the centerpiece in the grand carousel. All points of interest rotated around his every whim, his subtle gestures, his shifting gazes.

Although all eyes were on him at the present moment, no two opinions could have been more divergent in their conclusion than Jordan and Nick:

Jordan's eyes were heavy, his composure overthrown by earlier slugs of chardonnay and tequila. What he saw in Hedley's ghostly, shining apparition was complete corruption, a force that, at its core, had ripped apart some beautiful, untouched thing that had existed in the room only a few months before. In that sepia-lighted afternoon he met Nick, Jordan had seen his own youthful self in the younger man, felt again the pulse of those awakening feelings in the bubbles of champagne, the blurry lights of traffic down Halsted. The kiss that evening had been something enchanted in the red glow of Halsted street: a fleeting, backward look at his own innocent hopes. But, Hedley, in his serpentine way, had writhed into the condo and disrupted this arcadia. His presence, in that same room of weeks earlier, cast long shadows on the walls, ceilings, and faces of those gathered.

Division. Jordan thought of his own portentous statement many weeks before. The splits down Halsted, the haves and have-nots, the splintered mosaic of race and religion he had theoretically discussed were real. When he had come out, Jordan imagined that the world of gay was a perfect, unified Eden, a splendid paradise after the ghastly ordeal of adolescence, of fag, of queer. But in that room, staring at Hedley, he again saw that his vision was dead, that nothing in life, could be whole and perfect. As Nick smiled, arms crossed, muscles tensed, Jordan felt the tremble of division, the understanding that all could not be harmonious and equal. His romantic remembrance of the first, splendid afternoon – May wind rippling curtains, the pop of champagne in the background, a beautiful boy reclined looking innocently out the window – gave no signs of the rift of this present moment.

"Everything beautiful must be destroyed," Jordan said softly to himself, his tongue numbed by drunkenness.

Diametrically opposed to Jordan's tortured thoughts were the flowerings of understanding occurring within Nick's own mind. Standing next to Hedley he felt the radiance of his presence, saw the ripples of his muscles, the play of summer light on his sandy brown hair. As he spoke, competently, of the upcoming Red Tie League fundraiser, an event at Progress Bar in the coming weeks, Nick found that the world around him had receded. What a few months prior had been his cousin's city hideaway, was now a clutter of a middle-aged attempt at chic. Hedley's sun had thrown light on all of these objects, had made the posters of vintage films, the sparse modern kitchen, all seem a source of shame and pity.

They were trying, they were, but it was a shadow, an imitation of what Hedley cast out, what he represented. Peter's tight, red shorts, his oxford shirt gaping open on a chiseled chest, was only an echo of a true male form: the rippled, shaved core of Hedley. His button-up hung better on his broader shoulders, looked sharper and crisper in the afternoon sun. The others dabbling in local affairs was nothing to Hedley's leadership of The Red Tie League, his presence and power at creating change in their community.

His connection to Hedley had already begun to transform his position within the Halsted circles. The perfect men spinning through the turnstile at the gym were beginning to pause briefly, smile and nod in his direction as he sat at the desk.

"Saw you at Replay, right?"

"You were at Albert Devon's Pride party, right?"

The amorphous, slothful creature of his youth was now fully taking form. Dreams and hopes of his youth, of his college days and Stewart Johnson, were beginning to bud in the full light of day. While his life had once been a place of darkness, a tomb, it was now a garden, fully illumined by the light cast from Hedley's red sun.

For a brief moment, he had faltered in his devotion. Sal's shop, the old man's remembrances of a past Chicago, a past iteration of gay, had struck that far off chord that made him think that perhaps there was something else, that tearing up the roots of his past was not a solution to create a present. But, in the faded light of Sal's apartment, in the discolored pictures and dust of his shop, Nick had realized that there was only one way forward. What had started as a spark that first night he met Hedley, a slight pinprick of light shining on his dark past, a place darkened by the towering frame of his father, had now built to a steady, roaring fire. This past had to burn, wholly completely. In Hedley's eyes he saw the fire blaze, knew that it was only Hedley who could lead him on the path of ascent that was whispered in the swirling chaos of The Gala.

"What do you say then," Hedley said, handing his drink to one of his many followers. "Are we all done here?" The Set nodded in agreement and with a subtle acknowledgment, a smile in Nick's direction as he said: "Where to next?" Nick was brought into the group.

The Set, with Nick and a few others, bid quick farewell and disappeared from the party as rapidly as Hedley had appeared. Furtively, Jordan watched Nick say goodbye to Peter and George. As an afterthought, Nick politely turned and waved to Jordan as he rushed out the door.

Jordan got up and went to the window after they left. He watched the coterie emerge from the front of the building, drift away in their cloud of beauty.

On the street Nick thought only of the evening that was shaping up before him. He was moving away from the dull world of his cousin, of his tryst with Jordan, toward a future that, to him, only a few weeks before, had been as attainable as a fairy tale. His mind's eye now saw the possibility of his present and, from that beginning, projected a new future. The hunger that had begun on his first night in Boystown was now ravenous, unbridled.

His eyes followed the lights of Halsted as they disappeared into the horizon – the street lamps, endless copies of each other, projecting into the horizon.

Seven

Sunshine poured on the sands of Hollywood Beach in a generous, golden deluge. Bodies lay in repose along the strand, glinting in the burning light. In the midst of the sea of humanity lay The Set with their inner circle. Their eyes, screened behind Ray Bans and Guccis, assessed the seemingly endless mass of gay bodies lined up in tableaux. Mixed among the chiseled bodies of models and personal trainers were the girthy forms of bears and slim, aged gays, enjoying their sexual emancipation in tight, infinitesimal swimming suits.

Although no longer the resort destination it was at the start of the twentieth century, the beach retains a vacation atmosphere. The towering Edgewater Beach Apartment building watches over stretches of sand and water, its Miami-pink sheen glowing even after sunset. If one looks to the skyline, he can imagine the ghost of the sunrise-yellow hotel that used to look upon the sunbathing bodies in years long past.

The beach is one of the northernmost of the public Chicago beaches, a glittering gold and azure jewel in the crown of Chicago's public park system. It is one of the last points one can see manmade sands before crossing into the wild lands of Roger's Park, then further, the manicured, sweeping blankness of Evanston. Other beaches in Chicago, North, Montrose, Foster, contain a comingling of ages, races, and genders, masses of people out on the lake for days of amusement and sunlight. Hollywood stands as a partitioned stretch of sand, a land delineated between gay men to the south and families from the ethnically diverse neighborhood to the north.

Further in, the scene is fractured further, small camps of varying gays, all selecting into their crowd of choice, from Speedoed Asians, bears, and twinks with their older daddies, to the marginalized peasantry laying around the periphery. All come forth to worship the sun, parade their hard work in gyms, or flaunt their indifference to the mainstream gay aesthetic, hair and bellies fully exposed to those around them. A holiday atmosphere surrounds the beach on those scorching hot days in the summer, when all are gathered, eyes sweeping the sand for love, sex, and beauty.

Like any self-respecting coterie of gays, The Set had spent the early afternoon at the oldest member, Samson's, apartment drinking iced drinks in preparation for their day of leisure.

Samson, in an apparent moment of thoughtlessness, had moved north, out of the belly of Halsted and into the far away kingdom of aged gays in Edgewater. Among the towers, old hotels, and kitsch shops, he found a one bedroom that looked south to the city. From his southernmost window, Navy Pier could be seen. Closer to the building, Foster Beach was visible with its small lifeguard towers and swarms of families congregating during the heat of the day.

The move was a source of constant ire and consistent ribbing from his companions:

"To be so far from everything is despicable."

"How's the weather up there, Samson?"

"You are the oldest of us, but it's no reason to just roll up and die, is it?"

"Jesus do they even have electricity this far away from Lake View?"

Samson said he moved for a boy, one who had come and gone with the changing of seasons. It was only a few days after he moved into his high-rise apartment that he stated he was bored with the young architect. Their affair came to an end, and

Samson was left to explore the far northlands, always at the mercy of jokes tied to his age and virility.

"Viagra must be handed out on the street."

Samson's air conditioning purred as The Set, with their inner circle, Terrence, Lloyd, Jonathan, and, now, Nick, stood in tank-topped poses around the room. Sunlight flooded through the southerly window, bathing the walls in a patina of gold.

"It's so hot," Hedley said, taking a seat on the divan. "Just getting to the beach is going to be murder. Can you imagine how those alternative hipster gays will smell? They probably haven't showered in weeks."

A chorus of giggles rose in the room.

"Disgusting," drawled Skyler. Having just celebrated his twenty-second birthday, persons over the age of 25 were, in his opinion, geriatric. He remembered his mother's constant preening in her bedroom before leaving the house. She had instilled in him the importance of appearance in public places. "We better get a spot near the lighthouse. I don't want to be mixed up with all the rest. The riffraff..." He petered off, draining the last of his vodka and soda.

Terrence sat on the arm of the sofa, his husband, Lloyd, beside him. As was the case since news of the affair with Kinsey broke on Twitter, their interactions appeared unnatural, forced. Terrence did have his hand on Lloyd's shoulder, however, it lay as limp and idle as an old rag. Terrence's eyes were also empty and emotionless; there was little of interest to him in that room. He did occasionally watch Nick, who sat alone on a bar stool near the kitchen. Even though Nick had gained access to The Set, he was still somewhat reserved. Terrence took that as an indication that he too may have felt as an outsider, an incongruent piece in the dazzling puzzle of Hedley's creation.

"Nick," Terrence asked earnestly, "is Jordan coming today? I haven't seen him around much."

Nick shrugged indifferently. "He may. I texted him." He took a drink from his glass and set it on the counter.

"Are you two...still? Are we still beating that dead horse?" Skyler asked.

Rather than answer, Nick stood up and began preparing another drink.

"Let's just go!" said Samson, looking out the window. "We're going to all asleep if we all slough around here."

"The old man wants us to leave." Hedley laughed to himself. The rest followed with exaggerated chuckles.

"I want to get a good spot," Samson said casually. "We don't want to be by those bears again, do we?"

He threw a glance at Skyler, who waved the comment away. "It would be worse to be early. It makes us look desperate."

"For what?" Terrence asked innocently.

"What, what?" Skyler glowered. "We look dull, like we don't have anywhere else to go."

"Well, we don't," Lloyd said shirking Terrence's hand off of him. "Let's go and join a volleyball game or something – see if Nicky is actually athletic with all those muscles he's been working on this summer."

Lloyd walked over to Nick and jokingly grabbed his shoulders. The friendly gesture lingered for a moment. Terrence felt something catch in his throat. He blinked once, twice and then quickly went to the bathroom.

"I heard Kinsey was bringing in some boys from Montreal." Jonathan perked up. "Maybe we should go a little earlier."

"Well, let's go, then," Hedley said confidently. "We need more liquor anyway."

"Cheers!" Stephen, the middle Set member, said from across the room. Two empty cups lay at his feet and a labored smile was drawn across his face. "All the booze is the better."

"God, are you drunk, Stevey?" Hedley asked. "No wonder we're out of vodka."

Stephen dug into pockets and set his sunglasses on his face. "It's a Saturday. What else would I be?"

#

Jordan ran into Myrtle crossing the park toward the beach. She had been wandering down the bike path brandishing a bottle of cabernet and singing a boy band ballad that had played on the radio all summer. Her cover up was soaked in sweat, her hair a mess of moist tendrils.

"Myrtle?" Jordan watched her tottering form apprehensively. "Are you okay?"

"The best!" she wailed.

As she raised her bottle in salute, a scooter cut in front of her path, causing her to collapse forward into the grass.

Jordan lifted her up, her body shaking with mirth.

"It's the cab! The cab! Don't give this girl the cabernet, because she gets a little loopy!"

"God, you're a mess. It's barely two. Shouldn't you save this for the bars?"

"There's plenty of time for bar drunk, too, Jordy."

Jordan put his arm around her and guided her across the grass and back to the gravel path. Around them the park was alive with activity: children playing football, families picnicking, lines of gays heading toward the sands.

As they walked forward, Jordan felt his heart pound against his chest. Even though he knew that whatever had transpired between himself and Nick had expired, he kept coming back. It was a breach in his resolve that morning when, horny and hungover, he texted Nick and asked when he was going to the beach. Nick responded out of courtesy, and out of desperation, Jordan found himself putting on his suit and getting to the beach earlier than Nick had told him. He had enjoyed an iced drink at Starbucks on Bryn Mawr, heart pumping, thoughts clattering about how he could, possibly, maybe, pick their relationship back up.

Sweat poured from his forehead as he held onto Myrtle and crossed toward the beach. The heat was almost visible rising from the sand. The sun reflected off the water, a blazing, white disc.

The Set was camped at the south end of the beach, their towels strewn about, their bags concealing a large cooler of chilled drinks, when Jordan and Myrtle approached. Nick was standing to the side of the group, a sweating Solo cup held in his hand. His body was barely covered by a thin line of swimsuit that clung to his waist.

"Hello." Stephen waved from a small chair that was set off to the side from the group. He looked dazed, his sunglasses on the tip of his nose, his chest already turning red from the blazing sunlight.

"You should put on sunscreen, Stephen," Myrtle said primly.

"I just want more color," Stephen said draining the rest of his drink.

The others gathered paid no attention to the new guests. Skyler got up and walked toward the water immediately upon their arrival.

"I brought vodka," Jordan said dryly.

"Put it with the rest of the drinks," Hedley drawled from his sunbathing position.

Terrence got up and helped them find room in the cooler. He took out a piece of ice and gently rubbed it over his chest. "Jesus it's hot."

"I'm dying," Jonathan said, wiping his brow with his beach towel.

"It's perfect!" Myrtle put her half-drunk cabernet in the cooler and slumped over onto a towel. Lloyd happened to be too close to where she landed and felt her wet flesh rub against his own. Disgusted, he got up and walked toward the water, waving at Skyler.

Nick strolled casually over to Jordan. Jordan felt his heart slam against his chest.

While he had always been attracted to Nick, this new physical iteration of him he found addictive. It wasn't the newly added musculature, the cocky gait, or his new haircut and wardrobe but rather the estrangement, the moving away that made him want to cling. It was the absurd tension of loathing and loving The Set at the same time made incarnate in one person. While he, on some level hated Hedley, his corruption of Nick, he also recognized he had made Nick something more, something better, unattainable, and seemingly perfect. Nick became the incarnation of his own gay ideal, the possibility of ascent to the upper class, the crème that rises above the prejudice and fear of the rest of the gay proletariat. When he had first met Nick, he had seen something of his own youth and hopes reflected, but now, after his transformation, he saw what he might become, what was possible. It was the residue of his own time in high school purgatory, his desperate desire to be normal, accepted, cool. Jordan had been with boys, discarded them like tissue when he had grown tired of them. At the beginning of the summer he assumed Nick would be another one in this collection of used and forgotten men. But the young boy had begun to symbolize more. It wasn't the loss of a lover that Jordan found so heartbreaking, but rather the slipping away of a much larger ideal.

"How's it going?" Nick asked, leaning into the cooler to refresh his drink.

"It's good," Jordan said, forcing a lilting note of gaiety to his voice. "I escorted Myrtle here. I think she's fully ready for Betty Ford now."

Myrtle moaned from below.

"You go out last night?" Nick asked.

"No. I was with Kinsey, Aaron, and Todd. We me the Montreal boys and stayed in."

"How are they?"

The impersonal tone irritated Jordan. "They're fun – kind of into the leather stuff."

Silence fell between them. The sound of the sun's singeing heat was audible. Sweat trickled down Jordan's neck. Shouts came from somewhere far off, but for the most part the world had stopped, waiting for Nick to speak.

But he didn't.

Just as casually as he had entered the scene, Nick stalked away, taking a seat next to Terrence at the far end of their camp.

The afternoon drifted on in a hazy calm. Many came and paid homage to The Set throughout the afternoon hours. Soot appeared in long black trunks, his nose coated in a thick layer of sunscreen.

"It stops the aging process, you know," he said digging through the cooler. "No fruit garnishes? Well, that's fine. But you should all be putting on sunscreen, especially," he nodded toward Stephen, who was now a shade of scarlet, "him."

Hedley walked the length of the beach, collecting followers and dilettantes as he went. At each group he would pause, make casual conversation, thank them for some contribution to his charity, or reminiscence some drunken memory spent at Progress, Scarlet, or Mini. Jordan sat apart, watching the others and feeling his hatred build. He had stumbled into the middle of some drama in which everyone knew their part: Skyler, the prima donna stood in silence, his abs a mosaic in his white skin, his perfectly formed, youthful face scowling from beneath his sunglasses; Samson and Jonathan left the main group to join a group of bears and otters; and Stephen lay in his chair, passed out next to Myrtle, around his feet a collection of empty cups.

Heat rose up around them, as if the earth had absorbed all the sun it could and had begun to belch fire. Jordan felt sweat form on his neck and shoulders. Streams of salty water ran down his chest and soaked the waist of his swimming suit. Many had taken out ice and formed makeshift cooling devices from plastic bags. Water, whether from sweat or molten ice, ran down each of the men strewn about the beach.

Over the course of the afternoon, the rancor swelled in Jordan; it was exacerbated by Nick's casual flirtation with all those gathered. The intermittent teasing and smiling would have been fine, but it was the darted glances and stolen touches with Lloyd that made him fume. Terrence stood to the side, watching and knowing how the story would end. He had been cheated on and now knew how the full course of events would play out.

Perhaps it was the heat, the frustration, the complete disregard that Nick seemed to have for him, whatever the cause, Jordan found himself, arms crossed in front of Nick, his sunglasses taken off.

"Can we talk?"

Nick looked up, alone for the first time that afternoon, staring expectantly. "Why?"

"I think we need to."

"What about?"

"You know."

Silence peppered with shouts, laughter, the soft lapping of green waves filled the air for a fleeting moment.

"Okay," Nick said.

Slowly, they moved away from the camp. They climbed up the cement walling that lay at the south end of the beach. Atop these cement blocks was an open park. Above them leaves danced in the wind, throwing cobbled shadows on the ground. The lazy breeze and shade felt heavenly after an afternoon in the blazing sun.

Once fully removed from the vision of their company, Jordan felt the compunction to speak: "It's all over then?"

"What?"

"You and me."

Nick crossed his arms. "What do you mean?"

Jordan in aggravation put his hands behind his head. "What do I – Jesus, Nick... At least talk to me like I'm human. I know you and the others have some sense of absurd entitlement, but I knew you before you were one of those ridiculous bitches."

Whatever propriety Jordan cultivated on the beach, shattered. He rubbed his temples with his hands. He bit his lip. Jordan who had always been so cool, who had slid unnoticed in the Halsted scene, now trembled before a child, a boy.

"Bitches?" Nick asked harshly.

"I just mean – end it. Tell me you don't want to see me anymore. Say you're too good for me, or whatever you need to. I just want to stop thinking about it."

"What are you talking about?"

"Us! For the love of God, Nick, are you pretending like we didn't do anything, that we weren't anything?"

Nick stared calmly at Jordan, who now paced frantically back and forth in the shade of the trees. The casual relationship with Jordan had, in fact, receded from Nick's mind. Over the course of the last few weeks, he had viewed Jordan as some part of his history that needed to be ripped and burned. Vaguely, in the corner of his mind, their nights together clung like phantoms, like a child's memory of his ABC lessons, a distant, forgotten thought that had been assimilated into a higher mind. While Jordan impressed upon their relationship some emotional import, Nick had moved away, outgrown their serendipitous connection.

"It wasn't anything," Nick said finally. "We hung out some."

"But it..." Jordan felt his eyes grow damp. Instinctively, he put his sunglasses on his face. "It wasn't nothing. Didn't you feel something? I feel like you have abandoned me... us."

"What are you talking about?" Nick asked, beginning to lose his temper. "Can you just calm down? We hung out. We had sex. It's something casual – like most of what happens between dudes in Boystown."

Jordan remembered their first night – Nick's soft, uncertain voice. The sound he heard now boomed, echoed, from some far-off place.

"I've grown up this summer," Nick continued, "I've realized that I can be something other than the kid I came here as. I don't have to be awkward and uncertain and cling to people because I'm afraid to try new things." He hesitated. "I don't have to rely on others for some kind of support. I can be my own thing. You were my first guy in Chicago. It was fun – we messed around. Let's be adults about this."

Until that moment, Jordan hadn't even thought that Nick would be sleeping with others. But this is what his last statement meant: My first guy in Chicago... The first guy.

Jordan had been one of many.

He reviewed their summer evenings. Weeknights he spent alone watching TV while Nick was out with The Set were nights Nick rolled in sheets with strange, beautiful men.

Suddenly, all his pride faltered, shattered; he had thought he would stand beside Nick, that he could win him back, be the one on his arm at Sidetrack at Mini at Progress. But the idea of love, of possession of Nick in his prime, eroded into a fine powder. Jordan was alone again. He had lived a long time in self-imposed exile, but now he was rejected, broken – his own vulnerability now appalled him. The world transformed into a high school locker room, shouts, and jeers haranguing his ears. Again, he was nothing.

"Who else have you been fucking?" Jordan asked, his voice rising. The words were not aggressive but posed out of curiosity and bewilderment.

"You and I weren't dating."

"We weren't..."

"It's none of your business."

"It isn't." Jordan wished desperately for a cigarette, something small he could run through his fingers while he tried to think. It was one thing to confront Nick about their relationship, about where it was going, but it was quite another to hear that it had never been anything. Jordan's ideal of their coupling had been nothing but a shadow play. In that moment, the idea of Nick he had kept in his mind, the boy sitting across from him that first afternoon of the summer, was not real. But had he ever been? Had a new Nick ascended, murdered the old? Or was this man standing before him all Nick had ever been, the fully ripened fruit of which Jordan had only seen the seed. Had Hedley corrupted him or merely nourished the darkness that was already there?

Wind stirred the trees. Jordan turned to the water and stared at the waves lapping against the beach. He watched the other men along the sand, running, laughing, talking. Flirtations were occurring. In that moment hundreds of men were laying the groundwork for sex that night, or perhaps another. Nick had done the same, maybe dozens of times while at parties, while doing his rounds about Boystown in any one of the bars. Jordan had sat at home thinking he was with someone.

"God, I'm an idiot," he said at last, brushing a strand of hair out of his face. "So fucking dumb."

Nick sighed. "Don't be dramatic."

"Yes." Jordan felt something of his old self return. The armor was back up after its momentary loss. "A lady must always bring her own drama to any party."

Quickly, he turned, taking slow, steady breaths. He moved toward the beach. The fantasy, still not fully dead, manifested itself in a vision of Nick pursuing him down the beach, wheeling him around and pressing their lips together in a conciliatory kiss. But he knew that was not to be. This vision was one of many swirling through his mind – some visions of happiness, love, reunion, others of revenge, fear, and hopelessness.

He would work it out later; piece together the narrative of the day in a more rational state of mind. Now he knew that his course must take one direction and that was toward vodka.

The Set barely moved as he collected his things. He took no time putting on his shirt or folding up his towel. Clothing toppled into the sand as he scurried to get all his items and get away. The heat felt even more oppressive as he tried to put everything together. Sweat poured from his forehead and down his back in steady rivulets. The sand burned his feet – despite his desire to appear collected, he tripped through their beach camp in an awkward, post-modern dance.

"Off then?" Stephen, now the color of a cooked lobster, had awoken just in time to see Jordan groping for his bag.

"Yes," Jordan said. "I'm going home."

"Well, good-bye."

Nick didn't appear until a few moments later. He had stopped to talk to one of the boys he met at Soot's fundraiser.

"Jordan left," Stephen said pouring himself another drink. He had disregarded any propriety and filled his glass entirely with vodka. "He seemed to be in a hurry."

"I think something came up." Nick looked up and caught Lloyd's eye, a cockeyed smile crossing his face.

#

The Tweet actually went out shortly after midnight. Terrence's departure was estimated to have occurred somewhere between 1 and 2 am.

Gritty details were divulged at a later point, whether they had come from the source or been entirely mined from rumor and conjecture is still up for debate. Whatever their birthplace, the facts were as follows:

Directly after the beach, The Set, along with Terrence, Lloyd, and Jonathan all went back to Samson's for another drink. The sun had just begun to set and the group was in varying shades of inebriation. Terrence had an early brunch set up with Sal and left at approximately 9 pm.

The rest of the group decided that they would meet up and go out later. Lloyd, Stephen, and Nick left for Lake View in a cab at roughly 10 pm.

"They got out together," Stephen said later. "We were miles from Lloyd's place, but he insisted that he had to get out because he needed an ATM." Upon the pronunciation of the acronym, Stephen would roll his eyes with each successive letter.

The Set had made the plan to meet up at midnight at Sidetrack. Samson was the first to arrive, followed by Stephen, Jonathan, and Kinsey's boys from Montreal. Hedley came at 12:30, wearing a wry smile and speaking almost exclusively with Stephen.

"I told him that Lloyd got out with Nick. Of course, we all knew what happened. It had probably been happening for weeks. We all know that Lloyd can't keep his dick out of anything."

When Nick and Lloyd did arrive, it was noted that Lloyd was wearing a shirt that was too small, clearly taken from someone else's wardrobe. Who confirmed the rendezvous is unknown, however, after a large number of drinks the crew made their way to Progress, where it is believed over the thump-thump rhythm of Rihanna the confession was made.

In Stephen's version, a saintly glow hangs around Nick: "He felt awful, you could tell. He was just going through the motions. You could really notice him being out of sorts. He knew he'd double-crossed Terrence."

Other reports corroborate this, but some reveal an overt, flippant attitude in the young queen.

"He had his hand on Lloyd's back at Sidetrack. Jesus. The nerve."

Whatever the source of the confession, it spread like wildfire around the bar. Text messages filled every cellular network and before long it came to the ears of the mysterious Twitter power, who put it like this:

> *Hedley's new boy wastes no time. Another conquest for Lloyd. He's going for all the boys and all the diseases.*

Terrence was waiting for Lloyd when he got home. He had packed a large suitcase, which would provide a week's worth of reprieve from his cheating husband. Some say he slapped Lloyd when he arrived home. Others say there was an epic row with screams, shouts, and shattering glass heard throughout the condo building.

The most repeated tale, however, the one that was canonized, was that Terrence had been waiting, coolly drinking a glass of wine when Lloyd arrived home. When Lloyd staggered over to him, attempting a kiss, Terrence stuck up his hand and gently pushed his aggressive husband away.

"Someday," the rumors record Terrence saying, "you will look back on this – all of this – and be very sorry. Tonight," he said traversing the apartment, putting his hand on the door, "you have lost something beautiful and proud."

Eight

Nick didn't sleep the night of the incident with Lloyd. Word flooded Boystown flooded via texts, Tweets, and Facebook messages. Nick felt that his person was under direct attack. For better or worse, he now was known for a tryst with one of the most famous rakes on Halsted. The deed itself wasn't scandalous, but the fact that it was so overtly voiced in social media gave the incident weight.

At four in the morning, the July horizon turning blueberry in pre-dawn light, Nick took to the streets and up Broadway. Although initially he had no destination, with each step his resolve grew stronger. Each tap of his sandaled shoes upon the pavement took him more forcefully forward. He couldn't be absolutely sure that he would be awake, but Hedley's hours were never known. At times he would be out until 5 in the morning, but some mornings he would post a selfie paddle boarding on the lake at 7:30 am.

At 4:30 he crossed Pine Grove and walked down the abandoned street toward Hedley's, a towering high rise that looked over Belmont marina. It was an aged building, it's bricks and wrought iron fencing refurbished and scrubbed in the early 2000s. The inhabitants of the building were all moneyed, many of the boats in the harbor belonging to tenants of the soaring tower.

Hey. Nick texted, standing in the growing light. Although it was muggy, the temperature already beginning to pulse upward, he shivered in the early dawn.

What's up?

At your place. Can I come up?

Yes. Just tell the front desk to call me.

Nick passed on the request to the front desk attendant. The old man eyed Nick suspiciously as he held the phone to his ear and announced the arrival to Hedley. Once cleared of the gatekeeper, he walked down the magnificent hall, its gilded moldings and soft chandelier lighting, guiding him toward the golden grill of the East elevators. His heart was burdened with the weight of the evening. Guilt wasn't the source of his feeling so much as fear about his place within the social strata. It had already been reported that Terrence had left, although this wasn't the first time he had picked up and gone, the air was different, charged. Messages lit up his phone into the early hours of the morning from The Set. A group text message thread kept them all linked together. Lloyd, after Terrence's departure, had divulged more pieces of the rendezvous. Nick only sent messages in acknowledgment of incoming information.

"Homewrecker!" Hedley greeted Nick with drink in hand. He had not changed, but wore the same tight dress shirt and form-fitting peach shorts he wore that evening. Although not incredibly muscular, Hedley always carried his weight perfectly. Nick licked his lips as he took in Hedley's bulging thighs, cased in cotton.

"I'm glad you're up."

"I'm always up."

Hedley's apartment was vast and glittering. While a great number of the Boystown gays took to modernizing their apartments, Hedley's lent itself to a rococo design. Garish paintings clung to the forest green walls; huge, gold and scarlet carpets covered wooden floors, while swirling fixtures and sculptures decorated florid wooden end tables. Great cabernet-colored curtains were parted open to look at the rising sun over the harbor. The room appeared to be the stage for some grand party that was ready to begin. Even the table was pre-set with shining tableware, a vase of orchids overflowed in the middle of the oak table.

Hedley threw himself on his emerald sofa, a wry smile on his face. "You're afraid you're in trouble," he said sweetly. "Little Nick, you're fine."

"You think – I mean Terrence and Lloyd…"

"How many times have you been with Lloyd when he's cheated on Terrence?"

Nick relaxed slightly. "He does sleep with everything."

"Everyone. Everything. Terry is just kind of thick, you know. I mean, I'm all for his idea of monogamy or Christian bullshit, but he has to know that he married a whore. How does one not know they married a whore?" With the conclusion of this thought, Hedley used his fingertips to massage his nose. "Poor Terry was trying this open thing with Lloyd earlier this summer. It was an absolute disaster. The only good thing that came of it was the entertainment the rest of us got from Soot trying to figure out if they had a third."

Nick felt better immediately. The sun was just half peaking over the lake's edge. He took a deep breath and sighed. "You think Terrence is really leaving?" he asked.

Hedley shook his head. "No. They've been together forever. I don't expect he's going for good. Although, I think he is starting to figure it out."

"That Lloyd's a whore?" Nick smiled.

"More than that. He's figuring out the whole game, the whole ruin of his love."

"Ruin?"

In that moment, sunlight pouring into the scarlet and green room, Hedley's face illumined like some beatific image, Nick felt that some divine force had guided both men to that particular moment in time. It was everything Nick could do not to rise and sit at the feet of Hedley as he waited for the gay holy man to bless him or divulge a wise parable. The infinitesimal possibility existed, even in Nick's mind, that Hedley had orchestrated the event in its entirety: the cheating, the Tweet, the late-night messages, all forces of motion that had brought Nick to his door. Whatever it was, this morning became sacred to Nick, the final step in his symbiosis with the Gatsby of Boystown.

"Ruin." Hedley sat forward on the sofa. "I think it may be time you learned a little more about me."

In the growing daylight, Hedley told him the full, grandiose saga of Cedric and him, his self-proclaimed death and resurrection. This was the moment that the bones of his love story took on the full, animated life that would serve as a guide and gospel for Nick as he emerged into the full bloom of his gay manhood.

The demise of Hedley's love affair occurred one night in late August. School was about to begin and he planned to visit Cedric, surprise him with kisses in the flushing glow of autumn. New York was still alive with color and summer, although the subtle crisp of fall had found its way into the air. Hedley arrived at Penn Station early in the evening on a Saturday. In autumn twilight he headed into the city, the street lamps just beginning to glow as the sky turned scarlet from the setting sun. Moving down Fifth Avenue, crossing through the illuminated brilliance of Times Square, his enthusiasm burned, building into a feverish anticipation of his lover's embrace. Without being conscious of his body's movement, he found himself sprinting into the belly of Hell's Kitchen.

Cedric had subletted a cozy garden unit for the summer. When Hedley came in early June he quickly made it his archetype for a romantic New York setting: quiet courtyard, summer in New York, the acrid smell of the trash blending with the scent of blooming flowers. A small gate closed it off from 53rd Street. Crossing through the wrought iron portal brought one into a tiny, shared courtyard between two buildings. The owners of Cedric's place were an elderly Irish couple who had tasked Cedric with the job of keeping the overflowing geraniums and potted daisies alive throughout their summer holiday. The air reeked of the city flora, ivy and green cascading from pedestals set around the small courtyard.

As August had come to a close, the plants took on signs of age, their verdant foliage beginning to decay into streaked stalks of gold and dun. Leaves began to fall and litter the small courtyard. The slipping sun bled its dying red light on the cobbled stones.

In those days, Hedley had been a more superstitious person, a sensitive soul with vague dreams and aspirations of grand poetic ideals: youth, beauty, freedom, love, hope. Each moment was full of potential glory, each second a light foot forward into the direction of a bright and noble future. He read the air for signs of this greatness, of the unfolding brilliance of life that resonated in the dull echoes of footsteps on pavement and lilting laughter in the streets. The world in its fluid beauty was a bowl of tea leaves, in which his bright eyes had the perspicacity to read and divine greater truths. In this world of signs and predestination, Hedley made himself profoundly the center of the universe, however, it was an innocently constructed daydream, a beautiful faith in the goodness of this legible world that made him open to read it. In later years, he erected his world out of the skeletons and bones of these former ideals. What had once been an outward looking hope turned into a flood lamp of his own manipulations of others' visions. His view of life had once been a vista of golden morning, but resolutely turned to hopeless twilight: the inversion of his great faith. He no longer sought out the truth in the world, the mysticism in its russet tea leaves, but read the faith of others and spun his own web in which to trap them.

It was in that courtyard on that fall day that, for the first time, this sense of predestination betrayed him. The ailing leaves and blood-red sun told him that his path forward would be marred by some unseen horror. He paused on the cobbled stones, his head tilted keenly to one side. Ahead lay the door, his unseen lover perceptibly felt on the other side. In the brief moment of pause, he felt a sense of urgency rise up, no longer the striving, bursting enthusiasm of that first kiss that he had so innocently anticipated at their meeting, but a fundamental panic – a sharp pain that turned his blood to ice. With trepidation, he moved forward, stepped down the stairs and entered the building's foyer. Cedric's doorway stood before him, an ominous white specter in the fluorescent light. For some reason, whether his tea leaf perspicacity or blind luck, he chose not to text Cedric, but put his fist to wood. He knocked three times.

Cedric answered, his face turned away from the door.

"Our other boy is here," he said, his voice full of laughter. It was the same ringing echo of mirth that Hedley had heard on the streets, now turned to a throbbing gong, striking his temples.

Hedley artistically graces over the full brunt of the scene in his retellings. He focuses on the details of the courtyard, the changing leaves, and his sense of predestination – the trepidation of those steps into the hall. In an editorial decision made years before, he briefly mentions the image of Cedric in tight underwear, joined by another boy with dark, thick locks of hair. There was no fight, no tears, no ruckus. Hedley withdrew.

Fully.

He ran, trembling into the streets of New York. He got his head start, his phone blaring with calls from Cedric after he was a full three blocks away.

With a few strokes on the phone, the number was blocked and he stood shaking at the edge of The North River, his breathing coming in quick pants, his chest constricting around his aching heart.

He paused for a moment before moving on. Staring down at the ground, he forced himself to anticipate each movement, thinking only of the rat-tat of his own footsteps on the concrete sidewalk. With every breath the vision of Cedric and his storybook romance dulled and vanished into the grit of the city around him. The blooming June courtyard, under its halo of golden light, clouded, transformed into a sepulcher lit by a bloody sunset.

It was that moment when he was struck, the temple of his self ruined, laid desolate in the wake of infidelity. He had, over those months, created his alternate universe with Cedric. They were happy, moving toward some unknown but resolute future of bliss and sexual monogamy. The horrors of gay life that he had been taught growing up – the cheating, the sex, the promiscuity, and isolation – had been erased under the halo of Cedric's touch, his kiss, his charisma. In one swift motion this was destroyed, and he saw the whole wretched world for what it was. His sixth sight was gone, replaced by a barren cave, shadows racing over a stone wall.

Here Hedley turned to Nick and shook his head. "That desolation is what Terrence is too afraid to accept," he said. "Life has its baptism but it is a fiery one. It leaves only ash and bone. Terrence," he lifted himself on the sofa, sitting cross-legged and staring into Nick's eyes, "is afraid to grow up. His fear is a fear of life, of the desolation and despair of the unknown."

"What did you do?" Nick asked, still lost in the New York fantasy. "Cedric… What did you do?"

Hedley rose and moved to the bottle of wine at the dining room table. "That, Nick," he said, "is another story, for another time."

#

A few days later a prolonged brunch left Hedley, Nick, and Soot inebriated, garrulous, and wildly ambling between street lamps and buildings, their course a ping-pong trajectory down the sidewalk. The air had settled into an early August mugginess, a whispering breeze drifted from the lake, dousing the heated streets with a steady, lukewarm wind. The trio's wanderings led them past the growing crowds outside of Roscoe's and Sidetrack, the raucous brunch crowd beginning to emerge into the soft dusk with the ambition of being seen.

Hedley laughed as they crossed in front of a local coffee shop, grabbing Nick's hand and pulling him down a side street.

"I want to show you something!" he said gesticulating toward the sky.

Soot's cackle echoed from behind them. "Showing off, Hedders?"

"When have I ever shown off, Sooty?"

They staggered forward, the lamps above them beginning to turn on, the roadway illuminated in splashes of ghostly crème.

"There's someone you should meet, really," Hedley giggled again. "An old flame."

"Really?" Nick stuttered.

Hedley shoved Nick into the street causing him to stumble over a knee-high, wrought iron edging. He tumbled into the pavement, laughing and clutching at his knee.

"Children..." Soot said patting his blazer.

"Look up!" Hedley yelled into the night. "Up and up and up!"

Nick brushed himself off and stood. He drew closer to Hedley, their bodies almost touching. As their relationship grew, it was Nick who pressed at the boundary that separated them. Hedley had never, nor ever had any plan to sleep with any members of The Set. The manipulation of these inevitable, unrequited relationships, was one of his more masterful machinations as the leader of the small coterie. He fostered the closeness without crossing lines. These attachments were forged with fleeting touches, quick glances, and surreptitious smiles cast across rooms and parties.

"The ex," said Hedley. His finger was raised in the direction of the tall billboard, the one that Jordan had pointed out to Nick his first evening in Boystown. On that evening, it had carried the weights of some enchanted, distant object – a foreign representation of gayness, of some alien beings that Nick couldn't quite understand. Now, with Hedley breathing next to him and Soot looking on, the image took on the aura of something beautiful but terrestrial. The portrait was erased of its otherworldly power and stood as only a sign of something that had not yet occurred. Those two male bodies touching, their perfect faces locked in a sultry stare, no longer seemed unattainable but rather present and perfect. Hedley's tea-leaved views had not been erased from the world, but diffused and reborn in others.

Nick looked on in wonder.

"It was amazing while it lasted, but he had to move to New York. It's the inevitable migration for those who outgrow The Windy City." A huge smile lit up Hedley's face. "He's coming to visit next week for Market Days – that should at least be good for a roll in the hay."

"I think I shall move to New York soon," Soot said dabbing his face with a handkerchief. "It's the next thing, you know."

The men looked on for a while longer before their obligations to another party drew them away. From the silence of the side street they emerged in the garrulous herd of Halsted. Hedley's hand was in constant motion, waving to those he passed. Those higher up in the chain got a kiss on the cheek and brief hug before he moved down the sidewalk.

Their trajectory led them to Peter and George's condo. The last time Nick had been there was the party when he had left with Hedley. Since then he had been so busy he hadn't seen his older cousin. Now Peter and George were about to leave for a European vacation and it had been a matter of importance for Peter that Hedley and Nick show up at their last fete of the summer.

"We won't see you for oh-so-long, Nicky," George said over the phone. "Why don't you just stop by for a bit? It doesn't have to be long."

When they entered the condo Nick again felt that everything had been turned down, darkened in juxtaposition to the celestial glow of Hedley's world. What had been, in May, a world of modern color and light, flashes of spring green and gold, was now a diminished, dusty stage in the waning afternoon sun. Even the sounds were different: the bubbly tones of pop music were garbled by a bad speaker; voices coming from the dining room and kitchen were slurred, slow, devoid of the staccato, lively rhythms of the street.

"Come in! Come in!" Peter pointed to the kitchen. "Drinks are in there! Wine and gin as Hedley likes, if I remember correctly…"

Hedley entered with a generous hug and kiss for each of the hosts. Soot extended his withered hand with alacrity.

"Always good to see you both," he said smiling.

The rest of the party reflected the lethargy that Nick noticed upon entry. In the last hours of daylight people were scattered haphazardly around the room. The boy with enormous glasses from the earlier party was staring in awe at Hedley, a goblet clenched in his tiny hands. Hedley made eye contact with him briefly, causing the boy to tremble, spilling his drink on the hardwood floor.

In the far corner of the room, engaged in quiet conversation, was Jordan. He fit the scenery perfectly, his outfit muted, his hair no longer combed over in the latest fashion, hung limply over his forehead. His eyes were covered by the glasses that he religiously tried to keep people from knowing he had to wear. Upon sight of Jordan, Nick nodded politely and resumed discussion. Jordan reciprocated the social gesture and then gently guided the person with whom he was speaking out of the room.

All said, Soot, Hedley, and Nick stayed at the party for only half an hour. Nick spent most of the time talking to Peter and George, getting the overview of their trip to Germany and France. George was especially animated in speaking of a chateau he and Peter would stay at that had once been visited by Neil Patrick Harris and David Burtka. After much polite nodding and feigned interest, the three men quietly withdrew into the night, heading to a different bar, the world of beauty and color that had seemed so diminished in their brief time at Peter and George's, returned under the neon lights of Halsted.

When the door had closed behind them and they emerged back onto Halsted, Nick felt a kind of resolve, a final alteration within himself. The transformation was, in a way, complete. The diffident boy who sat upon the sofa and listened to Jordan espouse his theory of Halsted, had been slowly eroded, destroyed over the course of summer. He had been warned of the division and staunchly taken his position, secure and removed from the fractured world of Boystown in Hedley's garish tower. The world of Peter and George, and on further back, his own history in the dark bedroom trapped in shadow and self-loathing, had been erased at the gym, through parties, drowned in the cacophony of Hedley's world.

Soot left Hedley and Nick and disappeared into the night. Hedley, in one of his fleeting signs of affection, took Nick's arm and whispered into his ear. The words were some little something, a trivial statement, but carried with Nick the power of gospel. In their wake, all else was consumed, all history, memory of his life before their first meeting at his summer Gala was decimated. They continued, arm and arm, into the rambling, chaotic herd that filled the streets at twilight.

Nine

The day Terrence moved out, Lloyd was standing at the kitchen counter, drink in hand. There had been moments of violent emotion over the preceding week, but his doubts had been assuaged away by his friends in the darkness of the neighborhood bars.

Terrence was nuts. Always was.
You're lucky he's finally leaving.
You'll find someone much better. It'll take like 10 seconds.
He was old fashioned in every way – you were just two different people.

Helping Terrence move were Sasha, David, and Sal. Sal, in his old age, couldn't lift much but carried down odds and ends. His major contribution was preparing a large breakfast for all participating movers in his small apartment.

Lloyd awoke to them shifting large boxes. He forced his eyes closed and tried to shut out the sound until Terrence entered the bedroom and began moving out their writing desk. The wooden legs scrapped against the floor. The ruckus of writing utensils, papers, and books tumbling on the hardwood destroyed whatever peace Lloyd had tried to inculcate as the motley crew of movers slammed drawers and slid furniture in the room next door. Lloyd stumbled to the kitchen to get something hot, pouring a handsome sum of Jameson into a mug before filling it with coffee.

Sasha, ever abrasive, was the first to speak to Lloyd. His dark eyes glittered with mischief. "You look lovely, Lloyd. Your bulk from the gym is really showing. Is the Augustus Gloop look in this fall?"

Terrence immediately put himself between the two men, his palm against Sasha's chest, pushing him away from the kitchen. "Let's just go, Sasha. It's not worth it." He turned and limply waved at Lloyd. "We'll be out of here soon."

"The boys are coming," Lloyd said taking a draught from his coffee. "We're all going to brunch and I told them to stop by."

"This early?" Terrence almost screeched. He put a hand through his hair in exasperation. "You all are really going to brunch before noon?"

"Early start to the day. Hedley has a friend in town."

The slow drawl of Lloyd's response struck Terrence as especially cold. The indifference and calm were expected but still painful in their execution. There was something in the tone that made the day seem like any other. This morning, this end to their marriage, was just another thing to happen before brunch.

Terrence hesitated and rubbed the bridge of his nose. "I think there's some champagne in one of the cupboards there… for mimosas. For you all." His insides completely numb, Terrence turned and left the kitchen.

Around the corner from Terrance and Lloyd's, Hedley, Nick, and Stephen were approaching from Hedley's apartment. They stopped upon seeing the U-Haul parked in front of the building. Lumbering up the ramp into the back of the truck was Sal, laboriously lifting a box. Sweat stained his back and poured from his forehead.

"It's sad," Hedley said. "Terrence has lived here for, what, six years? The only people who show up to help him are an old man, a chubby guy, and that ridiculous Sasha."

"I met Sal and David," Nick said pointing to the old man. "I haven't met the other one, Sasha."

"You wouldn't. Sasha," Hedley said pointing to the African-American man coming out of the apartment, "isn't one of us.".

"Funny as hell, though," Stephen piped in, smiling.

"Aren't you chipper." Hedley said.

"I didn't drink last night," Stephen said, putting his hands in his pockets. "I met up with Mikey for some bowling."

Hedley was about to speak when Nick pointed.

"That's David, right?" he observed. The man he indicated was wearing khaki shorts that were entirely soaked through with sweat. "I saw him at a party or something."

"Probably at mine at the beginning of the summer. I saw him there. He's pining after Jonathan."

"I still can't believe that." Nick shook his head.

"A different life ago." Hedley smiled. "Jonathan is another one who rose from the ashes, shook of the dust of his old life. He made something better of himself, too." Hedley put his arm around Nick. "You remember when we met at my party?"

Nick nodded.

"That was a very good night," Hedley said.

"It was."

The three stood in silence, watching the moving men scuttle back into the apartment building. Hedley removed his arm from around Nick and clapped his hands together.

"If my party is the beginning of summer, then next weekend and Market Days is its perfect ending counterpart. It's absolute gay heaven: cute boys come in from out of town; the street is packed with people dancing and celebrating; for once in this weird town we all feel like one big group, rather than a mix of all kinds." Hedley smiled and motioned toward the U-Haul. "Shall we, Stephen?"

Stephen smiled and walked ahead.

"Nicky, go ahead to the restaurant. I'm sure Terrence would love to see you again, but you don't want to make a show…" He winked. "My friend will be there, too. If he's early you two can chat."

Hedley sprinted forward, playfully slapping Stephen on the back as he caught up to him.

It was Lloyd's direct request for them to come over at exactly this time. He phoned them immediately after Terrence called saying he would be picking up all his things in the morning.

"Hedley, please come over. I need to show him that I'm completely impassive – unmoved by all this. Bring as many of The Set as you can get."

Stephen had been the only one available. Skyler had been less and less present lately, his existence bordering on mist-like. He seemed to be always around but never fully present, the one who showed up to the party at its end or fled just after it began.

"Jesus – how desperate. He really wants us there that early to show Terry he doesn't care?" Skyler said in a quick phone call between the gym and a date. "Girl needs some lessons in ambivalence."

Samson had been preoccupied with non-descript Edgewater business, but, in truth, his ties to The Set had grown tenuous over the summer as well. There had been talk of him being cast out altogether, never by The Set itself, but by those in its periphery. His lessening attendance at parties and events, at Progress on Saturday, had been linked to a general indifference to The Set and a fall in the esteem of Hedley. Beard growth and the occasional appearance at SoFo Tap on bear night had further added fuel to the rumors.

When Hedley and Stephen arrived in the kitchen they were met with a tray of mimosas and a beaming Lloyd. "Glad we could start early today, boys!" he cooed.

The chink of their glasses only added to the mounting tension in the room. Terrence disappeared for a half-hour, while Sasha and David quietly worked on packing the DVDs from the entertainment center.

Sal smiled at the appearance of Hedley, sticking out his weathered hand in greeting. "Hedley! It's been a while. How's your summer going?" His voice dropped just slightly as he said, "I got your letter."

Hedley looked slight taken aback, his eyes briefly clouding over. It was just an instant, however, before his smile returned full force. The two men spoke for a short while before Hedley glided over to the window and quietly whispered to Stephen. Lloyd worked to keep up his air of serenity, chatting with all those present about the coming Market Days weekend.

"You'll all be at the festival, won't you?" he asked. "There's a lot of good music! 16 Candles is playing Sunday."

"Ah!" Sal smiled broadly. "Now, that is something I would attend if I weren't so old."

"You're not too old, Sal," Sasha said picking up a box. "Age is a number."

"And mine is very high!" Sal chortled.

Terrence slammed the front door, the sound disrupting the polite conversation. All the men gathered looked at the floor in one choreographed movement. A sense of shame rose as if it were dust, disturbed by the whoosh of the closing door. The group suddenly remembered the solemnity of the situation – the frivolity of the coming summer festival seeming inconsequential and puerile in the midst of a union dissolving.

"Are we about ready?" Terrence asked quickly.

No one said a word. Hedley and Stephen both turned to look out the window.

"You know what," Terrence said slowly, tears forming at the edge of his eyes, "fuck it. Drop it. Let's just go."

#

Lloyd left The Set and Nick immediately before brunch. He had sat down for only a moment at the table before he shot up, remembering he had forgotten to collect something from Terrence. The rest of them were relieved to have him go, his presence a tad too macabre for the bright, summer day. Once in the throes of brunch and another few drinks, Terrence and Sasha, David and Sal, Lloyd and his saddened eyes, disappeared into the realm of bad dreams.

At brunch, Hedley's ex, The Model from the billboard, joined them. To Nick, it was as if the heavens themselves opened and bestowed upon them a creature carved of sinew and light. Even Hedley's bright star was dimmed in the presence of the New York demigod. The rest of The Set had arrived also, along with Jonathan. They took a long booth table at Taverna for brunch, the other gays casting glances upon them, the whole line of beautiful men together resembling The Last Supper.

Nick found relief in being pulled back into the gravity of Hedley and his coterie. Hedley and Stephen told them all about the awkward tension between Lloyd and Terrance that morning. The crawling guilt he felt in the first hours after his rendezvous with Lloyd, writhed up again as he imagined the scene between the two lovers. But now that he was back in the constructed reality of The Set, with Lloyd gone, all was better. In the presence of these beautiful men he felt those creeping feelings disappear entirely.

He wasn't completely free of his emotions, however. In the place of his guilt, there were other pangs of feeling as he watched the scene at brunch unfold. These were manifested in jealous twinges whenever he caught glances between Hedley and The Model. He couldn't help but wonder if there was something he wasn't doing, if perhaps a few more hours at the gym, a little bit different wardrobe would draw The Model's eyes to him. Casually, he looked at his leftover meal and wondered if he shouldn't eat it all. They were going on a boat that afternoon – he didn't want to be bloated.

After leaving brunch, the group walked down Halsted toward Belmont Harbor. The air tremored with laughter, sighs, the sounds of fading summer. Leaves rippled overhead, soft music drifted from coffee shop and bar windows.

As they passed under Peter and George's condo, Nick wondered how they were doing, wondered whether they were on the Riviera. He imagined them staring at Grindr on their phones, their ghostly reflections on the screens. It would be a month before he saw them again. He wondered how their parties would be when he returned, whether Jordan would hang like a wraith around the periphery as he had the week previously. It didn't matter, really, but it was an annoyance dealing with him. Nick was altogether something different than he had been at the start of the summer, and Jordan only reminded him of the darkness from which he had come.

Perhaps he would have his own party. It couldn't be now, not with the embarrassment of his small studio, but at some point, in the near future, he could have a one bedroom. He would bedeck it like Kinsey's, a huge, white sofa filling the living area, a broad, platform bed inviting boys to his bedroom, shining steel counters, twined with greenery would decorate the kitchen. He'd mix in a dash of Hedley's style as well, windows would be dressed with scarlet drapes, and his bookshelves littered with garish, vellum volumes. Eventually, he would get a condo, something lavish in The Gold Coast, where Hedley had his sights now set. This would mean posher furniture, soaring chandeliers, thicker carpets, designer pillows, reflective, shining kitchen appliances and views of the city sweeping forward over the lake – that gleaming, azure surface that had given the city its life.

This future condo, this luxurious ideal, became a fixed point in his mind; the end goal of his offline fantasy adventure. He considered the point when he was wealthy enough to attain this status as the final stage in his gay, nay, personal evolution. He was now buried in the twisting, freewheeling streets of the city, but in his perfect future, he would be above it, staring down from the blank, black windows of a luxury tower. This future was his – his right, his entitlement. He would live among the beautiful and wealthy. He never pondered what his future home had once been: the site where Streeter defended his territory against the force of the Chicago police, a short distance from River North, where homosexuals, prostitutes and African Americans gathered in fear and celebration, in seedy back alleys during the early Twentieth Century. These histories made no impression; they were discarded as carelessly as his own.

This Gold Coast Idyll was at the forefront of his mind as he and The Set stopped on their perambulation down Halsted to look at a window decoration. In the shop, male mannequins, dressed in harnesses and chaps, were bent over in provocative positions. As the group talked, Nick saw his old ideal – a wonderful future, once an impossibility in the dark of his high school bedroom – staring back at him. He stood, muscled, toned, quaffed, laughing amongst an entourage of beings breathless with their own beauty. In the darkness of his room, years ago, yanking at his own self under the covers of his bed, Nick had imagined, forced himself into a vision of a future where he stood between men for which he desired, pined, lusted. Now these memories were crushed, reconstituted, forged into the form of his towering dreams of the Gold Coast.

This moment of perfection, of celestial motion upward and forward, broke, however, as individual pinpoints began to focus in his gaze. The Model, for one, standing taller than him, his rippling biceps stretching at the fabric of his shirt, bigger, thicker, than his own. Another, Skyler, his eyes shielded behind thick sunglasses radiated an aura of movie star charisma. His smile, when applied, spread across his face like a rough stone severed to reveal diamond. Third, Hedley's thick hair, his flowing mane that hung perfectly around his face, framing his light eyebrows, his bow-like mouth, and verdant eyes. Soaring, falling, crushing, rebuilding – the moment broke, as a fever, a flash of red, in their golden afternoon. The group moved from the window dressing, slowly pacing down the street toward the harbor.

"Wait until you see his boat," The Model said pulling at a loose strand of his hair. "Gorgeous. Yacht. They have two full bars – one upstairs, one down."

"It has to be better than that shitty barge Soot took us on a few weeks ago," Skyler scoffed. "I swear to God the thing was going to sink at the dock."

"When was that?" Nick looked anxiously between Hedley and Skyler.

Hedley laughed, a high ringing sound. "A few weeks ago? A boat of Trevor Johannsen, I think. He's a realtor in the city."

"It was distasteful," Skyler said.

"Well, this is not, and if you think it is you must be the fanciest bitch I have ever met." The Model turned down Belmont, walking them all toward the water.

"This one is definitely fancy," Stephen said, "a whore and not a prostitute."

"She is occasionally sober, Stevey," Skyler interjected. "So, one up on you."

The group laughed as one chorus, loud and resonant. The sound rebounded between the Catholic Church and the brick apartments along the street.

Over their heads the sun had climbed higher, bringing the temperature of the day to its soaring climax, the heat rose off the paved roads in concussive waves. As they drew closer to the water, sweat began to trickle down their brows and back, shirts were removed and thrown over their shoulders.

Across the street passers-by watched the group of men, images of masculine grace moving down the street, laughing in chorus at the barbs and antics of the others. Again, Nick rose to his heights, the fears, the nagging of the shop window's reflection erased in the joy of the afternoon.

At the boat they were met by a group of young men. In the midst of the crowd, Soot and another aged gay from New York greeted them with cheek kisses and flattering comments.

"Scorching hot, honey."

"What a man, covered in all this sweat."

"Thank God for heat and how it makes shirts go away."

The boat, *The IknowIm Gay*, was a yacht of immense proportions; its white, gleaming surface shining in the daylight. Soot poured cocktails while the New York man gave them a tour.

The day was quintessential for Chicago in August. The heat threw itself on the city like a blanket, a soft breeze rolling off the lake, barely stirred the trees. The other boats around them were alive with the sounds of laughter and music. Two docks down, a group of other gay men were preparing to go out as well. Among them were Clive, Kinsey, and Myrtle, caterwauling along to a 90's song. Myrtle managed to spot Nick from his position on the deck. She blew him a sloppy kiss, almost falling over the stern.

"It's so sad that summer's coming to an end," The Model said, a tinge of emotion rising in his baritone voice. "I suppose I'll spend most of the winter in Guatemala and Sao Paolo, but it's sad nonetheless."

Nick surreptitiously watched Hedley gaze upon The Model. For once Hedley's power was not absolute; small chinks were visible in his ample armor. Under the sweeping gaze of his former lover, Hedley was smaller, diminished, a dilettante in the presence of her matinee idol. He would gaze on The Model, eyes focused, looking so intently that Nick thought Hedley's stare may penetrate The Model completely, burn a hole through his chiseled torso and rip toward the horizon, a line of concentrated flame.

But these obsessive looks did little to diminish Hedley to Nick; the primary effect the raising of The Model in his esteem. In his worship of Hedley, Nick had not looked beyond his tutor and gay guide but remained complacent. Had he seen that there were more beautiful, more cultured, more magnificent men out in the world, he would have raised his own standards of achievement. In truth, he was now jealous, intermittently, but sharply when he saw Hedley's eyes fixated on The Model. His mind wondered to the dark place, that bedroom of his pubescent years where shame and feelings of unworthiness wrapped his body in a thick blanket. It was different, and in Nick's own mind, separated sharply by his own vision of who he had been, who he had become.

The boat pushed off, the large yacht drifting out of the harbor and into the open waves of the lake. The boys had stripped to their swimming outfits, most of them in tiny pieces of lycra, precariously stretched over their private areas. Soot remained fully clothed, a white, cotton shirt billowing in the wind. Around him soft, ash-like motes circled, believed to be from his new powder-based sunscreen.

Stephen was the one to turn on the music. With a martini in hand, he cranked up the yacht's stereo speakers and began to awkwardly dance through the crowd on the deck.

When no one would join him, he grew surly and shoved Skyler. "You all are all wet," he groaned. "Myrtle would be out here with me."

"Or passed out inside," Skyler quipped.

Upon this rejection, Stephen and a few others drifted into the main cabin to be closer to the cocktails. Hedley, The Model, Skyler, and Nick remained on the deck. The old New Yorker soon joined them.

Conversations batted back and forth. Most often the topic was redirected by The Model, who managed to force their flow into long diatribes about his most recent shoots in Sri Lanka and Brisbane. Those gathered minded little, as it gave them more time to imagine his life among other models, reclining on some foreign beach, his pouted lips pressed firmly together for the camera.

To the west, the city passed. Before them, near North Avenue, a long stretch of sand filled with sun worshipers drifted into their line of site. Castaways, the large boat-shaped structure that served as the bar and bandstand, stared back at them, an alien object between the saffron sands and waving green boughs of the park. Behind all this, the city appeared fully. The Hancock Building and the Drake Hotel's neon sign, dark in the blazing light of day, stared down at them indifferently. The Trump's peak appeared and vanished between the form of other skyscrapers. Overhead the sky spread in all directions, a deep, azure blue.

Waves lapped upon the bow of the boat in a slow, steady rhythm. Nick had moved and now sat on the edge, his feet hanging over the water as he stared critically at his own reflection in the rippling waves. The Model spoke on. The old New Yorker laughed. Hedley, sensing Nick had moved, looked over at him and caught his eye. A smile spread over his lips, one that Nick returned with uncontrolled joy.

The boat had come to rest, drifting up and down in the water, lost in its own isolation. The Model stopped speaking for a moment, taking a long draught from his drink. In that moment, the world hummed around them. The sounds of the city and urban life echoed between the towers rising and falling along the city's skyline. In the past there had been the sounds of riots and fire. A blaze had engulfed the whole world for one day, turning the city's soul to embers.

But on the boat, there had been no sound once it had come to rest. Even the music paused in the heat of the early afternoon. Fire on that vessel was rendered bone-chillingly quiet – past, present, future. It was drowned out by the quiet lap of water. The force of its history, its terror, its beauty, left silent in the wake of vague, ephemeral dreams. In the reflection of Nick's eyes nothing real remained; he saw only the quivering, hallucinated forms of Hedley and his former lover. In his mind's eye, he saw his idealized future – a condo above the city, a cage of glass and steel. Looking out from his windows, he'd see his kingdom spread out before him: reflection upon reflection upon reflection.

The Exodus

"A beautiful thing is never perfect."

– Egyptian Proverb

Summer 2015

Welcome to the Pity Party

It's just a flash, but I saw it over and over: an image after he left – cracked skin, red running out over my wrists and into water. The world was over and there was no other way to move on but to slash wrists and hear the clatter of the knife on the floor. The glamor of the idea, the thought of him missing me and sobbing at my gravesite, the look of slick blood on white porcelain tub and tile, verified that it wasn't a real wish, but a fantasy used to decorate stark reality. At first it had been more earnest, the details all crystal in my mind's eye. Over time dulled by space and time, it took on the grainy haze of old film. But I remember it. I go back to it at different times. Sometimes it's just alone in the early morning hours, a cold void in the bed we shared, or after I see him on the street, another boy holding tight to his hand. Then from the Halsted glow, from the brightness of early morning, it's back to cold fluorescent lights, ivory tile, blood.

He'll miss me.

I think those words, the fantasy warming the cold space created in my insides when I see him out, doing well, a smile cutting across the face I used to claim with a kiss. And I'm alone, the routine of my day desiccating the pain of his absence. Months have gone by, but the sting is there. And then he's out, laughing, smiling, he waves to me across the room – that's the point it comes back:

Knife, water, white, blood.

"And how are we, David?"

That's how my therapist would begin. He's old and has hair in his ears, but for some reason I found that reassuring.

Dr. Konstantin and I had had our relationship for about six months that one afternoon in May. I started seeing him at the behest of Sasha because my activities after Jonathan left had been reduced to pizza and Netflix with occasional sobbing peppered in. Being twenty-seven and knowing everything, I believed therapists were only for crazy people. For my specific demographic, strained homosexuals on the verge of buying cats number one, two, and three. But after I started seeing the good doctor, I had felt better (desires for cats two and three ebbing slightly). Like a valve slowly letting off steam, I had started to get back to normalcy.

That May day I was feeling terrible because Alexis was getting married. The following Friday afternoon I had to drive back to Michigan for the ceremony.

"I feel like it's the universe telling me that it's all hopeless. Like, just forget it and pick out a burial plot alone somewhere with enough space next to it for my collection of Precious Moments figurines," I said.

Dr. Konstantin didn't think I was funny, which just means he has good taste. Generally, after I told a joke he inserted a pause before his response to specifically indicate the spot where laughter should be.

The pause, then: "Why does the wedding make you feel like that?"

"Alexis, even up to six months ago said she was never going to get married. That it was an oppressive part of the patriarchy that she would never participate in. We made a pact that we would move in together and read literature and do crossword puzzles. Then she met a lawyer named Chuck and that's all gone."

"So, you're angry at her?"

"Not specifically at her, but more the universe in general. Like, love seems to happen to other people but never to me."

"Well, you haven't really been open to it lately. I believe your comment last week was that, 'all men are pieces of shit.'"

I'm not a nice guy, I would say. I'm kind of an asshole, but in general I keep that bottled up in pleasant company. Dr. Konstantin got all of it, though. When I was with him I was just an id. I cursed, I hated, and I loathed. I can only imagine what he told other people about me at his doctor happy hours.

That hateful queen was in today...

So today in white, affluent gay problems...

"They are," I continued, "but I want one. I want one who cooks and isn't a piece of shit. I mean, he can even be a piece of shit, but maybe rich, too? That could be fine. Sasha has one."

"You know you don't just want money, David." Dr. Konstantin stared at me, his aged face sagging into a frown. Based on a picture of his son he kept on his desk, I think he may have been a handsome man fifty years before. He still has thick, chestnut hair and one can see that his jawline used to be strong. I self-consciously stroked my own face, wondering when age would strike it and gravity do its hateful work.

"I know," I said. "But I'm just so tired of the bars, the meat market on Saturday nights. I want it to be over."

"Well, then, why don't you start dating again?"

Always this point. When we first started our sessions I just blubbered a lot and talked about Jonathan. Dr. Konstantin would nod as I told him about our third date for the 300th time.

I loved that date.

But sessions had turned into me complaining about my life, my weight, and how hot Jonathan had become. He's really hot now. He started his whole body sculpting thing the last few months before we broke up. That was probably when he was fucking everyone else – or at least the several I knew about. In retrospect, I should have left him, maybe those affairs were nice ways of him telling me that it was over. But I stayed. I pined, and then he left.

The doctor wanted me to date again and I wasn't sure. I'd never really dated to begin with. When I met Jonathan in college, we had been each other's first real relationships, and I didn't even know where to start. Sasha had suggested Grindr.

"Just for the needs, honey," he said. "It's not dating, it's just finding a place to stick your dick to keep it warm and virile. Just get on PrEP and wrap your dick. We don't want you upping that viral load."

So, I did fool around a few times, one awful sexual encounter with a closeted cop ended a brief run right after my break up with Jonathan. Then I deleted the app and was tempted by OKCupid and Scruff and Adam for Adam and on and on and on. But I didn't know – I wasn't over Jonathan and I was afraid.

"I don't know," I said getting sheepish.

"Rejection, I know." Dr. Konstantin steepled his liver-spotted hands. "But you have to face it sometime. There will be rejection. There will be men that have good chemistry with. There will be men that are terrible. You have to face it head on, though."

"Not just rejection," I said looking out the window. "There is so much awfulness. I mean look at what Jonathan did to me, but then look at my friend Terrence. He's married for fucksake and it doesn't end. It's lying a cheating and making excuses for someone."

Poor Terrence. One of my oldest gay friends, and one I'd seen struggle the longest. How many times would I have to lecture him before he dumped Lloyd and moved on? How many Tweets did everyone in Boystown have to get about Lloyd's latest bang before it sunk through his dull, optimistic head?

But then again, I'd walked that path. I'd been the one who cooked breakfast for the guy that had fucked the upstairs neighbor the evening before.

"We should try positivity, David," Dr. Konstantin drawled. He used one of his liver-spotted paws to wipe his nose. "Let's, for once, just pretend like everyone's not a horrible person."

I stood up and walked to the window. The office overlooked the Chicago River. Even the river's green, semi-toxic water seemed to be bubbling and laughing at me below. "Why can't it just happen?" I asked. "Like with Alexis, she just went to a bar one night and Chuck was there. Love happened to them. I don't really believe in that, but it's nice to think about. The idea that a sort of Swiftian Love Story can happen to you."

"Well, whether you believe or not, unless you are putting yourself out there, being open and vulnerable, nothing can happen to you. Life can't even happen to you."

I knew he was right. I moved from the window and plopped on the couch, the faux leather making a popping, flatulent sound. "I'll try. I will. This time I actually mean it. The Alexis thing is a wake up. If a vociferous feminist liberal can succumb to a white wedding, then I can go on a date with a banker named Chad."

"That's a start."

"A new beginning," I said looking out the window. From the couch the mocking river wasn't visible. All I could see was the city's beautiful, multi-faceted skyline.

I meant it. Why not? I'd find a boy and get married; we'd have nice furniture. That's the goal, right? That's what it's all about.

#

Sasha and Edward's apartment is not what you'd expect. Despite his vanilla exterior, Edward has a variety of odd habits, one of them collecting Egyptian-themed artwork and collectibles. Above Sasha and his bed, staring at them as they sleep is a rather ugly painting of Min, the Egyptian God of fertility, erect penis and corncob hat in tow.

"I wouldn't call it tasteful," Sasha said the day I helped them hang it.

"Honey," Edward had said, "if either of us had any regard for taste we wouldn't have ended up together."

Edward and Sasha met about a year and a half before. Unlike Alexis and her man across the bar, they had been in a volunteer group at the Center on Halsted. At a board meeting one night Edward had asked Sasha out. He said no – he had said no five times before committing to one drink at Wood on a Wednesday night.

"He completely underwhelmed me," Sasha said. "And it was exactly what I was looking for."

As their relationship grew, I spent occasional nights with them. When Jonathan began his, for lack of better term, transition away from me, I ended up on their couch more and more frequently. When he left, I was a permanent fixture.

"So, The Greek wants you to date again?" Sasha looked at me impishly over Edward's home cooked dinner. "Well, my God, for once I agree with him."

"He's wanted me to date for a while," I said. "I didn't want to bring it up, though."

Edward returned to the table with a steaming tray of mixed vegetables. Upon taking his seat he smiled broadly. "I love the feeling of putting the last piece of dinner on the table."

"Edward, it appears that David has ended his mourning and is going to start dating again."

"Oh!" Edward clapped his hands. "Gregory. I work with him; you two would be perfect. I mean he's a little older – my age," Edward winked and jokingly played with his eyeglasses, "but he's really smart and quite handsome."

"Oh no," Sasha groaned. "He's so boring! I talked to him at the Christmas party and he almost put my coffee to sleep."

"Let's be nice," Edward said shortly.

"No, no! I really appreciate it Edward," I said, "but I think I just need to go on bad dates. A lot of them. Get my skin back up, get back in the groove, you know."

"You've never had a groove, Sweetie. I've seen you dance." Sasha pointed his fork at me.

"Leave us poor white boys alone," Edward said laughing.

"You'll only get reprieve from me when you can handle The Macarena."

Edward laughed and reached across the table. He leaned in for a kiss, which Sasha gave him happily. "I'll practice at the weddings this summer," Edward said. "No guarantees."

Since the breakup, I had become repulsed by expressions of love. Being extremely single, it felt as if every couple on the street was making out or fondling each other to mock me. Every loving glance, every stolen touch served to point out what bliss I'd experienced with Jonathan. What bliss I'd experienced with Jonathan before he experienced much bliss, without me: on our sofa, on our dining room table, in our bed, and probably propped up on our throw pillows. But Sasha and Edward were immune from my judgment. Their natural, easy love was permissible since they had put up with my unnatural, difficult nature over the past year.

"I appreciate your help, lovebirds," I said plopping a filet onto my plate, "but I'll be fine on my own. I just wanted to make you aware that there will be more varied bitching in the future."

"Hear, hear!" Sasha raised his glass. "No more Jonathan bitching."

"To future bitching about Tom and George and Albert and Zeno and Zeus and any other man who proves to be offensive to you!" Edward clinked glasses with Sasha and then with me.

After dinner I helped Sasha clear the table and wrap up the remaining food. In the living room Edward had on a pre-recorded episode of The History Channel. The droning baritone of the aged narrator mixed well with the melodic clink of glasses and plates in the kitchen.

"This weekend's the wedding then?" Sasha asked as I put the last plate away. He was at the kitchen counter pouring us another glass of wine.

"Yeah, I am dreading it."

"The family part, the wedding part, or the Alexis, the rabid feminist, finding pure bliss part?"

"All of the above." I leaned petulantly against the countertop. "I was g-chatting with Terrence at work and he said weddings are new beginnings, so I should live in that moment."

"Sounds like he's doing okay after the Kinsey thing."

"We don't talk about the Kinsey thing."

"You white people love not talking about things."

"WASPs love our silence. Unless it's to talk behind your back."

"That must be why we get along so well," Sasha winked at me.

We returned to the dining room table. The room was fairly dark, two candles lighting up half the room, the other half illuminated by the TV projecting Edward's program. As the narrator's voice droned on, I fixed my gaze on the outside world. Their apartment building sits near the corner of Belmont and Sheridan and looks out over Lake Shore Drive and the twinkling lights of the harbor. Directly north and southeast one can see other high rises with dotted windows of light and dark. The glass panels stare dispassionately, some concealed behind closed blinds, others open with fluttering curtains.

"You ever see anything exciting in the other windows?" In my head I imagined some unfolding horror, Rear-Windowesque murder and mayhem. Perhaps behind one glass pane, a lone, blue-hued woman, watches nighttime television and paints.

"Oh," Sasha laughs and runs to the window. He cups his hands around his eyes and peers into the dark. After a few, brief moments, he sighs and leans back. "The shows not on tonight."

"Show?"

"Skyler," Sasha smiles, "that little tart who hangs out with Hedley? He fucks across the way. I mean, technically speaking, is fucked."

"By some pretty boy?" I grew hard thinking of Hedley's tiny, rippling henchman being plowed by a (lacrosse? football?) player.

"Oh, no," Sasha smirked. "Eddy, how would you describe Skyler's man friend?"

"Well-done?" Edward said. "Overcooked? I can never find the right adjective."

"What?" I asked.

"Yeah, huge, ugly, overcooked dude. Age unknown. He could be anywhere from thirty-five to sixty. Wears Abercrombie. Perfect body of course, but his skin is the color of V8 juice."

"What a fantastic descriptor, V8.'"

"You're welcome. Yeah, they fuck every week or so. Skyler sneaks in. We noticed one Saturday when we stayed in."

I looked across the street into the wall of other lives across the way. It would be so wonderful to be able to slip into the night and travel into another existence, just for a bit.

"He may be ugly, but you can't argue with The Set. Pretty much anyone would trade places with any one of them," I said.

"Well," Sasha said turning away from the window and traversing to the couch. "I can tell you that on the nights they break out the leather and V8 has him gagged and bent over the couch, I'm happy just where I am."

Tomorrow Comes Alive

I took him home. We drove through sparse farmland and flat roads, running toward their bleak infinity, the Midwest horizon. My parents greeted us with open arms and cheek kisses. My mother giddy as could be, set the table in shining silver and china plates that glowed like the moon. The evening crawled on in quiet talk, trivial discussion about his family and upbringing. As he told each anecdote I'd look over into his brown eyes and think, "He's mine. This one is all mine."

After glasses of wine and my mother magicking away the dirty plates, we found ourselves hand-in-hand walking out into the yard. Around us night had settled; the sky was pebbled with the lights of a 1000 stars. Hushed words passed between us, nothing important was said, but the moment seemed to wholly contain us. There were few other times that I could remember a moment and imagine it so fully down to the details of the grass – white moonbeams bathing the dark green stalks that swept up and down the shore of the lake. Frogs sang, an innumerable horde of them in their croaky chorus. Their music filled the night, their voices rippling through the moonstruck grasses.

The moment was silent but expanded outward. It had been my dream when coming out of the closet to take someone to that place, my home, my beginning, and show him how wild the night was. Outside of cities and landscaped college campuses, in the heart of it all, was this expanse of beautiful green and night and stars. We stayed silent while the moment expanded. I thought with each croak of the frogs' song that if the seconds continued their outward momentum I would be fine with my life being composed of this small piece of night, expanding outward, on and on, into perpetuity.

Mya smiled at me as I walked up to the church. A summer scarf was pulled around her milky white shoulders, her hair fell down her back in thick auburn curls. It occurred to me in that setting, heading to a straight wedding, hiding my new chubbiness under a suit a size too big in every direction, that in some alternate reality I might have married her.

"I'm so glad you're here." She threw her arms around me. "No one else could come."

"I thought Cat and Toby would."

"The baby, I guess." Mya laughed. "I don't know too much about that adult stuff. I guess the little things get pissy if you don't feed them."

"Like your pussy?" I asked.

Mya roared with laughter. The elderly couple next to us looked horrified.

"Shit," I whispered.

"I forget what it's like in rural public."

"That shit's still funny in rural public. Trust me."

Mya and I had stayed close friends through college and into our current phase of adulthood. In college we'd used Instant Messenger to keep in touch, after that it was trips between her home in Peoria, Illinois and Indianapolis, where Jonathan and I had settled after college. The doldrums, I called it. He was in grad school and I was whittling away at accounting work for a small firm in the downtown area. Neither of us knew what adulthood was then, so we stayed close, more out of habit than anything else. Mya would come visit and we'd stay up late in our apartment. Occasionally we'd go to a gay bar like Greg's, but most of the time we'd grab pizza or burgers and talk about nothing. At twenty-two and twenty-three, we'd wander the streets of downtown Indianapolis like a group of homeless Bohemians.

That seemed a lifetime ago as Mya and I entered the church and greeted Alexis's mother. Her father had run out on them when she was about six, an item that I believed contributed to Alexis's unshaved arm pits and Sylvia Plath obsession in 11th grade. Her stepfather, Grant, was about as big a farmer old-boy as you could meet. His cowboy boots shone white in the fluorescent lights of the church.

"Ah!" her mother, Gladys, gushed. "It's so nice to see Lexi's oldest friends! You know it says a lot about a person when their old friends are still around."

"Can you stop referring to us as old?" Mya winked at me, pulling back a strand of her hair.

"Oh! You know what I mean. You all are just kids!"

"Y'all are looking mighty handsome and purdy to me!" Grant inserted in his nebulous, (maybe?) southern accent. "It's a shame you two don't have dates." Grant stroked his salt-n-pepper beard. "David, ain't there any nice fellas up there in Chicago for you?"

I sometimes pine for a life in which my whole town isn't so accepting of my gayness. Everyone *loves* that I am gay. My mother told everyone when I came out in college. She's the kind of woman who would append "My son is gay" with "if you don't like it you can just suck on a bag of sweet potatoes." Somehow this idea had made its way around to everyone. Acceptance had become, not just being nice to me, but pressing for details about my dating and sex life. Everyone in town felt a massive overcorrection was in order for the ails of other communities that weren't so supportive.

"I've been dating around since me and Jonathan broke up," I said.

"Shame there haven't been any takers," Gladys said.

"Gladys and I were watching that TV show about the gays last week and we both stopped and said, 'we wonder how Davey's doin'?'"

Grant stared at me as if there was an appropriate conversational response to this. I nodded my head. When that didn't assuage the awkwardness, I began shuffling from side to side.

I was grateful for the feeling of Mya's hand on my back pushing me into the sanctuary. "We'll see you after the ceremony!" she called back.

The ceremony itself sashayed between awkward and heartwarming. Alexis and Chuck (well, Alexis) had opted for a ceremony "of the earth." The officiator was an androgynous toga'd person with garlands of flowers named Shalaya. Shalaya had obviously spent a former life as a Baptist minister as her "heart song" lasted roughly 45 minutes and wandered between ideas of unified gender and a poem by Wordsworth. The ceremony ended with a spirited drum solo and Chuck and Alexis kissing, united under their new chosen family name of Woodsmith, an innovative combination of their last names.

Pictures between the event and the, to everyone's relief, traditional wedding reception were at a local park, which allowed some time for Mya and I to head back to my parents' place.

My brother, Brad, answered the door in a tank top and cargo shorts, holding the latest of their brood. The tiny, wrinkled thing giggled at Mya's fiery hair.

"Sup?" my brother said.

Inside my mother was sitting at the dining room table with my brother's wife, Susan. I love my brother and his wife (and 2 of their 3 children), but communicating with them was probably analogous to the first settlers landing on North America and being confronted with the native people. Their days consisted of the minutiae of suburbia: groceries, work, mowing the lawn, talking about the neighbors. Meanwhile, my routine consisted of drinking heavily and talking to friends about whose dick they sucked the previous weekend. Trips home always made me a little envious of the quiet of their lives. While they had evenings at home listening to children laughing in the streets and cicadas, I was listening to bad electronic music and twinks crying over their lost lovers. It wasn't that either of them was better than the other – I certainly could never move back home – but I always wondered if there was some way to bridge the two worlds. It was probably a false hope, like the Egyptians thinking embalming their kings would let them take their bodies with them to the afterlife; just by getting a condo and putting up a white picket fence, I couldn't channel rural living into the heart of the city.

"There he is!" My mother leapt up and gave me a hug. Her hair was done up, as it had been since 1996, and dyed to the point that its color could no longer be described as a "natural." "Mya, good to see you, doll."

"Hey Mrs. Jenkins," Mya said. "You look great!"

"Oh!" my mother cooed. "There's that new lady gym in town. I've been going a half hour in the morning. No men allowed!"

By the grace of God, my brother and I hadn't inherited my mom's personality, which bordered on obnoxious. Somehow it was balanced by her small-town charm and the fact that she had looked fifty for the past 30 years. She wasn't the kind of woman who cared too much about appearances. The moment she married it was mom jeans and seasonal shirts and sweater sets. She was only fifty-five, but she had settled into AARP living in her early thirties.

My father was the typical, stoic Midwestern man. Lookswise, he was tall and gangly with a belly that distended over his high-waisted pants. He talked briefly, and when he did it was mostly about football or guns. On days when there would be visitors, like the day of Alexis's wedding, he'd make up a task to do to get out of the house. Today it was looking for a new fishing rod. For some reason it was imperative it happen exactly between the hours of three and seven when we'd all be gathered. My guess is that he was seated in a McDonald's doing a crossword puzzle.

Somehow, the mixture of my bald father and dowdy mother's genes, had created my brother, who basically looked like a movie star. From the age of fourteen on he was a matinee idol: athletic, handsome, studly. I counted it a blessing that I was a few years older and there wasn't the pressure to be any of those things. My brother was rather dumb, but this was easily forgiven in high school.

"Speaking of gyms," my brother said taking a drink of bottled water. "You're looking a little tubby, David."

"Now gosh!" my mom jumped. "Let's keep it friendly! We only get to see Davey a few times a year. Let's not scare him off."

"Your face looks fat," my brother continued. He then puffed out his own cheeks. "Swollen."

"City bees," I said quickly.

Mya laughed, as did Susan. My mother was wringing her hands, having not realized after thirty years of family life that our reunions were never as perfect as she envisioned them.

A silence blossomed in the room. Brad looked at me as if he still expected a response to his insult. I would have loved to tell him about eating feelings, but I didn't think it would be a concept he'd be familiar with.

Fortunately/unfortunately the loaded quiet was broken by my grandmother and Aunt Charlotte coming into the room. Grandma lagged behind Charlotte, her walker struggling over the lush carpet of my parents' foyer. Aunt Charlotte blustered in. She attacked me with a big hug, her ample breasts smashed into my face.

"Well, my stars!" she bellowed. "It's the prodigal son! Mom, look who's here!"

My grandma nodded. "Hey Davey," she said grabbing my hand. I helped her take the seat next to mine.

"Don't you look just so nice! And little Mya, too!" Aunt Charlotte clucked. "City boy coming home!" Aunt Charlotte barreled on. "Doing his fancy accounting work! You kids do all these things I can't even imagine."

Charlotte thinks accountants are gods. I don't know if there was some childhood trauma that ended with her being saved by a rippling Fabio-type accountant, but, to her, my job was on as high a pedestal as doctor, lawyer, or lesser deity. In general, everything amazed her: my mother's cooking, Priuses, tablet computers. Rarely did a conversation take place that she wasn't rambling on about modern science or how "amazing" kids these days are.

"Well, how was the wedding?" my mother asked.

Mya and I looked at each other and sniggered.

"Alexis is so weird," Brad said. "I thought she was a dyke for the longest time." Susan gave him a look, which promptly elicited a "Not that there's anything wrong with that."

"They had this Earth Ceremony… I think you call it?" I looked at Mya who was shaking with laughter. "The pastor let us all know that we are now *post*-post-feminist. So that was enlightening."

"The drums," Mya had her hand over her mouth. "Tell them about the drums."

"Oh! So, this fat white guy wearing traditional African garb played bongos. That was the backdrop to their first kiss."

"No!" my mother was laughing, fat tears rolling down her cheeks. "What did it mean? Did it symbolize something?"

"Bad drum music?" I said.

"You know it amazes me all these different traditions and beliefs," Aunt Charlotte said. "So many people on the earth – so many ideas!"

My grandmother rolled her eyes. "Liberals."

Susan, who despite her twenty-five years, maintained the naiveté of a small child, piped in. "I think it must have been nice. Were there beautiful flowers?"

"The flowers were lovely," Mya said.

"I would think so."

"The florist next to me makes the most beautiful arrangements. I don't know how he does it." Aunt Charlotte placed her hand on Mya's. "So many colors – some of them have balloons!"

"I think when I get married it will be really quiet," I said. "No hoopla, just like an exchanging of rings and a kiss, then lots of dancing."

"You gotta have a pastor," my mother grew deathly serious. "Pastor Bob will do the officiating. He did a great job for Joni and Pete's kids this fall."

"How's his wife?" my grandmother asked.

"Good, I think she's finally back to normal after the chemo." My mother scrunched her face. "Mom, was that you?"

"Can't help it," Grandma said. "You lose control in your eighties."

Brad gave Grandma a high five. "That was nice, Grams," he said.

"Are you looking forward to getting married?" Charlotte had missed Grandma's fart entirely. Her jeweled hand had not let go of Mya's since she clutched it regarding balloons. "I bet you want a big event."

"I don't think *I* do. My mother is a different story." Mya winked at my mother.

"Oh, Patty is going to make it a big event. Only child that's a girl? That's a big deal."

"I love big, white weddings!" Charlotte finally relinquished her grip on Mya. She needed both hands to wave her chubby fingers through the air in front of her. "Lace, and flowers, and something borrowed – the whole picture."

"What was your wedding like, Charlotte?" Mya asked.

Charlotte faltered for a moment.

My grandmother, still sharp as a tack, stepped in. "Rush job," she said. "Anybody want to join me for a cigarette?"

#

The reception was remarkably mainstream. A DJ played "Twist and Shout", they cut a (organic, gluten-free) cake, and Alexis's sister got drunk and hit on Chuck's cousin, Todd. Mya and I were seated by some of our other high school friends, which was less awkward than I had thought it would be.

When Jonathan and I had been together, I only stayed in contact with a few people from my past. Most I hadn't talked to since coming out. While I didn't care what they thought, I did worry about being in confined spaces and having to deal with awkward questions in person. As I mentioned, my hometown has good vibes about it, but it's uncomfortable when the couple across from you is talking about their four babies and you only have stories about how the bartender at Progress looks kind of like Matt Bomer and you mentioned this to him when you were vomiting in a urinal and he was beside you in the bar's bathroom.

As I watched Chuck and Alexis dance to their first song, something by Bjork, I felt genuinely happy for them. From afar it's easy to say that the universe is unfair and that your crazy feminist friend found love so why can't you, but when you see it in action, it's nice. I had only met Chuck one other time, but he was exactly what Alexis needed: bland, smiling, and totally in love with her. He could talk about everything, but didn't need to say anything. They looked pretty perfect swaying to the wall of Icelandic noise coming from the speakers. Alexis had her head on Chuck's bony shoulder. She looked radiant - plump and shining in her long, white dress, her big grey eyes staring into their shared future. Chuck, in his too big suit, bald head reflecting the tea lights, gave a thumbs up to a group of aged fraternity brothers that chuckled and cheered as he dipped Alexis.

At about eleven, Mya and I snuck out to the back of the reception hall and lit a cigarette I had taken from my grandmother. It was a running joke between us – when I'd been fifteen I snatched a whole pack from a lady who dropped her Marlboros at a restaurant. We smoked them in Mya's parents' backyard. We had also thrown up.

"This was nice," Mya said. "It was good to see your family, too. Especially Brad."

"Motherfucker somehow gets more attractive every day."

"Yessir."

Above us clouds obscured the stars. One of my favorite things about heading back to Michigan was the ability to see the constellations and remember that the sky wasn't a pinkish pastel smear of light pollution. Even with the starlight covered, everything looked calmer, less blurred and blended. "It's nice to get out of the Boystown bubble for a weekend," I said.

Mya handed me the cigarette. "You seem a lot better."

"I am better, I think."

"You still see Jonathan?"

"I see him out occasionally. We never talk, I just pine from afar. He is making his way through fucking all the hottest guys in Chicago."

"That sounds like it's a good way to get some STDs and HIV."

"It's always more about the venereal diseases than the people." I pulled Mya close in a hug. She put her head on my shoulder. The throb of music from the reception hall pounded behind us. I exhaled a plume of smoke. "You think it works? The whole marriage/love thing? I mean our parents made it work. Brad and Susan are making it work, but they're not like us. Are we wired differently?"

Mya was silent for a moment. "I have no fucking clue. Like, none."

"I'm glad I'm not the only one," I said.

An old couple stumbled out of the reception hall. The man was clearly drunk and the woman did not want to deal with him. She swatted him with her purse, called him "an old coot," then shoved him into their Buick. Their taillights were almost out of the parking lot when Mya said, "That doesn't look bad. Like, being married is basically having someone take care of you all the time, even when you're being an ass."

"Being married can suck just as much. You know my friend Terrence?"

"Yeah, he grew up around here, didn't he?"

"A few towns over, yeah. But his husband cheats all the time. Most recently the hubby went on a vacation with another guy from Chicago and Terrence didn't know about it. He thought he was at a 'conference.' Terrence was devastated as it was, but now word's out on the Boystown Twitter. Poor guy is in hiding now."

"That's so shitty."

"Yeah, he doesn't even really talk about it."

"Is he leaving him?"

"No, he just went away for a few weeks. He said he's coming back in town next month. We're supposed to get coffee."

The music inside grew quiet, a slow ballad beginning to play.

"I hope you're not letting that stop you, though," Mya said. "Just because there are assholes doesn't mean you need to stop trying."

"I am. I'm finally actually starting to try. There's a huge party next weekend. This important gay in Chicago puts it on. I'm going to go. I'm going to go and I'm going to get laid."

Mya pulled away from me. She looked into my eyes and started to slow clap. Before long she was slapping her hands together and laughing. "David is finally getting back in the game! The party is his coming out… again…or something!"

"Yes! Yaaaaassss!" I threw some punches at the air and then raised my hands up above my head. "The champ is back!"

"Fly like a butterfly, sting like a bee with a huge dick!"

"Big dick bee!"

"BIG DICK BEE!"

The clapping and bee talk soon turned into us pretending to fly around the back parking lot as bees. After a short circuit around a Town and Country van, we came to a stop. I pulled Mya into a hug. "I better not be the only one looking for love."

"I don't know about love," she said, "but I kind of want to make a move on that one groomsman."

"The short scruffy one?"

"Of course. You know my type."

The reception closed at midnight. Mya ended up, not with the groomsmen, but with one of Chuck's fraternity brothers. They danced to Prince's "Kiss." When his back was turned, she looked over at me – I gave her a very enthusiastic thumbs up.

Alexis's parents ended up driving me home. Grant told me about an episode of the "gay show" and how he "doesn't get fellers liking fellers" but he "sure as hell can't stand people being mean to other people."

As Grant and Gladys drove away, I flopped on the grass of our front yard and looked up into the sky. The clouds were lifting in patches and I could see an uncovered chunk of sky, tiny stars twinkling from millions of miles away.

For the first time in a long time I was seeing past the shadow of Jonathan. I thought about Hedley's coming gala, about the faces of a hundred unknown men smiling back in the dark. One of them might be a good one. One of them might be for me. Dew seeped into my back, I accepted the chill with a broad smile on my face. My heart beat against my chest. For some reason it pounded to the rhythm of a Shakespeare quote. Being home had sparked some memory in that unused, sophomore-in-high-school part of my brain.

Tomorrow, tomorrow, and tomorrow, it said.

"Tomorrow," I thought to myself, "is going to be a very good day."

That Gala Feeling

The first time was March. The last snowfall had dusted the ground like powdered sugar on grey, French Toast streets. The sky retained its winter bleakness, a ghostly sun lighting the trembling shadow of Chicago's empirical skyline.

I had gotten home earlier than expected and found his computer open. Only meaning to check my own Facebook, by clicking open the tab I found that his Messenger page was open. The thumbnail portrait was of a shirtless man, one I hadn't seen before. It took only a second of scanning the opening line of the first message to illuminate the full reality of our situation.

Last night was fucking incredible...

Then they came, like nits, lice, crawling over my bare arms and neck, the implications, the fears, the revelations bit hard on my skin, scrabbled across my back.

How many?

When?

I snapped the computer shut and went into our bedroom. The bed was pure, smooth and untouched; the sheets were starched and shone like talc in the wintry light. Shadows flew over it, like some sort of screen – bodies twined together, panting, sweating, the twisted noose of those sheets pulling around our relationship. The nits punched at my skin, each unaccounted for night, each of my long nights and away weekends suddenly becoming cavernous with possibility. Eyes that I paid little attention to that swept over Jonathan's body at the bars now became possible trespassers in my bed.

I trembled all over. In the bathroom I turned the water to cold, got in the shower in my clothes, attempting to wash away the doubts and unnumbered men who had, by proxy, touched my skin.

Water poured, coursed over my body, into every crevasse, over every part of me. But there was no feeling of clean. The water couldn't pierce the skin, drive through me and scrub away all – free me from the horrible blight which had come to fill the marrow of my very bones.

How many?

Later I would see that these first vile lice that filled the opening moments were but the harbinger of a great horde that would devour every thought that came into my mind for months.

What had I done?

What could I do?

How do you make someone love you, not just one instant, but on and on and on?

Sasha patiently waited in the living room as I tried on different clothes. Over the months since the breakup, while Jonathan grew trimmer and more muscular, I had swelled, my belly becoming the size of a basketball slung around my waist. I had definitely inherited my father's build.

I entered Sasha's living room in a dress shirt that was far too tight. My undershirt was clearly visible between the stretched button holes that attempted to cover my abdomen.

"Jesus, let's just stay away from the slim fit, David."

"I feel so fucking fat, Sasha."

"You're not a slim fit anymore, but it's not bad. Do you have anything a size up?"

"I have the olive shirt, but I didn't want it to come to that." Sasha smiled. "Sometimes you have to go with Plan B."

What had begun as a beautiful awakening the night of the wedding, had turned into a lot of fear, anxiety, and wine as the week progressed. The 100s of men that could be a possible boyfriend or lover, at the wedding, transformed into a sneering, grimacing mass – the faces of Boystown's elite. I swore looking out of Sasha's condo I could see Skyler and his orange, muscled lover laughing at me over vodka sodas.

I went to the bathroom and unbuttoned the slim fit, a nice checkered shirt that had fit perfectly only a year before. The olive shirt stared at me blankly from its hanger behind the door.

"Hey, hey!" it said in a Fat Albert voice. "Time to join The Chub Club."

Despite its hideous color, the shirt fit all right. Its bagginess was far from the chic, skin-tight tank tops the other men would wear, but at least it did cover my belly.

When I reentered the living room, Sasha clapped his hands once. "Tres chic," he said. "Now help me with this wine."

"I was looking forward to this thing only a week ago," I said taking a seat on the sofa. "I was even talking to Margaret about it at work. Now I would rather die than show up with all those queens. They just stare and gape and titter about everyone who comes in."

"That's why I hate them all."

"Well, I have to go in and find one who can tolerate me and who will be okay with the idea of coming home to only me for the rest of his life."

Sasha laughed. "I would save that kind of talk at least until date two."

"You think it's too much?"

We clinked glasses. The gala was set to begin at eight, just as the sun was creeping below the horizon. Sasha agreed he would again join the Boystown throng as my most illustrious and abrasive wingman. He had once been quite the scene kid, sexing scores of men in his late teens and early twenties. As he grew older and focused on school, this drive ebbed. We had met at the very end of this cycle, a few months before he found Edward. I think one of the reasons he found Edward so attractive was that he spent Friday evenings at art galleries and theater events rather than in the heart of Halsted.

"When are Tibbs and Donnie getting here?" I asked.

Sasha rolled his eyes. "They'll be here late. And they'll be talking about the last guy they fucked."

"They are the best open couple I've ever met. They literally are fine with fucking each other, fucking others, fucking others with each other."

The doorbell rang.

"Yoohoo!" Tibbs's dulcet tones sounded from behind the door.

"Entré, bitches! It's open." Sasha raised his eyebrows at me.

Tibbs stormed in first, his hairy belly barely concealed behind a mesh tank top. Behind him came Donnie, slim, tiny, his black bowl haircut flouncing as he sashayed through the entryway. The two of them together were quite the pair. Tibbs was tall, curly-haired and brash. He could barely keep his voice below a yell – after two glasses of wine, he was basically an air horn. His age was unknown, his chubby, boyish face the site of a number of gray hairs on both head and in his beard. His husband and sidekick was Donnie, who was as sleight a gay as you could imagine, barely 5'2", his body hairless, almost porcelain in its smoothness. They were one of those couples who seemed timeless – together as long as anyone could remember and happy and laughing whenever they filled the same space.

A third mystery guest was the last to enter the condo, a smiling, young man with wild, yet quaffed brown hair. He smiled rakishly as he followed the Tibbs and Donnie parade. I nearly jumped off the couch when I recognized him.

"Al! Oh my god! What are you doing here?" I ran over and gave him a hug. He laughed, his eyes sparkling.

"I see how it is," Tibbs brayed, "no love for the old folks."

"Not everything is about you, whore," Sasha said kissing Tibbs's cheek.

I ignored all of them as I squeezed Al even harder. "It's been forever! Al, how are you?"

Al gently pushed me away and gave me a five – we hit hands high, then windmilled around and slapped palms again about mid-thigh. "Fantastic," he said. "Just back from Berlin – I almost died when I found out it was the weekend of the gala."

Al and I had gone to school together – been in the same fraternity - hence the high five. When I was a senior he was a freshman. He came out to me, I bought him beer, we stayed up late smoking pot on the roof of our fraternity house. Over the course of college Al went from a geeky, skinny band nerd, to a taught, beautiful co-ed. Jonathan would comment on his continuing transformation each time he came to visit us – first in Indianapolis and then in Chicago.

Had I not known Al through the whole of his awkward and beauty phases, I would probably have dismissed him as a careless, gay twink. But I knew him like a little brother. On the roof of the frat house we'd talked about families, coming out, literature, poetry, love.

"How's smarty pants land and the Fulbright?"

"Oh God," Al pushed back a lock of hair. "I barely did any work. There were all the drugs and all the men. Berlin is a fucking riot."

"I've heard. Word on the street is it's very alternative."

"The most – music, graffiti, culture. It's stupid."

"So how many German STD's did you bring back to share?"

"None, I hope. The wall keeps them out."

We laughed together. From behind us, I could hear Tibbs bleating about one of The Hedley Set.

"Drink?" I asked.

Al put his arm around my neck and kissed my cheek. "It's so good to see you, David. Culture and graffiti are all well and good, but I missed all my boys back home."

The night became a percussion show: corks popping, wine glugging, silverware clattering. Outside the sun was sinking further and further below the horizon, a blanket of velvety night dropping across the eastern view from Sasha's condo. The lake went from green to a perfect shade of blue.

We had all gathered around the dining room table. Donnie sat on Tibbs's lap. Al and I had been jabbering non-stop. Edward joined the party late and looked on smiling as the rest of us drifted further and further into drunken revelry. When the clock reached 7:45 he gently tapped his wristwatch.

"Boys, you'll be late. It takes almost an hour to get there."

Sasha laughed. "You're just trying to dump us off. Is there a party at the Christian Science Reading Room, Lover?"

"Choir practice at the local nunnery, actually." Edward crept behind Sasha and gave him a hug. "But, seriously, you are all getting annoying."

"We can leave now," Tibbs said grandiosely, as if it had been his idea. "We don't want to be there too early, but I don't want to miss too much of the fun."

"What's the goal tonight, Tibbles?" Donnie asked. He reached into his pocket and pulled out two pills wrapped in Kleenex. "We going for a twink? Or a bear? It's been a while since we brought home an otter to swim around with together."

"No drugs in the house, please." Edward's face was red staring at the pills in Donnie's hand.

"Oh, honey bun," Donnie laughed. "It's just Adderall. We need it to keep up with the college kids."

Edward gave Sasha a look and then headed toward the kitchen. Al reached over and put a hand on my knee.

"Smoke outside, Davey?" he asked. "I could use some fresh air before we ride in the car with Tibbs for an hour."

We got up and headed to the door. Sasha began picking up glasses from the table. "Go in the back alley and we'll swing by on the way out of the garage," he said. "You may get through a whole carton before I wrangle up these assholes."

Tibbs and Donnie were in two similar, yet very different, states of oblivion. Donnie was in the kitchen, one hand flipping through Grindr, the other clutching tight to the final bottle of wine. Tibbs had Edward shoved against the wall in what appeared to be a very important and earnest conversation.

"We'll see you," Al giggled into his hand, "when we see you, I guess?"

Outside the night was clear, the street lamps bathing the pavement in ghostly pools. Traffic was roaring by on Lake Shore, revelers passing by on Sheridan Road, but compared to the riotous conversation inside, it seemed as if Al and I had landed on some serene alien landscape.

Al removed a joint from his pocket and lit it. He took a hit and passed it to me, a stream of smoke flowing out of his mouth. As he finished exhaling, his shoulders relaxed, his sparkling eyes growing even more luminous. I placed the joint in my mouth.

Al's eyebrows knitted together. "I was so sorry to hear, David," he said. "I mean, you know a break up is one thing, but what Jonathan did to you was something else entirely."

Smoke pushed out of my lungs. From the main road I could hear a group of partiers roaring with laughter. Once they had passed, the night settled into an eerie silence. I looked to the sky.

I knew I should have been saying something, but no words really came to mind. There was a lot to say, but then really nothing. What had been an open, bleeding wound had transformed into a nascent scab. Al had caused an odd reaction to the pain

– all at once I had completely forgotten Jonathan, forgotten that I would see him that night, forgotten that he had paraded the whole cast of gay Chicago through our sheets. On the other hand, the question from Al had made the wound pulse with a heat that was unique. It wasn't the same pain as earlier, before Dr. Konstantin, in those first broken times when I'd spent some Saturdays comatose on the couch, reviewing each instant of our relationship, running my hands over our union's glass looking for each individual crack and fissure. This feeling with Al was something that had only begun to emerge. Moving from the mid-twenties had brought on a wave of nostalgia, youth had slowly been slipping away and I'd suddenly started to notice it. Now with Al, our college memories were dimmer and dimmer moments in my psyche. Clear thoughts turning to vague feelings, emotions. My mourning for Jonathan was now aggrandized by mourning for a past life, a simplicity of mind that I hadn't been able to cultivate in a long time: memories of me, Al, and Jonathan happily atop the frat house, night slipping away in a stream of drugs, conversation, and jejune hope.

"It sucks," I finally said. "But what are you going to do?"

Al nodded. He reached for the joint. "If there's anything... You know..." He crossed his arms and looked embarrassingly at the ground.

"I'll be okay," I said. "If you know of any single men, who liked wounded, chubby dudes in their late twenties, then please, give out my number."

"Oh, shut up!" Al punched my shoulder. "You're lovely as always. Same smile, same person you've always been. If the gay assholes in Chicago can't see that, then you don't need any of them."

I threw my arm around Al. "You're right. Sorry – the moment of self-pity is over. Now that it's gone, I fully expect you to help me get laid tonight."

Al rubbed his hands together. "Now we're talking!"

No matter how far Al traveled, how many dudes he fucked or drugs he took, his optimism couldn't be quelled. When I had first met him his freshman year, his earnestness had bordered on obnoxious. He had come out to his family, which resulted in his brother railing against him, calling him a fag, and telling him to fuck off. The night all that happened, he ended up in my room telling me that the brother just needed some time and would come around.

It was his brother one hazy Pride weekend three years later who threw his arm around Al and proclaimed, "Fags are all right."

There was some halo around Al that I couldn't quite understand. He had it, The Set had it, and my brother seemed to have it, too. *30 Rock* called it "The Bubble", the protection around some beautiful people, a shield from the blinding pain of negative emotion.

"What about you?" I asked. "Any men? Many, I'm sure, but anyone special?"

A sheepish grin crept across his face. "Yes," he said. "A guy from Berlin. He was on a Fulbright, too."

"Al!" I raised my hands as if someone had just scored a touchdown. "Why did this take so long to come out? Details: where's he from, dick size, all the important points please."

I could tell Al's' face was red, even in the dim light. "He's from New York. He's actually going to Booth this fall, so we'll be moving in together."

I ran over and picked him up off the ground. "You little slut! Why didn't you tell me you were moving to Chicago?"

"Put me down!" he said laughing. "I wanted to surprise you, I guess. "

"Well, it's a really nice surprise!" I put him down and extended my hand. "Pics of your boy, please. I gotta see what he looks like."

"Don't you want to know his favorite book? His thoughts on Chaucer?"

"Right after I assess him shirtless, absolutely."

Al was giggling as he flipped through his phone. After a few clicks he was on Instagram. He held out a filtered picture of his new boy and him somewhere in Europe. Behind them the sky swirled with gold and scarlet brushstrokes, the sun beginning to set. They sat on a huge, marble fountain, leaning into each other, sunglasses on their faces. The other man could have been a mirror image of Al: his long, handsome face pulled into a wide smile, perfect, thick black hair soaring toward the twilight sky. I was happy for Al, I really was. But something in me couldn't help but feel deadened, defeated in the light of this magazine-caliber picture. In the eyes and faces of these two young men, far younger than me, was unbounded, adult happiness. My hand trembled slightly as I handed the phone back. I tried to keep the shaking out of my voice.

"Adorable," I said.

#

The house Hedley chose was impeccable. Climbing the sloping front lawn, I couldn't help but think of Dorothy and her motley crew meandering toward The Emerald City. All around us was opulence and the grandiose showmanship of drag queens, male models, and local celebrities. It was about ten by the time we arrived, so the main hordes had already come and emptied large parts of the bar. While the outside pulsed with music and life, the main foyer served as a marble beach of drunken flotsam and jetsam. An especially sad group sat in the drawing room, one of the men pounding a series of notes on the piano. Al and I peeked in curiously and were met with the pale, grey gaze of Lawrence Soot. Dressed, as always, to the nines, he wore a tuxedo with red cummerbund. He waved to us and shouted over the wailing of a young girl sitting next to him. Tibbs, Sasha, and Donnie scurried along as Al and I did our best to appear excited.

"Look at these troublemakers!" Soot bleated, embracing Al and planting two pecks on his cheeks. "Al, how long has it been?"

"Almost a year, I guess. Maybe longer."

Soot's botoxed face forced a smile. "Europe, correct?"

"Yeah."

"So cosmopolitan!" Soot had brought over a chalice of dark wine. He lifted it to his lips. "And David. I haven't seen you out and about."

"Winter blues, I suppose," I said.

Soot nodded empathetically. "I heard – I mean, we all heard via Twitter, but, you know, well, I'm sorry." He raised his tiny, manicured eyebrows as if expecting an answer. When I refused to say anything he abruptly twirled around. "Like my outfit? I was trying to live up to the party. Expectations were so high!"

"You look dapper as always, Sooty," Al said.

I felt a soft touch on my back. Before I turned I saw Soot's face contort into a look of pain.

"Larry! Why, it's been forever." Sasha's smile, if the nasty twist of his mouth could be called that, greeted Soot.

"Hello." Soot tapped his chalice with his ringed index finger. Around us the party throbbed with life. The girl from the drawing room continued to cry. From outside music poured into the windows and doors, filling the rattling hall with a bass-heavy soundtrack.

"Well," Soot said blankly. "I should go."

With a swish of his coattails, the older man turned around, his black shoes clacking away. Just before he sat down, he threw a worried, anxious glance back at Sasha.

"Piece of shit," Sasha said quietly, the same grim smile on his face. "I'm wondering when he'll go *American Horror Story: Coven* and start drinking in souls."

Al broke into laughter. "He and Jessica Lange do both dress well. Why can't you just bury the hatchet, Sasha?"

"I think it was the comments on my 'handsome, negro features' that still make me a little uneasy."

Sasha pushed us into the kitchen. The room was cavernous, a counter almost 15 feet long running through the center of the room. The marble countertop was adorned with a number of pitchers, tiny tags in cursive script explaining their shimmering contents.

"Like Hogwarts," Sasha said picking up a carafe and smelling it. "This is the cauldron of bad decisions," he said winking at me.

The party was filled with a variety of characters. Drag queens, bears, twinks, model-like, straight women, and a few flannel-clad lesbians, decorated the walls like a tapestry. Intermixed with the herd were some of the most beautiful men I had ever seen. Light reflected off their glistening skin, their cobbled stomachs creating deep shadows between their individually defined abs.

Sasha, Al, and I drank slowly. Sasha sipped on an Old Fashioned for the better part of an hour. Before long the room began to spin like a carousel, the tapestry and its cornucopia of characters coming to vibrant life.

A little after eleven, one young gay climbed on the long, marble counter, a carafe in his hand, its contents sloshing onto those gathered around.

"Shots!" he howled raising the pitcher. With a manic gleam in his eye he spun, splattering the crowd with the sticky, blood-like cocktail. Everyone bolted toward the center of the room. In the rush, Al, Sasha, and I were separated.

I was pushed into the middle of the wild herd, pressed tightly against a number of men. Despite my earlier hope of finding a love connection, even a hookup at the party, the alcohol had, sparked by the general torpor elicited from Al's questions about me and Jonathan, grown into a full flame of indifference. Behind me a muscled jock's, firm pecs shoved against my shoulder. Rather than being aroused, I fought forward, out of the crowd and rested by the back wall. My eyes shifted at just the right time to see The Hedley Set, minus The Hedley, making their entrance. In classical Set Mode, they posed in the entry foyer, their eyes sweeping the room, a searchlight of judgment.

Samson moved just slightly backward, his hand going to pull back a lock of his hair. The tiny movement revealed Jonathan to me, standing somewhat to the side, just behind the main three.

My body trembled, my fists clenched. I was jerked back in time to just a year earlier, when we had entered the party together. By then everyone knew what was happening between us, between Jonathan and dozens of other men in the Boystown scene. Our lives together had been unraveling at break-neck speed.

Jonathan, for one of the first times that spring, had debuted his new body via a tight t-shirt and short, plaid shorts. His firmer physique drew stairs, important ones, not just the riffraff, but Samson, Skyler, The Set, had sized him up as he walked by. I'd lost him before that, but that night, especially, seemed to be a kind of coming out for him. He had emerged from the winter as a different person – it was just over a month later that he disappeared, a note left on the table, and I had ended up on Sasha's couch, silent, cold, numb.

Without knowing my destination, I moved away from my view of the foyer and pushed my way through the growing kitchen crowd. By now a number of svelte men were on the counter, taking turns pouring new pitchers into volunteers' mouths. Behind them, through French doors, I saw the glorious, dark anonymity of the back porch, the pulsing lights and music pulling me out of the crowd and into the dead of night.

The bodies grew less dense as I drew closer to the back door. The screams of the kitchen and cackle of the twinks parading on the counter were replaced by the thumping club music on the dance floor. The rhythm and bass actually soothed me. The further I physically located myself from Jonathan, the more Zen I became. I thought of Dr. Konstantin's quotes: "Location is very important, not just physically, but mentally. You have to move yourself outside of thinking patterns that make you feel sad, lonely, depressed."

With relief I broke out of the throng and emerged on the back patio. Voices had diminished except for Ellie Goulding, who blared from the speakers. Above me I could see nothing but expansive sky and a few twinkling stars.

I was in the midst of taking a deep breath, moving myself from the pain of the Jonathan sighting, when I felt wetness cover my shirt. I turned to see a short, handsome boy standing before me. Even without meeting him, I could tell he was from the Midwest. His thick shoulders and neck acted like a corporeal GPS.

"Oh! Sorry…" he said patting my shirt.

"No, don't worry." I grabbed the napkin from his hand and patted the stain myself. "It's fine. This is an old shirt anyway." The music was so loud we were screaming at each other. "It always turns into a mess here."

The kid was accompanied by Jordan Barker. Jordan wasn't quite one of The Set, but rather one of the stragglers who formed its shadow. Every time I saw him he was a different kind of gay: queenie, sporty, lumberjacky. I noted he stood closer to the younger kid, a wolf-like gleam in his eye. Just like his wardrobe, Jordan's personality oscillated between genuinely friendly and horrendously bitchy depending on what time of day you caught him.

"Hello, David," he said dryly.

Today was bitchy.

"Oh! Jordan! It's good to see you." I took his hand. "I guess we've all been hibernating this winter. Time to wake up all the bears and get sloppy!"

"Yeah," a pregnant pause ensued. The kid was looking beyond me at a waiter in only his underwear. Jordan was examining his cuticles. "How are...things?" Jordan drawled begrudgingly.

"Things are fine. Going." I looked beyond Jordan and saw The Set enter. Jonathan was taking up the rear guard. Hedley was in front lavishing attention on each individual he encountered. Even though his face was obscured by a hood, you could tell that it was him. Say what you would about him, the man could make you feel like you were the only gay in the room. "I should go," I said quickly. "You boys have fun!"

I pushed my way across the dance floor to one of the huge granite staircases that flanked the back patio on the north and south sides. The dancers were lost in a mix of drinks and drugs, some reaching out and probing each other's bodies as if their sense of touch had just been discovered.

My attention was mangled, shredded between seeing Jonathan, being attracted to the kid with Jordan, wondering where my friends were, all these emotions mixed with the few drinks I'd had in the past couple hours, causing pure distraction. I was so lost in semi-drunk thought that I almost fell over when I collided with a man coming up the stairs.

"I'm sorry!" I said. "I'm a mess."

The man smiled at me. He wore a backwards hat, his brown eyes looked bottomless in the darkness.

"You should probably buy me a drink for the inconvenience," he said.

"They're all free."

"You should have one with me then."

We locked eyes. The man was cute. But, let's be honest, after drinking my sex drive is reduced to simple categories of "Yes, I'd fuck that" and "Who am I kidding, yes, I'd fuck that, too."

"Are you hitting on me?" I asked.

The man's laugh was high, almost girlish. He flipped his hat around so the bill faced forward and he sized me up. "Yes. I am. My name's Frank and I'm hitting on you."

"Frank, can you not be a whore for three seconds?" Behind him Frank was being pushed by a small gay with huge sunglasses and no shirt. Flash tattoos decorated his nude torso.

Frank was dressed diametrically opposite of his glittering friend. He wore a conservative, baggy gingham shirt and khaki shorts. "I'm not a whore," Frank said.

"That's disappointing," I quipped.

Frank and his friend both laughed.

"He's funny, but let's keep moving!" Flash Tattoos was pushing Frank up the stairs.

Frank extended a hand. At a loss, I reached out and shook it. "Consider this our Romeo and Juliet moment," Frank said winking at me.

In an instant they were gone, Frank carried up the stairs and me pushed down by a throng of girls that looked as if they were searching for the set of a Pitbull video.

I ended up sidestepping off the downstairs patio and sitting in the grass. The music was still pounding but it was slightly softer, enough to let my thoughts settle a little. What I really wanted was Sasha – or Al, Terrence, or Maya. Someone that I called friend to be there with me. I didn't want to talk about Jonathan, but I didn't want the silence that meant I would think about Jonathan.

The momentary thought of Terrence made me get out my phone. I typed a quick text to see how he was: *How's your night? A guy hit on me with a Shakespeare line.*

Poor Terrence had had no peace since the Kinsey Twitter story broke. As bad as it was to be the cuckold, I was out of the worst of it. Terrence was just caught in the eye of the storm.

"David!" I looked up and saw Hedley looking down at me. In the moonlight his quaffed brown hair was lit up like a Greek laurel crown. He wore a sleeveless hoodie, his toned bare arms laced with veins. "I don't think I've seen you since Myrtle's birthday."

"Hey Hedley," I stammered. I rose for some reason (respect?), plunging my phone in my pocket. "Great party. Is Myrtle here tonight?" Hope flickered in me. Myrtle was always fun at these parties – very drunk – but very fun. In my surprise at Hedley's greeting, I hadn't noticed that Jonathan was with him. he looked as surprised as I was at the encounter.

Hedley briefly flicked his eyes between my ex and me. My expression of horror and shock a clear social indication the conversation should end. "She's gone for a wedding," Hedley said. "You're having fun then? I saw Sasha upstairs. I think he's looking for you."

I couldn't focus with Jonathan looking at me. The most I could bring myself to say was, "Yeah, it's a good time."

"Excellent." He smiled broadly. "Well, have fun."

Jonathan nodded at me as they passed.

I flopped onto the grass. The composure I had managed after seeing Jonathan the first time had broken completely. Taking deep breaths, I squeezed my hands to try to keep them from trembling.

Fuck.

Fuck.

My head fell forward. Everything was fucked up. The feelings of earlier, the dull pain cause by Al, built into a full-blown panic. I was going to die alone – for sure. There was no one out there for me. The Frank guy? He was just making fun of me. Jonathan had moved on and left me in some desert of loneliness. Al was happy and going to be living with his new guy. Sasha was with Edward. Even Tibbs had Donnie. A tear formed at the edge of my eye. Again, I was in that bathroom and my thoughts turned to knife, water, white, and blood.

A tense buzzing entered my head. I massaged my temples with my palms. Following advice from Dr. Konstantin, I began to breathe like a woman giving birth. Rather than focus on any of these loose thoughts, I looked down at the grass and counted the shoots of grass.

Hold back. Hold back, I thought. There were no more nights in showers, on couches, crying into empty corners of my apartment. Those were gone. *"You have to move yourself outside of thinking patterns that make you feel sad, lonely, depressed."*

"Cinderella is leaving so soon?"

I looked up. I looked up and the tears of anguish suddenly were ones of joy. I leapt to my feet and pulled Sasha into a close hug.

101

"You showed up at the perfect fucking moment," I said.

Sasha recognized immediately what was happening. He saw my face then turned and saw Jonathan's broad back walking away from us. "Let's walk to down to the lake," he said quickly.

The tears were gone, the spell of sadness broken by Sasha's hug. We walked across the back deck. Invisible from the top level it was another concrete landing with several small tables and chairs. The crowd at this scene of the party was more subdued. A number of men in swimming suits, back from a swim in the lake, were gathered around one table. In a far corner, barely visible, I saw Al speaking to Kinsey, one of his old hookups, and public enemy number one to any of Terrence's friends.

"That piece of shit," I said.

Sasha followed my gaze. "That guy thinks he is God's gift to everything." Sasha licked his lips. "Heard his dick is tiny. It looks like a finger puppet."

I had to stop I was laughing so hard. "That is the absolutely best dick insult I have ever heard."

The roar of the upstairs party grew softer and softer as we trekked off the concrete and into the lush, manicured lawn. Along with the quieting of the party cacophony, my thoughts became less frenzied, muted. It was no longer the surge of fuck! and oh shit!, but a rising general calm, Dr. Konstantin's words softly whispering in my ear.

Tiki torches lined a path down to the lake, a few stray couples were making out, fondling in the grass. Sasha and I moved past them, over the rise in the lawn, and took a seat overlooking the black mirror of the water. The moon hung overhead, a single, white bulb.

I fell back on the grass and put my hands over my eyes.

"That fucking sucked," I said.

"Jonathan?" Sasha asked.

"Everything," I groaned.

"He looks good. Whatever, you look good, too."

"But he looks better," I whined.

We could hear the lake from our position, soft water lapping up on the manmade sand. A few years earlier I would have suggested stripping down, running to the water and plunging into the cold. Now I felt old and tired.

"If it means anything,' Sasha said, "I'm proud of you for coming out tonight. You knew you'd see him."

"I was so excited, Sasha. You know that Shakespeare quote – the 'Tomorrow, tomorrow, and tomorrow' one? I had that in my head. I thought of all the guys who would be here and how I could start fresh tonight – the start of summer, start of the dating life, everything."

"Well, first of all, that quote is fucking depressing in context, and second, at least you were excited. I remember a few months ago you were hoping for a quick, fiery death on the 77 bus rather than see Jonathan at the bars."

"I may have been overly dramatic."

"You, David?! Never." From the corner of my eye I could see Sasha smiling broadly, trying to get me to join him in the joke, but I was thinking too much to enjoy the humor.

I sat up and sighed. "It's not just Jonathan. I knew that would be fucking depressing. But it's everything. It's seeing Al – him taking out a picture of his hot boyfriend and me realizing that someone four years younger than me has his life together. It's everyone at this party looking so good half naked and me just being chubby and awkward. My friends back home are getting married, you are happy with Edward, Donnie and Tibbs have their… thing… Like, shouldn't it be easier than this?" I plucked up some grass and ran it between my fingers. "I mean, whatever *this* is."

With those last words, I fell silent. Waves, wind, and distant music filled the quiet moment before Sasha began: "So are you done feeling sorry for yourself?"

"No," I said.

"David, you know I love you. You also know I think you've been a fucking idiot about this Jonathan thing."

"Both things I do know."

"He cheated on you – over and over. You keep trying to go back and figure out why it didn't work and I can tell you why right here, right now." Sasha grabbed my shoulders and turned me so I was looking directly at him. "He's a dick head. That's why it didn't work. Even if he wanted out, he should talk to you. He shouldn't fuck everyone then leave a note."

"That was an asshole thing to do." Sasha's grip remained on my shoulders. I felt uncomfortable looking directly into his eyes and turned my gaze to the sky above his head. "But I wonder if I should want what he wants. I mean, look behind us. Hedley's mansion is everything you should want and we don't fit there. You and me are average guys, Sasha. We don't work out that much, we have okay jobs, we grab beers sometimes, but shouldn't we want that? Shouldn't we want the abs and the immaculate clothes and the perfect hair? Maybe Jonathan made the right choice."

Sasha stared at me. I didn't look over, but I felt his dark eyes on me, searching, blistering me with their judgment. His tongue flicked out and wet his lips. When it seemed as if he sufficiently scolded me with his gaze, he turned to face the water. "David, when I was growing up, it was just my dad and my grandma. My grandma didn't like my dad because he was black, and my dad didn't like being black – everything when I was growing up was mainstreamed and whitened to make me 'fit in.' My mother left us because she didn't want to be a mother – she got knocked up, got scared, and bailed. Grandma was from Russia. She hated Russia, Communists, the color red. I was raised in a home with no identity. Everyone hated who they were, who they'd been, who they were with."

"I know your childhood sucked." I put my arm around Sasha. "I'm sorry, I'm being really a spoiled white girl –"

Sasha lightly slapped the back of my head. "David, listen, I'm not done with my lesson. I'm going to be a professor for fucksake."

I laughed and hugged him tighter. "Sorry, please continue, Professor."

"My childhood sucked a lot, but the point is that everyone wants to be someone else. Everyone has some history that they think is the reason they can't be some ideal. Jonathan wanted to be free from you, thought he'd get ripped and get better friends. Now he looks like a fucking beat dog hanging around with The Set. Al says he has a hot boyfriend, but he's probably going to be sucking Kinsey's dick in about twenty minutes. You have the best friend in the world, a great job, and all you want to do is go back to the beat dog, who looks like he hates his new, glittering mansion life."

"I get it. Be happy with what you got."

"No," Sasha shook his head fervently. "Not be happy with what you got, but be satisfied with who you are. Things, people, fly in and out, but when you wake up in the morning, cheating whore of a lover beside you or not, it's you that you have to live with. You can't change your past, you can't change other people. If you want the abs, go for them, but don't go for them because you think they'll make you someone else. Be yourself doing whatever it is you want to do."

The wind picked up. "I know you're right," I said.

"I'm not going to let you fail finding yourself," Sasha said. "I'm pretty sure The Greek wouldn't be happy about it either." He put his head on my shoulder. Anyone passing behind us probably thought we were lovers.

Sasha had given me this speech over and over again for the past year. In the beginning the start had always been "Why doesn't Jonathan love me?!" At least now it was more a whole-picture concept. I knew why Jonathan left, but now I had to figure out what that meant for me. Did I need to change, too? Or did I just need to evolve a little, grow up, take what I learned and move on? I didn't really want to be like The Hedley Set. Jonathan could have them. But I also didn't know what I wanted to be. Did I really need to be anything?

"Did I change your life?" Sasha whispered in my ear.

I pushed him over. "Make this guy ABD and he thinks he's the head of the Dead Poet's Society."

"Carpe Diem, baby."

I hesitated just a moment, looking to my right and left. The knoll we were on was clear, the water was dark and empty, as still as a mirror. The talk, the silence, the camaraderie with Sasha made me feel young and free again. I had a brief flash to the rooftop, to me, Al, and Jonathan singing Mariah and Whitney "Miracles" as we talked about the stars and alternative universes. "Sasha," I said, "what do you say we strip down and go swimming naked?"

Sasha looked over at me and smiled. "My god," he said, "David fucking Jenkins, there you are."

We threw off our clothes and sprinted to the water. The cold splash made me shout. Sasha started singing a song from the movie *Frozen*. I started singing "Miracles." From the water we could see the house, it's glowing windows shining, impassively on us below. Behind us the sky was black, stars twinkling, the lights of distant planes flying into O'Hare intermittently flashing – red and white. We laughed and splashed and sang. A group of gays walked down to the water and saw us. They joined the chorus of *Frozen* and cat called us.

For a moment Hedley's glittering mansion faded away completely and we were just a group of boys in the water on a summer night.

"Come on in," Sasha screamed to the men on the shore, "the water's fine!"

Into the Woods

During the peak of it all, the apex of happiness, the world faded to white noise, a buzz that was easily ignored. Under our feet the earth rotated with its usual slow, monotonous pace, but our steps barely tread on the ground. Our bodies were suspended, hovering in eternal summer, when a look, a touch from the beloved was the only terrestrial, carnal reminder that we were not timeless characters painted on an ancient urn, but aging actors in a world made of flesh and blood and bone.

We met after junior year. Both of us had decided to stay the summer at school: me for an internship and Jonathan for time away from the drudgery of his usual summer job at home. By happenstance, the dots were connected, the stars aligned and on an evening in June, our paths crossed at a Charlie Peterman barbecue.

I saw him first, across the lawn. In those days he wasn't pastel and pasted on chinos, but t-shirts and cargo shorts. His chestnut hair hung loosely in his eyes, his thin arms flexed as he drummed the side of a Bud Light.

Who is he? I casually asked a bystander. That one over there. Jonathan? Communications major from Chicago. No, I haven't before. Is he a transfer? New? Haha. Yes. Yes.

Jonathan's gay bud had just recently opened. Our university was large and had gay scenes, but I existed only in their periphery. My friends and I stayed mainly away from electronica and ecstasy and enjoyed alternative rock and pot. Rather than hit the local gay bars in our plumage, we chose to hang in our favorite dive bars, play darts, and sip Miller Lite.

But, chosen exile aside, the gays knew each other. Grindr was on the horizon, Craigslist and gay.com made knowledge of the other gays open. The closet was slowly starting to dissolve into an electronic, open forum.

But I had never seen Jonathan before. And he was looking back at me in the way that a man looks when he sees something he likes. The current opened between us when the first words were spoken. Later in the evening, around the back of the house, when others had gone to the bars, I followed him to the side of the building when he went out to piss. Several beers and shots in, I watched hungrily as he shook off his dick in the shadow of the house.

Hey.

Hey.

The book opened, the first part of our love story writ with my hungry lips around his member in the shadows of Charlie Peterman's tenement on East 2nd Street.

Yeah, I have to meet friends, too. Cool – here's my number.

The next day he texted. We grabbed a drink and talked life, love, the closet, and politics at a tiny bar that served popcorn and played country music. His hair fell in his eyes and his smile lit up the dark bar with intermittent flashes of joy. That night we were drunk again and found ourselves in his small bedroom. The fan in his window beat out a steady rhythm. Sweat slid down our backs, thighs, and necks. I gently put him on his back, licked, massaged and prepped him so that I could take him completely.

In the morning, sunlight cascaded through the window. Its broad beams illuminated the dusty floors, our discarded clothes strewn about the room. He was laying on my chest, still asleep, his breathing in time with the blades of the box fan.

Above us I saw a fly, watched it trace a course across the room. Its buzzing was muted by the sound of the birds and the whir of the fan, but it seemed to be stopped in time. All my senses opened; the light, the fly, the world, grinded so slowly and perfectly that I could feel the rotation of the earth. I was above it, watching for the first time as someone who is in tune with the motion, the complexity of the universe. Moments as fleeting as this usually came under the influence of drugs on the roof of the frat house, but this was different, a stupor induced by my youth, after a night of passionate lovemaking.

Hookups had come and gone through my life, but none of them had been this easy. From first glance to sex, Jonathan and my trajectory followed a path of predestination. The world had slowed, the fan whirred, the fly hovered above the bed. Next to me Jonathan stirred, between the strands of his hair he looked at me, smiled, placed his lips together and pressed them on the base of my neck. When he had sighed and closed his eyes again, it occurred to me that the fullness of that moment, the simplification of the world's complexity into buzz and whir and broad beams of sunlight, must be love.

Of all the Boystown gays, Terrence had been my friend the longest. We actually met through our mothers; my mom knew his mom through a women's club in the neighboring town. When I came out, she demanded that we meet. Terrence was quite a few years older, a senior in college when I was coming out as a junior in high school. Because he was older, it was never about sexual chemistry, we were always just friends. There was something warm and welcoming about him that made me feel right at home. Over his tenure in Boystown his generous spirit became one of the few constants in the Halsted scene. No matter what bar you saw him at, what was being said about his boyfriend on Twitter, Terrence would meet you with a smile.

That was until the Kinsey news broke that May. Then he just disappeared. Sasha and I speculated why, whether it was a final straw or something else, but we never really knew. I kept in contact with him – I sent probing texts that he would respond to without any indication of his actual mental state. Example:

Me: *Hey, heard about the thing with Lloyd. You okay?*
Terrence: *Not great. It's definitely a "Say Something" hat day.*

We all knew Lloyd was a jerk from the beginning. I first met him when I went to visit Terrence in Chicago my junior year in college, right before meeting Jonathan. Even in those first days, I could see through Lloyd to his cheating core, but Terrence was smitten. Despite Terrence's charm and charisma, he didn't have much self-esteem. He never discussed it, but my mother said that his coming out was one of the main reasons for his parents' divorce. His father couldn't take it, disowned him. Being the youngest of four children, and the subject of his family's schism, didn't do much to his ego, which was torn apart in the incident. These were all things I put together later. The muscular brutes he dated, with tattoos and steely eyes, used him and discarded him, some leaving scars in their wake. When he met Lloyd, an East coast transplant with a winning smile, and slick fashion sense, he was lost in love.

Of all the men he dated, the muscular, the tatted, the cops and closeted jocks, the emotionally unavailable troupe that lit up his Facebook in the years that we knew each other, it was Lloyd who scared me the most. He was smooth as silk in speech, style, and presentation. He would sit in the corner, smile and nod, at the activities around him, but his eyes remained blank, removed. The first weekend I met him, he and Terrence were unofficial but "talking" and dating. In a moment of drunkenness, Lloyd's finger found itself tracing on the back of my neck. In smooth, dulcet tones he did all but ask me to go to bed with him.

At first, I had confronted Terrence, but so did everyone. The trap had been set, though. In Lloyd he had discovered some ideal, some concept that he had been striving and searching for: an exotic East coast ivy league boy with a refined vocabulary and perfectly manicured clothes and hair.

Likewise, in Terrence, Lloyd had discovered something that he probably had never had. Terrence was honest, loving, caring. I try very hard to believe that the best part of Lloyd loved Terrence but he couldn't overcome his promiscuity. Over the years there were moments of peace between them. There were kisses, touches that showed love. Even up to their engagement, several of us tried to put the pressure on Terrence, to make him see Lloyd for what he was. But there are some things people won't see. It was actually watching Terrence for all those years that helped me pull away from Jonathan with as much grace as I did. I tried to reform him, to make him go with me to therapy and counseling, but I knew when it was up. I mean, I clung more than I should. Jonathan had to cut it off entirely, but when he did I let him go.

It was this history that set the stage for Terrence and my coffee date the week after the gala. Since his vanishing, his texts remained the same. The night of the gala he wrote me back about 12:30.

Finishing important Netflix work. Shakespeare? At least he reads.

We met after work at the Starbucks on Addison. Around us were students typing up papers, awkward first gay dates, and a few beanie-wearing comedians working on sketches.

"David!" Terrence met me with a hug. "How are you?"

"I'm good. How are you?"

"Usual, I think. Did you want anything?"

"I got a coffee."

Terrence winked at me and went to the counter. He knew the barista by name. The two laughed over some shared joke. Coffee in hand, Terrence came back to me. He put his chin on the top of his coffee cup and looked at me intensely. "All right, Jenkins. Status."

It was an ongoing joke – the status thing. One night when we were drunk at the Market Days street festival, he had pointed at me in the middle of Hydrate nightclub. I had my tongue buried in Jonathan's mouth, shirtless, and sweating out the gallons of vodka we had drunk that weekend. "Status?" he had screamed. For some reason in that moment it was the funniest thing in the world.

"Well, let's see," I said. "Still seeing the doctor for my mental health issues. Still spending most free time with Netflix and ice cream, as you can tell." I squeezed my belly.

"It just makes you look jolly," Terrence said. "You're like a gay Santa."

"I'll update my Grindr profile name."

"You're on?! David – progress! Last month it was all about mourning and not being ready to get back in the game. I'm glad you're at least opening up some options."

"I'm trying to get back out there. Lately I've felt a new wind blowing."

"As long as it doesn't come from your ass." Terrence lifted his coffee and took a sip. Despite his casual airs, his light jokes and quick conversation, his eyes looked tired. His hair, usually a model of undercut perfection, was slightly unkempt, a few wheat-colored hairs out of place.

"Now you. Status?" I raised my eyebrow.

Terrence nodded. "I think you know a lot has been happening."

"It has. I'm glad you're finally saying it out loud. I've actually been watching the Boystown feed more closely just to see if you're mentioned. It's kind of dried up…"

"Yes," Terrence winced slightly. "Sorry, I know you've been trying to be a good friend and I've been pretty dismissive."

"There was an elephant," I used my hands to outline an invisible pachyderm, "in the room."

"I ran away from the elephant. I went home to Michigan and did some thinking. Then I came back and did more thinking." He paused here and took a sip of coffee. His mouth opened to speak again, but then it closed.

"Annnnndddd…"

"And, I think that maybe I'm being… too conservative."

"You did a lot of thinking and discovered you are a Republican?"

Terrence laughed. "Never! My god, David, I may be a lot of things, but NEVER that."

"Thank God."

"Glad that's straightened out," Terrence wiped away invisible sweat from his forehead. He suddenly grew serious. "Anyway, Lloyd called me after I was home a few days. He tried texting and I didn't respond. Then he called and I answered, when I had calmed down enough to not be a screaming mess."

"I like that level of maturity."

"Right?" Terrence winked at me. "So, we talked about it. And what he said made some sense."

"Did he say he was an ass? That would make sense." I tsked and wagged my finger.

"He apologized profusely. He had actually sent flowers the day before. He groveled as he should."

I nodded in approval.

"But in the call, he suggested that he needed more flexibility in the relationship."

"What the fuck does that mean?"

"It means he is more sexual than me."

I opened my mouth to speak, judgment visibly dripping from my eyes and mouth.

"Now, wait, David! Before you wag your finger at me again, let me explain. He just said that he thinks we need to assess what an open relationship would look like. I mean, in all honesty, I'm willing to talk about it. When I said conservative, I mean that maybe I'm putting a Midwestern gay filter on relationships and we need to rethink that."

"You really want to go hunting like Donnie and Tibbs?"

108

"It's not just them, David. It's Peter and George. It's common. We're sexual creatures and we need to use that in looking at dating and marriage in a gay context, not just follow what our parents did or what our churches tell us to do. Even with the Supreme Court decision coming up at the end of the month, we still need to be skeptical of the status quo. Those ways of thinking are on the table to be scrutinized."

"Listen," I leaned forward. "Terrence, you can do whatever you want. Grab Lloyd and fourteen people and get a room at Steamworks – that's fine. But is this what you want? I've never heard you interested in opening things up before."

"I've never thought about it. And, David, let's be honest, I've known that Lloyd has fooled around. It's never been as egregious as with Kinsey, but I'm not an idiot. I know some nights when he stays out there is at least a blowjob in a corner or an alley. But he comes home to me."

"And this would help, how?"

"If we bring it into the open, then it's not a… you know… 'sin.'" Terrence made air quotes with his fingers. "Sometimes Lloyd will go off and feed his need for sexual attention, and maybe, I don't know, sometimes we do it together."

"Have you talked to Sal about this?"

"No. I mean, I haven't seen really anyone for a few weeks. I've been doing the thinking. I did talk to my therapist about it."

"What does he think?"

"He says you should always be open to your partner: listen, compromise, bridge."

"Bridge? Does he say which one?"

Terrence stuck out his tongue at me. "You're a cunt today."

"I'm just a little surprised is all."

"Maybe I should try to be more full of surprises."

#

Dr. Konstantin again looked half asleep as I told him the latest in my string of complaints about my life. The hair in his ears must have been trimmed as it wasn't quite as protrusive as in the previous session.

"I'm getting ready for it, Doctor. I've been thinking and preparing for the jump into the void of dating."

Dr. Konstantin tapped his pencil on his notepad. "David, what has stalled you? You went to the wedding and saw your friend happily getting married. Now?"

"It's a mix of things. I'm definitely overthinking it. Part of it is this weird feeling of being trapped between two worlds. I don't know where to plant my flag." Outside the sky was a steely gray, a later afternoon thunderstorm ready to let loose. A bolt of lightning ripped through the sky.

"What two worlds?"

"Well, I was home, right? And I see my brother and his wife and kids. They stayed in our hometown and are doing exactly what my parents did. They have this storybook, Midwestern dream life. They take the kids to sports, they go to church, they have cookouts on Saturdays with my mom and dad. Their house has a white fence for fucksake."

"Hmmmm."

"Then in Boystown no one knows what they're doing. I have Sasha and Edward who are this settled, boring couple. Edward watches The History Channel at night and Sasha drinks wine and reads his books for his dissertation. Then there is my friend Terrence who is suddenly talking about getting fuckboys for him and his partner because his partner can't keep his dick in his pants. But also, you have Jonathan, who basically works out and fucks all the time, and to be quite honest that sounds great. Why not do that?"

The Doctor took of his glasses and rubbed the bridge of his nose. Rain began to pelt the windows. I looked outside, the view becoming distorted by the veins of rainwater dripping down the glass.

"David," Dr. Konstantin said, "in describing these other people, you aren't saying anything about yourself."

"What do you mean?"

"These are people doing a number of different things. Which of them do you want to do? What kind of relationship do you want right now?"

Thunder rolled in the distance. I thought briefly of all those things I'd said I wanted, all the things Jonathan and I had discussed in our evenings and afternoons together. When had we stopped planning a future? Why didn't I notice?

I sighed. "I don't fucking know. Everyone is a fuck up so I can't really decide."

"Sasha seems happy."

"He is, but Terrence did a few weeks ago. What if I go home tonight and Sasha calls me and says, 'Orgy at my place? Bring some lube!'"

"Then he'll have given you an invitation to an orgy."

Dr. Konstantin did this often. He would say a statement that didn't direct me or guide me or tell me anything but then clam up and wait for me to say something. I would always get flustered in these moments. I felt he was leading me to the middle of the woods and just fleeing the scene. Good luck, David! Figure this out yourself, you fuck! The sound of the storm added a perfect, ominous tone to the silence.

"So, you're saying… What? What if Sasha had an orgy?" I asked petulantly.

"Would you go?"

I didn't hesitate. "Absolutely not."

"This exercise," the doctor said licking his weathered lips, "where I ask you what you would do and then you reply with an answer…."

"Yes?"

"That's what you have to do to form your person."

"In the words of my friend Terrence, you're being a cunt." I half-smiled and looked to the window, the view now an impressionist painting, swirls of light and smudged, distorted buildings.

The doctor leaned forward slightly. He was scribbling slowly on his notepad, his eyes not lifting to look at me. "David, these answers don't come easy. You've only dated Jonathan. Date some more. Make mistakes. Go to an orgy – or don't. Do what it takes so that the answers you provide to these questions begin to build the person you are. Life is a maze that we have to cut our own way through. No one can get you out but yourself."

The maze: Doctor Konstantin had used this image before. In one of our first sessions he had even forced me to read the myth of Theseus in the Minotaur. Why couldn't the more applicable story for life be Dorothy and Oz? I was jealous of that pigtailed queen and her single, golden way forward. The decision to date again had been a momentous mental hurdle to overcome in and of itself, and now I was stalled on a number of real and imaginary minotaurs that kept me from moving ahead. It was looking fat in an olive dress shirt; it was realizing that I would never be the sexy, desired man that Jonathan had become; it was the split worlds of Michigan monogamy and Chicago promiscuity. When it came down to it, I saw myself as David, average, six-foot, brown-haired, middling education, stable and boring career. That was my main excuse for not making the leap, not putting on the ruby slippers.

After mulling this over for several moments, I finally said, "I think I'm afraid, Dr. Konstantin. I'm afraid that I have nothing really to offer."

"David," Dr. Konstantin sighed, "trust me. You enter the dating world and you will discover that there are a lot of awful, boring, awkward people." I could have been mistaken, but a hint of a smile flitted across his face. "Go out. Date. Come back here and we'll start asking those questions."

"To be or not to be."

Silence – then, "I think our time's about up."

#

When I had gotten home from the psychiatrist, I texted a number of friends to join me for my "Coming Out to Tinder." Surprisingly, on a Wednesday, there weren't a lot of professional adults willing to get filthy drunk with me and help me make online dating profiles. Al, however, had been willing and showed up with a box of wine.

"This seemed important," he said. "A bottle doesn't convey how important something like this is."

"You're so twenty-two," I said. I went into the kitchen and got a knife. "Should we cut it out of the box and just slap the bag?"

Slapping the bag was a college game that consisted of adult men and women ripping the bladder of a wine bag from the box and then raising it above the head. Others would gather in a line, slap the bag as hard as they could, then fall to one knee and chug wine for as long as possible. There are no goals. No prizes. Slap the bag is done exclusively with the goal of drunkenness in mind.

After a few rounds of the game and additional shots thrown in for good measure, Al and I found ourselves seated on the tile of my kitchen floor. Al was wearing a blue tank top, the shoulder hanging over his striated shoulder. He smiled at me and winked.

"David, thank you for also being a mess. I need someone to party with."

"How's the job search?" I asked.

"I'm kind of enjoying having a rich boyfriend paying half of my studio rent and hanging out in coffee shops."

"The life of a ne'er do well."

"I would say bohemian." Al pulled the strap of his tank up. He reached to the floor, where he had placed a Solo Cup of wine and took a long draught.

"Things are good with the boyfriend?" I asked.

Al put his head back. "Yes." The response was short, not short and decided, but cut off, as if thousands of words hung from the end, but he had lopped them off in an effort to keep the sentence tidy.

"That doesn't sound completely good."

Al smiled at me. "No, it's good. I just miss him and…," he licked his lips, "Chicago is full of temptation."

"Kinsey?"

"Ha!" Al cocked his head and gave me a dirty look. "That was so long ago, David. Give me some credit."

"You were cozy at the gala."

"No," Al bit his lip. "I actually was asking him about someone else."

"You didn't hookup that night, did you?!"

"I didn't. I was asking about Hedley."

"Hedley!"

"I don't know – he's gorgeous and that party and the atmosphere. There was something otherworldly about it." He began playing with the seam of his shorts. "I wasn't going to cheat. I'm not going to cheat, but I got caught up in the whole night. And Hedley is so, I don't know. He's epic."

"I didn't know you had a thing for him."

"Who doesn't have a thing for him?"

I took a sip of wine. "Yeah, we definitely all have a thing for him. He even talked to me that night. He remembered my name. He has that ability to make you feel like you're the only person in the room."

"He knows you pretty well, David. You hang with Myrtle sometimes."

"Yeah, but I'm surprised he thought enough to remember."

"Well, that's what I'm saying. If I had the chance, I'd bone Hedley."

"That's top talk, Al! You graduated from Bottom University."

"Girl, I do what it takes to get a dick."

The night had phased into hazy territory. Time had begun to drain off the clock at a rapid pace. What had been 7:00 was now 9:00. Wine and Jack Daniels gripped my brain and drained it of its full function, so that I felt comfortable opening up that avenue of talk that I had closed off from most people but Dr. Konstantin.

"I talked to Terrence." I stood up and reached for Al's glass to refill. He drained it and then handed it to me. "So, he and Lloyd are now in an open relationship."

"Oh," Al's eyes grew wide. "That *is* different."

"Terrence is going to open himself up to new possibilities."

"Okay," Al brushed back his hair, "open relationship is one thing. I feel like this is Lloyd telling Terrence that he has carte blanche to fuck anyone he wants."

"Bingo!" I pointed at Al and, in the process, slopped red wine all over the floor. "Shit! Sorry!"

We grabbed paper towels and mopped up the mess. Al sang "Working Song" from *Enchanted*. When the floor was about 1/3 clean, we both grabbed our cups and flopped back onto the tile.

"You know that I have no room to talk in terms of holding onto dying relationships."

"You are the king," Al giggled, his dimples showing in the side of his face.

"Well, all I'm saying is Terrence needs to let this die. Dead. Dying. Dead. Let it go."

Al waved his hands as if scattering ashes. "Goodnight, Moon!"

"I guess… that can be a thing? 'Goodnight, Moon.'"

We raised our glasses and toasted. Al fell over he was laughing so hard. "Like the book, asshole!"

"Okay, sure, Mr. Fulbright and his pre-school reading level."

"I fake it to make it."

Another round of shots, followed full glasses of wine. Al was barely propped up against the cabinets tapping buttons on his phone.

"Is that the boy?"

A dreamy smile decorated Al's face. "It is. He is just getting home from a club."

"Is he wishing you goodnight, moon?"

"He sent a dick pic." Al held up his phone and got caught up in another fit of giggles. "Modern romance!" He put down his hand, wine splashing from his glass.

"Messy, girl."

"I needed to let off some steam," he said. "It's been a bit lonely lately."

"I wouldn't know anything about that."

With a sudden jerk, Al was sitting bolt upright. "That's why we're here! The dating profiles – let's get you a man, or at least laid!" He stood up and stormed across the kitchen to grab my phone. "Open, please," he said handing it to me.

Before long I had Grindr, Scruff, Tinder, and OKCupid. Al was frantically keying in profiles and adding pictures.

"Try to make me seem classy."

"Know your audience. Do you have any sexy pics?"

"Holy shit, Al!" I took my phone and put it behind my back. "What are you doing?"

The look of disdain was searing. "David, you are being such a bitch. Grindr and Scruff – upload sexy pics, shirtless and play up your love of topping."

"People like that?"

"There's a shortage of your kind in Chicago."

"Okay."

"I know you're worried about your weight, but do like neck up. Maybe wait for a few days' beard growth. I think you'll be big with the Twinks."

"Yeah?" I couldn't help but smile. "You think?"

"You've got a little bit of a broey, older frat vibe – they like that." He put his finger to his chin, deep in thought. "OKCupid will be more work – you'll have to like create someone on that."

"Why don't I just be myself?"

Again, Al looked at me as if I was the biggest dumbass he'd ever met. "No one doesn't lie on OKCupid. You make up a persona and play it out."

"I'd rather be myself."

"Your funeral." Al grabbed his wine and leapt on the counter. "I think you're going to have a good time with this."

"Yeah?"

"Sex on-demand, at your fingertips. Create the new David on OKCupid and watch the messages roll in."

I took my phone and scrolled through some images. I still had a sexy pic from the closeted cop incident. In a second it was uploaded to my Grindr profile and being checked for decency by the Grindr Team. "Okay," I said, "here we go!"

"Yaaaaasss!" Al reached across the counter and grabbed the bottle of whiskey. He took of the cap and poured the amber drink into his mouth. "Your turn," he said, whiskey dribbling off his chin.

More shots, more wine. I secretly held back, doing about one-fourth the damage to my liver that Al did. It was 1 AM before he left my apartment. He wrapped me up in a big hug.

"You're my gay brother," he slurred. "Like, really always there, like a dad."

I was pretty drunk but Al was blackout. "Okay, sir. Well, you have an Uber on the way?"

"*Uber*!" Alan said affecting a German accent. "From Deutschland! Like me! Because I was in Berlin!"

"Okay, Goodnight Moon." I walked Al to the street. He fell over in the main foyer, taking a potted plant with him. The Uber driver game me a nasty look as I poured him into the cab. "Food poisoning," I said, slamming the door of the Acura.

When I got back inside I immediately sent a message to my boss noting that I would be working from home the next day. Margaret, my cube mate, would probably berate me with questions when I got in on Friday. "Late night on Wednesday, Davey?"

My second task was to open OKCupid and make a profile. My hands flew over the keys. Being drunker than I had thought, I kept laughing out loud to myself, an invisible David also in the room, scoffing Al's advice. "Ha!" I said. "A persona? I will be genuine, true! 'To thine own self be true!'"

Within twenty minutes I had the profile for Prometheus27 online. At the time the idea of me stealing fire from the gods seemed equivocal to beginning dating again. Prometheus was "A man looking for someone to share adventure with." Yes, I ended the sentence with a preposition.

I was about to close down my computer when I thought briefly of Frank from Hedley's party. Being so drunk and alive his words from the gala suddenly seemed the most romantic I had ever heard.

This is our Romeo and Juliet moment.

I scoured profiles but couldn't find him on the site. I laughed to myself after twenty minutes of blindly searching – just because one guy hit on me once, doesn't mean anything.

Before going to bed I went back into the kitchen, turned off the lights and grabbed my phone. There was one missed text from Al, letting me know he was home and had already thrown up in the shower. Below that text were a number of notifications from Grindr. It seemed my picture was approved and things were beginning to roll along.

Sup

This message caught my attention. Not because of the message, but because it was attached to a torso with two columns of abs prominently sticking out. What had Dr. Konstantin said about the maze? Cut my own way through?

I opened the messenger and typed a response: *Hey man.*

Into the woods, into the labyrinth, into the maze, ruby slippers on – Dr. Konstantin, here we go.

Grindrella

When I was a child I saw a Dateline special on Mad Cow Disease. In the program, a cow stumbled along, its muscled neck shaking, its legs sinking under its own weight. The idea, catalyzed in youthful imagination, became a ghost that prowled the depths of my consciousness. Staring into beef patties made by my mother, I would see the specter of this disease. I wondered if in a bite there lay the microscopic form that would flow through my blood into my brain. There it would slowly enflame the tissue, break down my motor skills, my head twitching, my body losing all ability to move forward. I would collapse, fall into death and darkness. Just as in the special, some man would stand up, take a gun and raise it in my direction.

That old exaggerated image emerged again after the break up. I was at home, driving with my mother, staring out the windows as we passed open cornfields and farmland. The bovine stench hit my nostrils as we drove further out into the country. Standing alone, isolated in a field, a brown, spotted cow was staring serenely into the horizon. Space and time twitched, infinitesimally, and I was seven again, sitting at the table, heart pounding, as I watched the burger drip fat.

At first, I laughed, reminding my mother of my year period of no hamburgers, that terrified age when I was sure that disease and death lurked under the processed covering of Wonder Bread buns.

But as the car rolled on, as aged thought took over, I contemplated Jonathan and me. I had known for a while. There had been attempts at counseling and reconciliation. In my most deluded state, I had awakened on a Saturday morning and made a large breakfast. I set the table with flowers and shined silverware and waited for him to awake. Hours ticked by, the food grew cold, and in its own poetic way, I had my answer to the repeated question of whether this was just a rough spot or the fated end.

We lumbered along at social gatherings, my own legs weak, my attention tuned for any whispers about the cheating. And it came, in hushed words, in faded sounds, in full stereo, around me. The list of his other lovers grew and I was witness to my own cuckolding. I wasn't like Terrence and his slavish devotion to his awful lover. What Jonathan and I had was real, worth fighting for. Years I'd spent with him and those good years were better than these months of bad. The scale was still tilted heavenward on the side of his fidelity.

I just had to wait.

But as in all such cases, the hobbling form of our relationship shuddered, twitched, fell. On one July morning it was Jonathan who raised the gun, leveled, and shot. I remember lying in bed, hearing the pop of the door slam and I knew, as one preternaturally knows when there are those life-altering events, that it was irrevocably over.

Tom was 5'10" and a yogi.

"It's liberation, the movements of yoga. I think I need to take you to the studio," he said drinking a glass of wheatgrass juice.

I had made a joke about him stealing picnic baskets that had fallen flat. As I watched his svelte form move to the bathroom, I made a brief list of our future trajectories.

Possibility One: I take up yoga. In tight stretch pants, I would watch the fat melt off of me in a sweaty gym several hours a week. We'd brunch after Saturday morning yoga, eating kale and vegetarian omelets at a trendy place in River North. Evenings I would spend in our two-bedroom Hancock condo watching documentaries as I waited for him to come home from late hours at the office. Eventually, there would be a biking trip through Europe, most likely on The French Riviera. I'd propose and we'd have a wedding with a vegan meal option.

Possibility Two: I continue to nod as he talks about his marathon training and how his juice diet was difficult to keep when he visited his parents in Madison. He had been flirty despite a rather dramatic disparity in our appearance levels. Him: fit, pecs twitching under a tight-fitting polo; me: in a loose shirt (the olive, of course), my eyes following meat entrees lovingly with my eyes as I grew angry at myself for ordering a salad after he asked if I had read processed meats give you cancer. But Tom was the kind who probably found my bigness exciting, who would sit on me and ride me with all the energy of a twink on Adderall. I just needed to nod for another thirty minutes to get us to the sweaty finish line.

Possibility Three: I kiss him on the cheek outside the restaurant. I'd say we'd meet up again, and make my way to McDonald's to get the meat and carcinogens I missed at the restaurant. He'd text me twenty minutes later and suggest we get drinks sometime over the weekend. I send a smiley face and then say that I would be out of town, but maybe sometime soon...?

Outcome: Double quarter pounder meal with ranch to dip my fries.

#

After the Hedley gala, I briefly had the idea to get "cut" or "ripped." I bought P90X DVDs from eBay and purchased a bunch of produce from Trader Joe's. Sasha rolled his eyes when I told him I was going to get back in shape, mostly because I had never really been in shape. My genetics had been a gift that was slowly being rescinded in my twenties. If I had ever had the urge to work out like my brother, I may have been as fit as he was, but, all told, that seemed like a lot of unnecessary work. I didn't want to die of a heart attack, but I also didn't care if you needed an abacus to count my abs.

Even before starting, I knew my desire wasn't there. Jonathan had gone from skinny guy to muscle head, driven by some wild, masculine impulse that had never really erupted in my own genetic code. By the end of week one P90X had been reduced to about P15meh, and by week two, I would just turn on the workouts while eating Pop-Tarts in the morning. Week three returned to my normal schedule of watching *Charmed*.

The only thing I got out of my fitness revolution was eating a little better. Not because I had a desire, but because I was so lazy that by the end of week one the only thing left in my fridge was spinach.

#

Tuesday CTA commutes are the stuff hell is made of. After Monday you have the satisfaction of making it through the day – likewise, Wednesday brings the satisfaction of completing Hump Day. Thursday there are drinks after work, so the train ride home is slightly drunk. Friday is Friday and all is right with the world.

But Tuesday.

Tuesday, the train compartments are hotter, there are still three full days in the week, and everyone is fleeing the downtown together, bodies bumping and rubbing against each other as the train rolls along in the darkness of the red line subway.

On one June Tuesday I ran into Myrtle Jennings. Sweat was streaming down her face, her sunglasses barely hanging on her ears. We uttered just a few words across the mass of bodies in the train car, but it was enough:

"Get off at Fullerton?" she asked. "Grab a drink?"

It was a relief to step off the train, the heat of the day giving way to a breezy summer afternoon, the sky a perfect powder blue.

"How are you?" Myrtle asked as we climbed down the stairs. "I feel like it's been forever."

"It has been. Hedley said you missed the gala?"

"I had a wedding. I heard it was a blast, though."

"It was fun. The usual gay mess."

"My favorite."

Myrtle smiled revealing a perfect row of white teeth. With the afternoon sun shining behind her, even with the sweaty forehead, she could have been a movie star in that one moment. It always amazed me when I ran into her on the street, not out in Boystown, the division between work Myrtle and bar Myrtle. If she had been at Hedley's, there's no doubt she would have been one of the drunkest, accosted some gay in a corner about her man problems, then most likely thrown up on the statuary. Work Myrtle, however, was business suits and quaffed hair. She had gone as Adele one year for Halloween and the resemblance had been dead on.

We went to Lincoln Hall – I ordered a summer shandy and Myrtle got a vodka cranberry. She slipped off her heels and rubbed her feet.

"I never understand drag queens. They choose to wear this shit."

"You seem really dressed up today."

"I had a client lunch. Tomorrow it's working from home and sweatpants."

The drinks came; the sides of the glasses were wet with condensation. The glass in Myrtle's vodka tinkled when they set it down on the table.

"So, you're back in the dating pool?" Myrtle asked.

"Yeah, I'm just lining them up and trying to get through them. Only one actual date so far – a yogi."

"Any good?"

"I ended up eating alone at McDonald's."

Myrtle laughed. "That's about right. I gave up after my last Tinder date told me he liked wearing his past girlfriend's clothes."

"That's made up."

"Couldn't make that up if I tried."

I raised my glass and held it out. "To being hopelessly single."

Our glasses clinked. The sun sank lower in the sky, traffic crawled by the outside windows, streams of college students from DePaul in tank tops and shorts drifted by, laughing and enjoying the sun and laziness of the afternoon. Around us the bar was slowly picking up with fellow happy hourers. Murmuring conversation mixed together with the light sound of car honking and laughter outside. Myrtle and I stepped outside for a cigarette. I took one, small puff as a contribution, Myrtle handling the lion's share.

One drink turned to four. One cigarette to three. Myrtle put her heels in her purse and had her feet up on the seat across from her.

"I just wish I hadn't met Brad," she said slightly slurring. "Like you spend three years with someone, then they just vanish. 'Sorry, Myrtle, it's not working out. You don't make me feel the way you used to.' What the fuck does that mean?"

"I didn't realize you and Brad were together that long."

"Yup."

"Jonathan and I were together six years. Things in Indy after college were this weird static happiness. I never expected he was looking for a way out. We moved to Chicago and he vanished, too – I mean, kind of. He all of a sudden was in the gym all the time and then started fucking everything."

"That's terrible. I actually ran into him a few days ago. He's hanging out with Hedley a lot now."

"I saw them together at the gala. Is he doing well?"

"Seems to be. I mean that girl is looking good." Myrtle pushed her drink to the side. She flipped a stray hair out of her eyes. "He and another little gay nugget are in Hedley's crew now."

"Oooh! Hedley's expanding The Set?"

"You know how he is, David. He takes a passing interest in someone and then who knows? That kid could be in The Set next month or Hedley could make him disappear socially. It's the razor's edge."

"Was he like that when you knew him in high school?" I never had the fascination with Hedley that others had, I guess Al included, but I found him interesting. I wanted to hate him, I really did, but then I'd see him at a party or on the street and he would say, "Hello" with genuine warmth and I didn't know what to make of it.

Myrtle leaned back in her chair. Her blazer was off and the last light of afternoon caught the spirals in her hair, causing them to shine. With the soft lighting and bustling ambience of summer, I felt like we were in a TV show. "You know," she said, "he wasn't like he is now, but looking back, I can see how he became the way he is."

I squinted my eyes. "I'm going to pretend I understood what you just said."

"You know what I mean! Like, he wasn't as popular as he is now, but when I think about high school, I can see how that would have developed into the kind of diva he is now."

"He's such a kind diva. He said 'hi' to me at the party."

"Let's just say..." Myrtle pursed her lips, "you aren't strategic. You're one who doesn't affect the outcome of the game, so he'll treat you nicely."

"I didn't know it was a game."

"All of it is. I get tired of it sometimes," Myrtle brushed a hair out of her face. "I'm not even playing with Hedley and his little Set, but I see it happen and some of it's painful."

"Like Terrence and Lloyd?"

Myrtle raised her glass. "Bona fide tragedy."

Before long the sun was down and we were stumbling back to the train. Myrtle smoked a cigarette on the way back to the Fullerton station, the smoke circling her like a halo. I was only going one stop, but we sat down on the train. Myrtle leaned her head on my shoulder. She took a deep breath and closed her eyes. "This is what I want," she said over the roar of the train. "Just this. A shoulder to lean on, a smile when I've had a bad day. That's all I want from a relationship. Why is it so hard to find?"

#

I awoke the day after I created my OKCupid profile to a throbbing headache.

Jesus, what had I been espousing to Al? I made a dating profile? My head drooped in the effort of staving off the rush of guilt, embarrassment, and swelling hangover headache.

Tentatively I went to my computer and looked at the Frankenstein-like effort of my profile.

I looked fat in the picture; my idea to be up front about my appearance was ill-advised and aesthetically displeasing. Al had been right about keeping my real self hidden.

About me:

Hey, I'm David. I'm not sure what I'm looking for on this but looking forward to seeing what happens.

Ughhhhhhhh. I sound like such an asshole.

I stared at the screen and the 0 messages I had received. The manic hope of the night before had turned to self-loathing.

Before Jonathan I hadn't even really dated. Going to the bars and winking at someone was all it took in college. Everyone was horny and I was twenty pounds lighter. Now I wrote stupid profiles and put up fat pictures.

When is it too early to start drinking?

#

Matt was out of my league. He had Allan hair and a smile from a toothpaste ad. We ended up going on a date the week before Pride. The only reason I snagged the date was the fact that when I updated my OK profile picture I strategically chose, literally, the best picture I had. In it I was at a charity benefit, wearing a suit. The soft lighting and camera angle had made me look like I could have been on ER in the glory days. This had somehow caught Matt, who was one of those gays who has it all together, and by that, I mean he has a creation of his future in his head that he crawls toward daily through his insane work ethic and gym routine. Everything about him was calculated from his outfit, to the GRE vocabulary he used during dinner.

Over our appetizers, I could almost hear his future self, speaking from the year 2025: "Persevere, Matt! We've got the Gold Coast condo and the boat, but we need the husband accoutrement. This one is too rotund and drudging. Ticked off the list – we need to update the screening process so we're not so disconsolate over here!"

As far as dates go, he was a solid B. He said some funny things and was very polite. When dinner ended, he got up quickly and headed to the door.

"It was very nice meeting you," he said emotionlessly.

I watched him walk away and wondered what it would be like to put my dick in his bubble butt. The pants he had meticulously picked were tight and cupped his buns so that they pushed out like two perfect hocks of ham. There was no way he would go on another date with me, but I don't think I'd even say yes if he asked. I could see five dates from now him picking out my clothes and tsking if I wore anything from a clearance rack.

One time Sasha had said he had been the same way as Matt in his younger years – this was after the whorey club Sasha and pre-opera Edward phase. It was when we had just started to become friends. He had said, "I came out, I was hot, and I tore through men like they were Kleenex. Even if I was with the hottest guy in the bar, I'd be looking at the door waiting for someone hotter to come in. But then I had my heart broken. I dated this guy for about two weeks, who by all accounts was my perfect man. He was handsome, charming, had a great job and had a dog named Milo. We went on a few dates, hooked up, and then he disappeared. He just stopped texting, stopped calling, stopped everything. I saw him at a bar two weeks later with a new guy. I got angry, cried, went to see my therapist and raged at the poor man for forty-five minutes. But you know what my therapist said? He said, 'Sasha, what if this isn't about the guy? What if you aren't mourning the loss of one person, but the whole ideal he represents? You had your idea of perfection for a minute and then it was gone. This guy doesn't sound like he was that great, in total, but what he stood for to you was. He was your future husband: smart, charming, physically your ideal. But you lost him – and in doing so you may have lost the delusion that this fantasy figure exists.'" Here Sasha looked to the bedroom and smiled at, what I assumed was Edward. "That meant so much to me. From then on, I was out of the cave. When I looked at guys I actually saw them. I listened to them. I realized it would take one or two dates to get to know them. I lost that zeal for dating, but I enjoyed it a lot more."

This speech ran through my head as I watched Matt walk away. I was suddenly seized by the urge to run and catch him and give him a hug.

"I know we wouldn't work out," I'd say, "but give these other guys a break. They may surprise you."

#

On the Fourth of July I went home to see the family. There was a festival, which culminated in my brother and his family, my mother, father, grandmother, Aunt Charlotte, and me sitting in the local park awaiting fireworks as evening approached.

"Can you believe it?" Aunt Charlotte's innumerable bracelets jangled as she waved her hands at the surrounding activity. "A celebration of America! Think of what Paul Revere did for us!"

As was the tradition with Aunt Charlotte's interjections, the comment was ignored by the rest of those gathered.

My brother was sitting with a beer clenched in his hand. On his lap one of the brood played with an empty bag of chips.

"I'm surprised you let her have that Brad. Shouldn't it be some sort of composted onion grass cakes?"

"All I can hear is the slap of your flabby chins, brother." He took a long sip from his beer and looked over at me. He tipped his sunglasses down so that his sparkling blue eyes could clearly let me know that he was not in the mood to fuck around.

"Now boys," my mother drawled. After three Bud Lights her image of familial perfection grew much more liberal. "Let's just enjoy. Enjoy!"

"I can enjoy and still let bro know he's chubby. Aren't gays supposed to be really fit?"

"Some of them," I said. "I enjoy wine and ice cream more than most, though."

Slightly offended, I rose and sauntered over to my grandmother. Her walker was leaned against a tree and a plume of grey smoke clouded her like Pig Pen from Peanuts. Unlike television grandmothers, mine really didn't care to see the whole family en masse. Whenever a large group was gathered, she very often crept to the periphery and chain-smoked cigarettes until the melee died down and the couch was cleared so she could nap.

"Brad giving you a hard time?" she asked.

"Always. How does my little brother run all over me, Grams?"

"He thinks you're gay and weak."

My jaw went slack as I fought to come up with a retort.

My grandmother looked at me and shrugged. "I didn't say it was accurate, but it's how straight men think," she said. She put a new cigarette to her lips and clicked her lighter. Once its tip was red, she drew a long, deep breath. "Men are stupid." The smoke blew out her mouth, her nose, "You look good with some meat on your bones."

I regained control of my jaw and laughed. "The other gays don't really think so."

"You shouldn't think in those terms, Davey. That's part of your problem."

"What terms?"

"'Other', 'them.' People are people – we're all one thing, there are no tribes, groups other than the ones in our heads. Some people are assholes. It sounds like assholes are giving you a hard time about being a little overweight."

"My brother is an asshole. This is correct."

My grandmother turned and nodded. In all the years I'd been her grandson, the number of smiles I'd elicited from her was in the single digits. Now she was looking at me with her standard look: eyes impassive, mouth pulled into a taught, straight line, right hand bent at the elbow, cigarette smoke pouring into the air. "He can be," was all she said.

At least, unlike Dr. Konstantin, she acknowledged my jokes.

Not much more was said as we sat by the tree. I could hear Brad's kids laughing as they chased each other through the fresh cut grass. My mother and father continued to move through Bud Lights with growing ease. Aunt Charlotte's chatter filled the air like a background vocal track in a pop song. The sun was almost down when I rose and began to walk toward the rest of the family. Grandma tossed down a cigarette and reached out to grab my elbow.

"Help me over, would you, doll?" she asked.

I grabbed her walker and led her towards the family. Mom's laughter was now bellowing above the children. We were almost back to the group when grandma gently tugged my elbow, indicating that we should stop. She didn't look at me, but licked her lips. "I meant that about you comparing yourself to those others," she said. "I don't know much about dating, never did. But don't try and go and be like a 'them' in order to get who you want. You'll be nothing but lost if you keep thinking about following some group. I see it already with Brad's little ones. They need this or that to fit in. They have to have those to be 'cool.'"

The noise of the families gathered had died down slightly as night approached. Kids were growing tired and reclining on blankets and parent's laps. "That's good advice, Grams," I said.

The night slipped away in a whirl of color. The fireworks blasted above us as John Philips Sousa blared. My brother grabbed me around the shoulders and apologized for being an asshole and said that he knew there was some guy out there for me. My grandmother farted and blamed it on the fact that she was in her eighties. Mom passed out as Aunt Charlotte trumpeted the genius of the Chinese and their gunpowder.

"Can you believe it? Thousands of years ago they came up with this stuff!"

I ended up sitting on an old Pokémon blanket with one of my nieces sleeping peacefully on my lap. For the first time in weeks I wasn't thinking about going out, being fat, meeting someone; my thoughts were preoccupied with the little body on top of me, the music of John Cougar Mellencamp, and the snores of my mother.

I wonder, I thought, if this is how you get out of the mess.

#

After the date with Matt, there was Mr. Perfect. Literally, he was perfect. Not in the Hollywood soft focus kind of way, but rather the way in which real humans can be really wonderful. In terms of looks he was a solid six – handsome smile, parted chestnut hair, and wide hazel eyes. When he laughed it was short and masculine, an abrupt roar of male strength. He hands were coarse, yet manicured, with slight hair around his knuckles.

And I had no interest.

He was a chemical engineer, a job he has wanted his whole life. Where others complain about their jobs, Mr. Perfect would detail the beauty and wonder of the petroleum refinement process in excruciating detail. Not excruciating enough to be annoying, however; he would pepper in questions about me and what I did so that he came off as completely genuine in loving his job and being interested in what I did for a living.

When I complained about my coworker, Mark, being too boring, Mr. Perfect jumped in to offer an alternative reading of Mark. Surprisingly poignant and thoughtful, this insight was enough to make me wonder if, perhaps, I hadn't worked with Mark for two years and didn't find him a personality vacuum.

"Maybe you have to get beyond the superficialities, you know," opined M.P. "You should get coffee and find out what's behind all his talk about mortgages and high-ticket furniture. I bet there's a lot more there."

After dinner, M.P. walked me to the Addison train stop and kissed my cheek. "Let's talk soon," he said, vaguely committing to a continuing relationship. But as I watched him walk away, I felt dead inside. Dead in one sense that I didn't care if I ever saw him again, but also dead in that I felt worse after being around his optimism.

It was fucking draining.

I waited for him to turn the corner and then I walked back to Halsted to get frozen yogurt. It was the kind of night when all the toppings are necessary. ALL OF THEM. Gummy bears belonged on top of Oreos, that deserved to be drowned in fudge.

Sitting alone, I found myself asking those questions that Dr. Konstantin had mentioned previously.

"Do I want someone who looks at the brightside always?"

No.

"Do I fucking care about petroleum refinement?"

No.

"What did we learn?"

Mae West nailed it. "When I'm good I've very good, but when I'm bad, I'm better." I don't have time for saccharine perfection – give me the fried beef of cynicism.

#

I ended up using my Grindr way more than I would admit to any of my friends. At some point I even lied to Al and told him it was deleted.

But it wasn't. Deep down I knew what a poison the app could be. On-demand sex anywhere, at almost any time was now at my fingertips. Gays used to have to go out, see someone, read them for our gay signs and codes, but now an entire queue of men sat in the interwebs and all I had to do was tap. Sex was everywhere, no longer in the bathhouse but a real possibility at any time, place, and with any kind of person.

BigBttm lived 874 feet away. His picture showed a furry torso that cut off just above his penis. We got together at 3 am on a Saturday after I'd been out in Boystown on Friday night. I could tell when he answered the door that I wasn't what he wanted, but we ran through the act of sex with medical precision. He had a condom and bottle of lube on the nightstand. Door to door the entire exercise lasted 35 minutes.

HauteJock was a closeted athlete from the local university. His fear of being discovered as gay opened the possibility of me sleeping with him. In two or three years he would be in one of the higher echelons of Chicago gays, maybe even a member of The Set, if Hedley didn't deem him too much of a threat, but in his current terrified climate, he was a muscly, brunette who came over at 10 am on a Saturday following his weight training sessions. I rhythmically pounded him, his expression aghast with his condition, shame, fear, but also liberation writ across his unblemished face. To my surprise, he was the one that kept coming back to me. Three or four times over three weeks we'd hit the sheets and go through the act of sex with him zipping his pants, nodding, and escaping immediately after it was over. It was weird to think, but HauteJock and I had the most honest relationship I had built that summer. We both knew we were using each other, and that was fine.

In an attempt to diversify my portfolio, I opened a conversation with Hung Top on a Saturday afternoon. He had a thick curly mane of hair and stood at 6'5" and 270 pounds. The size proportions excited me, in way that made me feel the impulse to bottom like I hadn't in years. I went over to his house and he opened the door. He quickly declared his policy not to kiss and led me to the bedroom where a towel was laid on the bed. No foreplay, no kissing, just a dab of lube, the sound of a condom being ripped open, and a painful entry and pounding of my unpracticed anus.

I got home that night and sat on the toilet. I had the feeling my insides were ready to drain out, mixed with the puckered heat and pain of my asshole trying to figure out why I had decided to willingly let a nine-inch phallus be inserted and removed from my butt for twenty minutes straight.

That night I went for a walk down Belmont and sat at the harbor. It was a quiet evening, away from the roar of Lake Shore Drive, the sounds around me were dogs barking, children playing, and couples chattering as they watched the evening sky. I thought of the queue of men in my pocket, that tone of message after message coming in to men all over the city. All their histories, stories, and lives reduced to a thumbnail picture, a line of text, if that, describing their lives, passions, and desires. In the lowest point I imagined my could-be husband thumbing through pictures. Years ago, when we didn't have our digital limbs that spanned continents, when we only had our small niches, we may have hooked up and talked into the morning. We could get to know each other and go to bars, join a team, go away on vacation together. A love story, properly nurtured, may have been able to grow, twining our lives slowly together.

Now he was looking at a screen, seeing my face or torso and scrolling on. Too fat, too boring, not in that kind of mood tonight.

That night I went home and had a glass of wine before bed. I deleted Grindr and brainstormed ways to encounter, get to know, living, breathing people.

Two days later the app was back.

#

"How long have you been seeing him?" I asked. I was in front of the TV, my phone held to my ear.

Mya thought for a moment. "I saw you at the wedding the last week in May? I guess we met like two weeks after."

"That's exciting! It's been a bit since you had someone you were even interested in."

"Yeah, we'll see. He's been traveling a lot this summer."

"I mean six dates is legit, nowadays. I really have yet to make it to two. This week was I dated this gorgeous, hunky man who was way out of my league. Ass for days. Maybe months."

"Months of ass is very nice. But there was no second date?"

"He was over me by the end of it. I don't think he could have run away faster from dinner."

Mya laughed. "What's your therapist say about these dating adventures? You should be self-actualizing?"

"Dr. Konstantin says he's proud I'm putting myself out there. Evidently the crippling rejection is good for me."

"Well, your ego was way too big. I'm glad these city assholes are keeping you in check."

Having Sasha in the city was wonderful, and having Al around when Sasha was busy was also great. But, especially in the heart of my dating nightmare, I wished I could just move Mya into the apartment next door. If there was anyone who knew about what a disaster the dating scene was, it was her. I had tried for years to get her to create an anonymous blog about her experience.

Her story was equal parts tragedy and comedy. She fell in love with a guy named John right after college. He convinced her that she was the most important thing to him, she lost her virginity to him, then promptly found out she was one of ten other girls that John had been banging over the eight months of their courtship.

Having been Christian and chaste, and then, destroyed by the spiteful ways of men, she did a 180-degree change and decided to have sex with everything under the sun. Sometimes successful, always awkward, she tallied a moderate body count over the course of the next year.

Following her sexual emancipation was a period of lukewarm and milquetoast men looking to settle down. Not all the pieces fit, however, and there wasn't even a guy that she was remotely able to stomach for more than five dates. (The record went to a personal trainer named, Sebastian, not because she imagined a future for them together, but because he was the most beautiful man she'd ever slept with. Eventually, his low IQ sank the scales against them, and she was forced to break up with him over a breakfast of protein powder and egg whites in his parent's house while they were in Branson on vacation.)

The current epoch of Mya's dating life was casual and intermittent dating with the few guys that trickled through her life. It was my hope to mature to her level of Zen when it came to dating. In her mental framework, she was a planet with her own orbit and spin, traveling through a sea of stars, comets, and other planets. Eventually she foresaw another body lining up to hers, falling into her orbit, but for the time being, it was drifting through space, sweeping through her usual arc around an impassive, emotionless sun.

"Have any of your friends offered to set you up?" she asked.

"I don't know if that would be great," I said. "I'm picky and bitchy. I think Al and Sasha both know better than to match me up with anyone in my current mood."

"Well, there have to be people they don't especially like? Maybe they can test that out?"

#

It was just at the start of the Fourth of July weekend that I ran into Terrence at Sidetrack. I barely saw him; he was in a back corner of the bar concealed in shadow. In one hand he had a drink, the other was under his chin, holding his face, which was so sullen it was in danger of drooping to the floor. I had come with Al, Donnie, and Tibbs on a whim that evening. They had gotten me drunk enough at an after work happy hour to diminish the fear of Jonathan seeing Jonathan at the bars. They convinced me on the grounds that we would be there quick and early. The next morning, I was heading home for the family events.

"Terrence!" I called across the bar. "Status?"

Terrence face pulled into a smile, it flickered on his face, before dimming and an empty gaze returned. "I'm same as always. Status?"

I took my drink and plopped down next to him on a barstool. "I'm struggling, but drunk, so we'll call it 'doing well.'" I looked around to see if anyone else was around. "Are you..." I stuttered, "here alone?"

With a flourish of his hand and a feigned attempt at his usual humor, Terrence pretended to flip his hair back. "Girl, my whole entourage is here. Lloyd, Jordan, and some of The Set went to make a fruit loop."

I cringed slightly, which Terrance noticed.

"Jonathan's not here. He's out with Kinsey, I think."

I let out a sigh of relief and put my arm around him. "How's things going with the new arrangement? You trying a new third every night?"

Terrence mockingly pushed me away. "A lady does not kiss and tell."

"A lady," I said, "also does not spread her legs and let four gentlemen pound her bouquet, but we're splitting hairs."

"Glad all your dating rejections haven't made you less cunty."

We both laughed. Al had walked into the back bar and waved at us. He had been FaceTiming his boy in the street.

"How is Mr. Terrence?" he asked giving Terrence a kiss on the cheek.

"Much worse now that I ran into this bitch," he said pointing at me.

"Well, I never," I said. "To make it up to you, let's do a round!"

I waved over the bartender and got a round of Rumple Minze. Al and Terrence rolled their eyes but agreed to take the shot. A round of shots and one of drinks happened before we saw Lloyd and his entourage re-enter the room.

Terrence, who had been bubbling back to his former self, suddenly diminished, his facing growing tight. Lloyd came over and gave him a kiss, slipping his hand around his husband's waist. The rest of the crew was a mix of The Set and some others I had seen out and about Boystown. Of particular note was the kid who had spilled his drink on me at the gala. He looked different, more confident. His hair was cut differently; the shirt he wore was pulled tightly across his chest. He was turned away from Jordan, who was pushing through the circle to be closer to him.

"Hey-o, David," Stephen, the only member of The Set I found enjoyable, waved at me. Like Hedley, he would actually speak to those who weren't part of, as Myrtle called it, The Game.

"Hey, Stephen. How are you?"

"All signs point to drunk." He winked at me and slid past the group to go to the bar. The bartender ignored the line of six people to get his order immediately.

"David, Terrence tells me you're out on the dating scene again," Lloyd had a sarcastic smile that I could never read. He was staring at me, eyes twinkling, a smug look plastered on his face.

"I am – hence," I said raising my glass, "why I'm here tonight."

The group gave me a polite laugh. I noted Lloyd's eyes flicked hungrily over to the kid with Jordan as he forced a laugh.

A pregnant pause grew after my little joke. Al politely tapped my back, a clear indication he was uncomfortable.

"Well, we're going to grab Donnie and Tibbs," I said awkwardly. "You boys have fun!"

The group politely mumbled a good-bye as Al and I made our escape. When we got to the main bar and were quite alone, Al held up his phone to my face.

"Check out the Twitter, sir. I think tensions with Terrence and Lloyd are mounting."

On the screen I saw The Boystown Twitter homepage: *Sidetrack or Savannah, the animals are out looking for prey, among them The Set and some very marry men.*

"I admire the cleverness," I said. "I wonder who writes it?"

Al shrugged. "A bitch who wants to be on the inside, I would guess." Al feigned mock surprise. "David… Could it be you?!"

I pushed Al through the crowd and toward the bar. "Buy me another few drinks and I'll Tweet anyone and anything you ask me to. Maybe I can get you into bed with Hedley yet."

#

"And how are we, David?"

It was Wednesday at six. and I was still hungover from the previous night. Dr. Konstantin stared at me blankly as if I didn't look like a gay trainwreck. After the date with Mr. Perfect and ice cream, Al had called me up and asked if I was interested in dollar drinks at The Closet. I had woken up in my apartment at 6 am with glitter on my face.

"I had a rough night, Doctor," I said.

"Oh," he said ambivalently.

"I don't know," I rubbed my eyes with my knuckles. "I went on a date with a guy last night. It didn't go well."

"Put it on the spectrum, where does he fall in the line of casual dates and…" Dr. Konstantin rarely lost composure, but he did falter with gay language, "Grindr encounters, I suppose we'd say? Is he the reason for your… current state?"

I thought it best to ignore the doctor's dig at my appearance. "By all accounts it was a good date. We met, talked, he told me about his upcoming trip to Colorado. I told him about the wedding earlier this summer, my friends…"

"But…?"

"He was so boring. Perfectly boring. Anything I said he felt the need to add some sort of optimistic spin on the story that made me angry."

"So, you don't want to see him again?"

I thought for a moment. "I want to want to see him again, if that makes sense. He was a handsome, nice, driven guy, and I wanted nothing to do with him."

Dr. Konstantin nodded. "That's a very good way to come out of a date. You know it's not what you're looking for, so you can move on."

"In general, I think I'm getting a better idea of what I'm looking for," I said. "I think between sex and dates and non-responses, I'm forming a picture of what I actually need."

"The problem," Dr. Konstantin said, "with that picture, is that it very often becomes the source of a whole new set of hang ups."

"Meaning?"

"People become pieces in a puzzle that we view as our lives. We no longer see a person but a concept that has to match a pre-conceived notion."

Matt, his bubble butt, and his future boat flashed through my head. "I know what you mean, but I think what I mean is that I'm learning more about dating people and the ones to avoid."

"That is a good way to think about it. Remember we're forming the answer to those questions: Who are you? What do you want? What do you like to do? Answering those questions forms the person that will find someone. You can't use a person to answer those questions – the answers must precede."

"Doctor," I said mockingly, "I like this whole you telling me what to do thing. We should keep doing this."

"You were on the way there," Dr. Konstantin said drolly. "I stop at helping with your Match.com profile."

There was a brief silence as I thought about this statement. The fan in the office whirred. "Doc," I said, "was that a joke?"

#

Sasha left Roscoe's before I did. It was a random Thursday night and he had humored me by getting a drink. I'd again gone over more stories of failed, sad Grindr and OKCupid conversations. Somehow, he was always willing to hear the stupid stories, despite them all pretty much being the same and ending with me finding some sort of food to eat.

Around us the bar was dead. A few stray groups were clumped together, but it was nowhere near the spring crowds when Drag Race was on.

During my discussion with Sasha, I tried to make eye contact and flirt with a man down the bar. He was a reach for me in terms of appearance, but he had let his eyes settle on me for a brief instant, which was enough to inspire me to creepily gawk at him the entire rest of the evening. But as I had gone on and on and on about my dating misses and bored Sasha to tears, my general mood went from flirty to hopeless, my eyes moving from staring at the guy to surveying the bottom of my beer glass.

The bartender walked over and politely asked if I wanted another drink. I declined, opting instead to stroke the condensation on my nearly empty Miller Lite, feeling sorry for myself, and my lack of dating success. This was all piled on top of going on a date with M.P. and hating every moment of it. Was it all just hopeless? Is dating something God invented to test how much humans can handle of the stupidity of our race?

The night before I had told Dr. Konstantin that I was learning more about myself, becoming a more educated dater, but really maybe I was just being a dick and looking for a hot guy to share Netflix expenses with. When it came down to it, I was just as shallow as the guy who posted "no fats, no fems" on his Grindr. Nice guys had come on my radar; I'd chatted with Henry, a balding thirty-five-year-old non-profit worker who had been sweet. I stopped messaging him when he sent me a shirtless picture and I just wasn't into it. Should I have been? Was it all me?

"Are we at Churchill Downs?"

A man had sidled up beside me.

"What?" I asked.

"The long face," the man said. "Horse-like. I thought maybe y'all were getting ready to run."

The bartender approached. The chatty man kissed the bartender's cheek and ordered two gin and tonics. There was something about him that was familiar, but after three beers and the gloomy, neon lighting of Roscoe's, I couldn't quite place it.

While the bartender made the drinks, the man turned to me again. "No, but seriously, dude, you look bummed. Why are you so morose this fine July evening?"

"Morose?"

"Sad, gloomy, touched by sorrow."

"That's a very smart and dramatic word."

"I'm in med school, I need smart and dramatic to get street cred."

I wracked my brain trying to remember where I knew him from. He was thin, a green V-neck tee loosely hanging from his shoulders. Despite him being skinny, his forearms were riddled with veins, and sinewy; the long thin fingers of his right hand drummed the bar. His other hand was propped under his chin, cradling, his baby face. On his lips was a dreamy, mocking smile – his brown eyes glittered with mischief. In other situations, other nights after a few more drinks, I might have found him crazy attractive – the mix of his young face with the sarcastic accents of his shining eyes and mocking mouth, made for a pleasant view.

I hadn't realized the length of our pause in speech before he said: "You don't remember me, do you?"

My face went red. "I mean, I know you look familiar, but I can't place you."

"Romeo and Juliet," he said drumming his fingers.

"The gala!"

"Yessir," he smiled and tipped his glass to me. "I was drunk and that was aggressive, but I do think you're cute."

"Wow," I said. "You just hit on me."

"I did." The bartender came back with a glass. "Again..." We stared at each other. His left eyebrow went up, while I looked at him blankly. The shock of his previous statement had reset my thoughts about him – it was one thing to hit on a guy at the gala, another to be flirty and direct at Roscoe's on a Thursday. Again, I didn't realize how long I was silent before he spoke again, "Barry!" The bartender nodded. "Can you get this gentleman a beer? He looks sad and lonely and wants nothing to do with me flirting with him."

"Sorry!" I said.

"No apologies necessary." He winked at me. "I should go back to my friends."

He walked to the small nook behind me and instantly began chatting with two other gays behind me. The nook was a Roscoe singularity, a small no man's land of space. Two pillars with a wooden plank that acted as a bar between them, blocked off a small gathering space just in front of the window. It was a cozy out-of-the-way alcove, the only object in it a carved Native American statue that looked onto the rabble of Halsted street through the front window glass.

It was weird that after a month and a half of flirting, messages, random sex, and drawn out dinners, that someone directly talking and flirting with me had left me completely speechless. Up until that moment I had kind of believed romance to be dead. If not dead, then an elderly man in hospice care at a nursing home. In the past two months I had met a number of men and had a broad range of experiences. At certain points, I was powerless to carry the romance forward – the yogi, the Al-clone not in my league, looking above and beyond me to their next date mid-conversation. But there was M.P. and Henry. Henry had said wonderful things like he liked listening to Glenn Miller because it reminded him of afternoons with his eccentric grandmother.

"I hear the first notes of 'In the Mood' and I'm back in her old trailer. There's dust on the windows and the shag carpeting has chunks of bone from her dog's chew toys."

It all seemed so precise, calculating, and antiseptic. There was a roll of men on Grindr available 24/7 for sexual relief; there were 100s more online looking for love, too. The whole experience ran entirely counter to the Disney mythology I was raised with – Walt didn't preach the idea that lives could intersect, in maze-like fashion cut through each other in the twisted stone confines of our day-to-day existence and mean absolutely nothing. A quick conversation with a boy while in the pursuit of love could be a meaningless jut in the labyrinth of my life story. I had come to this revelation before – in my post-college days, it became clear that the idea of a fated existence, of a preordered life that was made specifically for each of us by some higher being, was in fact bullshit. Entropy, chaos, disorder were the rules of the game and it was our job to run headlong into their ambling pathways and force our own way forward. There were no enchanted kisses, no towering destinies to fulfill.

As it does, this revelation had come and gone in my earlier twenties, and now came again. Being older, I grasped it as more hopeful. What had been a quiet admonition of life's randomness and my own lack of fated greatness, was now a chance to cut my own path in the stone of my life story.

But now there was a boy I had chanced on twice, who looked at me with a lovely, longing look and actually verbally said that he was flirting with me.

Perhaps romance wasn't all dead. He's on life support, but there's no need to pull the plug yet.

I asked the bartender for a pen and scrawled my number on a napkin.

David 555-7734, The Romeo

With all the confidence of an acne-covered eighth grader, I went over to green V-neck and held it out. He turned to me and looked with dun-colored eyes and a boyish smile.

"Oh, you were okay with the flirting," he said.

I nodded.

"Very articulate, too," his eyes sparkled with laughter as they had at that bar. They dimmed slightly and took on a warm glow. "David," he stuck out his hand. "I'm Frank – again."

"Nice to meet you – again," I said.

"I'll be sure to use this sometime," he said.

"I'd like that."

Frank's friends tried to look preoccupied, staring at a TV in the corner. I grew more and more nervous, finally taking a step backward and almost toppling over the Native American statue. Frank laughed, a high-pitched, loud sound that was infectious. Soon I was laughing, too, and we both had tears in our eyes.

"This wasn't quite as romantic as I thought it would be when I wrote my number down," I said.

"It never is," Frank said. "But I'm glad I finally found someone worse at flirting than me."

Dog Days

  Despite therapy and hours of self-improvement, the eternal question of my life, the central post the carousel of my existence turned around, was what had driven Jonathan away. Things had seemed fine – or perhaps the devolution into not fine was so gradual and soft a slope, that the change in earth was unnoticeable. Reviewing moments, from first courtship to the grand finale I could see him drift away – in quiet, almost imperceptible ways, he had started to drift after we came to Chicago. Prior to that was Indianapolis, the doldrums, what I had believed to be a homey, welcome stasis, was probably, to him, the horror of the future. I wondered if it was in Indy or some night on a trip to Chicago when he looked across the way and saw another man, saw a possibility of who he could be without me, and the seed started to grow.
  Mya described the collapse of her relationship with the personal trainer as "The Tell-Tale Heart." She said the first date was erotic heaven. They had met up, been instantly attracted to each other, and rushed dinner to get into bed. It was the second date, a less rambunctious affair that she had actually seen him for who he was. He was twenty-three, lived with his parents and didn't believe in reading.
  She tried to reconcile her physical desire with his spiritual being, but the moment the second dinner started, she said she knew that she heard the ticking. The time on their relationship counter was set to chime in a short time – inevitably, it would drive toward a conclusion of separation.
  What she didn't know was whether that conclusion was natural, evolutionary or rather her own mental sabotage. What if the trainer was a good match? What if her own prejudices were what had ended things, not a real problem with them coming together in a relationship?
  But she heard the ticking and had to end it – over eggs, in his parents' home.
  I liked the Edgar Allen Poe analogy, but I thought the real problems in relationships were more like boils. They fill up with puss, bacteria, the garbage from the time you spend together – unlike Mya, I think the problems are very real, tangible, festering in the relationship, not ticking phantoms under floorboards.
  I wonder what garbage had filled up under my skin that made me so abhorrent to Jonathan. What had time built up on my face that had forced him to look away?
  The boil analogy also gives some room for hope. "The Tell-Tale Heart" eventually ends in madness, disaster, but a boil is salvageable. It's disgusting and messy, but if you want to, you can lance it. The piercing takes some courage on both ends – the one to feel the pain, the other to attack the pustule and its inevitable oozing mess. It leads some refuse to clean up, but it can be erased. Some scars may remain, but that's life.
  What had been on me that Jonathan hadn't had the courage to remove? I would have gladly let him take it off – faced the pain and scar – but he had deliberately put down his lance and walked away. Something about a clean slate was more appealing than me. I was marred, scarred, pustualized by history. Not worth the lance. That is, I suppose, what lay under my floorboards – my faults that Jonathan hadn't allowed me to transform and change. Those were the things that drove me mad. In the middle of the night I'd wake in a sweat after dreaming of finding him cheating on me again.

*Sometimes 4 am.
Sometimes 2.
Tic.
Toc.*

Sal Henry's bookshop had changed little from its days in Lake View, according to his old friend, Clive. Sal had moved it north after his lover's death, partially due to the loss, but mostly due to rising rent prices in the area. It was a huge effort for the whole store to be moved in almost perfect order. Sal numbered books and shelves, spent almost six months in the different neighborhoods of the city looking for a space that most closely resembled his previous storefront.

He had grown reclusive after his lover's death. For the dozen or so years in the bookshop's previous location, Sal had been one of the friendliest faces of Chicago's gay scene. He served tea and hosted young gays and lesbians in his small shop; young people from all over the city could use the space for discussion, fellowship, and, most simply and importantly, safety. Clive had shown up bloody and beaten on Sal's doorstep one morning at 2 am after his father had found out he was gay. His brother drove him somewhere safe and told Clive to never come home again.

But in the years after his partner's death, there were no gatherings, no tea. His presence was so diminished in the gay social scene that the young men who had gathered in his shop, referred to him as "The Ghost." It was his closest friend, Gertrude DuBois, that was able to work him back to his old self. No one knew exactly how she was able to knead him back into his genteel, hopeful form, but in the early 90's there was a small gathering held in the tiny apartment above his shop. No one spoke of his disappearance or welcomed him back. Business went on as usual.

Over the next several years the gatherings moved to weekend evenings and evolved into something more. Sal opened his doors to dinner parties with new and old gays alike. Even as the Internet and email began to take over in the late 90's, Sal insisted on sending his small invitation cards out every week.

*You're cordially invited to this week's meeting of The Open Table.
Please only bring yourself and your most earnest ability to converse.*

*5600 N. Clark Street
Host: Mr. Sal Henry*

The group began as an extension of his work with young gays without places to go, but it quickly evolved into a political group. Sal's involvement with AIDs and eventually gay marriage equality, bled over onto all those who came to dine with him. Over the course of the 2000's, his health grew less robust. With gay culture becoming a mainstream reality rather than a shamed societal shadow, the need for the group diminished. The number of out men in Chicago exploded, with it, the need for quiet, safe gathering spaces, waning away. In the present day it had become a small gathering of his closest friends.

While I had gotten to know Sal when I first moved to Chicago, it was after Jonathan and my break up that I started going to his events regularly. Terrence knew how fucked up I was and suggested I go for the conversation. He hoped I'd meet some different gays separate from my usual haunts at Roscoe's and Sidetrack. The meetings were no longer a weekly occurrence but erratic, when someone wanted to talk – the garish dinners of the past replaced by sandwiches and soup or light brunch. It was still refreshing to sit in his upstairs cupboard and talk. Sometimes about relationships, sometimes about Boystown or Halsted, but, in some way, that small room felt removed from the garbage of the everyday. It was a space to talk about politics, religion, philosophy, and life. Very often the room would still, Sal's laundered shirts fluttering near the open window, and we'd simply listen to our host speak from the heart of his experience. It was difficult to find places like that, especially on the battlefront of Halsted, where the world only seemed to scream. In Sal's small corner of the world it simply, quietly hummed. It reminded me of the quiet nights in college when we'd all smoke and chat on the frat house roof.

The morning before The Pride Parade a group of us gathered to catch up. Brunch was cooking as Terrence and I waited in the dining room.

"Where's Gertrude?" Terrence asked. He placed a small bouquet of daisies on Sal's dining table and fluffed them out.

"Her family is in town." Sal placed a plate of eggs on the table next to Terrence's flowers. "Beautiful," he said leaning into smell. "Well, her grandson, gay as a rainbow, is in town for Pride. He wanted to take his old aunt to the parade."

"That's so cute. Where are they watching?" I asked.

"I think they are up north on Montrose. You know how it gets around Halsted."

"Miserable. Where are you watching, Terrence?"

"Albert Devon is having a party."

"Oh man," I laughed. "How is he? I haven't heard about him in months."

Terrence rolled his eyes. "He's been on vacation with his rentboy. I hear they were in St. Maarten for six weeks."

"You know," Sal said, "I sometimes think about following that school and being an old man with a young boy, but I just can't see myself doing it."

"Sal," Terrence lovingly touched the old man's shoulder, "I think you're passed the point of being able to handle a twenty-year-old."

"Perhaps passed," said Sal, "but not completely disinterested."

In Andersonville, Pride enthusiasm was all around us. People were out in droves, rainbow clothing, flags, and leather-wearing daddies surrounded us. The air thrummed with an electric current, pulsing from the heart of Boystown. I walked to the window and looked down to the street below. A pair of bears in leather vests and not much else held hands, their boots clunking against the pavement.

"I'm not a Pride person," I said, "but it does make you feel good to watch. I think of all these older men as poor kids trapped in closets ten, fifteen years ago. It's nice to see."

"You should have seen it back in the day, surrounded by controversy and protests. There used to be hundreds of angry religious zealots screaming at us toward the end of the parade. We even get to celebrate gay marriage this year." Sal sighed. "The dog days are over."

"It's so funny," Terrence joined me at the window. "You fight to get out of the closet and then no one tells you that the other side is just as difficult. Remember that *It Gets Better* campaign? I kept wanting to tell those kids that they should remember better isn't good."

"That's a very pessimistic thought from a usually obnoxious optimist," I said.

"Oh, no! I didn't mean – I just meant that Pride makes it seem like gay life is a huge parade, but it's difficult, too. You have to navigate relationships, the scene, heartbreak. It's just like when you're in high school and you think when you get out and move away from your parents that life will just be all wonderful all the time." Terrence looked between me and Sal, both of us staring at him intently.

"Something bothering you?" Sal asked.

"Sorry! No, nothing. Lloyd and I are good for the first time in a while. Sal, you've heard more of that than anyone, but we've turned a corner and there is definite progress." Terrence smiled, somewhat begrudgingly. "It got better."

"Are you fucking in threes now?" I asked.

Sal giggled. He looked between Terrence and me and suddenly realized that the question hadn't been completely in jest. "Wait," he said. "What does that mean?"

Terrence looked at me with an air of annoyance. This was obviously something he hadn't brought up with his old friend. The most likely reason being that he knew the whole stupid exercise was bullshit.

The pause went on for an uncomfortably long time before Terrence finally spoke. "Well," he said, "Lloyd and I are looking at opening up the relationship. He called me up after the apology and suggested we look at including other people."

"And you were okay with this?" Sal squinted his eyes he was so incredulous.

"Of course." Terrence regained himself. Color returned to his cheeks, the annoyance fled his voice and countenance. His voice was practiced, calm, rehearsed. "I think as we look at this very new world of gay marriage, we have to think outside of traditional boundaries. What worked for our parents and parent's parents won't work for our generation. In that I totally agree with Lloyd."

"Terrence, we've talked about this." Sal spoke slowly, tentatively. "You've never entertained this idea before. I mean, look at other couples like Donnie and Tibbs and you see people who make that lifestyle work. I thought you generally thought of relationships – love – in a more traditional sense."

Again, there was a pause. Terrence shrugged. "Thinking changes. I think that we continue to grow as people and have to grow to make marriages work." The end of this statement lost the rehearsed, powerful tone of his earlier speech. It dissipated into almost a whisper.

"Terrence," I said quietly, "we do grow and change," I hesitated, "but sometimes that isn't together. It's not a place that's best for both of you –"

Terrence had tears in his eyes. I did too. Suddenly I was alone in the bathtub again, going over and over Jonathan's evolution, how I had been left out, what I could have done to evolve in that same way. For the first time, though, the memory was taking on a sepia-toned hue. It was the past. Something had clicked and I now saw the ways we had evolved, the people we were, and how those trajectories could have never found a course together.

The room had taken on an oppressive air. Terrence bit his thumb. I looked out the window, lost in thought.

"Well," Sal clapped his hand. "Let's put this to rest for the moment," the old man went to Terrence and linked their arms together. "Let's talk about the parade."

He turned to me and linked my arm as well. "Let's talk about The Bud Boys strutting down the street. You know," he said smiling, "I was in San Francisco for the Pride Parade in 1980. You wouldn't have believed that scene. I had never seen anything like it. The enthusiasm of our entire people building into an atomic-grade, gay explosion."

"That had to be crazy in San Francisco." Terrence's mood instantly lifted. He allowed himself to laugh. "Were you out in leather and lace, Sal?"

I nodded and smiled along with them, but I sensed that a storm was on the horizon. My heart was breaking for Terrence. Before the past few months Lloyd had been an annoyance, a casual cheater who hurt one of my best friends. But now things had changed. His cheating had been blasted open and they were careening toward an impasse. I thought Sal's choice of the 1980's Pride Parade was an ominous one. A gay awakening in 1980, yes, but how had those eyes been opened in the following years? That bright, garish parade was the onset of a heartbreaking epidemic.

"Sal," Terrence said, "there's this new kid on The Scene, that I think would be interested in meeting you. He's been hanging out with us lately, but I think he could learn a lot from you. We could show him a little something different."

"Well, let's set it up then," Sal said.

"He'll be at the party today, I believe. He's been really close with Jordan lately. The kid – Nick – is a Midwest boy, I think he has a lot in common with all of us that ended up on your stoop, asking for advice."

"Oh, my," I said. "Jordan has been chasing that kid all summer. He was like a wolf around him at the gala."

Terrence nodded emphatically. "Everyone in that group is clamoring for his attention."

"Jordan's a good kid," Sal said, "but doesn't quite know himself yet."

"That's true," Terrence said, a note of sadness in his voice, "but really, who does?"

"Indeed," Sal said. "Who does?"

#

"You're a fucking ball of sunshine today."

Sasha and I had opted to stay in rather than go to the parade. We sat at his dining room table, the bright June sunlight filling the room. I had kept up my smiles and laughter for Sal and Terrence, but the more I thought about the whole conversation with Terrence the moodier and sullener I had become. The thought of going to the parade and seeing The Set and an innumerable number of gays, Jonathan included, half-naked and screaming made me ill.

My mild epiphany about Terrence and Lloyd and me and Jonathan – the whole changing, evolving, idea, had brought on a feeling of teenage-level ennui. All people change. How do we change together? Can we change together? With the Supreme Court decision just days before, it put a painful urgency on all of this. Everything about Pride in light of these ideas made the whole overblown affair seem stupid and hopeless. This was a few days before my date with Mr. Perfect, and even his innocuous, thoughtful texts reeked of future disappointment.

"Can we talk about your dating disasters?" Sasha asked. "You've said we can't talk about what you did at Sal's, the parade, or really any topic that I'd find interesting. What do lesbians talk about? Would that be okay to talk about?"

I sighed. "That was pretty funny. Sorry I'm not in the mood to laugh."

"You're being awfully boring."

"I'm being in pain."

"Can't you try to get drunk and numb it? You may be more fun then."

I walked over to the kitchen counter and lifted a full bottle of wine from the wine rack. The cork came out easily and I took a slug that lasted about ten seconds. "Let's try!" I said.

Sasha watched me. His eyes lost their ornery gleam and turned concerned. "But really," he said, "what's bothering you?"

I handed the bottle of wine to Sasha and walked to look at the view. Across the way, the window where Skyler and his orange gentleman would fuck, was dark. "It's Pride, everything. Everyone's so happy and I am – to put it simply - confused."

"Confused?"

"We were talking today at Sal's about Terrence and Lloyd. I just keeping seeing things fall apart around me. Jonathan and me, Terrence and Lloyd – even Al and his new man – that night at the gala with Kinsey. Everyone is super excited about gay marriage, but what's it all for? We're a generation of fuck-ups who are trying to chase some dream that we all were indoctrinated with as kids. We have to have the partner and the white picket fence. We have to have our babies and our lawnmowers and our golden retrievers. But we chase it, and in many ways, it just destroys us. We're not ready for it; we don't even want it – but we think we should." I turned from the window and faced Sasha. "But when it's gone, what do you do?"

Sasha got up from the table and put his arm around me. "David, you're having your first big boy crisis of faith."

"Faith?" I looked at him mockingly. "That's odd in a house full of pagan relics."

Sasha snorted. "Absolutely, faith. Well, I mean, that's the word we use for it." Sasha pointed at the wall in the adjoining living room where Edward's gold-plated print of Ra hung. His finger moved to the other side of the television, where its companion piece was placed, a silver print of Ra's queen. "Pagans had faith, too, David. For 1000s of years people have been getting through their lives by creating those things: their gods, their kings, their pyramids, their American, white-picket fence dreams. We make them to help us understand this world, to dumb down the annoyance of everyday living. Nowadays we've pretty much killed our gods, but we have that American dream, we have our Vegan diets, green living, and our CrossFit boxes that give us sanctuary. We cultivate new religions to fill the holes in our existence, the unknowing, the uncertainty of day-to-day. Our faith, whatever it is, shushes the 'why?' from rising up inside of us and driving us crazy."

I occasionally forgot that Sasha was in to a top-tier social science Ph.D. program – other times he would drop this kind of knowledge, and open up my tiny, compartmentalized accounting brain.

I nodded. "And my faith has always been that picket fence, but it's all bullshit and I believed it. I was chasing what my parents had, what my brother has – that rural, Arcadian dream of kids, dogs, home ownership, and a spot on the PTA."

"It's not bullshit, but if you take it away, you need to survive. It was always promised to you and now you're not sure. You may not get your fence and your dog. Your life may be different. You have to come to terms with the fact that for twenty years of your life, you were told a lie."

"Fuck," I said. "No wonder wine has become a cornerstone of my diet."

"She definitely helps." Sasha handed me the bottle.

I took a drink and then drummed the glass with my fingers. Outside the window I could see over Lake Shore Drive to the azure face of Lake Michigan. In the streets below, sunlight streamed down Belmont and lit up the cars that were stuck in the post-parade traffic.

"It looks pretty quiet down there," I said, "but you know two blocks away the whole world is a pile of blacked-out homo garbage."

"That would be an excellent title for my memoir." Sasha tapped his chin as if in deep contemplation. "*Sasha Williams: On Blacked-out Homo Garbage.*"

We laughed and took the bottle of wine to the living room. The sun sank lower, the lake fading from indigo, to velvet, to black. The few strong stars that could push their light through the Chicago pollution shone in the far distance, one of many of their kind to viewers across the lake in Indiana. Talk with Sasha turned to old times, to good times, to past Prides. It was a fitting eulogy to the chaos of the Pride parade.

"Can we go out for Market Days at least?" Sasha asked. "I don't go out much, and I hate it when I do, but I do love the nightmare of it, at least once a summer. Some gay festival where I can see gays frolicking, vomiting, singing, half naked; it's the talent of our people!"

I finished the bottle of wine with one last, long draught and set it on the table. "Yes," I said. "I promise you that we will be at Market Days and we will be just as sloppy as all those things you described."

"Edward loves it when I get festival drunk."

"Gurl, we all do."

Sasha smiled and laid back on the sofa. I pulled my knees to my chest and sat staring at the image of Ra on the wall. *A crisis of faith*. Sasha was absolutely right. He and Dr. Konstantin had been my spirit guides through the whole mess. I wasn't mourning a break up, I was mourning the fact that my life wasn't the dream I had been promised. I'd been in love and that love didn't last forever. Walt Disney and Taylor Swift had told me lies. The curtain was pulled back and my wizard was a portly, old Greek man.

I had survived coming out – that wasn't a problem. My family accepted me, my town accepted me, and I could survive that difference. In my head I was still striving for that happily ever after, though. After a few years with Jonathan, I just assumed that it would be us walking our dog in our middle-class suburb. That was the end game: Crate and Barrel furniture, 100K+ salaries, and babies genetically engineered from our semen.

Utopia.

But Utopia was razed with Jonathan leaving. Love was something altogether different than what I had imagined. It was pain, uncertainty, instability.

"You look pensive," Sasha said lazily. He was reclined on the sofa; his feet tapped my knees.

"I am," I smiled, a small one, but a real one. I hesitated, growing serious. "Sasha," I said uncertainly, "what was your crisis of faith?'

Despite our close friendship, Sasha and I never really discussed too much about our pasts that went further back than college. I knew snippets of Sasha's, enough to not know how much he would want to relive in casual conversation. My own background was as boring as drying paint. My parents were supportive of me being gay, my brother was really attractive and was living the American Dream, and my Aunt Charlotte thought I could literally move mountains with my accountancy powers. Sasha's past was checkered with emotional abandonment. I knew his mother left him with his dad after birth. His father was distant, cold, trying very hard to be the hard-nosed man his own father was. Down the street his grandmother had lived a Puritanical existence and helped raise Sasha, much to the chagrin of his father, who only acquiesced out of sheer necessity. While my family had been cohesive and wholesome, his had been fractured along lines of race, nationality, culture, and emotional insecurity.

"Ooooh, boy," Sasha clapped his hands. "I guess I do owe you that."

"I wouldn't call it owe. I was just curious," I said. "I feel like you've been dealing with yours for quite some time."

"A very long time." Sasha rubbed the bridge of his nose with this thumb and index finger. He was lost, deep in thought. I nervously pulled the neck of my shirt, wondering if maybe this was something Sasha would rather not discuss.

After, what seemed an eternity, he ceased rubbing and looked at me. His eyes, which oscillated often between sparkling with mischief and narrowing in judgment, now were relaxed open, brown pools. "I was seven," he said. "My grandmother and I had gone on a little weekend trip to Southern Illinois. If you've never been down there, it's gorgeous, especially in the fall. The foliage," Sasha puckered his lips, "gorgeous." He took a deep breath. "On the way home, we had to stop in a small town to get gas. My grandmother got out and filled the tank; I went into the store to look at some candy or some shit. When I got inside, the little bell dinged. The store clerk was chatting up some white lady in there – he was nice as could be. They were talking about the weather, about the football team, small town stuff. Anyway, he sees me and stops. The woman wonders what is going on so she looks over. Both of them were all of a sudden deathly serious. They saw a fucking black kid and had no idea what to do. Of course, then I didn't know what was going on, so I just walked down the aisle looking at candy. The bell dings and the white lady left.

"'Hey,' the storekeeper said. 'There something I can help you with?'

"I still didn't know, you know, so I said, 'No, I'm fine' and keep looking at stuff. Well, I love Reese's, so I pick up one and hold it in my hand. I walk towards the door and check to see if my grandma is coming in yet. The storekeeper sees that and he loses his mind – loses his fucking shit.

"'Hey!' he yells. 'What do you think you're doing?'

"I look at him confused again. 'I'm waiting for my grandma,' I say. Well, he looks out the window and sees an empty parking lot and only a white lady and so he says, 'There's none of your kind here. Give me that candy and get on out of here.'"

"Jesus," I said.

Sasha clicked his tongue. "Well, I'm confused as fuck, so I don't put down the candy, but, instead, turn to look for my grandma again. It just so happens she's coming toward the door, so I go closer to the door."

"Shit."

"Yessir," Sasha said. "The guy runs around the counter and grabs my hand. He tries to pull the candy out of it. I'm more confused than anything, so I resist, you know. I pull back. Well, the guy hates this, so he squeezes my hand, hard, and I drop the candy. My grandmother opens the door right as the guy says, 'I'll be damned if I get thieved by some n----r.' My grandmother hears, so she just looks at the guy. He's not paying any attention and walks around the counter. She looks at me – I'm starting to cry, of course, and she just really subtly points to the car, motioning for me to go.

"I walk outside and turn back. I see my grandmother and the man talking on like nothing has happened. She disappears for a minute and I walk back to the car. When she comes back out, she hands me an entire box of Reese's. She just breaks down, you know. Tears, streaming down her face." Here Sasha's voice caught. Tears welled in his eyes. "I had never seen her cry. Ever. She was this tank of a Russian lady. She picked up hot skillets with her bare hands. When my dad had something that needed fixed in the house, he called her, for Christsake. Anyway, she cries for like two minutes. Right after she starts, she pulls me close and holds me. The whole time just weeping. After a bit she stops, wipes her eyes.

"'Don't let him tell you who you are' she said. 'Don't let anyone, ever tell you who you are.'" Sasha turned and looked out the window. "It was that moment when you're separated from society; you realize the world isn't what was promised, it's fractured and broken and ruthless. We aren't part of some happy human family, but part of haves, have-nots, whites, blacks, tiny differences that make us outsiders – that make us tribal. For the first time I had to define who I was, realize that I was no longer protected, even by my badass grandmother. The veil lifted; I wasn't just a boy, but a black boy, with a white grandmother, in a small town, and I couldn't let other people tell me who I was. Just like now that you've lost Jonathan, you have to define what your future will be, who you are, what a relationship is. You're off script, Jenkins."

Sasha fell silent. He wiped away tears. I was wiping my own eyes. Out of nowhere he laughed, a loud seal bark. "In ten minutes my grandma was yelling at me for getting chocolate in her car." He smiled ear-to-ear. "Damn, I loved that woman."

We sat in silence for a moment. The apartment was remarkably quiet.

I grabbed Sasha's hand and squeezed it. "Well," I said, "you make my white picket fence tragedy look like complete bullshit."

"To be fair," Sasha said grinning, "it pretty much is."

I leaned across the couch and hugged my best friend. We both cried a little more. I felt Sasha's cool tears pelt my t-shirt. As we hugged, I couldn't help but think about the first few Prides. They would be mocked, teased, bullied – but I assume at the end, this is what they did for each other. Just held each other. Showed each other that despite everything they were loved.

We sat in silence for quite some time. I looked at the wall clock; it was getting close to eleven.

"Sasha," I said pulling out of our hug. "We're all going to be okay, right? Everything is going to end one way or the other, hopefully tipped in the direction of good."

Sasha pondered for a moment. He steepled his fingers in mock concentration. The thrum of outside traffic could be heard through the windows. Even a few shouts of late Pride revelers reached our ears through the cement and glass. "It will end," Sasha said, "and this moment is ending quite well. So," he pulled his legs off of me and sat up, "let's assume it will all end as beautifully as tonight."

B-I-N-G-O

I think of one night in particularly as my unraveling. For a long time, I was able to keep myself stitched together. It was painful needle work, a grimace pasted on to confront the world, heavy breaths in between painful stabs of memory that rose from seemingly benign, serendipitous occurrences, stealing into an empty bathroom stall and counting down from ten when a painful memory arose; this was the mechanism I used to keep from losing composure those first few months we were officially separated.

The panic moments came at the most random times - at the coffee maker at work, a scent of a particular Keurig cup brought to mind a weekend in Wisconsin the previous summer. In the scene Jonathan is shirtless, looking out our hotel room, a towel clinging to his waist.

A thoughtful invite to D.S. Tequila from Donnie: remembrance of me carrying Jonathan home from trivia one fall night. He'd gotten drunk after a rough day at work. "My god," he'd kept saying over and over again, "is this all we are? Drones working for the bees? Bees? Just wasting time working for some stupid corporate hive?"

Summer, always: I'd think about how we met that first night, those romantic first weeks together, the smell of fresh cut grass and the feel of air conditioning coming in from the heat. We'd meet after work at a Starbucks and get iced tea lemonade. That summer was free and careless. It seemed we'd found paradise in those quiet café moments. School was easy, the future was set, all we had were our passionate nights and days of leisure.

These moments came on, crippling before I started seeing Dr. Konstantin. I would see stars, lose breath, the world turning into a kind of broken, nightmarish carousel – all around, especially in Boystown, was color, music, and light, but the carousel's speed was broken. My hands strained to grip the whirling horses, their faces turned to horrifying grimaces, every one of them intermittently Jonathan, his face laughing from afar, his arms clinging tightly around another man, someone more handsome, richer, more muscular, more everything.

More – that's why he left, that's what I knew. When the chips were all down, I wasn't enough of anything. That's why Jonathan left, that's why they all would eventually. There was always more and more and more. Each night out, each picture on Grindr, each match on Tinder. These men opened up into a million possibilities, but I was only one. Other men were infinite for Jonathan, but I was finite, discovered territory.

Late fall I ended up on the doorstep of his new apartment. The world was chaos, a late fall storm whipping the trees. Raindrops were falling, mixed with hail. The sting of ice pelting my skin felt good, like penitents must feel with their cat-o-nine tails lashing against their skin. I was wasted drunk, angry, tired, afraid. Fear drove me to his doorstep more than anger; the fear of always being less in a gay culture of more.

I buzzed ten times – fifteen.
"Who is this?" he asked.
"Davey," I blubbered. "Fucking Davey."

The brief memory I have of waiting for him is of streetlights, flaring white in the dark night, hail, wind, rain pelting my skin. I had lost my coat at the bar and stood wet and dejected on the concrete slab outside of his building. Jonathan, a more massive figure than in our hotel in Wisconsin, came down to me. He was bleary-eyed, in a tank top. He smelled of sex and I found myself looking at him. I felt so tiny in that moment. One step below him on the stoop, an out of shape man, smelling of liquor and rain, looking up at a muscled god, reeking of sex and lust.

"David, how'd you get my address? You shouldn't be here."

I looked up into his eyes and knew he was right. He was looking directly at me, but saw nothing. The impassive blink of his lashes, his disinterested body language, leaning from behind the door, not even opening it for me to look in, were all I needed to see. The crushing was complete.

In the minute we stood out in the storm together, I said nothing. Slowly, I turned and began to stagger away from the doorstep.

"Call an Uber," he said over the rain. "For fucksake, get a cab on Broadway."

It wasn't out of care, but out of pity he spoke those words. His voice became a distant drone in the pounding rain and hail.

The lights continued to flare out in the night as I shuffled onward. I decided then to walk the ten or so blocks to my apartment on Wellington. My half-assed prayer that night was for the hail to swell bigger and the storm fill the sky with the fury of heaven. Hail would turn to fire – some beneficent being finding it right to send embers to tear me open, end the pain and misery of these days full of stinging memories.

The next morning, I woke up vaguely remembering the hail and rain. I told Sasha about what happened and that's the day he made me commit to Dr. Konstantin.

It took several months before I stopped praying for fire.

The bar, Sidetrack, on a Saturday is the hub of gay existence in Chicago, the central axis of our Halsted World. If you know anyone in the gay scene here and plant in one of its six or seven bars, you're bound to run into them at one point or another. This, of course, was one reason I had avoided it during my breakup. The time earlier in the summer when Al and I had run into Terrence was one of the few times I had entered the bar since the previous July when things fell apart. At other bars there was the pretense that I wouldn't see Jonathan or The Set or any of their satellites. At Sidetrack, it was guaranteed.

That is the reason it was a minor milestone when I told Sasha that I wanted to go out one Saturday and *I wanted to go to Sidetrack*. I had been texting with Frank a few days and suddenly Jonathan wasn't the bogeyman of Boystown that he had been. I missed the bar. I missed hanging out with my friends there, and Frank had, however slightly, pried open my daring and I was ready to go back again. Sasha sensed this turn of the tide and called our friend circle together, Sasha, Allen, Donnie, and Tibbs, for a party at his place. It was a week after The Fourth, but Donnie and Tibbs still dressed in matching holiday outfits: tight red pants, blue vests, and American Flag scarves. We all sat in Sasha's living room, an unremarkable pop song blaring from the speakers.

"Do it for America, faggot." Donnie was in his pre-blackout phase, which somehow seemed to be a leveling off point of drunkenness that he was able to ride through the whole night.

"David," Al said, pouting his full, red lips, "you know I never ask you anything…"

"Peer pressure!" Sasha popped open a fresh bottle of wine. "You can either join the game or join the game. Options are limited."

"Don't be a bitch. I know it's been a while since you've played, but Sidetrack Bingo is a staple of us getting wasted before and after the bar," Donnie said as he grabbed the bottle from Sasha and handed it to Tibbs.

Sidetrack Bingo was a Tibbs and Donnie specialty. It involved two bottles of wine. At the beginning of the night everyone stood in a circle and named someone they believed the group would see at Sidetrack. They'd then chug as many drinks as they bet on that "square." If that person was seen in the bar, then the group noted the sighting and owed that many drinks to the one who chose that person. Rarely was it a very scientific scorekeeping method, but we'd end up in the alley behind 7-11 on Roscoe about one in the morning chugging wine and claiming we'd seen everyone we selected.

"Sorry, Davey," Tibbs raised the bottle. "But I'm going to bet we see Jonny Boy with some muscly bottom." Tibbs took a drink. As he did, we all counted to three. "Annnnd," Tibbs smiled, "this is for the bottom." Another count to five was called out from the circle.

"Eight, love?" Donnie shook his head. "You're getting weak in your old age." Donnie took the bottle and raised it over his head. "I'm going a little more daring bet and I'm going to say Skyler's – what did you call him Sasha? Juicy Juice?"

"V8," Sasha laughed. "That's a good one. I just want to see him and Skyler in the same room in public. You can bet that little shithead won't even acknowledge him."

"To V8!" Donnie chugged for a full 10 seconds.

"Al?" Sasha chuckled. "Who do you want to see tonight?"

"I am going with a safe bet and saying Dear Ms. Myrtle."

Everyone clapped but me. "Unfair," I said. "Why don't you just say you'll see a queen drinking vodka soda?"

"You got something better, hot shot?" Al handed me the bottle after chugging to six.

I thought for a moment, drumming my finger against the neck of the bottle. "I'm going with a little off the beaten track," I said. "I'm going to say we'll see Terrence and Lloyd – together."

"Ooooh!" Tibbs clucked. "That's risky. I like that Davey."

I drank until ten and then handed the bottle to Sasha.

"You bitches thought Myrtle was a safe bet?" Sasha raised the bottle. "Sootie – for the win." We groaned, which turned to laughter as Sasha put the bottle to his lips. We counted a full fifteen before he put it back down on the coffee table.

"We all reaaaddddyyyyy?" Tibbs tightened the scarf around his neck. From his man bag he took out a pair of sunglasses decorated with red, white, and blue stars. "To Sidetrack!"

"Tally ho!" Donnie leapt and clung to his husband's back. He held on for about three seconds before toppling backward onto the sofa.

Edward entered from the bedroom smiling. "Sasha, I do adore your friends, but I'm glad these parties are few and far between."

"Eddy!" Al yowled. "Why aren't you coming with us?"

"Reasons of taste," Edward said. "But have fun for me. If you're single make bad decisions and forget their names before you can tell me in the morning."

Sasha grabbed his husband and kissed him sloppily on the cheek. "Patience of Job, my man!"

Soon Al and I were on top of Edward as well, our lips mashed against his face. Tibbs snapped a picture.

"This goes directly to Instagram," he said. "No doubt about it."

On the way to Sidetrack Donnie checked the Boystown Twitter feed and was able to confirm that The Set had taken dinner at Taverna. The account had also retweeted information about a drag show at Hydrate and reminded us that Soot's White Party was that night.

"Damn!" Tibbs bellowed. "We better hope that Sootie and Co. all come out after the party, otherwise bingo is going to be a bust."

"Should we re-do?" I asked.

"Ugh," Sasha groaned. "Like those scene girls won't be out after Soot's circle jerk. Of course, we'll see them all. It will just be a bit later."

We were walking in a line five abreast. Dorothy and her motley crew came to mind – Donnie, the lion, Al, the lovable Tin Man, Sasha, the ornery Toto, Tibbs, The Scarecrow, and me, clueless Dorothy, I guess. The night felt warm and promising; I wasn't regretting the decision to come out.

"Oh my gosh!" I pointed upward at the façade of The Closet. "You guys! Can we go in?"

Sasha pushed me forward. "After 2 am, only, Hon. Have you forgotten, our treaty with the lesbians? They keep it until our bars close."

"We have to go, though. It's been way too long."

"Not long enough." Al looked at me with disdain. "I expect more from you, David. I mean, really." A smile crept across his face.

"Oh, please, Ms. Scarlet. You can't judge me for my taste in bars when you dance with college boys three nights a week."

"I never!" Al groped at his neck as if reaching for a string of pearls.

The day had been hot and clear but the temperature was cooler, so I didn't have to worry about sweating through my shirt. Broadway wasn't particularly full, but there were groups of gays scattered about, all on the trek to Halsted. A group of twinks wearing pasted on jean shorts and tank tops turned their heads and gawped at Al as he walked by. As usual, Al was looking flawless: his hair falling perfectly, the wind blowing his clothing so that his shirt hugged the outline of his small, rounded pecs.

"Al, you sure you want to settle down with this boy you're dating? I just saw a half-dozen twinks you could bed before getting to Sidetrack."

"I think they were looking at Tibbs," Al said.

"No doubt," Tibbs said pushing us aside and catwalking down the sidewalk. "I could tell those bitches had good taste." Tibbs walked three steps ahead of us and then spun, putting his hand on his hip.

"God, my man can work," Donnie said.

As we cut down Roscoe toward Sidetrack, the trees overhead clustered together. We could hear shouting ahead and see the illumination of red brake lights. The ruckus was almost ominous, people screaming in the midst of some neon fire erupting up and down Halsted.

A line had not yet manifested itself outside the bar, so we were able to walk in with a flash of our IDs. Donnie and Tibbs knew the bouncers and exchanged cheek kisses and witticisms as we crossed the threshold and entered the bar's darkened exterior.

Sidetrack always astounded me in its sheer size. The bar we entered is a high-ccilinged room with two levels of platforms along the north wall. On a busy Saturday the main room will be packed, men standing shoulder-to-shoulder, the spillage falling into the entry way and then looping up a half-story staircase into the northernmost bar.

But these two bars are just the entry point. The main room is actually further in, the central hub of the vast labyrinth. From there, one can go upstairs, to the furthest back bar with the elevator, or take a seat on a large wooden table on the southernmost bar. In general, we usually would route through the two large rooms and find standing space or seats in the south bar. This was always less crowded and Donnie and Tibbs had a regular fuckboy who, more often than not, worked at that end of the Sidetrack bubble.

We were on our way to this bar when I felt a tug at my sleeve. I looked over to see Jack Freeman's eyes twinkling from under his thick, brown bangs. Sal had sent out an article he had written about Hedley from *The Windy City Times* a week before.

He's ornery, that one Sal had typed. *If you didn't know him, you wouldn't know he was being so cheeky.*

Jack and I had met a few times at Sal's, but didn't talk too much outside of those occasions. The longer I looked at him that night at the bar, the more he appeared to be on the verge of laughing uncontrollably.

"College Boy," I said, "you look like you're having a great time."

"It's not bad," he said. "I've been meaning to email you for the past couple weeks, but my schedule's been nuts."

"Email me?"

We were interrupted by an ebullient Sasha. "David, join us at the back." He reached over and rubbed Jack's hair teasingly. "Little Jackikins, you can come too if your mother doesn't mind you being out past nine."

Jack swatted Sasha's hand away. "Well, I think your mother is the one to ask. She's the one who takes care of me at night."

"You can have her!" he yelled disappearing into the next room.

Jack mechanically rubbed his thick mane of hair back in place. The younger man reminded me a bit of Al when he was in college, although, while Al had always been overbearingly optimistic, Jack had a sardonic edge that made him more fun to talk shit with. He had given up on keeping the laughter in and let out a loud guffaw. He was holding a tumbler full of a quintessential Sidetrack slushy that almost spilled onto the floor. No wonder he was slightly wacky; Sidetrack slushies are a little red ice mixed in a sea of hard alcohol.

"What is wrong with you?" I asked. "Do I have something on my face?"

"Maybe something from Terrence."

I squinted. "What?"

He crossed his arms (slushy almost spilling again) and leaned in close to me. "So, I've spent the last couple weeks writing this story about Hedley/Hank, whatever the hell you want to call him."

"Yeah," I said. "Sal sent it to us."

"Oh, no," Jack rolled his eyes. "It's pure drivel. The story was about his charity thing, but I was having more fun writing about all the made-up stories about Hedley, so it lacks focus." His nose turned up, clearly disgusted with his own work. "But I had some fun with it."

"Sal called it 'cheeky,'" I laughed.

Jack snickered. "That's absolutely what Sal would say." He took a long drink from his tumbler. "Anyway, my 'research' let me be a fly on the wall at some parties and…" Jack shook his head, giggling again. "Sorry, it's just – I know you and it's ridiculous."

"This has to be good." I couldn't help giggling along with Jack.

"Well, this week I was at a thing at Hydrate and Sootie was there."

"I don't believe Lawrence would be out and about!"

"I know! Can you believe it?" Jack wiped his mouth. "So, I'm there and listening to Soot drone on about Hedley and that new kid that hangs out with The Set, who Sootie claims is going to be indoctrinated or baptized, or whatever happens when you join the coterie, and Soot says, 'Now you know Terrence and Lloyd are opening up,' which, I didn't know."

"That part is true."

Jack shook his head. "Oh, brother. I can't see Terrence's asshole opening up that wide."

"You little cunt!"

Jack shrugged, his eyes twinkling rakishly. "So, Soot, says, 'I heard that he and David had been hooking up under the pretense of going to Sal's.'"

My mouth dropped. "What?"

"Yessir. Word on the street is that you and Terrance and Lloyd are some big orgiastic family."

"How would that rumor even start?"

"How does any rumor start?"

"It hasn't been on Twitter has it?"

"Oddly enough Twitter isn't interested in you banging Terrence and Lloyd. Maybe if you were part of The Set."

"I'm like that other girl that wasn't Monica Lewinsky."

Jack reached out and patted my shoulder. "That's all I wanted to tell you, but I've been dying. I just think of how awkward that hookup would be. I'm surprised the rumor mill didn't throw in Sal, too. He could be tied up with bungie cords while Lloyd watched."

"Is this a fantasy you've had in mind?"

Jack winked. "Well, with George in law school I have to do something."

"I applaud the imagination."

We chatted a bit more and then Jack went on his way. The crowd had grown in the thirty or so minutes since we arrived, so the atrium bar was a sea of boys all chattering about the most recent gossip. As I passed them I wondered how many knew about my alleged affair with Terrence and Lloyd.

With my friends in view, I saw that Sasha was already showing signs of fatigue. I grabbed him from behind, arms around his waist as if we were getting ready for a prom picture. "Already bored?" I asked him.

Sasha rolled his eyes. "I always think I'll have fun but then I get here and it's always the same shit I saw when I was a mess four years ago."

"The clothes are a little different – there are some man buns," I offered giving him a wink.

He shoved me off and pointed to a group of pretty white gays gathered in the corner. They weren't quite the caliber of The Set, but they were equal in their exclusivity. "Everything is the fucking same: pretty white gays run things and they decree that all blacks are tops and all Asians and Latinos are bottoms." He nudged me and pointed to the back corner where a small copse of muscle bottoms was gathered around a big black guy. "Everyone is window shopping, looking for the next fuck. When are people going to grow up?"

"You're just pissed," I said, "because you aren't surrounded by a crowd of muscle bottoms."

Sasha's mouth almost broke into a smile, but he held it back. "I'm glad I have Edward, that's all I'm saying."

"Well, how nice for you, Mr. HGTV and 10 pm bed times, but some of us have to come out to the market because our evenings are filled with ice cream, Netflix, and crying to Adele."

"How dare you invoke Adele to derail my argument." Sasha momentarily forgot he hated life and threw his arm around me. "And besides, you can do better than the messy gays in this place. I foresee you landing some very artsy guitarist or something. You'll grow herbs."

"Sure," I laughed and nuzzled Sasha's neck. "That's good. We'll keep our eyes open for a guy with a guitar and a bag marked 'Herbs.' Keep up hope! 'Tomorrow, tomorrow, and tomorrow,' Sasha!"

"Jesus. Your misappropriation of that quote is shameless." Sasha shook his head. "What did Little Jack want?"

I giggled. "Rumor mill. When he was working on that Hedley story he found out that people think I'm banging Terrence and Lloyd."

Sasha snorted. "Girl, you could do so much better than that used-up Lloyd mess."

I laughed and left our little group to order a drink. The wine flowing through my veins had put me on the verge of forgetting Jonathan and how much a failure dating had been over the summer. I looked around the room at the gathered crowd: tank top bedecked twinks, muscle boys chatting about the newest protein powders, towering bears holding court. I suddenly realized that I was looking for something specific. Frank had said he was going to be out of town Saturday day but may return in the evening. My intent turned to finding his smiling face, his backward hat, peeping from the crowd. It had been a while since I'd looked for someone at a bar out of anything but dread.

After ordering a drink I returned to the group. "What's the bingo score?" I called out. "The White Party has thrown off our game."

"No points yet," Tibbs said not looking up from his phone. "Let's hope the party is a bust so they start rolling in soon. I need my Jonathan points."

My heart leapt into my chest for a brief moment. My grandiose energy faded a bit, my hands slightly trembling.

Sasha caught my shaking and put his hand on my shoulder. "You okay?" he asked. "We can go – you know I wouldn't be upset about it, despite my show to keep you out."

I shook my head. "I'm good. It's just still a shock to the system."

Al raised his glass. "If the party breaks up that means Myrtle will probably be around, too. We'll need both bottles of wine at the end of the night."

Donnie had disappeared sometime during the previous conversation and returned with a tray of shots. His impish smile was never a harbinger of good things. "Joey, the bartender, offered and I couldn't say no!"

One shot turned into two. Before a half hour was up, the scene of Sidetrack had turned from crisp tableaux to the swirls of an impressionist painting. Waves of men ebbed and flowed through the back bar. I found myself looking into their faces – men I wouldn't have looked at twice an hour previously had transformed into shining beacons of beauty in the dull lights. Tomorrow, tomorrow, and tomorrow had become – now, now, and now. All the time I still kept my eyes on the bar for Frank. I glanced at my phone to see if he may text – say something…

More shots, more drinks. The impressionist painting went under a lamp – the colors melded, dripped swirled together in a soup of color.

With Sasha:

"But honestly, really, like when I think of it, it had to end," I said. "It had to. Me and Jonathan didn't have that destiny thing."

"Destiny, such a fucking middle-class nonsense thing. Only people with money can believe their lives have meaning. Farmers, laborers, their lives get meaning day-to-day, not through some garbage hope in a distant future. Carpe diem, Davey. Don't live your life for a possibility but for the now."

"Are you writing Hallmark cards in your spare time now? Is that what this is?"

"Spittin' truth here, Davey. My students have to pay tens of thousands for this kind of advice."

"I think I'm okay without a degree in Sashkatology."

Sasha drifted off. A fight broke out between Al and his boyfriend. Slumped in the corner I walked over to him. Wasted, in harsh overhead lighting he was still fucking gorgeous. His shirt hugged his chest, his bicep twitched as he ran a hand through his velvety hair.

"I'll be glad when it's not long distance," he said. "It's so fucking hard."

"You guys open until then?" I ask.

Al shakes his head. "I mean, I don't want to be…" He sniffs like a little kid and I remember again why we had never slept together, even when I was younger and prettier. "I don't know. Maybe we should be open but I don't want to be. I don't want anyone else. If he wants someone else… I don't know…"

I help him up and we go to the bar. Two boilermakers – good Indiana drinks, Al says. They go down easy – two more, Al asks. I nod – two more.

"It's good," Al says, "I think we're both drunk and stupid. I need to say I'm sorry. I need to say it. I mean it."

Al's on his phone and walks away before the next two come. I hear him talking "Sorry, yeah, I didn't mean to get upset – you can hang out with whoever you want. Yeah, baby…"

This conversation alone fuels my desire for both boilermakers. Down the hatch. Boom. I take a breath. "Baby" – no one ever called me baby. Jonathan, what did he call me? Speak of the devil.

Across the room Jonathan has peaked his head in. The White Party must have ended, or faded, which meant bingo scores were going to start going haywire. Jonathan was with Skyler from The Set and the new kid that Lloyd is in love with. I mean, I get why, he's so pure. Pure? Is that a weird way to describe someone? He's untouched, I guess is what I mean in my head. His face is so fresh, his body beautiful. I laugh when I see a tag hanging out of the side of his t-shirt. New. New wardrobe – moved to the city, new wardrobe, new life. Dress yourself up in Corduroy and Denim. I fucking love David Sedaris. That was a gay who understands life – not gay life or straight life but the absurdity of the whole motion of the universe. It's better to laugh than not, I suppose.

I catch myself looking at Jonathan – but I realize I'm really not looking at him. The sharp pains I used to feel have dulled – whether it's the alcohol or the emotional help from The Greek is up for debate, but it's not as strong as it was. Sasha across the way has seen us, seen me see him and catches my attention. I do need someone who loves me as much as he does – and Mya. They would fucking jump in front of a bus for me, die. And me for them – I'd do them for me. I mean the same thing. I'd jump on a bus.

In my whole staring at Jonathan he catches me looking at him and to my surprise politely nods. It's brief, fleeting and he's gone immediately after, but it happened.

Armistice. We'll get better. "I Wanna Get Better" is that Bleachers song I love. In the shower I listen to it thinking about finding someone who wants me to get better. Again, Sasha wanted me to – he convinced me to go to Dr. Konstantin and now I'm here. Maybe I need to get better myself, for myself.

Seconds drip by on the clock; dripping becomes a waterfall. It's 11:30, midnight, 12:30. Jack comes back and says hello. He's covered in slushy, eyes unfocused. The article was all right? He asks staggering.

Suddenly Myrtle is beside me. She looks gorgeous even with her make up dripping down her face. Adele in "Someone Like You." She's dabbing her eyes. Fucking how are you she says, then – I'm fine. Fine. Isn't that the only thing that is okay to say? Inhibitions gone, she says, Jonathan, fucking hell, he's here with us. Did you see him? Is that okay?

We end up talking, then outside for a cigarette. My world is starting to spin like the tilt-a-whirl, axis slightly off, the globe awobble.

My friends didn't come, you know, Myrtle says, the light making us all look cadaverous: harsh, spotlighted, wan, drunk. I have girlfriends but they don't come around much. Always with their boyfriends. Then I go with them and I'm the third, fifth, seventh wheel. Around here at least the boys are fun.

Everyone around us is a mess. Myrtle sucks down the cigarette furiously. Around us are wreaths of smoke.

But he texts. Myrtle stubs out the cigarette. He still fucking texts. Drunk and like 2 am but it's a "hey" it's a "how are you?" Another cigarette, the click click of the lighter. What is the point? What is he looking for?

Jonathan wasn't looking for me, I say.

Myrtle shakes her head. Jonathan just wanted something else. It wasn't that you weren't enough, it's the – he wanted something different.

Revelers are yelling, music from Roscoe's is pouring out of the open doors and into the street. A group of older gays pass us. Their muscles ripple in their tight t-shirts. One of them looks me up and down, smiles. I don't make eye contact, instead I reach out for Myrtle to hand me the cigarette.

Hedley and Skyler appear next to us. Somehow the horror-show lighting doesn't affect them. They glow in their white party attire. Hedley is in an immaculate pressed oxford shirt. His hair is slightly askew, a strand of it lifts slightly when a gust of wind moves by. I look at Skyler, face staring into his phone and wonder if V8 was out and about tonight. How many drinks do I owe?

Hallo, Hedley says. His voice is always precise, a note of cordiality, distant, but audible in his tones. Of all The Set, he's the one who rarely loses his composure. I suppose with his power, his prestige, one can't be sloppy at Sidetrack.

Where are the rest of the boys? Myrtle staggers. It was as if The Set had broken the bond of energy that had been flowing between her and me. Now we are just corpses standing for the attention of angels.

Hedley recounts the breaking up of the night's fellowship.

Samson had gone north to SoFo's Bear night. Stephen had evidently been too drunk to go out after dinner. Nick had gone off with Jordan: "A habit we have to break," Hedley says, his arms crossed over his pert chest. Hedley, despite his exclusivity, is always courteous. He says nothing about Jonathan.

Soon Myrtle is dragged away with her wards and I am left on the street. More men walk by, their eyes roaming over my body. With more dating, more time, with Dr. Konstantin, and some P15meh my weight had leveled off. I had lost the beginnings of just the sad weight. Better eating and less ice cream and cookies after 10 pm had helped. I sigh and look over at Roscoe's. My heart jumps and I think for a split second that maybe there – in that bar, I can find someone.

But the feeling quickly passes. I don't even want someone to go home with tonight. I'm fucking drunk and tired.

Hello – a voice from behind. I turn and recognize. Like some dream, the man has materialized from nothing. His voice, his manner is Frank. Frank.

You look wasted, he laughs. I texted, but you must not have gotten it.

He isn't wearing a hat today, so I see his sandy hair. He's wearing a polo that fits well, hugs his shoulders.

Sorry, I say. Sorry! Jesus, the one guy you're thinking of and – sorry. How was your thing?

It was good.

He is really cute, really. I can't think and stare at my shoes and look like a dope.

Good, I say not looking into his eyes.

Good, he says back. He's got that frat boy smile again. So damn cute. You know we should just go on a date soon, he says.

Genuine happy-shock feeling - I laugh and stagger, tripping on the curb. Frank's arms go around me.

You all right? Your friends here? Don't want to leave you here but also don't want to take your drunk ass home...tonight. He pecks me on the cheek and gently ruffles the hair on the back of my neck.

Another tilt-a-whirl feeling but this one outside the drunk. Goosebumps rise on the backs of my neck, along my arms, on my legs.

Al enters from stage left. He is laughing.

Davey found a trick!

That's Mr. Trick to you, sir. Frank is funny. He hands me over to Al, who guides me across the street.

We're walking away and he yells so everyone can hear – Thursday at 8 it is. See you then!

Yes! I yell back. Yes!

Al looking movie-star hot in the lights. Who was that?

A guy I met at Roscoe's.

Cute. Big dick? Al laughs and we end up in the alley behind 7-11. Tibbs and Donnie are there with the bartender. Bartender is attached to Tibbs, his fingers combing through his exposed chest hair. Donnie has a bottle of wine and raises it in the air.

We drink to the night.

Where's Sasha?

Home – he was done as soon as he saw you go off with Myrtle.

The drinks are counted – it takes two bottles of wine. Most of it goes to the bartender, the rest of us too drunk to play honestly.

We're exhausted but Al and I decide to head to Belmont harbor. The moon is out and the water looks like a bath of oil. Al and his boyfriend are okay – miscommunication it turns out. In the end, Al says, he thought it was cute I was so upset about the whole thing.

Fucking Al, I think to myself. Of course his argument would turn into a love fest. I wish I could see stars. I remember the night of the wedding earlier that summer. Alexis and her hubby were probably tucked in – thousands of maturity years beyond me drunk by the harbor.

Al and I catch up on the night.

Myrtle – what a mess, says Al, yeah, I say but the dude fucks with her. She's twenty-nine and all her friends are married. Those gays are all she really has to hang out with. Jonathan – Jesus, he's hot, Al says. Sorry, but didn't think he could go from point A to point B like that. I shrug my shoulders. Seems like he is okay with me. He nodded tonight. You think you all will be okay? Al drums the concrete on the harbor steps with his hand.

Maybe. I say. I quickly deflect and pucker my lips at Al. And how about your Hedley crush?

Al shoves me away. Me? What about you - that new guy? Al's eyes are big and staring at me.

I smile. Frank is all I say.

It's 4:30 before I get into bed. There is nothing to wake up for in the morning, so I flip my phone to Do Not Disturb. I haven't looked at it in a few hours and see a few messages from Frank Roscoe's. The last one:
Nice to see you tonight :) Thursday!

I smile to myself. It was weird to be in a situation where things were flowing in both directions. Frank was funny. Frank – quickly, I think of all the stupid things you should never think of with someone you just met. Meeting parents, wedding, hahaha! Laughing on a trip at some exotic location. I'm Taylor Swift and crazy is what I think hugging my pillow tight. I bury my face to keep from seeing the early dawn light. Birds chirp as I drift off to sleep.

Hard to Get

Funhouse mirrors in a long line began to circle around my memories of Jonathan. Having seen the new Jonathan, having a present light to shine on past concepts of my ex, I was unsure what reflection was really him. Here he is at my home, smiling at me, us making plans for the future. In another reflection is Indianapolis, quiet nights at his desk, a book opened, his face illuminated by lamplight. I turn and see him from another angle laying quietly in our Chicago apartment in those first few weeks after our move. What I had once seen as a fear, a hesitation about our new home, was maybe his own doubts about us as a couple, not about the city as a whole.

Romantic images from the past took on darker tones, sepia bleeding away to harsh monochromatic prints, even negative images. Where once I had seen us as happy, now I don't know what we were. I had been deluded during our whole courtship. If Jonathan, thin, smiling, quiet, had the capacity to evolve into the muscled alpha, maybe I hadn't been looking. Dr. Konstantin made me see this. He showed me that I wasn't really looking at the flesh and blood man that was my first lover. My thoughts and memories were clouded, diminished by the chorus of projections, ideas, and expectations that warped my perspective of him and us. This chorus screamed, strident noises, a cloud of locusts, chirping, whirling, drowning out the real voice, real image of the man I had loved.

Jonathan was the all-American boy. He was sporty, fit, and intelligent. He had a beautiful smile and came from a good family and a similar background. As gay marriage bloomed across the country he was what the media wanted us to believe in. Perfectly pressed and polished, gay marriage wasn't queer – it was normal. It was two white men in tuxes adopting white babies and moving to the suburbs.

As our relationship fell apart I held onto that and not to him. I was afraid of being alone, falling short of what I projected as my future. Thinking back, I couldn't know for sure what we really had in common, what feelings existed between us. We were young, it was a kind of love but maybe not the kind that really lasts. It was based on shared college interests, drinking and partying, blow jobs in a frat house and believing that the world had infinite possibilities. As that faded away, as years fell behind us and our college ties gave way to who we really were, this had to collapse.

Dr. Konstantin said knowing this made me better, more mature. Knowing that the cloud of locusts is there is part of the battle of emotional maturity. We have to wade through their chirping, their picking and gnawing, their destruction of the real person. We have to differentiate the real from the screeching that is our own obsessions and desires projected on the beloved. When we can see someone for who they truly are, we can love them. This was no longer about Eros but Agape. This was the love of two people in old age, sitting on a porch as a wind chime sings.

But knowing the cloud is there, that each person is a million reflections that have to be sorted through only terrified me. Jonathan's betrayal ran deeper than I thought. It wasn't about being rejected, it was about peeling back the layers of another person and seeing what's inside. When I'd done this before it just led to ruin. Was it really worth doing all over again?

Margaret, my cubemate at work, was a quintessential middle-aged office female. I wondered at times if the operations manager didn't hold casting calls rather than interviews when he hired her for our secretary position.

When they moved our office to the "open" format, I was pissed to discover that, it was not other accountants that would be in my desk spine, but rather Margaret, an intern, a person from finance, and Mark, who was on the design team.

The open format was meant to be a way to "unify" the office. Our COO had taken it a step further and moved people from the same teams apart so the office could be "fully integrated." What this meant, however, was that I was continually up out of my desk moving to talk to other people in accounting and consistently had headphones on to drown out general office sounds, as well as Margaret-specific noises, which included inane banter, tsks and sighs, and her constant phone calls with her friend, Debbie.

Along with me helping her with all computer-related problems ("David, sweetie, how do I save this as a PDF?"), she also treated me to concentrated bouts of nosiness twice a week. She would generally sidle up to my desk, her manicured hands twirling a strand of her fiery hair. "How are things with the boys? You know my daughter's a lesbian, so I know about these things."

I never specifically came out to Margaret, but I wore a pink polo to work one day, which was rightful cause for her to bring it up in the copy room.

"You know, David, if there's something you need to tell me, it's fine." Fifteen second pause. "You can tell me that you're gay."

This should probably have been reported to HR, but two weeks previously Margaret was out with her husband in Cancun, and I found I missed her horribly. The temp who took her place was a thirty-two-year-old hipster named, Fran, who was vegan and intolerable. Her haranguing me about my Chipotle one lunch break, led me to vow to protect Margaret for as long as it was possible. The week also made very clear that, despite Margaret's obnoxious tendencies, she was, in fact, brilliant at her job.

How she immediately knew about my date with Frank is beyond me. I think it may have been womanly intuition. The moment I entered the office, she slid her glasses down her nose and tsked.

"You look different," she said.

"Excuse me?"

"Yes. You get lucky?" Whenever Margaret laughed, her entire, bountiful rack jiggled. In this case, it was like watching waves rise and fall at the onset of a storm at sea. "Tell me!"

"I didn't get lucky. And Margaret, that's a pretty inappropriate question."

"I'm fifty-four, let me have some fun. It has to be a boy. No one looks that happy unless sex is somewhere on the table."

By this time Mark from design walked in. Mark was also gay, but he was too boring, even for Margaret. He was thirty, had been with his partner for six years and was in a constant state of complaining about his condo.

"Hey all," he said. He set his jacket over the back of his chair in a meticulous fashion.

"Marky, I think David's got a boyfriend but he's not telling me." Margaret's finger was in her fiery mop, twisting one of the strands of hair like mad. "Use your gay brotherhood magic and make him tell me."

"David, that's great." Mark said. "Is it a new guy?"

"I've got a date tonight." I sat down and groaned as if annoyed. "I've got a date, so, that's it." Despite my best efforts at being a grouch, a smile twisted the edge of my lip.

"There it was! You like this guy. Tell us more." At this point Margaret started doing the hand jive and singing *Grease*: "Tell me more! Tell me more! Did you get very far?"

I spun my chair around and looked as annoyed as I could. The façade, however, was breaking rapidly. "His name's Frank. We met at a party; this is the first time we're really going out."

"Is he a hottie?" Margaret had hit the mother lode.

"What does he do for a living?" Mark asked.

"Aw, gawd, Marky. Let's find out the fun stuff before we hear about his stock portfolio."

"He's very cute. He's in med school."

"Doctor!" Margaret fanned herself. "Sounding good, Davey!"

Probing progressed. As was expected, Mark stuck to a line of questioning regarding his home ownership status and Margaret skirted around queries about his dick size.

Frank and my texting over the week had built the anticipation for the date.

Mother Monster just asked me to do more charting. How's your day?

People say Monday is the worst but Tuesday is like the armpit of the week. Big plans today?

gif of Nicki Minaj screaming How I feel about it being hump day.

What had been a few texts before Saturday night became a frequent stream of texts and gifs back and forth. My interest in him had grown into full-blown stalking. I found myself on Facebook looking at his profile and public pictures. While not a guy that I would specifically call my type, he was extremely cute. Had I just been looking at online pictures I wouldn't have been interested, but the overlay of our few meetings, in addition to his picture at a Blackhawks final game watch, made him come alive before my eyes. For some reason, when I thought of him, it was that gentle touch on the curb outside Sidetrack that came to mind: the lightness of his fingers on my shoulder, the ruffle of the hair on the back of my neck, the light kiss on my cheek.

The day dragged on. Mark forgot about the date, but Margaret intermittently rolled her desk chair over and tapped my shoulder with further lines of questioning.

"What are you wearing?"

"You thinking about a kiss? You gays go French right away or is there a little holdback?" Fifteen second silence. "You guys just going to sex?"

"Where are you eating? Is it just drinks? Coffee?"

At exactly 4:59 I was logging out of my computer and packing my messenger bag. My heart thumped against my chest, the smile that had broken earlier in the day due to Margaret was now irrepressible.

On the red line I frantically texted Sasha. The night before I sent him a number of outfit options ranging from tan blazer and blue chinos to the olive shirt and bright yellow shorts. Sasha demanded pants due to the need for me to show the date that I could pick good shoes.

"Shoes are the windows to the gay soul," he said.

Sasha and my conversation on the train home was a ping-pong match of witty cut downs and prognostications about the date. I felt no need to explain to Margaret the complex flow of gay relationships: date then fuck, not date then fuck, break up then fuck, try not to fuck, then probably fuck, and no fuck then McDonald's.

In this instance, Sasha and I both agreed that this was a meet and greet/try not to fuck scenario. Sasha had held a kiss from Edward for almost three dates when they started seeing each other.

"He broke me down. He was so miserably adorable and caring. I didn't know which way it was going to go but then one night, snow falling down, he took charge and kissed me. It was the clincher. Next date was movie at my place and rounding third base."

I think that despite the pseudo-reality of gay men being sex-starved, nymphomaniacs, deep down we are really insecure high school girls looking for Mr. Right. A lot of us grew up with the idea of romance but were stuck in some kind of closet. Younger gays seem to take more easily to relationships but most of the gay men my age seem to be fucked up and carrying more baggage than a white family on a camping trip. We spent so long getting comfortable with our sex lives and fucking all the things, that when our loins cooled and we realized we needed to actually date, confusion and chaos ensued.

But Frank seemed promising. In the few conversations we had he was level-headed and funny. Over the course of my Grindring and OkCupiding, I had lost confidence in my appearance, but he seemed genuinely interested in me physically.

At 6:35 I was already dressed and pouring a glass of wine. I spent fifteen minutes on my hair, an exercise that, in reality, took one minute. I even used hairspray for no reason other than to give myself confidence that the time spent wouldn't be in vain.

6:47 brought a call to Mya.

"I'm so nervous," I said.

"That's good! It means you're really excited about him."

"I've realized during this whole return to dating thing that I never actually dated. In college it was just hookups which turned into Jonathan."

"Speak not his name. Tonight is about Frank."

"Frank. It's such a weird name, even. It's like a grandpa."

"Is he a grandpa?"

"No, he's younger, in med school."

"Dr. Love," I could hear Mya smile over the phone. "I already like this guy."

"What if it doesn't work out, like can you be an exit strategy? What if he turns out to be a psycho and talk about his exes or like eats his soup weird?"

"Who gets soup on a first date? If he gets soup at all, please text me and I'll abort it for you."

"You're a true friend." I was pacing in my living room. Against my better judgment, I had poured a second glass of wine which I sipped nervously. "How are things with you?"

"Work, sleep, diet, meh. The guy I had been dating is in Europe this month. He's texted, so I guess he's still interested." She paused, just for a moment. "This call made my week. I basically get home from the gym, put on sweatpants and turn on Netflix. This is a nice break."

"What are you watching?"

"Rewatching *Orange is the New Black*."

"I need to watch that. I'm glad you're my Netflix expert. What would I have done without Claire Underwood in my life?"

"You definitely would be under-educated on good bangs."

I took a deep breath. "Okay, I should probably get going. I'll text you after."

"Break a leg, or your dick off, whichever is better luck for gays."

"Thanks, Mya."

My finger ran around the rim of my wine glass. The sun was still high in the sky, casting long shadows in the street outside my building. Couples were walking their dogs down the sidewalks; a group of kids on their way home from basketball practice laughed and tried to chuck each other into the street. I pressed my head up against the window, forgetting the fifteen minutes I had spent fixing my hair.

"Here we go," I whispered under my breath.

#

When I got to the restaurant, Frank was already standing outside. He wore a salmon button-up, jeans, sneakers, and the backward hat that I remembered from our encounter at Hedley's gala. Nervously, I un-tucked my own dress shirt to appear less formal. He looked up from his cell phone and caught me mid detucking, leading me to awkwardly pause with my hand down my pants.

"Hey," he said. His smile was just as warm as I remembered. In the afternoon light, he appeared younger and fresher than what I recalled from Hedley's, Roscoe's, or Sidetrack. "You making sure everything's okay down there?"

"I – uh," I muttered, "I wanted to seem less dressed up."

"Well, you look good dressed up or down, so do what you need to do." He approached me and pulled me into a hug. Again, he gently reached behind my head and ruffled the hair on the back of my neck. "C'mon, let's eat – I'm starving!"

Wood on a weeknight isn't as terrifying as the weekend. On some Saturday evenings you'll enter and be assaulted with so much male beauty it causes vertigo. It was my belief the manager paid models to sit and whisper so that the real clientele felt as if they were in gay heaven.

"I love this place," Frank said sliding into a booth. "The food's good and I feel like I'm in some sort of 90's hot stud music video. Everyone looks like they were in 98 Degrees."

"I was just thinking that!" My eyes went wide. "I think the manger pays people to sit in here and be hot. I never see any of these gays in real life."

"They probably keep them in a paddock out back, Gay Jurassic Park. Nick Lachey donated millions of sperm to the project."

"Lachey-a-saurus Rex."

Frank's head went back; he let out his high, melodious laugh. "Can you imagine being trapped in a kitchen with Nick Lachey? Terrifying."

The waiter came over, seemingly concerned about the laughter at our table. "Everything okay here?" he drawled. A tiny lump of hair on his head was tied up in a valiant attempt at a man bun.

"Absolutely," Frank said. He pulled his hat up and down on the back of his head. I'd noticed he'd done it several times since we'd come in – a nervous tic I immediately estimated as "cute" but would most likely shift to "annoying" at a future point. "Let's do some appetizers. David, what sounds good?"

I frantically picked up the menu. "Ummm... the pretzel looks good?"

"Let's do the olives and the pretzel."

Waiter nodded. "Drinks?"

My mouth was preparing an affirmative statement, when Frank interjected: "No, thanks," he said.

Our waiter's man bun bobbed away. Frank leaned in conspiratorially. "Sorry about the no drinks thing. I just prefer first dates to be sober. It makes the pain or revelry much more transparent. I went on five dates with a guy once just because we'd get drunk and I'd have a blast. When we finally had an evening sober, he was boring as hell."

I felt a twinge of guilt for my earlier wine.

Around us the restaurant was coming to life. More people entered, and the ones present were finishing their first drinks, their lips loosening and shoulders relaxing into post-work poses of relief.

"How about you?" asked Frank. "How are your first dates?"

"Oh," for some reason the only thing that came to mind was the yogi and the shame consumption of McDonald's afterward. "I've had a rough go the past couple months. When I have a good date with a nice guy, I'm usually not interested. Of course, if I have a terrible date with a hot guy, I stare at my phone every five minutes the next day hoping he'll text."

"You like look at it so much you practically develop carpal tunnel? Then when your mom texts you hate her because she's not the hot dude?"

"You know the feeling?"

"Not at all – just trying to put myself in your shoes." Frank playfully licked his lips. His eyes flicked down to the menu, his long fingers tracing down the main courses. "I suggest one of the breasts, although all the food is really good."

"Breasts?"

"Duck or chicken. Does the word breasts make you uncomfortable?"

"Not at all, unless attached to 'feeding.'"

He laughed. "I'll lactate in private. Thanks for the heads up."

Dinner passed quickly. Frank ran through conversations nimbly. I had been on dates with guys like him before, although those other men tended to skate from topic to topic, conjunctions and transitions fired off with skill and alacrity, but Frank took his time, meandering through the course of each general discussion. The other men, despite their earnestness, lacked a level of engagement, one that Frank had mastered. Each word, each answer from me fell on attentive ears and kind, empathetic eyes that sparked briefly when he said something clever or ornery. When the bill came he deftly picked it up.

"Allow me, sir," he said.

I hesitated. "Don't – I mean, we can split it."

"David," his hand extended and gently cusped mine; his eyes flickered with that spark of his. "The first time we met I said some Shakespeare bullshit, then I bothered you at two bars and basically forced you to come out with me. This is the least I can do." His credit card fell with a thunk on the table. "You, however, get to decide if we do it again."

"Well," I said, "that's very thoughtful." I tried to keep my hands steady, my physical being from expressing the anxiety, hope, and joy that built steadily through our texting and now our in-person contact.

The term butterflies was not something I equated with my previous fuck and cum college relationships. Even with Jonathan I had been excited to see him, but any of the romantic, Disney-grade nonsense hadn't been present. Our bodies engaged before any emotion, nullifying the present feeling. Love songs took on a new gravitas as I felt the electric pulse of unspoken feelings, desires that simmered under our civil discussions. I wondered how Victorians engaged in olden time courtships held themselves together. Each light touch, each look, and smile was loaded with sexual energy. Invisible, subatomic particles vibrated at the frequency of old love ballads, songs of tortured romance.

Even when I had been with other men I found attractive, the current hadn't been moving in both directions. Reaching across the table to touch Matt and his perfect hair or his hand that signed for a $400,000 condo would have led to no spark or explosive reaction. But looking at Frank across the way, I was afraid of making physical contact. I feared that by doing so the feeling would end, the wild circuit created between us would vanish, the lights go out, and the particles cease to move.

My stomach turned as we moved into the street outside of the restaurant. The Thursday Boystown Set was out in force. I recognized Lloyd's little infatuation strolling with his hand in the pocket of a gym rat I had never seen before. Summer burned all around us, the fire of the neon lights, the slowly, extinguishing sun, the embers of lively conversations flowing out of windows and into the busy street.

When Frank and I got to my apartment, I couldn't quite remember what we had talked about for the duration of the walk. My heart had been pounding in my chest. I had been nervous about asking him up to my apartment. The David of a few weeks prior who had messaged HauteJock *ive got a big load for you* trembled like a child as we stopped in front of my building.

"David, this was really fun," Frank said. He leaned in close for a hug. Gently he pulled back and looked into my eyes, the spark and smile were both present. Without missing a beat, he leaned in and gently kissed me on the lips. The circuit flowed around, down, up and along my backbone, sending electric sparks over my scalp, between my toes. Our lips only touched for a moment before Frank pulled back. His smile was broad. "If you want to hang out again, let me know. Your treat next time."

He adjusted his hat and winked at me. His back was to me and he was halfway down the block before I was able to speak.

"Brunch?" I called out. "Saturday?"

Frank turned. "Jeesh, play a little hard to get, Davey," he called back. I felt hurt for only a moment before he said, "Saturday it is."

I stood in the street long after he'd gone. As he turned the corner and disappeared out of sight, the feeling of complete elation suddenly flinched, shook. A cloud passed over my emotions. A long, meandering road opened again, one I had known and struggled down before. Shadows of Jonathan, deceit, and betrayal seeded themselves in the fertile earth of this new connection. I thought of that night in the tub letting water wash over me; thoughts turned to Lloyd and Terrence engaged in some sexual escapade. I wondered at Terrence's expression – lost in sexual excitement or staring furtively at Lloyd and a conquest in the dark. The light of Frank's presence drifted behind clouds, its silvery lining dimmed by the haze of Jonathan's legacy, the poisonous belief that no couple could make it. The only thing love leads to is the slow entropic destruction of changing feelings, of desire for new, better, best.

Flip or Flop?

In the early hours the dark shifted from velvety black to an impenetrable, depthless obsidian. Beside me Al sat, staring into the pink lights of the city, the shine of his eyes and his loose, white polo the only things visible in the dark. Light pollution at Belmont Harbor is less present than other places. Near one of the trees hanging over the cement, one could feel as if the city had receded wholly into the twinkling lights of the loop.

Al sighed and I wondered what or whom he was thinking of. No doubt in moments his phone would rumble, signaling a message from his lover. The light from the text would shake the sanctity of the quiet, dark place, with news of a life from outside the shadow. My mind strayed, as it occasionally did, to the vodka-soaked fantasy of feeling Al's skin against my own. I imagined what my fingers would feel moving through his shining locks, dwelled on what his chapped lips would do once pressed against my own. These moments came fleetingly in dark night. Never would I act on such impulses, but Al's silhouette in the dark stood so holy, perfect, and unblemished.

Deeper down thoughts turned to Frank and his touch at the bar. His affectionate gesture lit a latent flame in my stomach. I remembered what it was like to have been touched in that way. Fingers slipped softly over skin, tapping a Morse code – love songs in syncopated rhythm. Jonathan and I used to lay in my bed, my roommates in college coming to life, stirring in the hallway. His eyes closed, his breath light and uneven, he'd reach out to me, lovingly wrapping me up in his embrace. These touches chilled as our relationship went on, dull warmth in Indianapolis followed by the frozen emptiness of the Chicago spring.

Just as night transitioned from calming dark to impenetrable blackness, so the light of Frank's touch extinguished and I was left staring at the cold pinpoints of pink shining from the buildings in the heart of the city.

Frank's touch transformed into Jonathan's. The secure embrace became claws on my bareback. What had moments before been the blooming idea of a future with another man, became the dead end of Jonathan and my rocky course – warm memories eroded by glacial uncertainty. Cold linoleum and warm tears, wine and painful nights on the couch with Sasha: these were at the end of love's beleaguered journey. I remembered the quiet emptiness of my bedroom, when Jonathan's empty spot suddenly became a confession of his months of cheating.

Al's phone then rumbled with the fated text from his boyfriend; he reached into his pocket and the spell of the darkness dissipated.

On the rest of the walk back home Al peppered me with questions about Frank, about where it may go, about how cute this possible boy was. By the time I got back to my apartment, the nagging fears of loving again were gone. There was only be the glowing screen from Frank's late-night text.

But the curse of the dark lay latent in the blossoming romance. Obsidian night, ready to mute, poison the spark of future feeling.

I felt bad for Frank. I really did. I was irrational and insane, but I couldn't hold myself together.

Date two had been the brunch. He was waiting for me at Kanela. This time he had no hat, his hair was combed back, freshly pomaded and shining in the dim lights. His thin muscled arms were exposed in a tight polo; he looked amazing and it made my stomach turn. Since our date Thursday, my tiny feeling of insecurity about him swelled into a disproportionately sized cyst that itched and consumed any and all thoughts about the possibility of an "us."

Friday night I stayed in, put on love songs, and sat on the carpet in my living room. I did the stereotypical yoga pose (legs crossed, index and thumb pressed into a circle), shut my eyes, and tried to remember the electricity running between us during the date.

There was the gala. We met on the stairs. He flirted with me, smiled, dropped a cheesy pickup line and then disappeared into the party.

Next was Roscoe's. He'd come over and been witty, bought me a drink, made it clear he was interested. I saw him, really, for the first time and he was adorable.

Third – drunk at Sidetrack, that irresistible rub of his hand on the back of my neck. I'd been looking forward to his texts, wanted nothing more than to hear the rumble of my phone, look at the screen and see "Frank Roscoe's."

Act four was the date. He'd been so good at conversation it seemed staged. He kissed me on the street and left the door open for me to ask for a second date. I did. The electricity was crackling, omnipresent, tangible in my thoughts about this new love interest.

Then…

Then…

I hadn't even called Sasha. There were only a few days between date one and brunch and I thought that the feeling would pass.

The feeling: a maelstrom of anxiety, fear, and unbelievably, a nostalgic burst of love for Jonathan.

The first time we went to my parent's house. I remembered the clatter of dishes, the shirt he wore, and the feel of his hand as we walked outside in the quiet country air. Summer reminded me of our first few months together, that budding romance in the dark corners of cheap bars.

There was a random memory of us meeting up with Mya while we were still in school. We did karaoke in a dive bar. The crowd of fifty people cheered as we sang "Reflections" by Diana Ross and The Supremes.

Our third date. That magical evening.

Indianapolis, the calm before the storm: quiet nights on the couch, dinner parties with our gay friends, and weekends driving to Chicago and seeing the fall foliage.

Walking home from the train after work, I passed by an alley we had pounded beers in before one of our friends' house parties. Suddenly the feelings of joy around Frank were a betrayal of, not just Jonathan, but capital-l, Love. If I felt that way before, it had to be real. It had to be a genuine, Platonic ideal-type feeling.

Could I betray that?

Why didn't Dr. Konstantin have a direct 911 phone line?

Dr. Konstantin's Hotline for Bitter, Insecure Queens, please state your problem…

Friday night I lay in bed, staring at the ceiling, counting these weird, white leprosy-like spots that were barely visible in the dark. I thought that if I tried hard enough to push out the crazy, that it would go away, evaporate in a cloud of gloomy-looking glitter.

"Hey, stud!" Frank stood up and gave me a hug. His body was warm, inviting. I smelled the scent of lotion on his smooth skin. "I've never been here. I'm excited to try this French toast."

I smiled and took my seat. My hands hung limply by my sides. Yearningly, I looked at Frank. He had toned arms. His hair looked great – he should really not wear hats so much. His countenance, again, looked fresh, youthful. When I arrived, his eyes stared deeply into mine. He winked. I was searching desperately for the butterfly feeling, but the butterflies were now ugly caterpillars, writhing and creeping around the insides of my stomach.

"How was the rest of your week?" I asked awkwardly.

"It was uneventful. I told you about that nurse that hates me. I brought in snacks and think I won her over."

I relaxed slightly. Casual conversation was good. It was easy. "What kind of snacks?"

"I actually am kind of a baker, so I made these snickerdoodle cookies. Speaking of," he reached down under his seat and dug through his bag, "these are for you."

The cookies plopped in front of me. They were in a red Valentine's Day bag with hearts on it. I looked from the bag to him – I'm sure my expression was illegible. We stared at each other for a moment. Frank's hand flew to an imaginary hat on his head. When he found it wasn't there, he dropped his hand and drummed his fingers on the table. "Are you like gluten free?" he asked with a smirk. "Anti-snickerdoodle?"

"Oh," I stuttered, reaching to take the cookies. The bag felt cold and lifeless in my hands. "No. I really like cookies. Probably too much." I pinched my stomach and laughed, half-heartedly. Frank smiled warmly, looking relieved.

He again turned his attention to the menu as I focused mine on my anxiety.

It was just a second date. One date. A meal. Why was everything so mixed up?

"Remember no drinks," he said. "At least until date three or so. Then we can just get hammered."

Again, I laughed in an awkward forced way.

He put his menu down and raised his eyebrow. His mouth twitched at the corner, a concern-filled smile tugging across his face. "You okay?" he asked. "You seem kind of... I don't even know. Were the cookies too much?"

"Heyyyaaa!" A bubbly blond girl arrived at our table. Her glasses slid to the tip of her nose. A high pony tail flounced as she emphatically gestured with her hands. "How you boys doing?"

"We're good," Frank said indifferently. He kept his eyes on me.

"Yeah," I kept my face buried in my menu. "Can I get a coffee?"

"Coffee?" The girl sounded as if this was the first she had heard of this thing called "coffee." "For sure, for sure: coffee. Why, we can certainly do that for you! And you?" She put her hands on her hips and smiled at Frank.

"I'll just do a water, please," he said.

"Water! For sure, for sure. Have you all been with us before?"

"Our first time," I said annoyed.

"Yeah," Frank seconded.

The blond rambled for a good three minutes about specials, goat cheese, and, her personal favorite, the pancakes. Frank continued to look at me, eyebrows raised, his brown eyes searching me for an answer to his initial question. "You okay?" Okay? Jesus, what was that? Had I ever been in a state of okay? I'd fucked like 5 people in the past few months. I thought I'd gotten over Jonathan and now stood even further mired in my painful longing for him to come back to me. Along comes Frank – handsome, clever, doctor, Frank, with his toned arms and tawny eyes – and I lose my mind remembering Jonathan. How did the one person who could possibly pull me away from Jonathan shove me further into the hopeless longing for days gone by?

"Sooooo," blondie continued, "if you're looking for something a little spicy, but really filling, that's when I recommend –"

"I'm a mess," I said.

The blond stopped mid-sentence, reaching up to pull at her ponytail. "I-uhhh…" she gurgled.

"Just the coffee and water for now," Frank said smiling at her. "Please."

"For sure," she said slowly. Then once more: "For sure."

Frank looked at me, his face relaxing, his eyes warm. "Whoa, boy. What's wrong?"

I sighed. Sometimes I was just honest. Not on Grindr, not on Scruff, not in-app when I could pretend to be a masc for masc jock into leather. But face-to-face, Frank's smile pulling me forward, the whole thing came out in a puddle of bumbled word vomit.

"Like, I like you, Frank," I said. "I do. I really, really like you."

"Are you just quoting Carly Rae Jepsen?" He smiled.

I smiled. A social valve released, let off some pressure.

"I just – I'm in therapy. I see a guy. I got out of this long relationship about a year ago and I'm still all fucked up."

"David," Frank leaned forward. "You're totally allowed to be fucked up. For me it's kind of a hobby." He again winked at me. "Anyway, so you're stuck on this guy?"

"Stuck… hopelessly so. Like, I see him in the weirdest places. I mean, 'seeing' isn't seeing, you know. I feel his presence when I'm out, when I go to a familiar place. He's everywhere. And I honestly thought it was getting better." I sighed and began to play with my fork on the table. "I had no trouble just going out and fucking. I was on Grindr, Scruff, just doing anyone who wanted it. But I met you and it's made things worse."

Frank laughed, his high, loud guffaw. "I didn't know I could cause such emotional devastation."

"In a good way?" I looked up and tried my best to smile. "I like being with you enough to make me think about an 'us' rather than 'a fuck.' This has made me totally confused and sad and insecure."

Frank nodded. His eyes looked skyward. "I dated a guy for a couple years and had similar feelings. It's confusing. Was this guy your first serious boyfriend?"

"Yes."

"Yeah, from my own experience and some of my friends', I know it's always a tough one. That's all you know about love, so it's hard to crawl out of the rubble."

I tapped the fork on the table. Blondie came back, set our drinks down, and opened her mouth. Frank halted her before she could speak. "We just need another minute," he said.

As her ponytail flounced away, I looked up at Frank and shrugged. "I'm sorry, Frank. I'm all kinds of crazy."

"You're honest," Frank said. He reached out and grabbed my hand. "It's no big deal, David. I really appreciate you saying something." He playfully drummed his fingers on my open palm. "I guess I wore my jock strap for nothing, though."

We both laughed again.

Brunch continued in a flow of casual conversation. I relaxed and words, stories, giggles came at more frequent intervals and with growing ease. At the end of the meal we stood up and went outdoors. The sun was shining brightly; it was a beautiful Saturday morning.

"Well," I said, "where do we go from here?"

Frank gave me a hug. "I hope you work this out. You'll be a good catch for someone some day."

"Do you want to stay in touch?" I asked.

He tapped his shoe on the ground. His tongue snaked out of his mouth and ran over his lips. "I've made that mistake before," he said quietly. "I'm not good at separating lovers from friends. I give a little too much." He held up the bag of cookies and shrugged. "But if you get over the guy and want to date and fuck," he said with a grin, "the Nick Lachey-Wood clones and I would be interested."

#

When I got home I cried a little bit. Anxiety levels remained high; I felt like a huge asshole. Why couldn't Frank have come along just a few months later? A different time, a different place and things would have been different. I could have...

But could I have?

When would the I could become I can?

I went to the kitchen and poured myself a glass of wine and pulled the ice cream out of the freezer. Within moments I had my pants off and HGTV on the television. It didn't make me feel better but the silence was filled. The clang of my own inner thoughts was dulled by the weekly adventure occurring on *Flip or Flop*.

I tapped around on my phone between spoonfuls of ice cream. My first thought was to call Sasha, but I knew how that would go.

Are you fucking kidding me? You dumped this stellar dude because you are still pining for that shithead, Jonathan?

The problem with having an honest, amazing best friend is that they call you out on your shit. And I knew my shit. And I hated it. The last thing I wanted to do was be mired in it. Mya would be the same as Sasha; she'd be gentler, but her subtext would be that I'm a daft cunt.

For a second, I thought about calling Margaret from work. I felt like she would give me that insipid, general advice older women excel at giving.

You know, Honey, you're fine. You've got things to get over and this whole thing will blow over. In a few months you're going to have the best, most wonderful boyfriend and you'll laugh at this.

Things weren't going well on the TV for Tarek and Christina when my phone jangled to life. I jumped up, unconsciously covering my junk, which hung sadly and limply in my boxers. The number was my call box. Who would be coming over at 1 pm on a Saturday?

"Hello?" I asked timidly.

There was silence on the other end, then Terrence's voice came on the line. It was forceful but shaking. "Status, Jenkins?" he asked. "Can I come up?"

Terrence looked as together as I did when he appeared in my doorway. His hair was askew; he wore sweatpants and a loose button up, ambiguous stains decorating both. After I threw open the door he looked sad for a brief moment before shaking it off in wonder.

"Jesus, what happened to you?"

I looked down and realized my own shirt was dappled in wine and ice cream stains. My dick hung limply in my boxers. "Oh, shit," I said. "At least we match."

Terrence reached in and pulled me into a tight hug. "Thanks for being you," he said. "I knew I could count on you."

"For being a mess?"

"We'll just call it empathetic."

I poured another glass of wine and got a second spoon out of the drawer. Terrence was already supine on the couch.

"Shall we commence with bitching?" I asked.

"You go," he sighed. "I honestly don't want to talk about it."

I lifted his legs and took a seat on the couch. "I'll just give a quick rundown. I was fucking lots of people, found a good guy, blew it."

Terrence nodded. "How did the blowing occur?"

"Not that fun. The farthest we got was a kiss."

"A good one?"

"Really good," I said. In that moment I was back on the street, the electricity running over my flesh and Frank's mouth turned up into a smile. "Really, really good."

On TV *Flip or Flop* ended in a triumph. Christina was giving us a recap. Terrence had his hands behind his head, elbows up; his eyes were on the screen. "How often do they flop?" he asked rhetorically.

We sat in silence for a moment, idle chatter and a commercial for Home Depot filling the silence. Terrence grabbed the ice cream and used my spoon to shovel a mound of Rocky Road into his empty wine glass. "This ice cream good?"

"Duh," I said. "It's ice cream."

He took a bite and shook his head. "Not good, but it stands in for the feelings I'm eating."

"Lloyd?" I asked.

He shook his head. His eyes were still on the television. When his mouth opened it was a surprise what came out: "Jonathan?" he asked.

"Sorry?"

He laughed, coldly. "Not me. You. Are you stuck on Jonathan and not able to move onto this guy?"

"You nailed it."

"I see the way you still look at him."

"You think that it's over when you call it quits, but it lingers. I was feeling better moving on. I looked forward to the date with the new guy, Frank." Terrence's laid down again, putting his feet on my lap. "But then we went on a date and I turned into an emotional shit show. I saw Jonathan everywhere. Every night out was another memory of him and me – the good stuff. It wasn't those nights in Sidetrack, seeing all the other guys stare at him, waiting for us to fall apart. It was the evening we spent in that back making out during Musical Monday. I was walking home and remembered the day we had a snowball fight in that schoolyard up near Seminary."

The images came relentlessly after my first meeting with Frank. I had no idea how the bile and anger of Jonathan and my break up transmuted into nostalgia and longing in only a few days, but it poured on my heart in an emotional deluge. Normally I could put my feelings aside and wait for Dr. Konstantin's assistance in meting through all the irrational flotsam and jetsam, but these were too strong, too possessing, too burdensome, to let fester.

"It's hard," was all Terrence said.

"So, I broke it off with Frank," I finished. "I said I wasn't ready."

Neither one of us said anything for a long time, other than to comment on something happening on the television. I got another bottle of wine. As the afternoon wore on, the ice cream melted down on the table.

Before long, it was dusk. My windows filled with warm, golden light. Our commentary on the television turned to casual discussion of our friends: Al and his boyfriend, who was set to appear in a few weeks for Market Days; Donnie and Tibbs and their frequent random hookups; general commentary on the intrigue of The Set. As we closed in discussion of The Set, particularly Hedley's new boy and, unspoken but near to the topic, Jonathan, we both grew more laconic, more intently turned toward the glowing television screen.

By the time it was night, the only sound in the apartment was the dull murmur from HGTV and the hum of my window AC unit. At the conclusion of *Caribbean Life*, Terrence stood up and stretched. "I should probably head home," he said yawning.

"We've had a big day."

"Huge – it takes resolve to watch six hours of HGTV and eat a half-gallon of ice cream."

"We're basically heroes," I said.

I walked Terrence to the door. He had crossed the threshold and was starting down the hallway, when he stopped and whirled around.

"David," he said softly, "there may come a time when I need you soon. Not just for ice cream and TV but for a whole lot more." His eyes were wet, his hands shaking.

"You know, Terrence," I said, "you can count on me. For anything."

He didn't want me to see him cry. His footsteps pounded down the hallway in staccato rhythm. Before I could process what had transpired between us, he was in the stairwell and out of sight.

I gently closed the door behind me. My apartment felt the emptiest it had ever been. Terrence and me, different but the same – heartbreak our shared language. He and Lloyd would be over soon – history, dead hopes, unwillingness to change the reason for their relationship's holocaust. Similar reasons to why I had to let go of Frank. That night I lay in the dark and counted those odd spots on my ceiling again. I had Adele on my iPod. A few times I thought of opening up my phone, sending a text to Frank – an "I'm sorry" a "Thanks for understanding" maybe even a "Best of luck to you", but I knew I shouldn't. I'd slaughtered our relationship and any hope of its future. At least tomorrow would be new and different. Tomorrow I could start fresh.

Everything Is Probably Fine

  Of all our memories together, the funeral home is one that sits morbidly at the heart of Jonathan and my time together. The call came while we were in Indianapolis. Jonathan was finishing up his grad school semester and I was coming out of tax season. We got into his old Buick and drove the eight hours to his home in the Chicago suburbs.
  The child in the coffin was a queer sight to behold. To see a perfect, tiny baby dressed as a doll in a marble box, surrounded by weeping adults, served as a counterpoint to all images of children I had ever encountered. Usually the center of joy and laughter, this child lay lifeless, his body untouched but destroyed by the specter of SIDs: one moment sleeping peacefully, the next gone to another life.
  Opaque curtains let in muted light; I paced in the annex room awkwardly glancing at pictures taken during the child's short life. Selfishly I thought of my own death, what pictures would be up, what memories and stories my friends would tell each other in the wake of my passing. This child had no history, yet its death crushed the adults that had witnessed its short life like a powerful weight.
  A long, gray day turned into a quiet evening with his family. His mother prepared an elaborate meal that sat mostly untouched. Emotional canines from this event had come out, begun to rip apart the seams of Jonathan's brother's marriage. The wife did not look at her husband during dinner. After the meal she escaped to the back porch, alone, to smoke a cigarette.
  "She hasn't smoked in years...," Jonathan's brother said as she clacked out of the room in her black heels.
  We stayed the one night and already I felt that the relationship had dissolved. At a time when I thought they would be weeping on each other's shoulders, they occupied separate, muted spaces, the silence palpably chilling the formerly warm home.
  It was only a few months later that the news came of their divorce. Jonathan said he had seen it coming, and I did too, but all that I could think of in the wake of the parting were those moments we had all spent together before: the baby alive, sitting on his mother's lap, Jonathan's brother gently massaging her bony shoulders. It was she who had transformed most; I saw it in Facebook updates. The formerly bright-colored girl, smiling, surrounded by a strong bond of family, had become something altogether different. Even in Facebook pictures, her formerly conservative dress was replaced by bust-bolstering dresses, her eyes looked wild and searching.
  For me it was a tremor, a sign of what destructive forces could eat away at the peace of everyday life. To see something so beautiful: a child, a relationship, a mother, become so horrifically altered, destroyed, immolated and reborn as tragedy, numbed my heart. I remember looking at Jonathan, for the first time wondering what would tear us apart, what serpentine force would set us onto divergent life paths. Children in coffins – purest hope destroyed. I tried putting the pieces of that heartbreak back together in the shape of redemption, but the scars didn't heal along fixed lines. When Jonathan walked out – when his truth became known – there was a new puzzle to put back together, new horror on which to force upon the shape of hope.

Dr. Konstantin looked up as I entered his office. He smiled, disinterestedly, and then looked back to his notebook. I settled on his leather sofa and he began as always: "And how are we, David?"

My exhale was dramatic, overly so, but it felt necessary. "Doc," I said, "It's all fucked up. I broke it off with Frank."

The old man's spectacles flashed. For a moment he looked up from his writing, but it was barely perceptible. "Hmmm," he said slowly. "And Why?"

I stared at the crown molding as I continued to speak. It came off as a bit rehearsed, I knew. "I couldn't handle it. I couldn't handle being close to someone again. After our first date I basically had a panic attack. All I could think about was Jonathan, how much fun we had, all our good times."

The doctor sighed. I could tell even he and his grandiose ambivalence were wearing down with my inability to do anything but whine. "Remember where that thinking got you last time, David," he said heavily.

The memory of Jonathan's porch, being stung by hail and rain, returned with a vengeance. "It's never a good place." I took another breath. "After I broke it off with Frank, my friend in marriage difficulties came over. It sounds like there's barely any life left in their relationship."

"In your opinion," the old Doctor wheezed, "is this good or bad?"

I faltered. "Good or bad? Isn't it always bad?"

"No," the doctor said, not even looking up from his notebook.

Terrence and Lloyd were terrible together, had been terrible together – I had been the biggest proponent of Terrence dumping Lloyd, but now that it seemed imminent...

Finally, after a lengthy silence, I said the truth. "Good. It's actually probably very good."

The old doctor nodded, barely moving. From the wall, the clock ticked unceasingly. Outside the late July sun cast long shadows in the city streets. I stood up and walked to the window, wanting to see the river, the impassivity of buildings made of glass and steel. I felt I should say something, but the only thing that came to my mind was how much of a failure I was. The Terrence and Lloyd thing made me feel like we were all failures – we were all doomed in this little gay society. Nothing was permanent, nothing held together for more than a moment.

Then there was my own, personal idiocy. I found a guy who may have endured for longer than a moment – he may have been something special. And I firmly rejected him.

I suck.

I blew it.

All I've done is complain about finding a man and I found one and choked.

"Do you remember what you told me was your happiest moment with Jonathan?" Dr. Konstantin yawned.

It took a moment for me to recall the night he had in mind. I had eulogized, praised, meditated on it 100s of times since it happened several years before. Over the past few months since I started seeing Dr. Konstantin and trying to get better, it hadn't been something I dwelled on. Even when I was mentally wandering and remembering Jonathan right after meeting up with Frank, it wasn't at the forefront of my thoughts. "Yes," I said finally, tugging at my shorts.

"Well," Dr. Konstantin steepled his fingers. "Tell me about that third date again."

"The story is the same as always, Doc."

"Humor me."

I licked my lips and glanced once more time at the city. It carried on as if nothing was happening outside of the flow of traffic and workers heading home in the late afternoon. The couch squeaked as I took a seat again and let my mind drift back to the night that had been so important to me for such a long time, the inner sanctum of the temple of Jonathan and my relationship. "We had gone to dinner.... Olive Garden," I said. "That was where couples went when I was in high school, so I thought it would be fun." Once I started talking, it all came back. Parts were shadowy, but they took form quickly. "After dinner we were driving back to my place. My hand was on his thigh and I was sure that we were just going back to fuck, but, halfway back to the frat house, he asked me to turn around." Despite my best efforts, I smiled broadly. "He started directing me. We went toward the outskirts of town, then down this weird country road. We drove for like twenty minutes outside the city. There weren't any lights. I was sure he was taking us to some weird place to have sex, but then he told me to stop the car."

Dr. Konstantin still looked as if he was on the edge of a long sleep, eyes fluttering up and down.

"But we got out and stood in the dark. He held my hand and told me this place was really special to him. He and one of his girlfriends had driven out there one finals week when they felt like they were ready to explode. They stood in the field and just screamed. All their emotions, frustrations, anger – they let it all out."

There was a slight pause. Dr. Konstantin rubbed his eyes. "And then you...?"

"So then we screamed. And the screaming turned to laughing. Laughing turned to kissing..."

The clock ticked. I took a second to bathe in the afterglow of the memory. It had been a while since I thought about it, and for some reason, the remembrance wasn't wounding or painful, but warm and emolliating.

"Did that moment make you happy?" Dr. Konstantin asked. "Or in another way, were you happy in that moment?"

"Yes," I said. I was standing on top of my beat-up car, screaming into the trees. Jonathan beside me, his body pressed into mine. He opened his mouth and let out a roar. Around us, the field, the trees were shining in white, bright moonlight. We later talked about how we felt so small in that moment. The screaming, the rage, was consumed by the darkness all around us. Our feelings were set free, destroyed by the night. They couldn't exist in that field, in what felt like the heart of the universe – they were too inconsequential.

"Was it Jonathan that was the source of your happiness?"

"What do you mean?"

The old man leaned forward, slightly. His nose hairs twitched as he took a deep breath. "In that moment – when you say you were happiest – what was the root of it? Was it Jonathan being there with you? Was he the reason you reached that feeling of joy?"

The memory had always been something tied to Jonathan, but in that moment, under Dr. Konstantin's lethargic gaze, I suddenly saw how they could be pried apart. Removing him from the memory wouldn't make the emotions any different. I would have still felt tiny, inconsequential, and more alive in that realization of nothingness. That's why the third date was amazing. It wasn't either of us, me or Jonathan. It was the being there.

"I never really thought about it," I said quietly, "but really it wasn't."

"Think back to those other moments you mentioned: the 'good times.' Was it the person?"

"I mean yes," I said quickly. "I wouldn't have felt that way otherwise."

"But behind it."

I thought then of the first time I took him to my parents' house. There was the clatter of china, the smile of my mother, and the singing of the frogs. That was Jonathan – or at least, what I wanted from Jonathan... someone like Jonathan. I wanted to share a part of myself, the thing I called home. Love did that, I guess.

"I'm thinking," I said.

"A dangerous pastime."

I looked quickly at Dr. Konstantin – that ghost of a smile was there but fled the moment my eyes focused on his face. "I mean, it could have been someone else," I said. "A lot of these feelings could have been with someone else."

Dr. Konstantin stirred in his great leather seat. "David, over the next week or so, I want you to parcel out those moments – deconstruct them. Look at the emotion inside of them and put them into perspective. How did Jonathan influence those events? Even in the dark times. Even in those moments when you were at the bottom, thinking about cutting yourself, causing a scene – where was he?"

"Well, in those moments he was the fucking reason." I said fucking as I would any adverb. I wasn't outraged, but rather pensive. I was examining the moments Dr. Konstantin mentioned through an emotional microscope.

"The reason isn't a person, David. The reason is always ourselves – how we put that person in relation to us. I have a feeling when you let these memories burn up, destroy the husk that you put carefully around them, you'll see things a bit differently."

With that, time was up. This was always punctuated by the doctor getting up and lumbering from his leather chair to his desk.

"Thank you," I said standing up.

While waiting in the elevator to be brought to the ground floor, I started to slowly burn, de-husk, those moments. Oddly enough, a prominent one in my meandering train of thought wasn't of Jonathan at all.

It was the night of a first date. Electricity filled the air; two men stood on the edge of something of consequence.

Burn it. Tear it down.

What was underneath?

#

Lost, utterly.

That was my thought picking up my pants from the floor of Ohiotter27, another Grindr conquest, on a Sunday afternoon. After seeing Dr. Konstantin, I was sure it was the start of a period of self-examination, rebirth, a return to the David I lost long before the break up, somewhere in the move to Chicago when I had let Jonathan come to define me. The morning started with the desire to get up, grab brunch, and head to church.

Instead I had sex with a stranger.

I invited myself over to Sasha and Edward's in the evening. Edward was on the sofa, The Discovery Channel taking him through the life of Nefertiti. Sasha was on the couch reading one of his textbooks. His reading glasses, usually kept out of sight of casual visitors, hung loosely on the end of his nose.

"Hey-oh," Sasha said. "How you doing?"

"I'm fine," I said. "I'm starting to just be fine all the time."

"That's good," Edward chimed in. "Fine is a perfectly...fine place to be."

He laughed. Sasha rolled his eyes. "I need to get him joke books or something."

Sasha filled me on his week, on winding down with his summer classes. Edward snorted when we brought up our plan to go to Market Days.

"That festival is such a mess," he said. "David, please take care of Sasha while you fjord the river of drunken, clothing-impaired homosexuals."

"Babe," Sasha reached out and grabbed his boyfriend's hand. "When have I lost control?"

"Do you want by calendar date or alphabetically by incident?"

"Recently!" Sasha suppressed laughter. "Receeennntttllly, when have I lost it?"

After the Nefertiti show, Edward got up and went to the kitchen. We heard the refrigerator pop open and then close. He reappeared, his hands on his hips. "I think I'm going to go for a walk. Would you boys like me to pick up some Thai on the way home?"

"At times like this I love you more than I ever thought possible." Sasha threw out his hands and Edward went to the couch to give him a hug. "My beautiful, Thai-loving, History-channel-watching boyfriend."

When Edward left Sasha jumped up and went to the kitchen. Wine was open and poured in a matter of seconds.

In a dramatic gesture Sasha took off his glasses and slapped them down on the countertop. "Tell. Me. Everything." His brown eyes bored into me.

I laughed. "I really don't know more than what we've been texting. You saw the Tweet last night. I texted as soon as I got up this morning but I haven't heard back."

"I hate it when he gets like that – all secretive and quiet. Just like when he disappeared earlier this summer. Did you try texting Sal? I bet he knows."

The TV was off, so the whole apartment was quiet except for the drumming of Sasha's fingers on the countertop. Outside we could hear the soft sounds of afternoon traffic. It seemed ominously peaceful in the wake of the previous night's cataclysmic event that severed Terrence and Lloyd's relationship.

I ran my finger along the rim of my wine glass. "No, I didn't. I'm going to let him cool off. Remember it took almost a week before he texted after he disappeared this summer."

"But I *need* to know!" Sasha dramatically clasped his hands as if in prayer.

"Patience, friend. Everything in its time."

Sasha shook his head. "This is a change of events – you telling me to chill out."

"Your job has basically been to keep me on ice for the past year. Don't get used to this."

"Speaking of..." Sasha came out of the kitchen and went to the dining room table. He pulled out a chair for me and patted the seat. "I think you had a session a few days ago." I sat and he flopped down in the chair next to me, putting his bare feet on the table. "Don't tell Ed I did this. He thinks it's uncivilized to put one's bare feet on furniture."

I reached out and tickled the bottom of his feet. "I promise this secret will follow me to the grave."

"Good boy!" Sasha rubbed his hands together. "Now, let's talk about your depression and this week's realization."

"God," I sighed. "It's really that predictable?"

"Maybe even more so." Sasha sipped his wine. "At least for your chiller-outer of the past year."

I chuckled and put my head down on the table. "I just like don't know," I said.

"Don't know about what?"

"Anything."

"That's the root of you feeling 'fine?'"

"I think so. Dr. Konstantin told me to start dissecting my memories with Jonathan. He said I should remove the husk and look at the emotions and where they came from."

"That seems like a worthwhile activity." Sasha's voice went high as he mimicked a grade school teacher: "And what have we learned, Davey?"

"I was making Jonathan more than a boyfriend. He came to stand for all sorts of things that weren't about the relationship. It was just like the guy I went on a date with earlier this summer."

"Please be specific. You've been a bit of a whore."

"That is wildly accurate." I again reached out and tickled Sasha's toes. "The banker guy – the one with the perfect body and perfect hair."

"We aren't talking about Al?"

"I mean, he's like Al. He's that type. It's those people, whether on Facebook or Instagram who project perfect lives. As Jonathan got hotter, I started clinging to that rather than him. I wanted to ride that wave – I saw him becoming some idea of perfect and it started to drive me crazy. Him rejecting me was about much more than just a break up. It was me not being what everyone thinks I should be. I should have the boyfriend with the good job, the Crate and Barrel apartment, and the six pack."

"But that's bullshit."

"I mean, as I've kind of thought about everything –"

"No, that wasn't a question, that was statement."

I smiled at Sasha. "That's bullshit."

"And that's why you feel 'fine.'"

"Perfectly. Fine."

A warm, sumptuous quiet enveloped us. Sasha and I both looked out the window. Across the street I saw the window Sasha pointed out earlier that summer, the view into the life of Skyler from The Set. Oddly enough it was open that day and the big, orange daddy was around, wearing only a bathing suit. Sasha and I didn't have to speak. He looked over at me and winked. I laughed quietly.

I wondered then what his history was – who he was. Unlike earlier when I imagined him and Skyler together fucking, the feeling that rose up that late July evening was something different. It was strange to even articulate; it seemed too Capraesque, too Pollyanna, but I hoped they were happy. In whatever life Skyler and his boyfriend had constructed, I hoped that when everything was burned away there was something real there.

"Sasha," I said quietly, sad to break the silence.

"Yessir."

"Instead of having horrible thoughts about V8 and Skyler, I thought something nice. I'm not sure how that makes me feel."

Sasha laughed. It was an airy laugh, wizened, tinged with sadness. "Fine. Nice thoughts about shallow people. Getting rid of all that crazy expectation garbage and looking at yourself and your emotions," he hesitated. "You know, David, I think you may be growing up."

"Well," I said sitting up in my chair, "let's not get too carried away." I chugged the last of my wine and stood up. "I'm still going to suggest we go out tonight."

Sasha didn't hesitate. In the blink of an eye he had his phone out. "I'll text Donnie and Tibbs – if they're not blacked out from brunch, they'll definitely go. You call Al."

#

In a couple hours' time we were full of Thai food and sitting at the back bar of Sidetrack. Al was beaming as he told of his boyfriend's impending arrival. Donnie flirted with the bartender, while Tibbs stood in the other room singing to show tunes. Sasha put his arm around me and whispered in my ear. I wasn't sure what it was, but I laughed. I laughed and realized I hadn't thought of Jonathan in hours. As Catherine Zeta-Jones filled the screens of the bar in "All That Jazz," I let my head bob along to the tune. The whole day had been peaceful. The random sex derailed my plan to get my life on track, but just because I hadn't gone to a physical church, didn't mean I had missed out on fellowship. It was a bizarre revelation to have at Sidetrack, drunk on slushy on a Sunday evening, but it was a similar feeling to being on that blanket with my niece on The Fourth of July. The maze's power was diminished, the struggle against the meandering pathways dulled in the wake of men laughing, ostentatious musical numbers, and the soft whisper of my best friend in my ear. I hadn't been thinking of Jonathan, but I hadn't been thinking at all. In that moment, emotionally, the storm quieted, the darkness receded, and the world was a soft murmur. Things were fine. Fine was good. If the maze had such wonderful diversions, perhaps it wasn't such a bad place after all.

A Farewell to Oz

   A few individual events in my youth confounded my understanding of the world.
   One was sitting on the couch with my mother and father watching television when I was a child. The screen projected a holiday special on one of the big three networks. In it, a family had been torn apart by tragedy. The youngest daughter moved away and came back home when her father was deathly ill. Through the course of the show she meets a neighbor, falls in love, rekindles her former relationships with her family, and manages to have a heartfelt and moving goodbye to her father just before he drifts off to eternal sleep. The final scene of the movie is a wedding where the bride takes a moment during the vows to express her renewed faith in God and family.
   My mother, eyes pouring tears, hugged my father and demanded my brother and I join them on the couch for a family embrace. This special, compounded with simple stories of superheroes and princesses over the course of my youth, eventually formed my concept of the future into a single, dug track projecting forward. There was family, God, and morality. You grow up and go through some trivial traumas before you celebrate all these things again. Your life can go off track, but ultimately there is one right, direct way forward into adulthood. It's projected on screens across the world – a singular, ideal way to live.
   The second event centers on a memory of me in the library when I was fourteen, before I was out and my mother was actively helping me find dates. Then it was still my secret and shame. One book in the library about the history of San Francisco helped me escape the fear. In it there was a photo of a Pride parade from the late 1980's. The image was black and white, but the men in it were all smiles, waving to the camera. In the background the sun shone, a huge, singular flare.
   Oz is often used as an image in gay iconography to represent the space of being out, being safe. In the library, even in college, when Jonathan and I would talk of our future, it was always consolidated around our image of that gay, urban center of solace. We dabbled in it a few weekends our senior year – attending pride, glitter and confetti filling our dreams. It became a fixed point: a heaven, a Xanadu, a home, we had both never had. Chicago in its seductive skyline, glittering towers, chaotic history, and welcoming spirit, fed into that vision. Coming to The Windy City then became a coming home – a new start in the place that Jonathan and I had always truly belonged.
   When Jonathan left, Oz was razed, the singular track broke into a fractured map of alleyways, meandering paths, and dead ends. Dr. Konstantin once said, sleepily and disinterestedly, "Let's not call it the break up; let's call it an awakening." I suppose this is the way to think of these things. The rhetoric does little to heal the pain, but it does something to gain perspective. By summer's end there was no longer a singular track forward. Looking around there was no wall of water protecting a path out of oppression and into a promised land. There was no yellow brick leading me to a shining city. It was more of the maze, more of the paths that lead nowhere and take you to dark corners you couldn't imagine.
   And yet…
   And yet, somewhere I think there had been an awakening. It sounds foolish to say, mawkish, but I think the realization caused me to take a keener interest in, not

the paths others told me were ahead, but in my own inner compass – heart and soul pulsing out coordinates to some undiscovered place. The road was no longer there – preconceived ideas and routes no longer pushed me forward – but for the first time I felt that I was moving on my own accord. I was heading home.

Al was sitting at Sal's dining room table. His legs dangled beneath him, his chin rested on his hand. Behind him Sal's shirts blew in the wind, their opaque whiteness creating a filter for the August sun.

"I'm like a little kid," he said. "I literally can't wait for Kent to get here."

"Young love!" Sal said from the kitchen.

I watched the shirts flutter in the wind. Sasha was beside me looking skeptically at Al. "You just want that D. How long has it been?"

"Oh, girl," Al chuckled. "I knocked some out on my own D this morning, but since I've seen Kent, it's been two months."

"The pain of monogamy," Sasha said.

"Most of the time I don't understand Donnie and Tibbs whole open, fuck-all ideology," I said, "but in this instance, just a little D dabble every now and then would keep you from going insane."

"Despite what you asses say, I'm actually looking forward to seeing him. I'll show him the city, we can talk about his move here…"

"Don't be crazy!" came the lyrical baritone from the kitchen. "Let that conversation happen organically. If you're at the airport today, see him, and have a list of apartments, he may flee."

"From that smile?" Sasha batted his eyes. "I feel little Al gets a wider berth on crazy than the rest of us."

"I feel like I ask for a second date and I push out the crazy vibe," I said.

Sasha examined one of his cuticles, smirking. "Frank wanted some more dates from you, but you opted for random Grindr dick."

"Did I know about Frank?" Sal asked from the kitchen.

"No," I said.

"He was perfect, but David wasn't ready for a commitment." Al looked at me feigning annoyance.

"It's a little more complicated than that." I gave Al a death stare. "I'm just basically a big fucking mess. Grindr dick is less… well, I couldn't quite handle the whole lovey-dovey dating thing right now."

Sal entered the room with a tray of food. "I think I may understand that feeling better than you know." He winked at me and set the tray of eggs, bacon, and fruit on the table. "However, there's always time for redemption. But, for now, let's just eat and gossip!"

We all took our places around the table. Sasha and I were dressed in schlubby workout clothes. We both agreed to help Terrence move that morning. Al had on a button-up shirt, slacks, and shined taupe shoes, dressed perfectly for the arrival of his man. I was impressed over the last few months that their courtship had not only lasted, but blossomed. Alan was radiant sitting at the table. At the beginning of the summer I would have wanted to reach out and smack the look off his face, but in my current state, I was mildly (ever so mildly) happy for him and his Instagram-perfect relationship.

Sal placed some syrup and butter on the table and then flopped into his own chair at the head. "I'm already breathing hard," he sighed. "I can't believe I'm helping with this move."

"You can carry the light boxes," I said.

"Did they pack Lloyd's sense of decency?" Sasha took a piece of bacon.

"Ladies," Sal said raising his arms into the air. "I know it's old fashioned but let's say grace before we resume conversation... and general bitchiness."

We all bowed our heads and held hands. There was a beautiful, brief, silent moment when the only sound was the wind rushing through the window and a few children's voices coming from the street.

"Dear God, bless this food. Thank you for fellowship with friends and for the joy it brings. Be with those who are not with us, who have passed, and who are struggling. Please be with Terrence in his time of pain and new beginnings. Amen."

We all dropped our hands and turned our attention to the food. Sal was not the best cook, but his meals always conjured images of crackling fires, wind chimes, and fluttering white and red picnic blankets.

"I can't believe you can get Sasha to pray," I said. "That is a miracle in and of itself."

"I didn't listen to a word of it!" Sasha had a glass of orange juice and shook it menacingly. "No God entered my ears."

"Your ears must discriminate more than your asshole, Sasha."

"Are you implying God can enter my asshole, Al?"

"I'm implying most things eventually do."

Sal had tears in his eyes from laughter. "Brilliant banter. The wit is much appreciated."

"My pleasure." Al raised his glass.

"Now, Al, that's the first good idea you've had." Sasha raised his glass as well. "Let's toast to our host with the most. Sal, thank you for having us over and for always being wonderful."

"Hear, hear!" I shouted.

After the glasses clinked together, we focused on our brunch plates. I knew that as Sal aged these events would become fewer and fewer, but I hoped I would always be in the small circle that was invited. Things had dwindled considerably from the mid-2000s when his parties were fetes on a much grander scale. His place now had dust and the food lacked panache, but I wouldn't miss a chance to sit at his table for anything. Being invited over to Sal's for friendly discussion had become monumentally more exciting to me than a raging party like the gala.

"We know Alan will be in Kent's arms next weekend for Market Days, but what will you boys be doing?"

"We'll be out," Al interjected. "We'll get all the sex out of the way early in the week so that we can be social during the weekend."

"I was planning on having people over Saturday," Sasha said. "Al if you and Kent come, please don't be too much in love. It's disgusting."

"I'll try to start an argument before we arrive."

"You're a peach."

I laughed. "If either of you get a talk show, please be each other's guests. I really appreciate these exchanges."

"Al usually doesn't come this hard at me," Sasha smiled. "I think he's getting braver now that his man is coming into town."

"I'm in a pretty good mood." Al's face turned red as he played with the eggs on his plate.

"Not to interrupt the flirting," Sal's eyes twinkled, "but David, will you be going to Sasha's?"

"Yes, sir. I wouldn't miss it. What about you, Sal?"

"Gertrude and I will venture out to the festival on Sunday; Clive is working so we'll stop by and see him. I always like to go during the day and see things before it gets too sloppy." His eyes looked to the ceiling in thought. "What would you boys think of coming here for brunch before we all go partake in the festivities?"

"Absolutely," Al, Sasha, and I said in unison.

Sal tapped his glass with his knife. "Then let it be done. We'll gather Sunday right around noon."

We all cheered in response.

I then turned to Sal. "I can't believe Gertrude goes with you," I said. "She really enjoys it?"

"Gertrude in her later years has discovered she doesn't mind looking at some beefy men in their underwear."

"Good for her!" Sasha snickered. "Better late than never."

"She does enjoy the festival," Sal continued. "I think after years of telling people what they should do and believe, she finds it liberating to enjoy the chaos."

"When did you all become close?" Al asked.

Sal massaged the side of his glass with a finger. "Hmmm," he said. "Our relationship was extremely complicated even up through Arnold's death. It was afterward that our real friendship started. We went from cordial adversaries to best friends."

"I feel best friends usually start out as adversaries." Sasha smiled and looked at me.

"Sasha and I hated each other at first." I shook my head. I remembered the first time I met him, dressed in tight, stretchy purple pants and shirtless. He had called me a cunt for telling him to go to the back of the line at the bar. "We got in a fight at Roscoe's. A week later we met casually through another friend. We made fun of our waitress together."

"Her terrible hair drew us closer."

"Kent and I didn't like each other initially, either," Al said. "I thought he was a stuck-up dick, and he thought I was a spoiled brat."

"Kent seems like a very good judge of character."

Al laughed. "He wasn't too far off."

Before long the table was cleared and Sal was giving Al a kiss on the cheek outside his bookshop. "Remember to try and bring Kent by this week. I want to meet this character you're obsessed with."

"We'll swing by." Al waved to Sasha and me.

"Bye, bitch," Sasha said.

Al headed toward the train while the rest of us piled into Sal's old Cadillac. Over fifteen years old, the inside still looked pristine.

The car rumbled down Clark Street toward Addison. In the late morning, up and down Clark, couples and families were starting their days and heading to brunch.

I sighed. The fun, loose atmosphere of brunch disappearing behind us. A knot started growing in my stomach the moment we left Al and started to Terrence's place. "This sucks so much," I said.

Sal peered at me in the rearview mirror. "We all knew it was coming," he said quietly. "It's probably for the best."

"You sound like my therapist," I said. "I told him about this and he just said: 'is this good or bad?'"

"Tell me you said good." Sasha had on thick, black sunglasses, his hand out the window.

"I did say good. But just because something is for the best doesn't mean it feels good, you know?"

"You're growing so wise with your therapy sessions," Sal chuckled, turning from Clark onto Addison. Wrigley Field loomed next to us. It looked abandoned with no one congregated outside.

"I just hope Terrence is okay. Did you all hear the story about the break up that's going around? It makes Terrence into some kind of folk hero."

"Sal, did he actually tell you what happened?" Sasha asked.

Sal took a deep breath. "Terrence and I have talked about this at length, several times. I was pretty angry at him earlier this summer when he embraced the idea of them sleeping around together."

"Are you getting judgmental in your old age?" Sasha reached over and gently massaged Sal's neck. "Are you and Gertrude trading prejudices?"

"Not at the sleeping around. My mantra has almost always been for free love, but, Terrence has always been resolutely against it. When he came to my place chirping about his future in a thrupple – well," I could see Sal raise his eyebrows in the mirror, "let's just say I wasn't buying it."

I laughed out loud suddenly remember Jack's story from Sidetrack. "Sal! I didn't tell you, but evidently, I was part of the problem. Jack Freeman told me at Sidetrack that Sootie said I had been a regular part of the thrupple."

Sal's laughing turned to snorts. "No! Really?"

"He said we were using you as a pretense to hookup. 'Just heading to Sal's' we'd say, and then go tie each other up and rub each other down with Crisco."

Sal shook his head. "I hope they didn't imply that took place in my apartment. I wouldn't tolerate that kind of messiness."

Gays were scattered on the street as we pulled onto Halsted. As I watched them my heart ached. August is always perfect in Chicago. The weather is hot, and Market Days roars in, a crazy, joyful way to send off the summer – but, it is always just that – the end. Last Market Days, Jonathan and my relationship over, I got home from the festival on Sunday afternoon and laid in bed, feeling my twenty-six years weigh on me. Everything seemed to be fading, turning cold and dark.

Sal parked on Halsted and we walked the block down Roscoe to Terrence and Lloyd's. When we arrived, Terrence was outside smoking a cigarette. A U-Haul stood ominously behind him.

"This is new," Sal pointed at the cigarette as he approached Terrance for a hug.

"Stress has a way of opening up new habits," he said kissing Sal on the cheek. "Myrtle got me into it."

When we arrived upstairs, Terrence had everything splayed across the floor. I had expected him to have it all neatly packed, but his jumbled mental state was on full display.

"I'm so sorry," he said shaking his head. "Just start throwing things in boxes. I'll deal with it later."

Lloyd didn't make an appearance until Terrence had to enter their bedroom and pull out his writing desk. He then emerged from the master suite wide-eyed and manic. It was the first time I had seen Lloyd even slightly ruffled. He was trying his best to remain calm, collected, but in his erratic movements, his overly emphatic speech, I could see him wondering what was happening, what was next, what he had done.

Sasha greeted him with the bile the rest of us tried to conceal: "You look lovely, Lloyd. Your bulk at the gym is really showing. Is the Augustus Gloop look in this season?"

Terrence pulled him back and tried to keep things civil. When Lloyd stuck in a barb about The Set coming over, Terence coolly offered them mimosas.

Hedley appeared and, it was, as always, like magic. He knocked lightly on the door, entering with a smile and cool greetings to all gathered. Stephen was with him and sashayed directly to Terrance. Hedley and Sal shook hands and spoke earnestly for a very brief moment.

I watched him furtively while packing Terrence's entertainment center. I liked Hedley. I did. For all the weirdness and awfulness that could accompany The Set and their activities – marriages ruined, shade thrown in the darkness of Sidetrack, Hedley remained somehow above it. He organized charity work; he said hello to people outside "The Game" at parties. I couldn't imagine him organizing something like Soot's White Party that raised money for ... a cause. Hedley actually participated. It was no wonder Al developed a crush on him.

Terrence slipped out for a cigarette. When he returned he was completely on edge. Tears in his eyes, he proclaimed he was ready to walk out and leave everything in the apartment. We spent twenty minutes outside talking him down.

"Terrence, as much as you'd love to give your asshole ex all your possessions, we're not going to let you do that," Sasha said sitting on the back of the U-Haul.

Sal was covered in sweat from what little activity we had done. He wiped his brow with a handkerchief. "I agree. If you feel this bad, give us a list of what to get and we'll take care of the rest."

"I just wish he'd go," Terrence said dejectedly. "Why does he have to have people over during the move?"

"He's trying to show you he doesn't care," I said. "It's a little game." It was, just as Myrtle had said it was. Everything was a game, all the men merely players.

"The Set is so good at their games," Terrence sighed.

"It's just a little longer, Terry," Sasha chimed in. "We'll be in there another couple hours then you don't have to go back."

"We can definitely do this." Sal crossed his arms over his chest. "We're all here for you."

Terrence shook his head. "Gah, such a nightmare. All of it."

He walked back toward the building. About three steps from the door he stopped in his tracks. The drop in movement was so abrupt that Sasha and I, following closely behind him, collided into each other. Terrence turned and licked his lips. "This isn't at all how I imagined it to go," he said quietly. "Not at all." Wind rushed through the trees that lined the walk. A bird chirped in the distance. "I don't know where it all went wrong."

The only sounds were the leaves, the birds, and a car driving by on the street. I thought then about saying something, something trivial, cloying, about how things will always turn out for the best, but in my recent way of thinking that didn't seem at all honest. Things were as things were – them being good or bad resulted from the mindset with which you met them.

It was Sal who broke the silence. He sidled up beside Terrence, gingerly setting his hand on his young friend's shoulder. "It always fucking goes wrong," he said jovially. "But you have friends, some good books, and good wine, and those always help turn things around."

I looked between Terrence and Sal, wondering if there was anything more that needed to be said. After a brief silence, Terrence started laughing manically. He grabbed Sal and cackled into his shoulder. The sound was mangled, a mixture of tears and laughter.

He lifted his head and motioned to Sasha and me. "Get over here assholes. I need a hug."

We embraced on the sidewalk. I don't think any of us knew what emotion the others felt. Sal, perhaps, having witnessed this kind of thing before, only calm; Sasha, no doubt, was relieved to be out of the quagmire of unsettled emotion; I was, placid, fine, happy that Terrence was seemingly okay; Terrence himself – I don't know. I guessed he was somewhere I had been in the previous year, whether hopeful and tomorrow, tomorrow, and tomorrow or hopeless in the dark of Belmont Harbor, I couldn't be certain. But he would eventually be fine. That I knew.

Terrence let us go and wiped his eyes. He smiled, genuinely, and cracked his knuckles. "Well, ladies," he said enthusiastically, "let's finish up."

Lloyd and The Set left after another twenty minutes to head to brunch. The rest of the move went smoothly after they had gone. By noon we had most of the stuff in the back of the U-Haul. Sal made some iced tea that we sipped in the half-empty living room.

"See," the old man said tipping his glass to the group, "we did it."

"Killed it," I chimed in.

Terrence surveyed the room. August light spilled through their large windows and illuminated dust bunnies we had exposed as we moved the furniture. He kicked an especially large one with his foot. "Who would have thought?" he asked. "You think you can just kind of push through, but I guess you can't."

"Sometimes it's better to let go," Sal said.

"Still painful but better." I walked behind Terrence and gave him a hug. "Trust me."

Outside the apartment we kissed each other's cheeks. Terrence's eyes filled with tears.

"Where to?" Sasha asked.

"Home," Terrence said sadly. "I'm going to take some time to get myself together. My mom and Step-dad have prepped the couch for me. My job is letting me work remotely. I know you all invited me to come back for Market Days... but I don't know."

"Well, think about it," I said. "In the meantime, I'm sure my mom will be by to visit. She'll probably bake you something."

"I'm going to get so fat living around there."

"I think the term you're looking for is 'insulated.'" Sal patted his belly.

It was surreal watching Terrence drive away. I still remembered the first time I came to Chicago to visit him with Jonathan. Only a few short years ago and it was me, Jonathan, Terrence, and Lloyd all bopping around Boystown. Now those threads had dissolved. We all were in very different, very difficult places.

"You want a ride, David?" Sal threw open the door of his Cadillac.

Sasha was already in the front seat. "I got shotgun, bitch."

I waved them on. "I think I'm just going to walk."

"Mr. Healthy!" Sasha said. "Don't lose too much weight, I want to stay the skinny one."

"I think I have too much insulation for you to worry about that." I patted my belly just as Sal had done.

The walk home was a pleasant one. I paced down Halsted to see the gays out in all their brunching paraphernalia. When I was almost to Belmont I saw, looking in a shop window, Hedley, The Set, Jonathan, and some other gorgeous men I didn't recognize. A few months ago the sight of Jonathan with The Set would have set my mind into an emotional free fall, but in that moment, I was completely indifferent. He was slowly evolving into someone I used to know.

Belmont was bustling with a distinctly more heterosexual energy. Ann Sather's windows were full of families getting a late brunch. The closer I got to home, the more meandering my thoughts became. I pondered over the whole chaotic summer. At the wedding in May I had imagined a brave new world of dating and fresh beginnings. There had been a handful of dates and fucks, but nothing permanent, nothing entirely hopeful. Tomorrow, tomorrow, and tomorrow had occurred, many new tomorrows, along with ambivalence and sad Sunday nights wondering where my life was going. It struck me then, as I walked up to my building, the one memory stood out more than others. It bloomed in my mind, a fresh flower in a remarkably dense thicket of brambles.

Two men standing in front of Roscoe's.

Frank, touched by sorrow...

It was followed by a succession of memories, moments over the last few weeks. I smiled, in spite of everything. I felt the ghost of his hand gently ruffle the hair on the back of my neck.

An Interlude

"When peace, like a river, attendeth my way,
When sorrows like sea billows roll;
Whatever my lot, Thou hast taught me to say,
It is well, it is well with my soul."

- Horatio G. Spafford, "It Is Well with My Soul"

I.

2009

China clattered in the dim lights. Around a large table, a cluster of gay men spoke loudly. At the head of the table, Sal Henry tapped his glass bringing the small crowd to a hush. In the brief silence, chairs scraped, silverware clanked, and eyes drifted around the room.

"Thank you all for your time and attention," Sal said. "It is a pleasure to invite you all to this meeting of The Open Table."

"Here, here!" a man bellowed. Older than most, his smile was the largest.

"Thank you, Clive, as always your enthusiasm is appreciated." The crowd chuckled. Sal used the time to take a sip of wine. "As it is the first meeting in the full glow of summer, I think it is fitting that we say thanks, to God, to Buddha, to whomever you desire -"

"Bacchus!"

Sal nodded. "Whomever you pay tribute to, we thank him, or her, or it for giving us the fortitude to survive."

The men cheered. Sal hadn't removed his laundry from the window. The white shirts billowed in the evening wind. From the streets below traffic rumbled over the pavement.

It was a varied crowd. A mix of races, ages, and social classes sat under the dim lights. From the table, the scent of fresh food drifted under the noses of the men gathered. Saliva formed at the back of their mouths in anticipation of the meal.

"Amen!" Sal said.

Another cheer rose up. Forks, knives, and spoons scrapped the china. In that moment, the table was a song of conversation.

Those gathered had come from a number of different places. Clive had been orphaned as a teenager. Even in Sal's dark times, he was a joyful presence. Others Sal met at parties, fundraisers, some at bars. Lawrence Soot was near the same age as Sal. His plump face shone under the lights, his grey eyes drifting around the room. The newest addition to the circle was a young man, a friend of a friend. He sat at the far end of the table, barely touching his food.

"Sal, do we always have to listen to this grating violin music at dinner?" a man with gold hair asked. "It makes me think of a funeral parlor."

"I think it's fabulous," another spoke up. "I see myself at one of those wonderful baroque parties with Glenn Close."

"*Dangerous Liaisons*, Nolan?" A man with highlighted hair snickered. "Is that just because you have an affinity for bareback?"

There was a smattering of laughter. A few gave quick looks to Sal.

"Have you heard about this new phone app?" a young man in a light sweater asked. "It's just come out. I saw something in *Out* about it. You literally get on it and can see gay men close to you."

"It's for sex?" For the first time, Lawrence was interested.

"It's probably for whatever you like, Sooty." Clive shook his head.

"Sex at your fingertips. How wonderful."

"Better on my phone than on my own dick."

Laughter overcame them. Sal stood up wiping tears from his eyes. He walked into the kitchen. A woman his age was at the sink. Her sleeves were rolled up. Deftly she dunked plates into the foamy water.

"Gertrude, go in and enjoy yourself."

"Please! This is me enjoying myself. You boys enjoy. I shall serve."

Sal leaned over the sink. Gertrude scrubbed a baking pan. "I believe you missed a spot," he said.

She playfully slapped him. There was a moment of feigned tension before the two embraced.

A noise from behind them broke the intimate moment. Standing in the door was the young man who had come for the first time. He was thin. His hair was shaggy, bangs falling over his forehead.

"Hello," he said quietly.

"Well, hello!" Sal reached out and shook his hand. "Gertrude, this is... I'm sorry, my boy, your name?"

"Hank."

"Very nice to meet you." Gertrude, hands wet, bowed slightly.

"Thank you for all of this," he said. "I haven't been in the city long. This is a lot different than Indiana."

"I would hope so. You're here with...?"

"Joe." He paused. "We met at Sidetrack."

Sal smiled knowingly. "A dangerous liaison?"

Hank laughed. His fingers drummed against the door frame. He was reticent to enter the kitchen fully.

"Do you like Chicago?" Gertrude asked.

"I do. There's lots to do."

"What do you do in the city?"

"I'm in marketing for a small company."

"Are you in charge of the billboards? Print ads?"

"Everything's digital now. Advertise on Facebook; how many clicks can you get?"

"Sounds like it," Sal said. "That new app sounds like we may all be reduced to clicks soon."

Hank half-smiled. Gertrude dried her hands and walked over to him. She gave him a hug. "Did you meet everyone?"

"Not everyone."

"Go in and try. I want a full report when you're done."

Hank nodded politely and withdrew. Gertrude winked at Sal and returned to the sink.

Their friendship had been long-lasting, uneven. He had been in love with a man, but Gertrude represented the most durable relationship in his life. He thought back to the first day he met her. They had both been teachers then. She stood in the hallway, rows of lockers behind her. The Sixties had brought a lot of changes, but none, stylistically or culturally, had touched Gertrude. Her hair was an ocean of small, golden waves. Every sentence she spoke was articulated perfectly, the words formed by her bright red lips. She retained the idea that God was the head of the household and a righteous voice was a silent one.

"How wonderful to make your acquaintance," she'd said. A conservative wedding ring circled her finger.

"He seems like a nice kid," Gertrude said. "I hope you take good care of him, Sal."

"If he comes around, I will. These young ones always dip in and out. You remember Stanley? Poor man is back home in East Lansing. He ended up 1000s in debt, his face devastated by meth."

Gertrude clicked her tongue. "Sad," she said. Water sloshed as she dipped another pan into the sink.

In the main room dinner was finished. Many had risen from the table and begun to mill about the room. Sal looked out the window and saw the usual crowd standing in the twilight smoking cigarettes. The central spoke of this fuming circle was Lawrence Soot.

Sal felt a light touch on his back. Another of the older crowd stood before him. His eyes were brimming with tears. "Joseph and I..." He stopped.

"Again? Was it a new one this time?"

The man shook his head. "I came home early from work to surprise him and found them together..." He dried his eyes. "Cunt."

Gingerly, Sal hugged the man. "It'll be okay."

"I always think about what you say, that 'immutable hope.' He'll change. He'll change. I don't know why I keep thinking that way. I don't know why I can't give up."

"Immutable hope." Sal smiled sadly. "It's good and bad. We believe in people even when we shouldn't."

"How'd you do it with Arnie?"

"He chose to go. I couldn't stop him."

"And he came back."

Sal was silent. He gently coughed. After the pause, he said, "When he came back he was much changed."

"But he did. He came back." The man's eyes were brimming with tears again.

Sal thought it best not to tell him all. It would do no good. Hundreds of men had passed through his door with stories, not just of cheating, but of drug use, of obsession. Sal's response was always to tell them of his own sad relationship. His phrase "immutable hope" had been transformed, from a cautionary tale to one that gave life to a specious belief that everything doomed could bloom again. But his story wasn't one that should be used as a guide. After years of telling men to turn back from their troubled courses, he had learned that their pathways were set. One day they would wake up from their respective nightmares and a new path would be open, but when they came to him they were in the trenches. Blind, in a consuming darkness, they moved forward.

"I should call him," the man said. "We had a terrible fight but I should call..."

He disappeared into the crowd flipping open a phone as he went.

The rest of the room bubbled with conversation. Hank sat attentively listening to one of the most attractive of Sal's group. The Adonis spoke animatedly to a circle of fawning listeners.

"Changes are coming quickly," he said locking eyes with Hank. "Sean Penn won the Oscar for Milk; Dustin Lance Black started a fire with his acceptance speech; Proposition 8 is here, but it is crumbling. We're headed into a new age, men. Gayness is coming fully out of the shadows."

"But are we ready?" Clive's voice was shaking. "Are we losing something in this process?"

"Losing?" the man scoffed. "I would say things lost would be prejudice, hate, disenfranchisement…"

"But we say we want all these things only because others have them. To me queerness is about difference, our exclusion from everyone else. As a group we create art, we create culture, but we want it all watered down – a suburban dream. I'm not saying it's bad…" Clive's voice softened. The attractive man looked on scornfully. "But…" Clive stopped abruptly.

Hank looked between them. Sal caught in his eye a mysterious gleam. The other men looked at each other pondering who should speak next. Clive's eyes stared at the floor. The attractive man smirked and shook his head.

"Progress is always painful," the man said, "but we shouldn't resist."

"Ah," Sal interjected. "Resistance. I think that's exactly what we should do, Martin."

"I guess it's young against old," Martin chuckled. "Tell us, Sal. What should we resist?"

"Well," Sal looked directly at Hank, "we need to think of how we create friction even as things put us mainstream. Gay is okay, but what about our queer black brothers, queer Muslims? Have you met Stephanie the transgendered girl who works at Macy's? Her life isn't shielded by the growing protection around white, gay men."

"Men!" Clive raised his hand. "Exactly."

"People aren't afraid of white, gay men. That's who is benefitting. Dustin Lance Black is an example of this. Queerness is fine as long as it looks lovely and is wearing a suit."

"You can't possibly be taking from his accomplishment?"

"Resisting it," Sal said quietly. "Not detracting from it but wondering what it means in a larger context. That is friction. That is resistance. When we refuse to look at a narrative as it is framed for us, we begin to awake."

Martin crossed his arms. "So, we should give up on marriage? We should politely say, 'No thanks'?"

"Absolutely not," Sal said. "But we should think about it, and think about who we leave behind when we move blindly forward."

Silence fell on the room like a curtain. Everyone hesitated to speak, caught in an awkward, social suspension.

The front door slammed. Lawrence and his smokers entered together. They looked anxiously around the room.

"Seems as if we've walked in on a funeral," Soot laughed. "Did someone die?"

From the dining room a clock softly chimed. Everyone looked from Sal to Soot, wondering who would break the tension. Gertrude, intrigued by the silence, entered the room, the floor squeaking under her high-heeled shoes.

Sal heard her enter and smiled sadly, thinking for a moment on their shared history. "Trust me, Martin and Lawrence, this," he said drily, "isn't what death looks like."

II.

1970

The bell clanged. Children screamed, rushing across campus into the school's pillared entryway. The grey façade looked down with stern judgment. Coming up the steps with his leather briefcase, Sal kept his head down. Only a few years earlier this had been a dream. The high school was an image of grace. Its regal face looked onto a beautiful grassy lawn. He needed to go north to find the school of his dreams, but he believed it would be worth the trek. Four years later, however, the institution's grace and mysticism had not marked him. The school from a storybook contained no magic.

Thirty. The number of years he'd spent on earth was hard to believe. It was hard for Sal to fathom. His friends from childhood were now on children two and three. His mother was long dead. His father kept to himself in an outer ring suburb. The most communication they had was a ten-minute phone call on Saturday afternoons.

Hello.

Funny weather we're having.

How's school?

Sal's father was a man from the old guard. Masculine indifference and propriety walled him from his son. At Christmas, Sal would bring him a poinsettia and a new sweater. His father would nod, horned-rimmed spectacles sliding down his nose. They would attend church. Dinner would be an elaborate affair with Sal putting his cooking gifts to work. Bubbling pots of warm stew were the appetizers. The leftovers of a golden goose provided meals for his father for months.

Sal had fallen into luck with the family arrangement. There were others like him who faced probing questions when they arrived home. Sal's father was content with only Sal's presence and a good meal at Thanksgiving and Christmas.

Passing through the school's wide hall, Sal nodded to familiar students. In his classroom, the wooden walls were the same as the year before. One of the windows was open, a warm breeze rippled the papers on his desk. He usually was enthralled with the first day of school. The air was always in transition, no longer the floral summer wind that splashed against his face, but a crisper, fall breeze, laced with the smell of changing leaves. New faces of students used to excite him, but today they were blank pools of idiocy.

What had changed?

A little, yet a lot.

He said a prayer: "Lord, help me be grateful for thy gifts."

The first few hours were hard. He went over introductions and the syllabus. On the blackboard, he wrote a quote from Keats. There had been a time he would leap on his wooden chair and perform the words. Today he was bothered by the chalk dust on his sleeve.

One doe-eyed girl placed an apple on his desk before lunch.

"Susie Everly," she said breathlessly. "I'm thirteen and already one year ahead. Pleased to meet you."

Throughout his opening lecture, she stared at him hungrily. He dropped the chalk feeling the voracious gaze on him. Susie Everly was desperate for so many things.

After that class, he needed to step outside. There was just one more period before the lunch bell, but he felt claustrophobic in the small classroom.

He stood in the middle of the lawn, using up all of the five minutes he was allowed. If he had more time he would have removed his shoes and let the grass stick between his toes. Behind him, the blank, scornful stare of the school burned into him. As soulless as the building's eyes were, they were less intimidating than Susie's spark-filled orbs.

"Hello," a man said.

Sal turned and looked at the young teacher walking toward him. The man's eyes were squinting against the sun. He was in the midst of trying to grow sideburns. The result was brown fluff in intermittent patches on the side of his face.

"Hello," Sal said. Handsome, he thought to himself. Young and handsome. "Can I help you?"

The man laughed. "I'm taking a walk. My first day isn't going well."

"They usually don't. You realize all your expectations are wrong."

"I had few," the man smirked, "but even those were misguided."

Sal nodded. "It gets better. I promise."

"It already feels slightly so."

An invisible jolt of electricity passed between them. Sal awkwardly rubbed the back of his head. He didn't break eye contact with the young man. Something in this new teacher's eyes brought to mind Susie. Hunger. It was rare to see it so brazenly looking back from another man. It was very rare.

"My name is Arnold," the man said. "I prefer Arnie."

"Sal. It's short for Solomon, but no one has ever called me that."

"Seems an awful waste for something so regal."

"I suppose."

"Hmmm," Arnie licked his lips. He tapped his foot on the cement.

#

Stolen glances and a few brief conversations were all that passed between Sal and Arnie over the course of the next few weeks. Arnie would occasionally stop by his office with logistics questions.

"Do you think I've been here long enough to ditch my sport coat?"

"Can you direct me to the football field? I'm not very interested but feel compelled to go."

"Are there any good restaurants around here? It's pretty juvenile but I'm dying for a good milkshake."

Sal remained stoic. It was not like him to let his imagination run away with him. He had tried long ago to conform to the social norm. Her name was Cindy Barlow. She was medium height, a little heavy, slavishly devoted to him. Their courtship last six months. He bought a ring. One month before the wedding he had taken her to a movie and at the end of the night broke it off in her parents' driveway. He could remember few times when he had shed so many tears. It wasn't only hurting Cindy that was difficult, but also the realization that it could never work; even with Cindy's slavish devotion, he couldn't make himself marry a woman. He could never work. Cindy called for almost a year after the break. The phone came to life at less frequent intervals over the course of the spring and summer of 1962.

After the calls lapsed, Sal let things drift. He wrote her one morning in the fall when he was reminded of her love of yellow leaves. After that first letter, epistles passed frequently between them. The written correspondence between them went deeper than any conversations they had while dating. Cindy had moved on. She had decided to travel. Her parents were rich and she saw Europe, Asia, and Africa. A few times she sent pictures. She wore khaki pants and silk head scarves just like the ingénues in the movies. Her last letter had not included information about a man. That note had been a Christmas Card. She enclosed no picture. The card contained only a few scrawled lines on paper.

The revelation of her engagement came that previous summer, right before he met Susie Everly.

"I just thought you should know…," she'd said over the phone.

Sal didn't realize this was the source of his tiredness, his boredom, his pain. She was lost. What had always been a possibility was now a known dead end. Sal always had friends, but with the loss of Cindy he felt, not just alone, but isolated.

Thirty. His parents had accomplished much before their thirtieth year: a marriage, stable careers, a stillborn followed by Sal. His friends were now entrenched in the same pathways as his parents, but Sal was not. He had a small garden and a little house that smelled old from the rot of wood and the stale smell of cigarettes that drifted through the vents from his neighbor's apartment.

But Arnie had provided some reprieve from the dull pain. Sal watched him in the halls. His heart beat faster when Arnie came into his classroom with an inane question about policy.

"Is it three tardies before a detention?"

Sal remained stoic, but his heart beat faster and his palms sweated. The feelings, the feelings he knew were part of him, burned hotter when Arnie was close by. It had been a while since he had felt them so intensely. There had been a man in his church. This man, Robert, had been a married father, though. There was never any tangibility, any possibility of a real relationship with him – erotic dreams were all that reminded Sal of his depravity.

Yea though I walk through the valley of the shadow of death.
Death.

Church filled his time after Cindy. People set him up on dates. Some people knew what he was, but they were all kind. Gertrude DuBois knew. Gertrude with her perfect family, her Sears Catalog husband, and her pink skirts. Gertrude, the upper-level English teacher, knew. Sal wouldn't use the word out loud, even in gossip, but nemesis was what she was. She ran the Bible study for the young adults at church.

One Wednesday evening she had asked for his help cleaning up.

"You haven't been going on dates, Sal," she said.

"I haven't."

"Family is so important, so godly. I know someone." She stopped and watched him.

Sal knew he had to respond: "Oh?"

"She's a little older but I think she may be perfect for you. She's quiet, settled."

"Hmm."

Gertrude walked to the door and made sure they were alone. She turned to him. Her high-heeled shoes spun on the linoleum. Her perfect quaff didn't move.

"Sal, I think I know what you are. You don't have to be a monster, though; you can resist. With God's help you can have a goodly, godly life: normalcy, children, a wife. Wouldn't that be nice?"

Tears formed in Sal's eyes.

"I have faith that you will be good." She reached out and grabbed his hand. "I know a man from my town who gave himself to the sinful life. His family never spoke to him again, as they shouldn't. I don't know why God has afflicted you with this demon, but he that gives can heal. Let me be your rock."

Sal thanked her and dried the remaining dishes.

The stoicism remained strong, except for within his own apartment. In that space Cindy and Gertrude were powerless to stop his imagination. It ran wild, free. Something about Arnie transformed him. Sal thought of Arnie's frame in his sport coat. One day after work he'd raised his hands to stretch and Sal saw flesh.

The thoughts sparked, caught fire, multiplied. Sal kept the darkest desires locked away, but others stretched toward the sun. He sat down and wrote lines.

Stag of the wood, regal, powerful, light;
Sun glints from thy pointed crown.
How you elude my touch.
Only my eye can cast its distant net
Over your graceful form.
But how I long to feel the cords
Of sinew beneath my hands.
How I long to feel thy bated breath
flow across my fingers.

#

"It's fully fall now."

"Yes."

"Do you ever go out? You know, grab a drink?"

"I prefer not to. I keep to myself mostly. Dinners with friends are all I really can get excited about."

"And Bible study."

"Yes, and that, I suppose. Although, you know how Gertrude is at school. Imagine her in her own fortress. It can be exhausting."

"Do you ever host? You could suggest it."

"I don't know…"

"Is there something wrong with your place?"

"It's cozy, in its way."

"'In its way' what a very Sal thing to say."

"'A very Sal thing to say' – what a very Arnie thing to say."
"I guess it is. I can't help my cleverness."
"You should be as clever as possible while you're young."
"Is your cleverness all dried up?"
"It comes and goes."
"In what way?"
"I write the occasional poem…"
"Oh, a *true* man of letters. I'm sorry if I think it's a bit cliché for the English teacher to write poems."
"You don't want to see my science projects."
"See, your cleverness isn't all dried up. You're not as old as you think you are. You look youthful."
"As long as I have my looks, I guess cleverness can just go."
"In a race I would guess they'd both travel about the same speed."
"Cleverness and looks?"
"Yes, you can be the most beautiful star of the morning but if you have no brains, you are limited."
"Do you know anyone burdened by this brain deficit and beauty surplus?"
"I had a friend. Gorgeous, but couldn't quite get life going."
"A woman?"
"A man."
"An old friend?"
"Not an old friend, but, I guess you'd say a dear one."
"You think he'll ever move forward? Or do you think it's hopeless?"
"I don't think anyone is hopeless. Truly hopeless. There is cause to cheer for everyone, I think."
"It's true. Some of my worst students are the ones I cheer the hardest. Some of them can't help where they come from, the hard lives their parents have."
"I think there are more reasons to cheer today than there ever have been. Even with Nixon trying to tear up our welfare state, we got Earth Day. The world shook when we invaded Cambodia. The youth are finding our voice."
"I hope you and your fellow youths are loud and indomitable."
"Indomitable. Now that is a fine word to describe progress."
"I think so."
"Well, I think I will be indomitable in getting you to join me for a drink. I have no friends and, quite frankly, you're the only one around here who interests me."

A hand placed lightly, gently on Sal's leg. In his head, a flash of feeling singed neural networks.

"I…"

"At least think about it! No one is hopeless, Sal."

"No… I think no one is."

#

Poetry wasn't enough at times. Alone in the apartment, the clock ticking, Sal's thoughts wandered. At first, he let it happen. He'd go to the bedroom and lay on his comforter. Shame kept him from removing clothing, but he would close his eyes and see Arnie in front of him. One night when they had met for drinks, Arnie wore an open shirt. His chest hair was visible in the light. Perspiration built along Sal's brow. Even the look of Arnie's hands, the weathered, masculine folds of skin, was erotic. That night Sal did not remain stoic. He let it slip. He girlishly laughed as Arnie spoke of his time at university. There was no possible way to keep his eyes from looking into Arnie's. He giggled. He smiled. Afterword he felt nothing but hot shame. To lose control like that was something he never did. When the feelings began, he buried them. The man at church he fostered the erotic feeling for was kept far away. He would not engage.

He knew that in the near future he would need to separate himself from Arnie.

But after the date, the full physicality of his desire became manifest. It was no longer imagination and poetry. He thought of Arnie and him across from each other. The erotic undertones burst open in his mind's eye:

"Aren't we naughty," the Arnie of his imagination said.

Sal reached across the table and ran his hand through the hair exposed below Arnie's collar. He did not get further than a vision of Arnie shirtless before the shivering ran through his body. Wetness formed on his crotch.

He sighed and opened his eyes. He was no longer in the dimly lit restaurant experiencing love, but he was awake: lonely Sal, sitting on a comforter in the light of the moon. That night he left his apartment in the dark. He threw his soiled bed clothes in a paper sack and put it in an alley three blocks away. If it was gone, it didn't happen. He could go back to life as it was before Arnie. *Feelings are faucets turned by the hand of God.* That's what Gertrude had said one day at Bible study.

Faucets.

But Sal's faucet dripped. After that first fantasy, the daydreams were unstoppable. He looked forward to getting home after school. He would go to the bedroom, lay, and let desire overtake him. At first it was the image of Arnie and his open shirt. After several weeks of imagining, Arnie's shirt was gone. After a month, it was Arnie in only his underwear. Sal imagined them, colored, like in advertisements he had seen. Blue. That was the end, however. He could never get farther than Arnie in blue, the whole restaurant gone and them alone in space.

The faucet dripped until one Sunday morning. The pastor spoke of adultery, but to Sal it was directly addressed to him and his warped sexual interest. Despite his age, he could not escape the vision of devils, pitchforks, and fire and brimstone he had been taught in his youth. The preacher drew from "Sinners in the Hands of an Angry God." Sal was prone to wickedness; he was condemned. Perspiration ran down his arms. He had to leave in the middle of the sermon to dab his face with water.

God is good.

I am made in the image of God.

I am burdened with feelings opposed to God.

But I can be good.

No one is hopeless – the phrase made him shake.

After church one of the older women from the service invited him to lunch at her home. She made a dinner of pot roast and warm cornbread. During the meal she discussed her gratitude that God would "fry up" the sinners. Her idea of justice was merciless. It desired fiery, broad punishment for all those who strayed from the path. Sal was sweating as the old woman cackled and told him gossip from the church. She listed all those she knew to be condemned. In her eyes, Sal remained safe.

Talk of hell gave way to a long walk. Fear kept Sal from going home to be alone with his thoughts. That day he didn't want to be sequestered with his fantasies. Relief washed over him when the old woman invited him to stay and watch *Bonanza* on her new color television.

It was 9:30 before he got home. He stood in the dark. The images of Arnie were relentless. He closed his eyes and saw him, shirt open. In the shadows he hallucinated Arnie's silhouette, his broad shoulders splashed along the wall.

To escape, he turned on all the lights. In the glow, he thought the passion would be extinguished. He shook. He collapsed. Tears ran down his face. Outside clouds gathered and thunder rolled.

I can be good.

No one is hopeless.

He mouthed the words and came to some kind of peace. In his later years, he would never quite know what the feeling had been. The most likely reason for the sudden calm was following the thoughts to their terminus: Arnie wouldn't have feelings like his. He was a friend and nothing more. It was only an infatuation.

Unreality. A phantasm. A devil.

Sal picked himself up and went to bed. The faucet, for the moment, patched, turned off. He went to bed without an erotic thought for the first time in weeks. Outside rain poured down. He watched it dribble down the window in tiny rivers. To him, it was a sign of the temptation being washed away. Baptism.

#

Gertrude DuBois organized the tea with Annabelle Crawford. It was Sunday afternoon after a church potluck.

"Wouldn't it be nice if you both came over?" Gertrude asked.

It was the first time that Sal had seriously entertained the idea of dating a woman again. After he broke it off with Cindy, he thought he would never attempt it. But there was real pain and fire if he didn't. He would be on the church lady's list of the damned. God had made him stronger in the baptism. The unreality was gone, burned up, and in its place was pale, smiling Annabelle. Her dress was black, her earrings white. Her voice was soft, uneven, discordant.

"There seems to be too much upheaval in the news," she said smiling. "It seems to me quiet is the best way to live in the world."

Quiet is the best way to live. The words for Sal, in that moment, were a salve. Live quietly. Sacrifice yourself, your desires, so that you add no friction to the world. God made us to be sheep, to follow the guidance of his hand. Praise be to him.

"You two even dressed alike," said Gertrude. "What a coincidence."

Sal had worn black slacks and a white shirt. The splashes of color he had slowly let into his wardrobe were inappropriate now.

Live quietly.

Annabelle left at five to get back to her mother and father's home for supper. Sal stayed back and helped Gertrude clean up the dishes.

"That went well," she said.

"Annabelle seems very nice."

"She is very nice. She's a very smart girl."

"She didn't go to university, though?"

"No, she thought it was best to work in Ms. Lehman's shop until marriage. I don't think she expected a decade to slip by. She wants kids as soon as possible."

"I admire people who know what they want."

"It's not always easy to know."

"Did you?"

Mr. DuBois entered the room. He was handsome, broad and square-jawed.

"Hello," he said. "I suspect tea went well?"

"Very well," said Gertrude. She paused for just a moment. "You know, George, aren't you meeting with some of the boys from the rotary club tonight?"

"I am, darling."

"Why don't you take Sal? He could probably use some time with the boys after a whole afternoon of tea with us girls."

George pursed his lips. "We'll watch *The F.B.I.*"

"Not exactly subject matter for ladies," said Gertrude.

Gertrude and George looked at Sal. A week ago he would not have gone. But a week ago he was a different person. He wore color. He veered toward loudness.

"Yes," he said. "I've never watched *The F.B.I.* but I think it could be very interesting."

#

"And her name's Annabelle?"

"Yes, we were introduced at church."

"Well, isn't that as all-American as you can get?"

"I suppose it is a very homey way of meeting."

"Very homey."

Arnie drummed his fingers on the counter of the pub. His eyes swept the bar. He thought for a moment. Another moment. Sal's heart pounded in his chest.

"I would have thought someone like you would have met a nice girl sooner," Arnie said. He licked his lips.

"I think perhaps it just never worked out. I was engaged once."

"Really?"

"Yes, not many people know. She's actually getting married very soon."

"Hmmm."

"What, hmmm?"

"It seems a very interesting coincidence."

"Why is that?"

"People at school said you didn't go out with girls much. Interesting you found someone right when your old gal found someone."

It was Sal's turn to drum his fingers. "I think," he stuttered, "that her getting married meant the world was moving forward. I had been stuck for too long."

"Stuck on her? Or something else?"

Arnie's eyes were large, full of life. They no longer swept the bar but rested on Sal. The weather was cool so he wore a cardigan; his chest was not exposed.

"I think it's a number of things. I turned thirty. Cindy is getting married. Time runs on like a river. I don't think it was just her; it was a lot of things. I need to be dislodged."

"Dislodged…"

Silence. It was one, brief moment. To Sal it radiated with electric, vibrant, uncertain power. It was a very different kind of quiet from Annabelle's silences. This was profound, full, rather than desiccated. This moment contained life.

Laughter. A clang of a glass. The silence ended. Arnie drummed his fingers on the pub counter once more. He smiled.

"I supposed we all get stuck," he said.

"I was stuck for a very long time."

"Hmmm," Arnie said.

"What, hmmm?" asked Sal.

"One too many beers. Muddled," he said softly. He pointed to his heart.

#

These parallel worlds, that can't unite,
Endless orbits circle far from light.
The sun distant, the worlds spin 'round.
In shadow, in fear, in shame they're crowned.
They drift close at certain times, brief moments,
Hoping, longing, for a sudden elopement.
If only they could spin away, touch, lightly,
A combustion of the heavens. Even tightly
Kept laws of what is and is not would break.
They'd be unbounded, unfettered, gloriously debased.
Would these worlds be, when met together,
Unified souls rendered light as feather?
Unknown. But bound they remain.
Fettered they stay.
These parallel worlds that can't unite
Still dream of union, touches, light.

#

Students lined up on both sides of the gym. A few wandered into the middle to dance. Sal paced near the door. His duty had been to make sure none of the students attempted "lurid" or "lascivious" dance steps. To Sal the new music the students listened to wasn't nearly as "lurid" as what the principal proclaimed.

"Raindrops Keep Fallin' on My Head" and "Bridge over Troubled Water" didn't induce gyration like the rock n' roll songs of his youth.

Susie Everly dressed in custard said hello. She watched him from the side of the gym. Four or five times she passed him on the way to the cafeteria to get punch. Every time she was clutching at the hand of her closest girlfriend, Charlotte. Susie's first theme that fall had been about Charlotte.

We have clandestine encounters since my father does not especially respect colored folk.

Clandestine... One night he and Arnie had gone out for drinks and the word kept running through Sal's brain. Susie's writing style left much to be desired, but her and Charlotte's secret friendship was a mirror of his own relationship with Arnie. Clandestine was a good word. Although nothing about Arnie and his friendship was truly secret, there was tension beneath the surface that couldn't be seen, only felt.

Muddled. No one is hopeless.

These words reverberated in Sal's head. Was he reading too much into them? Did it matter? He and Annabelle had been seeing each other for a month, living quietly. Sal had yet to cut Arnie off completely. He had rejected invitations to get drinks. No dinners, especially. He and Annabelle spent Sundays at church. One Saturday they had gone to Lincoln Park. They sat and looked over the pond. She put her head on his shoulder.

Since his baptism that fateful night he had only allowed himself sexual thoughts of Arnie once. It was three weeks from the day he made his decision to live in the quiet. He had spent the evening at Bible study. When he came outside onto Gertrude's lawn, a neighbor was playing basketball with his young son. The father was younger than Sal, probably twenty-eight. Sweat poured off him and glistened in the flood lamps that illumined the makeshift court. He was shirtless. Sal stopped on the front walk, hands in his pockets. His breath was taken away. The man looked up, smiled, wiped sweat from his brow.

"Beautiful evenin', huh?"

Sal nodded.

On the car ride home, his hands gripped the steering wheel tightly, his knuckles turning white. He closed his eyes. All of his energy was spent forcing the image of the neighbor out of his head. But the faucet had been turned on again. Steady dripping turned to a roar. It was Annabelle's ghost that tried to drive away the images. At first it was only the neighbor sparkling with sweat, but those turned to Arnie, the old images of him, shirt unbuttoned, smiling across the way. Sal saw Arnie's hands on the table, raw, tan knuckles; he saw the rough patches of five o'clock shadow. Annabelle's ghost sought to calm him. She appeared, the image of them on the park bench looking over the lake.

Water in such different capacities: the erotic drip of sweat on a man's brown, the placid face of a pond.

He went immediately to his mattress and cried as orgasm overtook him. Two feelings consumed him: release and panic. Can it be pushed away? Would it always erupt like this? Water – rushing, placid, deadly – currents, alternating within him. Would he never control it?

After the rush, he sat on the bed, head in his hands. It was that moment when he knew he had to cut out Arnie out completely. He needed to avoid him. There would be men like Gertrude's neighbor, but they would have less effect if he wasn't in such close proximity to someone that he truly... felt about. Feel about. How did he feel about Annabelle? To him she was a doll, a sister; he could protect her. When the time came, he could give her children. It could be worked out. Their life could be simple, calm, quiet.

But Arnie always appeared, breaking up that calm. Sal's stoic veneer eroded away; he was helpless before the image of Arnie's smile, his hands, his open shirt. The erotic was of the devil. Arnie wasn't a possibility anyway.

No one is hopeless.

Muddled. Muddled?

Arnie smiled at Sal when he arrived at the dance to chaperone. They exchanged pleasantries before splitting up. Arnie's task consisted of checking in the students at the front door. He looked dapper in a tan suit. His hair was growing longer. Strands of it were pulled back over his ears. Sal wondered if the principal would say something. Sal should tell Arnie to get it buzzed like his own. It was better not to start trouble.

"Hello, Sal." Gertrude appeared at his elbow. She was a vision in pink: pastels, high heels, high hair, rouged cheeks.

"Hello. Enjoying the dance?" Sal asked.

"I never do. You know these events are just an incubator for sinful behavior. I feel it's my duty to try to help keep it under control."

"I think today's crowd is tamer than we've seen."

Gertrude's blue eyes flew around the room. "It is better. I heard Arnold caught a group of boys trying to get in drunk."

"There's always those few who ruin it for everyone."

"The bad seeds." Gertrude crossed her arms. "What are you all reading this quarter? I feel like we never talk about work at Bible study."

"God always seems to get in the way."

Gertrude smiled, genuinely. "I suppose he likes to be the center of attention."

"We've just finished some poetry: Keats, Wordsworth, Shelley."

"I envy every student who gets to experience 'I Wondered Lonely as a Cloud' for the first time."

"'Ode on a Grecian Urn' still gives me chills after hundreds of reads."

"How do you top those? What's next?"

"We're dipping into American Literature." Sal suddenly felt uncomfortable.

"A rich pool to enter. What specifically?"

"Female authors is our next unit, I suppose."

"I tend to shy away from the women. They aren't quite as tried and true as the male masters. But there are good options. Who are you dipping into?"

Sal hesitated. "Chopin."

He felt relief when Gertrude looked on quizzically. "I'm not familiar. I don't think I've read her."

"We'll be doing *The Awakening*."

"Maybe I'll add it to my personal reading list."

"It's a slim book. I think it's good for young minds. I don't know if you'd enjoy it."

"Well, if she's that limited, perhaps you should rethink including her."

"Perhaps."

A student approached Gertrude. He stood before them, a rakish boy with piercing grey eyes. "Hiya, Mrs. DuBois," he said. "I think some girl's cryin' in the bathroom."

Gertrude politely bowed. "Duty calls."

Sal watched the boy and Gertrude cross the gymnasium. Quickly, furtively, the boy looked at her backside as they disappeared around the corner.

For a long time, Sal couldn't figure out the emotion he attached to Gertrude. They were friendly, but they weren't friends in the way that he was friends with other men and women. The mathematics teacher, Mrs. Reynolds, and he cultivated a very cordial relationship. He didn't feel the panic around her that always followed the clack of Gertrude's heels. One afternoon leaving Bible study, a strange word came to him: jealousy. For Gertrude, the world was a wound clock. It had a steady tick-tock rhythm undisturbed by the chaos around it. God was God and God was good. She had very quickly found it all: the church, the husband, the children, the posh house with floral-patterned furniture. Sal was thirty and had a small apartment with dying plants. Annabelle had some trace of Gertrude, which was perhaps what he had attached to. In her he saw the possibility of a painless future.

But chased to its inevitable conclusion… What?

The night wore on. More students loosened up and began to dance. Sal broke up a few couples who were getting too cozy with each other. As "Rock Around the Clock" boomed from the speakers he and Gertrude both politely tapped young men's shoulders who were letting let their hips move too freely.

During a slow dance, he remembered his own teenage years. It was before he recognized his affliction. Life had yet to teach him he was different, that he was broken. That came later. As his other friends picked up girlfriends, he stayed alone. Over time he slowly understood that the feelings his friends had for girls were what he had for them. He could pray and try, but otherwise he was powerless. What would a world look like where he could cross the floor and grab a boy's hand?

Standing alone in the corner of the gym, emotion overtook him. He, who remained stoic, was broken by The Righteous Brothers. Thank God for dark corners. A tear dripped down his cheek. He was afraid to wipe it away.

As he grew older the pain redoubled rather than ebbed. His other friends were married. They had children. Cindy moved on. Annabelle stood as a last hope. Was that what she was?

Sal splashed water on his face in the bathroom. The boy with grey eyes that had grabbed Gertrude earlier in the evening stood by the sink with his friends.

"Heya, Mr. Henry," he said.

"Hi boys. You enjoying yourselves?"

"I guess so."

"Enjoying more after, I think." A boy with buzzed brown hair laughed. One of his friends slapped the back of his head.

Sal sighed. He should reprimand the boy, but he was exhausted. "Well, be careful," he said half-heartedly.

As the night wound down parents arrived. Students filtered out to do what the buzzed-haired boy had been implying. The teachers helped pick up the gymnasium. In the end, there were a small group of chaperones and a few piles of crepe paper and used decorations. The banner that read "A Northside Dreamscape" lay on the floor.

Sal was in the middle of tossing the banner in the garbage when he heard shoes clack across the gym. He looked up and saw Arnie. No one else was near. His brown shoes made the only sound.

"I sent Annie and Mr. Gray home." He leaned over and picked up a pile of crepe paper. "It's just us to finish." His voice had broken.

Sal's heart pounded against his chest. Thump. Bump. Arnie wasn't thinking about that. He was being polite and sending the others home.

"Do you have a key?" Sal asked.

"Yes, Mr. Gray loaned me his. He was eager to get home."

"I'm sure."

The two men worked quickly to clean up. No words passed between them as they carried paper to the garbage and swept up bits of trash. Sal's heart continued to pound. He threw sidelong glances to Arnold, who was focused on his work. The squeak of the garbage can being pulled to the edge of the gym meant the end. Cleanup was complete.

Arnold flipped off the lights. Patches of moonlight shining from the upper windows and the square of light coming in from the main hallway were the only points of illumination. Arnie stood near the bleachers, just outside the glow of the door.

Sal walked toward the exit, but Arnie climbed up into the wooden seats, moving further out of the light.

"Want to grab a drink?" he asked. "Don't tell Gertrude but I snuck in some whiskey."

Sal hesitated in the doorway. Ahead of him was the golden glow of the hall; above him was the outline of Arnie, silhouetted in moonlight. "I'd feel uncomfortable drinking in the school."

Sal couldn't see Arnie's face. "One drink, Sal. I think we've earned it."

Sal stayed still.

Arnie sighed and clomped down the steps. As he drew near, Sal could tell that he had already been drinking. The tang of whiskey hung on his breath.

"One drink, old pal?" Arnie reached out and touched him. Touched. It wasn't the first time, but this touch was different. This caress had a motive; his fingers ran over Sal's skin, soft as rose petals.

Sal jumped. Arnie laughed. "See! You need a drink. You're too jumpy, Solomon."

Sal's heart beat harder. Arnie gripped Sal's arm. His hold was firm. Sal remembered seeing Arnie's hands across the table, their masculine, weathered look. He grew hard. His breath quickened. In the dark, Sal saw Arnie's face light up in a broad smile. He licked his lips.

Silence.

Arnie hesitated, then looked away. "I think you're on to me," he said.

"On to…?"

Arnie stared at Sal. He looked directly into his eyes. It wasn't the look of a friend; it was the hungry look he recognized from the first day of school on the lawn. They stared at each other for a tense moment. Sal knew he should be moving toward the door but he couldn't pull away.

Muddled.

Arnie ran a hand through his lengthening hair. He sighed. "Oh," he muttered, "why not?"

He pressed close. Sal felt his lips on Arnie's, smelled whiskey. Rather than pull away he relaxed. He leaned in. The calloused hand was on his cheek. Sal ran his fingers through Arnie's hair. His cock throbbed.

It was a 1940's movie kiss, tight-lipped, unsure. When Arnie pulled away, he looked terrified. He locked eyes with Sal. Words trembled on his lips, but were never spoken.

Silence.

"I'm… I don't know…"

"No, it's…"

"To be honest…"

"Be honest."

"I've wanted to for a very long time."

"You're?"

"Hmmm, nelly, yes."

"Hmmm."

"You?"

"Yes." It was a whisper, but it was said. It was said out loud.

The men stared at each other. Both looked frightened. Sal felt fully exposed, naked.

"What do we do?" Sal asked softly.

"I don't know."

"We should think…"

"Let's not think."

"Not think?"

"I want to hold you. I want to hold you in the dark."

"You…"

"I want to dance with you. I never get to dance at these things."

Sal remained motionless. Arnie stepped forward. He put his arms around Sal. Sal leaned in. He placed his head on Arnie's shoulder.

They were still.

Slowly, very slowly, Arnie began to move. He glided back and forth. The boards of the gym floor groaned beneath their feet. All was dark around them. They were far outside the golden light of the hallway.

They fell into rhythm: step, step, step. Arnie hummed softly. Sal gripped Arnie's back. He felt at home enveloped in phantom music and darkness. The faucet drip turned to flood.

III.

1980

    The tap tap of Sal's fingers on his suitcase drummed out an uneven rhythm. His nerves were shot. He hadn't been near an airport in three years. That time he had been picking up family for his father's funeral.

    This was his first flight. A colleague assured him that it would be simple. "People fly every day." The airport itself did calm him. The high windows made him think that a mostly transparent building couldn't be hiding anything malicious. He attempted to read a newspaper but his hands shook so badly it was distracting. Now, he drummed on his suitcase. A woman beside him eyed him uneasily.

    San Francisco. Since this was Sal's first flight he had felt the need to read up on as much as he could about his destination. He bought a book about its history and surveyed the glossy images of the steep hills and beautiful bay views. Prior to the book his knowledge of San Francisco was limited to what he knew about Rice-A-Roni.

    He wasn't sure why he had agreed to go. Arnie had been out there for almost six years. They exchanged letters over the course of that time. There was no hope, no thought that this was a romantic trip. Arnie had sent him Polaroids over the years of himself and his golden-tanned friends. They all looked stylish, young, and healthy. Sal hadn't sent a picture in a long time. He felt himself aging. He had grown fatter. There had been too much to do in recent years; his own health hadn't been of any importance. His concerns the last five years had been three: his father, the incident at work, the bookshop.

    A pilot walked by Sal in the terminal. He took a seat and crossed his legs. His face was chiseled and freshly shaved. He pulled out a newspaper and began reading.

    Sal imagined what the pilot's life was like. A younger Sal would have put himself in the pilot's life. For ten or twenty minutes, he would wear the pilot's skin. First, looking in a mirror at himself in the blue uniform; next, coming home to a wife in a suburban oasis and kissing a toe-haired boy and girl hello; finally, in a cockpit, looking at open, blue sky. But he had experienced too much painful reality and rarely daydreamed. Mostly it was logistics. *If he's single, how does he care for a dog?*

    He loved to listen to the young men who came through his shop. They still had dreams that expanded outward and upward. What better city than Chicago for them to come to? The Sears Tower stood as a monument to impossibility. Man could touch the sky.

    One boy with curly black hair and a high, nasally voice told him he wanted to lead the quest for gay rights. The younger generation of gay men had a fire that he had not had. They had Stonewall. The Chicago Gay Pride Parade had grown over the past decade. There was hope. Arnie had seized it by going to San Francisco. From his letters, it seemed that homosexuality in San Francisco was a common thing. It was becoming open. Homosexuals no longer had to live in such oppressive silence.

    There's this guy, Harvey Milk...

That's how one letter started. When Mr. Milk was murdered Arnie had written another epistle:

It feels as though I've lost a brother, or maybe something more. I don't think you can understand the change that's happened because of him. I wish my words came as easily as yours do. Maybe you can write a poem for me.

In Sal's corner of the world things remained stagnant. Heartbreak was followed by his father's illness. After resigning from the school, he opened the bookshop. His father had been his sole investor. The old man sold his house and moved into a small apartment so that his son could open a dusty store in Lake View. Sales were not great. They were not horrible. A group of lesbians held readings every Thursday. On Tuesday nights, a group of young gays gathered just to talk. Sal served them tea in an odd assortment of cups and mugs. So many were coming now he had to use a bowl for the newest addition, a small brunette who was obsessed with Olivia Newton-John.

It was this that had slowly brought him back to life. He loved cleaning his shop and listening to the young men and women discuss politics. They burned with hope and desire. Under his watchful gaze a number of young men had fallen in love. It was different from the complicated, taciturn affair he and Arnie had engaged in. Years of self-loathing, church-induced fear, and emotional stunting had led them to their impasse. The boys and girls that arrived at his store, though, were different. Love for them was earnest and uncomplicated. They stumbled into problems. Already two of the young men had screamed at each other in front of some of his other customers. But even in their screaming matches, they radiated this hopeful new life. Sal, on the other hand, felt dead. The part of him capable of the earnest love of youth had long since been washed away. In truth, he didn't know if it had ever been part of him at all.

One of Arnie and Sal's many arguments:

"You're so cold."

"I wouldn't say cold. I would say stoic."

"What are you afraid of? We draw the blinds; we hide in the dark."

"It's complicated."

"Is it your god? Your vengeful, fairytale god that beams down his hatred on all his loving followers."

"Please don't, Arnie."

"Don't what? Ask you to be human? Ask you to hold me, touch me?"

Silence. The ticking of the clock.

"I think you should get away from that woman, to be honest."

"What woman?"

"Gertrude. She's putting all kinds of garbage in your head. You need to quit that Bible study."

"I can't just stop believing."

"What has your god done for you? Name one thing."

"It's complicated."

"We're lovers. Help me understand."

Sal remembered taking a breath. He would allow himself to be vulnerable. "Hope, if that's not a cliché."

"Hope? The god of fire and brimstone, who tells you you are a queenie monster gives you hope?"

"Have you ever – seen God? Have you ever felt life around you that's so different from anything else that you know it just can't be the natural world? Have you ever been so gripped by emotion that you forget where you are? I once saw a man standing alone. He was old and he was feeding birds. The scene kind of rippled. It was so beautiful."

Sal knew he was babbling. He was trying to articulate that thing he couldn't ever find words for. Poetry came closer to describing it. During his father's illness, he wrote page after page of verse. Love, hate, confusion, conflict, Arnie: these were his themes. He couldn't quite describe that he saw a crack in the visible world. Through this crack there was something more than the ordinary. Poetry, in some way, helped him peer into this space, but it was never enough to fully pry it open. He wanted so desperately to see.

"That's a beautiful sentiment, Sal," Arnie said dolefully. "Listen, I think I'll go home tonight, but let's get together soon."

Sal watched him go. A romantic would have run after him, but Sal was not a romantic. He remained a scared boy in an adult body. Love for him was unformed. It slipped through his fingers. While the boys who entered his bookshop held love in its concrete form, Sal saw only could ever see a shimmering will o' the wisp.

A woman took a seat next to him in the terminal. Her hair was brown with gray streaks. Atop her head sat a large-brimmed hat. She put down her purse and gently coughed.

Sal thought then of Gertrude. This woman very well could have been a future version of his friend. Exquisitely dressed, hair perfect, she opened a compact mirror and dabbed at her nose. For a brief while Sal thought that he would abandon his friendship with Gertrude, as Arnie had advised. Her influence in his life was pernicious at times. But others it was not. On many occasions, the Bible study over, they would sit quietly in her front living room. Gertrude would take off her heels and rake her feet through the orange shag. Sal would sit upright, looking at the pictures on the wall. His gaze would drift to the window to see if the gorgeous neighbor would appear.

Their friendship was complicated. After Sal dumped Annabelle they did not speak for months.

"What you did to that poor girl…" She'd faded off and stormed away. At church for several weeks she refused to acknowledge his presence.

Annabelle had been easy to let go. At that time Arnie and Sal had begun to see each other. They had begun to see each other as much as Sal would let them. But as uncomfortable as Sal was with Arnie, it felt right to him. The chains of doubt had fallen away and he finally understood lust. It was not theoretical, seeing another man. It was tangible. He could feel the rough touch of Arnie's hands on his body. The first time Arnie brought him to climax, he lay in his bed staring at the ceiling as Arnie worked his mouth around his member; it was cold out but the window was open. The curtains fluttered.

Annabelle had wept when he broke up with her. Even in the moment, it was unreal to Sal. They had never been a true couple. Their quiet nights together were devoid of sexual energy. He felt more chemistry the nights he watched *Bonanza* with the old woman from church.

"Is it another girl?" she squealed. "You found someone else! Oh, I knew you were cold. Cold, cold, cold!"

Sal watched her cry. When she finished, she stormed from his car and climbed the steps to her mother's home.

Six months later her engagement was announced.

In the meantime, Sal enjoyed his few months of peace with Arnie. They would meet away from school at a small bar on Broadway. After a drink or two they would walk back toward the school and get in Sal's car. The anticipation on the way to his apartment was unbearable. Once inside the small apartment, windows drawn, they would attack each other. Sal still kissed in 1940's movie fashion, tight-lipped, face turned toward the neck.

Arnie showed him how to do it logistically. They used olive oil for lube. Sal should have known then, with the deftness of Arnie's fingers, the depth of his knowledge, but it didn't occur to him.

But after every bout of sex there was guilt. Arnie would leave and Sal would sit in his bed, dirty, covered in oil. At first there had been tears, but that only lasted for a short time. After the tears was deep, existential pain. He would sit, desolate and afraid on his beautiful comforter.

Muddled.

God is good. He could be good.

Sal was suspended between the physical and spiritual. He would shower and think that afterward he would emerge as a full person. He would not be separated, torn by the tension.

"Beautiful day for some traveling."

Sal looked at the old woman with the hat. She smiled at him.

"I suppose it is," said Sal. "I don't travel much."

"Ah! Are you nervous? You're shaking a bit."

"Very. I can't seem to keep my thoughts straight."

"Why are you going to San Francisco?"

"To see a friend."

"How very nice. How do you know this person?"

"We were very close, almost brothers."

"Good friendships are worth holding onto."

"I agree. I'm afraid to travel, though, so I haven't seen him in years."

"I'm sure it will be as if no time has passed at all."

"I hope so."

"Even if not, I think you'll like San Francisco. It's a beautiful place. It's almost perpetual spring there – it's warm in the sun, cool in the shade. I wear a jacket everywhere to keep from getting cold."

"Perpetual spring sounds lovely."

"It is. And you absolutely must see Alcatraz. My husband and I went the year it opened. It's fascinating."

"Is your husband traveling with you now?"

"No, he passed a few years ago."

"So did my father."

"Sad, but it's the way of things."

"It is."

The woman adjusted her hat. "I would also just say to stay away from The Castro and Tenderloin areas of the city. They're seedy, bawdy places. Chinatown, though, is worth a trip."

"Thank you for the recommendations."

A group of stewardesses passed by. The woman stood up.

"I think we're getting ready to board. I need to use the washroom."

Sal had been so lost in thought he forgot about the impending voyage. In less than an hour he would be suspended in the air flying over the city. His heart raced.

He knew he loved Arnie: had loved, loved, would love. The dread of flying had overshadowed this. Now as he saw the stewardesses preparing to board, as he saw his fellow travelers stand and begin to mill about, he realized that on the other side of the flight he would face new horrors. Arnie was with someone. Sal would watch them touch, kiss, smile at each other. He would remain stoic, but his heart would break.

His young wards at the bookshop had convinced him to go out to a few Chicago gay bars. The small brunette, who loved Olivia Newton-John, was possessed with the idea of finding love for Sal. They would see men in the bar and he would point.

"That one? What about that one there? That one looks a bit like the man in your pictures."

It was nice living more openly. The world was far from letting two men walk down the street, hand-in-hand, but in quiet, dark corners, men could brush up against each other, kiss, in relative safety. His own boys would scuttle to the shadows. Sal would sit with a drink and talk to anyone who listened. Over the course of the last several years, his group of friends had swelled. Meeting in a dark bar, the friendship would grow in the light of his bookshop. The local neighbors saw it as odd that his shop stayed open until ten, but that was when he did his business. In the late-night hours, the men could let go of their heterosexual posturing and relax over a cup of warm tea.

Sal stood behind the pilot in the boarding line. The woman taking the tickets smiled at the pilot as he passed. Sal also got a warm smile and an "Enjoy your flight!" The jetway was long, carpeted in gray. Sal wished it were some bright color. He was going to San Francisco, the heart of America's gay scene. The jetway should mirror that journey to somewhere bright, sunny, and flamboyant. But then, perhaps, gray was the best color for it. On the coasts gays had places in daylight to go, but in the country's heart their lives began at twilight. Their future as a people was unsure. Harvey Milk was dead. There were pockets of movement, but the shadows seemed the place they were destined to stay.

After the Bible study that Wednesday, he and Gertrude were the last two, as always. She ran her hand over her feet and looked accusingly at Sal.

"San Francisco next week?"

"Yes, I'll be gone."

"San Francisco."

"Yes."

She lay back on the couch and stared. "I know what San Francisco is Sal. Even watching the daily news, the world knows what that place is."

"It's a lovely destination."

Gertrude didn't smile. "I hope you're not backsliding."

"I would rather not discuss it now."

"George and the children are gone tonight. I made sure they'd be gone when we finished up."

"Gertrude…"

"Sal, I only say this because I care for you. You love God and he loves you and you cannot let this impulse destroy that."

"I haven't given into that impulse for a very long time."

"But how does one get to the impulse, Sal?"

"How does one…?"

"Temptation, Sal. You really think someone in your state should go to San Francisco, where the gay world is just a few steps away?"

"I think God would want me free to make that decision."

"I believe he'd hope you'd have the wisdom not to make it."

Gertrude knew nothing of his bookshop's after-hours secrets. "Gertrude, I will just say this, then let the matter rest. You live in a world built for you. The houses, the shops, the streets, the police, are structured to protect your interests, your way of life. This life itself comes naturally to you. You float through your days with the ease of bird through the air. I do not float. I do not fly here. Daily I battle demons that tear away at the fabric of a life that I struggle to hold together. While you see a smiling policeman, I see a man who may drag someone like me out into the street because he saw him expressing love for another person."

Gertrude raised her hand just as a student would do, to interject.

"Gertrude, I said this one thing, then let it rest."

Gertrude folded her arms. Her eyes narrowed.

"Happiness does not come easy to me. You know in the last years with father my well of joy has all but dried up." Sal stopped. He breathed. "But this trip will make me very happy. It has nothing to do with my impulses. It has everything to do with adventure. I have never been on a plane. I have not seen a dear friend for almost ten years. I have never seen the ocean. Gertrude, for you living comes pre-packaged in a box. Living for me is something I must search for. And, this week, I am going searching."

Silence fell. Outside the light in the June sky ebbed away, leading them toward dusk. Gertrude's pose relaxed. She turned to the window. Sal slumped his shoulders. He stared straight ahead.

"Sal, I'm not happy about this. But, I think what you say is valid. God put his children in the Garden of Eden so they would have a choice. Whether I like it or not, you go to Eden."

Sal sat next to the woman with the hat. She smelled of perfume. This must have been applied in the rest room. When Sal took his seat next to her, she turned and smiled.

"I'm very glad that this happened."

She reached out her hand. Sal took it.

"I think we'll make it just fine. Look out this window."

Sal looked out to the tarmac. The airport's windows were like eyes. The concrete structure looked imposing. It brought to mind a *Life* article he had read about East Germany.

"I think people try to think too much about it," the woman said. "They worry about the physics of flight, the turbines in the engine, the distance from the ground. It's a lot to think about. No wonder people are afraid of it."

"My fear is very simple. It's a long drop to the ground."

The woman laughed. "Well, terror is simple, the fear behind it is much more complicated." She pointed to a bird on the runway. "They fly with no problem." She pointed to herself. "I have flown dozens, if not a hundred times with no problem."

"This is very true."

"You should stop thinking about it and enjoy it."

"I think that's very good advice." Sal squeezed her hand. The woman turned to look out the window.

Sal relaxed slightly. Enjoy it. Perhaps that's what he should have been doing with the muddle the whole time. When the brunette boy pointed to someone at a bar, maybe he should walk over. They didn't have to kiss, become lovers, he could simply engage another person.

Arnie would be in San Francisco. He would be tan with his new longer hair and Tom Sellick mustache. He would be with his lover. Based on the most recent pictures, an African-American man with a beautiful body and wide smile. If they were happy that may be all Sal needed to see. They'd all been through so much. They deserved happiness. He deserved happiness.

Arnie had said they would go to the Gay Freedom parade. Sal imagined it as the smaller, jovial affair that took place in Chicago. There would be people yelling slurs at them. People like Gertrude would tell them that their happiness was not the right kind. On the other side would be people like him, free to ignore all of the hate for one afternoon. For a few golden hours they were protected in a refuge of camaraderie and fellowship.

As the airplane's engine roared, Sal slouched back into his chair. He was not thinking about the long fall to the ground, but ticker tape, confetti, and men walking together, hand-in-hand. "Perpetual spring", the woman had called it. A few words came to mind, verses. It had been a long time since they had come so easily.

Behold the sky, a rainbow of paper and light,
In jubilation, we walk forward, our hearts in flight...

IV.

1983-1984

Rasping, striving breaths came from Arnie. It was the end. Sal knew it. The doctors knew it. The man who showed up at his door less than a year earlier, tan, with a few purple lesions, was all but a corpse. It was all so fragile. Changing a few things here and there transformed youth and beauty completely. Arnie had devolved into a husk. His skin was only a case for what was inside. A few years ago, Sal would have been sure that the soul inside, the real person, would fly up to heaven. But now... But now.

Some things are hopeless.

It was a cruel twist. He had been through this with his father, in the trenches with death and disease. But here he was again; Arnie was just like his old man. He was kept alive by machinery. For someone so young, Sal had been surrounded by death for the better part of ten years.

Sal told only a few what was happening. When Arnie showed up at his door he didn't know what to say.

"Hello."

"Hi."

Two men stood six feet apart, like uncertain children.

They embraced. When Sal felt cold tears fall against his neck, he knew something was wrong. After he had been to San Francisco their relationship carried forward as a trusted friendship. Romance was never a possibility. He loved Arnie and Arnie respected him. An unscheduled arrival and tears meant that something was not good.

"It's AIDS." It was a few days after his arrival that he told Sal the truth. "I think the whole gay world is sick with it."

Sal had done what research he could. It was the world's dark secret. A hated populace was sick. Many thought it was for the best. In those first days, Sal chose to invest everything in Arnie. He had never been good at the game. When he returned from San Francisco he considered starting over. His boys took him to the bars and he looked for an opportunity. He imagined that someday a man would look at him and they would try to forge something long lasting.

Cold, cold, cold.

Muddled.

It was difficult to love in the way that Sal wanted. He lacked the easiness of his younger friends. Affection was difficult. After sex there was guilt. His psyche flitted between heaven and hell every second he was with a man. Time was taking its toll. He'd crossed from the panic of thirty into forty. He was not as affected in the new decade. Having experienced a love affair, he considered he may not be meant for a long-lasting coupling.

He told Clive, of course. One afternoon before Sal had to put him into the clinic, Arnie had collapsed and cut open his forehead. Sal found him on the floor, covered in his own blood. The next day at work he couldn't focus. Clive found him staring at a pile of periodicals in the back room.

"Arnie?" he asked.

"Yes."

"You know I don't like you two together."

"It's not that."

"What is it?"

Clive knew more about it than Sal did. He brought Sal brochures and even hosted an education night at the bookshop for the all the boys. They listened half-heartedly. They had youth on their side; for them, the disease was a ghost that haunted the gays on the coasts. In 1983 they were before Ryan White, before Rock Hudson, before *Life Magazine* told them "No One Is Safe from AIDS." Those days they were all just coming out of the denial; the virus spread, the mass media told them it was only for coastal homosexuals and intravenous drug users.

Gertrude knew. She pried it from him after one of their Bible studies. Now he never went to them; he had cut out God completely. To his surprise, Gertrude carried their friendship outside the bounds of the church. They got coffee early on Saturday mornings before he went to the hospital. She always looked perfect. He always dressed up for work, but on Saturdays with Gertrude he had to wear something even nicer. Saturdays he wore his Sunday best. Afterward he went to the clinic to sit with Arnie. Arnie's thoughts began to turn on Gertrude.

"Maybe I was wrong about her," he said once. "I think she does care for you."

"I think she's always been interested in things outside of her experience. I'm a keyhole into another world. I don't know if that means she cares, but I interest her at least."

"Here I sit dying and you are the one being cynical. Isn't that peachy."

It maybe was cynicism. Sal wasn't sure. Even in the depth of his gay despair he had never felt that his faith was fully tested. Homosexuality was something he pondered, tried to reconcile with God. AIDS was different. It was unbelievably different.

Death. Arnie's face grew more like a death mask every day. Sal saw the seconds of his life shed like dried skin. The lesions grew more abundant. Opportunistic infections plagued his daily life. He put on a happy face for Arnie. He'd sit quietly and recount the stories of the boys from the shop. Every evening for an hour he read from the book the lesbian book club had chosen for the month. Despite the low swinging scythe over the clinic, spirits were not low.

The clinic itself was a small sequestered room. Five beds were lined against the north and south walls. White curtains hung around them for privacy. When he read everyone hushed to listen. The curtains were pulled open and he could see all their faces. His voice would be the only sound some afternoons. Sal particularly remembered one October evening. An autumnal wind batted the window while he read from a story about the Stonewall riots. A nurse brought in lemonade and poured small glasses. There was ice; it tinkled.

The clinic had inadvertently become a haven. Almost every nurse who worked the floor did so voluntarily. The head nurse, a stalwart lesbian named Bea, often would come in after shifts, after Sal had left. She spoke rarely to him during the day. Arnie said she would sit and do needlework in the half-light.

"Tell me if you need anything," she'd said the first night, and little more after.

Sal made friends with all those men who lay beside Arnie in the clinic: Cedric, the African-American from Hyde Park; Joseph, the Mexican whose family disowned him at fourteen; Eugene, the most beautiful man he'd ever met. Sal became their friend, read to them, watched them die.

There were other visitors throughout the days. Cedric's mother, Lola, came every Sunday after church. She lied to her husband and said she had women's club. The old woman was a prolific knitter; she made sweaters and scarves for all the men who lay dying.

"You're all so skinny," she said to the men in hospital beds. "Wish I could give you some of my extra!" She'd shake her ample stomach and laugh. It was a contagious mirth; a chuckle from Lola meant the whole room erupted with joy.

Sal and Lola went outside together and sat. Often, one of them would cry.

"It's just a shame, Sal. It's just a shame."

"It's so unfair."

"Be careful thinking about fairness, baby. You keep putting yourself next to what you think is 'fair' you're always going to come up short."

"How do you keep from doing it?"

"I look to God. Only he can make you happy. He stops you from looking at everyone else and asks you to look inside yourself."

"I used to be devout."

"We all lose him now and again, honey. He keeps calling you back. Once you've seen him, you can't fully look away."

"I don't know if I'll pick up again."

"You will. Your Aunt Lola isn't going to let you keep pushing him away."

That same Sunday she told Sal a story about her pastor at church. He had grown up in The South. White people vandalized his home church as a child. They painted the n-word across the church door. They started a fire in the parsonage. The local, white fire department came and watched the house burn. Only when the fire threated to jump to a nearby municipal building did they turn on their hoses.

"But our reverend says his pastor was there at church that Sunday. He'd painted over all the bad words. That Sunday in his sermon he said that you could burn anything but hope. That, he says, is immutable, unchangeable, just like God hisself." Her eyes grew damp. "Our boys are in a burning building, but we have to look at the other side."

One Sunday Lola didn't come. Sal saw her later that week, decorated with a black eye and bruises up her arms.

"I'll make it when I can," she said. "Cedric's father found out…"

Sal led her outside and let her cry on his shoulder.

With Lola gone, Sal felt even more isolated. Bea would give him a polite nod every day but little more. Arnie grew more and more detached. He slept often. When he awoke, he was irritable. He was helpless, his body falling apart while his mind stayed sharp. Sal would read and be there. All he could do was be there.

In those moments, he was glad for his stoicism, his coldness. For years he thought it was a detriment. He couldn't hold onto a relationship. He was afraid of getting too close to someone, of being totally vulnerable. But with Arnie, and looking back, with his father, it kept him sane. It kept him strong.

One evening, on a cold night, he couldn't go. It was after he lost Lola. The previous evening Arnie didn't speak to him at all. Sal didn't know why he didn't go. The night may have been darker than usual; the sudden temperature drop may have unnerved him. Clive helped him close up the shop. After all was locked, Sal got out a bottle of wine.

"You're not going tonight?" Clive asked.

"Not tonight."

"You go every night."

"I know." Sal poured two glasses. "Thank you for helping out when I go."

"If it weren't for you I'd be on the street."

"I guess we're even then."

They spoke very little. Sal tapped his glass.

"Could you tell me some stories?" Sal asked. His eyes were wet. "What did you and the boys do last night?"

Clive looked at him. He hesitated just a moment and then didn't stop. "Well, last night nothing, but Todd had wanted to go out on Tuesday, so we just got a quick drink. He and Sam are kind of dating, but Sam is very odd, you know. It's a shame he's so handsome and so strange. I think we're all a little moody, though, with the holiday. Most of us have nowhere to go…"

"Oh, my. It's almost Thanksgiving, isn't it." Sal thought of his father, spectacles on his nose, and a goose cooking in the kitchen.

"It is."

The next day when Sal got to the hospital Arnie did his best to sit up.

"Sal! I thought… I was so worried…" his breath was short. He had to stop talking.

"No reason to worry…"

"Please, don't do it again. If I don't see you…"

Sal walked over and took Arnie's hand. He gently helped him sit fully up. Arnie's breath came in short, quick bursts.

"I won't do it again," Sal said tugging up his blanket. "Sorry to have worried you."

"I thought something happened."

"In the bookshop? The worst that could happen is getting a bruise from a falling copy of *Ulysses*."

Cedric had died that afternoon. Eugene, withered and frail, silently cried in the corner.

The time between Arnie's arrival in Chicago and the end was brief. He surfaced on Sal's stoop at the beginning of summer, thin but appearing healthy. They had a few months together in the apartment before he had to go to the clinic. One afternoon Sal came home early from the bookshop. Arnie was hanging his shirts across the room.

"There are dryers at the laundromat," Sal said.

"I know, but this is what we used to do in San Francisco," Arnie said. "The breeze would come in and shake them. My first roommate, Harry, had a never-ending supply of colorful shirts. When the sun hit right, it was like being in a disco. Everything smelled so fresh. The colors made our small place seem so alive."

They slept in the same bed but didn't have sex. It had never been the strength in their relationship. Arnie was also weak. In a little over a month after his arrival, his condition worsened. He needed to get a cane to walk properly.

"I come and wreck your life and can't even properly fuck you."

"I don't think I've ever been properly, enjoyably fuckable, so perhaps it's for the best."

Arnie grew tired early; Sal tucked him in. They'd kiss the way they always had. Sal, with closed lips, eyes shut tight. Arnie put his hand behind Sal's head and ruffled his hair. After the kiss, Sal went into the sitting room to read.

It wasn't even a year before he died, but the time stretched. In those sprawling months, Sal felt disconnected from his own being, as if he was watching his own life unfold on television. There were three acts to that tragedy. First: the two of them sharing Sal's small apartment. This was composed of good night kisses, quiet dinners, and, on Arnie's good evenings, walks to the lakefront to watch the sky turn from blue, to orange, to purple.

The second act was the hospital, the good parts of it. It was Lola laughing on Sundays; it was Cedric's soliloquys about his drag persona; it was Eugene, smiling brightly, giggling at the stories of those around him. These moments were before things were bad. Arnie asked daily when he could get his walking papers. There was still hope then.

The third act was the long winter. Arnie clung on until early spring. He wheezed and the machines hummed. Chicago was thawing. The birds woke Sal up in the morning. Sal put Clive in charge of the bookshop in the afternoons. Arnie could barely speak, but he would listen as Sal told him the usual day's business. Sal still read. He started *A Farewell to Arms*, but stopped at the first mention of rain. He hadn't thought about the implications of the book for those around him.

There were other flashes from that period, lamps in the darkness.

One was a sharp knock on his apartment door on a Saturday. He was dressed and ready to leave to meet Gertrude. His suit coat sat on the back of his living room recliner.

The girl at the door looked familiar, but Sal couldn't remember her. She was sheepish, but smiled uncertainly at the sight of him. She wore a thick, red coat. Her hair was covered by a knitted hat.

"Hello," she said.

"Hello, Miss."

The young woman hesitated for just one moment before she jumped forward and hugged Sal.

"I'm sorry," Sal said uncertainly. He did not pull back from the embrace. He missed the touch of others.

"Oh, I'm sorry! It's been years. Of course you wouldn't remember right off…" The girl removed her hat. A diamond ring flashed on her finger. "Susie Everly."

Sal smiled hugely. "Susie… It's been –"

"About ten years."

"Ten years."

Sal gently pushed her away. "Let me look at you."

Susie Everly retained her gangliness. Her smile remained exactly as Sal remembered it. Clive was the one who directed her to Sal's home. She stopped at the bookshop one rainy afternoon.

"Is this Sal Henry's shop?"

"It is."

"I'm an old friend."

Shyly, Susie put down her coat and looked around the room. Everything was in its place. She later described it to her fiancé as "spotless." It was not what she expected. It appalled even herself, but she was slightly disappointed.

"Everything is so orderly," she said. "It's just like your classroom."

"I can't believe you remember."

"How can you not when you had the books alphabetized. There were so many books. What did you call them?"

"It was a long time ago."

"Portals, I think it was." Susie crossed her arms. There was a trembling silence. Susie finished, in almost a whisper, "Portals to other worlds."

Sal nodded. He briefly remembered Susie's paper on *The Awakening*. She chose to write about Adele rather than Edna.

He had not had a guest in a long time. "Where are my manners? Susie, would you like some tea?"

"I would very much."

The two exchanged pleasantries. Sipping on the hot tea, they outlined what had happened in their lives. Sal provided only a bare skeleton; he avoided any piece of his history that alluded to homosexuality. Susie was engaged to a lawyer. She was a reporter for a small women's magazine.

"What kind of articles do you write?"

Susie looked at him blankly. "Mostly women's interest pieces. I've gotten in trouble several times for my 'socialist lean.'"

"I remember your papers in high school. You wrote about equal rights, for women, for blacks."

"You never said anything. There were others who did."

"We should let high school children think openly. The world tears them apart enough as it is. School should be safe."

"It wasn't for you."

Silence. Sal rubbed his mug. He pondered what she meant. What did she mean?

"You had to go. I know you had to go," she leaned closer.

"I didn't have to go. It was voluntary."

"It wasn't safe. You knew it. Not with what happened to –"

"I'd rather not talk about that. It's sordid stuff."

"I don't know the whole truth, but I imagine the rumors weren't completely inaccurate."

"It was complicated."

Susie leaned back. She took a drink from her mug. "We don't have to talk about that, if you don't want to."

"I'd rather not."

"But can we talk about the clinic?"

Sal's hands shook. It had to be a nightmare, something he could awake from. If he kept going and visiting Arnie, eventually he would wake up. It would be June and they'd both be healthy, intertwined in Sal's sheets. Arnie would laugh. "What do you think about this AIDS thing?" It would be a specter. It would be a *GayLife* headline and nothing more.

But Susie knew about him and Arnie. She knew about the clinic. She knew AIDS. She knew what AIDS meant about him.

"Mr. Henry...."

"Call me Sal, please," he said distantly.

"Sal, the people need stories. The press and the government are giving them abstraction. It's a deadly disease; it effects prostitutes, homosexuals, and drug users. That's what the world knows."

"Susie, I would rather..."

"Mr. He- Sal, here me out. I want to write a story about you and Mr. Bellows."

"I don't think anyone wants to hear that story."

"I think it could be a wonderful counterpoint to the awful, hateful..."

Sal coughed. Susie stopped and stared at him. He quietly said, "Susie, let's say I give you a story."

"That sounds wonderful."

"They'd find out about Arnie. They'd find out about everything that happened. Your tale of tragedy would be overshadowed by what happened at the high school."

"It would be anonymous –"

"It's not safe."

Susie pursed her lips. She smoothed her skirt.

"Susie, I know you want to help us. I know you want to change the world. You always have."

Susie's eyes gleamed. "I always have."

"But let Arnie die quietly. There are other men in the clinic with stories that aren't tainted like ours. I could introduce you to them. Make a hero out of one of them."

Susie looked up. "Really?"

"They may not talk to you. They may."

Susie stood up. Sal thought briefly that she was getting her coat to leave, but she began to pace the room. She wrought her thin hands as she walked in a circle. "Do you think I'm some silly girl, Mr. Henry? Do you think I'm the same girl who used to bat her eyelashes at you in class?"

"I never thought that."

"My fiancé and I went to visit family in Iowa. At a small diner they wouldn't give us service. In 1983. They said it was better for us to go somewhere else."

"People are cruel."

"So, we fight."

"When we can."

Susie stopped pacing and looked at him intently. "I wish there was more I could do. I wanted to help you. You of all people know the power of stories."

"The right story at the right time is a powerful thing."

"It's a beautiful thing."

Susie got her coat. She crossed the room and hugged Sal. Her bony arms squeezed him tightly. "I'm coming back to see you. I'll bring a book."

"I'll ask if anyone has a story to share with you."

Susie clutched his hand. "I know my situation is different, but we're all fighting together. I want to help."

"You have already."

Another light in that dark period was Thanksgiving. Sal brought some of the boys to the hospital in the evening. They made cookies during the day and brought them to the patients who were well enough to enjoy them.

Eugene looked exhausted but sat up. His smile was no longer the beacon it had been, but it was wonderful to see. One of the older patients, Lenny, had been taken to an intensive care unit after a heart attack. Arnie was frail, his eyes were beginning to sink in, his cheek bones grew more and more prominent. He munched on a cookie. After a few bites he set it down.

"I think I'd just prefer to admire the decoration."

It happened for only a short time that visit. When the small group arrived, it had been with solemnity. But at some point in the evening, for a brief moment, everyone forgot the reason why they were there. Sal realized it just too late. He was sitting on Arnie's bed, his hand on his lover's leg. Clive stood; he emphatically recounted a story from the previous weekend.

"So, at this point we'd seen the old goat at Lady Bug, Sidetrack, and Little Jim's. He kept making eyes at Roger, but, you know, Roger wanted nothing to do with it. So, he buys a round of drinks and sends them over. They come over and everyone just runs. I had no idea, because I was in the bathroom, so I get to the table with a tray of drinks and don't think anything of it. Then the old codger comes over, and that's when I realize it! He was my parents' neighbor! Mr. Goldberry with four kids and a wife! I obviously haven't been home since I was fifteen, and he doesn't realize it's me, but I feel obligated to tell him, you know, so I say, 'Mr... Goldberry?'" Clive giggled and put his hand to his mouth. "Well, Mr. Goldberry very slowly realizes who I am. I'm not sure how he knew for sure, but he acts like nothing is going on! He leans forward and says, 'Clive! I'm glad I ran into you, I'm looking for a degenerate.'"

"Degenerate?!" Eugene's voice squeaked.

"You won't believe it!" continued Clive. "So, he says, 'I came in here because my dog is sick and I think one of these degenerate lads could help him out with a good ...'" Clive's lip went up and he motioned the act of masturbating.

Arnie roared. "He asked you to flog his dog's log?"

"Yes. He asked as if it was the only question one would ask in a gay bar."

The other boys who knew the story laughed hysterically.

"Was it a joke?" Sal asked.

"I don't know! I could barely speak, for obvious reasons, and he said, 'Well, I'll tell your folks I ran into you!' And then he just disappeared. Poof!"

"Poof, for sure," Arnie quipped.

"But to have that story ready," Clive said in amazement. "He didn't miss a beat."

"I remember when I was young and would go out near Belmont Harbor looking for sex, I'd say I'd lost my dog," Eugene laughed.

"My parents found my muscle magazines under my bed," Arnie snorted. "I said I was failing gym class and needed to do extra research."

"What did you say about the pages sticking together?" Clive asked stroking his chin.

It was in that moment that it happened. They no longer were sick or healthy, or dying or doomed, but just men. Everyone laughed together. Arnie, without thinking of being sick took a nonchalant bite of his cookie. Sal tapped Arnie's leg and looked back at him with a large smile.

Then the spell broke and a nurse came in with some medication. The room grew quiet. Sal once tried to capture the moment in a poem, but the words never came. It was one of the cracks he had told Arnie about before he left Chicago. Through a crack in time and space, he briefly saw his image of God.

"I miss Cedric," Eugene said casually. "I can only imagine the stories he could tell."

"What he did at the balls. What was his drag name?"

"Hattie Bushnell."

"Emphasis on the bush," Sal, Eugene, and Arnie said together.

Sal and the boys only stayed a bit longer. The autumn night was clear and cold. Leaves crunched on the sidewalk as they took a seat in the car. Allen, one of the new boys, sniffled in the back.

"They're all going to die, aren't they?" he asked. "I used to see Eugene at Sidetrack," Allen said. He stopped.

Clive played the *Thriller* cassette on the way back to the book store.

In all their years of friendship Sal knew little more than the names of Arnie's family. Right after he arrived in Chicago he made it very clear they would not be involved in his final act.

"You're all I have," he said. "In San Francisco everyone is living in terror. Rick left me a few months before I got ill. I was tired all the time. He said I bored him. He's in New York. I needed to go to the place that most felt like home."

"Okay," Sal said.

"When all that happened, you never once blamed me. You never once said it was my fault or that I deserved it."

"I think deserve is a dangerous term."

"I was an asshole. I deserve this."

Sal went into the kitchen.

"Say it, Sal. Say I deserve it." He was weeping. He shook in the doorway. "Forgive me," he said. "Forgive me."

"It's hard to forgive what is forgotten," he said.

Why was it so easy to forgive? There was no way to describe Arnie and his first date, Arnie's unbuttoned shirt and smile. Arnie was the man who turned his faucet to flood. Words failed at describing their first day meeting on the grass outside of the high school. It was magic that bound them together. Arnie had said it, and it was true.

Home.

When Arnie arrived and the darkness spread, it was this invisible thread that wrapped them together. The last book Sal read to Arnie and the other boys in the ward was *The Wizard of Oz*.

There was fear and horror and sadness, but Arnie was the love the world had given him. Their brokenness together shaped something larger. This something bloomed in their seconds alone, in the quiet tick ticking of the clock in Sal's apartment, in the flutter of the shirts that were strung across his living room windows.

When they took Arnie out of the hospital room in a body bag, no one remained of the group he had spent the fall with. They were buried in the ground. Bea gently squeezed his arm in the hallway: "You'd think I'd be used to it now," she said quietly. "But each one of them is mine in a way."

Eugene's mother came three days after his death. She sat in a plastic chair, wringing her hands. She said very little.

"He said it was the end," she said. "I came too late on purpose. I couldn't watch..."

That was all she said for the better part of an hour. Outside it rained.

In that moment, Sal remembered he had never asked if one of the men would share a story with Susie. But it was too late then. All his friends' stories had ended.

The day Arnie died, April 4th, it did not rain. It was 48 degrees, wind speed 6 knots. Sal wrote this all in a notebook. Poetry had all but dried up so he recorded a simple list of facts from the day.

The Challenger I launched.

Gloria Swanson died.

It was Anthony Perkins' birthday.

That day, at the end of the column of figures he attempted a poem.

Home, where the heart is,

Where it finds its place to rest.

Sal put his notebook away. He had no energy left to write. In his imagination, all he saw were specks of dust, Arnie, drifting from an urn, into the blue of the lake.

V.

1980

Roaring, caterwauling, reveling: the streets were alive with the sights and sounds of gay freedom. A Ferris Wheel turned at the festival. Marching bands, floats, Episcopalians, and men dressed as nuns passed by in the parade. Someone told Sal there were 200,000 people there to celebrate.

It was all too much for him. He knew it would be when Arnie explained the festival to him in his letters.

Leather, drag, underwear, tits, the Gay Freedom Day hoopla is everything your mother told you to watch out for and more.

He arrived at the airport on Friday. Throughout the flight his nerves had been fine; he had almost forgotten that he was hurtling through the air during the middle of the voyage. When he peered out the window and saw the blue of the ocean, his nerves started to return. During the entire landing, the woman in the hat had to hold his hand.

It had been a relief to be on the ground again.

In the taxi ride to Arnie's apartment in The Mission, Sal briefly ran through the history of his weekend home from the travel books he had read: former home of the Ohlone people, spot of the city's founding, now known for its heavy concentration of lesbian people. Upon Sal's arrival, Arnie apologized for the lack of action the first night; the plan was to stay in and relax. He promised the rest of the weekend would be for drinking in the bars and heightened revelry.

In the small group gathered in Arnie's apartment, Sal could tell everyone was disappointed in him. Arnie was tan with long, shining brown hair. Sal wore slacks and a shirt he had clearly bought the day before. The other men made dressing seem easy. Their shorts clung to their toned thighs. Their shirts fell on their shoulders and hugged their chests nicely. They spent their evenings using nautilus machines, toning their lithe bodies.

Sal had spent the better part of an hour finding the shirt that now embarrassed him. It had been a long time since he cared what he looked like. When he went with the boys to the gay bars it was in his work clothing. He dressed dourly for work in the bookshop, as he had for school. Only on Fridays would he allow himself to wear something other than a shirt and tie. One day when he had worn jeans, Clive dropped a stack of books.

"Jeans? Sal, welcome to the 80's!"

The small two-bedroom Arnie shared was dingy. Mattresses were on the floor and cups lay strewn about. Arnie worked at a local mom and pop restaurant. He abandoned teaching. The thought of him getting any references was laughable.

That first night Arnie and his friend's smoked weed in the apartment. Sal put the joint to his lips but didn't inhale. He wondered what life would have been like if he'd come to San Francisco in his youth. The other men romanticized their home.

"My God," said one with a military buzz cut, "there will never be another parade like '78."

"'Give'em hope!'"

"That was the only night I drank as a political statement. Fuck Anita Bryant and her fucking orange juice."

"You drunk is quite the statement," Arnie said. "Slurred and incoherent, but quite a statement."

Sal laughed politely as he rose to use the restroom. It would be quiet in there.

Why had he come? Every bone in his aging body pushed against it. He didn't want to be drunk. One of Arnie's friends had already mentioned he would loan him some poppers for the "fucks" he predicted Sal would have over the weekend. The thought of random sex to Sal was unfathomable. Already there had been allusions to Crisco in the bathhouse, to turning over and letting an unknown body enter you. Far from judgment, the emotion he felt was fascination. He had no desire to join in with Arnie and his group of friends, but he enjoyed listening to discussion anyway. To be that free, to be that reckless and wild, was something he could never do.

Why had he come? He was in love with Arnie. That was why. But the reason behind that why was unknown. It perhaps was not a chance to act on the love, but instead to bury it. Arnie had alluded to his lifestyle and Sal wanted to see it. If he saw what Arnie was now, it would be an opportunity to let go completely. They were on other sides of the country; they were on other sides of understanding capital-l Love.

Sal washed his hands and went to the kitchen. Arnie followed him in. He smiled as Sal opened the refrigerator and took out a beer.

"They're calling you The Monogamist," he said.

"I think they're disappointed in your choice of friend."

"They are not disappointed. Confounded, maybe."

"Confounded?"

"I've been a little wilder here than I was in Chicago." He hesitated. "I mean, I've embraced a different idea of sexuality. Here we are stripped free of our psyche's oppression."

Sal felt sweat form along his brow. He felt ashamed. Arnie looked younger than he had ten years ago. He had bloomed over the past decade. Sal had receded; he had become his father. Arnie had trimmed up, grown into his face and features. Sal had grown fat, jowly. At one time it made sense they were lovers. Now, the only relationship strangers would draw between them was father and son.

Arnie grew shy. "I'm really glad you came, Sal."

"Hmm," Sal said smiling.

"What hmmm?" Arnie laughed. He looked to the floor. "But it's very good to see you. I know you may hate all of this, but I wanted to show you. I wanted to show you why I moved and why I stayed."

"I believe there were other reasons for the move, but I can see why you stayed."

It was silent for a moment. Arnie crossed the room and embraced Sal. He pulled him tightly. Before either could stop, they were crying.

"I missed you," Sal said.

"I missed you, too."

The others had heard the emotional exchange. Conversation paused for a moment before resuming at double pace.

Arnie pulled away and wiped his eyes. "Look at us old queens!"

"We obviously won't tell anyone about this little show of emotion."

Arnie grabbed some stray napkins on the counter and handed them to Sal. Tears turned to laughter as they dabbed their faces.

"Rick seems very nice," Sal said. "And quite handsome."

"We met at a bar. He was such a bitch, I couldn't resist."

"I see your type is the same."

"You were hard to replace, but I think I found a West Coast substitute."

"My figure is a little better, but he'll do."

In the living room the mood had changed. Another newcomer was being fawned over by the men. A Queen song was blaring in the background.

When Sal and Arnie entered, the men paused their flirtation and turned their attention to Sal. They may not have thought he was much, but they knew he meant something to Arnie.

"How is Chicago's scene, Sal?"

"I don't go out really that often. I do go to some bars close to my shop, but I never venture outside of that area. I've heard good things about Carol's. Some of the boys that visit the bookstore go to Unicorn or Man's Country."

"My friend, John, went out to Chicago about a year ago. He wasn't too impressed. He did enjoy Man's Country's breakfast," one of the men said through giggles.

"I'm sure it's not much compared to here."

"The bathhouses here are sensual experiences, Sal. I think after the parade you'll be drunk enough to enjoy it," Rick said.

"Do you know what fist fucking is, Sal?" One of the younger boys asked with a smirk.

"It sounds self-explanatory," Sal said uncomfortably.

"We could just take you to the Bulldog Baths. You could roam the cellblock."

"I think Sal is an adult and can make his own decisions," Arnie interjected. "After some drinking tomorrow, we'll see what he's interested in. Believe it or not, Sal, we could just go to one of the parties and have some drinks and dance. Not every night out ends in fist fucking."

"That is a relief."

With Arnie's polite rebuke, the boys backed off of teasing Sal. Talk turned to the parade, to the expectations of the floats and marchers, to a list of possible fucks over the next few days. Sal finished his beer and opened another. After their initial uncertainty over Sal, they began to warm to their Midwest visitor. Feelings for the other new addition to their circle also warmed; the fawning turned to open flirtation.

Sal looked at him through a slightly drunken haze. He was young, very pretty. He looked to be Mexican or South American, his skin a beautiful, coffee brown. His eyes were bright, chocolate-colored orbs, sparkling in the dim lights. It must be something, Sal thought. To come from nowhere, to not belong, to have your desires shamed and hated, and then sit in a room of beautiful young men who desire what you desire. Beautiful young men who desire you.

Sal knew why Arnie had stayed out here. Walking through the streets it made perfect sense. The entire city was a place of boundless hope. The streets rose higher, lifting to new horizons, different vistas. If you climbed to any height, you could see blue water, blue sky. What appears to be walls of streets surrounding you are actually pathways to different, unending views.

Timoteo, Teo, the brown-skinned boy leaned into Rick. It should have shocked Sal, but it didn't. They kissed passionately. Rick took Teo's hand and led him to one of the other men gathered. Teo and the other man kissed.

Arnie smiled and leaned into Sal. "Does it shock you?"

"Maybe a few hours ago," said Sal. "But I recognize now that the paradigm has shifted."

Teo, Rick, and the other boy walked to the bedroom. Arnie stood up.

"We'll be done in a bit, Sal. Do you need anything?"

"Actually," Sal said, "could I have your keys? A walk would be nice."

Arnie handed him the keys. Before he closed the door to his bedroom, Sal heard Teo moan. In his brief view through the open door he saw Rick standing nude, gently caressing his own nipples.

The other men who had not joined in the sexual encounter continued to smoke. The music had moved from Queen to Pink Floyd.

Outside was quiet. Sal was among residences that lined the street in an interesting variety of styles and colors. A cool breeze rustled trees above his head. He again thought of his book, of the history of entertainment, life and horror in this area. The native people were slaughtered, but now, from the ashes, a new, hopeful life blossomed for his own ostracized people. Out of fire, destruction, holocaust, there could be hope.

The trees continued their gentle song overhead. Voices drifted down the streets, some in English, some in Spanish. The stillness brought on melancholy in Sal. He took a seat on the curb.

If only I were more attractive, he thought.

If only I were younger, this lifestyle would be an open door rather than a snow globe I can only watch from above.

If only Arnie had stayed. If Sal had known this is what he wanted, maybe he could have been different. He could have gotten on the Nautilus machines and firmed and toned up. He could have gotten them some weed, membership at a bathhouse.

The curb Sal sat on was cool. He had always imagined California as heat and sunshine, but San Francisco proved to be cool and sharp. He thought of the old woman's words: "perpetual spring." Maybe again, this is what called the homosexuals out West. Even the weather was moderate, never extreme. After lives of extreme, why not someplace where the world was consistent and cool in the evening? In truth, Chicago still felt like a war zone for gay men. They were creeping into the open, but nowhere near the explosion in the light he had seen already in San Francisco.

If only.

He slept that night on one of the couches. His back ached the morning of the parade. Despite Arnie's promises, Teo and Rick's screaming was heard far into the night.

Some of those gathered got up early. Rick had pulled a bottle of champagne from his closet and gave Sal the first glass of mimosa.

"I don't think you're quite ready for this," he said.

"I've seen a lot," Sal said. "I think I'll be fine."

Sunlight shone through the windows. Sal thought of the sun's rays shining from the east, through Chicago, onto the cheap plastic table where he sat with his mimosa. Teo entered the kitchen in only a towel. He puckered his lips and took the seat across from Sal.

"Good morning," he purred. Overnight he had gone from boy to man.

"Good morning," Sal said.

"I can hardly wait. This is going to be a magical day."

"Truly magical," said Arnie. He put a dish of scrambled eggs on the table. "It's not much but a little sustenance before a day of drinking and merrymaking."

Teo devoured the plate. Sal didn't feel hungry.

The other boys dragged themselves into the kitchen. Their eyes were red, their clothes wrinkled. The lively characters from the previous evening had blurred and receded into the apartment's background. Sal let the undrunk mimosa sit in front of him. He delicately tapped the glass and watched the bubbles rise.

"Champagne seems too light for the morning, Rick. Where's the vodka?"

Rick handed the man a bottle. He didn't get a glass. The bottle tipped up and he took a long drought.

"San Francisco Breakfast," Rick said to Sal.

The Castro was wild. Gay men filled his view in every direction. Arnie led them down Market Street.

"I think Church and Market is the best place. It's right in the thick of it."

Sex was the word that described everything: muscle men, men in leather harnesses, women with their nipples exposed. Drag queens cut through the sex with comedy, but they were the exception and not the rule. In Chicago sex was a dripping faucet, here it was a deluge.

A large-bellied man in leather, wearing earrings grabbed Sal's ass. "Hey, baby," he said.

Sal again felt overly conscious of his clothes. He didn't have time to shame himself in front of a mirror as he had before he left Chicago. In the presence of beauty, glamor, and grotesque, he felt his tawny brown pants and checkered shirt stood out the most.

Arnie wore a loose-fitting red shirt and short pants. His legs were mostly exposed. All the other men wore sunglasses, while Sal covered his eyes with his hand. "Not much use for sunglasses in Chicago," he tried to joke.

"Don't you have the sun?" Teo asked earnestly.

Sal's understanding of the event was ripped into two halves. Around him was gay emancipation. A few boys who came to his own shop displayed such confidence, holding hands in the open, kissing in the open – the open. Juxtaposed to all this was a carnival of sin. Men wore nothing. Floats drifted by advertising sex. Behind the sex were Methodists. The San Francisco world was paradox, boundaryless. His joy was mixed with sadness. Love for him was his mother and father, sexless, sitting peacefully on the couch.

The gay world he had emerged into was chaos. Love was unbounded. Grab three friends and go to the back room. Lovers mix with lovers – the open. Sal wondered how Arnie felt when Rick caressed Teo's young body. He remembered Arnie and his sex together. It was jilted. In contrast to the gay freedom the parade celebrated, it was cold, dark. One night Sal had gotten up and wept. In that moment, he was torn again, experiencing love, but fighting the self-loathing the world had fused into him.

Muddled.

A PFLAG group walked by. An older woman, gray hair shining waved to all those gathered. The crowd roared. Sal thought about what quiet Annabelle would think of this crowd of men and women.

"You look so pensive!" Arnie yelled above the din.

"I'm thinking about a lot," Sal shouted back.

"That was always your problem, Sal! Don't think! Live!" He winked at Sal and turned to Rick. They kissed.

If he stopped thinking, he would cease to be. But perhaps he deserved an interruption. The woman on the plane had given him the same advice, and for the most part, it worked. Aside from the bumpy landing, he embraced his time in the sky. *You should stop thinking about it and enjoy it.*

When the parade ended, he walked with the boys to the festival. The sites of the simple, fun carnival rides and games helped calm his emotions. It wasn't all sex and shock.

The Ferris Wheel turned. The other boys went up but he didn't want to ride. It wasn't because he was afraid; he simply preferred to watch the wheel spin from afar.

It reminded him of Chicago. The Ferris Wheel had been at The World's Fair. He'd read about Burnham's white city and the beauty at Jackson Park. At the fair, goers had looked at replicas of Christopher Columbus's ships, they'd marveled at electric lights, and seen moving pictures.

The wheel was history, around him the present. But time was slipping by, their present moving to past. In a few decades, the world would not remember that Sal Henry stood at this spot and watched the wheel turn. All these boys living in the present moment, their sex, their lives, would be nothing but the memories of a few old men.

Arnie got off the wheel and ran to Sal.

"What next, Sal? It's your first time here. What do you think? A party? A bar? Disco?"

Sal laughed. "Let's do what Teo wants," he said winking at the young man. "I don't think I can have as much fun as him, but I can certainly enjoy watching you all."

"You're not dead, Sal!" Rick put his arm around the old man. "My job is to get you some sex tonight."

Arnie put his arm around Sal, too. The three of them, Arnie, Rick, and Sal stood in a line.

"Let's grab a drink!" Sal said. "We are gay and today is our day."

"It is most certainly our day!" Arnie kissed Sal's cheek.

It was the first time Sal said it out loud. "Gay." He would stop thinking for the day. He would stop thinking of the past, the future. Today was the present. He would sit back and enjoy the flight.

VI.

1990

Shwee-twee-twee.
Shwee-twee-twee.

Birds chirped in the early morning. The cement seat chilled Sal through his trousers. It had rained for days. Chicago spring entered as it always did, with a day too good to believe – sunny, warm, green shoots of grass rising up – the next day had been snow. Since then the wind and rain had been incessant. The sky was iron gray.

Sal moved north after Arnie. Lake View was getting expensive. His new shop and home were on Clark Street, not too far from where he had taught all those years ago. The boys came into his store rarely. The only one who stuck around consistently was Clive. They sometimes met for coffee or a drink after work. Clive acted as if Sal was normal. He mentioned the old boys and talked about his nights out, the new bars, the new boys.

Sal still kept his small home tidy. Out of habit he strung his shirts across the east windows to dry. He kept a few pictures of Arnie. They were old ones. The pictures he took in San Francisco had been burned. San Francisco poisoned Arnie.

Time was no longer separated in days, seasons, or hours. It flowed indiscriminately, unmarked. Sal kept no calendars and his shop opened every day. Business was fine. Investments and money left by his father helped him live conservatively. He made a large profit selling his old store, enough to give a cushion.

The outside world receded following Arnie's death. For a time, he pretended to move with his usual earnestness, but it was no use. God had abandoned him. His love story had ended. When he stopped seeing God, the poetry died away as well. He kept busy growing plants and going to art exhibits, alone. Behind his back Clive and the boys called him The Ghost.

"He doesn't seem sad," Clive would say, "but he's detached. I think you could murder someone in front of Sal and he would keep sipping his tea and remark on the weather."

Aside from Clive, the other threads to the outside world were Susie and Gertrude.

Susie's letters now came postmarked from California. Her letters were filled with stories of her exploits in women's groups, in protests, in her continued writing efforts. In one letter, she said it was her duty to open portals for others.

Susie's letters Sal put on his refrigerator. He would re-read them over and over again. Gertrude's letters he tossed out with other rubbish.

The anger that had burned through Sal during Arnie's sickness erupted full force after his death. God was the target of the ire. Since he had no terrestrial manifestation, Gertrude became the embodiment of injustice on earth. He thought of those conversations in her living room, her chastising and preaching in the years after Arnie and him had had their tryst. In her pursed lips over coffee, he knew that as hard as she may try, she would never accept him. His dying love in a hospital was an abomination to Gertrude DuBois. He was the freak that gave life to her dull, heterosexual lifestyle. To her, he was a carnival act, a side show.

But Gertrude had been relentless. After Arnie's death and Sal initially cut her out of his life, there had been silence. Then in 1985, the first letter. That one had been the hardest for him to ignore. It sat on his table for two weeks before, after a hard day, he tossed it into the garbage.

Then the next had come a few months later. In early 1987, they came monthly.

The monthly flow of letters wasn't interrupted for three years. The letter, with its address written in Gertrude's perfect script, came every month, and every month Sal tossed it into the garbage. At a certain point the act became automatic.

Then that spring she had showed up in his shop. She remained perfect. Her fair face had a few new lines, but, if anything, they only added to her glamor. Her head was wrapped in a scarf, covering her long, blond locks.

Sal's heart pounded in his chest. He expected her to be angry, accusing. She was not.

"Everything looks the same," she said. "I haven't been in your shop in almost 10 years and everything is in its place."

"I'm a creature of habit."

"Bad ones, I would say, based on what Clive has told me."

"You talked to Clive?"

"You didn't answer my letters; I had to figure out a way around."

Sal moved past Gertrude and began mindlessly handling a pile of books. "It's nice to see you."

"Is it?" Gertrude clasped her hands together. "Time has changed us both, I think. And in reviewing our relationship, I don't think it was ever nice."

"Well, then, what was it?"

Gertrude looked out the front door. "I haven't quite found the word."

Clive was not in the shop that day. He had moved on to a professional role at a marketing firm. His appearances in the shop were voluntary. Sal barely paid him more than he had when he started in the mid-70's. The shop was lonelier than it had ever been. In the awkward silence between himself and Gertrude, he had never wished more for Clive to pop his head in, for his old friend to crack a dirty joke.

"Sal, can we just talk?" Gertrude softened. "I want to talk about it."

"It?"

Gertrude rubbed a button on her spring coat. "You don't know?"

Sal shook his head.

"You didn't read any of the letters?"

Sal returned to pawing at the pile of books.

Gertrude looked out the door again. She took a deep breath. "I don't want to talk about this here. It's your place of business. Are you free this weekend?"

"I think I may have –"

"Stop pretending, Sal," Gertrude scolded. "Clive told me you only leave to buy food and more plants for your garden."

"I can make time."

"Saturday morning at ten – meet me over by the beach at the end of Bryn Mawr. We'll sit. We'll talk."

Before Sal could say anything, the door shut behind her. He trembled. For the first time in a long while his mind opened slightly, an empathetic light shone into the selfish gray waste of his brain. In the years he had received Gertrude's letters, he had never fathomed she needed him. It had always been a matter of her wanting to experience more of his freak life, compare it to her own unblemished existence. But when she mentioned 'it', pain had crept across her face; when Sal said he did not read the letters, it looked as though he had physically harmed her.

It was this sudden awakening that brought him to the steps near Kathy Osterman beach. To his left, the tiny lighthouse sat impassively. The water was turbulent, a cold gray-green. Along the horizon, the sky was the color of cinder blocks. Birds sang, tentatively.

Gertrude arrived exactly at 10. Despite the weather, she had on her full make up. Atop her head was a large lavender hat.

"Hello," Sal said. The rancor from their first meeting had ebbed.

"Hello, Sal," she said.

"I'm sorry for Thursday. I don't know…" Sal rubbed his hands on his trousers.

"Sorry about what?"

"I wasn't pleasant; I was mean. Can we please start over again?"

Gertrude politely nodded. "Let's do."

Sal weakly smiled. "Gertrude, it's very good to see you."

"It's very nice to see you, Sal."

"How is your family?"

Gertrude looked down at her shoes. "The children are very well, all things considered."

"What should they be considering?"

"George died. He passed about a year ago."

"I'm so sorry."

Gertrude clasped her hands together. "It was difficult. He was sick for almost two years – a little more."

"What was it?"

Gertrude gently took Sal's hand. "I think I should also apologize."

Sal balked. "What for?"

"I don't think I treated you like a friend. The whole time we were in Bible study together, I… I think I thought of you as charity."

Sal nodded. "It felt that way."

"And for that I'm sorry. You deserve more than sympathy. I was… not a wise woman in my thirties."

"I've never been wise. I don't know how to be anything anymore. I just live. One day at a time. It's simple, but day-by-day I wake up and I act out my life. I live quietly."

Gertrude squeezed Sal's hand. Tears were forming around her eyes. She tapped her thumb on the side of her leg. Her mouth moved to speak, but no sound came out.

"Gertrude, let's talk about it," Sal said. "If there's anyone who knows anything about losing loved ones it's me. Between Dad and Arnie, I've seen more of what sickness can do than…"

"It was AIDS, Sal. George died of AIDS."

Sal pulled his hand away from Gertrude's. He rubbed a hand through his thinning hair. "But… Gertrude – how? Is he –"

Gertrude shook her head. "No," she laughed, suddenly, loudly. "No, he definitely isn't like you."

"Then…?"

"Blood transfusion, they think, just like Ryan White. We went down to see Elizabeth at Stanford. It was her first year there. After spending the weekend with her, I suggested we visit Los Angeles or San Francisco. George loved the idea of Alcatraz, so we went."

"My god."

"It was a freak accident getting on a local bus. George slipped, he caught the pointed end of the fare collecting machine. It ripped open his shirt, gashed his arm. He's a hemophiliac, so I knew the drill." Gertrude spoke evenly. This speech was rehearsed. "We took him to a hospital. He got the blood, stitches – and a little surprise."

"Gertrude – I…"

"He was tired at first. He was very tired. He sweated in the night. Then it moved on from there. He got the purple spots. He died about two years after the bus incident of toxoplasmosis. Cats get toxoplasmosis."

The birds continued their wary song. The water slapped against the concrete wall below them. If Sal had heard this news secondhand, he would have felt vindicated. For so long Gertrude had made him the subject of her charity. He had been her entertainment. But now she was sitting before him. She was old, humbled. Watching her, Sal felt no sense of victory. They were all casualties in this war. The clock of Gertrude's steady ticking life had stopped chiming at its regular intervals. Life, Sal supposed, stops all of these clocks at some point.

"Gertrude, I'm so sorry."

"What killed Arnold? What small thing dealt the final blow?" she asked quietly.

Sal hesitated. "Pneumonia. He could barely breathe at the end."

Despite the weight of their revelations, the air felt lighter. Sal looked at Ardmore Beach beside them. It was desolate now, but in a few short months it would be full of people. There would be children, families. Summer would be at its height. The cold water of Lake Michigan would refresh, renew those who immersed themselves. Sal didn't care for summer except for the rain. Dipping one's toes in water was fine, but standing in the rain, letting the storm pass and feeling the world washed new was better.

"So," Gertrude said.

"So," Sal said.

"Now you get to tell my why you've become a recluse."

"I'm not a recluse."

"Clive said you hide away in your bookshop."

"I don't have many friends, so I do keep to myself."

"Well, then let's get you out. My new church…"

"New?"

Gertrude wrinkled her nose. "I couldn't stay where we were. Word got out… The rumors. You remember Mrs. Hinkley?"

"I used to watch TV at her house after service. She'd cook dinner."

"She was relentless. When word got out that George had AIDS… you can imagine. He was a sinful homosexual, and I was the wife that couldn't satisfy him."

Sal shook his head. "Why are we so cruel to each other?"

"When you see the dark side of God it makes you think."

"I've lived there. It does make you think."

The years between Arnie and the moment with Gertrude were darkness, slowly turning to gray. He did just as he said: day-by-day he woke up and acted out life. It was artifice – all the world's a stage. He often read Shakespeare. Hamlet was his favorite. To be or not to be… The lines were magnified in his depression. Despite the sadness, the constant dark, he never wanted to take his own life. His hobbies kept him interested. He loved caring for his plants. When some of the old boys would come to his shop, he delighted in their stories of the evolving Halsted landscape. He was not meant for the light, for the world above. His world was internal, obsessed with good. In San Francisco, he had realized that. These other men could play the game. They moved fluidly with their sexuality, between their relationships, through love. Sal was solid. He could not reform. What had happened with Arnie broke him, cracked him. His fate was paralysis in this state.

"Sal, let's start a book club," Gertrude clapped her hands together. "It will be like Bible study but minus the judgment and the God."

"Have you stopped believing?"

"Sal, I could never stop. At the very beginning, when the doctor spelled it out, 'H-I-V' – I went into a rage. I blamed God. I hated him. Hate evolved into a sort of acceptance. That's when I believed the disease was my punishment… for – you." Gertrude half-smiled.

"I don't think I warrant that tough of a punishment."

"None of us do." Gertrude stood up. "Can we walk?"

Sal stood. His bones were beginning to hurt. When his father had complained about these aches and pains he had laughed them off. He was quickly becoming old. Gray shot through his brown hair. He had lost some weight in his solitude, but his body had permanently lost the form, hardness of youth.

They walked together away from the beach and back toward Bryn Mawr and the large pink hotel. Sal offered Gertrude his arm.

The only sound was their steps on the grass, then gravel, finally the light taps of their shoes on the sidewalk. Sal had not spoken to anyone in a long time, at least not truly spoken: his own, honest voice. In fact, there perhaps had not been a time when he did speak without withholding some piece of himself from his friends, from his family, from Arnie, from everyone. Gertrude was the closest he had ever come to it. At Bible study she pried at him. Her questions were pointed. Even at school about his syllabus, she tore into him. She did not allow half-answers. She always drove at the truth. In her youth it had made her unnerving, insatiable. The natural evolution was the placid creature he saw before him. Truth breeds wisdom; wisdom breeds understanding; understanding births peace.

"Gertrude..." Sal stopped. In his head the next words sounded like a cold fact. It would be like reading from an encyclopedia. In the moment before he spoke them, though. He broke.

Sal sobbed.

The two middle-aged persons stood under the Lake Shore Drive overpass. Sal was on his knees. He was blinded by emotion. Gertrude stood, purple hat in hand, looking down at her friend. Her dream had been for this to happen. In reaching out to her friend, she hoped to wake him up, shake him from his emotional stupor. Now that it was happening, she was unprepared.

"Sal?" She leaned down and put her hand on Sal's shoulder. "Let's get away from the street."

She lifted him up to his feet. Sal's sobs turned to laughter.

"Are you...are you okay, Sal?"

"Gertrude..." Sal wiped away tears, "I hadn't cried. I didn't cry."

"When?"

"Since it happened."

"Not once?"

"No."

They walked slowly toward the old Edgewater Beach Hotel. The pink facade shone eerily in the gloomy, morning light.

"Not once," Gertrude said softly.

"No."

"How did you feel? When it happened – was it...?"

"I don't know. I think I'd been afraid of it for so long that I was just cold."

"Annabelle always said you were cold, after you broke it off."

"I think I always have been."

They walked down Bryn Mawr. In front of them a train roared by the station. Leaves were just starting to pop from the skeleton-like trees that lined Winthrop.

"Gertrude," Sal said slowly, "I don't think he ever loved me." The words he meant to say. The cold fact.

There was silence. Gertrude's short heels clicked on the pavement. It was the truth Sal had no one to tell. For years he had meditated on it, stewed, then forgotten it. Now it sat fully ripened in front of him.

"What do you mean? I'm sure he did," Gertrude said.

"We were familiar. He couldn't go home. I was the closest thing he had to familiar. I became home but it wasn't love. Arnold wasn't capable." Sal paused. "Maybe I wasn't either."

Gertrude wrung her hands. Before speaking she bit her nail cuticle, just as she had all those years ago in the school's break room. "Do you remember the hymn 'It Is Well?'"

"I do."

"That song always confused me."

"Confused?"

"So many hymns use more powerful language and imagery. But that one is very tempered – 'It is well.' It sounds plain."

"I suppose it does."

"I read and re-read the lyrics. In the poem the 'I' is very passive."

"The old English teacher isn't gone yet."

Gertrude smiled. "No, she's moved on to the dull task of dissecting three hundred-year-old hymns. But the 'I' is passive – he is saved by God, by the sacrifice of Christ. He waits for the final days. He waits."

"He waits."

They had crossed Broadway. The trees grew thicker. Their gnarled branches arched over the roadway. On either side of them the apartment buildings and houses looked on in ambivalence. Sal admired a few resilient rays of sun peeping through the clouds.

"For so long in my life I tried to be active, the agent of change. I fought my family, my husband," she reached and took Sal's hand, "my friends. I thought goodness and righteousness were forces to be pushed onto others."

"You were humbled?"

"Excruciatingly so. My husband was dying. The church I had thought would be there for me, turned its back. Do you know what I did?"

"You waited?"

"I began to wait. And the odd thing is, the more I waited, the more active I became. I reached out to you during that time. My first letter was an apology."

"I never opened any of them. I was angry at you."

"You had the right to be."

"Oddly enough, the group I focused so much ire on became my refuge. I joined a PFLAG group."

"Oh my," Sal said. "The scandal that would have erupted at church."

"Nothing more could surprise them. Maybe my lies to the PFLAG parents would have shocked them: I made George my child that had just come out. I sat and told those mothers about his new boyfriend at college."

They were in front of Sal's store. Sal motioned for them to go around the back to the alley. Gertrude continued with her tale of the PFLAG group. Sal led them up the back staircase. Gertrude settled into one of the dining room chairs. She set her hat beside her.

"These orchids are gorgeous, Sal."

"Thank you."

Sal went into the kitchen and put on a tea kettle.

"I became close to those women. A few of them I told what really happened. The real story about the bus and George and the transfusion. They were all lovely about it." She reached out and touched a petal of one of the orchids on the table. "But, through that process, I became vulnerable. I wasn't in charge; I didn't lead Bible study or press my opinions on others. I didn't hold a man hostage and force him to date one of my girlfriends." Gertrude looked at Sal. They made brief eye contact before her eyes fell to the floor. "I had given up on church, but one Sunday I was home and listening to hymns – 'It Is Well' came on."

"Were you well?"

"For the first time I could remember, I was well."

Sal took a seat next to Gertrude. He placed his hand on her leg. "I'm very glad to hear it."

Gertrude licked her lips. "I say all that, Sal, just to say that, of course Arnie loved you. He loved you in a way that he could. He loved you in a complicated, afraid way, and you loved him back in the only way you knew how."

"You don't know the whole story, Gertrude."

"I know enough, Sal. I was at the school when it all happened. I know what he did. I know why he had to leave Chicago and start over."

The kettle whistled. Sal stood up and walked to the kitchen. Gertrude drummed her fingers on the table.

"We're promised everything, Sal. We're promised heaven. We're promised true love. We think the demands are simple – follow God, follow the scripture."

"But the promises are broken," said Sal from the kitchen.

"They were never made, Sal." Gertrude bit her nail. "God doesn't want to give us things, he wants us happy – well..." she dropped off.

"I think that's a very nice way to think about it."

Sal plodded in with two cups of tea. They had not turned on the overhead lights. Grey clouds slid across the sky. The small beams of light that had broken through the clouds were battled back by the April storm.

"Be well, Sal. Arnie loved you. It wasn't what you expected, but it's what was given. Use it. Clive told me about your boys. He told me how they use to come to your shop. They would sit and talk and laugh. He said they loved you."

Sal felt his eyes grow damp.

"Clive told me about Thanksgiving. He mentioned the hospital and those dying men. He said it was the first time since he had been thrown out of his parents' house that he felt like he was home. 'Surrounded by death, I finally felt the love I was missing.'"

Sal stood. He walked to the window.

"That's who you are, Sal. Regardless of whether it's a storybook ending, it's your reality. Open yourself up to it. Arnie loved you in his own broken way. You were his home. You know why? Because he saw the good in you that all those boys see. He sees the good in you that I saw all those years ago. Why did I keep you after the Bible study? It wasn't to change you. I wanted to change you – but I wanted you. I wanted to talk to you, to get to know you. You were interesting, charming. You had wisdom."

Gertrude was breathing heavily. Her own eyes were growing damp.

"Gertrude, thank you. I –"

"Sal, you think you don't deserve some happiness. You've enshrined yourself here, but you deserve so much more. People need you. There are other boys with nowhere to go, with no one to talk to and no safe spaces. 'It is well' those words. Think about them. I'm not saying you'll be happy, but you may be at peace."

Sal was still staring out the window. Gertrude sat on the edge of her seat. With the final words out, she slowly slumped down. For a few moments, all was silent. Outside, cars drove by. Sal studied the tawny, brick façade across the street.

"Gertrude, thank you."

"You're very welcome."

Sal walked to the kitchen. He paused in the doorway. "Would you like more tea?"

"I would."

Gertrude stayed into the evening. To the east, the sky had begun to clear. Where the black and grey clouds met the pale blue, it looked as if the world was split into two perfect halves, one day and one night. Discussion turned lighter with talk of the weather, the old church days, and their favorite students. Sal asked Gertrude if she knew anything about Susie Everly. Gertrude said she did not, but that she never cared for her. She was a suck up. Gertrude's children were doing well. Her daughter that went to Stanford was married and expecting.

When the two parted, they did so with a hug. The darker side of history was behind them, forgotten by remembering.

"We should get coffee next weekend," Gertrude said.

"I'd like that." He began to close the door but stopped. "You know, I'm thinking about getting some of the old boys together – the ones who used to come to my shop. It would be small gathering. You should come if I do it."

"I think that would be delightful."

The door closed behind Gertrude. Sal went straight to the small writing desk in his bedroom. Dust had gathered on its top. He rarely looked at it anymore. In that moment, though, he was thinking back to the day he went to San Francisco. What had the woman said?

He began to write.

Behold the sky, a rainbow of paper and light.
In jubilation, we walk forward, our hearts in flight.
Freedom ignites the beauty of this celebration,
Where many stand, united hearts form nations.
Tenuously, some stand on the edge of this world,
Not fully accepting all that is unfurled.
For some have found that inside them lay,
Insecurity within the variegated fray.
But even they can't escape the air,
Its light, crisp, effervescent, a glorious snare.
Despite the manmade world around them,
They all feel earth, sky, rain when they can
Stand together. The earth moves uniformly, pulses quicken
Around them. Inside, they feel everything begin.
This moment goes on and on, although it ends quickly,
Contained in the fleeting seconds they live intensely.
Bells ring, voices in cacophonous chorus sing,
There together, hand-in-hand, a moment, perpetual spring.

VII.

1980

Silence – profound and sprawling –welcomed Sal as he strolled alone down Arnie's street. The afternoon went by in a blur of drinks and disco. At one point, Teo sat on Sal's lap, the young gay rubbing his crotch on Sal's. That afternoon Sal had forgotten his old clothes. He had forgotten about Arnie and his sordid past. In all his years, he had never been that drunk.

In one of the bars in The Castro, he tumbled down the front steps. The other men had laughed. For the first time since his childhood, Sal felt camaraderie. It was no wonder Arnie had stayed out West. If his evenings were always like this, it would be hard to tear oneself away. Here the party was ongoing, unyielding. His life in Chicago was a distant gray cloud on a multi-colored horizon. In one of the bars, a drag queen danced alongside a black man, who was kissing a Mexican, the scene overlooked by two lesbians. San Francisco was prismatic, Chicago a daguerreotype.

"I have friends from Chicago," a large man in pink said to Sal. "They say it's excruciatingly Midwestern, the whole WASP mentality pressed onto a whole city."

"It isn't like here," Sal said. "Here is explosive."

"It is! It's explosive!" The man leaned forward. He batted his eyes at Sal. "Have you been with any San Francisco boys?"

"A transplant," Sal said giggling. (Sal could giggle!) "That's who I'm visiting." He pointed to Arnie, shirtless pressed into another man across the way.

"Looks like he's not interested."

"He hasn't been for a long time."

"Well," the big man moved in. His lips splashed onto Sal's.

Gently, Sal pushed him away. "Thank you, but I'm not really in the mood. I'm very flattered."

The man turned and huffed away. Sal again giggled. His life had become the raucous party everyone had warned him about. He pictured Gertrude peering into the bar, shaking her head in disdain. Sal himself knew the moment was fleeting. This wasn't his life, but it was fun view into another world. He was Dorothy on the yellow brick road.

Stray words circled at the edge of his brain. Just as on the flight, words jumbled into rhythmic patterns.

In a weary world, a wanderer strays through fields of fallen.
The dismal light of day turns to a brackish evening sky.

At the next bar he found a dark corner. An old dandy in pastels drank beside him. Rings sparkled on the old man's fingers.

"And what do you do in Chicago?" he wheezed.

"I own a bookshop. I was a teacher."

"Oh, how wonderful. I owe a great deal to a teacher of mine, Mrs. Feldman. She always took extra time with me. She knew I was queer, you know. She made sure I felt special."

"I don't think I ever made much impact. I tried, but the students just don't care. I had good intentions."

"You never know who is really watching. I don't know if Mrs. Feldman knows she affected me the way she did." The old man ordered two whiskey and ginger ales. "My favorite highball," he said.

Sal and the older man were in a back room. Peering through the main doorway, he could see flashing lights and a piece of a disco ball. He was glad he wasn't in the shaking rhythm.

"Is that why you left teaching? You were frustrated?" the dandy asked.

"It's complicated," Sal said. "There was a bit of a gay witch hunt. Several of us thought it was better to leave under pressure from the administration."

"That is a shame."

"I had money, so I went into business for myself."

"I did the same. I started a little art gallery."

"How long have you been in San Francisco?"

"I came right after the war. That's when it all started here. We saw each other in the war; we couldn't go back to the old way of life. My family is from Minnesota. I haven't seen them in thirty years."

"Is that hard?"

"Of course it is. My partner of twenty years died a few years ago. But we have a community here. I have a group of people I host a dinner for once a week. We have transgender men and women, gay men, lesbians, even a few Republicans." He laughed. "I always keep an open table."

"You're lucky."

"You ever thought of moving here?"

Sal tapped the edge of his highball glass. "No," he said. "I don't think I'd enjoy life here. I don't know where I'd find happiness, but this place doesn't compel me. It definitely interests me." Sal smiled.

The dandy raised his glass. "To interest! May it ever be piqued!"

He went with the boys from bar to bar. When he returned to Chicago people asked him where he had been but memory failed. The entire day was impressions, blurred images of faces, bars, lights, fog, music. As evening came on, they walked back toward The Mission. Sal held the hand of one of the younger men from the night before. The boy tittered into Sal's ear about a love interest, one of several, he had met that day.

Arnie came from behind and linked his arm in Sal's. "How do you like my new home, Sal?"

"It's a rather odd kind of beautiful," Sal said. "It's not something I expected to enjoy so very much."

"Should I prepare a room for you?"

"I don't think we're there yet."

Back at Arnie's apartment the group further fractured. Two men they had picked up during the day's bar crawl began to make love on the sofa Sal was using as his bed. Teo stripped to only his underwear and flounced about the room. Arnie and Rick drank vodka straight from dusty glasses. One of the men on the verge of sleep dragged himself to the corner and turned on the tape deck. "Hot Stuff" began to play.

Sal stood in the middle of the room. None of the groups drew him. He realized that in Arnie's new world, he did not mesh with the surroundings, but rather ran counter to them. Earlier he had felt this as shame, tugging his old shirt, feeling embarrassed at his shoes, but that evening he felt like a soldier returning from war. Coming from the social battlefield of Chicago, it was odd to see young gays capering happily without a care in the world. He didn't feel integrated into their lives, but enjoyed the view into this different society. Again, the music, the flap of flesh, the clink of ice in glass, sung out a melody, a complicated rhythm.

> *He remembers how things used to be, the fresh pollen*
> *Of rare flowers blooming in a field once full of life.*
> *In truth, the world perhaps was never as he imagined.*

"Are you coming out, Sal?" Rick asked. "This afternoon was merely the appetizer."

"Now the fist fucking commences," Sal smiled.

"Indubitably!" Arnie raised his glass. "The whole city is having sex tonight. Women may get pregnant just from being in the 415 area code."

"No woman is getting pregnant tonight," Rick laughed.

Teo entered the room. He danced lithely in a circle around Sal. He swam through the air and started gyrating in front of Rick. Rick's eyes came alive. He slapped the young man's ass. Arnie chugged his vodka and stood. He wrapped his hands around Teo's waist. Rick pulled down Teo's underwear and began tonguing his hole.

Sal looked for only a moment before quietly withdrawing into the main room. The two men who had been having sex were passed out, half naked. Sal pulled a blanket over them.

Sal was shocked by his own indifference to the scene. It perhaps was the alcohol. Maybe it was the contact high from all the marijuana that weekend, but Sal was in a very calm state. The raucous, wild scene of San Francisco didn't shake him the way Arnie foresaw. It made sense to him. Boys trapped in closets for so many years were bound to break out and be wild. They were happy, though. Everyone was unbelievably happy. There were, of course, trivial arguments, lover's quarrels, but it was no different, other than in terms of scale, from his own boys in Chicago. The world was just beginning to normalize. Gay men had cracked open the closet door and light was creeping in. They *should* make the most of it.

A slap rang through the apartment.

"Not yet!" Teo bounded out of the kitchen. "The party continues! Who is going out with me?"

Arnie came into the room. He wrapped his arms around Sal. "Teo is mad about the cell block. I think he's always wanted to go to prison."

"If the coppers look like that, I don't see a problem." Teo slid on his small shorts and began buttoning his shirt. "Who's coming?"

"We are, obviously," said Rick.

"David and Alex aren't." Sal pointed to the two men asleep on the couch.

"You have to come, Sal," Arnie nipped at his ear. "If only to experience the full, vulgar life of San Francisco. I can't let you leave without going to a bathhouse."

Sal shook his head. "Arnie, I've been a very good sport, but I think the bathhouse is pushing my most liberal boundaries. What would Gertrude say?"

"I say we take a Polaroid of you greased up and see."

Sal walked to the windows. "I think I'll join David and Alex at rest, but thank you."

"Saaaaal!" Teo shrieked. "You aren't going to leave me alone with these two duds, are you?" He reached out and grabbed Sal's hands. "You don't have to have sex, you can just… explore!"

"No, thank you, really, but I'm going to stay in."

"Suit yourself," Rick said. "But we should be going."

The men all went to the bathroom for last minute preening. Sal briefly felt jealous of Teo, his wild hair swept to the side, his shirt wrinkled; he exuded effortless sex appeal. Teo caught Sal's eyes on him and winked.

"You sure you won't come, Sal?" Teo asked.

"Very! But…," Sal called to Arnie, "would you mind leaving the keys? I think I may go out for a walk. It is my last night here."

"You old devil," Arnie said. "No bathhouse, but you'll just find a dark room in one of the bars…"

"Something like that," Sal said.

When Rick, Arnie, and Teo left, Sal returned to David and Alex. He adjusted their pillows and again pulled the blanket tightly around them.

He had never been very sexual. His idea of love was always more complicated, mystical rather than carnal like these men. Perhaps in the past he may have been able to be a Teo. If he had moved from home, if he had gone to school out West, if, if, if. But he had not. And now he stood in baggy, dun trousers and a new shirt from Marshall Field's, a bizarre growth in the gay garden around him.

> *Were the trees a splendid green? Did the daffodils wave?*
> *Or had the world always been as now, abandoned?*
> *Had he imagined beauty or had he never been awake?*
> *The sky fully dark now, foul odor drifting, trembling trees*
> *Shake their bony fists at his own forgotten memories.*

Outside the air was cool. Drunkenness had warded off the pain in his leg after his earlier fall, but it was beginning to creep in. Sal walked beyond the spot he had sat the night before. People were still out running through Saturday routines. It felt like midnight, but it must have been seven or eight. Most people were just getting ready for the evening. In Chicago, he would be getting home from the shop.

Why had he come?

He was still in love with Arnie. Was it to dispel that love? Or renew it? He didn't know what he would find, but oddly, the chaos of Arnie's new life was expected. The other men tried to shock him. The baths, the fist fucking, the free sex in the apartment: to Sal it was a show. The wildness of Gay Freedom Day behind them, they would settle into their own routines. Rick would make breakfast; Arnie would go to work at the restaurant. They would walk hand in hand up the undulating San Franciscan streets.

Sal would go home. He would run his shop. He would read in his living room and go to church on Sundays. Some weekends he would mow the lawn for old ladies at the church. He would smell grass. Far across the country in their San Francisco home, Arnie and Rick would walk by the yard of a young family and they would smell the same, fresh odor.

But perhaps it wasn't what it was or could ever be,
The world that lived in his imagination, was curated in dreams.

He remembered the day the news broke. Susie Everly had looked at him strangely. After class, she came to his desk.

"Mr. Henry," she said, "how are you?" The words were uncertain. Susie was always certain.

"I'm fine, Susie. How are you?"

"I'm well, Mr. Henry." Her lips tried to form syllables, but no sound came from her small, bow-like mouth. "I'm fine."

She turned and left. It was third period. It wasn't until lunch that he went into the teacher's room. Everyone stopped speaking when he entered. Arnie, usually the first to arrive and have his lunch spread on the wooden tables, was palpably absent.

No one spoke.

Sal unpacked his lunch: a sandwich, a thermos of tea, an apple. He felt dozens of eyes on him. Sweat formed on his forehead.

Gertrude entered the room. She sat beside him.

"Do you know?" she asked.

"Know what?"

Her blue eyes flitted around the room. She bit the cuticle on her right index finger. "Come with me," she whispered.

The eyes followed them out of the room. The lounge door slammed shut as Gertrude hurried him into the hallway.

As they moved away from the lounge, Sal felt that the whole school was quieter than normal. The children stood clustered in groups. This was not the bawdy, loud cacophony Sal recognized as the lunch hour symphony. Outside of Gertrude's classroom, Sal heard footsteps approach. Gertrude's hand was on the door. Her manicured fingers gripped the knob.

"Mr. Henry," a voice said. "You will follow me."

Gertrude looked at Sal; her eyes were pools of fright. She said nothing. Her hand jumped from the knob. She realized she was now in collusion. Sal looked at her curiously. Before he could ask a question, the principal was walking past him, down the hall.

The principal's wingtip shoes clacked on the hardwood floors. Sal fell into step behind him. They passed through the art wing. Student portraitures glared down on the administrators.

When they arrived at the office…

When they arrived.

Sal's mind returned to San Francisco. He paused on the sidewalk, looking up through the leaves of trees.

Forgiveness, maybe. Was that the reason he had come? It was hard to pick it out in the swells of emotion. The reasons may have been many, an inarticulable mass.

> *Another look, closed eyes forced open reveals the sky*
> *Turning a lighter shade. He had, perhaps, been mistaken.*
> *Shaking trees were now standing, palms open, blithe.*
> *The gray, dead stalks in the moonlight turn, making*
> *Their haunted faces catch color: red, green, purple, blue.*

Forgiveness was a strange thing. It was given, a gift. Was God as tight-fisted as the others claimed? In church, he would sit and hear of the burning hordes in hell. He imagined them, faces twisted to an unhearing God. Could they be forgiven?

He had never lumped Arnie with those men. If he hadn't been down the road of his own life, he may have found it harder, but the natural state of Sal's heart was openness. He easily forgave. Gertrude in her plush, white-washed world, was forgiven daily. They were friends, but she transgressed the boundaries of propriety. She lectured him and told him he should change; there was a part of him she despised. But Sal never accepted surface action. It was what lay beneath that he held to. Gertrude, on the couch, asking him what he thought of the Fruits of the Spirit. Gertrude, hand on knob, the only one who took a chance to warn him.

He and Arnie had been complicated. Their letters over the decade had proven this. They loved each other, but the love was labyrinthine. It was not the love that ballads had promised. Sal remembered buying the record of "Unchained Melody." He would sit and listen to it repeatedly. In his head was the idea of two men, hand-in-hand, living out a life that was not labeled as sinful. It was after he and Arnie had danced.

It wasn't even fair to say they were fully together. They dated in the dark; they did their best to function, but fantasy could not support the crushing weight that pulled them down. Guilt, sadness, fearfulness: Sal was caught in their web.

"Do you know why you are here, Mr. Henry?" The principal asked.

"No, sir."

The principal did not make eye contact. "It is in regards to your," he clicked his teeth, "acquaintance, Mr. Arnold Bellows."

"I hope he's okay, sir."

"I'm sure you're concerned." The principal took out a ball-point pen. He began to scratch on paper. "Accusations have come to light."

"Accusations?"

"A young man, a child, came forward yesterday evening to his parents."

Sal felt his scalp grow hot. "He did," he whispered.

"It appears that he and Mr. Bellows have engaged in deviant acts."

"Sir, I…"

"Salacious, gruesome, unnatural acts, Mr. Henry. Vile, putrid, unholy acts."

Sal swallowed hard. "Is he…is the boy, okay, sir?"

"It is hard to say. But he came forward to accuse Mr. Bellows of seducing him into these acts after school."

Sal knew the boy without the name being spoken. It must have been Arthur Fletcher. He was a slight, loud-mouthed boy with a Botticelli mouth and sandy, brown hair. Arnie had mentioned him in passing. It was always in the context of Arthur's sexual teasing of Arnie. He would stay after class, draw close to the teacher, pass notes after class had finished. Or so Arnie said.

"His father is withdrawing him from the school. He won't be returning." The principal finished scrawling on the paper.

"That's horrible, sir."

The principal turned his eyes to Sal. "Your name was mentioned by this boy."

Sal put his hand to his mouth. Sweat flowed freely down his forehead.

"You were named as a close friend of Mr. Bellows."

Sal said nothing.

"Very often a blind eye is turned when such acts are kept behind closed doors, Mr. Henry, but the doors are wide open."

"They seem to be." Tears fell down Sal's face. They dripped. Oozed.

"It is expected you will resign. Mr. Bellows cleared his office this morning."

"Yes, sir."

"We didn't catch you before class, but Mrs. Jennings will be taking over for the remainder of the year."

"Yes, sir."

"I will make sure you will not be welcomed in the Chicago Public School System."

"Yes."

"Please sign this note of resignation and clear out your things."

Sal scrawled his name on the paper. A tear splashed on the white parchment.

"You have twenty minutes to clear your things, or I will call the police."

Classes had already resumed when Sal got to his room. Eighteen young eyes stared at him as he piled his belongings into a garbage bag. Mrs. Jennings stood, nose raised as he emptied the drawers. No words were spoken in the minutes he spent taking his life from the classroom.

He made it home before he broke down in tears. He stifled his wailing with a pillow.

Odious air, wind changing, turns to smells of pollen, leaves, water.
Did the world always exist in this trembling hue?
Had perhaps, the wanderer, imagined, senses faltered,
And the world bloomed, lit by momentary insanity?
Whatever the cause, it now was closer to the earlier dream.

Sal only had a vague idea of where he was in his San Francisco wanderings. Although he had studied the map like scripture, it did little good now that he was entrenched in the winding streets. He had walked by a hospital campus and passed under a highway. Everything was strange. It was comfortably strange. Sal thought of himself as a pioneer in a new land. Here the streets were quieter. He felt farther from the baths, from the untamed wild of The Castro and the freedom celebration.

Freedom. It was a strange concept. Liberty in the hands of some was terrorism to others. Imagine Anita Bryant looking at the sexual displays today. She would be horrified, affronted; the home and family were under direct attack by men in heels and leather. This was the apocalypse.

To other boys from Wisconsin, Kansas, Minnesota, this was freedom. Dressing in lipstick and heels in their parents' home, feeling the hard slap of society against their faces, they were finally free to express their innermost desires.

Sal felt somewhere between them. The acts of liberation were too much for him. He didn't hate them as some did. At the gay bars in Chicago some men scoffed at drag.

"They should just act naturally," some said.

"Why do they have to rub it in our faces like that?" asked others.

Each man is a territory with boundaries under attack. Sal had rested his arms at all fronts many years ago. Gertrude, with her dogmatic morality had made him see his own limitations. He didn't want anyone to feel the way she made him feel. No one should feel their natural state, their object at rest, is an assault to others. But Gertrude also loved him. She wanted to be around him. When homosexuality wasn't the topic, she was one of his closest friends.

For some reason, this night in San Francisco, Sal found peace with the duality. His best friend both hated and loved him. He both loved and hated himself. When he and Arnie had fucked, he had felt euphoria, then crippling guilt. It was evident his world was built on this tension; he occupied a fault line. It was a land meant to shake, on the verge of being torn.

But he had not torn.

The moon, the sky, the trees, in a state, precariously
Balanced, beautiful in a way he had not expected to see.
"Tonight you might be beautiful," the man said to darkness.

Arnie had made excuses. Sal had not wanted to bring it up. Instead of facing Arnie directly like a man, he cowered and hid. The weekend after they were fired, Arnie showed up at his door in the rain.

The day was gray. The afternoon was gray.

"We were never really together," he said. "I didn't know… You know how things were…are between us."

"How many were there? Should I be concerned about myself?"

"There's nothing serious. They would have told me. Your health will be fine."

"How many?"

"We weren't together, Sal. We had a few really nice nights. We had sex, but you were so fucking weird about it. They boy was a terrible mistake…"

"Why didn't you tell me?"

"There was nothing to tell."

Sal thought of both him and the boy, Arthur. They were bound now by fluid, blood. A mere boy. What had Arnie done? Was he a monster like they all said?

Gertrude: "I told you this was all bad business, Sal. You mess with the unnatural and it blows up in your face. Arnie was probably going around with everyone. That's how *they* are."

They. Them. He was one of them and not one of them.

Duality. Muddled.

"Look, I'm sorry I hurt you. I didn't know… Sal, you had to know it wasn't only you."

"I did." Sal ended it there. He politely asked Arnie to leave.

He knew. As he knew the week his father was going to die. It was palpable in the air. The world is full of signs legible under certain circumstances. He had an unnatural intuition. Arnie never mentioned anyone else. He was never late. He was busy some days with friends, but it was never glaringly obvious. Hadn't he been happy?

One day they had gone to Garfield Park Conservatory. They'd spent the afternoon there, and it had seemed perfect. In that moment, Arnie had probably been preparing for the night out. He had more boys on his mind. They'd had a rough go at it, but wasn't that afternoon perfect? Sal promised himself he would get the sex right that night. But Arnie dropped him at home and went out.

After the short, jilted conversation right after, they had not spoken for weeks. When Arnie called him after the new year to meet up for coffee, Sal had gone. Arnie had destroyed him, but he had been the one who let him live. In that second meeting, they only spoke of the incident with Arthur indirectly. It was alluded to and dismissed. They never spoke of it again.

It was not after that revelation that he had been wounded most. The day had come when Arnie told him he was going to San Francisco.

"You know I don't have a choice, Sal. I can't work in this town. I need to start over."

Sal drove him to the airport. Arnie sold everything. He went to San Francisco in a big-collared, mauve shirt with wayfarer sunglasses. He carried a suitcase that he'd taken from Sal.

That afternoon Sal wept. He drove to the city's south side and in an abandoned lot he cried until snot and saliva poured down his mouth and nose. While Arnie had been there, there had been hope. As muddled and messy as their relationship was, Sal could believe that they would end up together. Destiny existed as long as Arnie was in close proximity.

But he went away and the gray of the everyday consumed Sal. It overwhelmed him.

Even then the vision shook, death, life shifting before his eyes.
He sought to hold it, memorialize it, but knew the effort fruitless.

He said it quickly, before it could disappear into the brackish night.

And here he was. It had been ten years since he cried in the car, since his world turned a deep, unimpeachable gray. They had all survived.

Arnie was happy. He had found happiness with someone else, but Sal now understood that he could never make him joyful. Arnie's world was bathhouses and wild nights out. He naturally fell into a sexual rhythm with two other men.

Sal was not them. He was one of them but different. Perhaps it was learning this that had made him happy. The old queen in the bar came to his mind. That man had his meals, his friends, his partner. Hope smoldered again. It didn't have to be a man that brought him happiness; it could be, and had always been for Sal, community.

On leaving Arnie's apartment, Sal thought he would make it to the water, but he had stopped to ponder and grown tired. The alcohol and energy spent dancing had caught up with him. It made him happy all the streets in the area had the name of states. This made it seem as if he had gone very far.

Slowly, he stood up ambled back the way he had come; the pain in his leg was now throbbing. He was not sure how to get back, but he had a good idea. The boys would still be passed out, so he'd have to form a makeshift bed on the floor. This would cause some back pain for the next few days, but it was bearable. Before he went to bed he wanted to jot down the lines that had been floating around his head. In the peace of the evening, the words came quickly.

He whispered the words, afraid if he stirred the flowers and trees
That the spell would break and he would be
alone, beauty affright,
Returning to the earlier nightmare. "Perhaps this
vision is insanity,
But if this world be beautiful any night, then
I have seen it tonight."

VIII.

2009

A click of the door marked the exit of, what Sal believed to be, his last guest. He sighed thinking of the enjoyment of the evening. It would take work to restore his house to order. Gertrude grew tired early and headed home after doing a bulk of the dishes.

The brief conflict with Martin and Soot was a small low point in the evening. Things turned around when Sal put on his old record player. He chose to play an old disco LP to start. A few of the boys lip synced along with the words. It turned into a makeshift show. Sal jumped into music again in the early 90's. He collected stacks of records. His favorite was Whitney Houston. He made them play "How Will I Know?" as the closing song. In the moment, the boys threw arms around each other and sang along. He thought he would make it a tradition for the end of the gatherings.

In the beginning, the dinners had been tiny social gatherings. The first one had been Gertrude, Clive, and himself. Over the years, people came and went, but the group stayed consistently around ten people. Some weeks there were twenty, but mostly there were ten.

At that first dinner, he'd made a toast. It was symbolic in a way. After meeting with Gertrude, he had woken to a changed world: the 1990s. The 80s, and if he was honest with himself, the 70s had passed with emptiness and tragedy. It was time to live again. That night in San Francisco he decided that community could be his home rather than a romantic relationship. Love could be lived rather than contained in a love affair. That night a seed was planted in his heart. It took years to grow, fertilized by Arnie's death, and harvested by Gertrude in her coming to him in his isolation.

His toast mentioned something about The Great Chicago Fire. It was hopeful to know that an entire city could burn and be rebuilt with towers of shimmering glass. What was once thought to be destroyed, could become a center of life.

From that night on, it had proceeded. Clive brought friends. Sal went out more and met people in volunteer work at Horizons and work with AIDS patients. He looked up Lola in the phone book and got coffee. The old nurse, Bea, passed away and Sal put flowers on her grave. Old boys from the shop in Lake View began to pop up at the dinners. Susie Everly published a collection of short stories called "Voices in the Shadows."

"You may recognize one. Just because you didn't give me permission, didn't mean I couldn't use artistic interpretation," she said over the phone from California. He laughed to himself, thinking of Susie and her use of "clandestine" so many years before.

The world's current kept moving without Sal, but he reintegrated quickly. Before long, his days were full and his plants were becoming neglected. Gertrude told him about the joys of travel. During the late 90s and early 2000s, they roamed together. His fear of flying diminished with each journey, but on landings, he still put his hand in Gertrude's. They retained a glow of modesty on the trips, staying in separate rooms. Sal's favorite part of those adventures was breakfast: in Mexico chilaquiles, in California eggs with avocado (of all things!), in New York bagels from local bakeries.

The disco and Whitney Houston records put away, Sal plodded into his dining room. To his surprise, there was one guest left. It was the boy who had entered the kitchen, the newest member. He fingered Sal's shirts that hung in the windows.

"What are these?" he asked. With everyone gone, his voice took on an energy Sal hadn't noticed before.

"Shirts," Sal laughed. "It's an old habit."

"But why are they here? I saw you have a dryer."

"You're perceptive."

"I'm a reader," the boy said smiling, "not just books, but people, objects, homes. There are stories happening all the time if you watch and listen."

"I agree!" Sal pulled out a chair and tapped it. "Sit down."

The boy sat. "Will the story about the shirts really take that long?"

"No, look at the window, pay attention to how they are hung. When the light comes in from the east in the morning it creates a glow, a filter on the room. It's lovely. As I've gotten older, most of my shirts are white, but in my younger days there was more color. It was a bit like having stained glass, for people of less means."

The boy wrung his hands. "I can see that being nice in the mornings. It's interesting. You're very interesting." The boy cocked his head and looked at Sal. Sal had the feeling he was being looked through rather than at.

"Unfortunately, my life has been very interesting."

"I put it together – most of it. Lover lost in the AIDS crisis, an old teacher, bookshop owner, now single but very active in the community. Gertrude I assume is an old friend, a very old friend. Clive as well. Lawrence and Martin are more periphery; they seem, to use your term, 'resistant' to this little dinner event."

It was Sal's turn to cock his head. "Yes, that's accurate."

"Judging from pictures, you and your lover didn't have a standard relationship. I guess that's to be assumed in your generation. You couldn't post pictures with your lovers online. You couldn't hold hands in public."

"No, you couldn't."

"When did you come out? How bad was it?" the boy asked.

"Did you have trouble coming out?" Sal retorted.

"It wasn't coming out; it was the aftermath."

"Aftermath – how?"

"Broken heart – annihilated heart." The boy stood. "Do you mind if I have some more wine?"

"By all means."

"Do you want some?"

"Please – just a bit."

The boy went to the kitchen to get glasses. Sal watched him. It had not been apparent at first, but the boy had a magnetism, a certain wild charisma. He concealed this part of himself from the others. When all of them had left, he bloomed. Sal found it odd that there was something dangerous in it. In his direct, open gaze, there was some mystery that wasn't benign.

He reentered with two glasses and set them down. He took a deep breath.

"I was madly in love with my first boyfriend. I was naïve. My whole life I had spent in my imagination, spinning stories, hiding from my difference. I didn't know I was gay, but I knew that I didn't fit in. Creating a narrative was what helped me cope."

"Do you still write? I have a friend who had a collection published."

"No," the boy shook his head, "I haven't for quite some time. It began to seem childish. After the boyfriend, everything turned very angsty and maudlin."

"There's power in that."

"I suppose. But after that breakup, I fell into a dark place. People assume that's where you get your real inspiration, but I've found it strangled my creativity. I thought the world was one way, and it was another. There's no creative energy in that, just heartbreak."

"I've found that it's when I get renewed hope that I begin to write again."

"You write?"

"Poetry."

"Is it good?"

Sal smiled. "I think maudlin and angsty would be good descriptors. Was yours ever good?"

"No," he said standing and going to the window, "it never was."

The boy didn't move from the window for quite some time. Sal looked at the pictures along the wall. For a moment, he tried to look at them as the boy would have. It's true they revealed something missing. The pictures of Arnie he had in his living room were all old. He had one from his trip to San Francisco in his bedroom. It was of their full group from his first journey out West. Sal was not in the picture; Teo, Rick, Arnie, and the others were. Despite the following tragedy, he loved that picture. It always reminded him of the youthful zeal he had encountered in San Francisco – no one is hopeless.

The only picture ever taken of Arnie and him together was a school picture from a science event in the high school yearbook. Sal didn't know it was there until pointed out years later by Susie Everly.

"That's how I knew," she'd said. "That picture from the yearbook. You're talking at a school event, but there is such chemistry. The romance leaps off the page."

"To answer your question," Sal said slowly, "my coming out was long and painful but mostly self-induced. I was afraid of what people would think, what neighbors would think, what," he laughed, "God would think."

"I don't believe in God," the boy said.

"You will. When you see enough of the world, you have to believe something is holding it together."

"It's chaos, pure and simple." The boy turned from the window. He picked up a chair and spun it backwards, putting his arms on the backrest. He locked eyes with Sal. "There are only those who play God. No real ones."

Sal's eyebrow raised. "Who plays God?"

"Politicians, policemen, corporations, everyone. Everyone is always playing at it."

"It appears that way to young eyes, I suppose. But there is more to it than that, I believe."

"I respect that. I disagree, but respect it as an ideology." His gaze never strayed from Sal's.

"What brought you here tonight?" Sal asked.

"People adore you. I've been skulking around Halsted for quite some time and your name kept coming up. When I had my dangerous liaison with Joe, he suggested bringing me along to your dinner. I couldn't refuse."

"You came to see me?"

"Like I said, I read people, objects, books – you were required reading, so to speak."

"Why are you being honest with me? I feel that's not your style. Joe probably had no idea he was being used to get to me."

"Well, he wasn't at first. He was being used for something else," the boy laughed. He blinked, for what seemed the first time since he returned from the window. His posture relaxed. "I think you're genuine, which I've been discovering is a hard trait to find."

"The gay scene is full of smoke and mirrors. It's just like any group of humans, tribal and shattered."

"I know. I thought it would be something better. I believed in Oz," the boy said looking down. "Before everything, I thought I'd come out and there would be a group waiting for me with open arms. But it's not like that."

"There are places like that."

The boy again locked eyes with Sal. "That's what I wanted to see."

He stood up and drank the rest of his wine. Gently, he placed the wine glass on the table. His eyes ran over the object as if it was something of great worth.

"Are you leaving?" Sal asked.

"I was hoping you'd come with me."

"With you?"

"To get a drink. I like talking to you, but your place is a little... constrained. If I had guests, I would add a little more embellishment." He smiled. "Maybe add some scarlet and gold, open it up a little bit."

"A shopkeeper doesn't have much need for scarlet and gold."

"But you'll come? One drink? On me."

"I'd like that. It's a little selfish. I'm interested in knowing what else you've read in our tiny Chicago bubble."

The boy put on his jacket. "To be honest, not much of it is interesting."

"I feel Lawrence Soot would be an excellent study."

The boy laughed. "I thought so, too! There's something feline about him."

Sal put on his own light coat. The two made their way down the stairs and out the door to the back alley.

The boy went out ahead of him and looked up at the sky. "What's the most ridiculous place to go up here?"

"Ridiculous? Ridiculous, how?"

"Where would the other boys not expect to see you?"

Sal laughed. "I think I know the perfect place. There are go-go boys. They are a self-described 'dive bar.'"

"Perfection."

The boy extended his arm so Sal could take it.

"I'm sorry," Sal said. "With so much happening this evening, I've forgotten your name."

The boy smiled to himself. The mischievous gleam Sal had noticed during the heated discussion returned. "Hedley," he said softly. Then, more confidently: "My name is Hedley."

Judges

"It is a curious subject of observation and inquiry, whether hatred and love be not the same thing at bottom. Each, in its utmost development, supposes a high degree of intimacy and heart-knowledge; each renders one individual dependent for the food of his affections and spiritual life upon another; each leaves the passionate lover, or the no less passionate hater, forlorn and desolate by the withdrawal of his object. Philosophically considered, therefore, the two passions seem essentially the same, except that one happens to be seen in a celestial radiance, and the other in a dusky and lurid glow."

- Nathaniel Hawthorne, *The Scarlet Letter*

2015: Prologue

The scene was carefully constructed, on the verge of being artifice, but executed precisely so viewers were left with a sense of wonder. Hedley sat in the driver seat, his long, tanned legs exposed to the sun. Beside him was Stephen, cigarette in hand, fingers out the window strumming the air as if the currents were strings of a phantom harp. Samson and Skyler sat in the back seat. Samson, shirtless, his head thrown back, whole body arched toward the sky, glistened in the early afternoon light. The pièce de résistance, the focal point, which added the illusory, cinematic impression to the car driving down Bryn Mawr that warm, June afternoon, was Skyler. He sat on the back of the blue convertible, feet resting on the leather interior. Behind him a gossamer, scarlet scarf billowed in the wind. Passers-by stopped their forward momentum entirely to see the coterie drift down the road. The first impression most had was of fire, thinking in Skyler's hands a long pillar of flame was extending toward the sky.

Spectacle: in the beginning, it was not the most important part of joining The Hedley Set, but over the years the power of appearances overshadowed all else. Skyler's mother had perhaps put it best, a great many years ago, before Chicago, before The Set, before Skyler found himself at the center of Chicago's gay social scene. She sat stitching an ancient sequence dress, pins in her hair.

"It's how ya look, Sky. People don't care about anything except what they think you are. Think of Tom Cruise. They ain't thinking about Tom, but 'bout *Top Gun*, that guy from *Mission: Impossible*. That's what fame is."

Samson came to the show late. He did his best to meet the expectations set by his family, but at a certain point he had to awake from his somnambulant existence and choose. He had a relationship, an almost husband; his life had followed the patterns of the sideshow. One night ripped him in two – years building toward that fateful evening's climax, the lights of the city guiding him to a new, heartless world that he had somehow always known.

Stephen never had to learn the game; he was born a successful player. While most men of his age strove against the imperious resistance of the world, carving, forcing a shape of understanding on the monument of their existence, Stephen was born with fully finished statuary. Men and women bowed before him. Youth for him was a seamless, beautiful dance. His adulthood traced the same graceful path, rippling, scything toward a predestined, successful future. For him the understanding, the revelation, was in the shock of seeing himself unmasked. An unknown horror had knotted itself in his stomach; in his mind, the choice of living in two worlds, in the projection and in the shadow, was a daily choice, the weight of which tore the seams of his own consciousness.

Hedley alone had mastered the art of this duality. He was its commander, its chieftain, its god. While most people saw only the portrait of a car drifting down a road in the early afternoon, Hedley knew that it was so much more. The car itself was a sunburst and his eyes saw the full electromagnetic vision of its output; in his eyes, mind, and heart, the complex machinery of the social world could be tangibly felt, cultivated, and seen in electric pulses that flowed outward from his own carefully constructed hub. The scarf billowing, red, caught the eye, brought to mind fire. Heads turned, breath caught – the whole street seduced into asking the same question: What is flying toward the heavens? Skyler held it because he was the beauty of their group. Hedley knew each of The Set's weight and social value, knew when to play them like pieces in a game of chess: Skyler the queen, Samson the king, Stephen the rook. Samson sat shirtless beside him, in repose, because he was the necessary counterpoint to the camp of Skyler's scarf. Artifice and leisure sat side-by-side. He and Stephen would be ancillary in this scene, the driver and the passenger. Hedley knew he must always be near the fire, but never its source.

For many, this moment became a symbol of that summer. Nick, a new gay from Western Illinois, saw it with his friend, Jordan. He paused and watched the red fabric tear through the sky, ripple in the wind, and dance between the clouds.

"Isn't that…?" he asked.

"The Set." Jordan nodded. "They know how to make an entrance."

That afternoon, Nick watched them on the beach. His young eyes drank in the casual, magnificent flow of The Set on the sand. In his mind, a thousand lives filled the possible outline of each man. He dumped all his hopes, desires, and dreams into them, into the projections that glided down the beach. When Samson jumped on the back of a large, muscular man, Nick felt the heat of their skin touching. When he heard Stephen laugh, doubling over into the sand, he desired nothing more than to know the source of his mirth.

The infatuation Nick felt was contagion. It flowed through the neural networks of all the men on the beach. Even those who didn't desire to be immersed in The Set's existence, to stand at the pinnacle of the social strata, still found themselves feeling a pang of wonder at the ease with which they flowed through life. The scarlet scarf rippling in the wind was a symbol of The Set's own gossamer existences. While others strove, swam, fought the current of daily life, The Set flowed with delicate ease. How unbelievable, they all thought, for life to be so simple, so fluid. Imagine a life without friction, without the pain of resistance to the chaotic order of the social strata.

The world itself had become one of false lives, constructed humanity. Post only what you want others to see. Filter out your friction and present to others the sunny glow of an easy life. Nick and all the others watched The Set, not only on the beach, but with digital eyes across the internet. The Twitter feed told them where they were and with whom; Instagram revealed the excitement of their most recent memories; Facebook told their shining histories, pasts full of adventure and diversion. And now, in the light of day, at Hollywood Beach on a Saturday in June, they got to live in the intersection of The Set's digital life and the real.

A scarlet scarf, an afternoon in the sun, three posts from the day: one in mid-afternoon, Hedley on the deck of a yacht owned by a real estate broker and his new band of muscled boat boys; one in the car, Stephen snapping Skyler waving the scarf in the wind; the last, a group picture at twilight, four friends holding each other tightly in the magic hour before entering Samson's condo. The world sees them and imagines these lives of others. Imagine, it says.

Imagine.

But there is always the point before. Even Facebook's ubiquity ends at a certain limit. "Stephen Ripley joined Facebook." Under each beautiful picture on Instagram there are a thousand layers, tiny histories, 1's and 0's. When the computer is off, the world sped to the hour of death, what lies inside all of us, despite how

carefully kept and constructed our outer flesh may be, is the same simple mix of collagen, calcium, and protein.
Bones.

2000: Interior Hearts

Before looking at bones, it may behoove the reader to see all flesh and blood put before him. In our instance, we shall put them on the scaffold – a stage of wood stands before us, four figures against an early morning sky. Their shadows sprawl from the stage, casting an oddly menacing flourish to the crowd in the first few rows closest to the accused. Those behind the umbrage wish they were closer so that they could feel refuge from the sun.

It is a different shadow, thrown from their social figures, which sits on trial atop the scaffold. All of us have seen their faces in the crowd, felt the cold sting of their intrusion in our lives. At once we are forced to face ourselves as they would see us.

Too fat.
Too tall.
Too poor.
Too unconnected.

We would not know we were not if they were not to show that they are. The person next to you whispers of the night that the youngest called him "the slut of Uptown." Behind him you hear the soft mutterings of another who was forced to bed by the oldest, held down, blurred lines of consent marring the time earlier in the evening when they had laughed together at the bar.

They are careless, reckless, heedless, feckless; their crime is invisible, but we seek some sort of way to tangibly describe it in the early morning hours.

Is it justified?
Justice.

Careless people in a world that caters to frivolity. All eyes see the three, but there is one who stands for more than the others. If they are not guilty, surely, he is. If you cannot blame the leaves, then blame the roots.

But the magistrate admonishes the cries and hushed accusations bubbling up from the crowd.

"They shall have their defense. We are the avatars of our Lord and will enact his judgment on those gathered. Be they found culpable of the crimes or not, we shall hear the evidence and place the stones – to the left for guilty, to the right for innocent."

Silence settles on all those gathered. The town recorder shuffles to the scaffold holding a heavy tome, the record of those on trial. He wears a wig, it's grey curls bumping together jovially in the morning breeze. Those wise ones gathered lean forward, crane their necks to be sure they hear every word, weigh every fact. For many, the words matter little – the verdict, in their mind, resolute already.

The recorder adjusts his glasses, gently licks his shaking hand to turn the page. His voice is raspy, crinkled and worn as the pages of his book.

"I submit," he says slowly, "the objective evidence against the men gathered upon the scaffold, with judgment left to God, as delegated to his chosen people."

Skyler

Harmony View was a small trailer park settlement that strove to live up to its name. Its residents belonged to two major parties, factions within the small world with heavily competing ideologies. On one hand, there were the strivers, the dreamers, the wanting. Eveline Peavey worked two jobs in the local, Nebraska town of Dimmesdale to support her three boys. From 7-3 pm she waited tables at a local diner; from 5-midnight, she worked as a supervisor at a laundromat. Eveline taught her sons that hard work was the way to escape the island of Harmony View. She inculcated in her young children a natural urge to strive for life outside of set boundaries. They learned well from their mother. By the time each boy was twelve, he was working and studying, dreaming of a life as a scientist, as a banker, as the president.

Adjacent from Eveline's small plot of land, the other faction was represented by Siegfried Essen. The old man was born in Dimmesdale, worked in Dimmesdale, and retired to the outer world of Harmony View to escape the encroaching liberal agenda that a cable news outlet instructed him had circled its hands around fair Dimmesdale's pure throat. Siegfried believed exactly as the television hosts told him – never much of a religious man, his worship became self-righteousness in the form of racism and a perceived belief that the world of his childhood was being clawed away by African-Americans, homosexuals, and the deluge of Mexicans crossing the U.S. border.

The home between Siegfried and Eveline, the trailer where our story centers, was at the intersection of these warring ideologies. Georgina Shaw also subscribed to the belief that the non-white world was infringing on her abilities to rise above her station in Harmony View; she, however, also was determined to rise out of the rubble in spite of the momentum pushing against her. Her room was filled with pages of a play that she was perpetually in the stage of "getting perfect." It centered on a beautiful girl, struck down by the dramatic fist of fate, who rises above her station and becomes the star of a Broadway show. There were never more than twenty pages of it written at a time; the style varied greatly, but the quality was always deficient. Georgina's rural Nebraska, tenth-grade education was ill-suited for the construction of a stirring drama.

At twenty-five, she retained a hope that life was not all it seemed to be. She still imagined under its scarred surface, there was something more. For many, this belief is tied to God, to the promise of eternity behind the crust of the day-to-day existence; for Georgina, it was the dream of her own success, the idea that one day she would be in front of all those who had wronged her and be triumphant. Revenge and power were the sparkling suns on the horizon she looked to each morning. She always looked to not just any day, but one day.

One day they'll be sorry they treated me like they did.
One day I'll be the one they knew from high school.
One day ma will be sorry she threw me out.
One day, one day – a tomorrow at the long string of uncertainty.

In the evenings, she would put on her makeup and best dress and go into the city. Her son, Skyler, would watch her paint her lips and draw light color around her eyes. In the dim lights of the trailer, his mother would go from maternal to beautiful, years shaking from her like the skin of a snake. Pulling up her blond hair, she would tell her son life advice, small pieces of knowledge that she had gained over the years.

"Don' let anyone tell you that ya ain't something special," she'd say. "You're my boy and that's plenty special."

"There are people out there – mean people." She wiped lipstick from her teeth. "They'll use ya and treat ya like trash. But we ain't trash. We are not trash. Say that for me, sugar. Say 'We ain't trash.'"

"We ain't trash, mama."

"Good boy."

She'd leave him in the trailer at home alone, Eveline Peavey's number by the cordless phone. In those long hours by himself, the seven-year-old boy would put on his mother's collection of musicals. The cassette of *The Sound of Music* was nearly worn out; *West Side Story* was grainy and irregular during the "America" number. Skyler never imagined himself as the dashing male leads, but rather as the beautiful women. One of his most cherished dreams was awaking one morning as The Baroness from *The Sound of Music*; on nights when rain poured down, he dreamed of becoming Liesel, dancing from bench to bench as rain pelted the windows.

At seven, shame had not yet taken these dreams from him. Growing up in relative isolation meant that other children had not yet sought out this difference and gleefully destroyed it. In school, he was silent and taciturn. The other first grade children were yet to perceive Skyler's difference as malignant rather than simply unique. Many young boys and girls may grow up without this gay aberration shining through, however, Skyler was not one of these children. His soft, feminine voice, his porcelain face, swooped black hair, and love of pastels did little to conceal his flamboyance.

Siegfried Essen eyed him suspiciously from his porch on afternoons when Skyler would venture out to play. Preferring to stay inside on most occasions, some afternoons he would take one of his mother's hats and a stick from the ground and act out scenes from a formless musical that had attached to his imagination and grown like moss. The audience was compromised of a number of items he collected from the trailer: a mannequin head his mother kept one of her wigs on, a Toy Story doll he had received in a Secret Santa exchange, and a large canister of oatmeal he purloined from the kitchen. Skyler would soft shoe in the dust of their small driveway. If he performed well, he would bestow on himself a bouquet of weeds from their front yard.

On one fall day, Siegfried had enough of the show across the street. Hobbling forward, shoulder stooped, the old man waved his bony hand at the small boy blowing kisses to inanimate objects. In his left arm he carried a football, dusty and worn, retrieved from the depths of his closet.

"Boy, you shouldn't do that," he croaked. "They'll call you a sissy."

"Who?" Skyler asked innocently. His large brown eyes reflected the warm, red twilight.

"People. Everyone." Siegfried reached out and grabbed the stick from Skyler's hand. Deftly, he dropped the football to the ground and snapped the stick in half. "You should play with boys' stuff like this here football."

Skyler looked at the shriveled pigskin with abject horror.

"Oh, no," he said.

Siegfried stared at him darkly. To one born and imbued with the malignant strain of masculinity prone to racism and sexism, the site of an effete boy turning up his nose at a male relic, was an abomination.

"Siegfried," Georgina appeared behind the trailer's screen door. "What're ya doin' over here?"

"Brought your sissy son something to play with." Siegfried spit.

"He's fine," Georgina said thickly. Her stare burned into Siegfried for a long moment. "Sky, baby, why don't ya come inside and wash up."

Skyler ran up the wooden steps and disappeared into the dim light of the trailer. Georgina watched him scuttle down the hall; when the door softly shut behind him and she could hear the water run, she turned toward Siegfried. The old man was beginning to shuffle back across the street. Georgina picked up the discarded football and hurled it at his back.

Siegfried turned violently and sneered.

"You don't ever say shit to my son again, Siegfried," she hollered. "If I ever here ya calling him a sissy again, I will call up all fourteen of your ex-wives and we'll tear you to pieces."

"Ha!" Siegfried snarled. "I was trying to do that little faggot a favor. You see how he survives when he can't hide behind your skirt no more."

Georgina's lip quivered. Siegfried continued to cackle as he entered the barren dirt of his own yard. Across the street, Eveline Peavey looked up from hanging laundry and nodded at Georgina in commiseration. Georgina waved dejectedly and walked back toward the lurid glow of her own mobile home's door.

That night seeded in Skyler the first understanding of shame. It would take years before he would be able to name it, hate it, and cultivate it into a drive to burn his own history, to singe the ain'ts the what'res from his Midwestern vocabulary and bury a past of rejection and pain. But from that evening, pure pleasure in his diversions was no longer a possibility. Him being The Baroness, performing under the heat of the living room lamp, was suddenly questioned – it was shaded with a morality he had never known.

You shouldn't do that.
What, exactly?
Should I do...this?

Skyler was not one to let others erode his sense of self-worth completely; his mother was sure to inculcate in him a strong bearing, a proud understanding of himself as a person. But even the strongest character cannot fully disregard the comparison of social correctness against an individual's intuition of good. Siegfried made it very clear to Skyler that in Dimmesdale's paradigm, actions performed according to the more masculine side of the spectrum were rewarded, exalted, admired; him putting on lipstick, batting his eyes at the mirror in his mother's vanity every night, was wrong.

You shouldn't do that.

Skyler no longer took his shows outside. He performed for the doll, the mannequin, and the oatmeal in the quiet of the living room after dark. When his mother left the house in the evening he would draw the blinds and use the toilet brush as his cane. For all of society's power, it could not encroach on the safety of Skyler's own home.

In all the years of life inside the trailer, this safety was only broken once. It was the only time Skyler ever saw his mother reduced to nothing. No matter what her usual mood, she could always hide the cracks under eyeshadow, mascara, and a light layer of rouge.

Skyler was asleep. The evening had been quiet; he prepared a can of SpaghettiO's and picked the mold from some pieces of bread in the back of the cupboard. He enjoyed his meal in front of the television set; the stories playing out on the glowing screen were incomprehensible to his nascent understanding of the world. It amazed him to see adult men and women wearing fashionable clothes and living and working in a large city. The canned laughter instructed him when to be joyful; lachrymose music swelling notified him when to be sad.

He was snoring softly on the couch when his mother staggered through the front door. Her hair stood on end; her eyes flared out in tracks of mascara. On most nights, she entered like a ghost, Skyler not registering her soft steps on the shag carpet. But this evening, she was shaking. Never one to smoke in front of her son, Georgina held a limp cigarette to her mouth.

"Mama?" Skyler asked.

Georgina started, jerking back from an abyss of thought. She turned, slowly, toward her son and stared.

"Hello, baby," she said mechanically. "Come over."

Skyler reticently stood. In his child's mind, it was wrong to be up at this time of night. It was the witching hour, the hour that horror and mystery unfolded in the unsafe spaces outside of your home. When he did wake up at this time, he often covered his head with his ratted blanket, believing that the witches and monsters had to see you to be able to claim you as their victim.

"Don't be scared, Sky," his mother said absently. "Come over."

Skyler's bare feet padded across the living room floor. He paused in front of his mother. Drawing closer, he saw that her dress was ripped down the back. It flared out behind her like the plumage of a wild bird.

"Give me a hug. Hug your mama."

Skyler took a half step forward. His mother grabbed him, pulling him into her body. Her fingers clawed through his dark hair.

"We ain't afraid, are we?" she asked, her ringed hands pressing into his scalp. "We're strong. We are strong."

As suddenly as Skyler had been pulled toward her, he was pushed away. Georgina stumbled into the kitchen.

Buried in the back of a high cabinet was a shimmering fifth of amber whiskey. The bottle slammed on the counter; Georgina clawed through another cupboard for a glass. Skyler watched her pour the drink with a shaking hand. The shining spirit in the garish bottle glimmered under the pale lights. In the chaos of that evening, only that liquid carried calm in its gentle flow.

After a full glass, Georgina grabbed the counter. She staggered.

"We ain't afraid. Are we?" In the fluorescent glow of the kitchen, Skyler saw her eyes bleeding tears. He had never seen her cry before.

"They take it all. They take it." She threw her glass to the floor. Skyler jumped in the wake of the crash. He felt tears of his own form at the edge of his eyes.

"Mama?"

"Men," Georgina spat, "they're fucking the same. They all –," she waved her finger at him, "they all are the goddamn same." She ripped open a cabinet and found a book of matches. She lit another cigarette. "Your daddy…" Georgina's face darkened. "Your daddy…"

Skyler had only heard him referred to a handful of times. His father had been a shadow that hung at the periphery of his memory. Far back, way back, in some secluded part of his brain he remembered a large, rugged figure that once shared their space. He had come back once and yelled outside. Violence: that was the word which accompanied thoughts of his father. One rainy day he had pounded on the door. His mother had not cried that day, but she had screamed at the strange man through the flimsy screen door that separated them from the outside world.

Siegfried came over and pulled him back. "I'll call the police if you don't stop this hollerin'," he'd said.

"Your daddy was fucking lazy, violent..." She cut off. For the first time since her return home she locked eyes with Skyler. "You ain't him, though. No, you bury that, ya hear? You're a different kind of man. We're going to hide that piece. No one's gonna know where you came from – that you were the son of that bastard... No. You ain't like him."

Skyler stepped back. His mother was looking at him, but she was not seeing him. Her eyes had refocused and looked at her boy's unknown future. He was no longer the child with the effete manner, but the hulking mass of brutality that she associated with her old lover. For a moment, fear burned from her eyes and scorched the earth between her and her son. She put her hand to her mouth.

"Mama?" Skyler's eyes rained tears.

Georgina staggered around the kitchen. She threw unsure glances in the direction of Skyler, fearful that from his small shadow, a hulking brute would form itself from the darkness. Trembling she gripped the amber bottle and took a long draught.

"They take it all," she whispered, pulling a small, ripped piece of her dress over her womanhood. "You think they won't..."

The next morning Skyler awoke to his mother passed out on the kitchen counter. Relief flooded his heart to see that the frightened, shaking woman of the night before was gone. In her place was his mother; in the warm, dawn light, her face reflected the tranquility and peace of the early morning. Spilled whiskey and a few burned out cigarette butts surrounded her, like the halo of some fallen angel.

She felt his gaze and lazily lifted her head. The fiend present with them the night before was vanquished; the witching hour was over. Her son had stopped trembling between present and future forms, sending horror shivering down her spine.

"Good morning, baby," she said thickly. "Your mama was acting crazy last night. Did she scare you?"

Skyler nodded. "I thought you brought someone home," he said in his high voice. "You kept looking like there was a stranger here."

His mother shook her head. "No, honey. There wasn't anyone else here. It's just us. It's always just us."

Samson

If Skyler's childhood home rested at an intersection of competing ideologies, Samson's was built under a blanket of philosophical uniformity. Anyone wealthy enough to afford one of the palaces in his home suburb, prescribed resolutely to the American Midwestern ideal of hard work, family, and Judeo-Christian "correctness."

Few of these families engaged outside of their socioeconomic class – they did often help at soup kitchens or missionaried to exotic locations to read at schools for the less fortunate, but the fabric of their existence was bleached in white isolationism. They celebrated the blessings that allowed them to live removed from parts of the world that would bring into question their wealth, their idea of God, and their privilege.

Samson's father purchased his large, faux-mansion at the end of the Ohio cul-de-sac at the beginning of his marriage. In those days, the paint was fresh on the new facades; the sidewalks were new and smooth, and the tarmac on the street had not fissured, unwanted roots and weeds yet to creep out of the thick pavement. The subdivision took the name of the year of the signing of The Declaration of Independence. All families moving into its rolling green pastures looked to the idea of 1776, of Independence, as the perfect setting for them to begin a new generation of future leaders, scientists, and heroes.

The dream for Samson's family never came. When Samson was only two years old, his mother left them with barely a word spoken. One pale, gloomy October morning Samson and his father watched the back end of her Jeep Cherokee drive out of their dead-end street.

From that point on, it had been a household of slovenly masculinity. Take-out of varying Asian varieties littered the kitchen table; once a week Samson was tasked with cleaning up the empty containers and throwing them into the large trash bin outside.

Over time Samson's mother took on the form of a dim specter that haunted him at certain intervals but never in a capacity that elicited a warm emotion. Samson's father was so calming and loving a presence that the void she left was one of only bitterness and betrayal. Mr. Briggs did not need to rail against her; his dim eyes, and light sighs when she was brought up in casual conversation were enough to make Samson dismiss her and her memory as an unwanted shadow.

It was his maternal grandmother who redeemed the female sex for him. In disgust with her own daughter's actions, she made her presence a constant in her grandson's life. She and her husband moved to the suburb in which Samson and his father lived. She picked him up from sports practices, went to his choir performances, and made sure he was well-traveled around the contiguous United States. From his grandmother, Samson learned his love for camp, her wardrobe a cornucopia of colors and florals. When their whole family traveled to Disneyland when he was ten, many mistook the middle-aged woman for an older, kindlier Cruella deVil.

Between his grandparents and father, Samson's childhood was one of considerable ease. Were it not for the void of his mother's presence, he would have had a perfectly idyllic youth. Even when he turned thirteen and his father caught him with crusted muscle magazines under his bed, the family never broke its tight circle of love and understanding.

"I'm not upset, Sammy," his father said sipping a beer, "but it's going to be a tough road for you. Gay isn't the easiest way to go through life, but whoever you bring home, we'll welcome. Just wear a condom – and don't let anyone treat you shitty just because you're a guy who likes guys."

Despite his father's words of caution, Samson, in matters of love, always chose to pursue the course of greatest resistance. Rejection, betrayal, and indifference, were the traits that drew him to be attracted to the males in his life. In high school, there were few options for a young gay male in the mid-90's, but he found himself in constant pursuit of those who spurned him.

Vito O'Brien, a half-Italian, half-Irish boy was the target of his affection for most of his adolescent days. Samson joined O'Brien's small coterie as a periphery character. In silence, he watched his crush conquer women and talk about his pursuits for hours as they drove around town and smoked cigarettes stolen from the local gas station.

"Jessica had the best tits, but Hanna is the best pussy, hands down."

Samson watched in awed lust as he'd drape his muscular forearm over the steering wheel. When he'd look back in the rearview mirror and smile, Samson's heart would slam in his chest.

The other boys in Vito's group had no erotic attachment to their social leader but were drawn to his wild, alpha magnetism, cavalier attitude, and the endless funds from his doctor father and lawyer mother. Despite having no job and getting only C's in his studies, he was constantly rewarded with new gadgets, toys, and alcohol from his parents. Mr. and Mrs. O'Brien thought it best to nurture the id-like nature of their only son rather than tame it and pay with unknown repercussions.

Even though Samson spent his high school days chasing the resident bad boy, he remained, in all estimations, a star pupil and considerate son. He received straight-A's, sang in the school choir, and ran the 800 meter for the school's track team. When Vito and the rest of his acolytes would take a bottle of whiskey and stay out until dawn on school nights, Samson would give his regrets and drive back home to finish his homework, complete a science project, or merely keep his father company. His father's goodness compelled Samson, in turn, to be good. The thought of leaving his father alone on a Saturday night brought pangs of regret to even his young, reckless heart.

It took complete removal from his hometown to trigger Samson's first evolution. College offered the opportunity for him to exist completely on his own, free from expectations of family, and unburdened by the small-town stigmas that surrounded his sexuality. He was also free from Vito's spell. On his college campus, there were other out gays and he had the ability to pursue the pursuable, rather than pine after an unattainable ideal. The effect of this realization manifested in a new wardrobe, a new haircut, and a sudden desire to be desired.

Even with his look refreshed, however, the out gay men in his new social circle held little interest for him. Barry, the theater major with bleached tips and a Hollywood smile, excited him no more than the women who fawned over him at frat parties.

"You're gaaaaayyy?! No fair!"

Samson often used the other gay boys for sex and then quietly discarded them. The encounters were not malicious, but always accomplished after several alcoholic drinks, obscuring the emotional impact of the sexual contact in shadow.

"We were so drunk!"

"My gawd, can you believe we did that?"

Samson quickly realized that the out boys didn't draw him erotically like the dream of Vito. Something about an unspoken love, a constant pursuit, was what awakened his sexuality fully.

It was at a frat party at the beginning of his sophomore year that Samson found his first, true love interest. Joel was a Midwest, corn-fed boy with thick, auburn bangs and a square face. He had a girlfriend back in Iowa that he talked about intermittently, but Samson saw a mysterious gleam in his eye one drunk night at a frat party. One of the other fraternity brothers was shirtless, dancing with a girl. Joel's eyes were not focused on the shimmying female figure, but on the chiseled torso of the male.

Samson kept his eyes locked on Joel. After he saw him take several drinks, he casually went up to the thick Midwesterner and put a hand on his shoulder. The mysterious gleam was there again, this time turned on Samson, his brown eyes drinking in the sophomore's lithe, sinewy frame. Gently, Samson led Joel into an empty room.

"Ever done this?" Samson asked running his hands over Joel's thigh.

"Shit, dude – I'm not gay."

Joel fought little, however, as Samson deftly undid his jeans and pulled down the zipper. He wrapped his hand around Joel's throbbing member and gently began to rub.

The next morning Samson got a barrage of instant messages early in the morning.

shit
what happened dude
i was so fucked up

The following six months the two cultivated a heavily closeted relationship in the darkest rooms of Samson's dorm and the frat house. After nightfall and a large number of drinks, Joel became pliable enough to be used for his thick, masculine body. One night Samson pushed him to the limits, stripping down and bending over a palette of boxes in the storage room.

"Joel, it's just like a pussy. It's not cheating; it's not a chick. Just imagine I'm Julie."

In time the twisted relationship bore its ugly fruit. Samson began to imagine his and Joel's future. He knew it was an impossibility, but his heart was a playground for fantasies about them becoming a real couple: Joel would admit his love for Samson, they would go to Joel's home together and tell his parents. In time, they would move into together and begin a life. Samson imagined the two of them bringing a baby carrier and setting it on his father's kitchen table.

The fantasies clouded Samson's understanding of Joel's treatment of him. Their sexual exploits took on a darker shade as Joel's emotions erupted in violent outbursts during their encounters. One night he punched through a wall and threw Samson to the ground when he started to go down on Joel after a frat party. In another incident, a particularly violent one, Joel fucked Samson and slammed his head against the wall, causing a gash to open on his forehead.

"What's this, Samson?" One of the other gays asked him.

"It's nothing – I was drunk at a party."

After three months of hookups that grew more frequent, the situation exploded when Joel's girlfriend came to visit. A combination of too much alcohol and psychological confusion led Joel to be flaccid in the first sexual encounter of their reunion. Julie was accommodating, but Joel's feelings couldn't be calmed. After she left, he asked two of his frat brothers to help take vengeance on Samson.

"Dude fucking owes me money and isn't paying up," he said, keeping his eyes on the ground.

Per usual, he messaged Samson to come over. When he arrived, Joel was waiting in the basement, cracking his knuckles. The other boys waited outside the cellar door for Joel to whistle – the signal that they should enter.

"You play your faggot games with me and got me all fucked up, homo," he whispered, spit flying from his lips. "Lucky for you it was just a once thing and I gave it to my girl as good as ever. But I think we need to teach you what happens when you fuck around with people."

Joel whistled and his two brothers joined him. A sock was slammed into Samson's mouth and the three men threw him to the ground. They accosted him until he had three shattered ribs and his face was covered in blood. When he appeared to be broken completely, Joel's two thugs threw him into the backyard of the fraternity house, where a group of freshmen found him an hour later.

The bruises, marks, and blood were harder to explain this time around; "drunken night" failed to explain the magnitude of his disfigured face.

Samson's father picked him up from the hospital. Fall break was close at hand, so he was allowed to take the week off and return home to recover. The first few days of his respite he stayed in his room, refusing to accept visitors. His grandmother stood outside his door and begged him to come out for a game of croquet or a hand of Gin Rummy, but Samson politely refused. He kept his headphones in, lachrymose love songs flooding his ears.

His father finally forced his way in. He shoved open the weak, plywood door and stumbled into his son's sparsely decorated sanctuary. A few, stray music posters looked down from opposite corners of the room – dusty trophies glimmered on his rickety dresser. Samson, having spent most of his high school years attempting to assimilate into Vito's group, had done very little in cultivating his own personality. His first year of college was a learning experience, discovering gay culture and social norms. The short time he spent with his new, gay brotherhood, however, had not been enough time to fully developed an identity; Joel had cudgeled whatever nascent person was beginning to form. When his father entered his bedroom, Samson was an empty shell, sorting through the shattered pieces of his past and present selves.

"You all right, Sammy?" his father asked. He stood in the middle of the room, hands crossed, unsure of the state of his son. Sweat dribbled down his weathered brow.

Samson looked up from his chemistry textbook and nodded. "I'm fine."

"You want to tell me what this was?"

"I told you what I told the doctors and the police. I was surprised in the frat house basement. I'm not even sure who it was."

Mr. Briggs sighed. "That's your story, huh?"

"Yes." Samson kept his eyes down. "It was just being in the wrong place at the wrong time."

Mr. Briggs walked further into the bedroom. He gingerly ran his hand over his son's dresser. "One of your friends came and talked to me while you were in the hospital." He paused, looking at Samson with inquiring eyes.

The nerves in Samson's scalp rippled. His head grew hot.

"He said you have been showing up around school with some cuts and bruises. It sounds like this isn't the first time this stuff has happened."

Samson's mouth was dry. His hands shook; he closed the book.

"I wanted to see if there was something to talk about."

The air rushed out of the room. Samson felt himself gasp and slump over; there was no moment of uncertainty, no time to think. Without another word, tears began to fall from his eyes. They were copious, large, drops he could not hold back.

"Sammy?"

Samson was shocked by the force of the emotion. His body shook as streams of tears ran down his face. The sobs emanated from so deep within himself, that he felt his whole insides shake with feeling. For so long he had kept the two halves of himself separated: the one half was his daily life, his occasional gay hookups, the boy people saw in his classes and at the cafeteria for meal times; the other was his hidden self, the one that pined for Joel, that took his bruises and transmuted them into stories about their eventual future together. To have his father see them both, was a relief to all his senses. As tears fell from his eyes, he felt his horrible secret was being scrubbed from his insides, washed away in the wake of his father's love.

Over the course of an hour, Samson told his father the whole story: the relationship with Joel, the bruises, the attack that had left him as emotionally scarred as physically. His father rubbed his back and said nothing. When Samson came to the end of his speech, he stopped and the room fell into a peaceful quiet. He was afraid to look at his father, to see judgment, to hear him say that he was a fool.

The two sat in silence, the only sound the slight rustle of clothing as Samson's father ran his hand over his son's back. Mr. Briggs was deep in thought.

There were few times in his life that he felt he had an emotional opening with his son. When Samson came out, was one. This was the other. Coming out had only been a job of acceptance – there was never any question as to how he would respond to that confession.

This was an undiscovered wilderness of feeling.

Carl didn't know how to handle the conversation. His son was in the depths – the deepest recesses of the human condition. He had been there before; the divorce was the most vivid moment of human frailty he'd had to go through. How does one summarize despair? Acceptance he could do, but describing human pain in a tangible, hopeful way was beyond his emotional or intellectual vocabulary. Here there was nothing acceptance could do, there could only be understanding. His son, for better or worse, had grown up. The relationship they would have to cultivate was now entirely different.

"Sammy," he said slowly, "I wish I could say something really helpful here, but I got nothing. The one thing I will say is that when your mother left, I think I had a taste of how you feel now – you feel like the world is against you, and you trust nobody. You put your love into one person and then it's crushed up and thrown away – it's just garbage to them." He sighed. Gently, he stopped rubbing Samson's back and put his hands in his lap. "But it's not garbage, buddy. Your love is never garbage. There are people who don't respect it, but that's not your fault. When your mom left, I had nobody but you. Then your grandma came into the picture. All of us started up a new little family and I had more love than I ever did with your mom." For the first time Samson had ever seen, his father started to tear up. It was barely noticeable, a sparkling droplet at the corner of his eye, but his emotions were dangling in the open. "You're worth the world to me, your grandma, your grandpa, pretty much everyone in your life knows how great and valuable you are. So, don't feel like you have to fall for these guys who treat you like garbage." His father stopped abruptly. The teardrop fell down his face and followed the curve of his jawline. He sniffed once and put his arm around Samson. "Okay, guy? You got that?"

"Yes, sir," Samson said. For the first time since he was a child, he buried his face into his father's shirt. He wiped his eyes on the course, flannel material. His father smelled exactly as he remembered, of stale cologne, fried food, and burnt coffee. "Thanks for listening – and for giving me some space."

His father chuckled.

"What?"

"I wasn't giving you space. I would have come in earlier, but I had no idea what the hell to say."

"Did you tell grandma?"

"I told her you were in a jujitsu tournament and got the shit kicked out of you."

Samson laughed. "She bought that?!"

"She's smarter than that – I'd be ready for some interrogation over Gin Rummy."

"Jesus."

"In the meantime, I ordered us some Chinese."

"Crab Rangoon?"

"Triple order. It was an emergency."

That evening Samson and Carl ate in relative silence in the kitchen. In the dim lights, some ideas about relationships, obsession, and love, began to twist in Samson's subconscious. What was love but a pain that all kept returning to – bruises, abuses, and ultimately, tears slipping into Crab Rangoon? How could he assemble the lessons of his short life into a hopeful vision of future love?

Stephen

When Stephen thought of his childhood, the image that came to the forefront of his imagination was a still life of his father's church. In the almost-memory, he and his family sat in the fiery red pews, the smell of old women's perfume and wood polish hanging heavily in the air. Even though snow pelted the windows, the light in the sanctuary warmed his whole body, the stained glass transmuting cold, gray light into luminous beams of rich sunshine. The sanctuary was quiet, peaceful, and bright. He remembered that in those pre-sexual days, he was a whole person. It was before the world became fractured and non-contiguous. In the solemn glow of his childhood church, he was true to himself and his beliefs. The routine of church gave order and clarity to all.

Those Sunday mornings, everything moved like clockwork. The family awoke at 6 am, had a large breakfast, then dressed in their finest church clothes. Stephen's mother exuded supernatural powers, flitting around the house performing all morning tasks without the slightest appearance of exasperation: cooking breakfast, pressing clothes, dressing in the mirror, adjusting her make up slightly in the car ride to the church.

When the family took their place in the front pew, perfectly quaffed, the children a model of exemplary behavior, the rest of the congregation watched in awe and admiration. The old women fanned themselves and clucked in hushed tones about the orderliness of The Ripley Family, the perfect model of a Christian household with which George and Mary Beth had been blessed.

"God sees a true man of his word and blesses him daily," one of the old ladies said each Sunday when the coterie arrived. "That family is beautiful within and without."

Despite being the middle child, it was Stephen who shone the brightest in this weekly cavalcade. His older brother was brooding and inherited his father's heavy brow, thick, black hair, and deep-set eyes. David was averagely intelligent and chose to work at the local mom and pop restaurant after school rather than pursue extracurricular activities. When spoken to after church services, he gave the impression of being distant, withdrawn, and immersed in teenage listlessness.

Stephen's younger sister was only four, but she did not project the charm of her mother or the warm intelligence of her father. With other children, she followed blindly, always the girl in the back, waiting to be told which Barbie she could be or which Powerpuff Girl she could imitate.

While his older brother and sister passed by as quiet, benign children of God, Stephen shone as a holy beacon of heavenly success. He became a watermark which all other children of the church were held up against. As a fifth grader, many mothers saw him as already more successful than their older children and even their husbands.

"Did you see that Stephen won the regional spelling bee?"

"Stephen Ripley was named the lead in the school play."

"I hear that the teacher just uses his tests to do the grading. He never misses a question."

He inherited all the most admired traits of his parents. Physically, he resembled his mother. They both had light, blond hair, cherubic faces, and shining eyes that flashed different hues depending on the light. From her, he also got the charming laugh and gentle, warm smile that put everyone at perfect ease. His father had bestowed a lean, athletic frame, and sharp intelligence. In first grade, Stephen was given a third-grade textbook and told to study on his own.

At home his brother and sister were protective and kind to their middle brother. In some households, one sibling excelling in such dramatic ways would elicit jealousy and hatred, but in the God-fearing house of the Ripley's, Stephen's charms and triumphs were viewed as blessings only. His little sister strove to be more like her brother, and his older brother felt humbled to be able to protect such a gifted, younger sibling. The house had few fights and the family ran forward in a natural and easy flow.

Neighbors thought for certain that underneath the façade of the preacher and his family's perfect lives there was some dark history – an illicit affair, a fourth child chained in the attic, Mrs. Ripley secretly carrying on a second life as a lesbian or studying witchcraft – but these were all perfectly false. The Ripleys were exactly as they appeared on the surface: holy, God-loving, and simple.

One unforeseen effect of Stephen's wild successes as a child was a sense of isolation and seclusion from others his age. He had few close friends. The one, true companion he had was a neighbor, Davey Lucas, whose esteem he won, not due to his unimpeachable character, but because of their proximity. Often the boys would go on quests in the woods behind their homes searching for goblins, fairies, or elves. In the deepest part of the thicket, they would enact some drama, the play taking on the shape of everything from a superhero conflict, to Mario and Luigi exploring The Mushroom Kingdom. The two stayed over at each other's houses on weekends, playing video games, drinking Mountain Dew, and eating foods that weren't allowed during the more regimented weekdays.

At school children liked Stephen but were not overly friendly towards him. Lunchtimes were spent with a group of boys that, in a fifth-grade universe, exuded a sensibility of "cool." Kane Evanston's parents always had him dressed in stylish button ups or polo shirts; he bleached the tips of his hair when the fashion called for it. Ernie Hemsley was the quintessential chubby boy who made the cool boys laugh. These boys respected and liked Stephen, however, he did not fully merge with them socially. His father's vocation drove an odd moral wedge between them. When they started to talk about girls they liked, they looked at him suspiciously, assuming a preacher's son would not want to engage in so base a discussion.

When the school dance came around in the middle of the fifth-grade year, he and Davey both failed to find a date, or even group of friends, to go with. Stephen found it odd that, while he often heard his own name uttered by girls in the school, and once saw his name scribbled on a list of "Hot Guyz," that no girl talked to him or suggested he go to the event. The closest female interaction he had prior to the soiree was an altercation in which Sarah Kaplan called him a "slug face" at recess.

The night of the Fall Fling he found himself, again, in Davey's basement, eating pizza rolls and playing The Legend of Zelda. Davey's parents were gone and the house tremored with an unknown energy.

"Are you bummed you didn't go?" Davey asked.

"No, it was probably dumb, anyway. I don't know why they even have these things."

"Who would you have wanted to dance with?"

"I don't know… How about you?"

"All the girls at school are stupid. I can't wait for high school when they get really hot, like on TV."

Stephen chuckled. "Sarah Kaplan called me a 'slug face' on Tuesday."

"She did! I think that means she likes you. She calls me 'Gavey,' which I don't think is the same kind of thing."

"Everyone is mean sometimes. You can't help it if you're a Gavey."

Davey looked over at Stephen and snickered. "Oh, yeah?" He dropped his game controller and jumped on Stephen, putting his knees into his chest. "Say 'uncle' and I'll let you up."

Stephen laughed, shoving Davey off easily. With a quick movement, he had his friend's arms pinned behind his back.

"Say 'Gavey' and I'll let you go."

Davey squirmed, eventually wrenching himself free. The two boys tumbled over each other, crashing into the wall. They laughed, neither one of them able to get the upper hand.

Stephen caught the slightly acrid smell of Davey's body, his breath; he felt the sinew in his small arms flex under his hands. His heart beat faster. He felt blood rush to unpredictable parts of his body. Before any emotion could be attached to this physical result, the two boys had separated and lay panting on the floor.

"You're still the Gaveyiest," Stephen said, laughing.

"A Gavey who can beat you up!"

Stephen cocked his head. "If you weren't so tired, I'd test that out."

"Lucky for me," Davey rolled his eyes.

They went upstairs and turned on a movie. When Mr. and Mrs. Lucas came home from their dinner date, the two boys were fast asleep on separate sofas, a bowl of popcorn tipped over in the middle of the floor.

In his dreams Stephen relived the wrestling match, his mind beginning to piece together the physical sensations with emerging emotional connections forming in his brain. Stephen would remember the scene months later, after the physical changes in his body had begun to accelerate, his boyish fat beginning to melt away, small shoots of hair appearing in places they had never been.

It was just a wrestling match, he'd think to himself.

"But…," a buried piece of his psyche would pose in response.

But what?

Hedley

Hank didn't believe in the geographic boundaries that held him in rural Indiana. For him the world was unbounded, endless, a restriction-less, hopeful paradise explored in the pages of books and the glow of the silver screen. When his parents spoke of their entire lives spent in green, unending farmland, he was incredulous that they never fled. To them, the boundaries drawn around them as children in their quiet town, where they went to school, married, and started a family, were as limitless as the vast beyond in which Hank was in constant pursuit. In his youth, satisfaction with the doldrums of this quiet, rural existence seemed an impossible idea.

"You're always somewhere else, Hanky," his mother would say. "Come back to us." She'd playfully snap her fingers and laugh, her coarse, bark filling the house.

But Hank didn't want to return. He read his books; he watched fantasy and science-fiction films. While most children ambled and played through youth, Hank floated. He was barely tethered to the rough farmland his feet traced over every day; he was always above, looking beyond.

His fantastic inner life spilled over into the real as he began to feel his difference from other children. In his imagination, it was *his* face, *his* quest, *his* destiny, that replaced that of the legendary heroes. Internally, he cultivated a dream, a knowledge that he was the protagonist in a drama that played out all around him.

One day in a large bookstore, a name for his breed of person found its way to him: Indigo Children.

Kneeling on the sullied carpet, he read the words; his heart lifted as he finally understood what he was – that there were others like him.

> *"Indigo children are the future. They radiate light and will forge our world in the coming decades. They resist authority, shatter conventional boundaries, and represent the best and brightest of our next generation. They are thinkers, doers, empathetic souls who see the world as it should be, rather than as it is."*

Over and over he whispered the name quietly to himself. Finally, he had a label for the difference he felt compared to others. Unlike them, he resisted falling into the muted background. Hank read; he created. The moment he could construct words from his pen, he forged sentences and created imaginary worlds. He envisioned a separate universe which his friends and parents could not understand. For him, day-to-day existence was legible. If he looked hard enough, he could interpret the signs and signals his everyday reality presented. Two people talking was so much more than a simple, human engagement; the conversation was riddled with emotional fault lines, preconceptions, social cues, and unspoken words. In these invisible cracks, he saw a million different interpretations, endless possibilities he could explore in his imagination. Hank latched onto the idea of Indigo, used it as a mantra, a token that he placed in his heart.

In his sixteenth year, he began to, not just think of his difference, but to have the vocabulary to express it. As a member of the Enhanced Core Student Group his junior year of high school exposed him to philosophy, higher literature, and more complicated versions of human history. Every class brought Hank to a new understanding, a new revelation about the human condition and the blocks that built his world. Never one to speak out loudly in a room, he would listen to his parents talk and poke holes in their simplified beliefs and ideologies – did they even try to understand Marxist principles? Why would one read Tom Clancy when Chaucer was right down the shelf at the library?

In youth, his unfurling mind was, at its core, a fire of optimism.

"I could share these ideas. I can make people change their minds."
"People just need to know."

The expanding knowledge further diminished the geographic scope of his hometown– Kokomo, Indiana become a tiny, uninteresting speck in a world of unbelievable wonder. As he learned, read, and grew, he knew that he was destined for much more than the little town buried in America's heartland.

He confided this all in small journal, a bound, leather volume that was placed under his mattress. The glamor and Jane Austen Victorianism of the journaling, connecting him all at once to a beautiful past, and prismatic, dynamic future.

Journal,

Our extracurricular activity this week is a movie watch at Mrs. Anderson's house. The movie is Boys Don't Cry *– how sweet to engage with something queer, even if it's focused on transvestites and lesbianism. It's nice to not feel so alone; to remember that outside of The Mo there are varieties of different people, different lives, different love, and different pain.*

Education offered to Hank what his Catholic upbringing had never provided – hope. His mother and father found serenity in the idols and worship of their weekly church services, but Hank found them oppressive and destructive of his swelling egotism. When he discovered *The Fountainhead* at fourteen, he realized that some thinkers believed humans to be powerful, untamed, and capable of great achievements. The church made one think of themselves as vile, covered in sin, in constant need to apologize for their existence. His mother and father could slog through the weekly dance of up, down, kneel, down, up, but he would forge his own path.

With God successfully exiled from his psyche, coming out as gay wasn't as clouded in turmoil as many of those in Kokomo that would follow him. He still dreaded confessing his sexuality to his family, feeling the judgment and pity of their eyes on him. Inside he still trembled thinking of telling all his classmates, knowing that the boys would snigger behind his back and the girls would turn up their noses at his choice of lifestyle. But by sixteen, Hank was out to himself and had the courage to tell a few close friends. Anxiously, he awaited the day when he would go to college and be outside of the judgment of his small town.

His sister had been studying at Rose-Hulman for a few months when she returned home, bringing with her a spirit of change and growth – hope for life outside of Kokomo. As she recounted tales of college life, Hank listened intently treasuring stories about her classes, her roommate (a lesbian!), and the quirky coffee shops and restaurants in Terre Haute.

Journal,

Mabel's stories about college are under my skin, in my bones. I can't wait to get out of here, go someplace where living is exuberant, rather than muted. The Mo continues to stifle, to do its best to suck the life out of me. Just a few short years and I'll be free.

In the closet, Hank's affections manifested themselves in unique ways. His first crush was his rival, Brock Halloway. While Hank went through high school as lovable and geeky, the band nerd with a good heart, Brock skated through life on blades of hegemonic masculinity. Captain of the football team, muscular, and the son of two college professors, Brock was the smartest, most athletic, and most pursued boy in Hank's class. He and Hank sparred back and forth for the number two and number three spots in the grade. Florence Jones, a girl who had learned physics in sixth grade, was resolutely in the number one position.

Hank viewed Brock and his battle back and forth as a Ross and Rachel-style of courtship. Eventually, Brock would discover that he loved Hank – they would have sex in the locker room after an important football game.

It was at intersections like this that Hank's own perspicacity of the world and his effusive imagination tore him in two. On one hand, he understood people and their motivations better than anyone around him; if he removed himself from the situation he would have seen Brock as the flag-waving, testosterone-infused, heterosexual male that he was. But his own imagination, his visionary capabilities, obscured this reality, making him pine after the boy, dream of him at night, imagine their love affair with titillating clarity.

These two halves of Hank existed peacefully, until one night after marching band practice, they no longer could; even Hank's incredible imagination couldn't construct an alternative reading of Laura Pearson's story.

He was seated with Laura and their friend, Myrtle, in the football stands. Often, they stayed after band practice in the solitude of the abandoned sports complex. There was an incredible ambience those fall nights. This particular evening, it was already dark, the only lights the emergency floods on the side of the school. Above them stars winked in the velvety Indiana sky. It was early November, the final home game just a few days away. Myrtle shivered, leaning into Hank.

"You really need to bulk up so you can keep me warmer, Turner," she said, her teeth chattering.

"Or you could bulk up," he said.

"If you buy me donuts, I will bulk my heart out for you."

Laura stared at them, eyes sparkling. "You guys, shut up. I have so much news."

"News?" Hank and Myrtle asked together.

"Yes. About Brock."

Hank's heart lifted in his chest. Any anecdote about Brock was a window into the world of his unrequited love. He devoured stories about the football captain with relish. Imperceptibly, he leaned forward.

"Turns out after the Homecoming dance, he didn't go home with his date," Laura continued.

"Who'd he take?" asked Myrtle half listening.

"Annie."

"Are they together?" Hank leaned further in.

"Weeeeelll," Laura threw back her head and laughed. "They are! BUT, Mr. Brock ended up..." She awkwardly pantomimed a blow job, "with someone else!"

Hank's eyes went wide. "Someone else..."

Could the someone be...? Could it be a *boy*? Hank's mind raced.

"Is anyone surprised?" Myrtle flopped back in the bleachers and looked up at the sky.

"Who?" Hank whispered. In that fleeting moment, before the truth cascaded from Laura's lips, it could be anyone: another football player, the Homecoming King, some unknown boy next door... and always, the possibility, on another night, Hank himself.

"Cassie Wheaton."

"Gross," Myrtle made a gagging motion. "I've heard she is expert level at blow jobs. She does enough of them."

"Does everyone know?" Hank asked. "I mean, does Annie?"

"Annie thinks Cassie's lying to get attention. Of course, Brock isn't fessing up to it. All he said was that Cassie's last boyfriend is 'that fag Peter Bailey' so she probably wanted to look cool again."

Myrtle's eyes shot to Hank with a sympathetic glance. She was one of the few who knew his secret.

Hank shook slightly. He tried to maintain his composure. "That's pretty brutal," he said.

"You know Brock. Cassie is probably one of twenty girls he's letting blow him at school. I mean, I'd blow him if he let me." Laura shrugged.

Hank let out a fake, staccato laugh and stared at the blanket of stars. Something in him shifted. The story had done two things for his understanding of his own world. One, it had shaken him from his fantasy of ending up with Brock in a romantic capacity. For the first time, he saw clearly the illusion he allowed to veil his senses and blind him to the understanding that, not only was Brock not a viable romantic attachment, but he was also, a womanizing, vicious, homophobe. Two, it shook him from the safety which he liked to believe protected him in the closet. Kokomo wasn't the safest place to be, but he assumed that his silence was a protection from the gay-bashing epithets muttered by other boys at school. With this story, he was again exposed, frightened – vengeful.

That night Hank went home to think. Sitting cross-legged, his fingers steepled under his chin, he put his Indigo power into full effect. Tenuous lines began to form between all those around him:

Laura…

Myrtle…

Brock…

Cassie…

He traced the social threads which bound them all together. In this cartography, he looked at avenues between the players, roles he could pluck for each of them to play. Brock had crossed a line; he had violated the sacred form of their love Hank inculcated inside of his mind. For this betrayal, he would suffer. For Hank, this wasn't a vendetta, but a course of justice.

It wasn't the first time Hank had plotted in this capacity. He had manipulated his way into getting a dog when he was in first grade. When he turned fourteen, he convinced his grandmother to buy him a new PlayStation outside of the standard gift-giving season of Christmas. This incident, however, was complex – it wasn't getting what he desired, but orchestrating a scheme, which would bring others to act on his behalf.

A full week passed with Hank trying to put pieces together. In his journal he scribbled plots, ideas, and courses of action. A breakthrough occurred one afternoon in science class. That evening he went home and outlined a vengeful manifesto, a malicious flow chart with all his actors and possible outcomes. In the soft glow of his reading lamp, he looked at the completed plot and smiled to himself. He was ready, not only for one plan, but for several possibilities that would wreak vengeance upon Brock.

The following Monday, he went into action.

The first step was playing to Cassie. Laura had been accurate in her assessment of her character: even if she hadn't really blown Brock, it was believable she would have created the lie to get attention.

"Hey, Cassie!" Hank said kindly, approaching her at her locker. "What's up?"

"Hey, Hank. Not a lot," Cassie drawled. A mirror hung in her locker which monopolized her full attention. Delicately, she patted her cheeks, making sure none of her makeup had run during the early part of the day.

Written in Hank's notebook:

Player 1: Cassie Wheaton. Weaknesses - insecurity, vanity.
"Is that something on your lip?" he asked.
"What?" She finally gave him her full attention. "What is it?"
"I don't know, sorry. I thought I saw like a bump."

Cassie put her hand to her mouth. "Really?" she asked. Her eyes returned to the mirror with a new, manic energy. Nervously she sneered, exposing her lip. "You really think...?"

Hank smiled to himself. "It's probably nothing. Sorry! I just noticed it yesterday in biology."

The scene: biology class, so much for the imagination.

Setting was another crucial piece of the plan. In Hank's mind, the locations of the incidents were just as important as character. One could use the surroundings to add effect to anything. He likened it to Hawthorne using the dense forest in *The Scarlet Letter* to add complexity to Hester and the preacher's turmoil. In this particular instance, it was the centralized classroom that connected all his stray pieces: biology. He, Myrtle, and Cassie all intersected in that room every day. The shining coincidence for this meeting point was the fact that they were just starting to discuss viral infections.

Myrtle rarely studied, which made her the best target for the second step. This piece was also the biggest gamble. It would be skill and luck that triggered Myrtle to play her part at the exact moment it was needed. A missed cue meant Hank would be forced to break the seals on plan B or C.

After evening band practice, Hank laid his trap.

"Did you read the biology section for tomorrow?" he asked.

"Read? A textbook? You've got to be kidding."

Player 2: Myrtle Jennings. Targets: Brashness, inquisitiveness, low-interest in scholarly success.

"I didn't think you would, but there was some stuff on herpes, which seemed right up your alley."

The bait, the gamble: would Myrtle take it? Could he draw her to the conclusion which he needed her to arrive?

Myrtle roared. "Really cute, Turner. Yes, I need to know my STDs, obviously. I have so many men clamoring for my attention."

"I'm just saying, the book says it can live in your system for years before it pops up. Then your lip looks like football leather."

Myrtle raised an eyebrow. "Years?"

Hank's heart pounded. She was following script. His scalp prickled, chilled lines shooting over the top of his skin.

"Yes!" he laughed. "Like dozens of years. It's in the book."

"I don't care enough to look. But that is interesting."

"If you don't believe me ask Mr. Phelps."

Hank's heart stopped. It was a weird thing to say – it sounded unnatural. He would never give a shit about whether Myrtle read her biology homework. He may care, though, about: "In fact, why don't we bet? You ask Mr. Phelps – if I'm right, you buy my lunch tomorrow."

Myrtle shrugged. Hank held his breath.

"How many years? AND! If there is a special Mr. Phelps twist that makes you wrong, then I win!"

"Twenty years."

"Shake on it, Turner."

That night Hank lay in bed. It wouldn't work, he thought. It couldn't work. The wheels were in motion, he just needed the last two stars to align. The odds of them coming together perfectly were slim. The moments and actions were simple, but the game was not. People were unpredictable, but he needed both Cassie and Myrtle to be shamelessly predictable – he needed them to be themselves in a vacuum. There could be no variation.

The collision occurred the next morning after lunch. They all sat in biology, eyes barely open, Mr. Phelps droning about venereal disease in front of an old slide projector. Its dim light threw a herpes sore three feet high onto the wall.

Hank reminded Myrtle of the bet before class. Deftly, he tried to catch Cassie's eye and rub his lip at the same time, but she had not met his gaze. All the gears turned, but whether the clock would chime was still to be seen.

Myrtle threw a sidelong glance to Hank and raised her hand. "Mr. Phelps," she asked, not waiting to be called on, "is it true that herpes can live in your system for years before it makes your lips weird?"

Hank sucked in a breath. Myrtle's role was complete and perfect.

"Well," Mr. Phelps adjusted his glasses, enthralled that he had found a topic a student wanted to discuss, "it can lay dormant for two years, but the most common manifestation period is two weeks. You know, interesting fact, herpes can actually be dormant for forty years between outbreaks!"

Hank's scalp again prickled when he saw Cassie out of the corner of his eye. Her hand flew to her face. She looked anxiously at Hank. Hank, acting as he had rehearsed, looked innocently shocked at the realization they were both supposed to be having.

Everything had come together.

It only took two days to get full circle. He and Myrtle were sitting at the lunch table when Laura stormed over and plopped herself down on the plastic bench beside them.

"You guys," she whispered. "You. Will. Not. Believe. This!"

"What?" Myrtle asked.

Hank continued eating his lunch.

"Remember that rumor about Cassie and Brock?"

"You mean the one with the...?" Hank mimed a blow job.

"The very one!" Laura clapped her hands. "Well, turns out Cassie thinks that," she lowered her voice, "Brock gave her herpes."

"Herpes!" Myrtle bellowed.

A group of neighboring girls turned and snickered. They knew the rumor as well.

"Can you believe it? Cassie said she noticed this weird lip thing and it was *two weeks* after she hooked up with him. That's perfect herpes time."

"You really think it's true?" Hank asked coolly.

But he knew it didn't matter.

One thing this event solidified in his mind, a fact that he had begun to pick up on through his advanced classes and Indigo power, was that the truth rarely mattered. Perceived truth was what everyone was interested in – if you could reflect reality to others as you believed they wanted to see it, then you could shape their perceptions with any kind of lie.

Hank packed this revelation away. For now, he would celebrate: Peter Bailey, and his own thwarted love, were vindicated.

2005: Men in a Maze

The recorder pauses.

A woman in the front row beside you, who had held her nose high in the beginning of the trial, has shifted her gaze downward; in her hands, she frantically twists a silk handkerchief.

Eyes in the crowd flit between the men on trial – do they look younger than at the ceremony's commencement? Something is different, although they all appear to be frozen upon the scaffold; they do not blink, they do not smile, they do not cry or scowl.

You are growing thirsty, your throat clenching and saliva forming at the back of your throat. Should you move and get something to drink? How much longer can the trial last?

"It was sad that bit about the…"

"Excuses for perpetuating abuses, if you ask me."

The sun is higher; you put your hand to your brow and look upward, hoping a few stray clouds may skitter across its golden face and bring some solace from the heat. But no relief is in sight. Sweat flows down your forehead; the sticky arm of your neighbor presses against your chest. The men before you have sweat dripping down their bodies, their white tunics stir slightly when the breeze blows.

For a moment, with the recorder's silence, the blazing sunlight, and the parched feeling at the back of your throat, you forget the purpose of the gathering at all.

"Why are we here?" you think, brushing sweat from your cheek. "Why are we all choosing to be in this heat?"

It is only a momentary thought, however; the magistrate coughs and the recorder pushes forward with the evidence. Again, your attention is riveted to the stage, to the beings before you who have wronged you. They, too, were wronged in some ways, but it is the responsibility of this jury to break the cycle. The sun shines on all, but it is the duty of man to let his inner heart mete out grace and justice. Those hidden away parts are the whole, not the bags of flesh exposed to the sun. In broad daylight, we are perhaps all equal, but the shadows of the heart tell the true story of the man.

Skyler

Make up was no longer the biggest interest to Skyler as he stared into his mother's vanity. As a child he'd experimented with rouge, lipstick, and mascara. Over time, the interest in putting on face dwindled. Now it was the shape, the form of his mouth, which consumed his interest.

"The rain in Spain stays mainly in the plain."

One afternoon his mother brought home a cassette of *My Fair Lady* and forever altered his mirror-centric activities. It revealed to him the differences between himself and his favorite stars. He had the same dark hair and small stature as Tom Cruise, but something was missing. The new musical made it very clear that he needed to transform class, style, and diction to become his heroes. Maverick did not use "ain't"; he didn't staple "ya hear" onto the end of common questions.

"It is indubitably a surprise to see you, sir."

It wasn't just Eliza Doolittle who opened his eyes, however; Skyler's own experiences taught him a great many things about what he was and what he was not.

By the time he reached fourth grade, it was manifestly clear that he was poor. His clothing was old, faded, and ratted. Other students wore new clothes, had shiny sneakers, but Skyler had only the few items that his mother bought from Dollar General or Goodwill. Georgina did the best she could according to her taste and style; she utilized her skill in sewing to patch up clothing and erase as much age and wear as she could. When she could afford it, she bought him button ups, sweaters, and jeans, but no matter how hard she strove, no matter how stylish the clothing had been at one point, it was always worn, it always smelled lightly of mothballs.

Evidence of his penury was also glaringly evident in the school cafeteria. He had to get to school early so he could have the government subsidized breakfast; when he checked out and got his fish sticks and apple sauce at lunch, Mrs. Bailey checked his name on a special list that all boys and girls knew was for children whose parents couldn't afford to pay.

What else was Skyler? He was not like other boys. He did not envy Jonah Doran's new, slick Nike windbreaker, but rather, Charlotte McCafferty's floral print dress with the ruffles around the hem. During physical education courses, he sat with the girls in the bleachers to wait for mandated play time rather than running out with the other boys to pick up balls and commence immediate chaos. When Eliot Roth brought in his earthworms in a dirty mason jar, Skyler turned up his nose and refused to pass the jar to the student next to him.

At the intersection of these differences, these, in Skyler's mind, curses bestowed on him by the hand of fate, was the twisted moral seed planted in him by Siegfried Essen so many years before.

You shouldn't do that.

But he was born to do these things. He was born poor. He was born to love rouge and sparkles and high-energy musicals. If he shouldn't do these things, then why did he naturally tend toward them? If these were in and of themselves wrong, then why should other natural moral structures apply to him, either?

The progression of this line of thought ended in a ten-year-old Skyler becoming an artful thief. After school, he would make one excuse or another about coming home late and go into any number of stores and purloin a single item. The target always varied – sometimes it was chocolate, sometimes a shirt, sometimes a pair of sandals – but he always slickly let his fingers dance over the rows of items in the store, then *flick*, it dropped into his pocket, into his Pokémon backpack, into his coat. A childhood full of play acting made his escape a simple matter of smiling benignly and waving as he made his way out of the store. He marked days on his calendar and would only return when he was sure the missing item was completely forgotten.

Skyler's skill at thievery was second only to his cleverness. He knew his mother would be furious. For all her faults, she stood blameless in terms of simple moral mores. One did not steal. One did not lie. One did not slander the neighbors (apart from assholes like Siegfried Essen). Skyler hid his collection of items in a small bag that he kept under his bed. He would often take a shirt in his backpack and change in the bathroom once he got to school. Georgina loved her son, but her interest in the minutiae of his day-to-day life was limited. She made sure he was healthy, fed, and generally happy, but didn't probe deeply where it wasn't necessitated. Skyler, from a young age, took on the characteristics of his father, stoic, his face a screen on which illegible emotions were projected.

"Darlin', how was school?"

"Good, Mom. We studied a story about a boy and his dog in reading class."

"Was it funny?"

"It was okay."

They watched television in the evening before she went to work. Mostly he sat impassively, his face and dark eyes riveted on the screen. She only knew his internal thoughts when he'd turn occasionally, quietly asserting his feelings about the ghostly images on the screen:

"This is my favorite part – 'Shall We Dance.'"

In this manner, the two settled into a predictable, conflict-free relationship. Georgina watched him lovingly as she fixed her dresses and snuck glances at the pages of the unfinished script hanging on the wall. Every day, the white paper seemed to yellow, grow further into a part of some lost history.

Skyler shared specific pieces of himself with his mother and hid the rest. His life of thievery and his perfect grades, were things that he kept private and to which Georgina turned a disinterested eye. To Georgina, no news from a school administrator was good news.

"You doin' good in school, baby?"

"I'm doing well, Mom."

The balance was jeopardized one fall evening at the start of Skyler's fifth grade year.

Mrs. Jacobson, the art teacher, took a special liking to all her students who exhibited homosexual tendencies. Skyler was one of these, despite his best efforts to conceal his differences from his classmates. At school he hid pieces of himself that shined dramatically when he was alone in the trailer, his inanimate audiences watching his latest dance routine. When he was among his peers, Skyler turned inward, was taciturn, barely seemed to breathe.

Lunch was spent with his back to the rest of the cafeteria. Along with him in that remote corner were Jerry, a wheelchair bound fourth grader with his aid, Mrs. Stephenson, and Melody, a girl with rosacea and a stutter, who ate lunch with one of her My Little Ponies set on the table for company. Skyler found this crowd to his liking, quiet, indifferent, and outcast like himself.

This was the table that Mrs. Jacobsen took under her wing that year, stopping by and engaging them all in polite conversation during her tours as the lunch room attendant. Skyler reminded her of a number of gay men she had known in college. Even though he exhibited no promise in the visual arts, she believed he did, based solely on the evidence of his emerging sexuality.

"And how are we today? Melody, what have you got for lunch?"

"Bologna." Melody's answer was almost as reliable as ancient scripture. It was, would be, and only could be "bologna."

"Well, that sounds good! Any treats?"

"No, ma'am."

"Mrs. Stephenson, how are we today."

"Fine, Debbie. We're getting on along, aren't we, Jerry?"

Jerry rolled his eyes.

Skyler found it exhilarating when Mrs. Stephenson used Mrs. Jacobsen's Christian name. The breach in propriety, like his pilfering, made his heart quicken.

Although he never engaged Jerry directly, he counted him as one of his favorite people in the whole school. Jerry very often would flip Mrs. Stephenson the bird when her back was turned, an action that both Skyler and Melody loved dearly. It was one of the few times the three children came together over any particular point of interest, all of them giggling until Mrs. Stephenson's great rump turned around and they were confronted with her wrinkled face and withering permanent.

"Skyler, are you excited for art today?" asked Mrs. Jacobsen.

"Yes, ma'am."

"Your last watercolor was very nice. I think you'll like today's activity."

"Yes, ma'am."

This routine was acted out daily, the three students barely uttering a few laconic sentences over the course of Mrs. Jacobsen's interrogation.

Then one day, there was a shift. Instead of the casual stroll to the table, Mrs. Jacobsen showed up quickly, greatly agitated. Rather than exhibiting her usual lackadaisical confidence, she was flushed, her eyes rapidly flitting between Skyler, Jerry, and Melody. Her speech sputtered out in a more staccato rhythm. Even Mrs. Stephenson noticed the shift, her normally dead eyes looking up with a furtive gleam.

"All right, Debbie?"

"Yes. Why, yes! Why do you think – yes, of course!"

With that she huffed away. Jerry looked at both Melody and Skyler and shrugged indifferently.

Skyler discovered the reason for Mrs. Jacobsen's dramatic transformation immediately following art class. While the other students clamored to the exit, Mrs. Jacobsen called Skyler's name lightly.

"Could you stay after class a moment?" she asked wringing her hands.

Skyler approached her desk, his almond eyes full of questions.

"Skyler," she started once the last of the children left and the door closed, "I wanted to talk to you about yesterday."

"In art class?"

"No," she pulled at the ringlets in her grey and brown hair. "No, I went out shopping yesterday and I saw you in Tibbett's General Store."

Skyler's eyes went wide. Mrs. Jacobsen saw the confirmation in his face and slowly paced over to the window.

"Skyler, I don't think I need to tell you that what you did was wrong."

"Mrs. Jacobsen, it was an accident." Skyler's gift of performance took control of his actions. He was Maria confessing to the Reverend Mother. "I took the chocolate and put it in my pocket, but I meant to pay for it."

"Skyler," Mrs. Jacobsen turned to the small boy, "it's not the theft that really concerns me. Why were you out alone after school? Where was your mother?"

"She was at home. She is getting ready for work at that time."

"She works at night?"

"Yes, ma'am."

"What does she do?"

Deep down Skyler new the truth, the real truth. But that was never spoken out loud, even in the safe space of their home. "She's a waitress."

"I see." Mrs. Jacobsen clasped her hands together. "Skyler, I wonder if you would do me a favor."

"A favor?"

"Yes, you see, I help with the after-school program here. It's every day from 3:30 to 5 o'clock. I wonder if you would attend."

Skyler's cheeks flushed. In his embarrassment, the subtle twangs returned to his practiced speech. "Mrs. Jacobsen, I ain't got the money for that. I know it costs money. Laura goes and her daddy writes her a check for it. My mom couldn't…"

"Let me figure out the money, Skyler. There are ways to get around that obstacle. Will you go, though?"

Skyler hesitated. Part of him wanted to go. Despite his indifference, his quiet, his elation in being alone and living in fantasy at his home, he pined for a friend. When other boys ran and played after the final school bell rang, some part of him wanted that camaraderie. He wanted someone to sit with, to swing with, to tell his stories to.

Was there another boy or girl who dreamed of being The Baroness? Did a boy or girl who sat next to him in class ever dream up a musical number about recess?

But another part of him, the part that his mother unwittingly seeded in him in his early years, whispered doubts.

You shouldn't trust anyone.

The world was out to get you. You had to be self-reliant and strong.

We ain't afraid, are we? We're strong.

What would happen if he were to trust another person? If Mrs. Jacobsen found a way to pay, what would he find in the after-school group? Was the world really as his mother foretold? Or was there something more?

"You can think about it, Skyler," Mrs. Jacobsen smiled. "But I think you'd have a very good time and I don't want the cost to be prohibitive."

"Prohibitive?"

"I don't want that to stop you from coming."

That night, out of chance, Skyler put on *Bye, Bye Birdie*. During "The Telephone Hour" his heart leapt as he imagined himself in the middle of the chain of rumors. He could have friends to tell secrets and gossip. *Mrs. Jacobsen caught me stealing at the store.* For a brief, shining moment, Skyler didn't have to be in The Alps, in far off London, or in a pajama factory – he could simply live and it could be full of dancing, music, and hope.

Skyler didn't tell his mother he was going to attend the program. Just as he had done for many years, he made up excuses for getting home around 5:30 every evening. Mrs. Jacobsen let him out at the entrance to Harmony View and he quietly sauntered home. His first day he met a boy named Lawrence with thick glasses and a shirt several sizes too small.

"Hello," he said in a high, quavering voice. "You want to play a game?"

Samson

Samson's apartment was near enough to the Philadelphia Art Museum to require constant vigilance of baffled tourists. As they wandered around the museum, clucking about the Rocky statue, Samson kept his head down, his iPod cranked, and his hands buried in his pockets. It was his worst nightmare to be stopped by one of these listless beings and forced into a conversation.

"Which one is The Liberty Bell?"

"Y'all got good tacos near here?"

It was his boyfriend's idea to live in the city's downtown area. Samson wanted to live in the heart of the Gayborhood but Christian insisted they keep some distance between themselves and the other gays.

"No need to be in the thick of it. We can go to be with the gays when it suits us."

"Us" – the pronoun that came to describe Christian's tacit control over Samson. The older man got him to acquiesce through subtle language turns, by taking his voice. Samson was amenable to this after the mess in college.

After Joel and the abuses of his sophomore year, he returned to school an altered man. Sex rarely drove his motivations; his main concerns were in cultivating his physical appearance and generating friendships with those around him. When his sex drive overthrew him, it wasn't to his friends that he turned, but rather to craigslist, digging through the postings and finding some other closeted jock or local he could blow in seedy corners around town. In this way, he was able to satisfy his sexual impulses for the unattainable and still maintain a veneer of self-control and propriety. His clandestine sexual activities led many to perceive him as celibate, a kind of gay Mother Theresa, the holy homo who had been through abuse and now abstained from sex all together, awaiting the perfect man.

The tangential effect of this reputation was that Samson was one of the most desired men in the gay university clique. While he went in pursuit of his own unattainable conquests, he became the unattainable man to those around him. He spent hours in the gym, sculpting his physique. Although his grandmother's wardrobe was eccentric, it gave him an eye for color, style, and design. His obsession with fashion and his physical form contributed to his reputation of being the "it" gay boy on campus. When it was just an emerging fad, Samson was resolutely the campus metrosexual.

Every one of his suitors, however, filled him with a resigned indifference. Cody, the tiny, muscular bottom from Palm Springs, was attractive, but his assiduous pursuit of Samson only elicited sympathy from the target of his love. They spent one afternoon together, but the simpering, fawning Floridian couldn't crack Samson's indifference to dating. By the end of the afternoon, Samson sent the boy on his way, not even entertaining a haphazard hookup in the dorm.

Rolf, a German boy studying Physics his junior year, was slightly more successful than Cody. His pragmatism and lack of emotionality was much more attractive to Samson than Cody's sycophantic pandering. Over the course of the fall semester they engaged in regular sexual encounters, even going so far as to appear together at gay social events. Samson called it off in the spring when Rolf suggested they "make it official."

Samson didn't entertain a serious relationship until the fall semester of his senior year. While he was home for autumn break his grandmother and father both voiced concerns over his lack of a boyfriend.

"Don't you want to bring someone home, Sammy?" his father asked. "We could do dinner and take him around to the sites. It'd be fun."

"You know I'm getting old," his grandmother said adjusting her fur stole. "I'd like to see you happy."

The familial concern drove Samson to search for someone to date. In his mind finding a boyfriend wasn't a romantic comedy-style romp to find true love, but rather a logical quest to find someone he could tolerate for a prolonged period of time. His mother and father's relationship made this alteration in his mind from a young age – true love didn't exist. If it did, it was contained in the quiet sighs of his father whenever his mother's name was dropped into conversation. When his first "relationship" ended in assault, it doubly reinforced this concept in his own mind. His ideal relationship was the sexless union forged between his father and grandmother in the wake of his family tragedy. Their practical connection was an example of a relationship that could last decades; the frivolous love connections nurtured by his friends at school would burn out in a matter of months, if not weeks. Hearing conversations amongst his friends, in many cases, was like listening to conversations on a different planet.

"I just want a boooooooy! I need someone to cuddle!"

"Why can't I find someone to date?!"

His boyfriend, Christian, entered his life via a casual happenstance while he was interviewing for a job in Philadelphia. Samson flew out one Thursday evening for a Friday interview at a bank. Being removed from his usual circles, the thrill of a possible sexual encounter pulled at him throughout his flight. By the time he landed, his libido was on fire, his dick rock hard in his shorts. The first action he took upon arriving at the hotel was to use the business center to logon to craigslist.

M/M, sex only, no cuddling

The post included a picture of a hirsute torso with prominent abs.

By midnight, the mystery man was knocking on his door at the hotel. What followed was a dream-like sexual encounter for Samson. Christian entered wearing a tank top and cargo shorts. Having just come from the gym, he smelled of sweat. Barely ten words passed between them in that initial interview: Christian entered, pulled off his shirt and shoved Samson on the bed. The procedure was clinical, Christian flipping Samson over, pulling down his pants and prepping his asshole.

"Lube?" he growled.

Samson came within the first ten minutes, overwhelmed by the sheer force of masculinity that entered his hotel room. After Christian finished, he zipped up and put his hands behind his head.

"You're hot," he said. "Mind if I stay and we go again?"

That night they had sex four times apart from the first. Samson entered the bank for his interview with a pronounced, hobbling gait.

Coincidence built upon coincidence, with Samson getting the job at the bank and Christian offering him a place to crash until he could get his own apartment. Within a few weeks, however, the two men were sleeping in the same bed, going to dinner together, and, in all practical ways, boyfriends.

The thrill of the first sexual encounter diminished after a few months in Philadelphia. The raucous, closeted affair was replaced by bi-weekly sexual exploits that included Christian rolling over and pulling Samson close after coitus. It was never an actual decision or discussion for them to be an official couple, but rather a quick, unintentional decline into a relationship.

Christian, as a person, proved to be a completely different entity from the musky hunk who forced his way into Samson's hotel room. In the real world, Christian was a slightly effeminate gay with an obsessive-compulsive need to keep his kitchen clean. He ironed everything from his jeans to his towels; the task of doing his hair in the morning took roughly thirty minutes. Although Samson had initially been stunned by Christian's thick chest hair, he now realized it was shaved and kept with the avid attention the Japanese reserve for bonsai trees.

But, in the end, it was what his grandmother and father wanted. Samson was dating a handsome, successful man in a big city. They lived in a spacious apartment and hosted dinner parties for their friends. When Samson's father visited him his first spring in Philly, Christian bought him dinner and champagne at an upscale restaurant near Chestnut Hill. As Christian discussed global events, his 401K, and the perspective he had gained since turning thirty the previous year, Samson's father's smile almost tore the corners of his mouth.

The couple fell into faithful, taciturn step with Samson slowly merging his life into his first, official boyfriend's – his I became "us." When Christian told him to take off what he was wearing and put on something nicer, he always did. When Christian spoke patronizingly to him about the collapsed housing market, the neighborhood social scene, or current events, Samson nodded and considered it an educational opportunity.

The older gay man lulled Samson into a complacent sleep. If ever there was a moment to doubt the strength of their bond, Christian filled it with money, a dinner out, or a condescending speech about Samson's youth. Christian's friends reinforced the myth of the couple's happiness. Whenever Samson and Christian went to a friend's home for dinner, the host would wax about how wonderful it was that they had found each other; these diatribes generally twisted around to discuss Christian's superiority over Samson, his wisdom, his money, his upwardly moving position in his consulting firm.

The two carried on in this soporific state for two years before Samson collided with another man and his second gay evolution was triggered.

"Hi handsome," Edward Varos said one morning. The two were in line at a local coffee shop near Samson's bank.

Samson looked around nervously, not sure the well-dressed man was speaking to him.

"Yeah, you," Edward's magnetic grin lit up the room. "What's your name?"

"Samson..." he smiled. It was the first time in months someone had flirted with him. Christian rarely let him go out to the bars.

"Strong name." Edward gently gripped Samson's bicep. "Strong man." He winked.

Samson's skin flushed.

"I've seen you come in here for a few weeks. I like your shade of queer. No offense, but I can smell the gay on you a mile away."

"That's... a very interesting skill to have."

"I try."

Edward stared at Samson. The young man awkwardly put his hand behind his neck, scratched. He averted his eyes to the floor.

"I don't bite," said Edward finally blinking. "Unless you're into it."

The encounter ended with Edward giving Samson a business card. When it slipped into his hands, Samson could tell, just from the weight and the shine of the gold-embossed font, that Edward was someone important.

"I have a boyfriend," Samson said shyly looking at the token.

Edward shrugged. "I have boyfriends occasionally, too," he said with a wink. "Call me when you're bored."

That night Samson couldn't sleep. Christian had been too exhausted for sex, so the two parted ways at 10 pm, Christian to bed and Samson to the kitchen to make a snack. He took out a pan, dug through the freezer, but stopped short of pulling out the frozen broccoli and chicken breast. Outside he saw the shining lights of the city.

Had he ever looked at them?

Christian's snores from the bedroom kept the room from being fully silent. Samson studied the garlands of white, yellow, and red city lights that decorated the skyline. He thought of his walks home, the annoyance of the tourists. He suddenly understood them. How wonderful it must be to go to a new place, see a new skyline, look into a crowd and see hundreds of faces you have never seen before. In his youth, Samson never cultivated any interests of his own, too busy following, fawning over boys that aroused him. If he had looked into himself back then, he may have found he loved space, travel, or poetry, topics that took one to the end of their own understanding.

Edward Varos – the name shook him.

In the pale lights of the city, Samson saw a million tiny doorways, a dazzling, infinite number of worlds open to him. Each apartment lamp, each fluorescent light in an office, was a universe in and of itself. What would someone see if they looked into his and Christian's home? Would they see a happy couple; two men who, despite prejudice and social pressure, had forged a life together in a bustling metropolis? Would light shine through the cracks, the shellacked surface that Christian was so adept at applying to their relationship?

What had his mother seen when she shone the light on her life with his father?

The next morning Samson rose early and prepared breakfast for Christian. Feelings that had burned in the lonely dark of the previous evening made him feel dirty and ungrateful in the light of the sunrise. What would his grandmother and father say if they saw the creeping darkness that swept over his imagination? They wanted him to be happy. Christian made him happy. They were happy.

It was fall when the shadow took full root, its dark flower blooming. Samson was promoted at the bank. He was, at long last, dropping junior from his financial analyst title. At a dinner party with their mutual friends, Christian brought this up, not to celebrate his boyfriend's advancement, but rather to use it as tool of derision.

"He's finally dropped the junior," Christian said. "We'll see if he starts carrying some weight in the relationship."

Samson was not meant to hear it. Coincidence brought him out of the bathroom at the exact moment the words were uttered. It wasn't, though, the fact that it was said, it was Christian's reaction to Samson overhearing it that caused the shellacked surface of their relationship to fully crack.

"What did you say?" Samson almost whispered.

"I just think it's nice you'll be able to help out. I've been carrying us for quite a while."

There were few times Samson lost control of his emotions. Since the time he cried openly after the incident with Joel, tears were no longer the outlet his feeling took for release. As he looked at Christian in that moment, his feelings were manifested as raw, uncontrolled rage.

Slowly, he turned around. His hands shook as he walked into the bedroom to collect his coat.

"Childish," Christian said. "They may need to put junior back in the title."

In the years they had been together, Samson had not been childish. The best words to describe him with Christian were quiet, somnambulant, and acquiescent. There were nights when he would get drunk, but never had he done something that would mark him as in his early twenties. Never had he screamed or raged in a bar. Not once had he vomited in public company. Only rarely had he been drunk enough to forget himself.

His coat secured, Samson flew down the stairs and into the street. He couldn't control his breath, something wild in him had been set loose.

It wasn't drunkenness but emotional instability that caused him to totter down the street. Unintentionally, his hand found its way to covering his heart.

Single moments in a relationship, especially an unhealthy one, can ignite, combust trails of powder shed over the course of years. Childish had been the trigger – Samson was proud of himself, proud of his advancement and Christian found a way to turn it into humiliation. Suddenly he was crushed under a deluge of memories, vignettes from the past that revealed to him the true state of the affair:

You shouldn't wear that. It makes you look chubby.
I'll get this. I know you can't afford it.
Mr. Briggs, I'll take good care of Samson.
This is the best for us.
Us.

It wasn't his father and grandmother he thought of in that moment, but rather his mother. Had she been the one under attack? Would his father pit her against herself? Had she triumphed and he turned it against her? Is this what causes someone to just leave?

The lights of the Philadelphia skyline were shining. That night they appeared brighter than they had ever been before. He had lived his life in fear from the minute Joel struck him. When he was nineteen he had been beaten into a closet – not of fear about his homosexuality but his ability to be sexual at all. Sex was violence and danger. Christian showed him something contained, reliable, and protected. But at what cost?

The world spun violently, the city lights becoming flares in the dark. There were innumerable worlds to explore all around him, but he had hidden himself from them.

The figure of Edward Varos loomed large in his imagination.

Where was that card?

Stephen

Sweat dribbled down Stephen's chest and collected in the crevasse between his pectorals. The locker room was empty, the only sound a muted groan from the man with his lips wrapped around Stephen's member.

The other times he had engaged in these surreptitious acts it had required a much lighter tread. Davey Lucas had been his first male sexual encounter in eighth grade. The electricity that was a weak spark the night two years prior in Davey's basement, surged as their bodies entered puberty.

In the eighth-grade incident, Davey had come over after a post-soccer practice, weight-lifting session to hang out with Stephen, just as always. Stephen had taken off his shirt, reclining with his hands behind his head on the living room couch. That day, in the flush of physical activity, the whole downstairs empty, sexual tension pulsed through the room with a strange power neither boy understood. Davey looked to Stephen – it wasn't the look of a friend, but the look of one who anticipates lustful, physical intersection.

"Ripley, put your shirt on." Davey's hand slapped Stephen's leg. His heart tremored with an energy he had previously not known.

Most people assumed that Davey was gay: blond, effete, gangly Davey, with his arched eyebrows and bow-like mouth. He couldn't escape the "gay face" that the other children pegged him with the moment puberty started to bend his features. Stephen, on the other hand, presented as quintessentially straight. He wore baggy jeans and baseball caps. At soccer practice, everyone followed his lead; his face was a perfect combination of an emerging masculine jawline and slightly pudgy, boyish cheeks.

"I'm hot," was all Stephen said. He flashed a smile.

The two boys locked eyes.

Davey jumped up and fell onto Stephen. His scrawny arms put all their force into pushing Stephen into the couch. Stephen laughed – shorter and stockier than Davey, he quickly shoved Davey off and got his skinny friend into a headlock.

"You're too weak, D," he said. "I wouldn't mess with bigger dudes."

Davey fought with all his strength, finally shoving himself backward, forcing Stephen to crash onto the floor. The momentary shock gave Davey time to twist around and put his knees into Stephen's chest. In the rush of the moment, the heat of bodies twisting together, Davey leaned in and pressed his lips to Stephen's.

Right after, there was a throbbing silence. The spring breeze blew through the curtains; somewhere far off, the sound of a lawnmower rang through the air like the buzz of a large, mechanical bee. Davey was as shocked with himself as Stephen below him.

"I'm –," Davey started.

"Dude." Stephen gently pushed him off.

Davey looked down and saw Stephen was aroused. He lunged.

"Fuck."

Davey had barely gotten Stephen's shorts down before they both heard footsteps on the stairs.

"You shouldn't be fighting!" Stephen's little sister bellowed from above. "I'm going to tell Mom!"

The spell broken, Davey stood up, holding his head. "Dude, sorry – I…uhh…" He didn't make eye contact as he stumbled for the door. Retreating backward, his hand blindly groped for his backpack by the stairs. "See ya."

After the door slammed, Stephen leaned back and jerked himself off. The action took only a few seconds, Stephen imagining the heat of Davey's touch, the feel of his hands pressed against Davey's skin. When he was done, he stared at the ceiling.

For Stephen, at fourteen, the occurrence seemed benign. His entire life he had been desired by the opposite sex, by the same sex. He had somehow always tacitly known that Davey lusted after him; it was the same knowledge he had when Sarah Kaplan told him he was a "slug face" in fifth grade. Underneath the violence, the rage, he knew was attraction.

In just a few short years, now that they were in eighth grade, the desire no longer had to be sublimated under the guise of wrestling, the façade of name-calling and teasing. Sarah Kaplan, now wearing a B-cup, licked her lips at him in the cafeteria the week earlier; Davey jumped on him, tried to pull down his pants and take him in his mouth.

It wasn't a far step to that moment in the locker room two years later, the junior varsity coach on his knees, lips around Stephen's dick, bringing him to climax. At sixteen, Stephen's body had lost most of its baby fat. He still had rounded, boyish features, but his body was chiseled, athletic sinew. The same magnetism that had drawn teachers and parents to him as a child was now a shining beacon which drew others to him sexually. At the first soccer meeting of his sophomore year he and the new coach made eye contact. Within weeks, they fooled around in the locker room. The coach gradually led Stephen to their first kiss – here, a hand on his shoulder when the other boys were leaving; then, a meeting in his office, a hand on his own crotch, a slight rub.

Stephen was never his pawn, however. In a bird's eye view of the events, it was perhaps Stephen who had built the web, met his advances with openings to do more.

"This isn't gay; we did this in college," the coach said, the first time he had gotten Stephen naked. "Keep it quiet; it's just two guys having fun."

Stephen erected a partition between his sexual life and his emotional life out of necessity. Homosexuality was evil, but in the confined darkness of the locker room, in the warped display between himself and the coach, it remained quarantined in a realm of unreality. After Davey, it thrived in the darkness of his own bedroom. There was the shadow world of his sexual desire and the real world in which he was the star athlete, the favorite son, the preacher's child. As long as an iron curtain of good and evil separated them, he could confine his real desires to a netherworld, a trembling nightmare.

When Davey introduced Stephen to homosexuality, it had appeared benign, but the impact of the event opened a sore on his psyche. He had always known both sexes were in love with him, but now he began to fear he was on the dark side of that divide. Sex was natural in its God-given context. But in the days after Davey's advance, Stephen began to realize he could no longer contain its energy. What had been passing impressions and feelings, suddenly boiled over into an erotic flood of thoughtless emotion. Being good as a directive was no longer simple – it was poisoned by physical chemistry which took control of his thoughts and emotions.

Why, when he closed his eyes in the darkness of his own bedroom, was it Davey's bow-like mouth that he saw instead of Sarah's shining eyes? Why, when he was soaring to climax, was it the trembling muscles of Davey's arms that pulled to the front of his imagination rather than the soft, sumptuous curves of Sarah's feminine body?

Over time, the partition strengthened between his public-facing person and the shadow Stephen who came alive in confined, dark spaces – his bedroom, his bathroom, the locker room. He dated girls occasionally. They would go to second base and then he would blame religion for not wanting to take it further. There had been a mix of them since eighth grade. With the opening of his psychic sore, he believed the antidote was a relationship with a woman. By finding a home in the embrace of the female form, he would ameliorate the pain Davey opened so awkwardly in the impassive sunshine that one spring day. He dated Leslie, Jodie, Alex, Joy, and Annie. At first it was week or two long relationships going to home football games and getting food after school on Friday afternoons. Joy had been his most complex relationship, the two making it through an entire summer together before Stephen used soccer practice as an excuse to pull away.

He was able to believe that things just hadn't clicked – he hadn't found the right girl.

But then he met Pearl.

The fire that she lit in his imagination shed light even to the dark, shameful corners of his shadow life. She was not the glowing, pure, milquetoast vision that the church had raised him to believe was the image of a wife and mother. Pearl's smile wasn't acquiescent, but lively and warm. She understood uncertainty, just like Stephen; in church, she raised her hand and questioned the insurmountable protection around blind faith.

"But homosexuality is listed along with a lot of other sins. You're not supposed to mate two different kinds of animals. Do we give up hybrid vegetables and kill all the donkeys?"

Humor, wit, empathy – the sheer force of personality only found equal in the beauty of her physical form. Her elvish face had two, sparkling green eyes set into smooth, porcelain skin. Unlike the other girls of her age, she clipped her long locks and wore her hair short, adding to the fairy tale mystique of her depthless, verdant eyes. Looking at her in the Sunday School classroom, Stephen wondered if she would alight on one of the small desks. With a finger on her nose, she would shoot skyward like Tinkerbell, like Peter Pan.

She invaded the corners of his mind he thought were reserved for masculine fantasies only. He imagined her nude, her white skin reflective in a flood of sunshine. For the first time, it was a feminine body that he imagined running his fingers over in a private bedroom. While men occupied dark corners, Pearl was a being of the light.

She moved into town the summer before their sophomore year. Stephen, at first, had not tried to engage her; he assumed she would show some interest in him, as most girls tended to do. But as time went on, as he watched her make friends and blossom socially in the new school, he grew both fearful and awed. For the first time in his life, he felt unequal to a task. She was not blinded by his boyish good looks, his athlete shine, or his status at the church. Pearl unmoved, said hello to him on Sunday mornings, smiled at him in the high school hallways, and nodded indifferently if they passed each other in the school parking lot. It was rumored she pined for Jerry Dimley, a sophomore, second-string quarter back with jet black hair and blue eyes.

The soccer coach brought Stephen to climax. Stephen's eyes rolled back into his head, his mind illuminated by the glow of white oblivion sexual release always guided him to. In the dim lights, the coach wiped his mouth and stood up. He sat beside Stephen, pulling out his dick and jerking himself off.

Stephen stared straight ahead, regret and self-loathing exploding outward from his heart.

"You need a ride home?" the coach asked.

"I'm okay," Stephen said.

"Cool. I'll let you leave ahead. I'll lock up the office."

Stephen showered before he went home. The cold water washed over his skin, allowed him to forget the events of the previous fifteen minutes. As the water ran and the sexual energy ebbed, his thoughts turned to his homework, the evening's youth group, and Pearl.

#

"You out here all alone?"

"Yeah, it seemed like a good place to think."

"You're too good for the rest of us? You can't pray indoors?"

"They said we needed to find some place calming."

"Well, you're right there. This is calming."

Pearl turned her sharp chin sideways. The fall wind shook her auburn hair, made her loose shirt tremble in the breeze.

"Why are you distracting me from my prayers?"

"I had a question I didn't want anyone else to hear."

"What kind of question?" Stephen's indifferent expression broke. The corners of his mouth lifted into a smile.

"I heard something from my friend, Jenny."

"Jenny Oakley?"

"Yes."

"What did she say?"

"She said she heard from one of your soccer friends that you liked me."

"Oh."

"Oh?" Pearl snorted. "That's not what I expected you to say."

"It's not?"

"No, I thought maybe you'd say, 'Yes, Pearl, I do.'"

"Oh." Stephen looked up and directly at her for the first time. His face beamed. "So, you like me then?"

"Don't flatter yourself, sir."

Stephen laughed. "So, I guess we won't go to Homecoming together. That definitely won't happen."

"Correct. I just came to ask you if it was true. When I found out I was going to tell Jenny that 'Stephen The Loser' did like me."

"So, this is like reconnaissance?" The pressure lifted. They were talking around it, but she liked him. They were going to go together.

"Exactly! Look at you using big words."

"I'm smart, you know. I'm not just a pretty face."

"You're a pretty face?"

They both laughed. Pearl took a seat next to Stephen in the grass. They had spent the last evening at a retreat at the church. This morning was a last, private devotional before they were set loose to return to the world as wiser, purer beings.

"I liked what you said," Pearl went on. "Last night at the vespers service you talked about the different lives we lead. I think it's really true. I'm one person for my family, one person at school, one person when I do volunteer work. I wish I could pull them all together."

"I feel the same way." Stephen grew more animated. "I think I'm a few more million different people than you, though." He flashed back to the darkness of the locker room. "I do think that God somehow sees our whole self. I think to him we're full pictures instead of like stained glass or mosaic tiles, the way other people see us."

Pearl extended her hand, put it on Stephen's. "I like this side of you. I thought you were just a soccer jerk who smiled a lot."

"That's just one person."

"He's all right, but this one is better."

The breeze strengthened, shaking the trees, sending bunches of leaves falling to the grass. They sat in silence, but it was fully occupied by their two whole persons, if only for that moment. Stephen felt that Pearl had seen through him in his vespers confession. She knew that he hid a real darkness – it wasn't the slight fade, the blurred edges that plagued her. Stephen contained the full spectrum inside his psyche; his person was pure darkness, edging to white light. Pearl made the lightness more real in that moment than he'd felt since he was a child.

The door to the church opened. Mr. Ramsey, the youth pastor waved to them.

"Time to come in for the closing!" he called.

Pearl withdrew her hand from Stephen's. The two exchanged an awkward smile.

"So, I definitely won't pick you up before Homecoming and take you someplace nice for dinner," Stephen said.

"No, and you shouldn't make any reservations at Italian restaurants. I hate those."

"Good – I'll probably never talk to you again."

"Never."

Hedley

What becomes of an Indigo Child when he becomes an Indigo Man? Hank thought it queer that the self-help industry supported parents with exceptional children, but society-at-large did not support or care for exceptional adults.

The chaos of his first breakup made this the overriding question in his thoughts. Had the split been amicable, built on an argument or personal disagreement, the world would have kept its calibration; however, the dissolution was rooted in betrayal, lies, and deceit. What could make one person abuse another in such a tactless and heartless way? Hank was attractive. He was vulnerable in their relationship. He had been, in his mind, the perfect boyfriend.

And it wasn't enough. Exceptional wasn't enough.

At first, he had been destroyed. When Hank and Cedric met and their courtship began, a new Hank bloomed from the old. While in high school he had been petty, a dreamer, someone who always looked to tomorrow, to a better life, the Hank with Cedric was calm, collected, and energized by the everyday task of living. There wasn't a need to scheme, to create alternate universes in the heart of his imagination, like in high school. Cedric tamed that wild heart, turned its stony dissatisfaction into malleable love.

In the twilight of a New York summer night, however, this Hank was immolated. He caught Cedric cheating and fled the scene. His heart pounded as he pensively stared at The North River. If someone could have seen the spiritual world as Hank wept that night, they would have seen a blazing fire of blue – the calm, contented, vulnerable boy who was beginning to take shape, burned completely, the ashes of his soul drifting into the August air. That night and the few weeks after, Hank screamed. He railed against the universe, against Cedric, against a whole world that had spurned and betrayed him. The world of his youth promised so many things: career success, a family, children, Disney endings, and Prince Charmings. In Cedric that lie had taken full root, blossomed.

And then fire, destruction, and chaos.

The screaming turned to silence in the months after the break up. Like a caterpillar entering its pupa stage, Hank pulled away from the world, cocooned himself from all those that loved him. He no longer trusted anyone – friends, family, even casual acquaintances. When the world betrays you, a paradigm shift is required.

Just as when he planned his revenge on Brock in high school, now Hedley set his site on a much more colossal opponent, namely, society. Days were spent on his bed, fingers steepled, mapping the courses of action needed to move forward. The emotional pain of the breakup lasted barely a month. Hank's heart quickly bruised, stitched itself, and hardened into an impenetrable diamond of emotional stoicism. The few who kept in communication with him during this time were witness to Hank obliterating every trace of Cedric. He rebranded the breakup, referring to it as "The Incident." He used it only as a reference point in his social history.

Myrtle's was the one voice that called to him from the past. A Facebook post:

Hanky – I've been trying to get a hold of you. New number? Let me know! Christmas is coming up and I want to hear what's going on! Mine will be a quick update – average grades, no boyfriend, acquired a senior fifteen… (how's that's possible!?) Hugs!

A voicemail:

Hank, I'll be honest… Kind of getting worried here. I haven't seen you online. Your Facebook is basically just me posting at this point. I called your house phone but your parents didn't have much info, either. Please just give me a heads up so I can know you're not dead or something. Love ya, goofus.

Email:

Hank,

You're just being an asshole. You really going to ignore me forever? I'll be honest, you're winning. I don't think I can keep trying much longer. Don't be a total goober and send me something.

That was the last email and the hardest to ignore. Most of his other friends, even from high school, were easy to let go. Few knew him the way Myrtle did. She had been his confidant when he was terrified to even say the word "gay" out loud. He thought that arriving at college would let him shed his old life like the skin of a snake. On his way to freshman year orientation, he envisioned shaking hands with his fellow schoolmates, saying confidently, surely: "Hi, I'm Hank. I'm gay."

It wasn't like that, however. Months went by before he was able to say it with even a feigned air of confidence. These new people he didn't trust fully, but Myrtle he did. She had been one of the first he told and she kept his secret; she supported him. She knew him as he was and as he would become through college. When he saw her the previous summer, she was the only one he had let see the full force of his emotion for Cedric.

"He's probably the one, Myrtle. I feel it."

If Myrtle disappeared, then Hank was gone entirely. The new Hank was glad to see him go, mostly. The boy of his childhood was weak – he allowed himself to be crushed by someone who should never have been trusted. While he had been more present with Cedric in the real world, that real world was not reality. It was a shadow game Cedric's presence threw on the wall of Hank's imagination: two men standing in front of a white picket fence, baby carrier in tow.

The world wasn't ready for that. Gay men weren't ready for that – they wanted threesomes, sex permeating their entire existence. Hank prognosticated a future where gay marriage was legal and homosexuals would bend their vision of the world to fit with the heteronormative structure of mainstream society. It would fail. You can't make an entire race a subculture, a sub-species, and then expect them to conform completely and wholly to the world view that buried them under shame and grief. That would be just another war that gay men would have to fight internally, striving for an ideal that they were doomed to never achieve. Self-loathing and hatred would be reborn in their divorces, in their internal frustrations with wanting one partner, but then desiring everything beautiful. Some would succeed and they would only inspire more pain for the others.

But in his incubation, Hank saw that this was the story of society writ large. There was always the perceived mass, the constructed idea of society that the world wanted you to believe in. This was how order was retained. For centuries God and the Holy Scriptures kept this structure in place. Now hollow gods were rising from the Internet Age. On Facebook, he could scrub his image, create a new ideal, a new person that all could admire and emulate. For months, he could post backlogged pictures of himself and Cedric. He could make the world believe they were still together. Reality was becoming the most malleable substance on earth.

Myrtle was the last pinpoint of light in this darkness that eagerly and avidly consumed him. Even hearing "goofus" over the phone, brought to his mind the shell, the ghost of what was a possible reality: a nice boyfriend, a good job, The American Dream. For all the games he played in high school, the fantasies, and the machinations that he unleashed on his adolescent brethren, the relationship between himself and Myrtle had been real. When everything around him was turning to ash and bones, Myrtle's voice, her words made him see dawn in the deepest darkness.

But then Cedric's ghost threw his thoughts from this redemptive track. For the months they dated, he would have counted their relationship as genuine, real, the gospel truth. It may have been willing naivety, but he didn't see the betrayal coming. He had trusted Cedric implicitly during their courtship. When he said he was spending the night in his dorm room studying, Hank believed him. Now he imagined the sexual exploits he embarked upon during those lost hours.

If Cedric could betray him so easily, then Myrtle could also. It was just a new iteration of his love for Brock in high school – if you trust someone, if you give them power over you, they will abuse it.

Myrtle *would* abuse it also.

It was one lonely evening during his final spring semester at college that Hank left his room after midnight and went into the darkness. The decision had been made to clear Myrtle from his life and start fresh. Hank didn't know what that meant, however. In the next year he would go on Fulbright and enter into a research project in London. The distance from home, from the ache of the previous year's desolation, would make the experience worthwhile regardless of his project (a made-up endeavor about marketing in Victorian England).

He wandered away from campus, finding solace in the empty golf course. Stars winked in the night sky, the grass an emerald green, the fresh shoots moist with dew. Trees shook in the dark, a soft breeze brought the scent of lilac from bushes that bloomed nearby. In the peace of the moment, Hank was surprised that his instinct was to speak. The words were directed at God, but it was not a prayer, it was a chastisement.

"What is it all for?" The first words he uttered. His eyes rose and settled on a cluster of stars. They would stand in for the ambiguous God that clung to the edges of his imagination. "Why? It's a charade. A joke. We are born, betrayed, and die. What's the purpose?"

The stars did not answer. Frogs croaked ambivalently in the pond behind him.

Hank thought he buried God long before. In his books, in his academic pursuits and endeavors, God had no place. The sit, kneel, stand God of his parents rejected his gayness and, therefore, rejected him.

But, just as the old Hank was not easy to shed in college, so was God a specter that hung on to him, gnawed at his brain. The Guilt of God loomed large in the dark of his bedroom. On certain nights he would dream of hellfire and darkness, of the pit homosexuals were forced into on the day of judgment.

"Why…"

Hank began walking quickly. The night, so placid moments before, grew teeth, began to swirl and stalk him.

"You're afraid," he whispered, fear tightening in his chest. "You're afraid I've found you out. It's all a lie – your goodness, heaven, the kindness of strangers – it's all a lie."

He no longer was cognizant of whether the words were uttered from his mouth, or echoed only in his mind. Everything around him trembled, shook with rage: the trees rattled their leaves in the wind, frogs growled from the rushes, and clouds flew across the moon, throwing angry shadows over its gleaming surface.

"You're here…" He stumbled forward. Trees closed around him. When had he entered a wood? "You'll trap me. You trap everyone eventually. But eventually everyone sees you're nothing."

Branches and leaves obscured the moon completely. In the wood, it was total darkness. Hank stopped, panting. He covered his ears and shut his eyes tight, sure that some horror would consume him now that he had stopped running. The God-monster would bare its teeth and finish him corporally. His soul was already consumed by the world's indifference. This was the end.

But why, again, God? In high school, he had tossed off the intellectual shackles of the Christian deity and ascribed to Objectivism, Marxism, any -ism that unfettered his burgeoning mind.

And yet, there was always the difference, his innate feeling of being special, chosen, right. Despite everything, Christian ideals had been drilled into him, born their fruit. They told him he was chosen – just as Joseph, just as Israel, just as Abraham – he was destined for greatness.

Now the night laughed at him, stalked him. Cedric discarded him like a worn cloak. His technicolor dreams stripped of their color and revealed to be white, black, and gray. He was nothing to Cedric, nothing to God, nothing to the world.

"What becomes of an Indigo Child?" Hank muttered the words into the dried mud in which he sat on his knees. Tears were dry on his face. His eyes blinked, staring into the unknown shadows around him. He was chosen, but then again guilty – God crawled toward him in the darkness, stalked him in his despair. Why could he no longer believe – not just in God, but in the delusion of himself? Was he chosen? Was he a genius, a mastermind, something utterly unique and special? Or was this darkness the reflection of his own emptiness?

"What's the point?" Again, unsure of whether he spoke or thought the words. Unconscious of his own actions, he ran his hands over his forearms, felt the undulating tracts of veins in his wrists. A passing thought: *How easy to slip something sharp there – how easy to let the blood flow and die in some poetic fashion in a tub. The scene: white tile bathed in warm, fluorescent lights, a floral shower curtain sticky with gore.* It was a morbid daydream he had occasionally. It was never a real plan outside of pure darkness, when he felt the most alone, buried under the indifference of the world's pressing shadow.

How easy.

Then, a light. It was a small circle cutting through the trees. Feet crunched through the crowded wood, breaking leaves and sticks and kicking rocks as they came toward him.

"Dude," a voice said. "You okay? You were screaming."

"I was screaming…?" Hank whispered to himself.

"Yeah, some weird shit about God."

Hank saw a man appear from the darkness. He was followed by two other shadowy figures.

"You on some kind of weird trip?" a female voice asked. "Can we get some of what you're on?"

Laughter. The spell of the night was broken. God's teeth retracted; He retreated into the darkness of Hank's imagination.

"You smoke for the first time?"

Hank blinked into the light. He looked at his hands as if they were foreign objects. These strangers thought he was a stoner. Why couldn't he be one tonight?

"Yeah…" he said softly. "Yeah, I'm fucked up."

"I remember my first time. I ate like ten burgers from Burger King, bro. Not as cool as talking to God or whatever."

"You a freshman?" The girl again. From the glow of the flashlight Hank could see she had pink hair. A nose ring sparkled from the shadows falling on her round face.

Hank thought quickly of her story:

Chubby with a fresh dye job, she was clearly a freshman. Judging by her dusty shoes and faded track and field t-shirt, she had just begun to evolve into her post-high school form. At home she had probably been someone's fat friend – she sat in the periphery, making others laugh, but never was the center of attention. Now she was breaking free, becoming someone who stood out. *Yes, I died my hair. I'm different. Fuck YOU.* Predictably trying to escape prediction.

"I'm a freshman," Hank said. "I live on campus. I'm in Collins."

"The castle," the girl said. Her grey eyes sparkled.

"You all right, though, dude?" the guy asked again. "You seemed really fucked when we heard you screaming."

"Yeah," Hank said. "Yeah, just must have been bad stuff."

"We're headed to get some food if you want to come." The third figure emerged from the shadows. It was another female – she was pretty. Her long black hair was pulled back into a bun. She wore dark eyeliner and a Fall Out Boy t-shirt, but she had not committed as fully to the punk aesthetic as her pink-haired friend.

"That'd be great." Hank locked eyes with her. He flashed a smile.

She awkwardly looked away.

"Cool, dude," the boy said. "Well, let's keep walking. How you like Collins?"

The four of them crossed back over the golf course. The pink-haired girl, Kelly, was the leader of their small coterie.

"We just came out here to smoke. We've got to go back out to Headley, then back on campus."

"Headley?" Hank asked.

"That's the road that winds by the course."

They walked through campus and settled on a late-night sushi bar off 10th Street. Hank strategically targeted his questions at the pretty girl – Lucy – as soon as he found out she wasn't romantically involved with the boy in the group. She was from the Indianapolis area, the middle child of three. She liked riding horses. It was her first time having sushi.

At the end of the night he offered to walk her back to her dorm. It was near five in the morning, birds beginning to chirp, the world full of hope after the darkest hours of the evening.

"It was really nice to meet you, Joe," she said nervously.

"Same – I can't believe freshman year is almost over and we never met before."

"I know – what a funny way to meet."

Hank sized her up: middle child, nineteen, prone to fantasy. He could tell in the lights of her hazel eyes that she was imagining telling her kids about how she met their father.

He was alone, wandering on the golf course.

The children wouldn't know about the perceived hallucinogenic state he had been in or about Kelly and her nose ring. Lucy had already recast Hank, now Joe, as the quiet, thoughtful artist.

"I love paintings," Joe said earlier. "Monet – it's incredible how dried paint on a canvas can be a place *and* an emotion."

Joe put his lips to Lucy's. She withered under his touch, folding into his arms, letting him carry her full weight. Their tongues lashed together wildly. Hank felt her naiveté in the sharp bite of her teeth.

"Why don't we sneak in somewhere...?" Hank as Joe offered.

That night Lucy took Joe into her mouth and performed her first act of fellatio. Hank closed his eyes and remembered a football player he had seen in the hallway as he left the dorm. He ejaculated imagining the athlete's swollen chest in a tight t-shirt.

Joe gave Lucy a fake number and promised to call the next day. Lucy went inside, her emotions a knot of insecurity, wonder, and awe at her own power. Joe vanished, forever, in the dawn light – a figure as ephemeral and insubstantial as the mist rising from the freshly cut grass.

Hank went to the nearest convenience store and bought a pack of cigarettes. He did not smoke, but he also did not perform sexual acts with women. The night was full of new experiences.

He sat on the front steps of Collins, admiring the world coming to life around him. Students were beginning to emerge from dorms, birds soared overhead, and squirrels chittered in the trees. His heart hummed.

Joe, a wandering, drug-inspired artist formed in his imagination the moment he set eyes on Lucy. The ability he discovered in high school to read people, to know them from their thoughts and actions and bend them to his will, could be used another way. People wanted to see something in others – they wanted to believe in their own reality, their own projection upon them. Lucy wanted Hank to be mysterious – she wanted him to be dark with silver linings that allowed her to envision a future with him. If Joe was all darkness, cigarettes, and leather, it would be imperfect. Joe had to be an imperfect mixture of the profane and holy, a combination that spoke to wide-eyed Lucy's sexual and pragmatic desires.

The ability to manipulate the projection, to understand what others wanted and reflect it back... was a fantastic power to wield. Hank had come close to using this for his own means on a number of occasions. He pondered who he could become to catch the eye of a gorgeous gay on campus. *Just a little more masculine for Ernest. Craig prefers boys with a little swish in their walk.* He knew what they wanted but didn't yet know how to make them see it in himself.

Lucy inspired him to look closer and try harder. His encounter with God on the golf course stripped him down to his roots. When Lucy and her motley crew appeared at his lowest emotional point and perceived him to be a freshman in a drug stupor, it freed him to become someone else. If they believed him to be a different human, who was he to fight it? He would become their idea of himself and use it to meet his own ends. In this case, it was a shallow, simple goal: a blowjob at the end of a bad day.

But what else could he acquire, if he not only manipulated the projection, but actually guided it?

In the darkest hour of the night, Hank was buried in the ground. With the light of the new day, he was transformed. A new power shone in his eyes; it flooded through him and cast shadows on his soul. Gone was the optimism of his youth, in its place a mastery of human emotion and reality. He had forgotten his great imaginative mind – he, perhaps, was still chosen but not by God. No, he was something different entirely: malleable, changeable, a kaleidoscope of desires, dreams, and reality. He was Janus, a god himself. It was possible with his great powers of perception to present the face everyone wished to see. He had been himself once and failed.

Now he was many.

Now he was in control.

2010: Judges

  A delirium swept over the crowd by midday; everyone was relieved when the magistrate ordered those gathered to take a break for the noon meal.
  You gather with friends near the town well. No one ventured home, but instead, chose to wait with the crowd, fishing for opinions, conjecture, and details that will help when the ultimate decision is forced upon the people as jury. At that time, you will all step forward and place your stones. In your hand you will hold a pebble, which paves a pathway to freedom, or a course directly to death.
  "I had my mind made up in the beginning and it hasn't changed."
  "I can see why he did some of it, but there is something to say for responsibility. We're all adults."
  "They should be turning the other cheek, not wreaking havoc."
  You take a long drought of water and listen to the twittering of voices. Everyone has an opinion – every statement is followed by a "but..." or a "perhaps..." Some are still resilient in their beliefs about the accused's guilt, but their opinion is beginning to mean less.
  Your understanding remains nebulous – in the noonday heat, your judgment shook under the deluge of facts and personal stories told by the recorder. The static figures on the scaffold had begun to tremble before your eyes. All at once they were children, adults, teenagers, alternating visions in the light of the sun. Whether it was the delirium or the truth remains unknown. For so long these men had been ghosts, even before they were put on trial. Their lives were lived digitally, while you watched from your phone's screen.
  If you had been born more beautiful, more ambitious, with more cleverness, would it be you before them all? You would have taken every advantage as well. As it is, you were given enough, so you took that with alacrity.
  But it is true that God demands more. He exhorts mercy but imposes justice. In his eyes, all men are born the same – some great ledger, perhaps shown at the gates of the afterlife, will make this clear.
  Would it be better, though, if they were gone? With all men equal, their public force has elicited public shame. Should all men who rise above the average be struck down so that the mass experiences less pain?
  You don't know. These are large thoughts for a Sunday afternoon spent in intense sunlight.
  "You decided, then?" someone asks.
  "Yes," says one.
  "No," responds another.
  Soon the magistrate will again take the attention of the townsfolk and the stones will be placed. Each will have to walk to the scaffold and set their choice before the crowd. Guilty. Innocent. Two piles and each individual in the crowd held accountable for their choice.
  In the grand scheme, you think, you should all be on trial each time another man is put upon the scaffold. When the stones are down, the votes cast, is there really anyone who could stand innocently, before all gods and men, and claim to be worthy to be set free?

You have no time to ponder this question further. A bell is rung – the final act is ready to be told by the recorder.

With each ring of the bell, your opinion changes, your thoughts a muddle of fear and empathy.

Guilty.
Innocent.
Guilty.
Innocent.
All shuffle forward into the afternoon sun.

Skyler

At some point in his youth, Skyler began to pull away from his mother. Georgina was unsure when the separation began, but there were moments when she'd look at her son and feel he had become a stranger.

There were tangible elements to the distance. The shame was manifested in a number of ways: the hidden clothes under his bed, the relentless shining of his school shoes to erase signs of dirt and wear, the obsession he placed in his teeth, scrubbing them three times a day, and begging to be taken to the dentist, a calendar with the names of stores littered across different days. Did it all begin with the after-school program? Did other children tease and pester him about the way he dressed? About his ain'ts and yas? Was that why he spoke with such sharp elocution?

"Mother, I think it would be beneficial to find other ways to divide the household work."

Always, in the back of her mind, she wondered if the division began the night she had come home panicked, certain that the fabric of the whole world was unraveling. Had Skyler known then what she was? What she was afraid of? Had her drunken scene removed the permanent bonds of trust that were supposed to exist between mother and son?

She tried to rectify the occurrences of that night every moment since. In order to escape her nightly work, she banished her dreams of fame, fortune, and revenge to the wastebasket of their old trailer. It took several years, but she got back on her feet – she grew up. It started in a position as an orderly in the hospital. Within a few years, she was doing administrative tasks in the main offices; she had health insurance. She moved them away from Siegfried Essen and Eveline Peavey and rented a small, two-bedroom home near Skyler's junior high school.

Georgina was trying to do better. She was better.

But still Skyler stood apart.

Never was this more apparent than when Georgina brought home suitors. As she aged, her mental barrier against men began to crumble. While in her youth she sought mysterious, hyper-masculine men, in her new life in the hospital, she was drawn to the soft, quiet gentleman who littered the halls and said "hello" as they passed in the morning. This new kind of man teamed with Skyler's distance made her believe she could fill her loneliness with a lover, one which didn't cast long shadows of fear over her existence.

The affairs often started out well, but whenever the men met Skyler, things turned cold. There was something in the proprietary, dark gaze of her son which made the men doubt their place in the home – they became unsure of whether Georgina was who she claimed to be. Skyler, to the men, represented some other. The boy's primped hair and pressed clothes in a home with stained carpeting and wood-paneled walls unnerved them. This was Dimmesdale, a quiet conservative town – who was this woman and her queer boy? His effeminacy broke the sterility of their everyday life. It was as if in meeting Skyler, they were exposed to some other world of which they wanted no part.

Georgina hated that she was not immune to this same feeling of otherness; she wanted to understand its root, or not see the difference. But she felt it, palpably, in the air.

At school Skyler worked harder to conceal his queerness from the other students. He cultivated some friendships for a short time after starting the after-school program, but these faded away when he refused to open up. The ghost of Siegfried Essen haunted the boy – *you shouldn't do that*. He constrained himself so tightly that his personality couldn't escape. What started as the fear and uncertainty of allowing himself to be known, grew callous and cold over his adolescent years.

Physically, the slight chubbiness of his youth faded away, leaving Skyler lean and beautiful. In most ways he was average – height, musculature, intelligence – but, his face had the magnetism of a Michelangelo sculpture. Dark eyes peered from a porcelain face, electric lights in perfectly carved statuary.

In high school, he found a peripheral group, not much different from Jerry and Melody from his elementary school days. These peers casually hung out during the day, sitting on the steps of the school in the morning, the back corner of the cafeteria at lunch. They bonded over their position on the edge of high school society, mutual allies against villainous preps and jocks, overlords of nerds and band geeks.

Skyler found that his cleverness and natural coldness made him attractive to this group of lower-tier rebels. The rage he held inside of him was released in the form of vicious teasing of other, unwitting targets who had never done him harm. Especially easy marks were the overweight and effeminate students in his high school. He had no compunction in stringing together garlands of insults with which to hang these unsuspecting victims.

His homosexuality was concealed by a neutral-colored wardrobe and policed language and actions forced into molds just masculine enough to "pass." To protect himself, he was quickest to draw on those more effeminate than him. The affection he had felt his whole life for garish women's clothing had to be buried. Although he put energy into making sure his clothes were always clean and pressed, he did not allow any hint of flamboyance.

"Have you seen Alex Gross in his purple shirt?" he'd ask, snidely between classes.

The group found him fascinating enough to keep close: he was funny, dangerous, and mysterious. People knew Skyler, but no one could claim that they truly *knew* him. He rarely hung out with the crowd after school – occasionally, he and a few of the boys would walk home on the dusty streets and find abandoned corners to smoke cigarettes, but that was the extent of his social experimentation.

Skyler knew he needed good grades, a pristine record to escape Dimmesdale and find freedom.

The focus on escape and Georgina's rising prospects kept his darkest impulses at bay during his middle school years. But as high school moved on, as he grew antsy looking to the date of graduation, his dark side twitched. Stray thoughts began to focus on going into a local store and stealing again. It could just be once. The quick release was all he needed.

His impulse finally overthrew him one evening in early spring. He had taken the car to escape from being home while Georgina entertained another date. It was a clear night, and Skyler felt catharsis driving with the window down, yelling into the wind about the stupidity of the most recent suitor who had shuffled through their home. The screaming wasn't enough, and the thought rose up; the impulse burst forth in his mind with alarming clarity. In the distance, the fluorescent glow of a truck stop sign radiated red and blue in the late-evening sky.

Why not? He thought. *Just once on a night when I need release.*

He pulled their old Honda into the convenience store lot and took a deep breath. It would be just the same as in his childhood. He imagined going to the electronics section, letting his hand run over the headphones and speakers; at the perfect moment, he'd flick his finger, drop a device into his hand, then casually exit.

The door chimed when he entered. Tentatively, he walked through the store, scanning each shelf, each aisle to see where he could strike. His heart pounded in his chest as he eyed a cheap Mp3 player. It smiled at him through its plastic casing – *we belong together* – it seemed to say. Skyler committed then and there to that device and casually headed towards the restroom to make his final preparations.

Had he completed the act in that moment, the rest may not have played out as it did. But chaos, disruption, found him in the sterile light of the men's room.

"Hey there," a voice said from behind him.

Skyler turned, his brown eyes questioning. He had just entered the restroom and turned to see the source of the voice.

The man who had followed him was muscular, in his early forties. He wore a cowboy hat and tight, acid-wash jeans. His face was decorated with a mix of salt-n-pepper and red stubble. The hair above his lip was a shade thicker than the rest.

"Hello," Skyler said softly.

The man laughed. He moved his callous hands to his abdomen, where he scratched himself. "You're a skittish guy, huh?"

Skyler said nothing. He backed toward the line of sinks at the opposite end of the room.

"I'm not going to hurt ya," the man said. He glanced around the room quickly to be sure they were alone. He lowered his voice to a coarse whisper. "I wondered what a pretty, little guy like you is doing out here in the middle of nowhere."

Pretty. Skyler licked his lips. His heart beat faster. "I'm getting away from my mom."

"Oh... is that right?" The man smiled. He moved his hand to his crotch, scratched. "Whatchoo do when you're roaming around getting away from yer mommy?"

Skyler took a deep breath. The man was attractive in a generic sense. He was coarse, but his body was thick, masculine. As he drew closer, Skyler smelled body odor, lightly covered with aftershave.

Since his early teens he had looked at images of men to pleasure himself. He had purloined a few *Men's Health* magazines for the purpose of sexual release. In real life, he did not pursue sex at all. Fags were made fun of at school – he would have to wait until he escaped Dimmesdale before he was free to explore his sexuality.

But here was an opportunity. His heart raced. In his jeans, his cock throbbed to life, pre-cum beginning to leak from the sheer anticipation of contact with a living, breathing male.

The Mp3 player was forgotten.

"You ever seen a big truck up close?" the man asked. "I could show you mine."

Skyler followed him to the door of the convenience mart, trembling. As they left together, the young woman behind the counter looked up from her magazine. Her counterpart, an old woman restocking potato chips, shook her head knowingly.

In the cab of the big truck, the man showed Skyler the horn, let him turn some nobs. Chuckling, the man turned on the CB and let Skyler listen to the chatter.

Darkness had fallen completely around them. Skyler briefly looked out to the horizon, the velvety night calming his fragile nerves. His body pulsed with sexual expectation. The breath of the unknown man grew quicker; his eyes stared at Skyler with depthless hunger.

It was his big, hairy paw that initiated the action. Gruffly, the trucker gripped Skyler's thigh.

"Let's see what you can do with that pretty, little mouth."

At first, there was hesitation. Skyler didn't know where to put his mouth, how to kiss. He had never even played spin the bottle. But the trucker was in control. He forced Skyler back, mauled his already-wet member. In one fluid movement, he flipped Skyler over, ripped down his jeans, and put his tongue into the boy's ass. A flood of sexual feeling poured over Skyler – it was baptism, a surge of fire that consumed his body completely. He had been masturbating since his early teens, but the erotic pleasure he felt in this encounter overshadowed any feeling he experienced through self-manipulation.

The sex was painful. Skyler moaned, gripping the seat belt strap as the trucker took him fully. Tears formed in his eyes as the man thrusted into him. At one point, he shrieked from the force.

"Almost done," the man said shaking.

When it was over, the trucker patted Skyler's head and re-buckled his pants.

"Thanks, pretty," he said softly. "You're a good boy. Stay a good boy."

Skyler didn't cum in the cabin of the truck; the pain had crushed his sexual arousal. But the night provided an endless number of fantasies which fueled his dreams for the weeks to come. This first sexual encounter was everything he needed. It was darkness and duality, sexual passion mixed with an obscured crime that brought back memories of the high he felt stealing from those stores in elementary school. But this passion was physical, the contact erotic. It was ten thousand times the addiction his pilfering rush brought him as a child.

Within a month, he was driving to truck stops all around the area. He told his mother that he was going to visit friends and would vanish into the endless Nebraska flatlands, searching for more opportunities with men.

After a few weeks, he began to understand some of the code of the truckers. By his fifth encounter, he didn't even go into the convenience mart. A man would hop out of his truck and Skyler would slide out of his car. He'd casually lean against the Honda and make eye contact.

"*Hey there.*"
"*Well, hey, stud.*"
"*Look at you.*"

His beauty drew all to him, and Skyler felt no need to discriminate against any of the men that would press up against him and say hello. Some of them were young and muscular, some were fat and middle-aged. Every night was not a success but persistence paid off.

He kept a list, a diary that contained a description of every encounter. Skyler gave all the men names even though there had never been a formal introduction with any of them. He coded the actual activity with songs and lyrics from his musicals.

Frank – climbed every mountain.

Ernie – well worth the wait for this Henry Higgins.

Carl – loved you Conrad, and your giant Birdie.

The last half of his junior year into the summer, the list grew to over twenty. The encounters filled the shapeless hole inside of him. For the first time in his life his sex was expressed – there was no fear, no shame. No one was around to tell him he shouldn't do that. He was free to be himself in totality.

At school, his friendships strengthened. He opened up to others in ways that he never had in his youth. With his darkness and insecurity sated by the encounters, the lighter part of his life began to glow.

"Ya look good, Sky," his mother said one evening. The distance she always felt between them also diminished. "If I didn't know better, I'd say ya had a little crush or something. You can talk to your ma about it. Is there a special somebuddy?"

"No, mother," Skyler said smiling to himself.

For years, Georgina had wondered how to bring up his sexuality, but she had never been sure how to broach the subject. She did everything she could to express her indifference to gayness. She forced him to watch *Will & Grace* with her; they'd still put on *The Sound of Music* some nights and fall asleep on the couch watching it.

He had to know that she knew.

"You can always talk to me about anything,'" she said. "I love ya… and I think you should feel free to tell me anything… if you're dating someone… a person…"

Skyler rolled his eyes. "Thank you, Mother. I'll keep that in mind."

The high lasted through the summer.

Fall brought night sweats and chronic fatigue. After school, he came directly home and slept on the couch. He'd awake for dinner, then promptly start snoring again as the TV blared in the background.

Georgina watched, wondering if perhaps he'd contracted mono from the unknown love interest. She said nothing until the mouth sores appeared that made it difficult for him to eat.

"There's somethin' goin' on, Sky," Georgina said. "I'll drop you by the doctor 'fore school."

Georgina's motherly intuition directed her, not to make the appointment with Dr. Stern, the octogenarian, Skyler usually went to for yearly physicals, but the new doctor she had just met in her job in the hospital. He was young, from New York. Whatever was wrong with Skyler she felt was out of the reach of someone who had worked in cornfields for five decades.

But even knowing she wanted someone younger to assess Skyler, it never occurred to her or her son that something truly destructive was at work. Neither felt any twinge of fear as Dr. Roberts looked over Skyler. Medicine could cure whatever was wrong with him – he was young, beautiful, and healthy. Sickness preyed on the old, on the weak – they were safe.

Dr. Roberts, on the other hand, grew stoic, his jaw clenching as the young man told him his symptoms. His young doctor brain reeled trying to find another possible diagnosis. The effete, young man coming into his office was clearly … but it isn't always that. In New York young men could fall ill to such cosmopolitan diseases, not in Dimmesdale – not in the Podunk town his fiancé brought him to at the conclusion of medical school.

"Mrs. Shaw," the young doctor said warmly. "Would you mind stepping outside for a moment. I need to ask some man-specific questions to Mr. Skyler."

Georgina started. "Why, sure! I'm sorry – of course!"

His mother's soft shoes padded out the door and Skyler was left alone with the handsome, young doctor. For the first time since his gums bled, he started to feel afraid.

"Skyler," Dr. Roberts said gingerly, "I fear things may get a little awkward between us, but I need to ask you some questions." The doctor pulled up his clipboard. "Don't feel any judgment or apprehension in telling me. It's just us." He smiled and patted Skyler's knee. "Have you been engaging in any… high-risk intercourse over the past several months?"

Skyler grew numb. His mind moved quickly – the fear swelling to panic. Prior to that word – "intercourse" – the idea never occurred to him. He knew it could happen, but at seventeen, he believed he was invincible. The men who got HIV were old, ugly, deserving of the knife dropped by fate. When he was in the store, dropping small articles into his backpack as a child, he never believed that he could be caught. If he were, he could play the fool, smile his big-toothed smile and apologize. One could always apologize, smile, and escape.

"The symptoms seem to be pointing to a sexually transmitted disease…"

But if it was this…he could not escape. There was no escaping a virus – as tiny and as insignificant as it was flowing through his body, his blood, once there, it couldn't be apologized to. It couldn't be smiled at.

"If you don't want to talk about it, at least nod yes or no. I need to make sure to run the proper tests."

"Yes…" Skyler spoke barely loud enough to hear. "Yes… I have… done…" Tears formed on the edges of his eyes.

The week following the fateful day his anxiety swelled. For brief moments he believed that maybe it wasn't – but he'd begun to read about it. His "high-risk intercourse" over the preceding months had been the highest risk possible. His symptoms lined up exactly. The imagination of his childhood couldn't create an alternative ending for this story.

Skyler knew before the words were spoken out loud. He knew the moment his mother told him they needed to go back to the doctor's office.

"He got the results and just needs us to go over'em."

His heart slammed in his chest, with each alternating rhythm, there was hope, then resignation to his fate with the virus. It couldn't be... It had to be...

Sweat poured from his forehead and underarms as the diagnosis was stated in Dr. Roberts' private office. Skyler sat in a leather chair that smelled of newness – a clock ticked and his mother wept after Skyler allowed the doctor to let her know.

"It takes over the good things that fight disease," Dr. Roberts said over his vast, chestnut desk. "It turns them evil and makes them reproduce more of the virus. It's a scary little thing, but we can control it now. It's not like it used to be. You'll live a long and healthy life. There are grants and opportunities for medical assistance if you need it. If there's something I don't know, I have a network of friends across the country who can get me the information I need. We'll take this on – all three of us, together."

His mother put her hand to her mouth and said only, "Oh...my baby..."

How small a thing.

It turns them evil.

In his young mind, something broke that had always been tenuously holding back the flood of darkness in his brain. It could be perhaps traced to the moment long before with his mother, the instant when he saw what the weight of the world could do to another person. When she looked at him with her frightened eyes, he knew that something in him was innately evil, corrupted. Was it his father's fault? Had he passed on some dark force from which the son couldn't escape? Or was this the seed that Siegfried Essen had planted so long ago, bearing its unholy fruit? *You shouldn't do that.* He shouldn't have been gay; he shouldn't have stolen; he shouldn't have made fun of all of his peers to gain popularity; he shouldn't have solicited sex from wayward men at truck stops. His life was a chain of things he shouldn't be, but which his own soul couldn't refrain. Now his blood flowed with the power of death. If he went off of medicine, he could pass on something to destroy another. Siegfried Essen was right about him. He perhaps always had been.

"Honey," his mother asked anxiously tapping the steering wheel, "y'okay?"

They were outside the doctor's office. Skyler held a prescription crumpled in his hand. He didn't think beyond that afternoon. The idea of treatment, medications for the rest of his life, the technician at the small-town pharmacy finding out what the drug was used for and telling everyone in town – those things were all fallout that would come later.

For now, he simply looked to the horizon and a fall storm gathering. Menacing clouds rippled across the sky in waves of turbulent darkness. Skyler put his finger against the windshield and traced the distant clouds with his finger. He could try to tell his mother that the sky was how he felt: wild, chaotic, unyielding. But he doubted his mother would understand this explanation. How could he say he related to the coming storm better than he could understand his peers, his mother, or anything he had seen on television or in the movies? *I am the storm* – he wanted to say. But in the car, those words would be meaningless.

"I'm fine," he mumbled softly.

At home that night Skyler sat on the couch and looked at the blank TV. His mother sat beside him.

Georgina did not know what to say. Words in that moment were inadequate, tears inappropriate.

She had a word for herself – failure. She knew her son was gay – she knew there were risks associated with his emerging sexual orientation. Regardless of knowing, she remained silent. She had let the distance between them dictate how she treated Skyler – an arm length's away, always watching but afraid to engage fully. This night silence was consolation, but in the years before it had been violence. HIV, syphilis, gonorrhea, herpes: a good mother would have told Skyler about them all.

But it was too late.

She stood up and walked to the television. The DVD was still in the machine. She clicked the remote and the screen came alive. The scene was of the Austrian countryside, young children hanging from trees, the emerald green of the hills glowing behind them.

Georgina sat down on the couch. As she reclined backward, she felt her son's head fall onto her lap. He curled up on the couch, eyes forward, looking into a world they both knew well, one of safety, music, and magic.

Samson

Just as coincidence led Samson to Christian and The City of Brotherly Love, so too, it was happenstance that pulled him to Chicago.

The break up was simple. The night of the relationship's cataclysm, Samson called Edward Vargas and they writhed in naked, pagan-like abandon amid the waves of Edward's satin sheets. Whether it was Edward's gifts as a lover or the fact that Samson, for the first time in years, allowed himself to fully exist in a sexual encounter is uncertain, but the collision of Edward and Samson led to the best sex of Samson's young life.

"How's your boyfriend?" Edward asked the next morning as coffee percolated.

Samson smiled. He drummed his fingers on the expansive marble countertop. "Irrelevant," he said jovially. "As of last night, completely irrelevant."

Edward licked his lips. The boy before him tremored with new energy. In his own youth, he had evolved drastically, a series of dramatic life events hurtling him into adulthood, forcing his emotional maturity to take on new, fantastic shapes of which he had never dreamed.

"I think we might have a lot in common," he said. His honey-colored eyes sparkled with mischief. "Call us sluts, whores, or, what we really are, polyamorous, but we don't want just one meal our entire lives."

Samson was not looking at Edward, but to the translucent, cerulean windows that circled them in the kitchen. Endless reflections of the outside world met his gaze – buildings, sunlight, streets, clouds, and trees. Just like the day he met Edward, the world now seemed unquantifiable, a multiverse he never before had the courage to explore. The chaos and emptiness of this new world startled as well as excited him. Could one fall so deeply into the mystical portals of possibilities, that they were beyond redemption?

At the end of this line of thinking was a question. He did not know what he wanted as a response:

"Have you ever been in love?" he asked quietly, staring into the blue wall of the windows.

Edward's eyes flashed. "No, baby. Never went that way. I've been infatuated before, but the only person I've really ever loved is my abuela."

"Is she still alive?"

"Dead a long time." Edward poured a cup of coffee and slid it to Samson. "You're a direct one. Not nearly as shy as I thought you'd be the first time we met."

"I'm no longer junior," Samson said quickly. He was again looking at Edward, the mystifying world of possibilities closed behind him. There was fear and excitement alternating in the lub-dub rhythm of his heart, but that could be taken up another time.

"Can we fuck again?" he asked, shedding his underwear.

Two hours later, he left Edward's apartment with a kiss on the cheek and no promises or expectations of ever meeting again. As he left the loft, he looked at his phone for the first time since he called Edward the previous evening.

Eight voicemails.

Over the course of them all, Christian's anxiety grew steadily. The four the previous night had been calm, almost mocking. Then around 2 am one that revealed a more concerned tone. The three from the morning were conciliatory, apologetic, and loving.

"Hey, babe, I'm really sorry. You're right to be mad – I shouldn't get like that. I had some wine – listen, I just want to be sure you're all right. I don't know where you would have gone... Just give me a call, okay?"

Have you ever been in love? Just like Edward, Samson never had been. He knew that now. He was beginning to realize he may never be in real love – the sparkling, flamboyant kind his friends posted about on Facebook. The love his father and grandmother shared was love – he had never known the romantic kind to exist outside of heartbreak. Love was your mother leaving, driving out of a quiet subdivision; love was thinking a boy was your world and having him bash you across the face; love was coexisting alongside someone who belittled and secretly despised you. Love was a many-splendored thing, but the splendor was polished skulls and sparkling bones rather than glitter and gold dust as the world was wont to promise.

But how does one live a life without love? Without the drama, the pursuit of a perfect union? The world forces men and women into a steady tract pursuing this ideal endlessly. Samson knew his life no longer progressed down this rigid, phantom road. He did not have a pathway to follow. This was the reason for the erratic, cross-currents of thought that flooded his mind in Edward's apartment.

But another time.

Another time he would pursue the meaning of his new universe. Now, he would simply live.

He ignored the calls and instead went to the art museum for the first time since he had moved to Philly. On the Rocky steps, he proactively stopped overweight tourists and suggested that they get tacos at a place he knew downtown.

"Tacos are fine, but where is a really good cheesesteak?" one woman named Barbara asked.

Samson, in that moment, realized he had never had a cheesesteak in his two years in the city. His life with Christian had been devoid of any locality at all. They had existed in a glass box above the city, judging and ignoring the world around them. All those lights, those doorways to Philadelphia lives that he'd admired in the twilight, were never even considered in the years he spent with Christian. They passed nights having wine, dinner, and talking politics – what had they done with their lives? They'd left no imprint on anything in the city. For years they had been ignoring the sights and sounds of the world around them.

He received four more voicemails that afternoon. This time the tone went steadily from concerned and loving to pure anger.

"You know what? I'm glad I called you a fucking child. Run away like a little bitch. Just run. Don't expect me to be waiting for you to come back."

Samson got a cheesesteak that afternoon; he saw the Liberty Bell and went on a three-hour tour of Eastern State Penitentiary. In the evening, he went into the heart of the gayborhood and sat at the bar alone. The only man who spoke to him was a middle-aged businessman from Chicago.

"You like Philly?" he asked. "I'm only here tonight."

"Are you trying to hookup?"

The man laughed. He showed Samson a simple wedding band. "I'm straight, married to a schoolteacher. Only gay thing I've ever done is see *The Birdcage*. But I love to get drunk, so the wife only lets me go out to gay bars when I'm on business."

"She's a smart lady."

"That's why I married her."

Samson ordered two shots of whiskey. "To be honest," he said, "I don't know how I feel about Philly. I've been here a while, but I don't think I've really engaged the city."

"It's easy to get stuck in your routines," the man said twisting his wedding band. "I've been downtown in Chicago once this year outside of work. My daughter brought her boyfriend to visit. We went and saw The Bean, had brunch at some place that was way too expensive, then took an architecture boat ride. I learned about Prairie Style."

"Did you and your wife try that after the tour?"

The man roared. The shots had arrived, so he raised the glass and gave a small salute with his left hand. "To exploring what's around us every day."

"To that."

The two men took the shots. Within an hour, three more followed. By midnight, the older man had his tie pulled off, his sleeves rolled up, his head bobbing along to a Scissor Sisters song.

"I always liked The Village People," he said. "It wasn't manly but they were catchy as hell."

"My dad loved Steve Miller Band. I had to listen to it constantly growing up."

"Somethin' call me a Space Cowboy... Whhoooommmmm whoooooo!"

Samson laughed. In his years with Christian, he'd forgotten how joy could rush to his cheeks, flow through his veins, and make his toes tap. Even in college he was restrained, pulled into himself. Fear constantly dictated his emotions – when he went out with Christian's friends he couldn't be messy. He had to be the good boyfriend, the mature young man. If he slipped, he'd get a lecture, a school-marmish scolding in the morning about being an adult.

"Sammy," the man said, "you ever think about living in Chicago?"

Samson's heart warmed. Only his father called him Sammy. "Chicago?" he asked softly.

"Yeah, it's bigger than Philly – more to ignore, but a nice city."

"I never thought about it."

"Well, you should think about it. I'm in finance and we have openings for analysts pretty often. I like you, you're smart –"

"As smart as your wife?"

"No one is that smart," the man's eyes twinkled. "But you're pretty smart, so if you ever think about relocating, look me up."

He pulled out a business card and slapped it on the table.

"I definitely will."

Samson slept on the couch in the man's hotel room. He awoke to no more voice mails. He could thankfully consider that over.

He slipped all his belongings out of Christian's the following morning while his ex-lover was away at work. Even in the depths of his heart, Samson felt no desire to see him; the relationship was officially ended with a text message composed that evening:

Hey, sorry, I don't want to see you anymore. You were a dick and I think we should both move on. I'm moving to Chicago.

Despite feeling more alive than he had in years, the dread of telling his father and grandmother about his life transformation, hung over him like a shadow. In phone conversations and texts, he let his father believe that Christian and his relationship was flourishing. Concurrently, he was being absorbed into the Boystown social scene. Weekends were spent at Sidetrack and a variety of night clubs in Lake View or River North. The break from Christian was a break from responsibility, monogamy, and expectation. Nights were a whirl of alcohol and colored lights – days were powdered with cocaine to keep his eyes open in the cubicle farm that paid his rent.

Years slipped by quickly between the heat of the clubs and his excursions to Palm Springs, L.A., and New York. In Chicago he moved from Uptown, to Boystown, to a high-rise in Lincoln Park. There were a few relationships, but none that lasted more than a couple months. Samson wasn't cut out for a relationship in the long term. Buried inside of him was always the fear – the fear of one leaving, the fear of having your love turned against you in violence. Solace was found in the wild nights in the bars and quick sexual encounters when his body demanded it. His group of friends constantly evolved. Despite cultivating a crew of new faces, they largely came from the same mold – primped, stylish, hairless, and beautiful.

"You all kind of look the same, huh?" his father asked one afternoon while he visited. "Is this the guy you were dating last time I came down?"

"No, someone different."

"Hmm."

It was his grandmother's sudden death a year after Christian and his break up that triggered him telling his father the truth about their relationship. Samson was shocked when his father shrugged indifferently after the revelation.

"He seemed a little old for you. You're young with some mistakes to make yet. I wouldn't want you to fall into a trap like me and your mother."

By 2010, Samson was a fixture in Boystown. Casual evenings were spent in the dim lights of Minibar, the chiseled bartenders bringing him free drinks. Late nights ended at Hydrate, most often going home with a group of shirtless, molly-fueled men with wild eyes.

In the fall of that year he met Hedley. His future friend entered Minibar with a casual elegance that attracted all eyes to him.

"Who's that?" Samson asked.

"No idea," his date for the evening said. "Cute, though."

Samson turned to the bartender and nodded toward the new arrival. "You know who that is, Alex?"

Alex flipped back his shoulder-length hair. "Not fur shore. I thenk he iz mebbe Jason's frund."

Hedley turned and locked eyes with Samson down the bar. He winked and licked his lips. Samson gazed at him quizzically.

Once Hedley had his drink, the Boystown ingénue put down a ten on the counter. With vulpine grace, he made his way straight over to Samson. On arrival, he put his elbow on the counter and assumed a relaxed pose.

"I'm Hedley."

"Hedley?"

"Family name. I saw you looking and thought you wanted to know." Hedley leaned over and stuck his hand out for Samson's date. "Hedley."

The date nodded and stared.

"Can I get you boys a drink?"

"Uhhh – suuure…"

Hedley waved his hand at Alex. "Can I get three shots of Rumple Minze and two Malibu cranberries for my associates."

"Associates?" The date asked.

"Well, if we're not friends, why not be associates?" Hedley's eyes sparked with an ornery electricity.

Samson laughed, a loud, short note. Hedley, again, winked at him.

The date put his hand under his chin and looked at Hedley intently. He opened his mouth to speak, but then paused, sniffed, and turned away.

Samson scratched the back of his neck. "Thanks… for the drinks. Are you new in town?"

"My pleasure – and, not really, just becoming more visible."

The date fixed his hair in his blank iPhone screen.

Alex lumbered over, his pecs glistening in the dim lights. "Tuh-ew Malyboo Crunz and 3 Rumpz," he said. "Wuhld yuh like ta clooose or kup it open?"

"Open, please."

Hedley raised his shot and smiled. "To new associates – may they become friends."

Samson watched him down the shot. To his surprise, Hedley put down the empty glass, tipped an imaginary hat, and then slid back into the crowd.

"Strange bird," the date said. "I feel like he's playing at something… You think he had to do that as a bet?"

"I don't know." Samson smiled. "He definitely catches your attention, though."

Samson took home the date. Their bodies were full of alcohol and, by the end of the evening, poppers and a few lines of cocaine. The date progressed from masculine and withdrawn to sloppy and coquettish as the night continued. Although Samson knew their relationship was over after the first round of drinks, he had no issue with fucking him three times before the first lights of dawn stole through his blinds and splashed onto the hardwood floors.

When it was over, the date rolled onto his side and fell asleep. His snores rang through the apartment as Samson prepared a cup of coffee. In that early morning witching hour, he wasn't thinking about the date – the effete, interior designer from rural Wisconsin. The face that drifted through the forefront of his imagination – a salute, a smile, the word "associates" – was Hedley.

I feel like he's playing at something...

That's what the date had said. Samson smiled to himself. He intended to find out the rules of the game.

Stephen

Stephen spent most afternoons in a cloud of indifference on the university's main quad. Stella would sit beside him, pull a joint out of her purse, and they would discuss philosophy, politics, and love while watching co-eds scamper between classes.

"I feel like I wasn't alive until I read Joyce. He reshaped the world for me."

Stephen half-listened to Stella's marijuana-induced rants about whatever inspired or irritated her during the day.

"Sarah stayed up until 3 am last night. She just clicked on her keyboard and kept me awake; she's such a privileged bitch."

Stephen and Stella had fucked at a party right after his break up with Pearl. In his fog of grief and misery, he wildly scanned the frat house for someone to relieve his sexual angst. When studying possibilities lined against the dark, stained walls, the only criteria he had was "breathing."

After the party, he and Stella made a pact that they would not engage physically. Stella said his chakra wasn't aligned with her own. Stephen let that excuse carry the day and found another girl the next night. The friendship that was cultivated after sex was largely built on the need for both of them to self-medicate with alcohol and marijuana. Stella was the daughter of a lawyer and a doctor; she received average grades and studied art history. Her life was a constant stream of emails and calls from her parents checking-in, politely trying to steer her back to the path of the hard sciences.

Stephen's life lost its course the previous winter when he and Pearl ended things. He still had dreams of her standing in her white sweater, watching him leave through the golden panes of the living room window.

"Why won't you tell me why?" she asked through tears.

The root cause was Jimmy Gupta, the senior who lived next door to him in the dorm his sophomore year. Jimmy was from New York City; Stephen had never seen anyone so beautiful.

"Are you going to the party tonight?" Stella flipped back her curly hair. "I'm thinking about it, but I should finish up my paper on *Henri de Toulouse-Lautrec*." She said the name with a French accent.

"I may go," Stephen said indifferently. "I'm supposed to go out with Corey tonight."

"Do you still claim bisexuality? This is the fourth boy in a row you've gone out with."

"I'm indifferently sexual at this moment," he said flatly. "Corey is cute, though."

"He looks like he's right out of a toothpaste ad. Is that your type?"

Stephen thought briefly of Pearl, foremost her laugh when they were alone, a snort of pure mirth. "I don't know what my type is," he said.

"If you'd go for me and Corey, then I'm not sure I see a trend."

Stella was plump; she wore flowing dresses and had tattoos on her right forearm and left thigh.

"Sexuality is a spectrum, Stells."

Over the years, Stephen had only become more beautiful. His body solidified into statuesque perfection. Although the cloud of indifference settled over him, he still went to the gym to relieve stress; this, in addition to his place on the intramural soccer team, kept him trim and chiseled. His face retained its boyish charm but now was decorated with a manicured dusting of stubble. Even with the charm of Pearl and his relationship shattered, no one had noticed the magic had gone out of him completely. His eyes still shone with the rakish glow of youth; his smile still melted hearts that came in close proximity.

"I always wonder why you chose me that night," Stella said plucking grass with her ringed fingers. "You could have had anyone."

"You'd be surprised," he said coldly. "When you can have anyone, the world seems excruciatingly small."

#

After Stephen gave Pearl his class ring their sophomore year of high school, he had been good. The cloud of homosexuality only existed in the dark of his own bedroom when he was alone. Occasionally, it found its way into the light when a particularly gorgeous male specimen crossed his path and he couldn't control himself – in those moments, the bathroom or a secluded corner was where he found relief. But in terms of their relationship, he never strayed, never cheated, never flirted with other boys or girls.

They quickly became the exemplary couple in the church. Mothers and grandmothers would pat his arm and cluck delightedly whenever they appeared together at a service.

"Such a beautiful, young couple," the old women would say. "God blesses the good!"

Envious friends would comment on the success of their relationship with veiled acrimony.

"You two are just... perfect!"

And they were happy. Or had some general understanding of it.

Sex was kept to second and third base in all their years together. Only at the very end did Pearl begin to allow blow jobs. It was Stephen who broke the taboo, pulling her close one evening as they sat in the car. Deftly, he pulled down her pants and let his tongue explore her moist vagina.

But then, fire – a lightning bolt severing a pitch-dark sky, splitting open the partition that Stephen so anxiously cultivated inside himself.

Jimmy appeared in the hall the first week of his sophomore year in college. He was shirtless, his chocolate skin slick with sweat. Smiling he leaned against the frame of Stephen's open door.

"'Sup, neighbor," he said. "I hope you don't mind being kept awake with a little boom boom." Smiling he began thrusting the air with his hips.

His roommate, Corbin, appeared behind him, gripping him around the waist and throwing him to the ground.

"Don't listen to this ass," he said. "The last pussy he saw was his mama's when she pushed him out."

The two shoved each other around in the hall, laughing like children.

Stephen had never met anyone that exhibited the same traits others admired so much in him. Jimmy exuded charisma and charm. People were drawn to him, loved him, fawned over him after just one of his quick, ornery smiles. He had not lied about the fucking; over the course of their two semesters as neighbors, Stephen counted twenty different women who hit his messy sheets. Corbin became a fixture in Stephen's own room, sexiled two or three nights a week as Jimmy made his way through conquests.

Jimmy was his first boy crush. Other men had thrown themselves at Stephen: Davey, the soccer coach, and other boys in his classes. But aside from Pearl, Jimmy was the only other person he ever desired wholly. This was not a physical connection, it was a spiritual, magnetic attraction that burned between them.

Stephen remembered each of their moments together; he cataloged their social exchanges in his head. In solitude, he'd take out each memory and turn it over, savoring the minutes they spent together. Music made him think of Jimmy – slow songs led to him imagining them dancing together; fast songs brought to mind his nude torso and gyrating hips grinding to the rhythm.

Facebook/Jimmy.Gupta.11 appeared first when he hit "f" in the URL search of his laptop. Every morning Stephen would rise and scroll through Jimmy's images to see if someone had written on his wall or posted pictures. After spring break, Stephen feasted on pictures of Jimmy and his friends shirtless at the beach, drunk, wrestling on the sand, and making out with girls.

Jimmy brought Stephen to the end of his heterosexual delusion. Being raised in the church, Stephen imagined his sexuality as a spectrum; he sat somewhere just shy of the middle on the straight side. He appreciated men, he lusted after men, but he loved women. Women were to be loved.

But Jimmy sparked an understanding that his highest form of love – the complete fusion of lust, passion, and romance was, for him, with a man. Over the course of the first semester of his sophomore year, he texted and called Pearl less. The fantasies kept at bay for so long during their courtship burst forth in Stephen's imagination. It wasn't just Jimmy – the fire he started spread rapidly. On the floor of the rec center, Stephen ejaculated as he watched a muscled junior grunt out reps on the shoulder press. Between classes, after dinner, during library study breaks, Stephen was in a bathroom stall jerking himself off to the vision of men. It was never one, but the rainbow of them that crossed his daily path. The pot of gold, the epicenter of this quake, was Jimmy.

By the time he went home for Christmas, Stephen felt the impossible distance between himself and Pearl. Pearl recognized it as well; as they sat together on the couch, her soft eyes ran over him, tried to perceive what alteration had occurred during the few months they were apart.

"Are you okay?" she asked. "Do you want to talk?"

#

Corey was banal, as expected.

"I'm happy to say my first presidential vote was for Obama," he said. "We can already see the change. The Affordable Care Act is here. They sky's the limit." He flashed his toothpaste smile.

Stephen sighed. It was dark, but he kept on his sunglasses. They had driven out to a local park, Stephen under the impression that it would segue into a fuck. Corey had parlayed it into a never-ending discussion on American politics, healthcare (he was pre-med), and the rise of gay marriage.

"Are you always so optimistic?" Stephen asked, not unkindly. "You have on some intense rose-colored glasses."

"Is that what these are?" Corey leaned over and lifted the glasses off of Stephen's face.

Stephen saw it then, the subtle illumination which signaled infatuation, dawning feelings. Corey's eyes shone like embers in a dying fire. He licked his lips, puckered them subtly together.

Don't, Stephen said. The words did not escape into the air, but rebounded in his head, echoed across his heart.

Despite the revelation that he wanted men, he loved men, his soul still retained its recalcitrance to his homosexual pursuits. Fear in the form of rejection from his family, from God, from the church, from the coterie of fawning women whom he saved in his phone, kept him from embracing it fully. Part of him still saw these encounters with men as dalliances; he would find another Pearl. This thought grew smaller, dimmer, more hopeless, with every passing exploit with a man, but it was still there.

Don't.

What was at the end of this physical encounter? They would be sexually satisfied. He and Corey would be panting, tired, and lightheaded after climax, but this was a selfish end – a destructive end. The church had reasons for promoting heterosexuality; its ultimate conclusion was the creation of life, the most powerful, noblest pursuit for men and women in all the world.

Gays did not get to this achievement through physical union. They fumbled through the dark, pursuing better sex, better highs, and better men. The destination which homosexuality led them all toward was death. From their desires, their dating, and their need for companionship, nothing good, nothing eternal could arise. It led only to the reaper.

"Don't," the voice said again inside of Stephen. "Corey, don't come closer. Don't make this move and lash yourself to me emotionally. Don't believe in the possibility of us, in a future with adopted children and dual incomes. Don't fall in love. Don't believe in all you've been promised, because I don't. I am a dead end, as dead an end as your sexual pursuits. We end in death. The end is absolute and it is darkness."

Don't... the voice shattered in his psyche before it could be heard in reality.

It shattered the moment Corey pressed against him. Stephen felt Corey's lips touch his, followed by the taut sinew of his runner's body running under his hands. ("Doctors have to be the example of fitness for their patients.") Their tongues lashed together – Stephen gave in, his physical need overwhelming his spiritual and existential hollowness with blind lust.

After Corey, Stephen had one of his nervous breaks. They were much more controllable than they had been right after he gave up Pearl. They were preceded by his mind running over the futility of homosexual happiness; a speech that rebounded in his head before a sexual encounter with a man, a moment when his spiritual side broke through and tried to make him confront the truth, be the voice of reason to whatever person was on a collision course with him. He embraced the sex because he knew after there would be the desolate, cavernous oblivion of his emotions.

Don't come closer.
Don't fall in love.
Why?

Love was nothing. It wasn't an epiphany, seconds in time that showed you the certainty of forever. Love was complicated, desolate, unyielding, and uncertain. His love was against the church, the paradigm of good that permeated the bones of western society.

"I know it's crazy," Pearl said in a weepy voicemail immediately after the break up, "but I imagined us together forever. I thought of our children – I picked out wallpaper for our house..."

"How's Pearl?" he asked every time he came home now, every time he was on the phone with his mother.

"Her mom says she's doing good!"

"That's great. That's really great." Tears always formed at the edge of his eyes. His throat swelled and grew thick with emotion.

Don't.

Later she wrote the letter. It was a full year after they broke up. Stephen had drowned himself in sex, pot, and alcohol. Pearl had renewed her faith, switched majors, and gone into Christian counseling.

I took this class and it made me realize a couple things. One, namely, that I'll always love you. No matter who I marry, how many children I have, where I go, there will always be a piece of me that treasures you and our time together. I told my teacher it was a thorn in my soul – she said to think of it as a rose bloom. It was beautiful and brief and now lays flattened in the pages of my heart.

Two (which follows one), I'm sorry for the right after: the constant calls, the stalking on Facebook (that you will never really know about), the nervous scanning of all your pictures to see if there was someone else, if there'd be another girl beside you.

I'm not ready to see you again, but we had this assignment to write an "important letter." That was it, just to write it and call it important. I wrote one to my dead grandmother, one to God, one to Taylor Swift, for goodness sake. But the one that was really "important," was this one to you.

Stephen, I love you. I'm sorry. I hope you're well. I miss you. You're every part of heartbreak to me, but I think that you were right to break it off when you did. We were kids; we didn't know better, and I think we both have a lot of learning to do.

It went on, but that was the part Stephen mouthed to himself during his nervous breaks. The idea of love as terminal – it would never go away. The moment he broke it off with Pearl, Stephen went into a bottomless, shiftless depression. Slowly, he was recovering, or attempting to recover, but he always thought of one thing that sunk him back into the dark:

Two kids in a field after a church retreat. The world peaceful, calm.

Then Stephen believed in everything.

Could he go back there? How does one return to even one, isolated moment of innocence?

Hedley

A Manifesto on the Fractured State of Modern Reality
16 June 2010

THESIS:
    The present world is a convergence of presentation, interpretation, and understanding – lenses which the viewer is able to impose upon another person, with varying to no shades of "truth" regarding the "essence" of who that person is. Social media is the driving force of this new iteration of human existence. It is my conclusion that a measure of control can be placed upon these diffuse lenses, giving one a source of manipulation that can be forced upon a large population.

BACKGROUND:

Assumption:
    I'm starting with the presumption that within each person there is an actual form of person, which can be distilled into traits that would be their "essence." It is a broad assumption, but most humans have the same essence, built upon our fundamental animal instincts which keep us alive: fear, sexual desire, and self-preservation. Layered upon those core traits are varying moral constructs that society imposes upon the individual.

An example: Joe, a fictitious character.
    Joe is a father of two children. He and his wife, Jane, have been married for ten years and live in a small suburb of Chicago.

Primal Fears:
    Protection of his children, fear of losing his sales job, fear of mates competing for his wife.

Moralistic Fears:
   A fear of the Catholic God

Conflicts:
   *Joe is sexually obsessed with his neighbor, Elizabeth, a twenty-four-year-old wife and new mother.
   *Joe has had declining sales the past two quarters. He is on probationary status at work.

The Projection of Joe:
   To his friends and neighbors, Joe is an exemplary citizen. He attends church on Sunday, takes his children to baseball and ballet, and is regularly seen with his wife on cute, quiet nights at local restaurants

The Reality of Joe:
   Joe loves his children and wife. He has hidden the recent work trouble from Jane. He found Elizabeth's social media account and created a collection of photos from the mid-2000s when she was in college and wore revealing tops. He masturbates to these at least four times weekly.
   The guilt of both of these tacit lies has sent Joe into a more contentious, but also attentive, relationship to God. He prays nightly, begging for the sexual desires to be taken away, for his work life to turn around.
   Joe is morally at conflict with the world around him. He fights with God while keeping a veneer of normalcy. In his heart, he battles an onslaught of invisible demons.
   This is Joe's essence, every person's essence. We are at war with different expectations enforced by God, our family, and ourselves.

Projection v. Perception:
   Joe in the 1950's could keep up these local shadow plays with ease. He need only keep his household affairs private and stable his masturbatory and work problems in the dark, and everyone localized would only see his projection.
   In our current day, this localized perception can be blown out to reach the world at large. Joe can now keep up his appearances around town, but can also curate an image online that reflects the normalcy people see daily. It is possible then, to project this normalcy across friend and social groups. Now that Joe's mother is on Facebook, she can share pictures of Joe and his family in states of perfect happiness.
   Let's say one of the watchers of this activity feed is the mother of one of Joe's high school friends. This mother can share Joe's happiness with her daughter, Doris:
   "Have you seen Joe's wife and kids. They are just beautiful. He really has it together."
   Doris is recently divorced, in large part due to her inability to have children.
   Joe, indirectly, has exerted a manipulative power over Doris. He put a reflection up to her that doesn't exist but is only the veneer of Joe. No one, but perhaps God, could ever see the essence and conflict of Joe which may create a calming balm

upon the personal tribulations of Doris. Within the framework of this social interaction, Joe has shamed her, bullied her, told her that she is wrong. In reality, or whatever we can call the domain of our essences, Doris and Joe both live at the intersection of interpersonal and social conflict. War.

Manipulation for Other Means:
> But what if one could take this projection and make it a model of success rather than shame? What if, by artfully curating a media presence, one could create community and self-promote oneself to a place of invisible but omnipotent social power, for the purpose of a higher good?
>
> The Joe/Doris duality would be replaced by one in which Joe reflected something just shy of the unattainable. He need only slightly ratchet up the projection to make Doris, not feel rejected, but aspirational.
>
> "Why can't you be more like Joe?" would be replaced by "What is the world of Joe?" How can I rise to his heights?"

A Moral Interlude (I):
> Is presenting a false reality, in some ways, like lying? If Hank Turner becomes Hedley Renault and projects an image of an oasis rather than the vast desert most people encounter, is this untruthful – a rejection of Hank's own "essence?"
>
> I would pose that society needs this. Morality aside, if it is evil, it is a necessary one. Communities need heroes or else their moral compasses, as a whole, are useless. What is "good" if there is no example? What is success if there is no one achieving greatness? Is the preacher who fucks his parishioner in an adulterous affair rendered wholly evil if his sermons still inspire others to reach their true "essence?"

ON HOW TO CONSTRUCT A NEW REALITY:

What Is and What One Wants to Be:
> To return to Joe and Doris, an essential reason for Joe's power over Doris is that he has constructed a reality which perfectly conforms to a social understanding of "good." At a local level, Doris is put into contrast with Joe and manifests failures on major fronts of this "good" criteria: marriage, family, children, morality.
>
> But this small-town idea of good, can be magnified, exploded into something more. This simple, local good, can be manipulated into the "higher good" which makes others aspire to be more.
>
> For instance, with the World Cup coming to South Africa athletes are an excellent example. The media projects athletes as masters of their craft, the highest performers in their field. When an individual so devoutly manifests success in their work life, we want that to be a reflection of their essence. In the human psyche, we want the balance of perfection across all factors of that person.
>
> Michael Jordan is the most prominent athletic figure from my childhood. Everyone wanted to be "like Mike." In the mid-90's, he was the perfect symbol of masculinity – wholesome, talented, dedicated to family, handsome – Nike turned Jordan into a one-man marketing icon.

But can we put the lightning in a bottle? What are the factors that elevate good to higher good, and role model to icon? What are the significant factors that must be exploited in order to not only make other strive, but desire ascension?

My Experiment upon the Gay Community of Chicago:

Interpersonal manipulations have come easy and simply to me over the years. In high school, I could affect human relationships as easily as pressing the valves on my trumpet. It merely takes an understanding of the full network of human relations to see what notes need to be played to make the melody.

It is not simply manipulations. I have also discovered the merits of presenting oneself as a lie, a complete fabricated self in order to win trust and gain traction within the manipulation. In my first course, this was immaturely used to procure a blow job, in subsequent adventures, experimentation with new identities has yielded free hotel rooms, drinks, and successful sexual encounters with those who believed they were out of my league.

In my time at the marketing firm, our quickly growing social media department has impressed upon me the explosive potential of this new medium within the framework of my own interpersonal powers. If the networks of this new world can be seen and manipulated, who knows what kind of force one can wield over a populace.

The course of action requires a number of specific factors in moving the experiment forward:

1. Curated Media: The most obvious piece of this puzzle. I must create media profiles that leave others desiring what they do not have. Key factors: a toned body they strive to chisel out in the gym; vacations to exotic locations they desire to embark upon; friends of a caliber they wish they could gossip to; a personality that is not smug, but also exudes a charisma and intellect that is tantalizing.

2. A Morality: Surprisingly not amorality, but "a" morality. People like to feel that their role models do more than exist. They do the things that we do not have the time or energy to do. I must establish a cause, promote it, become a symbol of it. The gay community still has a number of shortcomings in terms of social stature and justice – this should be simple. Research into an elder gay man and his own cult of personality is a good reference point for this – see also, "The Key" below for more.

3. The Coterie: I need an entourage to be my support in this – whether knowingly or not. This may come to be something as predictable and diluted as choosing the personalities for a sitcom cast, but it must be precisely engineered to inspire envy and aspiration. All demographics should be appealed to so that even if they do not strive to be the sun, they can aspire to be the stars. In a generic outline, I expect to see – someone older, someone younger, the boy-next-door, and then perhaps a rotating member so everyone thinks they have a chance to be invited to be a part of this elite corps.

4. Real-life Interactions: With the coterie created, formed, and promoted on social media, there must also be a physical presence to make it real and tangible. To be seen as fully human and present, I must also occupy physical space within the Boystown community. It may come down to randomized locations so that it's not predictable. No one expects an icon to be at Sidetrack every Saturday. Even the "it" bars like Minibar have to be targeted for selected evenings and events.

5. A News Source: The trickiest piece is developing a third-party voice that speaks well of you, or at least inspires interest and fear in you. Instagram is extremely new but the possibility of a photo-sharing medium could develop into a localized paparazzi – could @Boystownnightlife be a thing? It may be better to sink more time into established media like Twitter and Facebook, which could publish quick news updates about my activities and comings and goings.

The Key: The Palimpsest

All these factors are important, but the real intangible key is, what I have taken to referring to as "The Palimpsest." As curated and targeted as the projection must be, there must always be the layer, or perceived layer, of the real essence underneath. It's hard to be in complete control and yet allow for some moments of spontaneity, but this is the goal. They must see me cry; they must know that I came from a small town and have farmers in my family; they, above all, must think that they can speak to me, that there is some direct line of empathy which runs directly between us.

Sal does not try to do this, but he is a master. His experience shines through the interpersonal so that everyone feels, in some way, connected to him. Whether it is his lover's death, his fag-hag best friend, or his own closeted experience, everyone feels there is some piece of him they intrinsically know and relate to. The master stroke is curating a palimpsest of which one does not lose control.

A Moral Interlude (II):

Is forming inter-personal friendships with the sole purpose of conducting a social experiment cold-hearted? Is it rude to use people in such a direct and manipulative way? Again, I would state a necessary evil. I have yet to make real plans if this succeeds and I can rise to become a powerful figure in the social strata, but I think it could be possible to exercise great "moral" force on the gay community if power is wielded in the correct way. Obviously, in every action there is the possibility of pure corruption – could I run a fascist regime out of Minibar that controls social and race relations in a way that is exclusionary and unprincipled? Of course – for every ying there is a yang. On the opposite side of a heaven, we always find a hell.

CONCLUSION:

The Action Plan resides above. I must first curate the media, the people, the morality, the news source, and work on The Palimpsest.

I already have some people in mind that could fill out The Coterie. Perhaps that's too bourgeoisie and can be refined to something more democratic – The Crew? The Flock? The Set?

These could all be pointless musings in a dramatic and manipulative twenty-six-year old's journal, but I think there is real opportunity to force my will on something larger than myself. I have always thought of myself as Indigo and there is power in that. Regardless of whether an Indigo Child is a real thing, the label, the possibility shaped my way of thinking in a number of important ways. It could be false, and the new man, Hedley Renault, will be as false – but, perhaps, that is the best analogy for this experiment. From deception we can create something greater than from any truth. God Himself is believed to be the greatest lie ever created by society to establish social control. But is that, then, evil if it inspires good at its core?

    Those musings are too much for one mind. I shall take control of what I can. I have my script written, now I wait for lights, camera, action.

2015: Epilogue

In late afternoon, the sky a Monet painting of running blues, reds, and violets, The Set returned to Samson's condominium. Pictures were posted and conversations ran rampant along the beach; news, rumors, and conjecture about The Set rippled up and down the strand in time with the hushed lapping of water on the shore. Out of the public space, The Set casted off the artifice and illusion of their earlier outing and embraced the quiet, trembling nature of their inner lives.

They arranged themselves in Samson's living room in dramatic tableau: Stephen sleeping soundly on Samson's recliner; Skyler pacing back and forth along the windows facing Foster Beach; Hedley at the bar watching Samson mix a drink. As he watched the vodka pour, he massaged his temples, reviewing how to put the pieces together for the evening: how long had it been since they'd gone to DS? Was it time to try something new? Maybe a bar in Wrigley?

"What a dull day," Skyler said. "Nothing new at all."

"Nothing is ever new," Samson called from the kitchen. He entered the living room with a fresh drink. "Chicago's gay scene is reliably boring."

"Maybe we should inject something into it," Hedley mused. "A large boat day or maybe some sort of second gala…"

"Soot would kill you if you stole the thunder from his white party," Skyler snorted. "We must respect our elders."

"My friend's coming into town at the beginning of August… Maybe we could do something for that."

"That's Market Days." Samson took a long drink. "We can't fuck with Market Days."

"I suppose not."

Hedley walked over the window and stared down at the beach with Skyler. Families were coming in from their days of leisure. Children laughed and jumped – mothers and fathers held hands watching the chaos unfold. If The Set's earlier adventure to the beach had been pure artifice, a reality built upon expectation, cultivated in the unreality of an internet world, then this view from Samson's window was its diametric opposite. Here was the essence of reality – a view made perfectly for an artist to render as still life.

"'After the Beach,'" Hedley said softly.

"What?" Skyler asked.

"That's what I'd call a painting of this view."

"Would you paint all the fat, bloated parents, or would you slim them down for art's sake?"

Hedley laughed; it was a low, mirthless chuckle – reactive, thoughtless. "I suppose we would have to think of aesthetics."

Stephen jolted awake. "Oh! You should have woken me up. Did I miss anything?"

"We were just discussing how boring everything is," Samson said.

I don't know…" Stephen rose, moving straight to the kitchen and vodka. "I think this summer has been interesting – maybe not, super eventful or amazing, but we have some new players – and… I don't know, there's some romance in the air."

"Are you talking about Lloyd?"

"Not particularly." Stephen, not finding a glass, took a drink from the vodka bottle. "I mean we've got Jonathan and there's you know…"

Skyler giggled. "You are dreaming about Mikey."

"Maybe," Stephen smiled as he took another drink. "I don't understand why you don't play around more, Skyler. When I was twenty-two it was anyone and anything. Girls, boys – it gets old, but I feel like we all need that time."

Hedley and Skyler exchanged a brief glance. "Well," said Skyler, "not everyone needs to be a whore, Stevey."

"Suit yourself."

Hedley returned his gaze to the families leaving the beach. The scene below relaxed him – it grew more common for him to go to quiet, out-of-the-way places and let the atmosphere wash over him. Sal was the one who told him quiet moments become more valuable as you age. Hedley mocked him one evening when Sal was late to a coffee date because he'd become engrossed with the Baha'i Temple and lost track of time.

"Someday you're going to find yourself walking alone to abandoned places for the sheer joy of it. There's something about it that allows your mind to unwind, drift, consolidate information rather than jumping from one thought to the next."

Here he was doing exactly that. Simplicity drew him more and more. At the beginning of his quest to control Boystown, it had been a game that he'd been steadily winning. Slowly he seized power and territory from the other cliques. Samson was a bargaining chip that solidified his place among the elite. Hedley, through attraction and some well-timed events, guided him away from the competing group of homosexuals, who had since disbanded. Stephen, when he arrived, was magnetic. Everyone wanted him, but it was Hedley who unraveled his knots and made him feel comfortable enough to stay with the group. Skyler was volatile – happenstance caused Hedley to stumble upon his secret, convince him he would keep it safe, and win his confidence.

But he was growing exhausted. There was now Jonathan, the newest rotating piece in the game. When he started to rise and physically change, Hedley toyed with making him a new kind of example – the before and after. Look what you can become when you put your mind to it! Hedley put hours into cultivating him, but he wasn't pure like Samson, Stephen, and Skyler. Jonathan had roots that went back to David – even though he had changed, he wasn't evolved. His way of thinking remained plebian. At the bars, he'd go after the easy targets.

"Why don't you go talk to him?" Hedley would ask casually.

"I don't know – I don't think he'd be into it."

The Set needed strong characters – alphas, to prosper. Jonathan was a Beta in a freshly minted Alpha's cloak.

The new boy Jordan introduced to the scene was a second chance – he couldn't let the summer go to complete waste, especially with Samson drifting so listlessly northward to the bears and muscle daddies.

"It's a sideshow, Samson. Are you sure you want to invest in that?"

"Hedley… Believe it or not, some people get tired of always being in the spotlight."

But Hedley knew. He knew more and more every day. It was exhausting and the quiet called him. What had it been? What triggered it? It was most likely the day with this family…sitting near his grandmother. He had begun to process that weekend in his journal. The thoughts were taking on the form of an epistle, but who was it to? Who was he trying to tell?

"God… I should go." Stephen put down the vodka bottle, now empty, and sauntered to the living room. "What's the plan?"

"Hedders?" Skyler gently shoved Hedley, who spluttered awake from his daydream.

"Oh – yes, yes. Should we do late dinner?"

"Wood." Samson said resolutely.

The other three nodded. "Perfect," they said in unison.

"See, you're still fun, Sammy. When are you going to leave us for the bears tonight?"

Samson laughed. "It's otter night."

"Christ," Stephen laughed. "Take what you like, but please leave me the perky-assed twinks."

"I can't help that I'm expanding my horizons, Stevey. Jonathan is going to join me. Someday you may pine for a musky, older gentleman."

"Musky?" Skyler's eyes went blank. He remembered the back of trucks, the smell of all those men as they straddled him.

Samson shrugged. "Are you boys leaving, too? I was going to walk Stephen out and then grab some groceries. You can stay or go."

"We'll stay," Skyler said quickly.

"Excellent. Help yourself to whatever you want."

Samson waved good-bye, collecting Stephen, who was idly staggering near the front entry. Once the door was shut behind them, a pregnant silence filled the room.

After a moment, Skyler sat dramatically on the sofa and crossed his arms. Hedley turned his attention one last time to the fading sky and the lively world below.

"Hedley, when are you going to gracefully sunset Samson?"

"Is that why you wanted to be alone?"

"One of the reasons."

Hedley took a seat next to Skyler. "It has to be done diplomatically. And we have to have a replacement."

"Is it going to be Jonathan?"

"No."

Skyler took a deep, dramatic breath. "Thank god. I've been worried all summer. I can be civil to him again now that I know he's not a contender. The thought of him joining; I was embarrassed for our brand."

"I'm definitely working on it." Hedley idly tapped out a rhythm on the coffee table. "Next line item for Skyler?"

"Stuart."

"Always Stuart." How many times had they spoken of the orange-skinned, quinquagenarian with whom Skyler spent all his free time?

"Yes," said Skyler resolutely.

"It's serious – dating serious?"

"We're complicated, but, yes, I'd say we're dating."

"You know what I've said."

"It's weird."

"You know how people will talk."

"He's got daddy issues; he looks like his grandfather; what is he doing with that old man?"

"Your other info may get out as well."

"Who would tell? You and Stuart are the only ones who know."

Hedley hesitated – he was tired. But, he was still in control; he remained the leader. As part of his duties he had to stay aware, to know everything, to always have a plan of attack, a plan B, a plan C, ad nauseam. For months, he held a smoking gun on Skyler's romance. As soon as the youngest Set member mentioned he was dating an older gentleman, Hedley went to work to prevent the PR nightmare. It was delicate, but he had done the research and held the key to destroying it.

"Stuart had a reputation," Hedley said slowly.

Skyler's eyebrows rose. Very slightly, the edges of his mouth twitched.

"Since you told me you wanted to unveil him as your boyfriend, I've been digging."

"And you've found?"

Hedley sighed deeply. "Pre-PREP there were rumors he was hiding his status. Some people think he gave it to them."

Skyler shook. "Yer lyin.' Stuart wouldn't do that…"

Hedley eyed his young protégé sympathetically. Heartbreak shattered the strength of his voice, caused the faint slip into his rural Midwestern dialect. With all Skyler had been through, he still believed in good, or to expect something good. His mother instilled that in him somehow, despite everything.

He remembered a night many months ago when they were very drunk. Hedley took Skyler up to his building's rooftop. They were alone, the rest of The Set disbanding earlier in the evening.

The roof wasn't accessible to everyone. Hedley schmoozed the building's manager into giving him a key one evening – he'd lied and said he was planning a first date. He argued that access to the roof, the view of the stars, would secure the affection of this other man. It was quick work to copy the key and keep his access forever.

Since that time, it had become his private office. People felt safe up there – they spoke the truth more than in his living room, in the bar, or in a café. Something about seeing the empty, black sky, the lake, the glittering skyline, allowed unrestricted conversation.

So it was with Skyler that night.

Drunkenly, he rose from his seated position near the access door. He hummed as he crossed the roof and leapt onto the parapet. The wall was two-feet wide, at most. Nothing stood between the boy and a five-second fall into oblivion. Smiling, he turned to Hedley. Very rarely was he like this, so brash, mischievous, and childish.

"It's fucking stupid, you know…" he said moving like a tightrope walker around the edge. "Everything, everyone. I get so fed up sometimes…"

He pivoted quickly, facing the darkness of the night sky, raising his arms as if preparing to fly. Hedley's heart beat faster. Below them, horns honked, an ambulance wailed.

"I've been in such dark places… After the HIV thing… I didn't know." He flapped his arms; he returned to the tight rope movement, watching his feet as he moved slowly along the stone ledge. "People don't see that – they don't look into the future and see deep empty space, no tomorrow. Unknown tomorrows –" He stopped moving and looked directly at Hedley, his brown eyes reflecting the building's floodlamps. "Samson hasn't been to that place – Stephen has – you can see it in his eyes; something is missing."

His head turned, exposing his perfect profile, the square jawline, and fluttering, black hair. A sigh from the depths of his petite body filled the quiet night. After a moment's pause, he took one more step closer to the edge.

Hedley resisted standing and moving closer to him; his conscience told him to go and take the boy's hand. But that would be weakness, of course. Skyler wanted to draw him out, wanted to feel that he was in control in that moment. *I'm just playing, Hedley. What are you so worked up about?* He would tell the others about Hedley's fear – they would assume Skyler had some special meaning to him. Skyler was on the roof. Hedley was afraid. Hedley was *protective*.

"I thought about jumping into that space, freefall. How would I do it? A gun? Electrocution? Or…" He spun dramatically. "Or a big fall."

Hedley's heart pounded. He knew he wouldn't jump – he didn't recruit jumpers, but he had also never seen Skyler fearless. His youngest protégé was always reserved, quiet, and calculated. He was not one to gambol along a parapet and discuss suicidal thoughts.

"You know what pulled me back, Hedders?" He took a step away from the edge. "Guess. One guess."

"Love," Hedley said dramatically. His eye twitched with the withheld desire to run and pull Skyler down.

Skyler laughed. "Maybe – that's part of it." He jumped off the ledge, back onto the roof. Dramatically, he raised his arms again, this time moving them into a position, as if to waltz with an imaginary partner.

"Was it Nietzsche?" Hedley relaxed. He could now jest – the storm was over.

"Ugh." Skyler laughed. "Not even close." He danced to phantom music around the roof. "Believe it or not, it was musicals. The day I found out about the disease I went home and watched *The Sound of Music* with Mom. And for some reason that makes me feel better. Like, the thought that reality could be something like that: colorful, lively, hopeful, romantic." He ended his dance and bowed. "It was musicals."

Back in Samson's living room, there was no music. Skyler and Hedley sat in ubiquitous silence.

"Who told you this?" Skyler asked. His eyes were dripping tears.

"Some of the old guard," Hedley said slowly. "In the early days of Grindr word got out. The HIV Bandit is the name they used." Just as on the roof, Hedley's eyes twitched. Two impulses tore him.

Skyler put his head in his hands. "It'll get out."

"I should have brought it up sooner but I knew… it would be a lot to digest." Gently he put his arm around Skyler. The boy shook under his touch. Hedley was tired of so much, this especially. He was tired of *this*. "I know he wouldn't do that to you – and this was, what, six years ago?"

"I just can't believe… he'd be like that."

"Used to be – I think is the best way to think of it. You and he have been together for a while, and I don't think he's ever cheated, has he?"

"Not that I know of…" Skyler's breath was labored.

Hedley's thoughts were chaos – thousands of threads extending in different directions: the beach, families, sitting next to his grandmother, quiet places, The Bandit, the gossamer scarf, Wood for dinner – what should he wear? – Skyler, the young boy from Nebraska, shaking under his touch.

The lie – the half-lie he had let fall from his lips.

In one, quick movement, Skyler rose.

"Sky..." Hedley said, "don't do anything rash."

"Fuck – I need to think. I need..."

He walked to the entryway. His footsteps stopped abruptly just as he opened the front door. When he looked back, Hedley saw the redness in his eyes, the sparkle of tears.

Skyler said nothing.

After the door closed, Hedley lay back on the couch and closed his eyes.

Breathe. Take control.

Slowly the chaos of his mind calmed. The beach, The Bandit, dinner, the different threads started to disappear, ravel back into the heart of Hedley's consciousness. When they vanished, he focused his attention on only the issue at hand: Skyler and Stuart – the relationship that threatened the purity of The Set.

The web shone in the dark of his imagination. It was all simple logic. In order to keep control, it had to be this way.

Stuart couldn't be a part of the The Set, even in the periphery, and Skyler was too valuable to lose. It was luck someone at the bar saw Stuart and said he looked like a guy they used to call "The Bandit" for his reckless sexual activities. It was the perfect way to alter the course of the game. He could withdrawal as Skyler and Stuart went to war with each other. Skyler would have to choose between love and his status being bleated about by every queen at Sidetrack.

It was vicious, but the game was vicious by nature. Hedley learned that early on.

Breathe.

All of The Set knew the game, but they were not masters – Hedley was the only one who could see down to the roots, the bones. Samson, Skyler, and Stephen could manipulate the pieces, but Hedley was the only one who could reach to the heart, grip its sensitive flesh, and force it to beat.

He was exhausted.

Hedley opened his eyes and returned to the window. Below, the very last of the families were coming off the beach. The sun was fully set, the horizon a deep purple fading to black.

He took a breath, sighed. The deep oblivion of the sky called to him. Slowly, his thoughts corroded; his memories flooded back. Which ones were real? Four men standing on the beach, 12,000 likes between them. Samson withdrawing and Skyler put at war with his lover. Could someone do to Hedley as he had done to Skyler? Was there any heart left to make beat?

The innumerable threads again exploded within his mind. There were a number of pieces to think about. He had to prepare for tonight.

Close your eyes, Hedley thought to himself.

He put his hand to the window's glass.

Don't think.

Breathe.
Breathe.
Breathe.

The magistrate has again taken center stage. Sweat streams down his forehead. Delicately he dabs away the grime as he solemnly begins.

"You have come forward to have your voice heard in this matter. Four men are before you, requested to be put on trial by the crowd so that we may weigh our collective grievances. They all have different histories, different pasts, which we, which God, tasks you to wade through to come to an ultimate conclusion. For although there is sadness and grief in each man, it is our duty to ask if their reaction to this grief justifies their treatment of others.

"They have called you names. They have defiled your beds. They have stolen your boyfriends on a whim. In early hours, you may have gone home with them and been promised love and adulation, only to be thrown out on the street the next morning. One of them may have spoken to you sweetly in the evening, then took you forcefully in the deepest part of night. Perhaps they called you an "ugly fag" or told your friends that you lack the social status or importance to be included amongst them. It is possible they came to you and called you 'friend' only to betray you when the opportunity for advancement presented itself.

"We have all been subjected to their sins. But do we, as the chosen instrument of God's justice, believe that there is enough guilt to convict? No man standing before his fellows is unblemished, except our God Himself, but we ask you to put aside prejudice, to put aside anger, resentment, and pain, and ask yourselves, whether the world is a better place with them in it."

The magistrate stops abruptly. Slowly, he raises his hands skyward and then, in a dramatic motion, clasps them together in prayer. He murmurs a benediction. When the prayer has ended, he turns and paces to the back of the scaffold.

The recorder, exhausted by his task, sighs, and then resumes speaking to all those gathered:

"Come forward. Grab a stone, and place it upon the scaffold. A stone to the left is a vote of guilt; a stone to the right is an assertion of innocence. We ask that you come forward one at a time only. Your voice shall be heard."

The first few rush quickly to the stage – three place their stones to the left, one places it to the right. People trickle forward as evening closes in around them. A woman beside you stands, eyes closed, mouth muttering prayers.

You think of the past. No sins were enacted against you, but they were against your friends. The youngest drove a wedge between your best friend and his lover. There are reasons for both final judgments.

But would the world be better?

More and more put down their stones. From where you stand it is hard to see which pile is larger.

With the sun almost set, the woman next to you finally moves forward. She does not make eye contact, barely breathes, as she skitters to the front and places a stone in a pile. The crowd has grown so thick at the front that you cannot see which side she has decided.

Before long, you realize that there are only a few of you left. All of you lock eyes and slowly start to form a final line to the front of the crowd.

"Don't look," one man whispers to the last of you. "Don't put that pressure on yourself."

"I think it's pretty well decided already."

"It's hard to tell with the piles – it could be closer; one could have slipped."

You file in behind them. The sun is set, the air grown cool. No wind stirs. All those around you barely breathe.

When the stone is in your hand, it feels cold, lifeless. It is strange such a harmless object could harbor such destructive power.

But then, perhaps that is the story of this judgment – the ripples, the wildfire caused by one life knitted together with both beautiful and horrible things. A heavenly face on a scaffold, benign to an untrained eye, can cause so much pain to so many.

You finger the rock in your hand. It rolls over your palm, onto your knuckles.

An epiphany strikes you in the final moments. Your eyes open and you realize your decision was never one of choice, but had always been an inevitability. With head bowed and eyes down, you place your rock upon the scaffold.

"We have our decision," the magistrate says calmly. "Our God has spoken."

A Modern Ruin in Deep Focus

"If you want a happy ending, that depends, of course, on where you stop your story."
- Orson Welles

Dramatis Personae

The Set
Hedley Renault – A Conflicted Leader
Skyler Shaw– A Young Twink
Samson Briggs– An Aspiring Bear
Stephen Ripley – A Lovestruck Drunk

City Folk
Nick Foster – An Assholic Transplant
Jordan Barker – A Quarter-life Crisian
Peter – An Aging Gay
George – The … Other Aging Gay
Myrtle Jennings – A Lonesome Thirtysomething
Lawrence Soot – A Worshipper of Youth

Exedosians
David Jenkins – A Protagonist(ish)
Dr. Konstantin – A Patient Therapist
Sasha Williams – A Best Friend
Edward – A Wise Boyfriend
Alan – A Coiffurelicious Friend
Frank – A Love Interest
Kent – A Coiffurelicious Boyfriend
Jack Freeman – A Person from Another Book
George – A Lawyer-in-Training
Mya – A Boisterous Redhead
Tibbs – A Boisterous Bear
Donnie – A Boisterous Bowl Cut

Interlutonians
Sal Henry – A Lover of History
Gertrude DuBois – A Faithful Friend
Arnold "Arnie" Bellows – A Deceased Lover
Clive – An Acolyte

Act I

SCENE I – PILLARS OF CLOUD

FADE IN:

EXT. CHICAGO SKYLINE – FAINT DAWN – 2015

Light is just striking the Midwestern city, causing it to shimmer like a line of uncut emeralds. We begin far out over the lake, slowly drawing closer to the coast, the skyscrapers taking on clearer form; they undulate, creating stair-stepped blocks of silver, blue, and gray. It is a moment of almost-silence, a light gust of wind and the distant cry of a gull the only sounds heard from so high in the sky. We slowly drift over the waves of Lake Michigan, the waters oscillating between azure and white. The city grows in magnitude as we drift nearer. It starts to speak to us through the bray of car horns, the light sounds of footsteps, and the distant chatter of voices in the streets.

DISSOLVE:

A SERIES OF PLACES WE HAVE SEEN BEFORE. THE IMAGES ARE FLAT, STAGNANT, NEARLY TWO-DIMENSIONAL IN THEIR PRESENTATION.

A PERSPECTIVE VIEW STANDING ON BELMONT AVENUE AND LOOKING DIRECTLY DOWN HALSTED STREET.

In the early dawn the street is almost empty. A single car drives northward, away from our view. A copy of the Windy City Times flutters across the street, its pages the only sound audible as the car's engine becomes quieter. Appearing from an alleyway, a homeless man shuffles down the street carrying a small bag. It is a more ruinous scene than our earlier views of Halsted, the neon glow, loud music, and cacophony of voices filling the senses.

DISSOLVE:

JONATHAN'S APARTMENT BUILDING

A benign, yellow-bricked apartment building is directly before us. A few urban professionals bustle out of the front doors and pass us, briskly heading toward their offices downtown. The longer we hold on the scene, the livelier it becomes. A dog-walker passes by, a veritable army of canines in tow. More and more individuals push in and out of the front entry. One man and woman leave the building arm-in-arm. Unlike our previous encounter with this location, hail and rain causing the vision to blur, the scene is bright, flooded by rays of sun, the colors glowing as if a filter has been applied over our vision.
DISSOLVE:

OUTSIDE SAL'S SHOP

Although the street outside Sal's shop is quiet, he is busily tending to his flower boxes on the front stoop. He hums a melody, paying excruciating attention to the amount of water he pours on each plant. For a brief moment he bends over, his plentiful rump exposed to our view. After he has finished the task, he rises and dusts his hands off on his trousers. It is at this exact moment Gertrude DuBois appears holding two plastic cups of coffee. They speak, but it is inaudible from our vantage point. Sal, in late-aged quickness, puts the watering can inside his small shop. He and Gertrude walk away from us.

DISSOLVE:

HEDLEY'S APARTMENT

On a great, golden-colored divan, Hedley's Market Days houseguest, The Model, is asleep. His huge height and musculature are highlighted by the lumination of the early morning light. He breathes softly, a thin blanket draped over his genitalia, but every other part of him is exposed to our gaze. It calls to mind a classic painting.

For the first time, our perspective moves. We turn slightly to peer across the room. On another sofa, Hedley is seated in a tense position, his body balled up, knees pulled in tightly toward his chest. His gaze is focused out the window. His expression is almost blank, however, in his eyes, by a faint play of expression on his lips, we see the beginning of what can only be called resolve.

The four previous scenes now shift over each other to compose one image, behind them all, the perspective looking down Halsted Street. In the foreground is Hedley's dim profile. Behind him, Sal and Gertrude stand outside Sal's shop. Even dimmer behind them is the doorway of Jonathan's apartment, which seems to be the entry to our infinite line of vision down Halsted.

This composite image lasts for several beats. The sounds from the different scenes – snoring, car engines, the flutter of the newspaper, and the tittering of early morning commuters, build to a single, loud, long note. It grows from faint to abrasive before cutting out.

CUT TO BLACK:

NOTE: Now begins the story proper, the merging and conclusion of the lives previously traced through earlier pages. It is the final weekend of summer, the Market Days festival, when all paths of the narrative are set, in one way or another, to intersect.

SMASH CUT TO:

EXT. BELMONT TRAIN STATION – AFTERNOON

The absolute silence of the blackout is destroyed by the loud sound of a train, the roar of voices, and the steady tap-tap rhythm of David Jenkins' shoes. Between the movement of the commuters, the cacophony of cars, trucks and busses, and David's tense expression, we feel a frantic energy.

An elevated train roars above Belmont Avenue into the station, just behind David. He is coming quickly and hurriedly toward us. As he pulls closer, visible from the mid-torso up, we see he is not looking directly at us, but rather at his phone screen. Anxious Chicagoans jostle each other moving quickly past him, heading home.

We hold our gaze on the street scene and David for a moment before our vantage splits into two parts. On the left is David's resolute face, on the right the image of his phone's screen, his thumbs poised over its glass surface preparing to compose a text message. The cursor on his phone's screen flashes. David quickly types.

MESSAGE:
David: *What's up? I wanted to say hi.*

The note is deleted quickly. On the left, David looks up and directly at us. He holds us in his gaze for a split second before looking skyward, consumed with thought. After a few moments looking upward, his head falls and he resumes staring at the screen. On the right, his thumbs twitch quickly over the keyboard.

MESSAGE:
David: *You going to Market Days? My friend's having a party.*

The would-be text message vanishes. Other phrases appear in chaotic bursts.

MESSAGE:
David: *How are*

MESSAGE:
David: *I wanted*

MESSAGE:
David: *I've been thinking*

On the right side of our view, the cursor pulses – one, two, three, four times. On the left, David rubs a hand through his hair. After a deep breath, his fingers fly over the keys.

MESSAGE:
David: *I fucked up, Frank. I really fucking fucked it fucking up.*

His thumb hovers over the send button. Before a final decision is made, he plunges it into his pocket. The right-side image of the phone screen is replaced by other brief flashes from David and Frank's past.

FLASHBACK TO:

EXT. THE MANSION OF HEDLEY'S GALA – NIGHT – EARLIER THAT SUMMER

David and Frank are on the stairs. Frank's flash-tattooed friend is pulling him away.

FLASHBACK TO:

INT. ROSCOE'S BAR – NIGHT – EARLIER THAT SUMMER

David and Frank are speaking in the bar's front window. David steps backward and awkwardly trips on the statue of the Native American.

FLASHBACK TO:

EXT. WOOD RESTAURANT – EVENING – EARLIER THAT SUMMER

Frank and David sit across the table from each other. Both men are laughing.

CUT BACK TO:

EXT. BELMONT AVENUE – AFTERNOON

On the left, David's face breaks into a smile. As the right-side image fades away, he again looks up and directly at us. His expression is peaceful, content.

FADE OUT:

FADE IN:

INT. DAVID'S APARTMENT – AFTERNOON

David enters his apartment and turns on the song "I Want to Get Better." He pulls down a bottle of wine but hesitates.

DAVID: A clear head. Doc is absolutely right.

FLASHBACK TO:

INT. DR. KONSTANTIN'S OFFICE – AFTERNOON – EARLIER THAT WEEK

Dr. Konstantin sits sagely in his large, leather seat, his finger steepled under his chin.

DR. KONSTANTIN: So, you want to try Frank again?

DAVID: Yes.

David rises from the couch and moves to the window. He looks at the river winding through the glittering city.

DAVID: I think he was a good one and I just threw it away.

DR. KONSTANTIN: I won't say that's not true, but I think it may behoove you to take a step back, a deep breath. Look at this with the clearest mind you can.

DAVID: You think some meditation? A power yoga class?

DR. KONSTANTIN: (pause) Perhaps just a moment of quiet. Relax into the silence and see what it tells you.

CUT BACK TO:

INT. DAVID'S APARTMENT – AFTERNOON

David is tying his running shoes. He wears a tank top and long basketball shorts. Atop his head is a grey sweatband. He jogs in place in his bedroom.

DAVID: I'll try a jog. Worst case I make it to Chipotle and grab a burrito.

CUT TO:

EXT. DAVID'S APARTMENT - AFTERNOON

Outside his apartment David stands uncertainly. He is framed against the door of his building. Young professionals pass by. A couple enters his building.

DAVID: A clear head.

He begins running down the street, away from our view.

FADE OUT:

FADE IN:

EXT. BELMONT TRAIN STATION - AFTERNOON

A large crowd of people is gathered waiting for the bus. Others mill about, laugh with friends, or speak earnestly in the rush-hour chaos.

David runs by the station. He is clearly winded, sweat soaking his shirt.

DAVID: Clear head and a heart attack...

After David leaves the scene, our perspective shifts slightly to see Nick Foster, dressed in neon shorts and a tight polo, leaning against one of the mosaic-tiled pillars outside the station. He is much changed from the boy who sat anxiously in his uncle's living room a few months before. Head down, staring at his phone, he appears to have no interest in what is happening around him: hustling commuters, lumbering busses, and a Human Rights Campaign worker attempting to catch the attention of distracted millennials on their way home from work.

As Nick types on his phone, a young gay man sidles up to him. We do not see this young gay's face; he is only a body. He does not say a word but pauses in front of Nick and crosses his arms.

Nick puts down his phone and smiles. His face is fully visible, but the young gay remains obscured, turned away from our line of sight. We lean closer, trying to discern if it is someone we know from the gala, Sidetrack, or another summer party. It is not clear if he is someone we recognize, so we again lean back and take on a full view of the train station.

It appears as if Nick is now speaking, but his words are drowned out by the sound of traffic. He and the young gay share a laugh before Nick picks up a gym bag and walks away with him.

We lose sight of them as the two head east toward the lake. More and more people pass us until the world becomes a blur of human movement. We turn our attention upward; above us a train shrieks away from the station.

FADE OUT:

FADE IN:

INT. GESTHEMENE GARDEN CENTER - DAY

It is a jarring transition from the sounds of traffic and voices to near-absolute silence. Behind us we can hear the soft flutter of plant leaves and the rhythmic rush of water falling into a fountain. From our vantage point we look down a row of green plants that shine in the daylight. At the end of our line of vision is Sal Henry who is scrutinizing a fern. He ceases gazing at the plant and puts a finger to his chin.

Around him all is green with a few points of explosive color. Warm, golden light filters through the greenhouse's glass. In the foreground a cherub lawn ornament smiles benignly, its attention fixed on an unknown event just out of view.

GERTRUDE: (from outside our view) I'm already bored, Sal. Sal turns toward the complaint. He is looking directly at us, down the row of plants.

SAL: I can't help you if you keep making the same poor decision to join me Gertrude.

GERTRUDE: I suppose not, but you *could* hurry up.

SAL: You can't rush genius, but I think I've made my decision.

GERTRUDE: Praise the Lord.

SAL: Daisies.

Sal walks down the line of plants. He picks up a pot of white and gold flowers.

GERTRUDE: I think that's an excellent choice.

SAL: (turning abruptly away from Gertrude) You know what, though. Maybe I should go back and take a second look at the hydrangeas. The boys may want some more color at brunch…

Gertrude sighs loudly. Sal joyfully snorts when he sees her reaction.

SAL: I'm just kidding, Gertrude. You'll get to your 3 pm bingo appointment. Don't get your adult diapers in a bunch.

Sal and Gertrude walk toward the cash register. We follow them but keep moving once they come to a stop. We step outside the greenhouse and peer into the street. Traffic moves leisurely except for a red sports car that roars past us.

CUT TO:

EXT. DAN RYAN EXPRESSWAY – DAY

A cherry-colored car zips through traffic. Sasha Williams is driving it, looking extremely disgruntled. A car cuts in front of him. Sasha slaps the steering wheel and makes strained, grunting noises.

SASHA: Suburban fuckheads! (he takes a breath) In a car for ten minutes and literally anger shoots out of my asshole.

He regains his composure. Just as he calms down, another car cuts in front of him.

SASHA: You've got to be fucking kidding me!

CUT TO:

EXT. O'HARE AIRPORT – DAY

The airport is a chaotic scene. A line of cars pulls up in the arrivals lane. People mill about, some serene, some trying to frantically flag down their friends and family driving by in minivans and SUVs.

In the throng Terrance stands disinterestedly, looking at the passing vehicles. From out of our view, we hear a shrill honk and faraway screaming. It grows in intensity.

SASHA: Bitch, pay attention!

Terrance turns and sees Sasha waving at him from the red car. Terrance laughs and picks up his bag, running toward him. He leaps between cars and throws open the passenger door, plopping down in the seat. He leans in and gives Sasha a kiss on the cheek.

TERRANCE: What a welcome!

SASHA: You're lucky I didn't just jump out of the car and slap you. These sloppy suburban drivers are giving me a migraine.

Sasha looks over and analyzes the tiny bag Terrance brought with him for the weekend.

SASHA: Is that all you brought?

TERRANCE: Packing light, my dear. I don't bring ten different costumes for Market Days anymore.

SASHA: Well, maybe not ten, but did you even fit one in that change purse?

TERRANCE: I'm not planning on wearing much.

SASHA: (laughing loudly) Yes, Girl! I'm so proud of you for coming. Back to the lion's den *after a week*. And ready (pause) to (pause) fuck. That's my boy.

TERRANCE: The plan is to take care of some drinking and sex *then* go back to Michigan and wallow in self-pity and cartons of ice cream.

SASHA: Well, my friend, if you want to merge everything together, we have some rocky road in the fridge.

Both men laugh as Sasha jerks the car out of the parking lane and into traffic. The red car roars away as our gaze moves upward to the blue sky.

FADE OUT:

FADE IN:

INT. ALAN'S STUDIO APARTMENT – DAY

We gaze with Alan at a square of blue sky visible from the small desk at which he's seated. The apartment is tiny. The living space consists of a desk, a couch, and a television.

Alan turns his attention away from the window and stares at his boyfriend, Kent, who is typing frantically on his laptop. Alan looks at him for a moment, his gaze piercing. The intensity in his eyes ebbs, however, and his focus shifts to something unseen beyond Kent.

FLASHBACK TO:

INT. ANN SATHER'S RESTAURANT – DAY – EARLIER THAT WEEK

Kent, hair ruffled, laughs loudly. He throws his arm around Alan and kisses him lightly on the cheek. Across from the young couple, a handsome man, Steve, laughs to match Kent. Alan forces a smile. He looks between his boyfriend and the new acquaintance.

KENT: I'd forgotten that. Things you do when you are horny and nineteen.

STEVE: Nineteen? Kent, be real, you were *maybe* eighteen.

KENT: A mature eighteen.

Steve clicks his tongue and shakes his head.

STEVE: Alan, I'm sure you've seen Kent be just as stupid. What did you two boys get into in Berlin?

Alan hesitates. We move closer to his face, focusing on his eyes, which look blankly into the distance.

FADE OUT:

FADE IN:

A SERIES MEMORIES OF ALAN AND KENT'S TIME ABROAD.

THE EIFFEL TOWER

The tower glows on a humid night. As it illuminates our view, a sepia-colored tint blossoms over our vision. Lights on the tower flare and blur like gold and brown waterlilies in a Monet painting. With our new sepia glasses, we are free to look down the tower to the base of the structure where Alan and Kent recline in the grass. Around them the night is an idyllic vision of Parisian spring. Vendors hawk wine through rows of tourists. The sky is an impressionistic swirl of violet, pink, and white.

The two sit idly for a moment before Alan sits up and digs into his pocket for his cell phone. Once it is in his grasp, he lifts his arm to the sky. The two men laugh as the shutter of the camera clicks.

DISSOLVE:

A BERLIN CAFE

It is a foggy morning. Alan and Kent perfunctorily glance at their laptops between stolen looks at each other. They giggle as the sound of a coffee grinder fills the small café.

KENT: We're not getting shit done. Let's go play. Alan slams down his laptop and leaps up.

DISSOLVE:

THE DUOMO, FLORENCE, ITALY

Alan and Kent are seated at a restaurant. Our gaze drifts around them, taking in the streets bathed in gold and the groups of tourists meandering around the towering church. When we again look to the table we see Kent idly looking at a map of the city. Alan has his hands locked behind his head and stares upward at the edifice of the Catholic temple.

SMASH CUT BACK TO:

INT. ANN SATHER'S RESTAURANT – DAY – EARLIER THAT WEEK

We pull away from Alan's eyes. He blinks several times before looking at Steve and forcing a smile. The sepia colors of the flashback drain away from our perspective as Alan glances at Kent. The image of his boyfriend tremors, shakes. Alan blinks again and clarity is restored. The sepia is gone.

ALAN: I don't know where to start.

KENT: The club in Paris? Should we tell them about the daddies who tried to take us home?

CUT BACK TO:

INT. ALAN'S APARTMENT – DAY

Alan takes a deep breath before looking away from Kent. He taps his fingers on the edge of the desk.

ALAN: Can you come with me to Sasha's tomorrow?

KENT: Oh, shit! (looking up) I'm so sorry, babe. I forgot. I made plans with Philip, Steve, and those guys.

ALAN: You'll be free later, though?

KENT: Of course. I mean, you're welcome to come with us. In fact, I planned on it. We had reservations at that Bird & Bloke on Clark.

ALAN: That works, but I have to go to Sasha's.

KENT: That shall be our first stop after brunch!

Kent returns to typing on his computer. Alan stares blankly again at that blue patch of sky outside the window. We hold our gaze on him for several seconds. Abruptly, he rises and walks away from Kent.

ALAN: I think I'll go for a jog, run a bit, get my thoughts straight.

KENT: Cool. But not too straight, I didn't buy all that lube for nothing.

FADE OUT:

FADE IN:

INT. STUART'S APARTMENT – DAY

Skyler Shaw is in bed, laying naked in the sheets. Beside him Stuart, his muscled, middle-aged boyfriend, snores softly. The interior of the apartment is modern: steel, grey, masculine. Blinds drawn across the towering windows block intense summer daylight.

Skyler gently moves Stuart's arm. Quietly, he stands and pads out of the bedroom and into the kitchen.

FLASHBACK TO:

INT. SAMSON'S APARTMENT – DUSK – A FEW WEEKS EARLIER

Skyler is looking at Hedley with tears in his eyes. They have just touched on the stark revelation that Stuart's past may have been not only sordid but deadly.

SKYLER: Yer lyin'. Stuart wouldn't do that… Who told you this?

HEDLEY: Some of the old guard. In the early days of Grindr word got out. The HIV Bandit is the name they used.

SKYLER: It'll get out...

CUT BACK TO:

INT. STUART'S APARTMENT – DAY

Skyler sits at the kitchen counter. A glass of water is in front of him. Gently, he runs his finger around the rim of the glass. His eyes look through us. A few stray tears glimmer on his cheeks.

FLASHBACK TO:

INT. SIDETRACK – LATE NIGHT – DECEMBER 2014

Skyler chats with Hedley and Samson. They share a joke before Skyler turns and saunters away.

He passes by us and crosses next to a group of older, gay men. Stuart is with them. The older gentleman reaches out and gently grabs Skyler's hand as he walks by. Skyler turns abruptly. A look of annoyance flees his face at the sight of the handsome, older man. There is a brief flicker of attraction that illuminates his features before he regains himself and puts on a mask of indifference.

STUART: Aren't you pretty. Want a drink?

Skyler turns to see both Hedley and Samson staring at the interaction. With a flick of his eyes, Skyler has assessed the situation and knows he must put on a show for his two friends.

He laughs in Stuart's face.

SKYLER: Gross.

Stuart smiles and demurely lets Skyler's hand fall away. With that, the younger man turns and saunters into the bathroom.

In the stall we see him take a deep breath. There is a flicker, a flash across our vision.

CUT TO:

INT. BEDROOM – DAY

It is Skyler's fantasy. Our vision is tinted black and white. Skyler straddles Stuart, his head turned up, a groan of ecstasy escaping his supple lips.

CUT BACK TO:

INT. SIDETRACK – LATE NIGHT – DECEMBER 2014

Skyler shakes himself. He rubs his eyes. From somewhere deep in the past we hear the familiar words of his old neighbor, Siegfried Essen.

SIEGFRIED: *You shouldn't do that.*

Skyler swallows hard. He wipes a drop of sweat from his brow.

CUT BACK TO:

INT. STUART'S APARTMENT – DAY – 2015

Skyler stops playing with the cup of water and stands. The windows facing across the street are open. The young man is nude, exposed for the world to see. He looks down and sees cars moving along Sheridan Road. He presses his hand to the glass, lost in thought.

STUART: (out of view) You giving the neighbors a free show?

Skyler turns, and we with him. Stuart stands in his underwear, a knowing smile on his face. Skyler's eyes are illegible.

Again, our vision flickers; it is another fantasy. Everything turns to black and white.

SKYLER: Did you do it? Are you the one who infected all those boys…

Just as quickly as the image has appeared it is gone. Color saturates our field of view and Skyler and Stuart stare at each other across the length of the apartment. It is a tense moment, broken after several seconds by Stuart crossing the room.

STUART: (wrapping Skyler in his arms) You're moody. I thought I fucked that out of you.

Skyler's face contorts as he tries not to laugh. But it breaks. He giggles as Stuart kisses his neck.

FADE OUT:

FADE IN:

INT. HEDLEY'S APARTMENT – NIGHT

Hedley's rococo inspired apartment is resplendent in the light of lamps and burning candles. The owner stands primped and preened, looking out over Belmont Harbor from the huge bay window in his living room. His gaze is distant, judging some dim object, just out of focus.

At the adjoining dining room table Samson and Stephen are well-dressed, Instagram-ready, speaking in hushed tones. The quiet of the room is disrupted when The Model enters from the kitchen wearing only a towel.

THE MODEL: What's the plan for the evening?

Hedley looks away from the window. He glances briefly at The Model. Our gaze mirrors his own, taking in The Model's chiseled torso and the towel, which hangs precariously around his waist, barely concealing his manhood. The Model stretches, his sinewy arms flexing in the dancing lights of candles.

Hedley looks away into the darkness of the window before speaking.

HEDLEY: We'll have to be at Sidetrack at some point, but I'm not sure where to begin.

THE MODEL: I would say Mini. That's where the "it" people will be.

STEPHEN: We are the "it" people, darling.

The Model and Stephen exchange a glance. It lasts one beat too long, causing Stephen to turn away. His previous confidence is erased as a blush colors his cheeks. The Model savors his flirtatious victory.

THE MODEL: Well, there have to be a few other boys in this city who are worth our time.

SAMSON: Very few.

THE MODEL: That is very disappointing. Hedders, you promised me more.

Hedley is lost in thought as he looks into the darkness outside of the window. His eyes flash sideways knowing that it is time to begin the show. He will turn on his charm and lead the coterie of boys into the night. He gently presses his hand to the window glass and draws a deep breath.

He spins, a wide smile on his face.

HEDLEY: Samson is being bitchy. Just because he's into bears now he thinks no one is worth his time on the main strip.

SAMSON: You're not wrong.

STEPHEN: (regaining his composure) I think Mini is the best idea. The out-of-town gays will be congregating and we should assess.

HEDLEY: It's decided then. (looking to The Model) I can't wait to see what New York couture you have to show us tonight.

THE MODEL: You'll have to wait and see.

SAMSON: I'm frothing with anticipation.

The Model winks at Samson and glides from the room.

Samson stands and joins Hedley at the window.

SAMSON: (whispering) He's unbearable. I think his ego has somehow gotten bigger over the past year.

HEDLEY: Unbearable, but gorgeous. And for Market Days we need a big-name cameo.

SAMSON: Always a step ahead with the show, aren't we Hedley?

HEDLEY: Usually two, Sammy.

The two laugh quietly.

Stephen approaches them.

STEPHEN: I think we need some champagne.

SAMSON: We do! And I think I will take a shot so Mr. Model becomes more interesting.

HEDLEY: You boys go pour and tell me when it's ready.

Samson and Stephen exit the room.

Hedley smiles broadly at them as they disappear. The moment they have entered into the kitchen, the expression vanishes from his face. His eyes dim and his brow furrows. Again, his attention turns to the window. Reflected back in the dark windows is his shadowy reflection, rendered muted and distorted by the thick panes of glass.

We admire Hedley's exquisite profile for just a moment before our focus drifts out the window.

CUT TO:

EXT. HEDLEY'S APARTMENT - NIGHT

We now slowly rise out of the window and away from Hedley's apartment. The owner's silhouette disappears as we climb up the surface of his tall, brick apartment building, eventually breaking over the parapet. We gaze for a brief moment on the roof, imagining the scenes of Hedley holding office. We can see the ghost-like forms of dates he's taken up here before; we remember Skyler prancing confidently along the balustrade.

Around us towering condos run along Lake Shore Drive. Strings of red and white lights float beneath us. As we look at the streets, cutting in zigzag and block patterns below, a voice speaks to us from the depths of the dark sky.

JORDAN: Division. The story of all people, but for our people its source is Halsted Street.

The voice fades. In our direct line of sight, we see the towering skyline of Chicago, a vast and glittering wave of lights on the horizon. The imperious Willis Tower glints from the darkness. The Hancock, The Aon, and The Trump stand impassively, looking directly back at us with their glowing facades.

Our vision tremors and we see time compressed. Three distinct images obstruct our view of the skyline. Layered on top of each other, we see time as one string of scenes.

DEEP FOCUS. WE SEE THREE DISTINCT IMAGES OF CHICAGO'S PAST, PRESENT, AND FUTURE OVERLAY OUR VIEW OF THE CHICAGO SKYLINE.

BATTLE OF FORT DEARBORN – DAY – 1812

Native Americans and settlers engage in combat. Blood sprays as the sound of gunshots and screams surround us. The settlers run, panicked as Native Americans whoop in victory. The victorious chanting lasts for just a moment before the image burns away, a gaping hole in the film of our imagination.

CHICAGO DOWNTOWN – DAY – 2015

We stand in the middle of Daley Plaza. At first, we only look skyward at the tops of buildings, the pale blue sky stretching behind them. Then, glancing closer to the ground, we admire the blank, uniform edifice of the Daley Center, the Mies van der Rohe design trying to lead our view upward – but we fight it to look on the mystery of the Picasso statue. Behind us there is chanting. Hundreds gather in protest, holding signs, which are blurred in the blazing sunlight. Streaking through this band of activists, men and women in suits skitter to work, their polished shoes clacking on the concrete.

NAVY PIER – AFTERNOON - FUTURE

The sky is grey, distorted. We see smoke rising all around us. The great Ferris Wheel is bent, shattered. Further past the pier itself, we seen the skyline much changed, chewed by time or war – we are unsure. The rows of buildings no longer rise, inspire, but tear across our field of vision like jagged teeth.

THE IMAGES FADE.

EXT. THE SKY ABOVE CHICAGO – NIGHT – 2015

We have returned to the present moment. We are high enough above the city that our view is obscured by clouds. The lights of the towers still shine, but they are muted by swirling grey and white.

Across the faces of these ghostly vapors, we see familiar scenes. They appear, like lightning, racing over the mounds of mist:

FAMILIAR SCENES FLASH ACROSS THE FACES OF THE CLOUDS.

SASHA'S APARTMENT – 2015

Sasha laughs as he and David toast.

CHICAGO HOSPITAL – 1983

Sal reads to Arnie as he lays, eyes closed, in the hospital bed.

THE GALA – 2015

The Set enters the gala. They assess the gathered crowds with icy indifference.

BOYSTOWN STREETS – 2015

Jordan, Nick, and Soot stand in the street. Ash volleys from Soot's cigarette as Jordan frantically digs in his pocket for his phone. Above them The Model's billboard looks on impassively.

DAVID'S APARTMENT – 2015

HauteJock surreptitiously grabs clothes as he flees a hookup.

KINSEY'S APARTMENT – 2015

Myrtle gazes out the window of the kitchen, her drink pouring on the floor as she holds it at an awkward angle.

DAVID'S PARENTS' HOME – 2009
David and Jonathan race through long grasses on a starry night.

OUTSIDE DAVID'S APARTMENT – 2015

Frank stands and smiles. He adjusts his hat.

PEARL'S HOME – 2009

Pearl weeps under the jovial glow of Christmas lights.

FRAT HOUSE – 2000

Samson is beaten in the darkness of a frat house basement.

The images race more quickly. We can barely comprehend each one as they tear across our field of vision. In the end we see only faces: George, Peter, Nick, Dr. Konstantin, Jordan, David, Sasha, Sal, Gertrude, Hedley, Samson, Stephen, Stuart, Skyler, Myrtle, Soot.

Everything distorts and blurs as individuals fly across the clouds so quickly they become nothing but swirls of black and white, blending into the night.

Then nothing. Silence. We see the dim lights of the skyline obscured by vapor for just one moment. The images gone.

FADE TO BLACK

SCENE II – REVELERS

INT. SASHA'S APARTMENT – AFTERNOON

It is Saturday of The Market Days festival. Sasha, Alan, David, Terrence, Donnie, and Tibbs are littered around Sasha's apartment in varying stages of drunkenness. The sun shines brightly through the large windows facing east.

David and Alan are gathered in a far corner speaking earnestly. We cannot hear any of their words, but Alan is driving the conversation. His head is down. He runs a finger over the rim of a wine glass. David nods empathetically.

Sasha is engaged in conversation with Donnie, Tibbs, and Terrance, but his attention is pulled toward David and Alan as he watches them grow more and more morose. Donnie's voice bleats over the noises of the party.

DONNIE: It's really too hot. I was begging for rain this afternoon.

He attempts to drink from his cup but spills on himself.

TIBBS: We couldn't have been to the beach if it weren't so hot, Donnie. We'd miss that parade of twinks in for the weekend.

DONNIE: It was a real rainbow of fresh meat. I can't wait to see them all out on the street today, hopefully shirtless.

TIBBS: Let's get ready for them – time for some Adderall and shots. You joining us, boys?

SASHA: I'm not going out tonight. I'm saving myself for the hot messes that hit the streets tomorrow.

TERRANCE: Not going out! Sasha, you have to!

TIBBS: Agreed! No question!

Tibbs leans over too far and nearly collapses on the floor. At the perfect moment, Donnie grabs him from behind and pulls him upright as if nothing is wrong.

DONNIE: I'll get this one a water, too.

Donnie and Tibbs leave the living room.

SASHA: (concerned) You okay, Terrence?

TERRANCE: Of course.

SASHA: I mean, really okay. Not just faking it to make it.

TERRANCE: I am totally fine. There are hundreds of gays at every bar, but even if I see Lloyd, I can handle it.

SASHA: You promise?

TERRANCE: I would prefer if you were there. You and David especially – strength in numbers…

Sasha looks as if he is going to retort, but David is rushing toward him.

DAVID: Sasha! Do you have any pot?

SASHA: Pot? No, I don't –

Sasha looks into David's eye and catches something in his expression. He flicks his gaze between David, in high spirits, and Alan, who stands looking dejectedly out the window.

DAVID: I thought you had a stash in your room…

Sasha has understood the secret meaning. He immediately turns with David toward his bedroom.

SASHA: The secret stash. Yes! (putting a finger to Terrance's lips) Don't tell anyone, Terrance.

TERRANCE: My lips are sealed.

Sasha pulls David down the back hallway and into the bedroom.

CUT TO:

INT. SASHA AND EDWARD'S BEDROOM – AFTERNOON

The room is immaculately kept. The bedspread is a golden color. Surrounding the bed are images of the Egyptian gods, who look on with dark, disinterested stares.

As Sasha and David enter the room, Sasha laughs jovially and gently closes the door. Both Sasha and David change expressions once the door is closed. Looks of fatigue and concern cover both their faces.

SASHA: We're not going to smell like smoke.

DAVID: No one will notice. Everyone's already fucking drunk, and it's not even five yet.

SASHA: Tibbs almost fell over.

DAVID: He'll be fine with some water and pills; he always bounces back.

David scratches the back of his neck. He looks at the walls and loses his train of thought. An old Egyptian painting of a green man with an elaborate hat sits next to the TV.

DAVID: (continued) What the fuck is that? An Egyptian Martian?

SASHA: That's Osiris, god of the underworld. They don't get much vitamin D in hell, David.

DAVID: The Egyptians didn't have multivitamins?

There is a brief pause. Sasha crosses his arms.

SASHA: Did you really fake my drug stash to talk about my wall art?

David looks to the closed bedroom door. He shakes his head.

DAVID: Al is having a meltdown about Kent. He doesn't think it's going to work.

SASHA: They've literally been back together for a week! Is it that bad?

DAVID: I guess Kent has been flirty with everyone. They've only been together a week, but he's drunk a lot is very handsy with his friends. Kent said he'd come this afternoon to your place but got too drunk at brunch and begged off to go to Mini instead. Beyond that, Al was talking about all the boys in Chicago this weekend – he has a crush on Hedley for fucksake.

Sasha flops onto the bed.

SASHA: Why can't those pretty, privileged fags get it together? They should go live hotly and happily ever after.

DAVID: They're young. I think I may be to blame for some of it. I haven't been a good role model this summer with the whining and pessimism about love and such.

David's gaze loses focus. He stares at the wall blankly.

DISSOLVE:

A SERIES OF DAVID'S MEMORIES OF JONATHAN.

DAVID'S APARTMENT – NIGHT – 2014

The sound of water rushing fills the empty apartment. We are standing in the dining room. The apartment is totally dark except for a pool of light coming from a door at the edge of our field of vision. Slowly, we move toward the light. The splashing water grows louder and louder. We hesitate for a moment at the door before peaking around the corner.

Inside the bathroom we see David, fully clothed, his eyes red from crying sitting in the bathtub. Water pours from the shower head.

DISSOLVE:

DAVID'S CHILDHOOD HOME – NIGHT – 2009

Frogs croak as Jonathan and David wade through tall grasses. It is dark except for a small glimmer from David's parent's house and the subtle twinkling of stars.

As the two young men cross through the grass, we see the moon reflected on a pond.

In close-up, David reaches out his hand for Jonathan's.

We stop following the couple and watch their silhouettes disappear into the dark.

DISSOLVE:

JONATHAN'S COLLEGE DORM – MORNING – 2009

David and Jonathan are lying in bed. Overhead a fan whirs steadily. David has his arm around Jonathan, who is sound asleep. David looks at him with an earnest, loving gaze. He smiles to himself.

DISSOLVE:

JONATHAN'S APARTMENT – NIGHT – 2014

David teeters on his feet – he grips the railing of the apartment's front entry steps to keep balance.

The sky weeps, a deluge of rain and hail.

JONATHAN: Call an Uber. For fucksake, get a cab on Broadway.

David turns and looks to the street. Car headlights shine in the distance. We move away from David and look back. Jonathan stands in the doorway, his shadow blocking the light from touching David on the street.

Our gaze tilts upward. Rain falls in our eyes.

FADE OUT:

FADE IN:

INT. SASHA'S APARTMENT – AFTERNOON – 2015

David's eyes remain staring into oblivion. Sasha leans forward from the bed and gently shoves him, causing him to jump.

SASHA: Well, David, I wouldn't say any of us are good role models.

DAVID: (smiling) That's fair.

SASHA: He and Kent had some sort of storybook romance over in Berlin, but now they're back to reality. You saw how pristine his fucking Instagram was while they were gone.

DAVID: Disgusting.

SASHA: Goddamn revolting!

David laughs and takes a seat on to the bed next to Sasha.

DAVID: I guess we're all just messes. Even pretty boys like Al and Kent. Everyone's a fuck up but probably fine.

SASHA: I'd say that's accurate. (pause) And what about you?

DAVID: What me?

SASHA: What's your plan for this weekend? Quick hookup? Orgy with some strangers at Steamworks? Self-induced orgasm while watching *The Iron Lady*?

DAVID: It's actually a mashup: Iron Lady orgy at Steamworks. It's their most popular event.

SASHA: Undoubtedly.

FLASHBACK TO:

INT. DAVID'S APARTMENT – DAY – EARLIER IN THE WEEK

Sunshine streams through the front windows. David bounces on his toes and shadowboxes the air around him. He holds a phone in his hand.

DAVID: This is it. Going to do it. (pressing the phone to his ear and taking a deep breath; there is a brief pause) Hey! Frank! Yeah, listen, it's David. I know. Yeah, *that*

David. I've been thinking a lot, a lot about us and where I left things and how, well, how fucking dumb I was. You're a phenomenal guy and handsome and smart and funny, and I'd like one more shot. I want one more shot to prove that I'm much less insane than I have let on this past summer.

He pauses.

CUT TO:

INT. OFFICE BUILDING – DAY

David's best friend, Mya, sits on her cell phone. She is nodding.

MYA: That was good. Dr. Love will appreciate it. I mean, maybe downplay the insane part, though – you know, say something like, "less impetuous?"

CUT TO:

INT. DAVID'S APARTMENT – DAY

David nods energetically.

DAVID: Yes! Impetuous! I mean, it is better than insane. Thanks for the test run, My. I need all the help I can get…

CUT BACK TO:

INT. SASHA'S BEDROOM – AFTERNOON – 2015

David slaps Sasha's knee.

DAVID: We should get back to the party. And to answer your question, there is absolutely no sex on the horizon. This weekend is about my friends and having a good time.

SASHA: That sounds lame as fuck, friend.

DAVID: You're calling yourself lame.

SASHA: I'm not going out tonight, darling, so everyone else is lame.

DAVID: (crossing his arms) I'm not telling you what you should and shouldn't do, but I think for Terrence's sake…

SASHA: (sighing) I have to be a good friend, don't I?
DAVID: I think it's for the best.

CUT TO:

INT. SASHA'S LIVING ROOM – AFTERNOON

The sun has fallen lower in the sky. In the kitchen Tibbs drinks a glass of water while Donnie and Alan exchange jokes in the corner.

Terrence sits on the couch, alone, on his phone.

The front door opens. Edward looks in apprehensively.

EDWARD: You're in much better shape than I thought.

DONNIE: Oh, Eddie! When have we ever been anything but the best of houseguests.

EDWARD: Do you want the list in alphabetical order?

Sasha and David enter from the bedroom.

EDWARD: There's mine! Sasha, will you all be heading out shortly?

SASHA: (laughing) Friends, that is Edwardian code for "Get the fuck out!"

TIBBS: We were bored anyway! Let's go, ladies!

It is a cacophonous exit. Tibbs carries Donnie on his back out of the apartment. Terrance chugs the rest of his wine and runs to the kitchen for a quick refill. Alan links arms with David and pulls him out the front door.

In the end it is just Sasha and Edward. They say nothing but give each other knowing glances. Edward raises an eyebrow. A slight upturn of his lips reveals he is not actually perturbed. Sasha stands, arms crossed, a large smile spread over his face.

We look intently at Sasha, his eyes gazing deeply into Edward's. The background blurs and Sasha appears to glow in the dimness. After the rush of seeing his friends, having his intimate discussion with David, and seeing the classically Edwardian entrance of Edward, he savors the moment.

The blurred background behind Sasha shakes, tremors and we three scenes compress behind him.

DEEP FOCUS. WE SEE THREE DISTINCT IMAGES OF SASHA'S PAST, PRESENT, AND FUTURE IN THE FADED BACKGROUND OF THE APARTMENT.

SASHA'S CHILDHOOD HOME – EVENING – 1993

Sasha's father slinks through the front door of their home. On the television a hip-hop song is playing. Sasha dances with the intensity and abandon of which only a young child is capable. His father shakes his head and clicks off the set. He places his briefcase on the ground and assesses his young son. A clang comes from the kitchen and he sighs heavily. Shaking his head, he walks toward the disruption. Sasha looks angrily after his father for a moment. He turns his attention to a row of action figures lined up on the coffee table.

A GRAVEYARD – EVENING – 2013

Sasha stands with Edward looking on a pile of freshly overturned earth. Beside them Sasha's grandmother sits in a wheelchair. She is greatly aged, her gray hair blowing wildly around her face. Sasha looks passive, reflective, appearing to stare beyond the grave, beyond the graveyard itself. It is with a sudden jerk that he begins to cry. He angrily wipes the tears away. With a sudden immediacy, he rushes toward his father's tombstone and kicks it. He yells into the sky. When the fit has ended, he bends over, panting. His grandmother looks to Edward and reaches out her hand. Edward squeezes it then moves behind her so he can push her nearer Sasha. Once close she rests a wrinkled hand on Sasha's back. She reaches out and, again, grasps Edward's hand. We are then behind them, looking at the three figures, a tableau of mourning.

EDWARD AND SASHA'S STARTER HOME – FUTURE

A small child runs through Sasha's legs as he and Edward carry in a large painting of Egyptian gods and goddesses. Edward is laughing so hard he gently drops his end of the painting. Sasha is infuriated for a moment before he also breaks into laughter. He slaps Edward playfully then runs toward the small child. Sasha picks the little girl up like a sack of potatoes and spins her in circles around the room.

THE IMAGES FADE.

SASHA'S LIVING ROOM – AFTERNOON – 2015

The background turns clear again. Sasha moves forward and takes Edward into an embrace. The couple looks into each other's eyes before they sensuously kiss. When they pull apart Edward is a slight shade of red, a childish grin on his face.

SASHA: I love you, baby.

EDWARD: Mutual, as always.
CUT TO:

EXT. SASHA'S APARTMENT BUILDING – AFTERNOON

Donnie and Tibbs walk ahead of the crowd skipping and singing a love song from the summer. Behind them, in pairs, David and Alan, and Terrence and Sasha speak in hushed tones.

Sasha has his arm around Terrance.

SASHA: You really are fine? I won't be handing you tissues later?

TERRANCE: Sasha, I feel fine. I will try to avoid him, but I am prepared for the worst.

David and Alan are a few steps behind Donnie and Tibbs.

DAVID: Are you headed to Mini to meet your man?

ALAN: Yeah, I should catch up with them. But keep me updated, and let me know before you head to Sidetrack! I want in on Bingo!

DAVID: Of course. We wouldn't dare leave you out. (David's expression grows serious) You know, it'll be fine. I think you just need to let things happen for a bit. Regain your footing in Chicago and see if being a couple is a good fit. You've been scowling for the past week. Have fun!

ALAN: That is the best advice you may have ever given me.

Alan pulls David into a hug. After the embrace they perform their windmilling fraternity handshake.

We drift back across the street and watch the men go by. Soon all have taken up the song Donnie and Tibbs have been singing.

SCENE III – THE MAGNIFICENT YOUTH

FADE IN:

INT. HEDLEY'S APARTMENT - NIGHT

The Set is gathered in Hedley's lair. Their numbers have expanded to include Lloyd, Nick, and two other homosexuals we have never encountered. It appears as if the crowd is preparing for something unpleasant. Everyone sits or stands in some approximation of comfort; however, all seem slightly nervous, onguard.

HEDLEY: Did you have fun at the festival, Nick?

NICK: I did. It wasn't quite as crazy as I thought it would be.

THE MODEL: I loved the eye candy. My senses were literally flooded with the sights, sounds, and smells of beautiful men.

The Model stretches upward, his chiseled torso exposed, his biceps flexing. It is a show for those gathered, a fishing line dropped into the pond of the other men's desire.

Although the moment is brief, the action slows and we see a few important expressions:

Nick lustfully ogles The Model and his sinewy body. His eyes convey pain in not capturing the Chicago visitor's full attention.

Across the room Lloyd looks on in concern as he watches his young lover's eyes lustfully drink in the body of another. His gaze shifts, however, and he stares out the window, his expression growing pensive.

Seated at the table, Stephen and Samson share a moment, their eyes locked, sly smiles tipping up the corner of their mouths. They know what there is to know of Nick's desires and Lloyd's sudden taciturn state.

Skyler is flanked by the two new gays. They are obscured in shadow. Their lips move but we cannot hear what is spoken. We focus on Skyler's vacant stare. He appears to be totally disengaged, deeply lost in thought.

The final expression is Hedley. He glances at everyone in the room. Something like fear fills his eyes but vanishes just as quickly as it appears. Skyler then becomes his sole focus. He looks on thoughtfully at his youngest protégé. He wrings his hands.

The action resumes full speed again when The Model turns to Hedley and softly laughs. His long fingers scratch his abdomen.
THE MODEL: You weren't impressed by the hot bodies on the street today, Hedders?

Hedley rips his gaze from Skyler.

FLASHBACK TO:

EXT. MARKET DAYS STREET FESTIVAL – EARLIER THAT DAY

Hedley is behind The Model and Nick, walking purposefully to catch up with them.

NICK: Hedley likes to think he's still in charge but he's not. Things aren't the same.

Hedley stops abruptly. Nick and The Model continue pacing forward.

Stephen grabs Hedley from behind and cackles loudly.

STEPHEN: You hear that, Hedley? The little one is joining the game.

CUT BACK TO:

INT. HEDLEY'S APARTMENT – NIGHT – PRESENT

Hedley's eyes flick to Nick then back to The Model.

HEDLEY: They were fine. I think I just still have my standards.

The Model bites his lip. He winks at Hedley.

THE MODEL: Always the cunt.

STEPHEN: Hedley's right. It's all the tired boys we always see.

SAMSON: Oh, shut up, Stevey! We all know that you've only had eyes for fresh-faced Mikey all summer. Since you stumbled across his Christian ass at Hydrate... of all places.

SKYLER: (awakening from his stupor and smiling) Our Lady of Hydrate puts so many boys on their knees, doesn't she, Stevey?

For a moment The Set is one again; it is the Last Supper before their Gethsemane. All four men share a warm, garrulous laugh.

NICK: Who is Mikey?

STEPHEN: Mike—

SKYLER: (loudly interjecting) Mike is a hottie from a church group who is trying to bring gays back to Jesus.

SAMSON: Very holy.

Samson puts his hands together as if in prayer. Skyler laughs and comes forward joining him. Hedley follows suit.

HEDLEY: (assuming a prayer pose) He has a perfect eight-pack, so blessed.

SKYLER: (crossing himself) She's Boystown's Sister Mary Clarence.

Skyler, Hedley, and Samson look at each other and grin.

ALL TOGETHER: Aaaaaaammmeeeennnn.

Stephen is gasping for breath from laughter.

STEPHEN: My god. Can we refer to him as Sister Mary from now on? That's too perfect.

SAMSON: (with a small bow) As you wish, sister.

The Model and Nick share an awkward look, wondering when they'd been pushed aside. The two other gays shuffle to the kitchen to fill their drinks.

HEDLEY: Well, we need a plan.

NICK: Did anyone check Twitter?

SKYLER: Oh, honey. (looking at Hedley) He doesn't know?

HEDLEY: He doesn't. (winking) But I think we should check anyway.

STEPHEN: (leaping to his feet) Oh, you're right!

Every man gathered stares downward at their phones. There is a brief moment of silence.

ALL TOGETHER: Sidetrack!

The other gays peep into the living room.

BOTH: What's happened?!

SAMSON: Twitter is back for the high holy holiday.

THE OTHER #1: She's been so silent!

Hedley laughs and heads toward his bedroom.

HEDLEY: Well, we can't be seen at Sidetrack first, so I suggest a drink on the street and then head in.

THE MODEL: The street! My god, Hedley Renault is such a man of the people.

HEDLEY: (disappearing from view) Everyone deserves to see the queen.

FADE IN:

EXT. HEDLEY'S APARTMENT – NIGHT

The coterie walks away from the apartment building. Streetlamps cast a lurid glow over all the men, bathing their faces in buttery light so they appear drained of life. Samson and Stephen have their arms around each other, laughing loudly at nothing of note.

Hedley wears a white linen top and form-fitting red shorts. The Model sidles closer to him as they move away from Lake Shore Drive toward Halsted. Barely noticeable, he lets his hand fall onto Hedley's back. He whispers a trivial observation about Nick into his host's ears.

Skyler is behind all the other men, hands in his pockets. The sounds of the night fade away as we draw closer to the youngest Set member and see a smile creeping over his usually icy features. He looks up and laughs at his friends ahead of him. His gaze does not stop there, however, it lifts higher to take in the ghostly buildings and starless sky that hang over them. Skyler then slides to the left side of our field of vision. The right side becomes a projection screen for a number of fused images, a collage of his life as it was, is, and will be.

DEEP FOCUS. WE SEE THREE DISTINCT IMAGES OF SKYLER'S PAST, PRESENT, AND FUTURE PROJECTED ON THE DIM STREETS BESIDE HIM.

DOCTOR'S OFFICE – DAY – 2010

Pale autumn light filters through curtains as Skyler sits in a plastic chair. It is totally silent. Skyler listens to a young doctor. His words are inaudible, but as we watch his mouth move, a swelling, high-pitched tone grows in intensity. Skyler's head falls on his chest as the unheard words bombard him. The tone swells louder. We pivot our gaze and see his mother, Georgina, in blurred silhouette behind him. She is weeping, her hands covering her face. Skyler's eyes have grown red; tears drop down his cheeks.

SKYLER'S STUDIO APARTMENT – AFTERNOON – 2015 – MONTHS BEFORE

Skyler and Stuart stand on opposite sides of our field of view. Skyler's arms are crossed. He nervously smiles, looking away from Stuart, who stands outside the apartment. Tentatively, Stuart enters. Skyler's smile fades as the older man draws closer. They are only inches apart when Stuart stops. Skyler keeps his gaze away from Stuart, looking out the window. Gently, Stuart takes a finger and caresses Skyler's collarbone. Skyler's eyes close. His head goes back. Stuart lightly moves his hands down Skyler's chest. Finally, Skyler fixes his attention on Stuart. There is one tense moment, both men gazing longingly into each other's eyes. Skyler is the one who moves – he reaches out and takes Stuart's face into his hands. They kiss.

BELMONT HARBOR – UKNOWN TIME – FUTURE

Skyler paces along the cement wall at the edge of the harbor. The sky is gray. It is unclear whether it is muted day or approaching night. Lightning ripples on the horizon. With each crash of thunder the clouds roil and reveal a new image:

THUNDER CRASH 1:

Skyler and Stuart are sound asleep in each other's arms.

THUNDER CRASH 2:

Skyler looks shocked as he catches Stuart fucking someone else in their bed.

THUNDER CRASH 3:

A church. Georgina is dressed in all her finery as she watches Skyler and Stuart come down the aisle.

THUNDER CRASH 4:
Shadows creep over an unknown boy's face in the cab of a truck. He looks up at Stuart, tears staining his cheeks. His clothes are ripped. He is nude from the waist down. The mystery boy shuts his eyes as Stuart forces himself upon him. In the faint darkness of the window behind the boy, we see the dim reflection of Georgina in a ripped dress, a bottle of whiskey beside her.

THE IMAGES FADE.

EXT. CHICAGO STREETS – NIGHT – 2015
The smile on Skyler's face fades away. Instead of looking skyward his eyes focus on the pavement in front of him.

SAMSON: You okay, Sky? You look fucking sad.

Skyler takes a deep breath. He clenches his fists. When he looks Samson in the eye, he is smiling.

SKYLER: Just wondering when you'll skip north to the bear orgy, Sammy.

SAMSON: Oh, the orgy is tomorrow. Tonight I may have to settle for whatever twink comes calling at Hydrate.

SKYLER: (laughing) That's if any of the twinks will even talk to you, old man.

Samson throws his arm around Skyler and pulls him toward the main group. The younger gay joins in the singing and the raucous discussion. For a fleeting moment we see a brief expression of sadness in his eyes before he again looks skyward.

SCENE IV – XANADU

FADE IN:

INT. THE SLEDGE BAR – LATE NIGHT

The bar is dying out. Several drunks hobble tenuously toward the exit.

Alan and Kent are making out in the corner, their hands running through each other's hair. David and Sasha lean on the bar watching them kiss.

SASHA: I remember when I was a hot youth. You fight but then get drunk and horny and all is forgiven.

DAVID: I didn't stand a chance with Jonathan after his six-pack came in - no hope for make-out reconciliation.

SASHA: You were fucked.

Sasha and David clink glasses. Terrence joins them at the bar. His clothes are completely disheveled.

DAVID: And where have we been, Terry?

TERRANCE: The Hole.

SASHA: My god, I'm proud of you. I really thought I'd be taking you home at 10 pm in tears.

TERRANCE: I told you. I'm a reformed man. I've given up on love stuff for now. I'll just go into a basement of a bar and get a what I need.

DAVID: Is this what happens after a week at home? Zen-like state? Self-actualization?

TERRANCE: (pause) You remember when we got coffee at the beginning of the summer? I had all those ideas about trying to get into threesomes and going along with Lloyd's new open thing?

SASHA: Of course. David, Sal, and I talked shit about it all summer.

TERRANCE: What great friends. (rolling his eyes) Well, it kept not working. Then it totally broke when I found Lloyd was fucking that college kid Peter and George brought into town – who I tried to befriend! The little bastard... Anyway, the day you all helped me move, after Lloyd paraded everyone through our apartment in that ridiculous show, on the way home to Michigan, I just woke up. Lloyd's an asshole. He's always been an asshole, and you can fuck a pile of dudes together every night, but it doesn't mean he's not an asshole. (abruptly pauses) Wait... has it been last call?

DAVID: No.

TERRANCE: Well, then let me get some shots and a round of drinks.

Sasha looks at David and covers his mouth to stop the eruption of laughter. As Terrence orders a round with the bartender, David turns to Sasha.

DAVID: I fucking love this bar. I come here once a year, and it literally is like Xanadu; it appears from the mist as a post-drinking utopia where anything goes. Terrence, goody-goody gay gets a blowjob in the back; Alan and Kent's relationship on the precipice, fires back to life; Sasha Williams stays out past midnight for the first time in years, actually *excited* about Market Days…

SASHA: And! David Jenkins brings up his ex-boyfriend after months of saying he's over it.

DAVID: I'll have you know Dr. Konstantin says I'm doing very well. And…

SASHA: And what?

DAVID: So… (pause) I'm going to call Frank and apologize, and see if we can give it another go.

SASHA: Wait. Stop. Why didn't you tell me?

DAVID: I thought you'd call me a "dumb bitch" again, and I wasn't in the mood.

SASHA: Well, you are a dumb bitch. Everyone knows that, but – wait – when are you going to call him?

DAVID: After the weekend. I talked through it with Mya and I'm going to apologize next week.

Sasha takes a step back. He raises his hands and begins to slowly clap.

Terrance turns around and looks at David earnestly just as his ordered drinks arrive.

TERRANCE: Did I miss something?

SASHA: (stops clapping) David is done being a dumb bitch – for the time being.

DAVID: A momentary lapse into good judgement.

TERRANCE: Well, here's to that!

Terrence, Sasha, and David all take their shots. Terrence throws a five on the counter and then spins around.

TERRANCE (continued): Where was I? I was telling you my revelation?

DAVID: Yes, evidently Lloyd is an asshole.

TERRANCE: He is! Right!

SASHA: And...

TERRANCE: And what I realized on that ride home is that I've been a huge fucking asshole, too. Not an external asshole like Lloyd. I don't destroy people's lives with joy and then dance on the tombstones of their emotions drinking mimosas.

SASHA: That certainly is a visual.

TERRANCE: Right. But I've been an internal asshole – ignoring the signs, being deluded into thinking that a cancer like Lloyd is worthy of my own asshole love. It's fucking not. I'm better than that. I can choose not to be an asshole. And someday, I'll go back to my boring Christian ideals of having a husband and some adopted babies from Asia and Africa, but that's not this summer. It's not while we're getting divorced. For this interim time, I'm going to get blowjobs in backrooms and have reckless, Truvada-taking, condom-wearing, adventurous missionary sex. Because I can only adventure so far before my boring calls me back.

David looks at Sasha. He raises his hands and both men begin to clap together. Soon all the drunks in the bar have joined in. Alan and Kent stumble over laughing. Kent covers Alan's neck in kisses.

ALAN: What did we miss?

DAVID: Nothing you two love birds need to worry about. (he ruffles Alan's hair) Jesus, you move it and then it just springs back to ruffled perfection. This fucking hair.

KENT: Isn't it flawlesssssss?

DAVID: I'd say obnoxious... but, sure.

SASHA: (waving at the bartender) Can we get five shots, please?

The bartender ambles over.

BARTENDER: We already called closing time. You're lucky I'm getting laid tonight; this is the last one.

SASHA: Absolutely!

The bartender sloppily pours five shots of Fireball. He grabs Sasha's card and gives him a wink.

Alan grabs a glass of the whiskey, almost spilling it. Kent laughs loudly and pats his boyfriend on the back. When Alan has regained his composure, he raises his glass in the air.

ALAN: Here is to friends and boyfriends and everyone who makes us who we are.

DAVID: That's surprisingly deep for Al at 3:40 am.

ALAN: I, sir, am a Fulbright Scholar... soooooo...

Alan downs his drink. As he finishes the shot, the bar lights come on. For a moment all five men stand dazed in the harsh, fluorescent glow. The growls of the more drunken patrons echo from the dark corners of the bar. Men appear from the basement in various stages of undress.

ALAN (continued): I feel like I'm in a memory. Like, I'm already remembering this.

SASHA: You need better memories girl if this late-night mess is what you're going to remember from this weekend.

KENT: I kind of feel like it, too.

CUT TO:

EXT. THE SLEDGE BAR – EARLY MORNING

The group is standing on the street. Kent stretches and yawns loudly. Terrence, Sasha, and David gather to the side.

TERRANCE: Let's get breakfast and watch the sunrise. We only have an hour or so. We can eat then watch it from Sasha's roof.

DAVID: I'm down. It's been a long time since I've been up this late – let's keep it going.

SASHA: (playfully annoyed) You assholes convince me to come out, and now I have to watch the fucking sun rise. This is why I don't ever do this.

DAVID: Let's live in a memory, just like Al.

The three men watch as Alan and Kent giggle and climb into an Uber.

TERRANCE: (watching Kent and Alan leave) Ahhhh – young love.

SASHA: Fucking gross.

Terrance skips away from Sasha and David.

TERRANCE: Pancakes, Sash? On me? You have to follow me; I'm your guest!

Sasha groans as he stomps after Terrence. David starts skipping, linking arms with Sasha and Terrance as he passes them.

DAVID: We're off to see the wizard…

CUT TO:

INT. UBER – EARLY MORNING

Kent has already fallen asleep against the window, his chest rising and falling as the car drives down Clark Street.

Alan watches him. A sad smile is on his face.

ALAN: (softly) Just like a memory.

Gently, he reaches over and brushes a strand of hair away from Kent's eye. He turns and looks out the window, the images passing by suddenly growing cloudy, transforming and compressing into three scenes spreading toward the horizon.

DEEP FOCUS. WE SEE THREE DISTINCT IMAGES OF ALAN'S PAST, PRESENT, AND FUTURE THROUGH THE UBER'S WINDOW.

THE ROOF OF HIS FRATHOUSE – NIGHT – 2011

David, Jonathan, and Alan lay on the roof, looking up at the night sky. Jonathan takes a hit from a joint and passes it to Alan, who gratefully accepts. He takes his turn then passes it to David. We draw closer to Alan's face. His expression is placid, calm. He closes his eyes and sighs deeply.

BERLIN NIGHTCLUB – NIGHT – 2015

Alan and Kent make out with reckless abandon in the hall of the club. Women and men in varying costumes pass by them. An especially tall female in a blue wig with a riding crop, slaps Kent across the back. Both boys laugh. Kent pulls away from their kiss. He runs quickly down the hall. Alan follows him through a number of twisting corridors. From different rooms in the club there are audible screams of pain mixed with groans of ecstasy. Kent turns into a room and Alan follows him. Within are two men, one bound to a bed, the other, wearing a leather harness, fucking him. For the first time, Alan's expression grows conflicted. Kent laughs and grabs his hand, pulling him toward the sex display. He drops his hand when they get close. Kent licks his lips, holding eye contact with Alan, but backing toward the man in the harness. The two men fucking barely notice. Kent leans over the bed, beginning to run a hand over the body of the man strapped to the bed. Alan's breath speeds up; his eyes look concerned, confused.

ALAN AND KENT'S BEDROOM – MORNING – FUTURE

Alan and Kent sit on opposite ends of the bed. The room is drenched in white light. Alan stares at Kent, who sits placidly smiling at his lover. There is a flash and Kent is no longer alone; he is surrounded by different men, who caress him and kiss his neck and cheeks. Alan's face returns to the conflicted look of the sex club. Kent beckons him to come closer. As he motions for Alan, he also turns to one of the men caressing him; they begin to kiss, their tongues thrashing wildly. Alan looks away to the window. The sounds of sex grow louder. Alan flicks his eyes toward Kent. Their eyes lock in a meaningful stare.

THE IMAGES FADE.

EXT. KENT AND ALAN'S APARTMENT – EARLY MORNING – 2015

Kent opens his eyes when they arrive. His groggy gaze finds Alan's.

KENT: That was fun.

ALAN: It was.

KENT: Feels like a memory.

Alan punches Kent playfully and drags him from the car.

ALAN: Don't make fun of my drunken brilliance.

KENT: No, it was very true. I liked it. Nights like this, when they like blend together, you feel time slipping a little bit. It's like we're actually moving from present to future – from today to tomorrow.

ALAN: See! You're also waxing poetic.

KENT: Just when I have my muse.

Before entering the apartment, Alan turns back and looks to the sky. It is not yet morning, but night is burning away, purples and blues beginning to swirl along the eastern horizon.

One foot inside of the building, one foot out, Alan smiles.

SCENE V – WORLDS AT WAR

FADE IN:

EXT. TAVERNA RESTAURANT – DAY

It is the next morning. Lloyd is running down Cornelia Avenue; he is late for brunch. He arrives at the door to Taverna breathing heavily. Sweat drips down his forehead. He takes out a paper towel and mops his brow. Nervously, he peers inside the large glass windows.

CUT TO:

INT. TAVERNA RESTAURANT – DAY

We see Lloyd peering through the front window then suavely enter the restaurant as if he isn't late at all. He waves to the host and heads toward the back of the dining room. Hedley, Samson, Skyler, Nick, and The Model all sit in silence. They are seated in the far back corner in a long booth able to fit eight people.

Lloyd eyes everyone at the table nervously. No one speaks. All have their heads bent down or stare forward, totally disengaged with their surroundings.

FLASHBACK TO:

INT. SIDETRACK – THE PREVIOUS NIGHT

The bar is packed – it is a mass of bodies. Near us, we see Nick and The Model standing away from the rest of the group. Nick pulls himself against the body of The Model. The older man gently shoves him away. Nick whimpers and slaps his hand on the bar.

NICK: Why? Ollllddd Tired Hedsleys? You been flirtin' inna weekend…

The Model turns a deep shade of red. Demurely, he takes Nick's hands.

THE MODEL: Darling, that's what I do. Don't take it personally.

NICK: Issa Hedley? Why? He does unt care. He does unt give a fuck 'bout you, me, 'bout anyone. (grabbing The Model's hands, he shoves them into his pants) Is yours, if you want it…

CUT TO:

EXT. SIDETRACK – NIGHT

Skyler is rushing down the street away from the bar. Hedley runs after him.

HEDLEY: Skyler – wait! Let's at least talk.

Skyler stops abruptly. Hedley almost collides with him. His young protégé whirls around, his gaze menacing.

SKYLER: Get. Away.

HEDLEY: Skyler – I'm just doing this to –

SKYLER: Do what, Hedley? Do fucking what?

People have stopped on the street. A small crowd gathers at the door of Sidetrack.

HEDLEY: I just don't want you to be –

SKYLER: Oh, it's me. It's fuckin me? Yer just looking out for me, clearly, Hedley. Clearly, you care so fucking much. So much. Thank you for your fucking generosity. See how much you... (shoving Hedley, then turning to the crowd) Hey Fuckers – yeah! All you fuckers dying to know what's going on, I'll tell you: I'm fucking an old man. He's hot and he's just turned fifty, and I let him lay his old dick inside my ass.

The crowd is perfectly silent. One young gay turns and whispers to his friend.

YOUNG GAY: Shhhhhhit...

Skyler stomps back to Hedley his arms raised in triumph.

SKYLER: There Hedley. Everyone knows. Everyone fucking knows. Put it on Twitter – put Stuart's big, old cock on Instagram and tag me. Everyone fucking knows.

Tears form at the edge of Skyler's eyes. His resolve seems to be breaking. Hedley sighs.

CUT BACK TO:

INT. TAVERNA RESTAURANT – DAY

Lloyd slowly takes a seat at the table. Once seated, The Model turns to him.

THE MODEL: Can you pass the crème?

Lloyd hands him the crème container and nervously looks around at each man.

LLOYD: Rough night?

SKYLER: Nice of you to join us, Lloyd. Thought you may be finding someone to fuck in front of Terrence, just for old time's sake. (turning and grabbing Nick's arm) Maybe just repeat? Lloyd stutters. Hedley looks down at the table and waves his hand.

HEDLEY: Boys, let's cool off. I think it was a rough night for all of us, but there's no sense in taking it out on everyone else.

Skyler nods at Hedley but stares, darkly, at Lloyd.

LLOYD: (stuttering) It *was* a rough night. Messy girls?

STEPHEN: I think everyone was a bit overserved. (passing a menu to Lloyd) It was Market Days Madness, let's say.

LLOYD: Looks like not for you, Stephen. You're beaming.

ALL BUT LLOYD AND STEPHEN: Mikey.

Stephen flushes and takes a sip of his drink. He opens his mouth as if to speak but then stops and shrugs.

A waiter comes over anxiously assessing the local celebrities at the table. He's new in the role, sharply dressed. Out of anxiety he continually grabs his collar.

WAITER: How are we? Ready to order?

LLOYD: I'll definitely be having the bottomless brunch special. Bring two mimosas and that should get things started.

WAITER: Yes.

SAMSON: I think we'll need a moment on food. We're all a little slow today.

WAITER: Sure. Yes. Well, I'll get this sir's – this man's drinks going.

The waiter scuttles off. The group remains silent. Lloyd drums his fingers on the table. His eyes roam over the faces of all the men gathered. Nick does not meet his gaze. His own attention is riveted on The Model, who clutches his coffee as if he's afraid it will fall through the table and onto the floor.

Around them conversations are ebullient, men and women excited for the final day of the festival. A few gays at the table directly behind them are already intoxicated, cackling at the least provocation.

LLOYD: Well, if last night was a bust, what's the plan for today then?

SAMSON: I think we may need sustenance before committing.

HEDLEY: (attempting lightness of tone) Some of us are going to the beach, then Samson's, then out again to the fest. There are some shows tonight. Everyone is welcome to join, of course.

THE MODEL: (leering at Hedley) I may go prowling.

FLASHBACK TO:

INT. HEDLEY'S APARTMENT – THE PREVIOUS NIGHT

Hedley and The Model enter the apartment together. Hedley is distracted. He sets his keys on the counter then rushes out of the room. He returns, running his hand through his hair, deep in thought.

THE MODEL: Finally alone, Hedders. Fancy a drink?

Hedley does not hear him.

THE MODEL: Hedley? You're not thinking about that shit show, are you? Everyone was wasted. None of this is your fault. They'll go home, sleep it off, and tomorrow will be fine. Are you upset the little muscle boy called you tired?

HEDLEY: (as if just waking) What?

THE MODEL: The little one who said you were tired and uninteresting? The little social climber?

HEDLEY: Nick… We made sure he got home…

THE MODEL: Jesus, Hedley! Are you okay? Maybe the baby butt plug is right about you losing your edge.

HEDLEY: Baby butt plug?

THE MODEL: Nick! Fuck! Here… (pouring a glass of wine, he hands it to Hedley) Drink. Relax for fucksake.

HEDLEY: Thank you. Sorry… I…

THE MODEL: You lost control of your henchmen tonight. There's nothing wrong with that. It happens.

HEDLEY: Not to me… Skyler almost found out…

It is perfectly silent. The Model takes a swig from the wine bottle. Casually, he removes his shirt, begins scratching his muscular torso. He clicks his tongue and stares at Hedley.

THE MODEL: So… you're upset…with…?

Hedley barely notices his guest. He stares into nothingness. Slowly he returns to reality. He drinks all of the glass of wine.

HEDLEY: (not looking at The Model) What do you think about at night when you're alone?

The Model is surprised. He stops his subtle seduction and shrugs his shoulders.

THE MODEL: At night? I mean… I suppose I think about my plans for the next day. What will I do, you know. When I'm traveling I'm on Scruff and Grindr a lot, seeing what local delicacies I can tap into.

The joke is wasted on Hedley. He continues to look down at the kitchen counter.

HEDLEY: Are you happy? With that. Does that make you happy?

THE MODEL: Yeah, I mean… I make good money. I travel. I get to go to exotic parties in LA and New York. It's a good life.

HEDLEY: Good…

Hedley walks from the room. He returns to the living room and stares out the window. The Model apprehensively follows him.

HEDLEY: Tonight… A lot of nights… I feel like the party has ended… The crowd has left, and I have nowhere to go.

A tear forms at the edge of his eye.

The Model softens seeing the emotion on Hedley's face. He moves toward his old lover. He places one hand on Hedley's back and rubs sensuously.

THE MODEL: There are ways to make you feel better…

Hedley glances at The Model. He sadly smiles then resumes looking out the window.

FLASHBACK TO:

EXT. HEDLEY'S PARENTS' HOME – 2015 – EARLIER THAT SUMMER

We have taken the point-of-view of Hedley as he sits on a grassy hill. Beside him his grandmother is seated in a lawn chair. Our eyes turn toward Hedley's sister and her children as they roughhouse in a patch of worn earth at the bottom of the hill. A small pond is just beyond them.

Hedley's nephew runs up the hill and stops in front of his uncle. He looks up at Hedley.

HEDLEY'S NEPHEW: Uncle Hank, you want to come see the fish? They keep swimmin' but they don't drown.

CUT BACK TO:

INT. TAVERNA RESTAURANT – DAY

The Model, behind his designer sunglasses, stares at Hedley. Hedley makes brief eye contact then shifts his gaze to Lloyd.

HEDLEY: How's your weekend been, Lloyd?

LLOYD: It's going. Last night was tame after seeing you all. I went with Kinsey and the gang to get dinner then to Seven for a drink. Even it was crowded, if you can believe it.

SAMSON: These truly are crazy times.

The waiter brings two mimosas for Lloyd. The glasses barely touch the table before they are both in Lloyd's hands.

LLOYD: (chugging down both) Bottoms up!

WAITER: Are we ready to order then?

CUT TO:

EXT. TAVERNA RESTAURANT – DAY

It is two hours later. The tension has melted and The Set and their coterie have fallen into a reverie once again. We jump between social pairings as conversations and apologies come quickly.

NICK: Hedley, I'm so sorry. I shouldn't have said those things to your friend. It wasn't…

HEDLEY: Nick, people do stupid things when they're drunk. It's fine. Don't make it a habit, though. Sloppy isn't cute. It's not us.

Nick awkwardly reaches out and takes Hedley into an embrace.

NICK: I just I got carried away – I wanted him to be into me...

Hedley pats Nick on the back. Across the sidewalk he catches Stephen's eye and winks.

Lloyd is watching the peace reinstated between Hedley and Nick.

The Model is in the middle of another rambling speech.

THE MODEL: ...But you know how The French can be. I generally love Paris, but there are moments when they're all so petty. I actually prefer my work in Southeast Asia. They're all so friendly. I was at a shoot in Batayan and it literally felt like I was home...

Samson and Stephen have their heads together and speak in hushed tones.

STEPHEN: And where did you go, Sammy?

SAMSON: My pans changed... I was north, engaging with a different kind of set. And it sounds like you were balls deep in Mikey?

STEPHEN: The girls exaggerated. I was sharing a drink with him in the middle of Sidetrack.

SAMSON: You're not even hungover. My guess is he has you pretending to be a responsible drinker?

STEPHEN: We had fun.

SAMSON: (mockingly) We had fun.

Hedley claps his hands to get the group's attention.

HEDLEY: Are we all ready? Whoever wants to head north, we can just take a few Ubers.

NICK: I'll get one!

THE MODEL: (whispering to Stephen) Looks like he's trying to get back in good graces.

NICK: I'm getting a plus!

SKYLER: We'll need one more. I can grab it... Hedley, want to ride with me? We can...

Hedley nods. The two exchange a conciliatory smile.

When the first Uber rolls up, The Model, Samson, Stephen, Lloyd, and Nick scramble inside.

CUT TO:

INT. UBER - DAY

Nick takes the front seat and buckles himself in. He glances in the rearview mirror and watches his friends fall into their places. His gaze lingers on Stephen's broad smile, on Samson's cool demeanor, and on The Model's thick shoulders.

As he turns to face forward, we see the background fade. Around him are three scenes compressed into this one moment, Nick's past, present, and future.

DEEP FOCUS. WE SEE THREE DISTINCT IMAGES OF NICK'S LIFE ROTATING CLOCKWISE AROUND HIS HEAD.

NICK'S PARENT'S LIVING ROOM – AFTERNOON – 2015

Nick is less physically fit. His clothes are shabby. He looks bored as his father paces in front of him, gesticulating earnestly. We do not hear the words, only muted, distorted conversation. We see Nick's eyes focused forward, looking at some unseen, distant object.

HOLLYWOOD BEACH – DAY

Nick stands, arms crossed on the hill overlooking the beach. In front of him is Jordan, who looks broken. He is hunched over. Although he wears sunglasses, tears are visible on his cheeks. He is looking at the water. Nick stands impassively – he does not falter in his stance. Jordan turns to him one more time, pleading with his eyes for a reaction. When he gets none, he suddenly stands tall. He says a few inaudible words, turns, waves over his shoulder, and walks quickly away. Nick does not change his posture. We watch him standing on the hill as Jordan awkwardly rushes away.

MINIBAR – NIGHT – FUTURE

Nick enters the bar at the head of the coterie. Behind him are Skyler, Stephen, Samson, and in the rear of the party, Hedley. Nick walks around confidently, saying hello to all those gathered. He kisses cheeks, slaps men's asses, and steals a shot from a girl's hand to take for himself. At the end of the bar The Model waits. He smiles at Nick and winks. Nick sidles up to him and puts his arm around his waist.

THE IMAGES FADE.

INT. UBER - DAY

Nick again looks into the rearview mirror. The Model is on his phone, soft blips from Grindr can be heard under the thumping rhythm of the car's sound system. Nick eyes The Model's pecs that peak out from his teal tank top. His gaze moves up and settles on The Model's blood-red lips.

ACT II

SCENE VI – THE WHISPERING WAVES

FADE IN:

EXT. BELMONT HARBOR – DAY

David and Terrance walk along the lakefront. It is just before noon. Both men are disheveled. They have bags under their eyes, ruffled hair, and the same clothes from the night before. They hold carry-out coffee cups.

A few joggers and bikers are on the trail getting in their morning workouts. Birds twitter in the trees, and the water shimmers in the rays of the morning sun. It is a peaceful day after the chaos of the previous night.

Two-foot high stone steps lead down to the water near the harbor. A few people are littered about – some reading, some reclining, soaking up the sun.

TERRANCE: I'm glad you couldn't sleep either.

DAVID: I'll be honest, it was mostly a combination of Sasha's snoring and this hangover from hell.

TERRANCE: Keep drinking that coffee. You'll get some good greasy food at Sal's, too.

DAVID: How are you not hungover?

TERRANCE: Wisdom. I consumed one-third of the shots you all did last night. (pause) Sasha's snoring was really bad. Who would have thought such a skinny guy could make that much noise?

DAVID: No idea. Maybe snores are tied to the size of the personality and not the person.

The two men stop and look to the horizon. Far in the distance Navy Pier's Ferris Wheel is barely visible in the morning haze.

A young man and woman rush past Terrence. The man's pants are undone. The girl is flushed and laughing.

DAVID: Young love. Enjoy it while you can, kiddos.

TERRANCE: Kiddos? Are you like sixty now? So wizened by your first breakup.

DAVID: Definitely not wise but less stupid… If that's a thing.

TERRANCE: Less stupid, I like that. I think, if anything, I feel more stupid.

DAVID: More?

Terrance takes a seat on the cement steps that lead to the water.

TERRANCE: I feel like the first part of my life was trying desperately to be one thing. I didn't do stupid then, so now it's time for it. I just want to fuck and forget.

DAVID: You're really over him then? It's not a show?

TERRANCE: Not a show. But I'll never be over him.

David watches as the young man and woman scamper up the concrete steps and disappear into the trees.

FLASHBACK TO:

EXT. FRAT HOUSE ROOF – NIGHT – 2009

Jonathan and David sit on top of the roof, passing a joint. David puts his arm around Jonathan and kisses his cheek.

CUT BACK TO:

EXT. BELMONT HARBOR – DAY – 2015

The young couple is gone. David takes a seat next to Terrence.

DAVID: Would you do it all again? Knowing what you know now, would you date Lloyd?

TERRANCE: I still love him, if that's any kind of answer.

DAVID: Yeah, I'd say the same about Jonathan. We were happy once – or I was. I was happy. Then we moved to Chicago and he saw too many things he liked.

TERRANCE: And now we're both here.

DAVID: And hungover…

Both men stare at the lake. The surface is calm and sparkling. The haze of the morning is starting to melt off. Around them birds sing in the trees.

Terrance looks into the distance. We hear the sound of a door opening.

FLASHBACK TO:

INT. TERRENCE AND LLOYD'S APARTMENT – NIGHT – A MONTH EARLIER

Lloyd enters the apartment. It is completely dark. Gently, he closes the door and tiptoes toward the kitchen.

A light clicks on from the corner. Lloyd turns, a surprised look on his face.

In the light from the table lamp we see Terrance. He is seated and fully dressed. A packed suitcase sits by his feet.

LLOYD: Hey –

TERRANCE: (softly) No.

Terrence stares at Lloyd. Lloyd looks as if he is prepared for a rebuke; he cowers slightly. But nothing comes.

An eerie silence fills the space. Terrance sits, his eyes locked on his husband.

LLOYD: Are you going –?

TERRANCE: (holding up a finger to silence Lloyd) Let me have this moment. You've taken everything you've wanted, but this moment is mine.

Terrance steeples his fingers and leans forward, his eyes never pulling away from Lloyd's face. Lloyd grows visibly uncomfortable. Awkwardly, he changes his standing position – first, crossing his arms, then moving to the wall and leaning against it.

Terrance doesn't move.

LLOYD: Jesus. What is this, Terry?

Terrance finally blinks. He sits back in the chair and takes a dramatic breath.

TERRANCE: I was looking for something.

LLOYD: What? I had to borrow this shirt from –

TERRANCE: Nick. I know. I know what happened.

LLOYD: What? I went to Nick's and...

TERRANCE: You fucked him.

LLOYD: Terrance...

TERRANCE: I got texts. Many.

LLOYD: Listen, you said you wanted to try the –

TERRANCE: Right. This is my fault. It's never yours.

LLOYD: You said that –

TERRANCE: You should fuck everyone? That you should stay out late and leave me at home? That you shouldn't call? You shouldn't think of me?

Terrance stands and grabs his suitcase.

LLOYD: Why do you have that suitcase?

Terrance walks toward the door. He does not stop as he passes Lloyd. He steps outside.

Lloyd calls to him just as he reaches back to close the door.

LLOYD: (pleadingly) What were you looking for?

Terrance turns his head halfway around. He doesn't speak.

LLOYD (continued): You said you were looking for something...

TERRANCE: (sighing as he pulls the door closed) Remorse. Guilt. Love. (pause) Something to make me stay.

CUT BACK TO:

EXT. BELMONT HARBOR – DAY – 2015

TERRANCE: I don't know what happened the night I left him. It was a relief. Earlier this summer when I left, it was so painful, but that second time... It was like I saw him, truly, really saw him. I can't really describe it.

FLASHBACK TO:

INT. FUNERAL HOME – DAY – 2011

David and Jonathan are sitting next to a collection of pictures of Jonathan's nephew; mourners are milling around the room. David looks up as he sees Jonathan's sister-in-law shove away her husband. David looks over at Jonathan, scrutinizing his face.

CUT BACK TO:

EXT. BELMONT HARBOR – DAY – 2015

DAVID: It's like you suddenly see depth. Before it was just images and colors, but then there is perspective, a vanishing point.

Terrance puts his arm around David.

TERRANCE: Yeah, a vanishing point. I saw the end for the first time.

Both men enjoy the ensuing silence. David looks to the horizon with a contented smile on his face. Terrance lays back and rests his back on the concrete step.

DAVID: You remember the day you came over and we ate ice cream?

TERRANCE: That was a good day – sad, but good.

DAVID: It was. The boy I dumped that day, I told him I never wanted to see him again. But I do. I want to see him.

TERRANCE: Details?

DAVID: Doctor-in-training. Skinny-fit, brown hair, good smile. He's super funny.

TERRANCE: Like, he's cute so you think he's funny or legitimately funny-funny?

DAVID: Do you think so little of me?

TERRANCE: Well, we're looking at vanishing points now, David... And... Jonathan was your last choice... so....

DAVID: He was pretty awful, huh?

TERRANCE: If he were a food, he'd be flavorless custard.

DAVID: It's no wonder he turned into a meathead, he always had the brain for it.

TERRANCE: At least he committed to it.

DAVID: Ugghhhhh. He's getting to fuck such hot guys now.

TERRANCE: But it's like a pool of boring custards slop-fucking each other. The one thing I did learn from this whole mess is that when the fucking is done, the thing I want in my next boyfriend – or husband, for that matter – is good conversation. I want to care about what he has to say.

DAVID: Did you care about what Lloyd said?

TERRANCE: At first, you know. Then it mostly turned to boring chitchat – clothes, work, who's who in Boystown, Hedley, blah blah blah.

DAVID: I would kill myself. I don't think Frank knows who Hedley is.

TERRANCE: Frank?

DAVID: The guy.

TERRANCE: Call him. Ask him to Sal's this afternoon.

DAVID: That seems like a lot. I also feel like death.

TERRANCE: Well, get some food in your stomach then ask to see him at the fest. We'll all go after.

DAVID: I want it to be a nice gesture, though, an apology. I think it's best to wait until next week and then follow-up.

TERRANCE: What if he meets the man of his dreams this weekend?

DAVID: When has anyone met a guy other than the man of right now at Market Days?

TERRANCE: I think you should go after it.

DAVID: I'll think about it. (suddenly leaping up) Fuck! Terrance! We're going to be late for Sal's!

TERRANCE: What time is it?

DAVID: Almost noon. I still need to shower and dry my olive shirt.

TERRANCE: Yes! And text the boy.

DAVID: That's a maybe, but the shower is a definite yes.

David starts awkwardly climbing the concrete steps. Terrance laughs and bounds up behind him.

TERRANCE: You really need to get back in the gym, Jenkins.

DAVID: Please. I ran on Friday night and that was plenty. My ass is still sore.

TERRANCE: Sure. That was the run.

The two men laugh, mounting the final step and starting to run in the grass.

Terrance looks around at the park. As he watches the couples, dogs, and joggers, he smiles to himself. As our view comes back to his full face, the background around him tremors. We suddenly see the lake and the park melt away. Three scenes lead our eyes to the horizon.

DEEP FOCUS. WE SEE THREE DISTINCT IMAGES OF TERRANCE'S PAST, PRESENT, AND FUTURE.

INT. COFFEE SHOP – DAY – 2008

Terrance is seated at his laptop typing frantically. A chime rings as Lloyd enters the cafe. Terrance does not acknowledge the new visitor; he is distracted by his work. Eventually, he looks up from his computer and stares into the distance, deep in thought. His attention then turns to a light bruise on his forearm. Delicately, he runs his finger over the purple and black skin, a concerned look on his face. He is deep in thought until he hears Lloyd clearing his throat. Terrance looks up and sees him rakishly smiling, looking Terrance's direction. Terrance is surprised. He glances behind him then, again, at Lloyd. Lloyd smiles even more broadly and points at Terrance. He mouths the words "You" and "Cute" before abruptly turning around to order from the barista. Terrance turns his attention back to his computer and prepares to type – he hesitates. He looks back toward Lloyd who has his coffee and is putting in crème and sugar. Terrance thinks several moments, his fingers hovering over the keyboard. He takes a deep breath then rises and makes his way over to Lloyd.

EXT. TERRANCE AND LLOYD'S APARTMENT – NIGHT – EARLIER THAT SUMMER

Terrance stands under a streetlight. He is perfectly still. In the background we hear the chime of text messages coming from his phone. They start sporadically but then grow in frequency. At long last he breaks his pose and digs into his pocket. He pulls out his phone and glances at the screen. We see a number of bubbles. He scrolls upward. We see enough to piece together what has happened.

MESSAGE:
He's with Nick.

MESSAGE:
They came to the bar really late.

MESSAGE:
He's fucking the little twat.

MESSAGE:
Have you heard?

MESSAGE:
The little fucker just told me what happened.

Terrance slowly puts the phone into his pocket. Indifferently, he stares into the night. He finally turns and sees someone else out in the street smoking a cigarette. He holds up his hand and bums one from the stranger. The stranger lights it then politely turns and walks away. We focus on Terrance. His face remains impassive, but his hands shake as he puts the cigarette to his mouth.

INT. TERRANCE'S MOTHER'S HOME – DAY

Terrance sits alone on his mother and stepfather's couch. His parents stand behind him in the shadows. A clock ticks steadily in the background. We move closer to Terrance. His expression changes, in an inhuman way, emotions run over his face like a screen: happiness, sadness, joy, fear, anger, elation, terror. Every small step closer we take to him is a new emotion, a new Terrance. When we are close enough to just see his face, his eyes snap shut. The clock stops. After a full second, his eyes open again. His expression is blank.

THE IMAGES FADE.

EXT. SASHA AND EDWARD'S APARTMENT – NOON - 2015

David and Terrance bid farewell at the doorway to Sasha's apartment. David goes to his phone, tapping to get an Uber to take him home for a quick shower.

Terrance starts to enter the revolving door of Sasha's building but stops just before the vestibule. Laughing to himself, he pulls out his phone and taps on Grindr.

TERRANCE: Why not? (swiping through a number of nude torsos) I can reheat something at Sal's.

SCENE VII – THE OPEN TABLE

FADE IN:

INT. SAL'S DINING ROOM – DAY

Sal bustles in and out of the dining room, shuttling in trays of hot food: bacon, pancakes, eggs. Seated at the table are Alan, David, and Sasha. They are all engaged in quiet conversation. David rubs his temples; he is clearly still feeling the pain of his hungover.

Sal sets down his most recent dish and apprises the table. He nods, satisfied with himself, and walks quickly to the kitchen.

CUT TO:

INT. SAL'S KITCHEN – DAY

Gertrude is wiping sweaty strands of gray hair from her eyes. She smiles as Sal enters.

GERTRUDE: We're getting too old for this, Sal. Next time let's just order it from somewhere.

SAL: Well, I feel like until I'm totally useless, we should try to cook.

GERTRUDE: I reheat lasagna for my kids. Pop in the Stouffer's and we're good to go.

SAL: That menu isn't without its charm.

GERTRUDE: Mr. Judgment. You have to give me a break; I did all my party planning when I was young.

SAL: Those fetes were lovely. Main dishes of judgment, hypocrisy…

GERTRUDE: Touché…

They both laugh as Sal grabs a tray of pastries from the counter.

CUT TO:

INT. SAL'S DINING ROOM – DAY

David shakes his head when Sal enters.

DAVID: I don't know if I should eat or throw up. Why did I drink so much? There were so many shots. So many.

SASHA: Oh, come on. If old Sasha can make it the day after, you can too.

DAVID: I really don't know if I can…

ALAN: I don't even remember the end of the night. I think I'm still drunk now.

SASHA: Where's Kent?

ALAN: He had a brunch with some friends in Boystown then is heading straight to the fest. We're going to meet up after.

DAVID: Ugh. There's going to be an after. (slams his head on the table)

SAL: (to Alan) I'm still disappointed you two didn't stop by this week… And speaking of missing homosexuals, where is Terrance?

SASHA: Dick.

SAL: Is that a friend?

ALAN: He means penis. Cock. Getting it put in – or putting it in. Not sure his preference. Judging from Lloyd's latest indiscretions, I'd guess bottom? David, do you know?

DAVID: I think they flipped. I don't think there was a lot of sex the past six months, if we're spilling tea.

ALAN: I'm a very moody verse. (he starts) Shit, I am still drunk.

DAVID: Sasha, while we're going around?

SASHA: Edward loves being penetrated. Was that the question?

ALAN: In so many words.

All the men laugh. Gertrude enters with a tray of mimosas.

GERTRUDE: In case anyone was in danger of sobriety.

Alan greedily reaches across the table for a glass. David looks as if he's going to vomit.

DAVID: I felt bad this morning, but now it's worse. These mid-twenties hangovers are brutal.

SASHA: (handing David a glass) Hair of the dog, girl.

GERTRUDE: I wish my nephew could have come in for this. He had so much fun at Pride.

ALAN: Has he been to Market Days?

GERTRUDE: No, he's young. Sal suggested he at least be twenty-one before being introduced.

ALAN: That's fair. Although, I did have some good times before...

DAVID: Slut! (chugging a mimosa) Let's just throw caution to the wind, huh?

SAL: Well! Before we get too far in the bag, let's all say a quick word of prayer. Sasha, you can close your ears.

SASHA: (reaching for a mimosa) I can handle it. I'll pray to the god of champagne. All gathered lower their heads, even Sasha. For a moment the room is perfectly silent.

SAL: Our Father, thank you for all those gathered. Thank you for the freedom to join together in fraternity and fellowship and to be free in places that were once unsafe. Bless this food and protect these gays as they go out into the world in varying states of inebriation. In these moments of celebration, may we take pause and remember those who came before.

ALL: Amen.

SAL: Let's eat!

Everyone attacks the food.

ALAN: Sal, where's Clive? I thought for sure he'd be here.

SAL: He was out with Kinsey last night and volunteering at the festival today. I'm going to meet him when he gets off duty.

DAVID: Is he being flogged in chains at the leather installation?

SAL: He has his bulldog on display today for the pet tent. I think he'd rather be being flogged, though.

SASHA: Speaking of, David, I didn't say anything last night, but I think your old boy Jonathan is... experimenting.

DAVID: Experimenting?

SASHA: I perused the leather store next to Sledge and saw him in a harness with some... rough trade.

DAVID : Are you serious? (looks around the table as if expecting someone to give him an explanation; when no one speaks, he grabs another mimosa) I thought he was going the Hedley-preppy-boy way.

SASHA: I guess it's a short skip to the furry, muscle daddy way.

SAL: Well, to each his own. And, let's not forget, David has successfully moved on from Jonathan.

ALAN: But has he, though?

DAVID: You better still be drunk, cunt.

The group, except David, laugh raucously. Tears are falling down Sasha's cheeks. David looks agitated and crosses his arms.

DAVID (continued): If you all must know, I'm going to call the guy that I stopped seeing earlier this summer.

SAL: The really nice one?

DAVID: Yeah, Frank.

GERTRUDE: (wiping her eyes) Ah, well, David, we're laughing *with* you! I hope it works out with the new guy.

SASHA: Don't fuck it up again!

DAVID: Jesus! Can everyone just leave me alone!

SASHA: Fine. (turning to Alan) Alan, how's your rocky relationship?

Alan stops before taking a drink. The glass hovers just in front of his lips.

FLASHBACK TO:

INT. ALAN AND KENT'S APARTMENT – MORNING

We see the open door leading to Alan and Kent's bedroom. It is silent for a moment before we hear the sounds of sex.

ALAN: Uhhhh!

KENT: Fuck, baby.

ALAN: Yeah, baby. Harder. Fuck.

We hear the groan of a mattress, the clunk-clunk rhythm of the headboard slamming against the wall, and the subtle, intermittent sound of flesh hitting flesh. The noises build before we hear release, a chorus of pleasure, the "uhnnns" and "oooowwwwws" that signal both men have finished.

There is heavy breathing and the shuffle of feet. Alan leaves the bedroom, wiping his abdomen with a dirty shirt.

ALAN: Damn, Kent! Someone was ready to go.

CUT TO:

INT. ALAN AND KENT'S BEDROOM - MORNING

Kent is seated on the bed. A corner of the blanket covers his nude body.

KENT: Looking at you all night gets it going. Especially when everyone in the bar is checking you out.

CUT TO:

INT. ALAN AND KENT'S BATHROOM - MORNING

Alan is on the toilet. He smiles to himself.

ALAN: Same.

Alan flushes the toilet and stands up. He looks in the mirror. At first he smiles, checks his reflection, as one does before going out for the night. As our gaze lingers, however, his smile melts and he is expressionless. Tentatively, he touches his face: he runs a finger over his jawline, lightly touches the corners of his eyes, traces a line across his forehead.

He sighs and turns away from the glass.

CUT BACK TO:

INT. SAL'S DINING ROOM – DAY

ALAN: (pensively) I think it's fine.

Sal and Sasha exchange glances.

SAL: Only fine? Last week you nearly fell out of your chair talking about him.

ALAN: I think I'm still waking up from the Berlin dream. We've hung out with his friends and I realized that … I don't know… it's weird, but I realized that he's this person, with a story, with a past, with this life I didn't know.

Alan looks as if he will say more but then shrugs. He takes a drink.

SASHA: Awww! Our little Ken doll is growing up!

ALAN: Is that what it is?

DAVID: Well, you won't grow up like normal people, Al. You'll like have one problem in life and then get married and get a BMW. The rest of us will settle for a sad, middle-class existence jerking off to Instagram celebrities.

SASHA: Someone's drunk again already.

DAVID: I mean, it's fine! I'm fine! Everything is fine!

Gertrude and Sal lock eyes and smile.

GERTRUDE: It's more complicated than that, David. It's happy and sad but never dull.

SAL: Hear, hear! To it never being boring.

All raise their drinks into the air and toast.

CUT TO:

INT. SAL'S LIVING ROOM – AFTERNOON

The shadows from the sun have grown long. Sal is in the living room. From our vantage point, we can see that the dining room is littered with used dishes. A soft breeze blows through the windows, making a white shirt slung over the window dance in the wind. The record player is on low volume, softly playing in the background.

Over the music we hear the click-clack rhythm of Gertrude's shoes as she enters the living room. She crosses her arms and takes a deep breath.

GERTRUDE: I know I said it earlier, but we're too old for this.

SAL: I kind of enjoy the cleanup. It's a nice quiet task. You can think while doing it.

Gertrude sits on the sofa and removes her shoes. She rubs her feet.

GERTRUDE: Seems like eons ago we started these dinners.

SAL: Another lifetime to be sure. So many boys passed through these doors. I sometimes wonder what they're all doing now.

GERTRUDE: Do you hear from them?

SAL: Some. Others disappear into the gay ether.

Gertrude gently places her shoes to the side of the couch. She pats her hair, making sure everything is in the proper place.

SAL: I actually heard from Hank – Hedley, the other day.

GERTRUDE: I remember when he came here the first time. He got you to go to Atmosphere for goodness' sakes. I'm surprised he didn't charm you onto the go-go stage.

SAL: It didn't go that far. He does have a magnetic personality, though. It's no wonder he's become so popular.

GERTRUDE: Oh, this old girl just needed to see his jawline and she knew he'd be *very* popular.

SAL: (pause) I'm worried about him.

GERTRUDE: Is he sick?

SAL: No, he... he wrote me a letter. It was very deliberate, thought out. I think he's coming to the edge of himself.

GERTRUDE: The edge?

SAL: You know that place when who we are – or thought we are – disappears.

Gertrude takes a deep breath. She hesitates a moment before responding.

GERTRUDE: When George died, I'd hear them whispering behind my back at church. The people I called friends...

SAL: After Arnie died and you found me and brought me back. That moment. When I cried on Bryn Mawr. I think he's there. He's seeing the world differently.

GERTRUDE: Isn't that a good thing? I think my life got considerably easier when I let that tide roll in.

SAL: It is better. But it's not easy. I haven't heard from him in a long time. I wonder why he doesn't talk to his friends about this...

GERTRUDE: Maybe he doesn't have any. I didn't. (pause) You know ten years ago we saw gays pile in here every week. They'd go through friends like tissues. The boys here today have the advantage in that respect. They have each other. Sometimes being surrounded by smiles doesn't mean you can look to a single friendly face.

SAL: I should call him.

GERTRUDE: You should. (glancing at her watch) And speaking of should, Clive is going to be off-duty soon, we should go collect him.

Sal shuffles toward his bedroom. The door closes softly behind him. Gertrude walks into the dining room.

CUT TO:

INT. DINING ROOM - AFTERNOON

Gertrude stands by the table. She watches the single shirt dance in the wind. Around the table the plates of leftover food are covered in paper towels. Flies are beginning to buzz around them. The buzzing builds to a single tone, swelling in intensity. The background of Sal's apartment goes dark, and Gertrude stands before three images of her life, projecting behind her. The tone stops as the images become clear.

DEEP FOCUS. WE SEE THREE DISTINCT IMAGES OF GERTRUDE'S PAST, PRESENT, AND FUTURE.

EXT. CHURCH – DAY – 1985

We see Gertrude in her car. She takes a deep breath, her hands gripping the steering wheel. She sits still for a moment before digging into her purse and pulling out a compact mirror. Distractedly, she looks at herself. She touches up her mascara and puckers her lips. Once she is satisfied, she puts the small mirror back in her purse and again sits still. We see her bend her head over and mutter a prayer before pushing open the door and rapidly getting out of the car. The world spins for a moment as she gains her balance on her heels. Others are staring at her: couples near their cars, children who had been playing, a line of individuals who are about to enter the church. Gertrude falters for a moment. She takes a step back toward the car. It is silent except for a light wind and the uncertain clack of her heels. Her hand is on the car door. She lowers her head and again mouths a prayer. Small tears in her eyes, she turns toward the church. She slowly and methodically walks toward the building. The unfriendly gazes of everyone around her following each step she takes.

INT. GERTRUDE'S BEDROOM – DAY

Gertrude is digging through her closet as a Katy Perry song blasts in the background. She throws up scarf after scarf before exalting when she finds a garish, sequin one. She exits the closet and enters her bedroom where her young grandson dances with wild abandon. Gertrude throws the scarf around him and they dance together. Sal enters the room and laughs loudly at the scene. He joins them, awkwardly and erratically moving to the music.

EXT. BEACH – DAY – FUTURE

Sal and Gertrude sit in chairs, viewing a wedding. They gently squeeze each other's hands. Tears drip down Gertrude's face as she looks to the front of the ceremony and the two men whom everyone has come to celebrate. One of the men, her grandson, now grown, turns toward his grandmother and smiles.

THE IMAGES FADE.

INT. SAL'S DINING ROOM – AFTERNOON – PRESENT

Sal re-enters the room, ready to leave.

SAL: Are we ready?

GERTRUDE: We are. Let's collect Clive, drop off his dog, and go see the hunks strut down Halsted.

SAL: Does your nephew know that you probably have the same taste in men?

GERTRUDE: He's a bit too young. But you can bet his grannie will take him to the next Captain America movie.

Sal heads to the door. Gertrude takes one more moment in the dining room. She traces a hand over the table and smiles to herself.

SAL: Hurry up, slow poke!

GERTRUDE: I was just thinking about old times…

SAL: Well, let's forget those and think about the new ones. I'm sure Clive has a lot to tell us from his shift today.

SCENE VIII – THE SOUTH END OF THE WORLD

FADE IN:

INT. THE DRAM SHOP – AFTERNOON

We are in a dive bar with dim lights. It is one long room with the bar extending along the north wall. Aside from two bar flies, it is empty except for the group coming from Sal's. David, Terrance, and Sasha order drinks at the bar. Alan and Kent are huddled alone near the jukebox in the back corner. Everyone has slipped into varying states of drunkenness.

DAVID: I can't believe you skipped Sal's for a hookup. Was it at least good?

TERRANCE: (laughing) No. He was super weird. He put on porn and then wouldn't take off his pants. We just ended up watching two jocks blow each other for a while. I jerked off myself and left.

SASHA: He didn't even want to make out? He just… sat there?

TERRANCE: Yup. He wasn't as cute as his picture, though, so it was kind of a relief. Terrance shrugs his shoulders. David grows agitated. He runs his hands through his hair.

DAVID: Dating is the fucking worst! People are terrible and dating is terrible, and it's just a fucking mess.

TERRANCE: That is why you should stop wasting time and just text the Frank guy.

SASHA: Agreed!

Sasha clinks his beer can against Terrance's glass.

DAVID: I think I need about three more drinks before I decide on the Frank question.

SASHA: Bartender! Three more drinks for this guy.

David and Terrance laugh hysterically.

The moment of mirth is interrupted by hollering coming from the doorway. George Anderson and Jack Freeman are entering the bar. They bound in together, hand-in-hand.

JACK: How are you boys?

GEORGE: We appreciated the text, Sasha.

SASHA: We needed to add some life to the party. We were out all night and are losing steam.

JACK: Well, we need some excitement, too. We were just at the beach watching The Set hold court.

GEORGE: It was a snoozefest.

FLASHBACK TO:

EXT. HOLLYWOOD BEACH – DAY – EARLIER THAT AFTERNOON

Our perspective never settles but spins quickly toward the north, east, south, and west. In all directions we see gay men of all varieties: slim, young twinks, large, burly bears, and all body types inbetween. A cacophony of laughter, music, and shouting fills the air. The Set is visible close to the water; they stand at odd intervals. Although they are speaking to others, all of them carry an air of distraction, looking to the horizon, back to the beach, down at their feet, not focusing on anything for long.

CUT BACK TO:

INT. THE DRAM SHOP – AFTERNOON

JACK: Odd choice for a bar, but I like it.

DAVID: We decided to start at the southern end of Halsted and then make our way up to the festival.

SASHA: What he's saying is we're hungover and not quite ready for the full festival yet.

GEORGE: Understandable.

As Jack and George order from the bartender, Terrance tips his glass toward Jack.

TERRANCE: Jack, is Hedley speaking to you after your article?

JACK: I don't think he gave a fuck about it. He does wave to me at parties now, so that's a thing. (pause) The weirdest thing to come from that was Jordan Barker starting to write for The Windy City Times with me. He said my article "inspired him."

DAVID: That guy is such a dud. I wouldn't read his signature, for what it's worth.

JACK: He's working on a book about Boystown. He says he needs to be on the front lines.

GEORGE: Jordan's going to beat you to the publisher, Jacky.

JACK: He let me read the first few pages – it's…pretentious.

DAVID: Like I said, a dud.

SASHA: How about we all do a shot to celebrate – whatever. It doesn't matter. I'm getting shots.

They are interrupted by a ruckus heard from the entry to the bar.

The Set enters followed by Lawrence Soot and Lloyd. The pace of the scene slows as David and Sasha assess the effect of Lloyd's appearance on Terrance. Sasha shoves Jack and George in front of him and pulls David close. He then forces Terrance to sit next to one of the bar flies so that he is blocked completely from view.

DAVID: Status, Terrance?

TERRANCE: Fine. But let's get some air.

David and Terrance skulk toward the back. There is an emergency exit they push open. Lloyd hears the door slam shut and throws an anxious look to the back of the bar, just missing their escape.

Sasha takes a sip of his beer and winks at Jack and George.

SASHAL: I feel like Market Days drama is rising from a soft five to a frantic ten.

JACK: (poking George) This would be such a great short story.

GEORGE: How handsome would you make me in it?

SASHA: (playfully slapping them both) Can y'all take a chill pill? You're almost as disgusting as Alan and Kent.

CUT TO:

EXT. THE DRAM SHOP – AFTERNOON

David and Terrance stand in a fenced-in blacktop. Both look anxiously at the back door.

DAVID: I bet we can use those crates…

David picks up some plastic crates from a pile and builds a makeshift tower. Terrance climbs up and over the fence and lands in an alleyway on the other side. We see from Terrance's perspective as David follows behind him. He awkwardly straddles the fence before collapsing in a heap in the alley. Terrance tries to stifle laughter as he helps him up.

TERRANCE: I'm telling you, not as an aesthetic critique, but you need to get some flexibility at the gym, Jenkins.

Terrance helps David dust himself off as they both laugh. Terrance relaxes.

DAVID: Jesus, that was close. How in the hell does The Set show up at the fucking Dram Shop?

Terrance smiles to himself.

TERRANCE: You really think it's random?

DAVID: Yeah, like the most random.

TERRANCE: (chuckling) You didn't check Twitter?

DAVID: I don't anymore. The Boystown account has been so sporadic lately, I haven't bothered.

TERRANCE: It's back online. It said I was here.

David rips his phone from his pocket. In a few clicks he is on the Boystown feed. His eyes scan quickly.

TWEET:
Terrance returns: it looks to be less than triumphant. Is he awaiting a new prince or the old? #lonelyheartatthedramshop

David stares intently down the alley.

TERRANCE: It was only us there.

DAVID: Right – so that means…

TERRANCE: Do you need some more help?

DAVID: Fuck. (looking at Terrance, shocked) You?!

TERRANCE: Me.

David shakes his head. He whistles.

DAVID: That explains why it has been disappearing this summer… But (pause) you released your own breakup news… You…

TERRANCE: Cognitive dissonance. I could know without knowing. It's fucked up.

DAVID: I'd say fascinating, actually.

TERRANCE: My life was getting more and more partitioned. I was seeing and not believing; things I accepted as facts were proven to all be lies.

DAVID: Can we stop with the vagaries?

TERRANCE: (taking a deep breath) At first Lloyd was kind. He was sweet. But even six or seven months in I knew it was getting bad. But it was what I wanted… What I thought I wanted.

DAVID: Hot guy from a good family.

TERRANCE: Right, and you know my past – you know I was actually beat up before, so when Lloyd would disappear for hours, when he'd come home smelling like some other guy…

DAVID: You were always thinking it could be worse.

TERRANCE: It could be way worse. Lloyd was good to me. There was some cheating, but he said nice things. He kept moving forward with our relationship, with me. It never felt separate. When the wedding happened, that's when it got bad, you know? I was heading toward the best day of life with the best-looking guy I had ever met, and still I felt conflicted. Half of me wanted it so desperately, but this deeper part – what I've come to know is the right part – was fighting against it with everything I had.

DAVID: Shit… Is that when your Twitter started?

TERRANCE: After the honeymoon it got way worse. Lloyd would go out with "friends." On weeknights he'd come back after one in the morning. He'd smell like booze. He'd smell like boys. So, I started to go with him. I got involved. People started texting me. I was never the drunk one. I was always the voice of reason, so they'd let me know the plans, the details, the gossip. I started to morph into this hub of information. Even The Set would text me – they trusted me.

DAVID: And you turned it into the most watched account in Lake View.

TERRANCE: It was more than that. When Stephen would text me at eleven on a weeknight about he and Lloyd being out at Progress, I knew what was happening. But I couldn't tell myself the truth, right? So I started telling everyone else. The account became a protection, another Terrance, the one who was plunged in the drama of it all.

DAVID: Shit… I would never have guessed.

404

TERRANCE: It doesn't fucking matter anymore. That was the last one I wanted to send out.

DAVID: Why?

TERRANCE: I wanted to see if he'd come... I wanted to know if he thought I was unhappy if he would come.

DAVID: And he did.

TERRANCE: He did.

Both men look away from each other to the end of the alleyway.

DAVID: So... What does that mean? He showed up.

TERRANCE: He cares. That's what I wanted to see. I needed to know if anything was real. I looked for the same thing the night I left... Fuck, I was two different people while we were together. I don't even know if I was real – who I was.

FLASHBACK TO:

INT. DR. KONSTANTIN'S OFFICE – DAY – EARLIER THAT SUMMER

Dr. Konstantin is seated in his leather seat. He sighs.

DR. KONSTANTIN: David, over the next week or so, I want you to parcel out those moments – deconstruct them. Look at the emotion inside of them and put them into perspective. How did Jonathan influence those events? Even in the dark times. Even in those moments when you were at the bottom, thinking about cutting yourself, causing a scene – where was he?

CUT BACK TO:

EXT. THE DRAM SHOP - AFTERNOON

DAVID: Sometimes you have to look back and not just see him but see yourself. I've been doing that a lot with my memories of Jonathan lately.

TERRANCE: Seeing myself... Seeing that whole mess would be really something.

The two men laugh and then lean in for a hug.

TERRANCE: Earlier this summer when I told you about doing the open relationship, that was the low point. That was me dividing further. It wasn't just Terrance and Twitter Terrance. It was Terrance, and Twitter Terrance, and anyone Lloyd wanted me to be.

DAVID: Grindr Whore Terrance? (pause) So what broke the Terrance photocopier?

TERRANCE: I honestly couldn't tell you. Time. That's the best thing I can say.

DAVID: Time. I think I've been finding out the same thing.

There is a loud jolt in front of them. Jack has tripped on the corner of a dumpster. He, Sasha, and George are coming toward them from the other end of the alley.

JACK: Oooooh! Did we interrupt a romantic moment?

DAVID: Yes, we were just heading behind the dumpster to trade BJs.

GEORGE: Romance really is everywhere on Market Days.

SASHA: Now that we've successfully escaped, I think it may be time to go to the festival. I am shit faced for the second day in a row, so I probably have one more hour before I just collapse in a heap. Time to see the gay garbage swept up and down Halsted.

TERRANCE: Well, let's go party!

Terrance bounds away from the small group down the alley and toward the street. Jack, George, and Sasha follow closely behind.

David stays behind for a moment. He hesitates then opens his phone. We see him scroll down his contact list.

PHONE SCREEN:
Edgar
Finnegan's Bar
Fiona
Frank

We see him select the Frank contact then quickly type.

MESSAGE:
David: *Hey.*

CUT TO:

INT. DRAM SHOP – AFTERNOON

Alan and Kent are now speaking with Hedley, Soot, and Lloyd. They are discussing trivial matters and cackling loudly. Lloyd looks half engaged, tittering at a joke but then looking away quickly to scan the bar.

From the far end of the bar, Samson and Stephen sip on vodka sodas. They watch the scene unfold passively.

SAMSON: I think this may be one of the last times.

STEPHEN: (looking at Hedley) He knows.

SAMSON: What are you and Mikey doing later?

STEPHEN: I'm going to go with you all to the fest then head over to his place for a movie.

SAMSON: How boring.

STEPHEN: Thanks for noticing. And what's your agenda?

SAMSON: Some boys from Fort Lauderdale are in town. Every year they get a few hotel rooms downtown and it's a free-for-all. We do some lines, take some poppers… There's a big party in this abandoned factory near Fulton Market.

STEPHEN: You know in the end it all makes sense, you parading off to fucking adventures and me finding the youth pastor to play board games with.

SAMSON: And Skyler heading off to his geriatric boyfriend.

STEPHEN: …And so the fellowship breaks.

Both men are silent for a time. They look fondly across the bar at Hedley.

SAMSON: I'll stick around for a while. We owe that to Hedley. He's a good guy. I was there when he started this thing, so I feel like I should be there at the end.

STEPHEN: He'll land on his feet. He probably has a shortlist of twenty to replace us.

SAMSON: I don't think so. He's getting tired of it himself. This may be an excuse for him to move on – retire, if you will.

STEPHEN: (raising his glass) To The Set. May we prosper from places outside the limelight.

They clink glasses.

The scene then splits, both men moving to the sides of our field of vision while the bar around them fades to black. Before us, two groups of images project, one of each man's past, present, and future, extending into the darkness.

DEEP FOCUS. WE SEE SIX DISTINCT IMAGES OF SAMSON'S AND STEPHEN'S HISTORIES.

SAMSON'S BEDROOM – DAY – 2000

Samson sits alone in his bedroom. His face has a blank expression; it is bruised. There is a soft knock on his door. He begins to breathe heavier. A second knock comes and he starts to shake. He closes his eyes to compose himself as we hear the door open in the background.

CHURCH SANCTUARY – MORNING – 2000

Stephen is seated in church. His attention is fixated on his father, who preaches dramatically from the pulpit. The light is golden, illuminating the blood-red sanctuary as if it is afire. There is a sudden tremor and we see an apparition of Davey smiling at the front of the church. The image fades quickly. Stephen's expression changes. He is nervous, sweat trickling down his brow. The ghostly image appears again. This time it is the memory of Davey on top of him, wrestling. Stephen blinks and it is gone. He sits shaken in the church pew. His mother gently leans over and whispers something in his ear.

UNKNOWN HOME – NIGHT – 2015

We are in the living room of a house. A sliver of light spills from an adjoining room. The sounds of sex pour from the cracked door. Behind us, another door opens. We turn and see Samson come from the bathroom. He is nude. Just as he approaches the half-open door leading to the orgy, a man exits. He smiles broadly when he sees Samson and pulls him into a deep kiss. As their lips part, the man shoves Samson through the door.

HYDRATE BAR – NIGHT – 2015

Stephen is dancing with The Set. The lights are dim, lasers cut through the dark as a disco ball spins. Laughing, Stephen moves away from his friend group and walks through a curtain to the main bar. He pulls out his wallet and is tapping his credit card on the top of the bar. He looks up and sees Mikey across the way. Mikey is dressed in an oddly formal way, a button up tucked into pleated pants. Stephen is momentarily entranced. The bartender asks for his order. Stephen looks passed him and stares again at Mikey. Mikey looks up and sees Stephen for the first time. They share a shy smile. Stephen hesitates for just a moment before waving the bartender away. He walks toward Mikey.

SOUNDSTAGE – DAY – FUTURE

Samson is sitting in a chair in the middle of a stage. He has a huge smile on his face. Behind him is a scene of the Parisian skyline. He is flanked by two muscled men. The lights go out but instantly come back on. Samson is still seated, but the background has changed to New York. The muscled men are replaced by beautiful, androgynous beings flanking him on both sides. The lights flash again. Now he is in front of a scene of London. Two handsome, athletic men are beside him. We move closer to his face. The lights continue to flash with new scenes behind him: Tokyo, Moscow, Florence, Chicago, San Francisco...

OUTSIDE OF STEPHEN'S PARENTS' HOME – DAY – FUTURE

Stephen stands hand-in-hand with Mikey. Stephen looks nervously at Mikey as he raises his hand to knock on the door. They both stand in uncertain anticipation. Mikey turns to Stephen and mouths "I love you." Stephen smiles and squeezes Mikey's hand. The door to the house opens. Stephen's mother and father stand in the doorway, looks of judgment on their faces.

THE IMAGES FADE.

EXT. HALSTED AND BELMONT INTERSECTION – EVENING – 2015

David and company have arrived at the festival. The scene is chaos and revelry. A line of gays in varying wardrobes, from short shorts and vests, to drag queens in full regalia, sprawl out of the tent that serves as the entry point to the festival. The thumping rhythm of the bandstand rings in everyone's ears as laughter fills the air.

Sasha, Terrance, Jack, and George push through the line to pay for their entry to the festival.

David stops briefly. He takes in the moment, looking around at all the excited men and women around him. He smiles to himself. Just before he gets to the entry point his phone buzzes. Surprised, he pulls it out of his pocket.

MESSAGE:
Frank: *Well, hey to you. I'm at Market Days on something of a date.*

The money collector at the gate looks annoyed as David giggles to himself and types out a response.

MESSAGE:
David: *Don't be. Tell me where to find you.*

Act III

SCENE IX: A TOUCH OF EVIL

FADE IN:

EXT. HALSTED AND BELMONT INTERSECTION – EVENING

Hedley is not far behind David at the entry tent to the festival. Lloyd, in an effort to escape the disappointment of the almost-encounter with Terrance, has drunk himself into a stupor. He is led by Kent and Alan toward the festival money collector. Soot bobs along beside them, examining his complexion in his phone screen.

KENT: You're going to have to pull it together, Lloyd. You can't be this drunk.

LLOYD: I'll be – fin. Fine.

Lloyd shuffles forward, reaching into his pocket and fruitlessly digging for his wallet. Samson and Stephen are huddled together, whispering. Hedley sees them together and intuits their desire to leave the group.

HEDLEY: You boys going to escape early?

STEPHEN: I – I mean, we're going to stay – we're going to be around…

HEDLEY: Don't apologize. Go forth, I'm actually going to take a detour. I may not make it out myself.

SAMSON: Oh! Hedley, did you and your model make up? Are you going to have some fun and a fuck back home?

HEDLEY: Something like that.

Quietly, Hedley turns from the group and proceeds down Belmont. Soot jumps to life as Hedley melts into the shadows.

SOOT: Hedley? Hedley? Are you going to join up later? You are coming back, yes?

STEPHEN: He'll be back. (turning to see Lloyd being lectured by a security guard) Oh, shit.

The security guard returns a twenty-dollar bill to Lloyd's hand and points him to the exit. Alan and Kent rush over and put their arms around him.

ALAN: We can walk him home.

Soot joins them. He shakes his head.

SOOT: No, my boys, you go in and enjoy! I'll walk our little tippler back to his abode. I have some other business to attend to, anyway. I'll see you all out at the festival in a bit!

Lloyd growls as Soot gently gives him his arm and helps him step away from the entry tent.

CUT TO:

INT. DINER – NIGHT

Clive, Gertrude, and Sal sit together, sipping cups of coffee. They have just shared a joke and are all shaking with laughter. Gertrude wipes a tear from her eye.

GERTRUDE: That I wouldn't want to see. Although, there are some I wouldn't mind seeing in a jockstrap.

CLIVE: Well, you won't have to worry about it. I politely declined the invitation to the locker room party, even if it was for a good cause.

SAL: A better cause is you not being in a jockstrap.

CLIVE: That is something we can all agree on.

The three friends clink coffee mugs together. Gertrude discreetly looks at her watch.

GERTRUDE: Oh my. It's time for this old bird to head home. A few hours of mimosas and walking in crowded streets is too much excitement for one day.

She digs through her purse and pulls out a small comb. Violently, she plunges it into her dyed, blonde hair and teases out her wiry locks. When she is satisfied, she replaces the comb and pulls out lipstick.

CLIVE: Home? (pointing to her lipstick) From this little display, I'd say you were going to meet a boyfriend.

GERTRUDE: Please, I haven't had a boyfriend since the 60's. I prefer the company of you old codgers. Less work.

She stands and Clive follows, his great weight requiring effort to pull himself out of the booth.

CLIVE: I need to get home to the dog. You want to split a cab, Sal?

SAL: No, I think I may actually take another lap out at the festival. I love the live music, and I never get out to hear it.

GERTRUDE: If you want to call that caterwauling music then Godspeed, Mr. Henry.

Gertrude leans over and kisses Sal lightly on the cheek. Clive roars with laughter, pointing at the lipstick mark that has appeared on Sal's face.

CLIVE: She left a mess, Sal, just so you know.

GERTRUDE: Consider it a souvenir!

Clive and Gertrude both throw bills on the table and walk away, still laughing.

SAL: Good-bye!

When the door to the diner has closed behind them, Sal sighs and wraps both hands around his cup of coffee. He looks to the window and takes in the pedestrians walking by.

DISSOLVE:

FADE IN:

INT. BAR – NIGHT – 1970

Arnie enters the bar in his open dress shirt, his chest hair visible. It is silent but we watch as he takes a seat across from Sal. He winks. Gently, he reaches across the table and squeezes Sal's hand.

DISSOLVE:

EXT. SAL'S BACK ALLEY – DUSK – 1995

Gertrude and Sal sit in chairs looking down the alley at the horizon. Gertrude's hair has its first strands of white. Her dress blows lightly in the summer wind.

DISSOLVE:

INT. HOSPITAL – NIGHT – 1984

The beds are barely illuminated around Sal. He sits, reading a book, as Arnie sleeps. Bea, the nurse, approaches him and pats his back. She moves away into the dark.

FADE OUT:

FADE IN:

INT. DINER – NIGHT – 2015

Sal is silent, his eyes unfocused. We hold our gaze on him for a few beats longer than comfortable. Sal finally awakes from his stupor and pats his pockets, looking for a pen. When he finds one, he pulls a napkin from the dispenser and begins to write. In the background, the diner door rings indicating someone has entered. As we hold our attention on Sal, from behind, we hear the pop of the plastic booth signifying the arrival of the mysterious newcomer. Sal finishes writing a line on the napkin and then lifts his gaze. A warm smile spreads over his features. His eyes twinkle.

Hedley sits across from him.

SAL: I didn't know if you'd come.

HEDLEY: I didn't know either. Did I miss Gertrude and Clive?

SAL: Yes. Those old fogeys have gone to bed.

HEDLEY: A good rest sounds wonderful.

A waiter approaches the table. Hedley motions that he wants a cup of coffee. For the first time, we see Hedley at ease. He haphazardly wrings his hands. The tight control he has maintained prior to this moment is slipping away. He appears almost childlike.

HEDLEY (continued): You're writing? That looks like the beginning of a poem.

SAL: I was inspired. It's been a very long time since I've wanted to write anything.

Hedley stops wringing his hands and leans back in the booth.

HEDLEY: You got my letter?

SAL: I did. I was digesting it. It had a lot of content.

HEDLEY: I tried…I tried to organize them, the thoughts. I've always been good about organizing everything – in high school I kept a journal, you know – and then later I'd write thoughts, pages, manifestos… self-indulgences.

SAL: What about?

HEDLEY: How I saw the world. What I wanted to do… What I wanted to – to conquer, I suppose.

The waiter returns and sets coffee in front of Hedley. Hedley looks up and nods in thanks. His mouth tremors, but he stops short of forming words. Instead, he gazes down and begins to draw lines aimlessly on the table with his finger.

SAL: I think the letter was very organized.

HEDLEY: (not hearing him) Do you remember the first time we met?

SAL: I do. We ended up at the go-go bar as I recall.

HEDLEY: I was so sure then, Sal. I was sure of so much. I thought I knew things. In a moral way, if that makes sense. I was driven; it was vocation; it was right.

SAL: What was?

HEDLEY: The plan. The plan to make something of myself. Hank Turner from Kokomo was going to do great things. I had seen... (pause) I had understood what I was supposed to do...

There is a moment of silence. Sal sits quietly staring forward. Hedley looks down in defeat.

HEDLEY (continued): When I met you that night I thought I finally understood how it all worked, how to control it to some positive end. But it got so corrupted. It was never good – it was always broken. And it ran away with me.

SAL: I don't think it was never good. I don't think a thing can ever be truly bad if you look at it from all sides.

Hedley sighs. He looks up and holds Sal's gaze for a moment before his eyes fall on the table again.

HEDLEY: I wrote to you, and I told you how things were different now.

SAL: You did.

HEDLEY: At the beginning of this summer I went home and I saw my family. I don't see them often – my sister, her children. But we all were on the back porch. It was a Sunday afternoon. My grandma was sitting with a glass of iced tea, and my brother-in-law and the kids were playing out in the backyard. (pause) I had been inside, on the phone – constantly on the fucking phone – making plans with Samson, Stephen, and Skyler for the next evening. I came outside and sat next to my grandma. My mother and father were down by the pond getting out fishing equipment. And –

Hedley stops. His voice catches. Sal looks on patiently.

The entire diner is quiet. A soft clattering is heard from beyond swinging double doors to the kitchen, but it does not break the peace.

HEDLEY (continued): Sal, it was an incredible moment. It was this tiny piece of perfection. (his face relaxes and he leans back) Then it started. It was a flood of memories. Some part of my brain had been closed off, but the stone rolled away, and I remembered those days, like that. I was six, in shorts with no shirt, running through the dandelions, kicking up their white seeds. I remembered rolling in the backyard in fall leaves and the crispness of the air. I saw the Christmas lights blinking on the house, then in a moment, I was sledding down that hill in the backyard and skittering across the frozen pond in my toboggan. I remembered the taste of apple cider, the sound of the grass in our Easter baskets, the coarse fabric of the suit I wore going to church…

Hedley stops abruptly. His breath shaking, he wipes a tear from his eye.

SAL: You remembered home. You saw through the cracks of life to something larger…

HEDLEY: (smiling) Yes. I had been working so hard to build this world, to control, to guide what others think and know. I left all the life out of it. In that silent moment outside, I… felt. I felt so much. And for the first time (pausing briefly, choked with emotion) I looked at my nieces and nephews and wanted to give that gift – that life – to someone else.

He stops, fully. Sal also is growing emotional, his eyes beginning to sparkle with dewy tears. Neither can say a word. There is a moment of uncertain silence before
Sal reaches over and grips Hedley's hand.

There is an explosive light that shines from their joint hands. Our vision is only whiteness. Slowly, the frozen portrait of Sal and Hedley comes back into focus. Along with them are scenes from their lives extending from the foreground, into the distance – Hedley and Sal resolutely in the center of the images.

DEEP FOCUS. WE SEE THREE DISTINCT IMAGES OF SAL AND HEDLEY'S PAST, PRESENT, AND FUTURE.

SAL'S HOME – NIGHT – 1960

Sal's hands tremble as he sets down his keys on an entry table. Arnie enters the apartment behind him. Arnie moves past Sal and enters the living room. Adoringly, he walks by the shelves of books. He lovingly runs a hand over their spines. Sal stands awkwardly watching Arnie. Arnie takes out a single book and flips through its pages. Sal watches with rapt attention. Arnie snaps the book closed and looks toward Sal. Sal tenses, turning his attention out of the room. His lips tremble as if words will form, but he is too nervous to speak. Slowly, Arnie moves across the living room and approaches Sal. He reaches out and strokes Sal's cheek. Sal calms. Arnie gently leans in and places his lips on Sal's.

HEDLEY'S PARENTS' HOME – DAY – 2004

Hedley and Myrtle have just finished discussing something. She leans in and gives him a long hug. When she pulls away she is laughing. Joyfully, she bounds away from Hedley and disappears from view. Hedley turns and looks toward Cedric, who stands surrounded by a group of Hedley's friends. Hedley's expression is pure love and adulation. Hedley's mother brings out a soda and hands it to Cedric. He takes it and thanks her profusely. When she has left, Cedric turns and waves at Hedley; he blows him a kiss.

HOSPITAL – MORNING – 1984

Sal stands by Arnie's bed. Bea gently lifts a sheet over his lover's face. There is a prolonged silence. Sal does not move. He reaches out to touch the body but stops short. He pulls his hand back and looks on in silence. Slowly, he turns to leave. He paces towards the door but stops. Turning back, he marches to the bed and extends his hand outward. The hand falls short of making contact with the body. Sal puts his hand to his mouth. Bea stands beside him. Gently, she takes his hand and leads him to the side of the bed. She sits him in a chair and pulls Arnie's hand from beneath the sheet. She places their hands together and squeezes. Sal looks at their linked hands and nothing else. Bea quietly leaves the room.

HEDLEY'S APARTMENT – NIGHT - 2010

Hedley is manic. He paces frantically around his small studio wringing his hands. Against one wall he has pictures of men displayed with descriptions written next to them. It looks like a murder investigation. Hedley assesses the wall and then runs to his desk where he scribbles down notes. He returns to the wall and looks at all the men. He pulls a few photos down and discards them. A photo of Samson is one of the few remaining pictures. Hedley rushes back toward the desk and scribbles down another line in his book. He suddenly pauses and relaxes. When he turns, it is toward a wall with a mirror. He looks at himself in profile for a long moment. Slowly we see changes spread over his features and body: he stands more erect, his face pulls into a blank, serene stare, he pushes his hair away from his face. When he turns away from the mirror, there is nothing of the manic man that first appeared in the scene. He looks resolutely forward and locks his gaze on the photo of Samson.

NEAR HOLLYWOOD BEACH, CHICAGO – FUTURE

It is twilight. Clive is standing before a group of gay men, including Sasha, Edward, David, and Al. All the men look older and grayer than we have seen them previously. We hear half-phrases, silent muttering. They laugh quietly. Clive has tears in his eyes. Edward holds Sasha, who chokes on sobs between laughter. For a moment they are silent. We watch them from far away, five men gathered on the edge of Lake Michigan. David bends down and turns on a speaker which begins to softly play "How Will I Know?" Again, soft laughter is heard. It is mixed with sniffling; Al takes out a handkerchief and wipes his eyes. As the music plays, Clive leans over and picks up an urn. It is silver and shines in the last light of the day. He takes off the top. With a quick look to the group, he smiles and dumps the ashes into the lake. When it has been emptied, he stands motionlessly. There is a brief moment of silence before he is wracked with sobs. First David, then the rest of the men, come forward. They place their hands on Clive's back. All stand still before Clive turns and pulls the men into a group embrace. We drift far away, atop the water of the lake, watching ashes dissolve, the men standing, holding one another.

RUSH MEDICAL CENTER – FUTURE

Hedley runs into the hospital. His polished shoes clack on the tiled floors. Frantically, he runs to the nurse's station and is directed to an elevator. A few moments later, we see the elevator doors open and Hedley is inside. He places one hand on the doors to stop them from closing. The other hand he puts on his heart. Sheer terror rests on his face before being replaced with a flash of a smile. Once he has his breath, he bounds down the hallway. He glances at room numbers as he sprints by. Finally, he pauses outside one of the rooms. About to enter, he hesitates and steps back; he runs a hand through his hair. With a final look of resolve, he enters the hospital room. Inside our view is blurred, distorted. We see a woman in a bed, and next to it, a bassinet. Hedley walks to the bassinet. We see his face peer over the side. The look is one of childlike wonder, eyes wide, expression earnest. His hand moves forward and delicately caresses the baby in its bed. A man approaches Hedley from the side of the room. He embraces him and kisses his cheek. He then lifts the child and puts it in Hedley's arms. Hedley is shocked at first but then relaxes. The man, still not fully visible, gently adjusts the blanket around the baby. Both men, both fathers, look on their child with wonder.

THE IMAGES FADE.

INT. DINER – NIGHT – 2015

Sal squeezes Hedley's hand. Hedley still looks youthful, lost in his own revelations. Sal is smiling broadly.

HEDLEY: Sal, I don't know what I'm going to do next. I tried for years to forget the past, to ignore it, to pretend it had no function. And now it's the source of my pain… and my hopes. (laughing) It's fucked. It's absolutely fucked.

Sal laughs along with him. Slowly his face relaxes. Resolve and understanding cross his features. He drops Hedley's hand and clasps his own together. He doesn't make eye contact with Hedley but begins to speak.

SAL: In all of this – the pain, the memories, the muddle – there is a need, a deep desire in all of us to destroy the past, to move on from it, break free from it. But that can never really be. The past molds us, shapes us, gives us the framework we have to live in.

FLASHBACK TO:

INT. HOSPITAL – DAY – 1983

Lola stands in front of her son's bed. Her arms are bruised, tears stain her cheeks. Sal is sitting beside Arnie, who struggles for breath. From the shadows we see the eyes of Eugene. He watches, despair written on his features.

CUT BACK TO:

INT. DINER – NIGHT – 2015

Sal is still not looking at Hedley. Emotion is creeping into his voice.

SAL: I think you know I studied literature and poetry in my younger years. The old poets, the Alexander Popes, the Shakespeares, the Marlowes, they moved within a set group of rules: iambs, soliloquys, free verse, heroic couplets. But within those limits they were able to explore infinite, unfathomable truths about the human condition. And I've come to truly believe that is how it should be with our lives, tethered to a place in history, fighting and overcoming our parents' influence, our social prejudice, our chaos… We cannot escape who our lives have made us, but we can look to the possibilities our history imposes on us. (pause) Hedley, who we are is the sum of who we have been, but who we become… (reaching for Hedley's hand and looking into his eyes) Who we become we decide every moment we live. We are restricted but it isn't hopeless – nothing is. It's a boundary we push, we expand. Keep looking back to that moment at your parents' home this summer. Remember the leaves, the cider, and the snow, and from that build the life you want. Expand your world to what you need. You've hidden in a cave for long enough. You tried to give other people what they wanted, what you thought would bring you the adulation you needed to survive. But now it's time to embrace your whole self and create something new.

Hedley's gaze falls to the table. It is silent for a moment. Even the clattering from the kitchen has ceased. After a few seconds, Hedley perfunctorily opens his mouth to speak. He closes it as he realizes the power of the silence. Tears fall from his eyes. Abruptly, he pushes away the mug of coffee and stands. He does not leave the diner, but, instead, remains motionless near the table. Sal looks up at him, surprised. Uncertainly, he climbs from the booth. Sal has barely stood when Hedley pulls him close. A vice-like grip encircles the old man. Hedley buries his face in Sal's shoulder. It is not long before Hedley begins to shake. Sobs wrack his body as tears pour down his cheeks.

SCENE X: A TOUCH OF GOSPEL

FADE IN:

EXT. HALSTED STREET – NIGHT

The scene of the Market Days festival is an exuberant explosion. David spins within the crowd, looking at all the varieties of men and women gathered. To his left a man in leather has another gentleman pressed against a food tent. Beside them a lesbian in a basketball jersey dances wildly with a trans woman with thick, curled hair. Music booms in the distance, a mash of techno, pop, bass, and synthesizers. David looks right and sees a number of men, shirtless and decorated with flash tattoos glimmering in the lights. Behind them, a group of preppy gays wear polos and shake their heads, judging everyone. In the windows of bars, gays gyrate to the sounds of the city.

David is with Sasha, Terrance, Jack, and George. He follows the group at a distance, taking in the chaos of the street. Strangers bodies press against him. His senses are overwhelmed by the lights, screams, and smells assaulting him as he walks by art booths and food vendors.

An older gentleman stops him. He winks then reaches around and slaps David's butt.

OLDER GAY: Hey, sweetie.

David awkwardly laughs as he scurries to catch up with Sasha. All around he sees familiar faces, people from the past, from parties, from the gala, and others who seem vaguely familiar.

DAVID: Is it even worth finding Donnie and Tibbs? The line at Sidetrack will be awful.

SASHA: I think Terrance wants to. He's looking for one more Market Days dick, I think.

David laughs. Terrance turns and raises an eyebrow.

TERRANCE: My ears are burning. (to David) Status, Jenkins? You too drunk for this? Despite what Sasha says. I could head home.

David puts his hand to his ear. He can't hear anything as a speaker has boomed to life beside them. He shrugs his shoulders and points ahead to Jack and George, who are pushing their way to closer to Sidetrack.

As they resume their march, David turns and sees Jonathan. His face registers shock as he takes in his ex-lover bedecked in a leather jockstrap and studded harness. Jonathan's body glistens in the dark. The man he is with is pumped full of some form of hormones or steroids. His salt-n-pepper hair sparks like glitter in the dark. He runs his tongue over his lips as he gyrates on Jonathan.

David's breath slows. The noises around him dull. He focuses on Jonathan, then turns and stares at the muscular man who is dancing with him. David puts his hands to his head. He closes his eyes. The only sound is the lub-dub of his heartbeat. Around him the insanity of the festival ebbs into a haze of colors and lights. We are suspended in this state for a moment, David's heartbeat throbbing, the external world muted.

Suddenly, Sasha's hand grips David's shoulder. Abruptly, the noise returns and the haze is gone.

SASHA: I told you! From frat boy to leather pup in just a few weeks. He's cycling through the scene.

DAVID: (running a hand through his hair) That's on the verge of fucking me up.

SASHA: Well, don't let it. Be fine. Be normal. Let's go to Sidetrack.

Sasha pulls David forward. Terrance is ahead and turns back giving a thumbs up. Both David and Sasha nod in return.

CUT TO:

INT. SIDETRACK – NIGHT

Music screams from the speakers, but it is barely heard over the shouts and drunken caterwauling of the patrons inside. The bar is packed wall-to-wall with every kind of gay, straight, man, woman, and all inbetween.

Terrance, Sasha, David, Jack, and George stand before Donnie and Tibbs looking exhausted. Donnie and Tibbs, however, are in much worse shape. Donnie is being held up by Tibbs.

TIBBS: We've had *a day*. I've been trying to send Donnie home for two hours, but he says he doesn't want FOMO.

DONNIE: No FOMO, no homo!

Donnie laughs drunkenly and begins to slide out of Tibbs's grip. Tibbs quickly pulls him up and reasserts his hold.

SASHA: (to David and Terrance) Drunken idiots.

TERRANCE: I'd say one more drink then we all go home.

DONNIE: Never too much! (seeing Soot across the bar) That's eight! Eight for Soot! BINGO!

JACK: (concernedly) How many rounds of bingo have you played?

TIBBS: Three – give or take... five or so.

Both Donnie and Tibbs roar with laughter. Donnie's mirth is short lived. He throws a hand over his mouth and grows green in the face.

GEORGE: Oh, Jesus. Jack, grab him. Let's get him to the trash can before he blows.

Jack, George, and Donnie disappear into the crowd. Tibbs shrugs.

TIBBS: Cunt is getting old. We used to go to Hydrate 'til 3 on Market Days Sunday.

Sasha and David lock eyes.

SASHA: One more drink then we all go! I'm tired, old, and I'm not babysitting you assholes the rest of the night.

DAVID: I'll get this round. Tibbs – water and a whiskey ginger ale. Sasha – vodka soda. Terrance... (looking around) Hey, have you guys seen Terrance?

SASHA: We'll never find him in this mess. Did he text?

DAVID: I haven't gotten anything...

Tibbs claps his hands together twice, loudly.

TIBBS: Dumb. Bitch.

DAVID: What was that for?

TIBBS: Cell phones aren't working. There are two thousand horny homos looking at Instagram, Grindr, and Twitter right now.

DAVID: Fuck!

SASHA: Shit.

DAVID: I have to...

SASHA: Go see about your man, girl. If you have time change your shoes!

DAVID: Windows to the soul, I know!

David throws a hasty wave backward as he shoves his way through the crowd.

TIBBS: That bitch better bring me back a drink!

CUT TO:

EXT. SIDETRACK – NIGHT

David tumbles out of the front door, falling to the curb. A number of gays laugh at him maniacally.

GAY 1: Yes, bitch!

GAY 2: Worrrkkkkk that drunk body!

GAY 3: Boy needs to get to his Grindr dick!

David laughs as he picks himself up. He throws glances left and right, frantically deciding where he can go to find cell signal. He decides to head right and stumbles through the crowd, moving down a closed street flanked by portapotties.

DAVID: (to himself) Fuck, fuck, fuck.

He runs out of view, holding out his phone, checking for signal.

CUT TO:

EXT. BROADWAY AND ROSCOE INTERSECTION – NIGHT

David crosses the intersection at a sprint, not checking for traffic. A car honks. Nearby a crowd screams and laughs as he narrowly avoids plowing into a man walking a dog. Once through the intersection, he slows down and looks anxiously at his phone. He doesn't see the sidewalk is uneven and trips over it, his phone launching out of his hands and out of sight.

DAVID: Of fucking course.

He rises up and dusts himself off. It is very dark outside. It appears his phone has been thrown into a small garden full of flowers and a few bushes. He sighs and methodically moves aside the branches of the shrubs to find his phone. A man and woman walk by and see him digging through the brush. They pause only for a moment before shuffling quickly away.

DAVID: Where are you, you little piece of shit?

He sighs and stands, looking into the pitch darkness of the shrubs and weeds. There is a moment of silence on the street. It is absolutely quiet. A lone car appears; it slows as it nears David to go over a speed bump. Then there is a noise. It's soft, a slight buzzing. David spins, arms akimbo, trying to find the source of the sound. A light flashes from under a small shrub. Quickly, he digs it out of its hiding spot and holds it high into the air.

DAVID: YES!

Nimbly he clicks through screens pulling up his messages.

MESSAGE:

Sasha: *Bitch let me know when you're fine.*

MESSAGE:

Jack: *Sooooo we got kicked out with Tibbs. Currently shoving Mexican in his face.*

MESSAGE:

Frank: *The knight errant seems to have lost his way. Well, I'm listening to the main stage show at 8 if you want to swing by.*

DAVID: Forty-five minutes ago…

From somewhere, whether a nearby party or passing car, music swells. David leaps away from the small garden and stands in the middle of the street. He starts running back toward the corner.

CUT TO:

EXT. HALSTED STREET BANDSTAND – NIGHT

David is back at the festival. A stage is set up in the parking lot just off of Halsted. David assesses how to find his could-be lover. Between him and the stage is a sea of bodies gyrating to the sounds of the 80's cover band. He scans left and sees a small opening leading toward the food tents that line the main street. Resolutely, he takes a deep breath and plunges into the crowd. He is pinballed around muscle bears, women, young gays, and drag queens as he makes his way toward the edge of the throng. Once he breaks through, he stands at the line of tents looking toward the band, plotting his next course of action.

TALL MAN: Hey, dude, you lost?

The man has dilated eyes and moves to a rhythm much different from the one blasting from the speakers.

DAVID: I am! Could.... I... Could I hop on your shoulders and see if I can find my friend?

TALL MAN: Shit, dude, that is so rockstar.

David is hoisted into the air and his view of the stage is clear. His gaze sweeps from left to right then back left. On its route back to the stage, he sees Frank. He is wearing a backwards hat and tank top, singing loudly to the girl next to him.

DAVID: I found him! You can put me down!

The tall man lowers David to the ground.

DAVID (continued): Thanks, big guy!

TALL MAN: No problem. See ya around, rockstar!

David stands still for a moment, looking nervously into the crowd. He is lost in thought, but the tall man shoves him forward. The crowd pushes him as well; no longer is everyone keeping him from getting to Frank but rather propelling him toward him. David's breath comes in short gasps.

FLASHBACK TO:

INT. COFFEE SHOP DAY – 2009

David smiles across the table at Jonathan.

FLASHBACK TO:

INT. INDIANAPOLIS APARTMENT – 2012

David watches Jonathan, his head buried in a book, studying.

FLASHBACK TO:

INT. CHICAGO APARTMENT – 2014

David sits in the bathtub, water pouring over his body.

FLASHBACK TO:

EXT. DAVID'S APARTMENT – 2015

David and Frank look at each other. Frank leans in and kisses him.

CUT BACK TO:

EXT. MARKET DAYS FESTIVAL - NIGHT

David pushes through the crowd with more resolve. People give him dirty looks as he squirms his way closer to the stage. When the gyrating bodies part slightly, he sees Frank. He hesitates again. He looks down, then back toward the tall man, who sees him and waves. His gaze turns to the night sky; he takes a deep breath. When he glances back toward the stage, Frank is looking back at him. He stops dancing and gazes at David expectantly. David pushes through the last line of bodies and stands before Frank. He is breathing heavily.

DEEP FOCUS. WE SEE THREE DISTINCT IMAGES OF DAVID'S PAST, PRESENT, AND FUTURE FORMED AROUND HIS HEAD LIKE A HALO.

INDIANA FIELD – NIGHT – 2010

David and Jonathan stand on top of David's car. It is a rural night sky. Stars pepper the dark in every direction. We hear both men screaming into the darkness as we watch from afar. As we slowly draw nearer, we see them standing hand-in-hand. They are looking toward the heavens, both lost in separate thoughts, gazing in opposite directions.

SIDETRACK – AFTERNOON – 2015

David is with his friends at Sidetrack watching musical numbers on the bar's TVs. Donnie flirts with the bartender while Tibbs sings. Al is jubilant discussing the arrival of Kent. David smiles ear-to-ear. Sasha puts his arm around David and whispers something. David laughs turning his attention to *Chicago* on the screens.

INDIANA FIELD - NIGHT - FUTURE

David stands alone on top of his car. He is looking skyward but then turns his gaze downward. He is looking directly at us.

THE IMAGES FADE.

EXT. MARKET DAYS FESTIVAL - NIGHT

David is looking directly at us. It is not us, really, but Frank beyond us. We step back and see both men gazing at each other intensely.

FRANK: Is this how…?

But before Frank can say more, David takes Frank's head in his hands and presses their lips together. The music of the 80's band swells behind them. When their faces break apart, Frank is beaming.

FRANK: Well, that was nice. I should probably introduce you. (awkwardly pointing to those gathered behind him) This is Sarah, John, and Abby. That man (pointing at a stocky man disappearing into the crowd) was my date.

Frank smiles again, but it melts into a look of earnest emotion.

FRANK: (softly) I'm glad you came.

Frank reaches out and ruffles the hair on David's neck. They lock eyes. They smile. Frank pulls David close. Their lips hover an inch apart before meeting again. And again. And Again.

SCENE XI: THE END IS THE BEGINNING

FADE IN:

EXT. PINE GROVE AVENUE – NIGHT

It is silent. Hedley wanders aimlessly down the empty sidewalk, hands in pockets. He looks toward the sky, takes in the facades of each building as he passes. His face his peaceful. When he comes to the intersection of Pine Grove and Byron, he hesitates on the corner and looks down both. His face breaks into a smile. He then closes his eyes and turns around in several circles. When he opens them, he is facing north. Resolutely, he steps forward.

FLASHBACK TO:

INT. SAL'S APARTMENT – AFTERNOON – 2010

Sal sits, sipping a cup of coffee. Hedley is across from him, looking disinterestedly out the window.

SAL: As you get older, the destinations become less and less important. The spaces between come to take on a life of their own – the restaurant you never noticed, the two-flat with Christmas lights in July. And you appreciate it. The silence starts to draw you. Before long you'll be sitting beside me on Montrose beach, watching the tide roll in.

CUT TO:

EXT. BROADWAY STREET – NIGHT – 2015

Hedley turns from a side street onto Broadway. His head is down. The joyful look of earlier is gone; he is deep in thought.

FLASHBACK TO:

INT. HEDLEY'S STUDIO APARTMENT – NIGHT – 2011

Hedley is pouring drinks. Samson is in a small sitting room looking through a stack of books.

SAMSON: I thought we were just going to have sex…

HEDLEY: And I told you it could be much more than that. Not an us, a royal we, a hegemony.

Hedley slams a drink down in front of Samson. Samson looks up intrigued.

HEDLEY (continued): Imagine control. Imagine walking into a bar and everyone already knowing who you are and why you're there. We could shape Boystown. Not just socially but politically.

SAMSON: You have a plan for this?

HEDLEY: Multiple. (a prolonged pause) Do you think I'm completely crazy?

SAMSON: (smiling) I wouldn't say crazy. Sociopathic, maybe.

The two men clink glasses.

CUT BACK TO:

EXT. MONTROSE AVENUE – NIGHT – 2015

Hedley comes to the intersection of Broadway and Montrose. Ahead the road vanishes into the city, but to his right, it leads toward the lake. He turns down the dark path toward the park and water. We see him in profile. Around him are shadows of images, barely visible. It is The Set. Their ghost-like images walk with him. The apparitions begin close to him but then start to trail away, taking other turns, vanishing down alleyways.

CUT TO:

INT. STUART'S APARTMENT – NIGHT

Skyler sits cross-legged on the floor of the apartment. He is looking out the windows that face the row of towers across the street. Stuart is sleeping peacefully on the couch. We hear his snores and Skyler's heart beat in syncopated rhythms. Skyler looks at his lover with a penetrating gaze. Slowly, we draw nearer to him. We inch toward his face, eventually growing so close that we fall into the darkness of his pupils.

FLASHBACK TO:

INT. A TRUCK CAB – NIGHT - 2010

Skyler is nude below the waist. A mysterious figure is thrusting into him. Skyler's eyes are closed. His face flashes between expressions of pain and pleasure.

SHADOWY FIGURE: Unnngghhhhhh…

The shadow shudders, leaning forward over Skyler. The boy opens his eyes and looks into the dark. For a moment, the face is illuminated – it is Stuart hunched over him. As quickly as the face appears, however, it is gone. Skyler sits, shaken, looking into the shadows. The face is gone, withdrawn into the darkness.

CUT BACK TO:

INT. STUART'S APARTMENT – NIGHT – 2015

Stuart is still snoring. Skyler reaches out and gently touches the older man's skin. He is looking intently for something invisible. His finger moves over Stuart's torso and up to his face. He gently draws a line down the older man's jaw, swooping around and lightly tracing over his forehead.

FLASHBACK TO:

INT. SKYLER'S APARTMENT – DAY – 2015

Stuart stands outside the apartment with flowers. He raps on the door. Skyler answers. His face registers surprise seeing the bouquet.

SKYLER: Hi... (looking at the flowers) You... What are these?

STUART: A gift. Is it stupid? I never do this romantic stuff, but I wanted to see you again...

SKYLER: See me...

Skyler waits in the doorway. He looks away from Stuart. The two men do not move. Skyler grips the door – it is unclear whether he will let Stuart inside.

STUART: Well... (laughing) Can I come in?

Skyler keeps looking away from Stuart, no emotion on his face. He glances back, sees Stuart's weathered smile, and concedes. Gently, he pulls open the door.

As Stuart enters we see the studio apartment through his eyes. It is a very small space. Skyler's bed is covered in clothes, which he haphazardly picks up to clear room for his guest.

SKYLER: I didn't clean. I thought we were just going to...

Stuart holds out the flowers. Skyler looks at them with an air of disgust. For a moment they hang suspended between the two men. Neither is certain of what to do next. Skyler finally forces a smile and takes them. He clambers over some ramshackle furniture and sets them on the kitchen counter. We see his face. He licks his lips. His back is to Stuart.

SKYLER (continued): Listen, I was just thinking we... you know...

He turns. Stuart looks young, inexperienced. His eyes focus on the floor.

STUART: I'm sorry – it's – it's weird. I... umm... usually it is just a fuck but I thought... (speeding up his speech) I think you're gorgeous. I've never seen... when I grabbed you at the bar, I never thought you'd come back around and actually talk to me.

SKYLER: Well, I obviously thought you were also... gorgeous, I guess. I like that you... said that – that you grabbed me. Guys my age play these games. Stupid games. I like when someone is direct.

Stuart smiles. Both men remain silent. Skyler, who was gaining energy, draws back. He sighs.

STUART: I wasn't completely honest. It was so fucking... I thought if I were honest that you wouldn't want to do this.

SKYLER: You weren't honest... About...?

STUART: I brought the flowers as a kind of apology. Man, this is so – I'm sorry, I just had to see you again. It's dumb. I didn't tell the full truth so I could come over and I brought the flowers because I didn't think you'd want to fuck if you knew I was...

SKYLER: If I knew... what?

STUART: That I'm poz.

He looks plaintively at Skyler. Skyler stares forward. He shows no expression. After a deep breath, he bites his lip. He crosses his arms.

STUART (continued): I knew I... I'm sorry. It was really dumb – childish...

Stuart turns around and heads to the apartment door. Skyler hesitates. His expression turns from blank to pained. He looks to the door as Stuart is opening it to leave. Conflict is written in Skyler's expression. He closes his eyes, takes a deep breath.

SKYLER: Wait...

Stuart stops; he is outside the apartment the door nearly closed.

SKYLER (continued): I... uhhh... If we're being honest. (pause) I am, too. I have it... I have it, too.

There is a moment of silence. Stuart turns slowly.

STUART: And... You weren't going to tell me?

SKYLER: I don't... (laughing) I don't put out. I just suck guys off. I was just going to suck you off. I'm a lady.

There is another quiet moment before Stuart begins laughing. In a matter of moments, both men are laughing uncontrollably, tears running down their cheeks.

STUART: Well... we both have secrets.

SKYLER: We do.

STUART: What would the lady say to dinner, then?

Skyler smiles awkwardly, looking out the window.

CUT BACK TO:

INT. STUART'S APARTMENT – NIGHT – 2015

Skyler smiles to himself. He stands up and grabs a blanket that is thrown over the back of the couch. Gently, he places it over Stuart.

CUT TO:

EXT. MONTROSE AVE – NIGHT

Hedley walks in a zigzag line down the sidewalk. There are no people on the street. On his left is an open park. A few cars pass by him, their headlights casting a doleful glow over his face as they pass.

CUT TO:

INT. NICK'S BEDROOM – NIGHT – PRESENT

The Model and Nick are nude. The Model shoves Nick onto the bed. After the younger man lands, he is flipped over in one, deft motion. The Model slaps Nick's ass and laughs coldly. From the shadows of the room, two other figures join. Groans of pleasure erupt from Nick as one of the shadows approaches him from behind. We cautiously slip from the scene as the forms begin to merge. Limbs extend in all directions forming a shapeless mass in the darkness.

FLASHBACK TO:

EXT. HEDLEY'S APARTMENT – NIGHT – EARLIER THAT WEEK

Hedley and The Model are seated at Hedley's dining room table. They are at opposite ends, as far as possible from each other. Hedley stares vacantly as The Model chatters.

THE MODEL: But you know Zach and Rob have done quite well with the Instagram thing. They are (making air quotes) "influencers." They are adorable, but in a way it's sad. I always appreciated that you didn't do all that, you know. I mean, if you're attractive make money from actual modeling.

The Model motions to himself and smiles. Hedley keeps looking ambivalently across the room.

HEDLEY: How's Rob's mom? Didn't she have cancer? I thought I saw something on Facebook.

THE MODEL: Did she? I'm not sure. But we were all in Cabo just a few weeks ago. We took turns taking quite a few pictures, you know – hashtag t-b-t for later…

The Model continues to speak, but it becomes muted in the background. Hedley plays with one of the placemats on the table.

CUT BACK TO:

EXT. MONTROSE AVE – NIGHT – PRESENT

Hedley waits at a crosswalk. His expression is sad as he watches the signal turn from stop to walk. Even when it says to go, he remains still. He sighs before stepping forward.

CUT TO:

INT. MIKEY'S APARTMENT – NIGHT

Mikey's apartment is a small studio. It is cozy with none of the sterilized modernity of Samson's home or the pompous grandiosity of Hedley's. Stephen pours two glasses of sparkling grape juice in the kitchen and then moves to the adjoining living room.

STEPHEN: (handing a glass) Your juice, milady.

MIKEY: What chivalry.

Stephen takes a seat on the couch as Mikey aims the remote at the TV.

MIKEY (continued): What's good? What should we watch?

STEPHEN: I'm tired of Netflix. Do you have any actual movies?

MIKEY: Under the couch. In the long, flat storage bin.

Stephen jumps from the sofa and pulls out the container. He begins rifling through the movies, silently at first, then with sudden bursts of giggling.

STEPHEN: Wow… Veggie Tales?

MIKEY: It's for the kids, jerk! I didn't buy them for my own benefit.

STEPHEN: You already know all about God, of course.

MIKEY: You are so critical!

STEPHEN: I'm gay; it's my sworn duty. (examining one of the movies) I think I may have one.

He crawls toward the TV and inserts a disc into the player. There is a soft click then a hum as the movie begins to play.

MIKEY: What did you choose?

STEPHEN: Something romantic. Something to put us in the mood…

MIKEY: Naughty boy… (puts his hand on Stephen's leg)

FLASHBACK TO:

EXT. CHURCH – MORNING – 2005

Stephen is sitting on the grass outside the church. Pearl is beside him. It is silent except for the slight whistle of the wind. No dialogue is heard, but Pearl erupts into laughter. Stephen smiles. We see them from afar, the young couple, sitting an awkward distance apart in the grass.

CUT BACK TO:

INT. MIKEY'S APARTMENT – NIGHT – 2015

Stephen looks over at Mikey as the movie begins. It is almost silent, the only sound muted music coming from the television. Mikey turns toward Stephen and smiles. It is a slow, serene moment. In a second it is over. The TV roars to life and Mikey's lips begin to move.

MIKEY: Good movie choice, Stevey.

Stephen nods, his eyes growing wet.

STEPHEN: I have good taste. (abruptly standing) I'll be right back.

CUT TO:

INT. MIKEY'S BATHROOM – NIGHT

Stephen stands over the sink, his eyes red and damp.

DISEMBODIED VOICE: *Don't*.

Stephen looks up and stares at himself in the mirror.

CUT TO:

EXT. CHURCH – DAY

Young Stephen is now alone on the church's lawn. He looks toward the building; its imposing façade casts a long shadow in the grass. The bell of the church tower tolls ominously. Suddenly, Stephen's family appears – mother, father, sister and brother. They stand, expressionless. Stephen stares at them apprehensively, when from behind, a blurred form approaches. When Stephen turns at the sound of footsteps, he sees Mikey. Mikey's hands are in his pockets, a contented smile on his face.

CUT BACK TO:

INT. MIKEY'S BATHROOM – NIGHT

Stephen wipes tears from his eyes. He turns on the faucet and lets the water run. He takes several deep, shuddering breaths then looks into the mirror.

CUT TO:

INT. WAREHOUSE – NIGHT

Bodies move, shadows across a neon backdrop. A tribal beat blasts from speakers. Jets of water from the ceiling coat the gathered party in a sparkling sheen.

VOICE: WELCOME TO THE TROPICS. WE WILL TAKE YOU INTO THE HEART OF DARKNESS.

Samson has just arrived. As the water rains down on him, he tilts his head skyward and opens his mouth. He returns his gaze to the gathered mass of bodies. No face is clearly visible. He sees dimly illuminated profiles peer from the dark. Green lasers fly above his head, cutting through the pitch blackness. A face erupts from the shadows. It approaches Samson. Separate, disembodied hands run over Samson's body.

SHADOWED FACE: Room 1312 in the hotel across the street, if you want to join.

The face leans in and sucks on Samson's mouth. It is a quick, passionate kiss, lasting a fleeting moment before the sound swells, the lasers sweep, and the man disappears into the writhing mass. The crowd of people no longer moves in a quick, syncopated rhythm, but rather gels, twitches, bubbles like light in a lava lamp. As Samson searches the faces, we see some familiar visages: Kinsey, Jonathan, others from the gala. They are visible for only a moment before shadows obscure them. The water turns on once more. The jets spray the crowd, which moves as one mass, like a wave in the ocean. Samson looks skyward and raises his hands toward the heavens. We slowly climb higher, above the crowd, swimming through the jets of water, drifting through fog and lasers. We see Samson, only briefly, before he disappears into the cloud of bodies below.

CUT TO:

EXT. MONTROSE FIELDS – NIGHT

Hedley has come to the end of the busy street and into the dark of the park. Ahead of him is Cricket Hill, standing isolated in a field of green. He climbs its sloping surface. We see him from far away, his ascent slow, plodding.

FLASHBACK TO:

EXT. KOKOMO FOOTBALL FIELD – DAY – 2000

Brock stands in his football uniform, a smug smile plastered on his face.

FLASHBACK TO:

EXT. NEW YORK STREET – DUSK - 2004

Young Hank is outside Cedric's summer apartment. The door opens and he sees Cedric and his lover. He runs away into the twilight.

FLASHBACK TO:

EXT. INDIANA UNIVERSITY CAMPUS – EARLY MORNING – 2010

College Hank is walking home Lucy. They kiss in the doorway. Hank whispers into her ear. She tugs Hank's hand and pulls him into the dormitory.

FLASHBACK TO:

INT. HEDLEY'S OLD APARTMENT – NIGHT – 2012

Hedley's old notebooks are littered about. The chart with names and places is on the wall. Occasionally, this younger Hedley closes his eyes and mutters to himself.

CUT BACK TO:

EXT. CRICKET HILL - NIGHT

Hedley stands in silent contemplation atop the hill, looking toward the darkness of the lake. The world is quiet. A few stars are visible in the night sky. Behind him we see the lights of the city spreading to the north, west, and south. A siren suddenly breaks the silence. Hedley turns and looks toward the buildings, their impassive windows and lamps showing no knowledge of the emergency the ambulance flies toward. His expression is annoyed at first, but the look fades to one of wonder. He turns away from the lake to look fully on the sea of lights that extends toward the horizon. We see him from afar on the hill, between the darkness of the lake and the glow of the metropolis. Above him a plane flies overhead. Hedley laughs to himself. He waves hello to the aircraft passing through the sky.

CUT TO:

EXT. HALSTED AND BELMONT – NIGHT

Myrtle Jennings rushes down Belmont. She pulls out her purse and tries to put on makeup before getting to the festival. Around her gays walk, zombie-like, away from the street and toward their homes. Myrtle shoves her makeup into the purse and pulls out her phone. It is blank.

MYRTLE: Does anyone fucking stay out late anymore? Somebody has got to still be out…

Just at that moment her phone chirps to life.

MESSAGE:

Soot: *Outside Town Hall, darling. I hope you are bringing cigarettes.*

Myrtle claps her hands gleefully. She quickens her pace as she heads around the corner and up Halsted.

CUT TO:

EXT. TOWN HALL BAR – NIGHT

Soot checks his appearance in his cell phone as Myrtle bustles toward him.

MYRTLE: Sooty! Thank gawd you still know how to keep the party going.

SOOT: Everyone has been a bit of a party pooper this evening. But, dear Myrtle, it's delightful to see you!

They kiss each other's cheeks. Although the festival is dying, the streets are still crowded. Vendors are packing up as gays jump, dance, and laugh between the stalls.

MYRTLE: And How was it?

SOOT: A triumph, as always. Shame you had to miss the most important part of the activities.

MYRTLE: I know! Family duty called, though. I had to pretend to be a good aunt, daughter, sister, and niece.

SOOT: And how was that?

MYRTLE: Well, let's see. Mom, Grandma, and Aunt Lucille asked me forty-five times each if I was dating anyone. After time thirty I went straight to the liquor cabinet and helped myself to some of Dad's gin. My brother is good; his kids are good; I am unbelievably grateful to be back.

SOOT: Hear, hear! And we are very glad to welcome you back.

A boy in a hoodie sidles up next to Myrtle. He says nothing as he inches closer to her. Myrtle faces him, amused, and extends one of her manicured hands.

MYRTLE: Can I help you, love?

The boy wipes his nose. He looks awkwardly around, trying too hard to be casual.

GREG: I was hoping to get a cigarette.

Myrtle looks at Soot and shrugs.

SOOT: Myrtle?

Myrtle hands both the boy and Soot a cigarette and helps light them. It is clear the boy is not an experienced smoker. Myrtle and Soot exchange looks of amusement, just as the boy's hood falls and his face is revealed. He is very young. Light, pubescent stubble dusts his face.

MYRTLE: My god! How old *are* you?!

The boy jumps, the cigarette falling to the ground.

GREG: I'm... I'm going to be nineteen next week.

Soot chortles and pats his hair, sending a cloud of dusty product into the air.

SOOT: Nineteen? I'm old not blind, young man.

The boy looks between them. Myrtle and Soot both wear expressions of warmth. The boy relaxes when he sees their calm expressions.

GREG: My name is Greg Hanover. I'm... (speaking more softly) seventeen. My parents are staying at the hotel over there and I snuck out when I found out about this festival.

MYRTLE: See! Isn't the truth nice?

GREG: I dunno.

Soot takes another drag from his cigarette and exhales white vapor. He stares penetratingly at Greg.

SOOT: Are you out, my boy? Curious?

GREG: My parents don't know... No one knows, I guess. I just... I wondered what it was like.

MYRTLE: (placing a hand on Greg's shoulder) Where are you from, Greg?

GREG: Topeka. My dad went to DePaul, so we got this hotel and came up to see the campus and the museums and stuff.

SOOT: You've never been anywhere gay?

Greg shakes his head.

SOOT (continued): Well, then, the more important question I have for you is do you have a fake ID?

GREG: (looking between them) You aren't cops or anything, are you?

There is a brief pause before Myrtle and Soot both explode with laughter.

MYRTLE: A cop! I've got my tits hanging out talking to the oldest man in Boystown, and he wants to know if we're cops!

SOOT: I would watch that show, darling. Lawrence and Myrtle: the silver fox and bombshell unit!

Greg laughs uneasily. Myrtle shakes her head and puts her arm around him.

MYRTLE: Greg, we are not cops. Do you have a fake?

GREG: It's my brother's...

SOOT: Fantastic. Let's go across the street. You need to be somewhere gay.

GREG: To…a bar?

MYRTLE: We'll give you a little taste of what you're missing in Topeka.

The three cross the street and get in a long entry line. Greg is shy, laughing uneasily. He scans the line, the street, the windows of the bar, taking in all the varieties of gay men around him.

GREG: I've never seen anything like this.

MYRTLE: Well, welcome!

CUT TO:

INT. BAR – NIGHT

Soot, Myrtle, and Greg sit at the bar. Soot is looking disgusted as he assesses the beer in front of Greg.

SOOT: Honey, never order a beer again. It's so unbecoming.

MYRTLE: Oh! Don't listen to him. He is just jealous. He can't have carbs.

Greg barely pays attention. His eyes focus on the cornucopia of men in the bar. Most of the gays are getting messy, leaning heavily on each other or slumping over in chairs. Some throw glances his way. His response is to turn away, flushed and take frantic drinks from his beer.

Time begins to move quickly. Soot, Greg, and Myrtle talk animatedly to each other and laugh. Their drinks disappear and are replaced by new ones. Gay men drift behind them, streams of color in the background. Suddenly, time slows, then stops completely. The three are all caught in a moment of laughter – Myrtle has her head reared back, her hand on her stomach; Greg is leaned over, his head pressed against the bar; Soot is cackling, his hand extended gripping Greg's arm.

DEEP FOCUS. THE THREE TREMBLE AND MULTIPLY SO THAT THERE ARE FOUR SETS OF THREE. THREE SETS DRIFT BEHIND THE PRESENT SOOT, MYRTLE, AND GREG.

BLURRED GRAY BACKGROUND – PAST

The three are frozen in their look of laughter, but they fade and new characters come to the foreground. Younger versions of Soot, Greg, and Myrtle are all in a row. Young Soot sees an old couple, his parents, shaking their heads in shame. His father disappears into vapor and his mother reclines on a bed. Soot is beside her. She turns away from him; her bed is then consumed in darkness. The early-20's Myrtle is holding onto a businessman, locked in a loving embrace. They look happy for a fleeting moment before the man suddenly fades away and Myrtle is left alone. Greg is an early teenager in his bedroom. He lays on his bed, his hand down his pants, stroking himself toward climax.

THE BAR – PRESENT

The young versions of our merry band fade away as we pull into the midground. The present Myrtle, Soot, and Greg are still frozen in their look of laughter. Behind them a neon light glows. Slowly, the three figures come to life. They are recovering from their mirth, wiping their eyes, and clutching each other's hands.

GOLDEN BACKGROUND – FUTURE

A last movement takes us beyond the present figures and pushes to the background. The neon light behind the contemporary Myrtle, Soot, and Greg grows brighter and turns golden. It tremors, becoming a screen on which a blend of different images drift before us. We see beautiful men of all ages dancing; confetti bursts as disembodied hands extend and toast with overflowing glasses of champagne. Couples in silhouette hold hands and multiply and divide. Soon the whole golden landscape is nothing but men and women, men and men, and women and women, embracing and kissing in a phalanx of love that ripples and divides. When there are too many, they all sparkle, flare, and fuse into one single point of golden light.

CUT TO:

EXT. HALSTED AND ROSCOE – NIGHT

Outside the bar Soot and Myrtle flank Greg, their arms locked together. A conversation passes between them, unheard. They drift away from us, disappearing into the darkened streets.

SCENE XII: PILLARS OF FIRE

FADE IN:

A SERIES OF VIGNETTES. QUICK, LAST GLANCES INTO THE CHARACTERS' LIVES AS WE CLOSE THE PRESENT NARRATIVE.

CHICAGO SKYLINE, ABOVE HALSTED STREET – DAWN

Below us, the night is ending for some and, for others, the day beginning. A few stray boys wander aimlessly in the empty streets, their feet leaded with drunkenness. Others walk briskly to work or a fitness class, their line of movement precise in the growing dawn light.

DISSOLVE:

GREG'S PARENTS' HOTEL ROOM

Greg slinks cautiously back into his parents' hotel room. His father snorts as Greg slips beneath the covers of his own bed. When he is settled beneath the layers, he looks up to the ceiling. As he stares into the empty, white stucco, the image of Chicago's skyline appears. It is a tiny, pin-sized version at first, but it grows so large that we are consumed by the image, adrift in a sea of skyscrapers. Below us cars and people move in erratic patterns. To our right and left, huge towers rise from the concrete and stretch toward the sky. Slowly we drift backwards out of the vibrant metropolis and rest just outside of downtown on the lake. It is the same perspective Nick took a few weeks before, rolling on the waves in the old New Yorker's boat. The buildings shine a pale red as the sun sets.

Our last glance at Greg is him staring upward, eyes glowing bright. A smile spreads over his face as he becomes lost in the phantom reflections of steel, water, and glass.

DISSOLVE:

DINER

The inside of the diner glows a welcoming, amber gold as we watch Soot and Myrtle sit across from each other, mugs of coffee between them. We can't hear the words spoken, but they both look calm, relaxed, and comfortable, as if coming home after a long journey. Myrtle flips back her hair and adjusts her ample breasts in her shirt. Soot's botoxed face glows with laughter.

DISSOLVE:

BROADWAY STREET

Turning away from the window we see the long line of Halsted cutting away from us and disappearing into the maze of the city. Neon lights glow as day breaks to the east. A few gays from the festival, drunk on the last droughts of summer, are in the streets. We are not static, as in the opening pages of this drama, but rather organically drift from one vantage point to the next. To the right a businessman brusquely pushes past one of the drunks as he hustles toward the train. We hear the rumble of the train's engine as it rolls into a station, just out of sight.

DISSOLVE:

GERTRUDE'S KITCHEN

Gertrude is already awake, per her usual routine. A warm cup of tea is in her hands, her eyes looking out to the street. On her refrigerator we see a smattering of pictures. One of them is her and her grandson at the Pride Parade, another her and Sal swimming near dolphins on their most recent vacation. Before leaving the kitchen, she takes a fleeting glance at the images, straightening one of her and her husband taken before San Francisco. A gentle look sparks in Gertrude's eye when the picture is set aright. She pauses only briefly before bustling into the living room. Clicking on the television, she dramatically stretches upward toward the sky. A woman comes on screen encouraging her to get ready for the prerecorded yoga class.

DISSOLVE:

HOTEL EXTERIOR

Samson emerges from the hotel staggering from sex, drugs, and alcohol. A commuter on his way to work smokes just outside the entrance. Samson asks him for a cigarette and a light. Once he has taken the token, he gives thanks via a pretend tip of an imaginary hat. He takes a long drag from the cigarette, a plume of smoke flowing from his mouth as he exhales. Rather than walking down the sidewalk, he skips into the street and raises his hands in the air. He looks victorious as he strolls down the road toward the rising sun.

DISSOLVE:

THE IMAGES COME FASTER, MORE EARNESTLY AS THE SUN CLIMBS HIGHER INTO THE SKY.

JORDAN'S APARTMENT

Jordan has on his glasses and sits at his desk. He is dimly illuminated by the light from his laptop. Deep in thought, he puts his hands behind his head and sighs. Above his desk a poster from Baz Luhrmann's *Great Gatsby* imperiously glares down at him as he works. After a brief moment of inactivity, he suddenly jerks back to life, his fingers clattering over the keyboard of his computer.

CUT TO:

NICK'S APARTMENT

Nick, nude, looks down from his window at three men emerging from his apartment building. He waves and shouts to them below, but not one of them acknowledges him. When he turns away and looks back into his apartment he smiles. The sun is now coming over the horizon, painting his room the color of blood.

CUT TO:

STEPHEN'S APARTMENT

Stephen is sound asleep in his bed. There is no one with him. Clutched to his chest is a letter. The only words visible are a salutation "Dear Mom and Dad" written tentatively in black ink.

CUT TO:

STUART'S APARTMENT

Stuart and Skyler sleep peacefully. The bedroom window faces east, the rising sun covering the two lovers in golden light. Skyler's eyes open briefly, looking at the sky, before they close, and he goes back to sleep.

CUT TO:

SAL'S BOOKSHOP

Sal is already at work, watering all his plants in the shop and straightening piles of books as he makes his way through the small aisles. When he is satisfied with the look of the store, he walks back to the cash register. He smiles as he picks up a postcard from Susie Everly and pins it on the wall. He sighs contently and turns on a radio. Light, classical music begins to play.

CUT TO:

THE ROOFTOP OF SASHA'S BUILDING

Sasha and Terrance sit on chairs near the edge of the building's roof. They look at the rising sun. An empty bottle of wine sits between them. The two speak in hushed tones. Sasha puts his hands behind his head and sighs. Terrance smiles at his old friend, extending his hand to pat Sasha on the back.

CUT TO:

MONTROSE BEACH

Hedley is alone sitting cross-legged on the beach. His eyes are red. He sniffles like a child, then laughs to himself. The laughter turns to a stifled sob, then back to laughter. With a sudden manic energy, he rises and raises his hands to the sky. He lets out a loud, gleeful yell. Soon he is stripping out of his clothes. Our last glimpse of him is running, naked, into the waters of the lake.

CUT TO:

BELMONT HARBOR

David is awake, looking toward the sky. Frank is asleep on his shoulder, breathing deeply. The sounds of the waking city swell around them – the crash of waves, the twitter of birds, the sounds of morning traffic. David turns to take a look at Frank. He smiles to himself and pushes the hair back from Frank's forehead.

DAVID: (barely audible) Tomorrow, tomorrow, and tomorrow…

We take one last look at the lovers before our perspective lifts from the ground toward the sky. The park grows small as buildings rise before us, their windows winking silver and blue in the morning light. Once above the line of the highest condo towers, we take in the view fully. We see sparkling lake water, box-like buildings below our feet, and gold and gunmetal skyscrapers.

After this moment of respite, we rise higher.

There is a moment when we are in the clouds, when we see nothing at all. From here there is only the sound of wind, even the noises of traffic not lifting so high to the sky. It is a moment of quiet before we fall back.

SMASH CUT TO:

CHICAGO STREETS

Like lightning we drop back to earth. The downward trajectory stops inches above the pavement. We turn rapidly, assessing the many paths, the numerous avenues, boulevards, and streets which we can use to traverse the canyons of the city. With a quick jerk, we turn and fly north, the buildings, individuals, and cars turning into blurred, variegated streaks as we sail northward into Boystown.

When we arrive at the intersection of Belmont and Halsted, it is fully light, the street bathed in a golden glow. There are no longer any fest-going revelers present, but instead, commuters heading to work, parents and children capering toward schools, or others, old and young, perambulating to enjoy the sounds of the waking city. Our flight is paused as we take in the street. The image tremors for an infinitesimal moment and it is night again. The gentle sounds of early morning are replaced by the raucous noises of the street fest booming around us. But we blink and the flash to the past is over.

Our minute of pause ends, and we sail down Halsted, veering down Clark Street, diving into the heart of the city. When we slow and emerge on Michigan Avenue, we pause briefly at the base of the Hancock to look skyward, to take in the endless reflections, blue sky, and towers of steel around us. Superimposed over all is a ghostly image of Hedley. He writes, deliberately, at his desk.

HEDLEY'S VOICE: I think we often look to the heavens as our means of hope, the limitless and vast beyond, tomorrow, next, what is to come. But those dreams always burn away. Perhaps I have been thinking of it incorrectly, though. The fire is not outward destruction but internal purification. The world around us is never destroyed, just our vision of it. Our soul's landscape is fragile but filled with the most malleable of all substances. From ashes we can re-build towers. From barrenness, new hope.

As Hedley's voice fades, we take a final journey out to the lake, the placid blue water drifting below us. When we turn, we see the city fully. From the south, to the north, it is an undulating, three-dimensional vision of man's claim to the earth. Just as on Halsted, our vision trembles, and we drift momentarily into the past – we see a wooden city, smoke and fire rising above the line of buildings and darkening the sun. This image disappears. We again look upon the modern metropolis shining in the early morning light.

Where we leave the story is just above the water. The waves lap around us, covering our eyes as we bob up and down. The skyline is visible for brief moments, just before blue and white foam obscures our vision. Rising above the water in stolen seconds, we see the glowing windows of shimmering buildings. Like tiny fires they stretch from north to south, as far as we can see. In the end we fall further beneath the waves, but even in the dark, we still see shards of light flickering on the face of the city. They shine, even as all turns to darkness, even as we

FADE TO BLACK

Appendix: Sal's Poetry

Untitled
Stag of the wood, regal, powerful, light;
Sun glints from thy pointed crown.
How you elude my touch.
Only my eye can cast its distant net
Over your graceful form.
But how I long to feel the cords
Of sinew beneath my hands.
How I long to feel thy bated breath
flow across my fingers.

Parallel Worlds
These parallel worlds, that can't unite,
Endless orbits circle far from light.
The sun distant, the worlds spin 'round.
In shadow, in fear, in shame they're crowned.
They drift close at certain times, brief moments,
Hoping, longing, for a sudden elopement.
If only they could spin away, touch, lightly,
A combustion of the heavens. Even tightly
Kept laws of what is and is not would break.
They'd be unbounded, unfettered, gloriously debased.
Would these worlds be, when met together,
Unified souls rendered light as feather?
Unknown. But bound they remain.
Fettered they stay.
These parallel worlds that can't unite
Still dream of union, touches, light.

Perpetual Spring
Behold the sky, a rainbow of paper and light.
In jubilation, we walk forward, our hearts in flight.
Freedom ignites the beauty of this celebration,
Where many stand, united hearts form nations.
Tenuously, some stand on the edge of this world,
Not fully accepting all that is unfurled.
For some have found that inside them lay,
Insecurity within the variegated fray.
But even they can't escape the air,
Its light, crisp, effervescent, a glorious snare.
Despite the manmade world around them,
They all feel earth, sky, rain when they can
Stand together. The earth moves uniformly, pulses quicken
Around them. Inside, they feel everything begin.

This moment goes on and on, although it ends quickly,
Contained in the fleeting seconds they live intensely.
Bells ring, voices in cacophonous chorus sing,
There together, hand-in-hand, a moment, perpetual spring.

Tonight You Might Be Beautiful
In a weary world, a wanderer strays through fields of fallen.
The dismal light of day turns to a brackish evening sky.
He remembers how things used to be, the fresh pollen
Of rare flowers blooming in a field once full of life.
In truth, the world perhaps was never as he imagined.
Were the trees a splendid green? Did the daffodils wave?
Or had the world always been as now, abandoned?
Had he imagined beauty or had he never been awake?
The sky fully dark now, foul odor drifting, trembling trees
Shake their bony fists at his own forgotten memories.
But perhaps it wasn't what it was or could ever be,
The world that lived in his imagination, was curated in dreams.
Another look, closed eyes forced open reveals the sky
Turning a lighter shade. He had, perhaps, been mistaken.
Shaking trees now stand, palms open, blithe.
The gray, dead stalks in the moonlight turn, making
Their dead faces catch color: red, green, purple, blue.
Odious air, wind changing, turns to smells of pollen, leaves, water.
Did the world always exist in this trembling hue?
Had perhaps, the wanderer, imagined, senses faltered,
And the world bloomed, lit by momentary insanity?
Whatever the cause, it now was closer to the earlier dream.
The moon, the sky, the trees, in a state, precariously
Balanced, beautiful in a way he had not expected to see.
"Tonight you might be beautiful," the man said to darkness.
Even then the vision shook, death, life shifting before his eyes.
He sought to hold it, memorialize it, but knew the effort fruitless.
He said it quickly, before it could disappear into the brackish night.
He whispered the words, afraid if he stirred the flowers, trees,
That the spell would break and he would be alone, beauty affright,
Returning to the earlier nightmare. "Perhaps this vision is insanity,
But if this world be beautiful any night, then I have seen it tonight."

Reading Notes

Introduction:

It came to my attention that 1) few may read this entire book and 2) even those who soldier through may have no idea what is going on in terms of style and content. To help slightly I'm writing a few notes to aid people along and perhaps give insights into my intent as the author. Whether my foray into different styles is successful is entirely up to the reader's own experience engaging with the novel, but this may at least give shape to the hidden form if it is entirely unclear.

To give some brief history, in the beginning, the book was going to be a *Love, Actually*-style romp, taking on the perspective of new characters throughout the course of the novel, culminating in their mixed interactions at the Market Days festival. I planned on using a very similar narrative style as my first book, *Faggit*, in creating a light-hearted, enjoyable read about the lives of gay Chicagoans.

The first draft of chapter one, however, made it clear that the novel had other intentions. Things grew dark very quickly, and I was forced to reexamine the intent of the work as a whole. My own personal experiences also took me to places emotionally that I had never been, in terms of the people I met, and the Boystown world that I grew more and more accustomed to.

Below I outline each individual section and the basic intent of the stylistic choices made for the part/novella's form. In general, there are two main structural/thematic elements for each piece:

*A literary counterpoint, which was chosen to highlight some thematic element within that section.

*A Biblical counterpoint, which is also chosen to examine theme within the book.

If you are looking for the reason I imposed these structures on the text, the best answer I can give is to listen to Sal.

Hopefully the below adds some clarity to why these choices were made.

General Structure:

The structure seeks to draw the reader through an empathetic metamorphosis during the journey through the text. In the most basic sense, I hoped to take the reader from simply accepting the written word and the authorial intent, to imposing their own understanding on the world of the novel.

The first section is meant to be superficial in its portrayal of the Halsted world. It feeds the reader prejudices and half-truths with an authorial authority that is, at best, disingenuous. The second section uses the "I" to move to pure subjectivity, removing the biased filter present in the first section. In the third section artifice is stripped out with simpler prose and quotations. Allusions are presented with reduced context to give the reader control over what they choose to understand. In Judges the reader is narratively made an adjudicator, taking in the stories of The Set and asked to deliver their verdict on their culpability within the Halsted world. The final section attempts to give the reader as much control as possible. The author's voice is pulled back and images are presented from the perspective of a camera. Judgement, context, and emotion are the work of the reader, bringing whatever life they want to the final pages.

Individual Sections:

City Lights
Narrative Style: F. Scott Fitzgerald, *The Great Gatsby*
Biblical Parallel: Genesis

The Great Gatsby is one of my favorite books, and its structure and style are gorgeous. In engaging the text, I was more interested in writing an inversion of the original narrative – what if Nick comes to the city and is utterly corrupted rather than disillusioned? What if he embraces the destructive culture rather than shunning it?

In terms of a Biblical construct, my intention with this section fit well with the narrative story of creation in Genesis, specifically the fall. The red fruit calls and with one taste brings about man's collapse into sin.

The Exodus
Narrative Style: My Own
Biblical Parallel: Exodus

This section was meant to be the light part of the novel and engage readers with a more direct narrative than other sections.

Structurally, each chapter opens with an introductory section meant to parallel one of the plagues of Egypt. The final chapter is the crossing of the red sea.

An Interlude
Narrative Style: Ernest Hemingway, *A Farewell to Arms*
Biblical Parallel: Song of Songs

The moment Sal is introduced in City Lights, it is with music. The structure of this piece mimics a song, with each chapter representing a part of the musical construction.

I've always had complicated relationships to love stories and this section encapsulates that well, mixing the imagery of the Bible's great love story, *The Song of Songs*, with the stark disillusionment of *Arms*. I wanted to present a different kind of romance.

The disillusionment piece not only applies to the love story within the text, but also to the social standing of gays within the era in which it's set. LGBTQ men and women were making advances in rights: Harvey Milk had risen to prominence, Marsha P. Johnson and courageous others rioted at Stonewall, and nationwide gays and lesbians were beginning to emerge from the shadows. But, as the cause gained momentum, so too did the AIDS epidemic. I cannot fathom what it would be like to have lived during those years – but I can only imagine the sense of abandonment, hopelessness, and frustration that a whole generation of gays felt. I thought Hemingway and the Lost Generation – a generation of men who also, saw many of their brothers die on the battlefield fighting for a war that appeared to have no purpose – was a poignant historical mirror to look into for this period in gay history.

Judges
Narrative Style: Nathaniel Hawthorne, *The Scarlet Letter*
Biblical Parallel: Judges

    Fitzgerald was taxing but I couldn't even come close to mimicking Hawthorne's incredible prose. I did lift the ideas of judgement, the imagery of the scaffold, as well as tried to make the natural world/setting represent mental states of the characters.

    Hawthorne's text also deals closely with the idea of empathy. The epigram from this section is meant to call that out. While Hester has to wear The Scarlet Letter, those around her impacted by the act of sin, suffer immeasurably as well. Reverend Dimmesdale must suffer in private. Roger Chillingsworth lets revenge destroy him completely. To me the book is ultimately about seeing beyond what we wear, our positions, our surface motivations, and trying to perceive the soul within – hate and love live in a delicate balance, and if we understand and try to empathize with our fellow men – attempt grace and mercy rather than justice and revenge – we can ultimately live fuller lives.

    Within the text I wanted empathy to be stewing in the reader's brain. The goal was to have people have faint impressions of The Set – I would assume negative associations – and bring these over to this section. As the stories unfold, I'd hope readers would not only view them with new understanding, but also develop some sympathies for them – new perspectives to take back and re-read the first section of the novel.

    The Book of Judges is a brutal read, but I found the idea of cycles fascinating in its structure. Essentially, the Israelites slide into wantonness, are sent a Judge, have a moment of redemption, then fall back into their moral quagmires. This idea of moments of salvation became important in the later drafts of this section.

A Modern Ruin in Deep Focus
Narrative Style: Orson Welles and Herman J. Mankiewicz, *Citizen Kane*
Biblical Parallel: The Gospel

    I couldn't get the idea out of my head that the final section should be an overblown, post-modern explosion. Orson Welles was a young genius, and this section strives to achieve a unique, stylistic voice, outside of the literary realm the previous four sections inhabit. Citizen Kane was a brash, explosive piece of art from an auteur on the rise; I tried my best to channel that energy in this section.

    Welles' use of deep focus, or a single frame with multiple layers within the image, was especially poignant in the context of the rest of the novel and its obsession with personal history and empathy.

The Gospel allusions stick to themes of revelation and redemption – the breaking of the old order.

Closing:

I hope the above gives some additional guidance in reading the piece. It is an ambitious 400+ pages that I can't say is entirely successful but does strive to unravel some of the mystery of early adulthood. Love isn't always elation; relationships are never simple; life is unceasing in its disappointments; friends are lights in constant dark; and honest life is often most palpable in the simplest and smallest of moments.

In the end, although much darker than originally intended, I sincerely hope the reader finds some salvation in the pages of this book. Although life may not always take the course we had set in our sights, it does not mean the destination can't be its own kind of paradise.

Sincerely,
T. Hawks

Acknowledgments

This book has been a remarkable journey through my own young adulthood. Along the path there have been many who shaped its construction, its meanings, and its heart. There are too many to name here, but I am always indebted to my family, Emilio, and my closest friends who knew little about this project but always asked about its progress.

A very special thanks to Jess, Melinda, Steph, and Kyle who waded through this mess when it was at its most unrefined. Your support meant more than you can ever know.

In terms of literary inspiration, I've enumerated the books this text draws inspiration from. It's also worth noting my obsession with James Joyce and David Mitchell's *Cloud Atlas* shaped a lot of this construction. I'm also forever indebted to Randy Shilts' work *And the Band Played On: Politics, People, and the AIDS Epidemic* which forever transformed the pride, love, and grief I feel as an American gay male.

Endless gratitude to the staff of the Gerber/Hart Library in Chicago, who assisted me in researching those brave gay men and women who came before.

And, lastly, to all those who dreamt of better, got worse, and found purpose. I hope this story can act as a commiseration, a small lighthouse in the midst of the storm.

Made in the USA
Monee, IL
11 July 2020

36332938R00267